WRATH OF MARS

THE FOUR WORLDS

BOOK 3

SKYLER RAMIREZ

eBook ISBN: 978-1-964457-26-0

Paperback ISBN: 978-1-964457-28-4

Cover design by: Persephone Entertainment Inc.

Printed in the United States of America

Published by Persephone Entertainment Inc.

Texas, USA

Don't ever miss a new release!

Sign up now for Skyler's newsletter and get access to new release updates, free content, and great deals.

Just go to www.skylerramirez.com/join-the-club

FOREWORD

When I started writing The Four Worlds, I intended it to be a trilogy. However, as I wrote the third book, I realized there is far too much story to tell in three books. So, while *Wrath of Mars* ties up many of the storylines from the first two novels, there will be a fourth and final book in the series. I promise that the wait for that fourth book will be shorter than the wait for this one.

As the title suggests, in *Wrath of Mars* we finally get to spend some time with the Martians. I loved creating their society in my mind and on the page, and I wish I could write a dozen books just exploring the red planet and its fascinating people. I hope you enjoy getting to know them as much as I have.

Skyler Ramirez

CONTENTS

PART SIX
INVASION

PROLOGUE

October 2, 731 P.D. (Post Diaspora)

One month after escaping the Crater

The sand was coarse under the old woman's bare feet as she walked across the unbroken plain. Above, the sky was dark with thunderheads, and the occasional flash of lightning lit her otherwise dim view of what lay ahead. It was in one of those flashes that she finally caught a glimpse of the object she sought.

As she drew near, she could make out the details. It was a door, just as it always had been. The setting changed each and every time. Sometimes, like now, it was dark and cloudy; at others, it was sunny. The strangest had been an all-black landscape with a sky colored to match so that the horizon was impossible to see. She'd had to feel her way across the plain that time and had almost missed the door.

The only common thread each and every time—she actually couldn't remember how many times she had done this; had it been a few dozen, a hundred, a thousand?—had been the door waiting for her at the end of her journey. As she neared this one, she could see this particular door was obsidian black and spider-webbed with cracks across its face as if it were a mere push away from shattering to pieces.

Like the plain, each door was different. But the *presence* of the door was a constant, as was what happened next.

When she was almost to the door, she saw the man blocking her path. It was always a different person, but never the one she sought. She breathed a sigh of frustration for the fiftieth, hundredth, thousandth time.

"Who are you?" the man asked in a raspy voice. He had a rugged face, covered in worry lines, with bleach-blond hair above green eyes that gave the impression of deadness. She sighed again. Something told her this one would be more difficult than the others.

"I seek Jinny Ambrosa," she said, ignoring the man's question. It was the same thing she said first every time, and it started the game. The only problem was that she didn't know what game she was playing. Next, he would pretend not to know the—

"What do you want with that simpering nakusha?"

The question stopped her. Had he just . . .? This one was *different*. The rest—at least those she could remember—hadn't acknowledged knowing Reader Ambrosa. They'd all feigned, or maybe honestly expressed, ignorance even of her existence, which was frustrating in the extreme, considering where they all were.

But this man *knew* Jinny, or at least purported to. That changed the game drastically, though she didn't know how yet.

"I am here to save her," the old woman told the man, hoping for a reaction.

He threw back his bleach-blond head and laughed, revealing straight white teeth. Stunned again, she stood there in silence, not sure what to do next, as the man roared until tears came to his eyes. When he looked back at her, he wore a wicked grin.

"You're a fool," he said in a matter-of-fact tone, at odds with his fit of laughter. "She can't be saved. I'm not even sure she exists anymore."

The woman known by her title as the Majko—the matriarchical leader of all Earth's readers—swore silently. This was going to be far more complicated than she'd thought. The last one had been much easier: a man who'd been the victim of a horrible crime. Jinny had read him after death to help the Colonial Guard solve his murder. Like all the others, he had claimed not to know who Jinny was. And all the

Majko had needed to do was listen to the terrible details of his death, letting him vent until he'd finally seemed to find some peace and had opened the door for her.

This one was different. Not only did he *know* Jinny, but he was already giving her signs of a level of opposition she hadn't encountered with any of the previous doorkeepers.

"I must save her," she said simply to the blond man.

He shook his head. "There's nothing left to save, stupid woman. I've seen to that. All this is mine now." He swept his hand as if to encompass the entire desert wasteland they shared. "And you *can't* have it!" He yelled that last part, causing her to involuntarily take a step back.

But squaring her shoulders and looking him in the eye, the Majko settled herself in for a long fight. She hadn't come here, after all, to give up. She had to save Jinny Ambrosa, even from this monster.

Even, if necessary, from herself.

Two weeks earlier

The Majko stood in the brightly lit hospital room, looking down solemnly at the figure of Jinny Ambrosa on the lone bed. The young reader was hooked up to so many IV lines and monitoring wires that she looked like a science experiment gone wrong. It had been two weeks since she'd arrived in Perth, but she had still never awoken, despite the care of the best doctors the reader community had.

It was strange. Jinny's body appeared to be sleeping peacefully. But the leads and wires hooked up to her forehead and temples recorded a flurry of round-the-clock activity as if the reader was fully awake but trapped inside her own mind.

"Are you sure about this, my Majko?" Doctor Jolee Sinema asked from her place at the Majko's right. "It's dangerous in ways we can't even begin to understand."

The older matriarch smiled. "Has anything else worked?"

Sinema frowned. "No. Her body has healed just fine, but nothing we've done has changed anything about her brain activity or given us any hope of her waking. There's more we can try, and sometimes, the best thing to do is simply wait. These things often resolve themselves, given enough time."

The Majko shook her head slowly. "Time, Doctor, is the one thing we don't have. The Sol system is at a crossroads, and this woman will be the deciding factor in what is coming."

Sinema's frown deepened. The doctor was a woman of science and put little stock in things she couldn't measure or analyze directly. But the Majko knew that some things just had to be taken on faith. Like what she was about to do.

An orderly entered the room, pushing another wheeled hospital bed. The two women moved out of his way as he maneuvered the bed to a place right next to the one that bore Jinny Ambrosa.

"I still must again formally advise against this, my Majko," Sinema said as they watched a nurse enter and start to set up IV bags and monitors next to the new bed. "We feel there is a high likelihood that, rather than you helping her, she may drag you into whatever state she's in. There's simply no way to tell what might happen, especially if she truly bears the nightmare sickness. That is bad enough for most readers, but with her special abilities, we have no idea what to expect." She didn't elaborate further; of all those in the room, only the Majko and Sinema herself knew the full extent of Jinny Ambrosa's capabilities.

The old woman turned and laid a gentle hand on the doctor's shoulder, giving her a warm smile "As you've already said, Jolee. But it's my choice, and I believe it must be done. The fate of all of humanity may very well rest on what we do here today."

Sinema's frown did not abate, but she straightened her spine and was abruptly all business. "Okay. We'll be monitoring you the entire time. If it looks like your vitals are waning, we'll administer kopelmentarizine, which should be enough to wake you if you end up in a comatose state." Left unspoken was that the same drug had not worked to wake or even stir Ambrosa from *her* coma.

The Majko nodded in reply, then moved to lever herself up onto the second hospital bed, arranging the pillows underneath her for some semblance of comfort.

The nurse quickly moved to her side and started applying the sensor leads to her forehead and chest, and one to each of her hands. Then she started an IV line in the Majko's left forearm, on the side opposite Jinny Ambrosa's bed. The nurse double-checked all of her work and, once satisfied, stepped back and nodded to Sinema.

"All right," the doctor said, her tone one of professional detachment but her eyes still containing a trace of her trepidation. "Whenever you're ready, Majko."

Despite her assurances to the doctor, the old woman had a fleeting moment of doubt and fear. What if this didn't work? What if she got stuck in the same state as Jinny?

She steeled herself. It had to be done. Regardless of Sinema's words, the Majko knew there was simply no other way.

So, resolved to do what she must, she closed her eyes and reached out her bare hand to grasp the limp wrist of Jinny Ambrosa. And then the Majko screamed.

PART ONE
LANDSCAPE OF THE MIND

CHAPTER 1

Present Day; October 2, 731 P.D.

Tyrus Tyne was pacing the floor of his small quarters in Olympus Mons Government Center, a massive installation carved into the side of the enormous, *active* volcano that was the geographic and political heart of Martian society.

It had been an entire month since he, United Earth Congressman Corey O'Leary, Cal Riggs, and Toby Haight had arrived on the red planet after rescuing Jinny Ambrosa from the infamous Crater prison on Luna. And Tyrus was growing increasingly restless.

On Earth, the government and military—especially the military—had kept him extremely busy, sharing intelligence on the Council and their warship capabilities, as well as grilling him nonstop on their technology and general tactics.

He'd expected the same when he'd arrived on Mars; it had been the entire reason O'Leary had asked him to come to the red planet instead of going to Australia to watch over Jinny. But so far, the Martians had seemed completely uninterested in Tyrus or anything he had to say. It had confused even Corey, who reassured Tyrus daily that he was working on it and it would only be a matter of time before the Martians would seek his advice.

After a month, Tyrus had lost any optimism. Even O'Leary's assurances that, eventually, the Martians would seek his expertise rang hollower each day that passed with Tyrus essentially confined in this small apartment.

His companions on this mission were no help either. O'Leary spent virtually every waking hour in meetings with Praetor Aphrodite Starshadow, one of the rulers of Mars and clearly an old flame of the congressman's, though O'Leary wouldn't talk about it.

Riggs was, like Tyrus, essentially confined to the apartment the Martians had given him. But unlike Tyrus, he gave no outward indications of even wanting to leave his quarters. When he was sober—an increasingly rare occurrence—Riggs was moody and sullen, still mourning the loss of his best friend and copilot, Jynx, in the Luna mission to rescue Jinny a month ago. Tyrus didn't blame Riggs for how he'd chosen to handle his grief, but he hoped he would soften with time and rejoin their society, if only so they could help him through it.

Toby Haight, the newest member of their group, was also mourning Jynx. The two had formed some kind of relationship when he'd helped Jynx evade and hide from a police dragnet on Earth. Her death had obviously rattled the boy, and he was almost as quiet as Riggs about it, withdrawing into himself and pointedly avoiding every member of their party except for O'Leary.

Or maybe it was more that Toby was avoiding Tyrus specifically for other reasons. Perhaps he sensed that Tyrus suspected him of some sort of duplicity after he'd been caught trying to sneak a holdout pistol into Phobos Station when they'd first arrived in Mars space. But, despite watching the boy carefully in the month since, there had been no further signs that he was anything other than what he purported to be: an Earthborn orphan who just happened to be in the right place at the right time to help Jynx.

Either way, it meant that even at dinner time—the one time each day when the four members of their group got together to eat and talk about their situation on Mars—Riggs and Toby mostly kept to themselves, and only Tyrus and O'Leary did any talking.

In the times in between? Tyrus had nothing to do. It left him with far too much time to think, which, for a man with a past like his, wasn't necessarily healthy.

He mostly thought of Jinny. Had the doctors in the United Earth reader community at Perth been able to wake her from her coma? Was she awake and sitting there in the city of readers, feeling as useless, cut off, and bored as Tyrus? Was she still alive?

The most frustrating part was that he probably wouldn't know the answers to those questions anytime soon. Which led to the second problem he dwelled on alone in his quarters: the Council invasion was coming. They didn't know when, or how many ships the enemy would send, but Tyrus knew it would be more than enough.

Together, the various Four World navies boasted close to 750 ships. But the Council had forty-seven entire planets and their respective industries to devote to the war effort. Tyrus didn't know how many ships were in the Council Navy, but he guessed it would be a lot more than 750. He expected that when the Council's forces finally arrived in the Sol system to do more than recon, they would come in such overwhelming numbers that they would run right over the various defensive forces scattered around the system.

Only by working together could the Four Worlds hope to stand against them. Europa seemed open to allying with United Earth—Earth and Luna—in a common defense. But Mars and Earth had been in a state of cold war for virtually the entirety of the nearly six centuries since the Four Worlds had driven the Council government out of the Sol system. At various points—fifty years ago and almost again two years ago—that cold war had turned hot, but even without there being any overt hostilities now, the two planets didn't trust one another. So much so that they each actively jammed any transmissions sent from the other, cutting off any and all contact between citizens of Earth or Luna and citizens of Mars. Supposedly, the highest-level leadership of each nation had somewhat regular contact, but all Earth's messages to Mars asking to discuss the impending Council invasion had gone unanswered.

Which was exactly why Tyrus and Corey O'Leary were here now. O'Leary had conspired with a political ally, Mikael Gorsky, to come directly to Mars as Earth's unofficial emissary after they'd rescued Jinny from the Crater prison. Gorsky himself had stayed back on Earth, getting himself elected president when the former UE president, Pereira, had been removed from office in shame over Jinny's arrest and the false reports that she'd died in custody. After obtaining power, the plan had been for Gorsky to formally recognize O'Leary as United Earth's ambassador to Mars.

However, thus far, they'd heard nothing from Gorsky or Earth. Nor had the Martians seemed to be swayed in the least by O'Leary's passionate arguments that they needed to ally with their ancient enemies.

Thus, Tyrus and his friends were at a stalemate, with the specter of an enemy attack always threatening to take what little time they had and abruptly end it.

At least dwelling on Jinny's fate and the Council's inevitable invasion kept Tyrus's mind mostly off of the thing he feared most: his own past. As a former enacter and alpha—an elite assassin for the Council—he'd done and seen things that he knew would haunt him forever. Unbidden, his thoughts turned to those things now as he paced the small apartment. His already dark mood soured further.

He was relieved beyond measure when the chime for his door sounded and interrupted his self-recriminatory musings. Tyrus hurried to the apartment's door and opened it.

There, he was surprised to find a tall figure—just under his own two-meter height—in a head-to-toe black exosuit, the type Martian warriors wore to augment their strength and allow them to survive and fight in near-Earth gravity. The suits also had incredible stealth capabilities, which Tyrus had experienced firsthand when meeting Centurion Parn, a member of Mars's elite Praetorian Guard, in the cockpit of the *Blind Monk* just after docking at Phobos Station.

This visitor wasn't Parn. Tyrus took that in at a glance; this was definitely a woman by her shape, and she was quite shapely even under the exosuit, especially for a Martian. The denizens of the red planet trended toward tall and preternaturally thin, given the low gravity they grew up in.

"Can I help you, soldier?" Tyrus asked when the woman at first said nothing.

The visitor made no move or sound but must have sent some sort of command to her suit, as the opaque helmet covering her head and face seemed to disintegrate in front of Tyrus—it might be a while before he got used to Martian nanotech. The disappearing helmet revealed a long, attractive face, the woman's olive skin indicative of the melting pot of races that had originally colonized Mars. She had full lips and wide, aqua-blue eyes that contrasted sharply with her tanned complexion, and her short hair was lustrous and deep black.

"Visitor Tyrus Tyne?" she asked formally, using his full name and quasi-title as was the Martian tradition for nonfamiliars.

He nodded in reply.

"I am Optio Domitia Felix of the Praetorian Guard." She kept an impassive expression as she spoke. Her soprano voice betrayed no emotion but oddly reminded him of a set of wind chimes he suddenly remembered from his early childhood home.

"Welcome, Optio Domitia Felix," Tyrus said, returning the formality. Mars had a lot of strange traditions and cultural mores, and O'Leary had coached him, Riggs, and Toby on the basics. One was that, if in doubt, one should always use a Martian's full name and title when addressing them.

"Thank you," she said in the same even tone. "I bring the compliments of Centurion Marcus Parn of the Praetorian Guard, who asks if you would be amenable to joining him this afternoon for a sparring session."

Tyrus was surprised. He'd only met Parn once, when the *Blind Monk* first docked on Phobos Station. He hadn't even known the man was on Mars's surface. The invitation was unexpected and strange. Though, Tyrus had to admit, given the alternative of sitting in his quarters and reliving past sins, it was also highly welcome.

"Of course, Optio Domitia Felix. You may tell him that I would be honored to join him."

Still no smile from the tall woman. "Good. He requests that you meet him at 1400 hours in the Gorgon Training Gymnasium. Any of the wall terminals can give you directions there."

She started turning to leave, her message delivered and her duty done, and Tyrus blurted out the first thing that popped into his head. "Optio Domitia Felix, wait . . . please."

The Praetorian Guard paused and turned to regard him.

"Would you . . ." How to say this? "Would you perhaps wish to join me for lunch while I await the sparring session?"

"Why?" The sharply spoken one-word response caught Tyrus off guard. Why indeed? He decided to just go with the truth.

"I'm afraid that I have been alone in this room for quite some time, and I would appreciate the company. I would also like to ask some questions about Martian society so that I may better acclimate myself during my time here."

She seemed to consider this for a long moment. Then she nodded. "As long as you bear no romantic intentions, then I will join you for lunch, Visitor Tyrus Tyne."

Tyrus sputtered. He hadn't been expecting *that*. But O'Leary had continuously warned him of how blunt and straightforward the Martians were. "I, uh, I assure you, Optio, my intentions are strictly professional."

She frowned slightly at his breach of etiquette, using her title alone without her name, but seemed to forgive him quickly. Domitia Felix nodded again. "Then I will return in an hour to collect you for lunch." Without another word, she turned and walked away.

Tyrus watched her go and caught himself admiring how the exosuit clung to her curves as she walked. He shook himself, turning around to go back into his room. According to O'Leary, if a Martian woman caught you looking at her in a manner that suggested attraction, it kicked off a complex series of rules of interaction that could just as easily end with the offending man married to the woman or dead by her hand—or the hand of her designated champion—in an honor duel.

Keying the door closed behind him, he sighed. Martian society was proving to be extremely unique and complex. Maybe Optio Domitia Felix really *could* help him learn how to navigate it. Or maybe not. But at least it would beat another lunch alone in his quarters.

The man—she'd learned his name was Hendrix—glared at the Majko from just a few meters away, where he stood, nervously fidgeting. She, on the other hand, sat still on the coarse sand, her legs crossed, projecting an outward calm that didn't quite match up with the turmoil inside of her. But she had found that *appearing* to be calm unsettled Hendrix. And she needed him unsettled if she was to convince him to let her through that door.

The cracked, obsidian-like door was still there, just behind the man, mocking her with its presence. She had no idea what lay beyond it, only that she had to get through it if she was to have any hope of saving Jinny Ambrosa. She'd already been through many like it, however, and was forlornly positive that there would be many more to come. Still, one had to take a long journey one step at a time.

"Why are you here?" the Majko asked Hendrix with forced casualness. It was not the first time she had asked the question, nor had he answered it on any of the previous occasions since she'd arrived at his door a few—hours, maybe?—ago. But given how much the man was fidgeting now, perhaps this time would be different.

Hendrix sneered, but she was getting used to that. It seemed to be his default expression, as if he thought himself so much smarter than her or anyone else in the galaxy. But the sneer had lost some of its bluster as time had worn on. This was most definitely a man who abhorred sitting still or being under anyone's scrutiny, a man who preferred to operate in the shadows and slip in and out as he pleased.

"I told you before," he said, "this place is mine now. The reader is dead."

He grinned as if expecting his pronouncement to shock her, even though he'd said as much when she'd first arrived. The Majko fought to keep her face impassive, though she wasn't actually shocked. Instead, she had to work hard to keep from smiling. He was finally engaging with her again after his initial outbursts.

"If she were dead, you wouldn't be so intent on keeping me out of that door," she said simply, and from the scowl that passed across his features, he knew as well as she did that Jinny was still alive.

"What would you know? You don't even belong here!" Hendrix snapped.

"Nor do you." She let herself smile now, sensing it would throw him further off balance.

He shook his head rapidly as if trying to shake her words out of his ears. "Of course I belong here," he said angrily, though she thought she detected a slight note of pleading as well. "This entire place is mine. Jinny was weak, like all women, so I took it from her and made it my own. It's mine now!"

The Majko shook her head and clucked her tongue as if scolding a small child. "Why do you tell me lies? Jinny Ambrosa is many things, but weak is not one of them."

His eyes widened slightly as he further lost control of his features, and they told the story for him. Hendrix was *afraid* of Jinny. This man who had, by his own admission to her early on, killed a dozen women in life, was scared of one little reader. Which meant Jinny wasn't just still physically alive but also mentally alive somewhere here in the landscape of her mind. It sent a surge of hope through the Majko.

She spoke again, cutting Hendrix off just as he opened his mouth to reply, doing her best to keep him off balance. "I imagine she's not even on the other side of that door, is she? You are far too unimportant a memory to be the gatekeeper to her directly, so there must be more doors after this one. I'm right, aren't I?"

He shook his head violently again, which only confirmed her accusation. "No, no, no!" he growled, looking everywhere but at her as spittle collected on his chin. "She's dead! I killed her. Just like I'll kill you."

His threat was empty. The Majko hadn't spent her seventy-seven years of life reading others without becoming an excellent judge of human character and behavior. This man, Hendrix, would happily kill a defenseless woman, most likely by sneaking up on her in a place where she felt safe. Even if killing her in this strange dreamland were possible, he would never try it with her eyes solidly on him and her guard up. He was too much of a coward.

With every other door and every other guardian she had met in her long journey through Jinny's subconscious mind, the trick had been to help them find closure. Even the criminals Jinny had read over the years who now inhabited these depths were mostly looking for justification, for someone to listen to their side of events. With many of them, it had been difficult to pretend to sympathize, but doing so had been a small price to pay for access to their doors.

But Hendrix was different. He was a criminal of the highest order—a serial killer who had murdered only those weaker than himself—and he was also clearly a sociopath. He wasn't looking for justification or forgiveness, for he had no doubts, no guilt. He only understood one thing: fear. And she could work with that.

"You know, if Jinny does die, then you're dead as well," she said evenly, then studied his reaction.

He quickly hid his look of surprise under his usual sneer, but the curl of his lip wasn't quite as pronounced as earlier.

"In fact, the *only* chance you have at staying alive is for me to reach her," she continued.

"You lie!" Hendrix snapped back, though with less conviction.

She shrugged. "Believe me or don't, but if I don't get through that door, Jinny will eventually die on a hospital bed in Perth as her body continues to shut down. And when she dies, so do you."

She let the silence torment the man as he tried to come to grips with what she had said. His hands opened and closed repeatedly, his eyes widened, and he again avoided her gaze. She could see his mouth silently forming words of denial, but his voice wouldn't come.

Hendrix stayed like that for several minutes—it could have been longer, but time worked strangely here—fighting an internal battle that was obvious to the Majko. Then, finally, he slumped to the ground. He was on his hands and knees, staring at the ground in front of him and shaking his head again as if he needed to vomit but was fighting to keep it down.

"No, no, no, this place is mine," she barely heard him whisper. "All mine. Just mine."

"This place will *never* be yours," she said harshly, drawing his gaze back to her, gratified to see his eyes go wide with shock; he was far past the point of being able to control his emotions. "But if I save her, then I save you too, and you may keep existing here, as much as you don't deserve it."

Hendrix opened and closed his mouth several times as if trying out different responses in his head. He broke from her gaze again and stared at the sandy ground, his features going slack.

It was time to take a chance. Slowly, carefully, the Majko stood. It wasn't just for want of not shocking him out of his stupor, but somehow, the joint pain of her real body had transferred with her to this dreamscape. It didn't seem fair at all, but she wasn't going to let it get to her too much—just the hazards of being old in mind as well as body.

Not even looking at Hendrix, who remained on the ground, muttering silently to himself, she stepped around him toward the door.

"No!" he choked out, but he made no move to stop her.

She reached out, hoping, and pushed on the door. To her immense relief, it opened inward at her touch, revealing an inky blackness beyond. That had been the final moment of truth. Before, none of the doors had opened for her, no matter how hard she pressed, until she had overcome their guardians. That this one opened for her now was the final confirmation that she had guessed Hendrix's weakness correctly.

She stepped through, and like all the others, the door did not close but simply disappeared behind her.

The Majko stood for a long moment in the darkness, waiting. Gradually, a light began to build around her, and she could make out her new surroundings. Then she heard a sound: the lapping of water. Feeling wetness around her ankles, she looked down and saw that she was standing in a shallow lake that spread all around her, as far as she could see.

She walked forward, sloshing through the water, which was cool but not overly cold. Above, the sky slowly resolved to a dazzling blue unblemished by clouds, the light seeming to come from everywhere in the heavens, without a sun or other single point of illumination.

The Majko knew from experience that she would have to walk a short distance before she would be able to see the next door. After sloshing through the water for a time, she saw a speck on the horizon. A few long seconds more and that speck resolved into two specks. As she got even closer, they resolved into the image of a door and a man.

He was tall, with jet-black hair, and as she neared, she could make out his olive complexion and bright green eyes. But what really surprised her was the broad smile he wore and the twinkle of mirth in those eyes.

"Huk watukuq," he said in a language she didn't recognize. When she showed no comprehension, he spoke again. "E ny sai tait u."

She shook her head at him.

"Hadda ma I fahantay?"

She frowned.

"Aur ab?"

Another shake of her head.

"How about now?" he asked in English.

"I understood that," the Majko said.

He smiled broadly in response. "Ah, good. I was worried that you Earthers had come up with a language that even I didn't know," he said. He motioned toward her feet, and she glanced down, surprised to see that a small, dry patch of ground had appeared in the water between them, a campfire cracking at its center.

"Please, sit," he said in a friendly tone, settling cross-legged on the far side of the fire. Behind him, she could see his door, cracked and cheap-looking like she'd expect in a low-income apartment building. On its worn surface, two tarnished metal figures declared it to be apartment 7C. She briefly wondered if that had any significance to this man—or to Jinny.

She lowered herself to the ground across the fire from him. Though she knew it was all an illusion, the warmth of the fire felt good to her and lent to the cheeriness the man displayed.

He didn't wait for her to speak, as many of the others had. "I'm Ryder, a good friend of Jinny's. I'm the man who brought her into the rebellion."

"A speaker?" she asked, guessing from his earlier use of so many different languages.

Ryder nodded.

"Why would a speaker join the rebellion? I thought you ruled the 47 Colonies?"

He shrugged. "Is every reader the same? Do all of them universally accept every decision you've made as their leader? Such it is with speakers as well; not all of us believe in the Council's lies. And some of us want to make a difference in the galaxy."

He raised his eyebrows, inviting her to speak next.

Given the strangeness of this encounter, the Majko decided to try something new: the direct approach.

"I'm here to save Reader Ambrosa. How do I get through your door?" she asked him.

Ryder smiled even wider and shrugged. "It's open to you whenever you want to go through it." He waved her down as she started to rise from beside the fire. "But first, there are some things you'll need to know if you truly want to save our friend."

She lowered herself back down and nodded for him to proceed.

"Jinny is broken," Ryder said simply. "You no doubt knew that from what you've experienced already. But you likely don't realize just how badly she's been fractured." He paused, inviting questions.

"Tell me," she commanded with all the authority of her station, though she recognized she likely didn't need it with this man. Still, she had certain habits when dealing with speakers on Earth, and long-formed habits tended to assert themselves in stressful situations.

He didn't look offended; his smile didn't even lessen. "I'm her friend. And if you're here to save her, then I *want* you to succeed. Even if it means she loses me. But there are others who will defend her to the end, and they will not be as accommodating as I am. You met one already. Hendrix. He defends her because he seeks to dominate and control her. That you got past him speaks to your abilities and fortitude. However, those that remain defend her for entirely different reasons, and they will not be so easy to subdue."

She leaned forward. "Then tell me how to get past them; tell me how to save her."

The speaker gave his head a slow, single shake, though he kept smiling. "If I knew, I would tell you. But that part of her is sealed off even from me. I can only give you two pieces of advice."

The Majko leaned forward further, risking drawing too close to the dreamed flames but excited to hear what Ryder had to say.

"First," he began, "you are sure to meet her father, Frank Ambrosa. Their relationship is . . . complicated. And not just in the ways of most father-daughter relationships. He will defend her with a passion born not of fear as with Hendrix or of friendship or familial love"—here he gestured at himself—"but of much more sinister designs. I can't really tell you much more. Jinny only shared a few things with me when I still lived, and she has chosen to keep more hidden from me even here."

"Then her mind—her personality—still lives?" the Majko asked anxiously.

Ryder nodded. "She still lives. But it will take time to put her back together, and I doubt she will *ever* be the same as she was." For the first time, he frowned.

"You said two pieces of advice," she pressed. "What is the second?"

His frown deepened. "At the end, you'll have to face *him*." He left the last word to hang in the air like a death sentence. A long time passed—it could have been hours—and he said nothing more.

The Majko finally broke the silence. "Who is *he*?"

Ryder just shook his head. "I won't say his name. It . . . upsets her. But he will defend her to his last breath. I fear that no one can get past him."

"Why?" she insisted. "You seem to know that I am here to help. Why would *he* prevent me from doing so if he truly wants to defend her."

Ryder sighed and raised his eyebrows. "It's complicated. *He's* complicated. He loves her. And he feels like he failed her before, which makes him obsessed with not failing her again. It goes beyond rationality. Even if he believes, as I do, that you are here to save her, he cannot be certain of that or of whether or not you truly know *how* to save her. So, he is unlikely to let you pass. And if you cannot get past him, then you can't save Jinny."

"So what do I do?" She didn't hide her impatience as she struggled with his cryptic comments.

He shrugged. "What you've been doing. Just hope that it works." Ryder stood, nodding to her, and started walking away from the fire and from the door. Dry land seemed to form under his feet as he did, then disappear just as quickly as he left it behind. He said nothing more and didn't look back, and after a moment, the air above the water shimmered, and he was gone.

Sighing, the Majko stood, walked around the fire, and pushed open the apartment door.

"It appears to me, Praetors of Mars, that this war of which Congressman Corey O'Leary speaks is one of Earth and no concern of ours. When the Council Navy sent through their scouting force, was it not Earth's forces they attacked at the Front Door? Did they not travel toward Earth before fleeing back through the Rift? At no point did they threaten Mars. So I must ask, Praetors of Mars, why should we ally with our ancient enemies against a threat that is to them alone?"

Corey O'Leary frowned across the large round table at Martian Praetor Kol Tiberius. The stocky—for a Martian, at least—man with thick caterpillar eyebrows glared at him, the expression on his long face amplifying the challenge of his words.

Corey took a moment to consider his response. It had taken weeks for the Quorum of Praetors, the ruling body of Mars, to even allow him to address them. And in the just over two weeks since that had first happened, it felt like the praetors continued to make the same arguments.

That was especially true of Praetor Tiberius. The man was, as near as Corey could tell, the leader of what passed for the opposition in the Quorum. And given that the petition to allow Corey to address the Quorum had come from Tiberius's chief rival, Aphrodite Starshadow, the man seemed dead set on arguing with every point Corey attempted to make to convince them that an alliance between Earth and Mars was the *only* way for the Four Worlds to survive the coming Council invasion.

"Praetors of Mars," Corey began formally. "I ask, did this Quorum make a deal with the Council to support their invasion of Earth?"

"You know we did no such thing!" Tiberius snapped, standing from his seat. The man's tall Martian stature meant that he loomed over Corey from across the table. But before Tiberius could challenge him to some ridiculous duel to the death over his words, Corey took a risk and interrupted.

"I know that Mars would never ally with the Council government. I ask the question rhetorically. But during the scouting mission of which you speak, the Council Navy sent an encrypted message to Mars implying that such a deal had already been struck, did they not? I must ask, Praetors of Mars: if Mars would never dishonor herself by allying with the Council government, then why was that message sent? And why send it in a way that United Earth could not only intercept it but decrypt it far more quickly than should have been possible?"

A quarter of the way around the table, to Corey's right, another Martian spoke up before the red-faced Tiberius could argue again. "They did it because they wanted to sow further discord between Earth and Mars." Praetor Gale Sunsbane glared at Tiberius as he spoke.

"You are most wise, Praetor Gale Sunsbane," Corey said, nodding to the man and using Sunsbane's full name and title as was tradition on Mars between those who were mere acquaintances. "And most correct in my estimation. Praetors of Mars"—he turned to look back at the group as a whole—"we stand on the precipice of history. The Keeper and his false Council government would have Mars and Earth at odds with each other in the very hour in which we *must* stand united. I urge you to make an overture to Earth and . . ."

Fifteen minutes later, Corey sat nervously fidgeting in the antechamber alone while, behind closed doors, the Quorum of Praetors voted on whether or not to send a message of peace to Earth—to start a proper conversation with Corey's government about an alliance before the Council Navy returned in force.

The inner doors to the Grand Hall of Praetors finally opened, and Corey stood respectfully as the various praetors passed. Their black-clad bodyguards—all members of the aptly named Praetorian Guard—seemingly appeared out of nowhere to fall into step with their protectees. He watched as twelve of the praetors exited through the outer doors. A few seconds later, the thirteenth emerged. When she saw him there waiting for her, Aphrodite Starshadow sighed.

Martian politics had always been a black box to anyone on Earth. The red planet was secretive in the extreme, and no one outside Mars ever seemed to know who was in charge. Corey knew Aphrodite from years before when he'd spent a school year on Mars as an exchange student during a rare period of peace and semi-open relations between the two worlds. He'd been surprised to arrive on Mars again with Cal Riggs, Tyrus Tyne, and Toby Haight to find that his old friend, Aphrodite, was not just one of the Quorum of Praetors but actually its titular leader. As consul of Mars, she had some vague authority above that of the Quorum, but Corey still hadn't been able to tease out which decisions were hers alone and which required a vote of the other twelve praetors. He wasn't even sure when he was supposed to address her by the title of consul or as a praetor, as he'd heard the other praetors refer to her as both in different situations.

It was all making his head spin.

"What was the vote tally this time?" he asked as she reluctantly approached him. "Did I sway anyone?"

"Eight to four against," she said heavily.

"Great!" he said, trying to sound happy about it. "That's one more in our favor than last time."

Aphrodite's startling blue eyes regarded him skeptically. Then she shrugged her narrow shoulders. "That may be, Congressman Corey O'Leary, but the remaining eight praetors are staunchly opposed. They favor Praetor Tiberius in this debate, and you are unlikely to sway them." Corey didn't miss that she used his full title and name while she omitted Tiberius's first name, showing more familiarity with her political opponent than with her old friend from Earth.

He swallowed and put on the best fake smile he could. "I have to keep trying, Consul Aphrodite Starshadow," he said, purposefully returning her formality. "It is vital that Earth and Mars present a united front when the Council attacks once more."

She frowned. "Perhaps."

Optio Domitia Felix returned to collect Tyrus from his room for lunch exactly one hour after she'd first left the door of his quarters. She was still dressed in her exosuit, but the helmet was blessedly retracted—or maybe the right word was disintegrated.

With few words, she led him through the base's tunnel system to a small cafe that jutted out of the side of the massive mountain on a platform that appeared to have been built solely for that purpose.

It was one of the few times Tyrus had experienced the open air of Mars after a month in the underground warrens of Olympus Mons Government Center. The air on the cafe's outdoor patio was crisp and clean, with a chill that even the multiple orbital mirrors he could see reflecting additional sunlight to the planet's surface couldn't completely dispel.

They took a seat near the edge of the platform, which gave them a stunning view of the large city that covered the foothills of the massive mountain. Buildings glittered in the midday sunlight. At the edge of the city, closest to them, he could see the older ones that represented the planet's first colony, which he knew had since been converted to the campus of the University of Olympus Mons, the red planet's foremost educational institution.

Around them, the cafe was crowded, with almost every seat occupied; the optio must have called ahead for a table, given how quickly they'd been seated. Tyrus picked up the menu and focused intently on it, both to take his eyes off Domitia Felix before she noticed and took offense at his gaze, and so that he could avoid gazing at the other denizens of the cafe.

Despite the colder weather in comparison to most areas on Earth, Martian fashion tended toward the revealing. The men, at least those not in a military uniform, preferred shorts and sometimes little more, while the women wore clothing that would have been considered scandalous on Earth and even on the more liberal colony worlds.

Which made it very difficult for Tyrus, as an outsider, to *not* let his gaze linger, hence his aggressive focus on the menu.

"What's good here?" he asked the optio after they had both studied the menu for a few moments.

She furrowed her brow. "Why do you ask me that? Surely, we have different tastes; what is pleasing to me is unlikely to be so to you."

Tyrus resisted the urge to shake his head. Martians were a strange lot—so literal, despite symbolism and ceremony being woven heavily throughout their entire culture.

Again, he decided on the honest route. "As you may know, I was a spy in the colonies. I am used to going to new planets and blending in with the citizenry there. Part of that is learning to appreciate the local cuisine. Perhaps you could share with me your favorite dish on the menu so that I may begin developing my own taste for it."

She sat, considering that for a little while. Then she nodded curtly. "I understand. I am partial to the paella. It is an Old Earth dish adapted to Martian ecology and tastes. I will warn you that it is considered quite spicy, even by local standards."

Tyrus hid a grimace. He'd never shied away from spicy food, and the food the Martians had been bringing to him and his companions since they arrived had seemed to be as near to Earth cuisine as they could expect—he suspected they had done that strictly for their visitors' benefit—but he had already noticed how much Martian cooks tended to use hot peppers and other spices liberally. A few of the dishes had stressed even his pallet, and most of them made Riggs sweat profusely as he ate. But, nothing ventured, nothing gained.

"Thank you," he told the dour woman. "I will try that."

A server came to the table, and they both ordered the paella and glasses of water to drink. While they waited for their food, Tyrus tried to make small talk with Optio Felix, but he was able to coax little from her aside from one-word answers.

Finally, just as he felt the awkwardness build to a crescendo, the food arrived, saving him.

He waited until she had taken the first bite, another Martian custom, and then took one of his own . . .

. . . and almost spit it out. 'Spicy' didn't even begin to describe the dish. His entire mouth felt as if it were on fire, and the flavor was highly unusual. Tyrus had had paella several times in his life—it was a delicacy on Mendoza, where he'd spent six months undercover—and this was nothing like it. First of all, the dish didn't appear to have a single piece of seafood in it; instead, there were chunks of spicy, dark meat in an even spicier red broth, all poured over something that appeared to be rice but had a different texture than what he was used to. And it *burned.*

He grabbed his water glass and took a long sip, the coolness of the liquid doing little to douse the fire but giving him at least a small measure of momentary relief.

Across the table from him, he heard a small snicker, almost too quick to notice. He looked up and over at Domitia Felix, who wore what looked like the merest beginnings of a smile at his discomfort. It was subtle, and she didn't look like a woman who had just laughed, but it was the first outward sign of emotion he had seen from the warrior, and it looked exceptionally good on her.

"You weren't kidding about the spicy part," he said through gasping breaths.

She cocked her head and furrowed her brows at him. "Why would I kid about such a thing?"

Tyrus shook his head. "Sorry, figure of speech. It certainly is spicy, much more so than anything I've eaten before, with the exception of a potato dish I once had on Reunion."

"Reunion, settled by those of the Latino cultures of Earth's Central America. First surveyed in the year 98 post diaspora, terraforming completed in the year 145, and the first permanent settlement established in 147."

He gave her an appraising look. "Yes. I believe that's all correct. But I am surprised you know so much about the colonies, given the long schism between them and the Four Worlds."

She raised an eyebrow. "I studied all the colonies in primary school. Do you not study the Four Worlds in schools in the colonies?"

He shook his head. "Actually, the Council government teaches that everyone in the Four Worlds died in a plague in the year 173. We learn nothing else of Earth, Mars, Luna, or Europa except that they are supposedly still barren wastelands devoid of life. It was a shock to all of us to discover that life and society continued to flourish here."

She cocked her head again. "How odd. Tell me, what is it like on Reunion?"

He set aside the spoon with his second bite on it, grateful for an excuse to keep talking and delay shoving more of the deadly dish into his mouth. "What would you like to know?"

She shrugged. "Language, culture, or anything else you deem important for me to know."

"Okay. They speak mostly Spanish in their homes on the planet, though everyone knows English in the cities. There are even a few carried-over ancient languages in some of the outlying towns. Supposedly, they're evolved forms of the languages that the original inhabitants of Earth's Central America spoke before those areas were settled by the Spanish.

"As for culture, they're a very friendly and open people. But also very scared. The Council government has not been kind to them—or to anyone, for that matter. Being in the Coreward Rim, Reunion has a fairly stable economy, far better than planets on the Edge, but nowhere close to the prosperity of the Core planets."

He paused to see if she was absorbing the info, but her impassive expression gave nothing away. So he kept going.

"Family is important on the planet. It's planets like Reunion that have kept the Council—the Twenty, really—from outlawing marriage as an institution. They tried a few times in the past, but many of the planets ignored the edict, and some saw active rebellions. Reunion was one of the latter, and there is a whole portion of the planet's northern hemisphere that is still uninhabitable, the leftover impact of the Guard's orbital bombardment of the rebels."

He saw her mouth open slightly as if she wanted to ask something, so he paused again. She opened and closed her mouth a few times, debating something with herself. Finally, she met his gaze. "And what about the women?"

Tyrus did not answer immediately. The question was extremely open-ended, and there were a variety of answers that he could think of —and a whole host of others he couldn't—that were sure to get him in trouble. But in the end, he decided to continue with his policy of open honesty, at least in dealing with Domitia Felix.

"It depends on what you're asking. The women there are as educated as the men, on average. But they tend to play more traditional roles, if you will: teachers, homemakers, cooks, raising children, and the like. When I first arrived, I expected them to be unhappy as a result, and some certainly were. But on the whole, they actually seemed just as happy as the women I encountered in the Core worlds. I never could figure out why that was, and I was only on the planet a short time before my mission was complete, and I was called to another planet."

She nodded slowly, clearly considering his words. "Thank you," she said simply. "I am now more informed than I was at the beginning of this conversation. Such knowledge will help if we are ever to go to war with the colonies. Are you going to eat more of your paella?"

The abrupt change in topic took him by surprise, and he looked down at the angry red dish in front of him. Even the scent was making his eyes water. "Uh. I must admit it is altogether too spicy for me. Maybe once I've acclimated better to the local cuisine, I will be able to eat more of it, but today, I believe the food has bested me."

Another small hint of a smile graced her full lips, but it disappeared quickly. "That is why I sent a message to the server asking him to have the cooks prepare an alternative dish for you." She nodded to someone behind Tyrus, and their server appeared as if by magic, wordlessly taking away his plate of paella and replacing it with what looked like a sandwich, though he couldn't identify the meat, and there were sliced hot peppers instead of cheese.

"Thank you," he told her as he lifted one half of the sandwich and took a tentative bite. It was spicy, but nowhere near the heat of the paella.

They said little more for the rest of the meal, and afterward, she led him to the gymnasium, where Centurion Parn was waiting for them. There, Tyrus learned that one of the favorite activities of all Martians was to spar, with full contact and full consequences.

CHAPTER 2

One Week Later; October 9, 731 P.D.

"Try again."

Doctor Jolee Sinema frowned and turned to face the man who had spoken. He was of medium height with a bald head and a hawkish nose, upon which perched old-style reading glasses. He wore a business suit that was slightly frayed at the joints and cuffs, battered and worn, like so many things in Perth.

"As I've explained to you, Factor Lamkin, I have already administered multiple doses of the drug. And none have so much as stirred the Majko from her coma. To administer more would be—"

"I don't care!" the man snapped, looking down at the still form of the aged Majko, lying in her hospital bed next to Jinny Ambrosa. The older woman's hand still rested on Ambrosa's wrist, taped firmly in place there per the woman's instructions. "Try again. We must have our Majko back. The Speaker of the House is insisting on a meeting with her. Can you imagine what will happen if we admit that she is comatose at this juncture? Do you understand the urgency?"

The man's demanding and condescending tone put Jolee's hackles up. "Of course I do!" she retorted. She didn't, really. Jolee had long ignored politics, content to focus all of her mental faculties on medicine, leaving that dirtier social science to the Majko and her small Council of Factors, like this man. About all she understood that the Speaker of the House was the Majko's equivalent among the speakers who lived in Sydney.

Now, the Council of Factors was panicking. The Majko had lain next to Ambrosa for the better part of three weeks, not moving and making no sign that she was even still alive save for her brain activity, which fluctuated madly on the doctor's monitors.

"The Majko left very specific instructions," Jolee said, turning to glare at Lamkin. "Go back and tell the Council of Factors that I will *not* risk her life further just because the lot of you have gotten nervous!"

The man frowned. "We'll see about that." He turned and stormed out of the room, leaving Jolee alone with her own fears and doubts.

"Why would I let you through to corrupt my daughter and turn her against me?" the man asked with a sneer. He was shorter than the Majko and strangely wore a white lab coat rather than the plain clothing the other guardians had worn in the dreamscape. But, of course, she knew enough of Jinny's story to know that her father, Frank Ambrosa, had been a top scientific advisor to the Council government. *And* that he had been the one to engineer in Jinny her extraordinary powers.

The Majko stood a couple of meters away from Frank Ambrosa now on a plane of stark white tile—no cozy campfire this time. The sky was also a featureless white, as if they were both inside a giant laboratory clean room. And maybe that was exactly what it was.

She considered her response carefully. She had gotten through a few more doors after Ryder. One had been Jinny's mother, Virginia, who had only let her through after she had appealed—mother to mother—to the woman's worry for her daughter's well-being.

Another, a girl named Sakura, had almost not let her through, until the Majko had ferreted out the girl's death by suicide and convinced her that Jinny had never healed from the event and that only by letting the Majko through could she help her friend start to mend.

But Frank Ambrosa was proving to be a much bigger challenge, just as Ryder had said he would be.

"I don't intend to turn her against you," she replied cautiously. "I'm only here to save her, which, as her father, I would think—"

"You know nothing," he interrupted with a dismissive wave. "You think I care about Jinny's sanity? She's only in this situation because she refused to listen to me for all these years. I could have helped her a hundred times over if the stupid girl hadn't cut me out of her life for some imagined slight."

Like killing her mother, the Majko thought wryly. Frank was clearly in denial about the evil things he'd done to his family. But instead of voicing a direct challenge, she chose another tact. "If you choose not to help her now, as you tried to so many times before, she'll never leave this state."

He laughed. "So what? Let her stay like this. She did it to herself!"

Obviously, this man wasn't going to respond to any plea for sympathy for his daughter's plight. Nor could the Majko simply appeal to his ego by insisting he help her just to prove himself right that Jinny should have accepted his help before.

"But how will you learn about the full extent of her abilities if you can't talk to her?" she insisted, trying to push on his curiosity as a scientist.

He shook his head and smiled wickedly. "I don't need her *mind,* you idiot woman! I only need her blood. Jinny was weak. My next creation will be far more resilient, able to take full advantage of the wonderful gift I give him. It was a mistake to use a stupid little girl as my first subject anyway."

Okay, thought the Majko. *He's stubborn and a blatant chauvinist. This may take a while.*

CHAPTER 3

"Doctor." The insistent voice of one of her orderlies broke into Jolee's silent vigil by the Majko's bed. She looked up at the man, whose worry was evident on his face.

"Yes, James?"

"It's Factor Lamkin," the man replied. "He's on his way up with a formal order from the Council of Factors to sever the Majko's connection to Reader Ambrosa. And then to try again to bring her out of her coma."

Jolee sighed. It had been four days since Lamkin's last visit, and she should have been grateful that the man had given them that long. But the Majko was still showing no signs of waking up.

She looked at James. "Are the Majko's personal guards still in the hall?" she asked quickly.

"Yes, Doctor, but what can they do? They won't defy an order from the factors."

"Tell them to *stall* the factor. Then come back, and bring Carl and Jessica with you."

Five minutes later, Factor Jurgen Lamkin was yelling in the doctor's face.

"What do you mean, you lost them?" he screamed for the third time.

"As I told you, Factor, when I returned to the room, they were just—"

"Gone! Yes, you've said that. But how could you lose the Majko with her guards just outside? You're either a raging incompetent, or you're hiding them so that you don't have to follow the Council of Factor's orders. And I choose to believe the latter."

Jolee pretended to look offended, which wasn't actually too hard in the face of this blowhard. "Sir, I assure you that I have done no such thing. You are welcome to search the hospital, as I will also be doing."

Lamkin stepped forward and glared over his glasses at her, shoving a skinny finger in her face. "Oh, I *will* search the hospital, Doctor. And when I find the Majko, I will have you arrested for kidnapping our leader. Not even she will be able to defend you when she wakes up!" He didn't wait for her reply but spun and left the room, slamming the door.

It opened a moment later, and James stepped through, shutting it softly behind him.

"It's done?" Jolee asked.

He nodded. "I thought we were going to sever the connection a couple of times, moving them so quickly down the halls." He looked over at the now *single* empty bed that occupied the room. Jinny Ambrosa and the Majko were sharing the other bed so as to better fit down the halls and into the elevator. James and the other orderlies Jolee had called had taken the two comatose readers down the freight elevator even as Factor Lamkin had ridden the passenger elevator up to their floor. The two comatose women were now stashed in a random storage room in the hospital's expansive basement.

"Good," she said. "That should buy us some time. Go down and stay with them, and get them hooked back up to the monitors. But first, tell Carl and Jessica to make themselves scarce. The constables will be here soon, and it would be better if they're not around to answer any questions."

James nodded, then left the room the way he'd come.

Jolee sighed. She had just blatantly broken the law, and she wasn't entirely sure she'd done the right thing. Perhaps removing the Majko's physical connection with Ambrosa *would* rouse her from her coma. But somehow, she doubted that. Rather, she was afraid that doing so would lose *both* readers forever. She couldn't let that happen.

It had felt like hours, maybe even days, and Frank Ambrosa was no closer to letting the Majko through his door than he had been when she'd started. Multiple times she had tried appealing to him as a parent (that never got far), playing to his own arrogance (that got only slightly further), and trying to convince him that waking Jinny would be a step forward for his science. He just laughed at that one every time. She'd tried several more tactics, but none got her anywhere.

She'd long since stopped standing, sitting instead on the stark white floor, even though it allowed him to glower down at her from a position of power. Her old legs simply couldn't support her weight for that long, even in a dream world where they didn't actually exist except in her own mind and perceptions.

But now her legs were cramping from the awkward sitting position on the hard ground. After he rebuffed her latest attempt to convince him, she paused and stretched. Then, she pushed herself back up to her feet. And in that very moment, as she stood, she saw something flash in Frank Ambrosa's eyes.

Fear.

It was gone almost before she could register it, but she was nearly certain she had seen fear. And it hadn't been from anything she'd said but from her simple action of standing up.

Could it really be that simple? she thought in utter disbelief. Was this man really that similar to the serial killer Hendrix?

She took a single step toward him. He flinched. That was when she knew she had him.

The Majko walked right up to Frank Ambrosa, a man roughly half her age, and slapped him hard across the face.

He yelped and took a step back, both hands flying up to hold the cheek she'd hit. Then the Majko did something she hadn't done in anger since she'd been a young girl on the schoolyard. She made a fist.

The next blow was a solid punch to the man's gut—at least as solid as a near-octogenarian could deliver. But it had the desired effect. Frank hit the ground, clutching his stomach in pain.

"I'm going through that door right now, and you will do nothing to stop me," she growled, standing over him. "Understood?"

The man said nothing, tears streaming down his face, his expression a rictus of hate and shame. But after a moment, he nodded.

I guess he can't handle women who fight back, just like Hendrix, she thought with a growing disdain. If only Virginia had had the strength to truly stand up to the man, Jinny's mother might still be alive, and Jinny's life may have been quite different.

Now, with Frank whimpering on the ground, the Majko calmly turned her back on him and walked up to the door, this one stark white and perfectly clean, just like the rest of the plane they were on. It opened at her touch, and she stepped through.

Just before she left, she heard Frank say in a low voice, "It doesn't matter. You'll never get by *him*."

"Doctor, this will go far easier for you if you just tell us where you've hidden the Majko and Reader Ambrosa." The constable detective's voice was friendly, even conspiratorial. But Jolee knew when she was being played. The red face of Factor Lamkin behind the man offset any fake friendliness the detective tried to show her. They weren't here as her friends; they were out for her blood.

"I'm sure I have no idea where they are," she replied, parroting the same words she'd already told everyone who had tried to question her on the topic.

The constable detective sighed and shook his head. In an instant, all friendliness was gone. All this man knew was that she had conspired to hide away his Majko from the Council of Factors, the duly appointed rulers, in the absence of the Majko herself. To him, Sinema was a criminal, nothing more.

"My men are searching this hospital room by room," he said, his voice hard. "They *will* find the two patients, and then I can do nothing for you. Let me know if you change your mind."

Without waiting for a response, he turned heel and began issuing orders to the few men who had remained on the hospital's top floor with them. The hospital was large, the largest on the Australian continent, but Jolee knew that the Majko only had an hour at most before they found her and forcibly separated her from Jinny Ambrosa. At that point, who knew what would happen to the two women?

CHAPTER 4

On the other side of Frank Ambrosa's door, the Majko found herself in a dreamscape unlike any she'd seen thus far. The rest had been almost bland in their appearance, usually centered around one theme with a uniform landscape, the only structure a single door.

But this one was far different. It was a suburban neighborhood, with a tree-lined avenue separating rows of similar cookie-cutter houses in various shades of beige, gray, and tan.

Only one house stood out from the rest. The Majko stood on the sidewalk, facing across the street toward a house that was painted a deep and vibrant blue with a startling red door. Unlike the other homes, which sported simple lawns, this house was surrounded by planters full of verdant flowers of every color, casting a bright and cheerful glow on the otherwise drab neighborhood.

Strange place for an assassin to be waiting, she thought with a frown. From Ryder's comments and even Frank's, plus a few more from Virginia and Sakura, she was pretty sure who she would be facing as the last guardian before she finally—hopefully—found Jinny Ambrosa: Tyrus Tyne.

It made perfect sense. Tyne was Jinny's traveling companion and friend, the man she'd somehow turned from perfectly loyal enacter to a rebel against the Council. The Majko had never met Tyne, but she'd heard the stories of what he did to rescue Jinny in the Crater prison. The little hacker that had come with Jinny to Perth—she called herself the Neon Mouse, of all things—had been quite distressed as she'd recounted how Tyne had practically stormed the prison on his own, killing anyone who came between him and rescuing Jinny.

That Tyne would, therefore, be Jinny's last guardian in the prison of her own mind should have been obvious from the start. The Majko scolded herself for not realizing it much sooner. The big question now was whether or not she could get past the man and open whatever door he guarded. And whether she could do it fast enough. For some reason she couldn't define, she had the overwhelming feeling that the time to reach Jinny was running out.

Hesitating only long enough to gather her nerve and her wits, the Majko walked across the street and up the front walkway of the brightly colored house to meet with a ruthless killer, who himself was likely just as mentally fractured as Jinny Ambrosa and was sworn to protect her against all others, even to her detriment. It would be her hardest challenge yet.

She expected to find the big assassin standing just outside the home's front door, but when she arrived, the porch was deserted. Frowning again, she tried the front door, but it would not budge under even a hard push, and there was no handle on this side, just as none of the other doors had had any outer hardware to open them.

Confused, she stood there for several moments. Then, almost timidly, she reached up and knocked on the door.

She didn't have to wait long. The door started to swing inward, and she braced herself to face the two-meter-tall, dark-skinned man who had once been the Council government's most effective killer.

But to her surprise, Tyrus Tyne did not look back at her from inside the door. Instead, she faced a smiling man with light skin, thick brown hair, and hazel eyes. He was tall but nowhere near Tyne's height. To her further surprise, he stepped aside and gestured for her to enter.

She stepped through the door cautiously, not taking her eyes off the man. "Please, have a seat in the living room," he said in a friendly voice, motioning toward a couch in a reasonably large room just to the left of the entryway.

Not knowing how else to respond, she did as indicated, and he took a seat facing her in a comfortable-looking armchair.

"You're the Majko?" he asked simply, crossing one leg over the other and regarding her with a relaxed expression.

"I am," she said, trying to keep confusion out of her voice. "And you are?"

He smiled. "Oh, you were probably expecting Tyrus. Is that right?"

She nodded slowly.

He shrugged. "Well, believe it or not, Tyrus isn't here. He hasn't been around here much since he rescued Jinny from prison. Most of the new ones aren't. Didn't you notice that everyone you've met here is either dead or long gone from Jinny's life?"

That answered one question that had lingered with the Majko throughout her journey in Jinny Ambrosa's subconsciousness. She had expected to encounter Tyne and the man called Riggs at some point—both of them were important in the young reader's life—but never had. Apparently, Jinny had decided that they no longer belonged in this prison of the mind—something to do with their being still alive outside of it. Or maybe she had never read them? No, that wouldn't make sense.

"Who are you?" she asked again.

The man cocked his head and looked amused. "I'm Alan Daily." She looked at him in confusion. Then it came to her. Jinny had mentioned an Alan Daily. He was a cop, or the Council equivalent—a guardsman, that was it! And he'd somehow helped her get off Nova Tejas but then died at Tyrus Tyne's hand before they got far.

More confusion filled her. Alan Daily had sounded like little more than a minor player in Jinny's story in all of the news reports and biographies they'd done on her when she, Tyne, Riggs, and Jynx had all arrived on Earth. But apparently, he'd been something more.

"Where is your door?" the Majko asked, deciding she was done with anything but the direct approach with any of these dreamscape phantoms. She still felt a strong nagging that her time was limited.

Alan shrugged. "It's here, but you won't be getting near it. Sorry."

He didn't elaborate, so she leaned forward and fixed him with her gaze, putting all her years of authority into her next question.

"Why do you want to stop me from saving Jinny?"

He looked surprised at the question and shook his head slowly. "No. You misunderstand, ma'am. I'm not here to stop you from saving Jinny. I'm here to stop you from killing her."

Now, it was her turn to be surprised. She sat back on the couch and regarded him. "I'm not here to kill her, I assure you."

Alan shrugged again. "Oh, I have no doubt that that's not why you *think* you're here. I believe you truly do want to help her, though your reasons for doing so are at least partially selfish. No, you have relatively good intentions. But unfortunately, that doesn't change the fact that letting you through to her will kill her."

"How?"

He leaned forward now. "Tell me, how many doors did you have to come through to get to this point?"

The question confused her, mainly because she really had no idea how to answer it. Time and numbers had lost meaning in this place, and she legitimately couldn't fathom the count or even an approximation.

"Quite a few," she answered carefully.

"And why do you think the doors were there in the first place?"

This she *had* given quite a bit of thought to since first arriving in Jinny's dreamscape so many hours—days, weeks, years?—ago. And Alan Daily seemed earnest, so she decided to give him her straight answer.

"They've been constructed by the fractured remnants of the memories of others whom Jinny has read in her lifetime. You each built your doors to keep her from escaping so that you can live on in her split personality."

It sounded clinical, even to her ears, but Alan didn't seem to take offense either at her language or her accusation.

"Wrong," he said with another smile. "Not a bad guess, but completely wrong. *We* didn't build these doors." He leaned forward further, and his smile disappeared. "Jinny did."

The Majko shook her head. That made no sense. "I don't believe you."

His smile returned, sadder this time. "It's the truth, whether you believe it or not. These doors, even this house"—he gestured to encompass the dwelling in which they sat—"were all built by Jinny herself. She built them as protection against what was happening to her—a way to keep all of us separate from her consciousness, if you will."

He paused, and when she didn't speak, he continued. "Jinny knew she was going mad—that her personality was, as you put it, splitting. The doors were her last-ditch efforts to separate all of the memories of those she's read from her own consciousness, keeping all of the others in their own separate places, far from her core memories. It was her way of preserving what little sanity she had left when Tyrus rescued her from the prison on Luna."

Now, the Majko was truly confused. It couldn't be, but the earnest way in which Alan delivered the news made her trust that he was telling the truth, at least as he saw it.

"But each person I met was the guardian of their own door. Doesn't that defeat the purpose, giving them control of their own means of separation from Jinny?"

Alan shook his head. "Again, a good guess, but you've read it wrong. The others you met were never the guardians of their doors, just like I'm not the guardian of the last door in this house."

"Then who let me through the doors . . ." She trailed off, the answer coming to her suddenly. "Jinny. It was Jinny herself letting me through, wasn't it?"

He nodded appreciatively. "Now you're getting it. She's been watching you, and she let you through each door when you showed that you were honestly coming to help her. She really liked the way you dealt with Frank, by the way. That guy gives even me the creeps." He shuddered visibly. "And Hendrix . . . well, he's almost as bad."

"But, how? Why?" She wasn't even sure what she was trying to ask, but Alan seemed to get it anyway.

"Like I said, Jinny is protecting herself. She never intended for you to get as far as you did, but when you showed you really were here to help, she decided to let you come all this way so that I could at least explain to you why you can never finish what you started. She felt she owed you that much."

He frowned now. "But she won't let you through the last door. You have to understand that. Because you've opened all the other doors now, that last door is the *only* thing protecting her from the others. And even those with good intentions would destroy her as they subsume her memories and personality with their own."

"But she's in a coma. How can that be better than letting me in?" The Majko was frantically trying to find an answer to this final obstacle, but nothing was presenting itself to her mind.

Alan nodded. "Believe me, if there were any other way, she would take it. But by turning her entire consciousness inward, she had just enough strength to build all of those doors in the first place. Now, she needs to rest so she can attempt to do it again. And under no circumstances can I let you disturb her."

"But I'm here to help." Her mind raced, and still, no answers came. "I can get her out of the coma *and* help her deal with all that's happened to her. I know I can, especially after what I've learned here. I *know* I can make things right."

"Sorry," Alan said simply, holding out his hands in a placating gesture. "She can't take that risk. And it's partially your fault."

The accusation, delivered in such a matter-of-fact way, with no resentment or anger, surprised her greatly, and it took her a moment to process the words.

"My fault? How?"

He shrugged. "You told her that her powers could save all the readers. And your nephew, Charles, he told her they could also be used to destroy. That she'd either be the savior of the readers on Earth or their undoing. In her fractured state, she lacks control to even choose which one to be. So, she chooses not to be either. If she stays here, she won't have to take that risk, and she won't let you talk her into it."

"But I can help her!" the Majko pleaded.

"And what if you can't?" Alan demanded, his voice suddenly hard. "What if bringing her back to the real world only makes things worse? Do you realize that she has in her head all of the knowledge and training of an alpha? Two alphas, in fact—Tyrus and an even worse one named Collins she read back in the colonies. She also has dozens of killers, including more than one psychopath, rattling around in here. What if, when she wakes up, she does so with all the skill of those alphas and all the morals of men like Hendrix? Could *you* stop her then?"

Knowing that a lie wouldn't help her case, the Majko shook her head.

"That's what I thought." He settled back into the chair, the hardness gone from his face and voice. "And she just can't take that chance. It's safer for everyone if she stays here. Because if she did wake up and start working destruction, she would have only one choice: to use the last bit of her consciousness and willpower—the last bit of her that *is* Jinny Ambrosa—to kill herself before she could do too much damage.

"So, like I said, letting you into where she is would kill her, not save her."

The Majko shook her head emphatically. "But what if she's wrong? What if I *can* save her?" She was pleading now, knowing now that this man, Alan, like all the others, was just a manifestation of Jinny's fractured mind. Maybe she could get through to the woman if she tried hard enough. "Think of all the *good* she could do. Think of all the people she could help!" She wasn't even trying to keep her voice calm. The time for half measures was over; now was the time to throw caution to the wind and do everything she could to reach Jinny.

"She can't take that risk," Alan repeated evenly but with a hint of frustration in his voice. "I'm sorry. *She's* sorry. But it's far safer for everyone involved if she just stays here, where it's safe, with the rest of us on the outside, where we can't hurt her, and she can't hurt you."

Tears started to run down the man's face, and the Majko had a startling realization as to why Alan Daily was the last line of defense in Jinny's troubled mind. She'd been in *love* with the man. And hadn't part of the story been that Tyne had . . .

She loved him, and Tyrus Tyne killed him. Yet she forgave Tyrus. She . . .

And suddenly, it all came together for her.

"What if I can guarantee she won't become the destroyer my nephew worried about? What if I can absolutely prove that she will only use her abilities to help people?"

Alan looked at her through wet eyes but raised his eyebrows slightly. She took this as a sign to continue.

"You're a detective, right? A guardsman?"

He nodded slowly.

"Then you've made a career out of following the evidence, am I right?"

He nodded again but said nothing.

"Okay, so let me present two pieces of hard evidence for you to consider. First . . ." She thought of the brief note that Tyne had sent along with Jinny's medical capsule back to Earth. It had been light on the details, but she could reasonably fill in a few of the blanks. "First, in the prison, when one of the others—I'm guessing Hendrix—tried to get Tyne to kill that guard, Jinny exerted her control just long enough to tell him to stop. Am I right?"

Alan had wiped the tears out of his eyes and was regarding her now with the calm look of a law enforcement professional, evaluating her words carefully. He nodded again but still said nothing.

"Don't you see?" she asked him, her exasperation plain. "She stopped Tyne from killing the man who helped torture her! Even though she could have simply let Hendrix, or Frank, or any number of the others take control and keep her away from the dirty work. But no! She fought to get back to herself and stop Tyne from taking a life that she should have, by all rights, *wanted* him to take. Why did she do that?"

Again, Alan Daily said nothing, but she decided to wait him out this time. Finally, after several long seconds, he spoke slowly. "Because Jinny is a good person. And she wanted to save Tyrus from the guilt of a needless killing on her behalf."

"Right," the Majko said excitedly. He was getting it. Which meant, she hoped, that *Jinny* was getting it. "Like you said," she continued, "Jinny is a good person. No matter who else is in her head with her or what control they have over her, she is a *good* person. She proved that in the prison. You can't dispute that." He could; it was a subjective argument. But she was really hoping he *wouldn't*.

To her relief, he nodded. "Jinny is a good person, but she can't guarantee she will always have that kind of control. It took everything she had to break free of the fog just long enough to stop Tyrus from killing that guard. There's no guarantee she'll be able to do that the next time. Sorry, but *you* can't dispute that."

The Majko shook her head and smiled. "Actually, I can. I can dispute it with my second piece of evidence. This conversation."

She was gratified to see Alan look momentarily confused, but then his face became impassive, and he motioned for her to continue.

"Alan Daily is dead." She saw him wince but pushed onward. "You are here only as a manifestation of the memories she read from him. Do you argue with that?"

He frowned but stayed silent. She took that as assent to her point.

"And if Alan Daily is dead, and none of the others are here either, and—as you yourself said—it was really Jinny herself choosing to let me through those doors, then that means that I am talking to *Jinny* right now. Sure, she may use you as her latest manifestation to face me, but this entire time, through all of the others, I've been talking to her."

She decided to keep going before Alan—or Jinny, really—could argue with her "Let's recap. In the course of the last few hours, or maybe days, or longer, I have spoken to dozens of killers, including one very unhinged serial killer and Jinny's own father, who murdered her mother. And do you know what every single one of those killers had in common?" Again, she didn't wait for him to answer. "They left me alone. I'm a seventy-seven-year-old woman. Any one of them could have easily overpowered me and kept me from going through the next door or even somehow killed me in this dream and driven me entirely from Jinny's mind. But they *didn't*! And why? Because Jinny stopped them!"

"So you're saying that she maintained just enough of herself to keep you safe on your journey here?" The guardsman's voice betrayed no emotion. She couldn't tell if he was incredulous or agreeing with her.

"No, I'm saying she maintained *all* of herself that really mattered: her moral code."

Alan frowned.

"No! You can't. It might kill them both!" Jolee's voice was much shriller than she could ever remember it being. The constable detective—his name was Ghisemmi—had led her down to the basement and straight to the room where she'd had the orderlies hide the Majko and Reader Ambrosa. It had taken them only forty-eight minutes to find the hidden patients. She'd been lucky it had even taken that long.

Now, inside the room, Factor Jurgen Lamkin was red-faced and indignant.

"Remove that woman!" he cried, pointing at Jolee.

Ghisemmi shook his head. "Every doctor and nurse I've spoken to says that only Doctor Sinema can safely bring the Majko out of her coma. None of the others are even willing to try."

"But she's the reason they're down here in the first place!" Lamkin sputtered.

The constable detective was unmoved. He turned to Jolee. "Doctor Sinema. We need you to cooperate. Otherwise, one of my men will be forced to do what they can to awaken the Majko, starting with separating her touch from Reader Ambrosa's."

Jolee looked in desperation at the two women piled together on the narrow bed, the Majko's hand still taped to Ambrosa's wrist, where it had been for the last three and a half weeks. Both women were thin and gaunt. Even with the IV-fed diets, they were losing body mass fast.

"I can't," Jolee almost whispered in response to the constable's request. "She left very specific instructions that I not remove her touch for any reason. It will undermine everything she's trying to do. You *must* listen to me."

Ghisemmi frowned. "I'm sorry, Doctor." His eyes pleaded with her, though his voice remained hard. "It's the only way. Please. You have a much better chance to keep both women alive if you help us."

Jolee was silent for a long moment. Her resolve hardened, and she was about to rebuff the man again. But then, she had a thought.

Turning to one of the nurses who had followed them into the room, she said, "Carol, please get me 50 ccs of DPM." It wasn't the right drug, really, but it would buy her some time. She could only hope it would be enough to let the Majko finish what she'd gone in there to do. At best, the woman would only have two to three more hours to do it.

"Don't you see," the Majko pleaded with the apparition of Alan Daily, whom she now *knew* was merely a mask that Jinny Ambrosa wore. So really, she was pleading with the extraordinary young reader. "Jinny has been struggling with the nightmares for months, well before she even met you. Possibly years. And in that time she has done exactly *zero* things that would go against her moral code. On the contrary, she has become the one shining hope for a galaxy about to go to war."

"But what if she's the one who plunges them *into* war?" Alan asked in a low voice. "What if she succumbs at long last to the memories in her head, and the split is too much for her? She's only read a few people since coming to Earth, but it's enough. If she took what she knows back to the Council, they'd be unstoppable."

The Majko shook her head emphatically. "How? She was at the lowest point of her life in that prison cell. She'd been tortured, physically and mentally, and left without hope. The memories *had* taken over, for all intents and purposes. Yet she still retained enough of herself to stop Tyrus from killing that guard. And enough after that to put herself into this coma in the hopes of saving everyone around her." That last part was a hunch. "Tell me those aren't the actions of a moral woman in control of herself."

"But she put herself in the coma because she *knew* she couldn't maintain that control any longer," he said, confirming her hunch.

"No. Look around you. Look at this carefully constructed universe she's created to keep herself from being awoken for the wrong reasons. Look at all she's done to still protect her friends and the rest of humanity, even after all that has been done to her. That *proves* she is still in control. And if we take her out of this coma, she won't break, especially not with me and the other readers there to help her."

"But what if she does?" Alan's voice cracked now, and tears came back to his eyes. Then those eyes slowly changed color from hazel to a deep brown.

"But what if she doesn't? And what if she is the only hope we have to stop the war, or at least win it? How many more will die if she doesn't wake up?"

She couldn't explain why she felt so strongly that Jinny was the key to freedom for the readers and other enhanced on Earth, or why she was the only one who could stop the Four Worlds from being pulled into slavery. It didn't make a whole lot of logical sense. Sure, the young reader's special abilities spoke of a power that could topple governments if used the right way, but a lot would have to happen to get to that point. Regardless, the Majko had known from the first time she'd seen Jinny Ambrosa on the news, just a week after the girl had arrived on Earth, that she was the key. She knew it as much as she knew her own name, even if she couldn't explain how.

The Majko leaned forward on the couch and stared into Daily's eyes—no, not *his* eyes. "Jinny, I know you're in there, and I know you're scared. So am I. But you *must* wake up!"

Suddenly, Alan Daily was gone. In his place was a barely recognizable young blond woman with stringy hair and dull brown eyes ringed in sunken shadows. Her whole face was gaunt. She wore an old-fashioned straitjacket, her arms tied behind her in an archaic way that hadn't been used in human space for over a thousand years but still managed to be the popular way to depict the insane and unstable.

This is how she sees herself now, the Majko realized. *As a hopeless, worthless, insanely dangerous person. Oh, my dear.*

"Jinny," she said softly, putting as much warmth as she could into her tone. "I can help you, Jinny. I promise I can. But I need you to wake up with me now."

The young woman started rocking back and forth on the couch, her feet drawn up under her, refusing to meet the Majko's gaze.

"Please, Jinny. Please wake up."

"What if you're wrong?" she asked in a whisper so quiet that the older woman had to strain to hear even from less than two meters away. "What if I kill them all? You can't know I won't."

The Majko sighed and shook her head. "Jinny . . . you're right," she admitted. "I can't *know* that you won't do harm. But I *do* know that we stand a much better chance with you than without you. All of us. Your friends on Mars, those you left behind in the colonial rebellion, the enhanced here in Australia, and every other person in the Four Worlds. We all need you.

"Without you, we're almost sure to lose. But with you . . . With you, we just might stand a chance. And that's a risk I'm willing to take, because the reward is so much greater. How about it, Jinny? Will you take a chance with me?"

She reached out her hand toward the younger woman, who finally looked up at her, a glimmer of hope in her eyes. "And the nightmares? What if the nightmares come back?"

"We'll attack them together," the Majko promised, smiling at her. "I'll be with you every step of the way."

Slowly, Jinny shifted arms forward, the straitjacket releasing its hold on them. Hesitantly, she pulled back one of the sleeves, reached her hand out, and put it gently in the Majko's outstretched hand.

Constable Detective Ghisemmi sighed loudly and shook his head. "Constable Peters. Please remove Doctor Sinema from the room."

Jolee felt her heart sink. The drug she'd given the Majko had quickened the woman's heartbeat, making it appear on the monitors that she might wake up soon, but that was all it had done. It had been a desperate ploy to buy the old woman a few more hours on her mission, but it was over now.

"No, Constable Detective," she said in surrender. "I'm ready to wake her up now—for real."

The man shook his head. "I'm sorry, Doctor. I just don't think I can trust you. I . . ."

He trailed off, looking past her at something. Jolee whirled around to the bed that bore the two comatose readers. The Majko was stirring. And then, a groan. From Ambrosa!

"I'm sorry, Doctor. It appears I misjudged you," Ghisemmi said in an awed whisper.

Jolee rushed to the side of the bed and held the Majko's wrist in her own hand, feeling for a pulse through the thin rubber gloves she wore.

"My Majko, can you hear me?" she asked.

"Of course I can hear you," the old woman said, sounding mildly cross. She started coughing, and one of the nurses rushed forward with ice chips. Next to the woman, Reader Ambrosa's eyes also fluttered open, and she looked around as if in disbelief. Another nurse started tending to her. Jolee, hands shaking, reached down and untaped the Majko's hand from Ambrosa's wrist.

When her coughing fit was done and she regained her voice, the Majko looked back at Jolee. "Doctor, can you explain why we appear to be in a storage closet?"

She smiled for the first time in three weeks. "It's a long story, my Majko. But I promise to tell you all of it."

CHAPTER 5

Four Days Later; October 17, 731 P.D.

Creighton Horvath, Assembly speaker and secret member of the ruling cabal known as the Twenty, read the latest report on Project Epsilon and frowned. Doctor Hiroto Takahashi, the project head since the disappearance of Frank Ambrosa, had promised to deliver two million ready-made enacters within one year, and Creighton had made sure the man understood that he and the 'Council' expected the first million within six months. Now, three months later, the program had only delivered three hundred *thousand*. It wasn't looking good for the doctor to hit his required milestones in time.

Epsilon had been created by Frank Ambrosa under the direction of the Council government with one goal: create an army by transforming regular unenhanced citizens of the 47 Colonies into loyal enacters via specially engineered food and water additives.

For a while, it had appeared successful, managing to transform several hundred thousand people across the nine worlds where it had been tested. But then, a rash of suicides on those same planets led to the program being exposed in those blasted Revelations.

The Revelations still rankled Creighton. He'd known Kendra Siefred well. He'd even been the one to recommend her to the Keeper as a member of the Twenty. That she had betrayed the Twenty and shared their secrets—the death of the true Council generations before, the habitability of the Four Worlds, the secret Council Navy, and Project Epsilon—felt to him like a personal betrayal as much as one to her nation.

Worse, the so-called Revelations had forced them to make changes to Project Epsilon, further prompted by Admiral Chen's reports that the newly created enacters were often passively resisting their new situation. Enacters might not be able to disobey direct orders—with some notable exceptions such as the cursed Alpha Tyrus Tyne—but they could resist in other ways. Having to order your warship's crew to bathe and do other small things was not conducive to a navy's efficiency or morale.

Still, they'd managed to recover, shifting Epsilon testing to other planets and areas and pressing forward. Even without Frank Ambrosa, who had fled after the Revelations alleged he'd performed illegal genetic experiments on his own daughter, they'd managed to create a total thus far of 517,400 enacters already shipped to the secret naval base at Delta 3. With Chen's officers—all born enacters—that left another half million still needed in order to fully crew the Council Navy. But they'd been optimistic.

Now, however, it seemed impossible that Hiroto Takahashi and Project Epsilon would meet their deadlines. It meant they would have to delay the invasion of the Four Worlds, not-so-tentatively scheduled for early in the next year. Either that, or they'd have to go in with less than their full naval force, which was *not* something Creighton thought would be even remotely wise. Unfortunately, from the way Keeper Ian Petrov was talking these days, the man would almost certainly go for the second option.

Creighton sat back in his chair and let out a long sigh, turning to look out his ten-centimeter-thick reinforced window, which still managed to give him a stunning and sharp view of the New Brussels skyline. The capital city of the 47 Colonies, located on a planet of the same name, was home to a billion people and was the single largest city in human space. At night, it was an incredible sight. The white, green, and red flashes of hovercars zipped in lines between towering buildings that rose in some cases two full kilometers into the sky and were themselves ablaze in lights.

Those kinds of building heights wouldn't even be possible without counter-grav technology, and even then, they were altogether unnecessary. One thing the colonies *didn't* lack was usable land. Even on the capital planet, there was enough open space to build dozens of cities of the same size as New Brussels.

No, the towering skyscrapers were not *necessary* but were rather monuments to human ingenuity—and pride, if Creighton was being honest with himself. Probably more of the latter, in fact. And as he gazed out on their heights from his own astoundingly high office on the 258th floor of Assembly Tower, he worried that soon it might all come crashing down.

They'd known for decades that the enhanced bloodlines were weakening at an exponential rate, but they'd first suspected it over a century ago. What had then seemed a distant hypothetical to the members of the Twenty, those who truly ruled the 47 Colonies in the name of a nonexistent Council, was now a very real problem for Creighton and his associates.

Every day, it seemed, they got reports of new instances of enacters disobeying orders given to them in the name of the Council. Fifty years before, even twenty-five, that would have been unthinkable. Now, it was becoming increasingly commonplace. Some of the members of the Twenty thought it had all started with Tyrus Tyne. But Creighton knew better. As part of the Keeper's innermost circle, he knew the truth: they'd started getting reports of disobedient actors fully three years ago. They had been extremely rare back then and, therefore, easy to write off as mistakes or outliers, even to suppress the news of them altogether. But in the last year alone, hundreds of new cases of enacter disobedience had sprung up, including an astounding number among even the loyal Guard in that rebellion on Panamar just four months before.

Creighton knew it was only going to get worse. All of the enhanced skills were wearing thin. A secret report from the Reader Corps leadership noted that the newest inductees in the Academy could only read eight hours of a subject's memories on average, making them almost worthless for the mission the Twenty used them for. Likewise, it was now taking newer blenders up to two *weeks* to change their appearance enough to truly mimic another human being.

And speakers like him . . .

When Creighton entered the Speaker Academy at the age of five years old, he had already known six languages fluently. By the end of his first year there, he knew twenty-two and could perfectly mimic dozens of accents and local affectations of speech. But even the young speakers who worked on his staff now knew less than that. What was worse, they were starting to fall short of the most important skill a speaker could have: mimicking individual speech patterns.

Creighton remembered the first time he had seen that particular skill set at work. It had been in his third-year lessons at the Academy when he was only seven years old. They'd been shown a live broadcast from a Guard holding cell on the other side of the planet, where a man suspected of committing two murders was being interrogated. Both murders had happened months before, making readers almost useless in ascertaining the man's guilt. So the Guard had sent in a speaker.

The speaker had been a man who looked unassuming. He had reportedly watched a few hours of vids of the suspect talking to investigators and a few more hours from the man's social media profile. That had given him enough to do what needed to be done.

The speaker sat down across from the suspect and smiled at him. He didn't start by asking him any real questions; instead, he started talking to him about his hometown and his upbringing. As he did so, the speaker perfectly mimicked the man's accent and his speech patterns, sharing a few anecdotes that would have only made sense to someone from the same corner of Osiris as the suspect, and even shared a few jokes that young Creighton hadn't been able to understand, but the suspect certainly had. Within just fifteen minutes, the suspect and the speaker were trading banter and laughing uproariously with each other. Ten minutes later, the suspect made a full confession, delivered in a conspiratorial fashion as if the speaker were an old and trusted friend rather than his interrogator.

The man had seemed genuinely surprised when the three guardsmen burst into the room and took him away as soon as he finished telling the speaker all about strangling the two women. It was as if he'd forgotten where he was and had really thought he was just chatting with a confidant rather than sitting in a Guard station.

From that day forward, young Creighton Horvath had studied everything he could on how speakers could use their special gifts to manipulate those around them. Except while many speakers used those skills to settle simple disputes in the courts, reassure local citizens angry at government actions, or help the Guard find the truth in criminal investigations, Creighton had always had his eyes on a larger prize.

Within one year of graduating from the Speaker Academy on his home planet of Nova Tejas, he had managed to land a job as a junior speechwriter for the planetary prefect. The woman he worked for was not a speaker herself but an enacter—prefects *had* to be enacters by law so that they would never guide their planets in a way not in keeping with the Council's commands. He did so well at his job, even writing a speech that had, according to later polls, helped the planet's public almost completely forget that the same prefect had been caught in bed with a man half her age, who most definitely wasn't her husband, on two separate occasions.

After that, the prefect had made him her chief speechwriter, an unheard-of position for a then twenty-year-old. And within a year after that, she had made him her press secretary. No longer in the background writing speeches for someone else, he was now in front of the press core *and* the public on an almost daily basis, and he quickly had them all eating out of his hand.

It took only a few years for the Council—or so he thought—to notice him and bring him to New Brussels, where they made him the junior Assembly representative for Nova Tejas. From there, his meteoric rise continued, as he was able to make angry crowds almost swoon within minutes and even helped the Assembly cover up several scandals by simply distracting the public to other topics.

It took him three decades to rise to become one of the most influential Assembly Speakers, chairman of three different important committees, and a leading speech maker for the carefully choreographed public Assembly meetings. By that time, he was also a respected voice *within* the Assembly, drawing several to his pet causes in the unbroadcasted secret meetings where all the real decisions were made.

That was when Ian Petrov, the top Assembly speaker, also known as the Keeper, and supposedly the only man who knew the Council's identities and spoke directly with its members, reached out to him and invited him to a private lunch. In that meeting, Creighton had his eyes opened to the *true* nature of power in the 47 Colonies. From that day forward, he was a member of the Twenty, the actual ruling body of human space.

Even back then, his rapid rise had been impressive, but by today's standards, it would have been downright impossible. New incoming speakers to the Assembly lacked the polish of the older members by a large margin and often struggled to sway the public to their way of thinking. That, coupled with the increasing disobedience of the enacters and the reduced capabilities of the readers and blenders, was cause for panic. The enhanced bloodlines had grown too weak over the centuries. But the Twenty relied on the enhanced to maintain power; without them, anything could happen. It would be pure chaos across the 47 Colonies and make the debacle at Panamar look like only the opening act.

Worse, on top of everything, Creighton was now entirely certain that Ian Petrov, his longtime friend, mentor, and leader, was insane. The man had become increasingly secretive and erratic, even by the standards of the Twenty, and Creighton had caught some of the newer cabal members whispering that new leadership may be needed.

Unfortunately, removing a Keeper from power was next to impossible. So rarely had it ever been done that there weren't even reliable historical records to guide them. No, Creighton needed Petrov to stay in power, at least to get them through the current crisis and in control of the Four Worlds and the undiluted enhanced bloodlines on Earth. Then, he could quietly find a way to remove Petrov and install new leadership—his leadership.

He stared far down at the street below as the lights of a single hovercar turned from the line of hundreds of others and into the no-fly zone established around Assembly Tower. The mere fact that the car wasn't immediately blown out of the sky by the automated defenses was enough proof that the driver had transmitted the proper clearance codes. The car made its way slowly through a corridor from which, despite it being invisible to the naked eye, even a meter's deviation would result in the vehicle's instant destruction.

Creighton lost sight of it when it circled around the side of the building to one of the parking bays. Then he checked his watch. Five minutes later, at *exactly* the appointed time, his office door chime rang.

"Open," he said to his office AI, and the door dutifully slid open to admit a striking woman with a shock of bright red hair. She wore a black dress that could best be described as 'slinky' and spiked high heels that accentuated her long legs.

Lara Owens winked at him from the doorway and then looked back out into the antechamber. "Don't wait up," she purred at Creighton's assistant, who threw her a glance of disapproval before Lara entered and shut the door in the other woman's face.

For two years now, Lara Owens had visited Creighton three nights a week in his office and sometimes on the weekends at his private suites. She always did so wearing attractive clothing and was often seen coming and going in a state of mild inebriation. Whenever she left his presence, her clothes and hair were always just slightly more disheveled than when she'd arrived.

It was the worst-kept secret in Assembly Tower that Creighton and Owens were having a torrid love affair. Since Creighton was a lifelong bachelor, it wasn't exactly a scandal, except that Lara was forty years his junior, *and* she happened to be a midlevel staffer in the Keeper's office. No one really minded, though they all whispered about it where they thought Creighton couldn't hear, and even Petrov himself would often make oblique little comments to rib him for sleeping with one of his staff.

It gave them all a little pleasure to be 'in the know' about the personal life of one of the most influential people in the 47 Colonies. But it gave Creighton even greater pleasure to know that they were all wrong.

"I don't think Kim likes me," Lara said as she kicked off the spiked heels and settled into an overstuffed leather chair against one wall of the office, curling her bare legs underneath her as she did.

"Don't take it too personally," Creighton said, moving out from behind his desk and walking over to the identical chair next to hers. "She's secretly a monogamist—thinks I should have settled down with one woman a long time ago. Doesn't really like that I'm supposedly sleeping with you and two other women on a regular basis."

"And how many of those affairs are actually real?" Lara asked with a little smile.

"That, my dear, is none of your business."

She shrugged as if to say that she really didn't care what he did with his personal life, which was probably true. "I do have to say, I'm surprised you employ a monogamist at all. That's one step away from *religion*."

He laughed lightly. "What can I say? She's the only assistant I've ever had that I didn't want to murder after six months. She keeps my calendar perfectly, plays an excellent gatekeeper, and even gets my coffee right every time. On top of that, she has two PhDs, so she actually knows her stuff. Quite frankly, she's wasted here, but I think she likes the proximity to power, so I let her stick around."

Lara shrugged again.

"What do you have for me tonight?" he asked her, moving the conversation along.

"He's still having daily conferences with Admiral Chen," she reported, her tone all professional now. "And I still haven't been able to get an ear in the room—he's obsessive about having his office swept for listening devices three or four times a day—but I think he's getting antsy about launching the invasion."

This wasn't exactly news to Creighton, but he nodded along. "Anxious enough that he might launch the attack on the Four Worlds early?"

She frowned. "Two days ago, I would have probably said no. But he made a comment yesterday that has me wondering."

"What was it? Word for word, please."

Lara stopped and thought for a moment, though he knew she really didn't have to. Lara had an eidetic memory but seemed to have learned long ago that demonstrating her instant and perfect recall tended to make others uncomfortable. Instead, she always pretended to have to take a moment to remember the details.

"He said, 'Rolston had better not complain about getting me those four Guard Space Force squadrons.' It was practically under his breath, but some of us heard. He said it during a discussion about pirate activity near Nea Mykonos."

"Hmm. That could mean anything. In fact, it's probably more having to do with the false flag operation Chen's been urging him to allow for the last several months."

Lara cocked her head to one side. "The coming out party for the Council Navy?"

Creighton nodded. "Chen wants to get some real combat experience for her people, something I fully support. But your boss has been reticent to expose the Navy's existence to the public—he thinks doing so will make them wonder what other parts of the Revelations might be true."

The woman frowned. "So you think he's approving Chen's plan?"

He nodded. "Based on what you just told me, I do. There's a merchant fleet full of relief goods going to Panamar in nine days. It will pass right through Nea Mykonos on its way there."

She frowned, bringing up a hand to brush a strand of hair absently out of her face as she always did when thinking hard. "By relief goods, I assume you mean another Guard invasion to take out the rebels there?"

He eyed her but didn't respond. Panamar was another major irritant for the Twenty. Just four months ago, what should have been a simple Guard suppression of a small planetary rebellion had turned into a disaster when a good chunk of the Guard Paramilitary Forces sent there, including a healthy percentage of the enacters, defied their orders and joined with the rebellion. By all accounts, they'd mostly left the planet since, but Petrov had been grumbling about teaching the inhabitants left behind a lesson ever since.

Seeing that Creighton wasn't going to answer her question directly, Lara asked another. "You think he's going to somehow get the pirates to attack the convoy and then use the Council Navy to heroically swoop in and save the day?"

This time, Creighton graced her with a small nod. "And then claim the pirates were part of a rebel attempt to stop supplies from reaching war-torn Panamar. It's the perfect 'coming out party,' as you put it, for the Navy. And it will let Admiral Chen get her wish of operating more openly in the Colonies, giving her people more experience ahead of the invasion of the Four Worlds."

Then he looked at her sternly. "But shouldn't *you* be the one telling *me* all this? It's your job to keep me appraised of what your boss is up to."

Lara grimaced. "I've tried, but he's becoming more and more paranoid. I even took a risk later and asked him, in private, if he wanted me to follow up with Guard Commissioner Rolston on redeploying the Space Force. He looked at me like I had just stomped on his big toe and quickly told me no. Then he said, and I quote, 'Ebby is already handling the GSF.'"

Creighton frowned. Ebby Hall was Petrov's chief of staff and quite possibly one of the top ten most powerful people in the colonies. She was an enacter, not a speaker, and the Keeper trusted her completely even aside from that. For that reason, Petrov only gave the most critical assignments to her. A simple Guard redeployment to combat pirates certainly didn't meet that criteria. And Ebby was also the only one on Petrov's staff who officially knew about . . .

"Wait," he demanded, "you think he's deploying the GSF to Moloch?"

Lara nodded. She only knew about the Moloch system because Creighton had told her, which put her in a very small group of living people. Moloch wasn't the system's real name, but it was the one they all used for the location of the entrance to the Goat Path.

For centuries, humanity had believed there was only one path through the Castilian Rift, the strange sphere of space around the Sol system and Earth that made faster-than-light travel impossible. But just over a hundred years ago, they'd finally found another path. The aptly named Goat Path was the twisting, ever-changing, and dangerous navigational route that emptied out in Sol's outer system. For the last century, the Twenty had used it to silently infiltrate the Four Worlds by sending scout ships carrying spies to Sol. Now, it was to play a critical role in the invasion by allowing them to deliver a part of Admiral Chen's Navy to the system, bypassing the heavy Four Worlds forces guarding the more well-known path through the Rift at the so-called Front Door.

"That's exactly what I believe," Lara confirmed. "It would make sense, then, why he had Ebby handling such an otherwise mundane assignment. If they're talking about deploying the Guard to Moloch, it would track that they're planning to rotate out some of the Council Navy forces guarding the system."

"Which they'll have to do if Chen wants to use them at Nea Mykonos," Creighton finished for her.

She nodded again, and he frowned. "This is troubling," he said, steepling his fingers in deep thought. "Letting the Guard get anywhere near Moloch—if the existence of the system leaks to *anyone*—could be disastrous for the invasion."

"I don't believe he's thinking rationally about it anymore," Lara said, her own face turning troubled. "If Chen asked him to make her a member of the Twenty and somehow convinced him that doing so would move up the timetable to invade Earth, I think he'd give it to her."

Creighton stood up abruptly and moved back to his desk. "Thank you for this," he told her sincerely. "I will take it from here, but I need you to try and find out, subtly, exactly which units of the Guard he plans to send. Can you do that?"

She frowned. "I can try, but I think Ebby might be getting suspicious of me lately."

That was new and troubling, and he gave her a sharp look, which she pretended not to notice.

"Do what you can," he told her. "And the other thing we discussed?"

She shook her head emphatically. "No, I still don't know exactly who he's been talking to in the Sol system. We know he's somehow managed to install a quantum comm there, but I don't know who's on the other end. Nor do I think I can dig more into it without arousing his suspicion. With how paranoid he's been lately, all it would take is a little bit of doubt on his part to land me a date with an alpha."

Creighton nodded. "Very well." He sat down and started pulling up information on his desk holo.

Lara took the hint and stood up from the chair. She ran her hands through her hair a few times, mussing it up, and pulled a tissue from her purse, which she used to smear her lipstick at one corner of her mouth. Then she bunched up her dress and let it fall back into place, adding several new wrinkles to the fabric. Not bothering to put her heels back on, she picked them up and held them over her shoulder by the straps and headed back to the door.

Then she was gone from Creighton's office, the door closing behind her after revealing the disapproving scowl on his assistant's face once more.

Creighton frowned to himself and turned his chair to look out over the bustling nighttime of New Brussels below. All they needed was six months—maybe a year—and victory in the Sol system would be assured. In the grand scheme of over seven hundred years of Council rule, another year was nothing.

But something was driving Keeper Ian Petrov to push too hard and too fast. If they weren't careful, it would only lead to disaster. Because without the pure enhanced bloodlines on Earth, the Council government—and the true rulers, the Twenty—were on borrowed time.

"I am humbled by the trust you have shown in me by electing me to be your president." Mikael Gorsky looked out over the packed Congressional Hall, at all the members of the United Earth Congress in attendance along with their staffs, a bevy of reporters, and even those regular citizens lucky enough to have gotten seats in the upper galleries. He smiled. His outward expression was crafted specifically to show his humble gratitude to all of them. But his inward smile, the one only for himself, was at their gullibility.

He slowly took on an appropriately somber expression. "Like all of you, I am deeply saddened by the events of the last few months, and especially by the actions of those we used to call colleagues and even friends. Former President Luis Pereira committed heinous acts that betrayed our trust. He imprisoned an innocent woman, Reader Jinny Ambrosa, and did that which no president must ever do: lied to the people."

If they believe that, they really are *idiots.* Inwardly, he still grinned. If only they knew just how incompetent Pereira had been, to let all of that happen right under his nose and not even suspect Mikael of pulling the strings.

"But that pales in comparison to the sins of another individual we trusted," he continued. "Corey O'Leary, a man I once called a personal friend and confidant before we took different paths so many years ago, did not just betray that trust we gave him. He betrayed the sacred Constitution and our nation when he defected to Mars. Can anyone now doubt that the Martians are not to be trusted?" He had to tread lightly here; he didn't want to start certain things *too* early.

"But former Congressman O'Leary is worse than the Martians. For they are as scorpions; we know what they are, and we expect them to sting us. But Mr. O'Leary pretended to be one of us, a patriot. Which is why his traitorous actions cannot be forgotten nor forgiven, for they represent the ultimate betrayal."

There were a few mutters at this from the right side of the chamber, where members of O'Leary's Red Party sat. But they were drowned out by shouts of agreement from the other parties.

"My commitment to all of you, as your president, is simple. I will never betray you. I will never take your trust and grind it into the ground as Luis Pereira and Corey O'Leary have done. And even though we may not always agree on each and every issue"—he looked pointedly at the right side of the chamber for this part—"I can promise that we will always be on the same side: the side of United Earth and the Constitution!"

Every seat cleared as the members of Congress in attendance, starting with his own Blue Party, stood and applauded. The noise crescendoed as the members of the Red Party fought to celebrate louder than their Blue Party opponents—everything was a contest to these fools. If only they both understood how soundly he had played them.

The applause continued for a full two minutes as he made half-hearted gestures to quiet the room, all the while wearing a look that he knew would appear to those who watched live and on the vids as one of near-embarrassment at the unspoken praise they heaped upon him.

Keep clapping, he thought. *The better to not hear your doom as it sneaks up on you.*

"Have you finally come to your senses, girl?"

Jinny looked up at the sharp-toned question to see the Majko peering into the small dormitory room she'd been staying in for the four days since awakening in the hospital. She frowned, understanding the old woman's question but not wanting to answer it yet.

The Majko regarded her coolly and, without an invitation, walked through the doorway and into the room, sitting on the small bed and regarding Jinny, who was seated at the smaller desk.

"By now, you must understand that your friends are out of reach," the dour woman pressed.

Jinny swallowed the instant argument that threatened to spring to her lips. Four days ago, just hours after waking up, the Majko had insisted on starting her 'training,' expecting her to just jump on the old woman's offer from months ago now that Jinny was back in Perth. She kept talking about Jinny being some kind of savior to the readers on the Australian continent, but that only *she,* the Majko, could provide her the training that would unlock her full potential to become such, through a skill called Read Learning.

If the Majko were to be believed, Read Learning was an ability all readers had, but it took training and practice that the Council government had purposefully withheld, most likely to keep their readers from becoming too powerful. Supposedly, it meant that Jinny could learn new skills just by reading those who already had them, skipping all the messy learning and practice.

She highly doubted it.

So, four days ago, Jinny had turned the offer down flat. She was grateful, of course, to the Majko for saving her from the prison of her own mind. But she felt an overwhelming need to find Tyrus, Corey

O'Leary, and Riggs. She'd even wanted to find Jynx and had been devastated upon learning that the mercurial woman had died rescuing her from the Crater.

Unfortunately, four days spent trying to think of ways to find and join her friends had yielded absolutely nothing. She knew Tyrus and the others were on Mars, but there was no way to get a message to them—Earth and Mars jammed any and all interplanetary communications—and even attempting to send one would be like throwing up a beacon telling the United Earth government exactly where she was. So far as she knew, elements in that government still very much wanted her in prison or simply dead.

The two men who might have been able to take her to Mars—the pilot who had brought her to Perth and the blender, Jordan Archer, who was so instrumental in her escape from the Crater—were nowhere to be found either.

But despite all these setbacks, Jinny wasn't ready to concede defeat. On the contrary, she was still as adamant now as she had been four days ago to find a way to reunite with her friends. The Majko must have seen her resolve in her expression, because the old woman looked for a moment like she was sucking on a lemon.

Then, abruptly, her face softened, and her bony shoulders slumped. "You're stubborn," the Majko said with a shake of her head. "Too stubborn to see the truth in front of your face. That there is no way to reach your friends while they remain on Mars, and the best thing you can do for them—for *all* of us—is to allow me to train you."

Jinny sighed. "I can see why you believe that. And I'm certainly grateful for all you've done for me, but you can't expect me to just sit around while I'm not even sure if Tyrus, Riggs, and Corey are alive."

The Majko stood and started pacing the room. "Of course I don't expect you to just sit around, girl! I expect you to learn about your abilities. I expect you to become more than what you are. So that when you *do* find your friends again, you'll be a help to them instead of just a liability." She stopped, glaring down at Jinny, who involuntarily shrank from her gaze.

The old woman, knowingly or not, had hit a sore spot. Thinking back on their time on Earth, Jinny had been little more than a liability for Tyrus and the others. She had allowed herself to be arrested while Tyrus and Jynx managed to escape their captors. Even Riggs managed to free himself with the help of Jordan Archer, posing as an attorney.

But not Jinny. They *all* had to put their lives on hold to come and rescue her. And, in the process, Jynx had died.

"You're not going to let this go, are you, girl?"

The question snapped Jinny out of her slow spiral back into despair, and she looked up at the Majko again. "No, I'm not."

The old woman chewed on her words for a moment and then licked her lips. "How about I make you a deal? You train with me for 90 days. During that time, if you find a reasonable way to reconnect with your friends, I won't stand in your way. You'll be free to go at any time. But if you stay the full ninety days, and you still want to go gallivanting off into space and probably get yourself killed . . . then I'll put all of the resources at my disposal into helping you do it."

The offer surprised Jinny. Unconscious though she may have been, she'd read the Majko constantly for the weeks they were literally tied together at the hospital. She knew that the normally irascible woman wasn't one to strike many compromises, and this one gave much more than it required. She thought over it for a few moments, wary of a potential catch. Not detecting one, Jinny nodded slowly.

"Good! It's settled then," the Majko said with a grim smile. "Let's go." She started moving toward the door.

"What, now?" Jinny asked in surprise.

The leader of Earth's reader population turned back to her from the doorway. "Of course, now!" she snapped, all traces of her earlier conciliatory mood gone. "I only have ninety days with you, girl. Not a moment to waste."

Sighing again, Jinny stood and followed the Majko from the room and out of the dormitory building that serviced the University of Perth. They walked side by side across the large campus in silence, the old woman seemingly lost in thought and Jinny not feeling she could interrupt her musings.

Finally, they arrived at a nondescript building. The Majko marched Jinny right past the front doors and around the side to what looked like a service door. There, she knocked twice, and it was quickly opened by a young brunette woman around Jinny's age, who looked at the two women in timid fashion.

"Reader Ambrosa, this is Reader Kelly Martin, my assistant," the Majko said, pushing by the younger woman to enter the building and beckoning Jinny to join her.

Jinny gave Kelly Martin a nod and a friendly smile. The brunette returned Jinny's smile with a shy one of her own but quickly broke eye contact and dutifully followed her boss down the interior hallway. Shaking her head, Jinny walked after them.

The Majko led them to what looked like a martial arts dojo, complete with sparring mats and a variety of weapons on racks that covered three of the four walls—the fourth was all mirrors.

On the dojo's center mat stood another woman. She was shorter than Jinny by at least eight centimeters, with a build so thin and frail that it looked like a stiff breeze could blow her away. The woman's Asian facial features gave her an ageless quality. That, combined with her small frame, made her seem almost like a child. But there were laugh lines around her eyes that belied her true age, which Jinny guessed to be around forty.

The Majko inclined her head toward the small woman. "Yamiko is your first teacher. To pass her test, you must fight her and pin her to the floor."

Jinny shook her head slowly, regarding Yamiko with skepticism.

"Before you speak," snapped the Majko, "bear in mind the agreement—the promise—you made just moments ago. You're giving me ninety days to teach you, and during that time, you *will* not question my methods."

Jinny was about to open her mouth and protest that she'd never agreed to that last part, but the Majko stepped out from between her and Yamiko and yelled, "Fight!"

Yamiko inched toward Jinny, who shrugged and began to think of ways that she could take the woman down to the mat without hurting her. As her opponent neared arm's reach, Jinny stepped forward and extended both arms to encircle her so she could gently pitch her to the ground.

But to her shock, Yamiko suddenly wasn't there anymore. The

small woman expertly sidestepped Jinny's grasp. Then, while Jinny's focus was on Yamiko's arms, which didn't move at all from their place clasped behind her back, she missed the sweep of the older reader's leg. As Jinny fell to the ground, bruising her tailbone in the process despite the mat, she knew she'd been duped.

Before she could react or fight back from her now-seated position, Yamiko jumped on top of her. Jinny saw the diminutive fighter's right arm swinging rapidly downward. She tried to throw out her left to block the blow, but the gloved palm connected solidly with the side of her head, and she saw stars as she fought to maintain consciousness. An instant later, Jinny found herself gasping for breath as Yamiko planted a knee in her chest, pinning her to the ground and restricting the expansion of her lungs.

"Enough!" cried the Majko, and the small woman on top of Jinny was suddenly gone. When she lifted her head to peer around, Yamiko was standing several meters away, not looking tired in the least.

"What was that?" she tried to yell, but it came out in a hoarse gasp. "She could have killed me!"

The Majko shook her head with a frown. "No. She didn't even come close. She was instructed to go easy on you."

"That was easy?" Jinny had some of her voice back now, and the question came out in a closer approximation to a shout. "What was the point of all that?"

"To show you how far you have to go. I happen to know that you've read your friend, Tyrus Tyne, on multiple occasions. As an ex-spy and, if the rumors are correct, assassin, he is no doubt trained in a wide variety of martial arts. *You* have his entire memory in your head. Every lesson he ever took, every fight he ever got into, and every blow he landed or blocked. It's *all* in your head. But until you learn to access it, it's utterly useless to you or anyone else."

"So, you send me against an expert the first time? How about easing me into it?" Jinny ground out the words through clenched teeth as her anger surged. She wasn't sure if she was truly still upset about the swift beating she'd received or if she was defensive at the Majko's supposition that she should be able to fight like Tyrus after no more than reading him. Either way, she felt anger and resentment surging inside of her, all aimed at the old woman in front of her.

To her surprise, the Majko laughed. She pointed a finger squarely at Jinny. "*You* were the one who wanted this done in months instead of years. That means there is no time to take it easy on you. *Every* lesson has to land hard the first time. Or would you rather I coddle your tender feelings and not show you how utterly unprepared you are?"

Jinny clenched her teeth harder but didn't respond. The Majko continued.

"Yamiko is *not* an expert. If you could access even a small portion of Tyrus Tyne's training, you would have no problem dispatching her. In fact, Yamiko has never had a lesson in person."

She said the last part without raising her voice, but the emphasis was clear that this was the point of the entire affair. But Jinny had to ask herself at first if she'd heard the woman right. The Majko obviously saw her eyebrows furrowed and knew her shock tactic had gotten through.

"That's right. Yamiko has never taken a single martial arts or self-defense lesson in her entire life. But six months ago, she decided it was something she wanted to learn. So, every weeknight, she reads her niece—with the girl's permission, of course. Her niece takes daily lessons in Taekwondo, an ancient form of martial arts. Yamiko and her niece spar a few times a week, using what the girl learns in her classes. As you've just witnessed, that is all it has taken for Yamiko to become quite proficient."

Jinny stared at the Majko in shock. She'd thought she understood what the old woman had been speaking of in their first meeting when she claimed Jinny could use her reading ability to master skills others knew. She'd also assumed that it was hyperbole, this entire concept of Read Learning that they'd explained to her.

"No lessons herself? Just readings of her niece's lessons and practice?" she asked, her voice returning to normal.

The Majko smiled and nodded. "That's it." She waved a hand. "That is essentially all there is to Read Learning. We always combine the readings with a little bit of practical application to help drive the lessons home. Muscle memory is important, and practice can also prevent the memories from fading before the lessons have sunk in. There's only so much room in even a reader's head, after all. I'm sure even you start to forget the memories from your readings after some time if you don't have a specific reason to recall them. The memories of other people simply don't stick as well as our own."

She paused, and Jinny nodded in response to confirm that it was an issue she shared, though she'd always considered it a blessing not to indefinitely retain most memories of those she'd read. Unfortunately, it was always the most shocking memories, especially of the criminal nature, that seemed to stick—that took root and formed new personas in her head.

Jinny had been sitting on the floor during the entire conversation, propping herself up on her elbows. Now she levered herself to her feet and stared into the Majko's eyes, her fists clenched and her face full of resolve. Next to the old woman, Kelly Martin flinched as if Jinny's intensity shocked her.

"Okay," Jinny said, "show me how to use Tyrus's training to defend myself."

To her surprise, the Majko laughed louder than she ever had before. And to her chagrin, the laughing continued for several seconds, with the woman even brushing a tear out of her eyes. When the older woman looked back at Jinny, she shook her head with a half smile.

"No, my student. What you just saw will be part of your advanced course. First, you must learn to knit."

CHAPTER 6

"Why should we listen to you when your own people declare you a traitor?"

Corey stood in the Grand Hall of Praetors—they hadn't invited him to sit this time—and swallowed his first response, doing his best to ignore the angry, self-righteous glare of his questioner, Kol Tiberius.

Just two days earlier, Corey had secured yet another vote in the Quorum in favor of sending an overture of peace to Earth. One more, and he would have had a tie among the twelve praetors, and *maybe* Aphrodite could have voted as the tie-breaker in her role as consul—he wasn't actually sure how that worked.

Just one vote left.

Then, Mikael Gorsky's denouncement had come and shocked them all, but no one more so than Corey himself. The plan had always been for Gorsky to declare his backing for Corey's mission to Mars as soon as President Pereira was removed from office. That would have given Corey immediate status as the UE's official ambassador to Mars and allowed him even greater status with the Quorum of Praetors to negotiate a joint defense agreement for the coming invasion.

At the very least, it might have been enough to get him that one more blasted vote.

But Gorsky had betrayed him.

Part of him desperately wanted to believe that his old friend was improvising, changing the plan on the fly based on information he had access to and that Corey could only guess at. But he knew that wasn't the case, nor did he even have a way to ask Gorsky why he'd thrown Corey under the proverbial bus. The Martian praetors had staunchly rejected his every request to contact Earth since arriving.

It wouldn't have mattered. Corey had the sinking feeling that his 'friend' had never been anything of the kind, that to the big Russian, Corey had been just one more tool in his rise to power as the new president of United Earth. And if that were the case, it meant that Gorsky had been pulling Corey's strings all along, sending him to Mars so that Gorsky, and not Corey, would be the clear choice to replace Pereira. And so that Corey couldn't defend himself against the false allegations when Gorsky claimed that he'd come to Mars without his knowledge or blessing when it had been Gorsky himself who had suggested the necessity for the trip.

Of course, he couldn't tell the Martians any of that. Not only would he lose any formal status he had with them, but by allowing himself to be used so brazenly by Gorsky, he would lose *perceived* status, which in the twisted Martian system of social honor would be even worse. So, he had to improvise and tell just part of the truth.

"This was always part of Mikael Gorsky's plan," he said slowly, finally responding to Tiberius's question. "He is holding together a fragile alliance as the new president, replacing the corrupt Luis Pereira and hoping to mend a fractured government. He cannot speak in favor of an alliance with Mars until he is assured that such an alliance is possible. Which is why you *must* send him the overture of peace we have discussed. Then he can make it known that he is in favor of it, and we can unite before—"

"We *must* do nothing," a dispassionate voice interrupted, and Corey involuntarily clenched his jaw in frustration to see Aphrodite Starshadow, the person who should have been his staunchest ally among the praetors, eyeing him sternly. "Mars will do what the Quorum decides," she continued, still betraying no emotion. "You may give us your thoughts on the matter, Emissary Corey O'Leary, but we will decide what Mars *must* do."

Corey inclined his head toward her and then toward a smug-looking Tiberius, but in his heart, he felt a surge of hope. After Gorsky's public disavowal, Corey was no longer a congressman of United Earth. But by calling him 'Emissary,' Aphrodite had effectively given him a new status almost on par with his former one. He could work with that.

"I apologize for my poor choice of wording," Corey said, fighting to keep his own voice as even and emotionless as Aphrodite's. "What I meant to say is that our top military minds, including Fleet Admiral Horatio Krishna Lopez, do not believe that United Earth can stand alone against the might of the Council fleet. And if Earth cannot stand alone, I would argue that logic dictates neither Europa nor Mars could do so." There were a few harsh looks at that statement, but Corey was gratified to see some heads nod around the table. Mars and Earth had always been close to evenly matched.

"If you would," he continued, speaking carefully, "Tyrus Tyne, who accompanied me here, has firsthand knowledge of the Council Navy, and I would implore you to allow him to speak to you directly in order to—"

"Visitor Tyrus Tyne has no status here on Mars," Tiberius interrupted. "Therefore, he cannot address the Quorum. And speaking of status, esteemed Consul Starshadow"—he nodded deferentially to Aphrodite—"I would move that, in light of the denouncement from his own government, former Congressman Corey O'Leary also be stripped of any status as Emissary."

Corey sat back in his chair, feeling defeated. He'd hoped that Tiberius would have been so happy at Aphrodite seeming to take his side that he would fail to notice her slip in the title. But no such luck. He was one step now away from being stripped of all status, just like Tyrus, and being either confined to quarters or possibly even killed by some archaic Martian procedural law.

He looked around the room for support, but as always, the majority of the Praetors maintained stony expressions that betrayed nothing. Only one, Praetor Sunsbane, gave him a slight but reassuring nod.

"We must discuss this matter," Aphrodite said, authority ringing in her tone. "Emissary Corey O'Leary, you will leave us now and await our decision."

Corey opened his mouth to argue and plead his case again, but he thought better of it. To dispute or delay in following a direct order from a Martian consul or praetor, even with good intentions, would do nothing to help him win over the Quorum. He'd picked up on that much. So, instead, he nodded respectfully to Aphrodite, stood wordlessly from his seat, and left the chamber.

He waited in the antechamber for almost an hour and then for another several minutes while the praetors and their bodyguards exited. Then, again, he watched as Aphrodite reluctantly entered the antechamber and made her way over to him, regarding him with the same stony expression she'd worn in his presence since he'd arrived on the red planet.

"Has the Quorum of Praetors reached a decision in regard to my status?" he asked, trying and failing to keep the stress out of his voice.

"We have," she replied, betraying nothing. "At this time, you will retain the title of Emissary, though it may be revoked at a later date." Without waiting for him to respond, she walked out of the antechamber, following the other praetors. The four silent praetorian guards that had been standing sentinel over the quorum chamber's entrance moved to surround her on all sides, leaving Corey alone in the room, where he slumped back down onto the hard chair and rested his head in his hands in a mix of relief, frustration, and despair.

"Why are we starting with knitting?"

The Majko frowned. Jinny's question was a valid one, but it wouldn't do to give her student too much leeway at the start. She was going to have to trust the process . . . and her teacher. Otherwise, this wouldn't work. She didn't answer the younger woman's question.

"Reader Ambrosa," she said instead. "Please read Reader Sanz." She nodded toward the elderly woman, even older than her, who was sitting on the couch with her knitting needles.

"Come on," Jinny continued to argue. "I thought you said I would be reading people who are *taking* lessons. This woman looks like she's been knitting since before I was born." She looked sheepishly down at Sanz. "Sorry. No offense intended."

Sanz just smiled in a grandmotherly way while the Majko fought the urge to sigh in frustration. Jinny was stubborn, as most women her age tended to be. She was set in her ways and had firm beliefs about what she could and couldn't do with her abilities, all of which worked against her when it was time to learn something new. It was why they typically started training readers in the art of Read Learning from a young age, essentially from the time they first demonstrated reader capabilities.

She met Jinny's stare and decided to answer her question. "Reader Ambrosa, I do not make it a habit to explain my methods to my students. However, out of respect for your unique situation, I will explain myself this once. Reader Sanz is not a student of knitting but rather a teacher. She taught three knitting lessons today and countless thousands in her lifetime. If you can harness the ability of Read Learning, then she will be a far better subject for you to read than a young student."

Left unsaid was that the Majko wasn't yet willing to let Ambrosa read any of the younger readers. The skin-to-skin contact would always result in a two-way reading; those Ambrosa read would also read her—if only for the normal twenty-four-hour period or less. But given all the young reader was going through, it might be dangerous for *anyone* to read her, much more so a young, impressionable student.

"Okay," was Jinny's simple response. At least the girl could be persuaded. She reached over and took the older Sanz's outstretched hand, holding it with her eyes closed for about five seconds before withdrawing the hand and looking back up at her.

"Ready to try knitting?" the Majko asked.

Jinny shrugged and looked dubiously down at the needles and yarn that Sanz had placed on the small coffee table. She plopped down on the apartment's small couch next to the old knitting teacher and picked up the needles, testing their slight heft and inspecting them closely. Then, she tried to start with the yarn.

The Majko could see Sanz watching her with distress as Jinny tried and failed three straight times to start her knitting. It was clear the old woman wanted to jump in and help the young reader, but the Majko shook her head silently to stop the intervention. If Jinny couldn't learn this on her own from reading someone with decades of experience, then they would have to try again with another skill, but they needed to *know*.

A full and frustrating hour later, Jinny threw the needles down on her lap in disgust. She'd *almost* gotten something started a couple of times but had ended up tying the yarn into a few knots and nothing more.

"I'd say this is a gigantic failure," the young reader muttered.

"No!" snapped the Majko. "Even the youngest, least skilled readers in Perth can do this. You are experienced and have abilities they don't even dream of. You *can* do this. You *will* do this. Now try again."

For a moment, it looked like Jinny was going to argue once more, but she only frowned and then started awkwardly manipulating the needles and yarn.

Students in Perth, readers all of them, were able to graduate high school years ahead of their non-reader counterparts elsewhere in the world, all by dividing the class load across multiple students who would then read each other at the end of each day. By afterward doing every class's homework, the readers were able to learn three to four times the material as non-readers over the same time period.

For some reason, the Council government and their pet readers in the Council Reader Corps had suppressed all knowledge of this ability in the colonies. Most likely, the Majko believed, they did it to keep their readers from getting too powerful and becoming a threat to the speakers who truly ruled there. She had been so certain that all it would take was learning about the ability to break through Jinny's mental block against it.

But regardless of her beliefs, when she finally let a frustrated Jinny take a break three hours later, the young woman was still hopeless with the knitting needles.

Yesterday had been knitting. Today was drawing.

"That doesn't look like a bowl of fruit," Jinny said, wrinkling her nose in disgust as she compared her sloppy sketch with the example provided for her to copy. By the look on Reader Howell's face, her attempt truly *was* terrible, even if the art teacher had enough tact not to call out her student's failure.

"Art is more than knowledge," the middle-aged man soothed. "Art is feeling, emotion, and practice. Even my best students didn't learn all they needed to know in one day. Give yourself some time."

Jinny looked beyond the kind man to see the Majko frowning from her seat in the corner of the room. The old woman obviously didn't share the art teacher's optimistic assessment of her capabilities. Nor did Kelly Martin, the Majko's assistant, who refused to even look at her.

Sighing, Jinny did her best to smile at Howell. "Can I try it again?"

CHAPTER 7

Five Days Later; October 24, 731 P.D.

"This one requires no physical skill," the Majko explained, her voice even and not giving hint to the frustration she had to be feeling after so many failures.

It wasn't that Jinny wasn't trying. For a week, she had sat with and read various instructors at the University of Perth, some of them professors at the school and others brought in from local high schools and even elementary schools. She'd read nearly a dozen of the teachers at this point and had failed just as many times to pick up the skills they were meant to impart to her.

The latest spectacular failure, just the day before, had been archery. She'd read Reader Crabtree, a dour woman in her fifties, and then set about trying to hit a stupid little target with a stupid little arrow. In her mind, she could see and hear the endless instruction Crabtree had given her students throughout her life. She knew the mechanics—how to hold the bow, nock the arrow, pull back just so—but her first several shots hadn't managed to come close even to the bail of hay upon which the target was mounted.

Several hours later, she was doing somewhat better. She'd even managed to hit the bullseye once. But when the Majko excitedly questioned her afterward, the old woman was disappointed to find that the shot had been mere luck rather than any actual learned skill.

Jinny's disappointment was probably even greater than the Majko's. After a week of trying various skills, she should have at least found *one* she was naturally good at, but it was almost as if the pressure of trying to accomplish each one took away any natural skill she might have had. She might know the theory of how to hold a bow or move a paintbrush, but the actions felt unnatural and stilted to her. Her brain couldn't understand why her body didn't already know the movements and refused to allow it the luxury of figuring it out in its own.

"You're still anticipating the shot and flinching as you pull the trigger," Reader Jershon chided. "You need to stay relaxed and let the pistol do all the work. Squeeze the trigger, don't pull it."

Jinny nodded and turned back to point her gun down range, firing off another few shots toward the not-so-distant target and missing it with almost every one.

"You're not trying hard enough!" the Majko snapped when she had emptied the latest clip. "You need to relax and let the skills of those you've read come to the surface."

Jinny frowned but didn't respond to the seeming contradiction in the old woman's words. Or the tone, though it was enough to make Kelly Martin—the assistant had become ubiquitous in these sessions—wince. Then, the voices in Jinny's head started up again.

That's right, Jinny, let go. Let me take control, and I'll do everything these sniveling abnorms want. She shook her head, trying to banish Hendrix back to the fog, the ever-present fog that roiled in the back of her mind.

For the first several days after waking up in the hospital next to the Majko, Jinny had thought the fog and its inhabitants were gone. She'd woken up each morning to find that she was blessedly alone in her own head, the myriad of voices silent.

But four days ago, the fog had been there when she'd awoken from a fitful sleep full of nightmares. The voices were back, too, albeit muffled. She'd cried for fifteen minutes, until the Majko had come to fetch her for the day's lessons. Ever since, the fog and the voices within had grown steadily stronger, taunting her with their presence. She hadn't told the Majko yet—she wasn't sure she could. After all the old woman had done to save her from her own psyche, she couldn't admit to her that it hadn't worked, that things were just as bad as before and getting worse every day.

"I'll try harder to relax," Jinny said to placate her now. "Let me go again."

"We're going to try knitting again." Those had been the Majko's first words to Jinny this morning, nine days into her training. "Perhaps a repeat reading of Reader Sanz and another try will solidify the learning in your mind."

Jinny didn't argue. In fact, she said little to the Majko the entire walk from the dorm back to the small classroom where they'd met the knitting instructor before. Last night's dreams had been particularly bad. She'd relived a few of Hendrix's murders and then again relived Alan's death in the alley on Centauri II. Jinny had woken up several times in a cold sweat, screaming aloud, terrified of what was happening to her.

She only hoped that the Majko didn't notice the bags under her eyes.

They arrived at the classroom and found the old knitting instructor already there, smiling at Jinny as they entered. Kelly Martin was also there and, as usual, said nothing as she shyly avoided Jinny's gaze. Jinny had tried on multiple occasions to draw the other young reader out in conversation, but the brunette rarely answered her questions with more than one word, if even that.

After a few small pleasantries, Margaret Sanz held out her hand for Jinny to take. The reading lasted only seconds, again, and then Jinny set to work, trying again to manipulate the needles in a manner that might come close to the way she saw it in her head.

You're a failure! Hendrix's voice mocked her. *You can't even do what five-year-olds can master.*

She tried to shove the thought aside and push the serial killer's voice back down into the fog, but he kept mocking her while threatening the things he would do to everyone around her once she slipped up and gave him control.

Don't listen to him, Jinny, Alan's voice soothed. *You're trying your best.*

The words, comforting as they might be, gave her no good feeling. Even Alan's welcome voice was a stark reminder that she was losing her mind again.

Then, another voice spoke from the fog. A new one. *Deary, you're doing that wrong. Let me help you.*

The Majko watched as Jinny Ambrosa once again failed. She'd seen three-year-olds knit better than the reader after just a few lessons. Jinny, on the other hand, had gained *thousands* of lessons, both taken and given, when she'd read Margaret Sanz. Even without the Read Learning capability, she should have been able to simply recall the lessons to her memory and, by following simple instructions, do *better* than she was. It was as if her mind was completely rejecting the knowledge.

It had been the same for every one of Jinny's attempts at Read Learning. Reading expert instructors in each skill seemed to actually make her *worse* at the skill. It was baffling, as was the return of the young reader's nightmares.

No doubt Jinny thought she'd managed to hide the resurgence of the nightmares and the voices in her head. But the Majko's people had enough cameras in her dormitory to capture it all as it happened, and the young woman's appearance this morning spoke of someone who wasn't getting any sleep.

The Majko hadn't discussed it with Jinny yet. She was hoping the young woman would bring it up of her own volition, but she hadn't thus far, and the Majko was almost ready to force the issue.

Why should I trust you? Jinny demanded at the voice of Margaret Sanz, which emanated from the fog.

You're the only one who can answer that question, deary, the old woman replied. *Surely, you've read enough of myself and the others to know which of us you can trust and those whom you shouldn't.*

The simple statement caught Jinny off guard, and her fingers paused their clumsy attempts to knit, drawing curious gazes from both the Majko and the real Sanz. She swallowed, thinking hard.

Jinny, sweetheart, Alan chimed in, *what have you got to lose?*

What *did* she have to lose? Her not-so-slow descent into madness had begun after only a short break, and whatever she was doing with the Majko certainly wasn't working.

She suddenly recalled a conversation she'd had with Professor Tichner in her first weeks on Earth. It had been toward the end of her time staying with the man before he'd sent her to stay with the O'Learys. He'd been explaining to her why he had to leave for a while. In the conversation, he'd been short on details as to his trip, insisting that the less Jinny knew, the better. But he'd given her the distinct impression that the old power broker's trip was directly related to their joint effort to prepare the Four Worlds for the coming Council invasion. When she'd asked him outright about it, questioning why he didn't just stay and help her and Corey spread the message to allies in Congress, he'd given her a sad smile.

"My dear," he'd said, "I trust you and Congressman O'Leary to spread the word here. But I'm afraid I have seen enough of our government to know the uphill climb you face. And as a very famous pre-Diaspora scientist, Albert Einstein, once said, trying the same thing over and over again while expecting different results is the very definition of insanity."

She reflected on his words now. Since arriving on Earth, she'd been trying everything she could think of to stop the nightmares and the voices in her head. She'd ignored them, tried to suppress them, even tried staying awake to avoid the nightmares.

None of it was working . . . so why *not* try something new?

Okay, she told the disembodied voice of Margaret Sanz. *Help me.*

The Majko was about to ask why Jinny had stopped her attempts to knit, but she was brought up short by the abrupt transformation of the girl in front of her. Jinny closed her eyes briefly. When she opened them, her shoulders hunched forward, and she squinted down at the knitting needles as if she had trouble seeing them. Then, without any word of explanation, she started to perfectly and quickly knit a line of yarn.

The Majko and Sanz watched in amazement as Jinny continued moving the needles as if she'd been born using them. In just a few seconds, she had gone from hopeless to a far better knitter than even Read Learning should have accounted for without *weeks* of actual practice. But oddly, she kept her shoulders slumped forward, and her eyes squinted.

"How are you doing this?" the Majko asked. "So perfectly, when before you couldn't make it work?"

Jinny squinted up at her now as if surprised by her presence. "What did you say, deary?" she asked, her voice shaky.

"I said . . . Wait. Reader Ambrosa? Jinny?" the Majko demanded, a terrible suspicion growing inside her.

"Why, my Majko, don't you recognize your dear friend and knitting teacher?" Jinny said, her voice still shaky. Next to her, the real Sanz turned white in shock.

"Margaret?" the Majko asked, still looking at Jinny.

"Of course, deary," Jinny responded. "Who else would I be?"

"What about Jinny?" she asked, fearing the answer.

"She's still in here, deary," Jinny said with a smile. "She says not to worry. She's in control. But she's letting me come out to do the knitting. It was frustrating her so. Poor dear."

The Majko's mouth fell open, and next to her, Kelly gasped in horror.

CHAPTER 8

Three Weeks Later; November 11, 731 P.D.

Jinny stood on the edge of the mat, her bare feet making indentations in the soft surface. Across from her, Master Kurihara, one of Perth's foremost martial arts instructors, bowed to her. She bowed back. Then, he went into a defensive stance.

Jinny attempted to mirror the stance but found her arms going to the wrong places as she shuffled her feet, trying but failing to get them to the right distance apart.

Kurihara watched her solemnly, not attacking yet.

She sighed and closed her eyes. She was still a little creeped out at this part. When Jinny had first let the knitting teacher take control of her three weeks ago, she'd done so out of desperation. She hadn't expected it to actually work. And once it did, she'd been even more terrified that the old woman wouldn't give back control to Jinny when the time came. But at the end of the lesson, the persona of Sanz in her head hadn't argued; she'd simply retreated back into the fog, leaving Jinny completely in control of herself once more.

Encouraged by that first success, She had tried the same thing with several more of the personas living in the fog, mostly instructors she'd recently read or other benign people from her past. She'd strictly stayed away from the emotionally charged personas—the dark ones like Hendrix as well as the ones close to her like Alan or Tyrus—but each time one of the personas faded voluntarily back into the fog, it increased her confidence.

Now, facing Kurihara, she parted the fog and invited one of its denizens to come forward.

Instantly, she was sharing her head with another person. Paul Kurihara looked out through Jinny's eyes at . . . himself. This was always so weird.

He attacked, and the real Kurihara jumped back, barely dodging an expertly placed roundhouse kick.

What followed was a sparring match for the ages. Two absolute masters of their craft going at each other. In the end, the real Kurihara won—his longer reach and stronger muscles made sure of that—but he was sweating and gasping for breath.

"That was interesting," Kurihara said once they'd both recovered some of their breath.

Jinny gently pushed aside his persona in her head and answered with her own voice. "It's no picnic for me either. I can remember making every one of those moves against you, but if you asked me to repeat any of them on my own, you'd laugh out loud." And he had, earlier in her training, when she'd tried just that. "It's just so weird."

"I bet," Kurihara replied, looking at her wryly. "This is a very strange ability you have. And it's so odd to think that I now have a double living inside your head." His smile grew broader. "Please don't tell my wife. I can't imagine what she would do to me if she knew that I now live full-time inside the mind of a woman half my age."

Jinny laughed. She had taken an instant liking to the master. He reminded her a bit of Corey O'Leary with his ready laugh and his self-deprecating humor. But as far as deadliness went, he was much more like Tyrus.

Tyrus . . . That brought forth another thought, one that she had avoided until now.

"Master Kurihara," she said hesitantly. "Can we try once more? I want to attempt something different."

He looked at her with his eyebrows raised, but when she didn't volunteer anything further, he shrugged. "Just let me get some water first. You should hydrate, too."

Five minutes later, they squared off again across the mat. This time, instead of channeling Kurihara, Jinny took a deep breath, thought hard, and summoned another one of the personas inside her head. She brought Tyrus out and gave him control.

Dropping her arms to her sides instead of mirroring Kurihara's stance, she caught the man looking at her oddly. Then Tyrus struck, lashing out with Jinny's right foot as she—or maybe it was he—hopped forward with the other leg. Kurihara went to dodge, but it was a feint. Instead of trying to connect the kick, Tyrus planted Jinny's right foot on the mat directly in front of the martial arts instructor and used it as a pivot point, turning her body and lashing out with a closed fist that connected with the stunned master's jaw.

Tyrus brought up Jinny's other leg, which came around and connected with the instructor's knee. At the last possible instant, Jinny overrode Tyrus and pulled the strike so it wouldn't do any permanent damage. It still sent Kurihara to the mat.

Jinny stepped back. Or rather, Tyrus stepped back—it was all so surreal to her. One moment, Tyrus was on full attack and completely in control of Jinny's body, and the next moment, she was pulling the ex-assassin's kick and giving their opponent time to recover. Even more surprising, Tyrus didn't fight her on it, not even a little. Somehow, she was in full control even when she *gave* him control.

Furthermore, she did it instinctively. That had been the breakthrough she'd had three weeks before with Sanz. Jinny could choose to give over conscious control of her mind and body to any one of the people she'd read over the years. But somehow, *she* always stayed in control, as long as she didn't try to force it. If she stayed mentally relaxed and didn't fight the other persona directly, but rather guided them and channeled them where she wanted to go, then she remained in charge. But when she fought against them head-on, it was like the other personas chafed at the attempt and refused to bow to her authority inside her own head.

Little risk there with knitting, but a lot more on the martial arts mat. Still, she'd managed not to hurt Kurihara badly, even though she was fully aware that Tyrus could have done so through her. The logic of the entire thing made her head spin.

"That was incredible," Kurihara said from the floor, rubbing his jaw and looking up at her. "Those aren't moves you got from me."

She shook her head. "No. Someone else. A friend."

"The alpha?" he asked with raised eyebrows. "Tyrus Tyne?"

Sheepishly, she nodded. "I'm sorry."

"Don't apologize, Reader Ambrosa," he said with a grin. "I got complacent, assuming I was just going to face myself again. You took me by surprise. I'll be more ready this time."

She looked at him in confusion. "You want to keep going?"

He leaped back to his feet, testing the knee she—or rather, Tyrus—had kicked and seeming to come away satisfied. "Of course I want to keep going. I really want to learn what the Council is teaching those alphas. Can you bring Tyne back?"

She nodded.

"Would it be possible for me to speak with him?" Kurihara looked embarrassed to ask the question.

Jinny grimaced but nodded. She'd expected problems bringing Tyrus out, given the emotionally charged nature of their relationship. But surprisingly, she'd felt just as in control with him in the driver's seat as she had with Sanz and the other instructors in her head. "Sure. It's no different giving him control of my voice than any other part of my body."

She closed her eyes for a moment, then opened them and nodded at Kurihara.

"Very nice to meet you, Sensei," Tyrus's persona said through Jinny, and she heard her voice go lower as she tried subconsciously and unsuccessfully to mimic her friend's natural baritone.

Kurihara shook his head and smiled.

What followed felt to Jinny like she was a spectator to two masters comparing notes. There were even a few more sparring matches where Jinny didn't have to pull Tyrus's punches; Kurihara was a quick study.

Three hours later, exhausted and sore—she'd gotten Tyrus's skill but not his musculature or stamina—she begged off any further sparring and left the small dojo, bidding Kurihara a fond farewell on her behalf and Tyrus's.

Outside the room, she found the Majko watching through the two-way observation glass.

"How long have you been standing there?"

"Long enough," the older woman answered with a frown. "You could have really hurt Paul."

Jinny nodded. "I could have. But I didn't. Even when Tyrus was at peak control, I was able to moderate him, just like I've done with the others. I'm not in control, but I am. It's hard to explain."

The Majko surprised her with a smile. "It's the oddest thing I've ever witnessed. But perhaps the most important as well. There's so much I wish we understood." She looked solemnly thoughtful for a moment but then shook it off and looked Jinny in the eyes. "There is still much for you to learn, and we are late to your next lesson. Come along, then."

Jinny rolled her eyes but didn't argue as the old woman led her rapidly across the campus to her next encounter.

"No Kelly today?" Jinny asked, more as a way to make small talk than out of any real interest in the shy assistant's absence. It was a welcome change, in fact. The other young reader had clearly developed both a fear of and a healthy worship of Jinny's abilities. Unfortunately, that hadn't broken the ice between them, and the Majko's almost ever-present aide was still reticent to engage Jinny in conversation. Having her around so much had grown awkward.

The Majko ignored the question. "Your next lesson will be in the Watkins Student Center. We're going to try your hand at cooking again."

Jinny frowned. "Didn't we already have a session with Chef Johansen this week?"

"We did, but I want to understand how repetition of readings and . . . your manifestations of the individuals you read might change your behavior, if at all."

Jinny shrugged as she walked. "I call them personas, not manifestations. But fine, they're your ninety days. Spend them how you will, but I still intend to leave and find my friends when this is over."

The Majko didn't respond, falling silent as she always did when reminded of the time limit she had agreed to. As they turned a corner toward the student center, Jinny caught a whiff of something on the light breeze and stopped in her tracks. The Majko stopped a few steps later and looked back at her in confusion.

"Okay," Jinny said, wrinkling her nose. "Tell Chef Yoro that we're going to be a little later still. Before I meet with *anyone* else, you need to let me shower and change."

As she turned and walked in the other direction toward the dorms, leaving the Majko behind staring after her, Jinny thought back over the past three weeks. When she'd first let the persona of Margaret Sanz take control so that she could knit, it was like a dam had broken. Since then, she'd allowed more than twenty of the personas stuck in her head to take control at various times, each time calling them forward out of the fog, and each time bidding them farewell as they surrendered full control back to her without argument.

Thus far, the signs were good. Even her nightmares had diminished, though she still had one or two every evening instead of half a dozen. It was progress, though she was impatient for more of it. Now, she couldn't help but wonder if what she'd done today, letting Tyrus take control, would further bring forth the sanity she so desperately sought. Was she finally making peace with the others who inhabited her head with her? Or was this simply the calm before the storm, and would she wake up a few days from now having completely lost her mind? She feared the latter but desperately hoped for the former.

The questions weighed heavily on her, and she did her best to shrug them off as she arrived at the dorms and quickly showered and changed. Something in the act of letting the hot water pour over her and then donning fresh clothes felt like she was shedding the worries of the morning. When she walked back toward the student center and the waiting Majko and Chef Johansen, Jinny found an unexpected bounce to her step as she allowed herself to feel the first barest strands of hope that things would get better.

UE President Mikael Gorsky squared his shoulders as he walked into Joseph Blackmont's lavish office, hidden in the depths of a fake water tank in the middle of the desert near the Utah-Nevada border. From outside, the water tank looked old and rusted. Inside was a far different story. The facility housed not only the very comfortable office he now stood in, but also the most groundbreaking piece of technology anywhere in United Earth.

"You're late," Blackmont said with a scowl from behind his desk. "He won't be happy."

Mikael didn't reply, only glared at the man. He was gratified a second later to see Blackmont, head of the largest mercenary organization in the Sol system, flinch under his gaze.

Without further conversation, the two men moved through the door that slid open behind Blackmont's desk and entered a room that appeared straight out of science fiction. Using interactive holo technology unique to the 47 Colonies, the mercenary leader accepted the incoming connection request, and the disembodied head of Ian Petrov, Keeper and true ruler of the 47 Colonies, appeared to float in the middle of the room.

"Status update?" the Keeper asked without preamble.

"The reader's training proceeds as hoped," Mikael said, cutting off Blackmont's aborted attempt to speak first. "Our people in Perth say that her abilities have surpassed even the Majko's optimistic expectations. In a few more weeks, she will be ready."

Petrov smiled, an expression that always looked predatory on him. "Good. How do you plan to recapture her for further study?"

Mikael looked over at Blackmont, nodding to give the man permission to speak.

"Uh . . . getting people into Perth has proved difficult, Your Excellency. If I may—"

"I don't want excuses," Petrov snapped. "Just get it done!"

Blackmont opened his mouth to argue but thought better of it and inclined his head. "Yes, Your Excellency."

"And what of our other plans?" the Keeper asked, turning his steely gaze back on Mikael, who was trying hard not to smile at Blackmont's discomfiture.

"All proceed as anticipated," the UE president responded. "Corey O'Leary has been discredited on Mars. I assume that if they haven't killed him by now, he is in a cell somewhere. The Martians should already be suspicious by now, and we are on schedule for when the next mining shipments leave Nyx."

Petrov smiled again. Then it disappeared. "What of Tyrus Tyne?"

The hatred in the man's voice almost made Mikael take a step back, but he held his ground and fought to keep his face impassive. "He is on Mars with O'Leary, Your Excellency. I have no doubt that the Martians will view him with the same suspicion as O'Leary now. In fact—"

"Do not underestimate him!"

The force of Petrov's shout broke even the president's composure, and this time he did take a step backward. So did Blackmont.

"Tyrus Tyne is not a man to be trifled with," the Keeper continued in a low growl. "You never should have let him survive the rescue of Jinny Ambrosa."

Blackmont gulped visibly. That had been *his* job, and he'd botched it, sending only a single team of special operators to take out the big ex-alpha, practically ignoring the Keeper's warnings that Tyne would surprise them all with his skill and ferocity.

"No matter," Petrov said, his voice and face suddenly softening. "Since the two of you have proved unable to handle Tyne, I have sent another to do so. He should be dead soon."

Mikael shuddered. He had met the young alpha named Toby when the boy had first arrived on Earth. Since then, Mikael had made it a point never to visit the desert quantum comm facility when Toby was there using it to speak to the Keeper. The young assassin with dead eyes gave him the creeps.

"The day of the invasion nears," the Keeper said, oblivious to his discomfort. "You both have your parts to play, and I expect you to play them to perfection. Do not fail me, or when my Navy comes, you will be among the first to die."

With those final, blunt threats, the holo flickered out, and Mikael and Blackmont were left alone in the high-tech compartment, frowning at each other. In a prior communication, Keeper Petrov had told them that he would share the timing of the final invasion with them soon, surely within a month's time. But one month had come and gone, as had most of a second, and the Keeper had shared no further details on the timing of the conquest except to consistently say it was near.

Something had changed, and Mikael worried that he wouldn't like it when he found out just what it was.

PART TWO
TRIALS OF MARS

CHAPTER 9

Forty-Two Years Ago; 689 P.D.

Corey O'Leary, twenty years old and ready for adventure, stepped off the shuttle that had brought him down to the surface of Mars and fell up and forward and then flat onto his face.

They had warned him; they really had. The shuttle crew, the captain of the unarmed passenger liner that had brought him here, and even his parents had all tried to warn him. But what did he do? His first moment on Mars, and he forgot all about their warnings and put too much power into his first step on the lower gravity planet, launching himself in a strange, flailing, slow-motion fall that ended with him face down on the shuttle port's tarmac.

What a great way to make a first impression.

At least he heard no laughing. He looked up sheepishly and saw that while a few of the impossibly tall and thin Martians were looking at him strangely, none of them were laughing. How odd.

Corey picked himself up carefully and brushed off his clothes. Then he picked up his carry-on bag; the shuttle porter had said his other luggage would be delivered to his new dormitory. All sorted out, he headed toward the most official-looking Martian he saw, whom he hoped was the one waiting for him.

He stepped more carefully now and managed not to fall again, settling into a clumsy half-skipping motion that made him feel like he was back on his family vacation to Luna two years earlier, when his father had insisted he come along for a space-suited walk on the moon's barren surface.

It was unnerving to experience the lower gravity now without the bulky space suit. Other than the reddish tinge to everything, there were plants and trees aplenty that almost made him feel like he was back on Earth.

But he wasn't. A stark reminder of that was just how tall the official who greeted him was. She looked down at him from at least twenty centimeters above his respectable—for Earth, at least—177-centimeter height. And she was just so *thin*. It looked like someone had taken a normal Earth woman and stretched her out, like a character he'd seen in a comic book once. He couldn't help but get the impression of a scarecrow, but he stifled the laugh that came to his lips. At least he remembered *that* bit of guidance from his parents. Most people didn't like being laughed at; Martians, apparently, viewed it as a mortal insult.

"Visitor Corey O'Leary?" the scarecrow—no, the Martian woman—asked in a high-pitched voice that threw him off again, coming from someone so tall.

"Uh, yeah. That's me," he answered, looking for a name tag on her strange uniform but seeing none. "And you are?"

She looked him up and down with what he thought was a disapproving glare—he was used to those from his father—and answered him. "I am Emissary Lea Parvina. I will be your liaison during your time here on Mars. I will help you settle into our culture, find your classes, as well as make any other necessary arrangements or"—she looked him up and down again—"adjustments while you are here for the next nine standard months."

"Oh, uh—" He wasn't sure how to respond. "Thank you, I guess. Look, I'm just really tired. It was a long trip. Any chance you can take me to my dorm?"

She frowned and looked confused. "Of course there is a chance I can take you there. The chances are quite high, in fact." Then she stopped as if she felt she had already answered his question and was waiting on him for the next part.

"Uh, okay. *Will* you take me to my dorm? Please."

Her eyes widened. "Of course. Follow me, please."

He did, and they walked in relative silence for about ten minutes across the campus of the University of Olympus Mons. It looked like it could have been a college campus on Earth or Europa, except that the only building materials he could see used were concrete and red stone. Plus, the doors were way too narrow and far too tall. He'd read that the university had been built on top of the remains of the first colony on the red planet, and he thought he saw that in the age of the buildings, but he couldn't be sure. For all he knew, the archaic-looking structures were the latest in Martian architectural style.

When he wasn't studying the buildings, Corey spent the walk trying hard not to gawk at his companion. Parvina's long legs moved in a sweeping, swinging motion that reminded him even more of a scarecrow he'd once seen in an animated movie or of the stilt walkers his parents had hired for one of their garden parties. *Those* had actually been meant as a way to make fun of Martians, a popular pastime on Earth, but they weren't all that far off from how Lea Parvina actually moved.

She caught him looking despite his best efforts and stopped, glaring down at him. "You look too much, Visitor Corey O'Leary," Parvina admonished him in the same tone his mother often used. "To gaze at a person as you do now on Mars is considered an offense. We do not examine each other. Doing so with anyone other than me is likely to result in you being challenged to an honor duel or ending up married."

Without waiting for a response, she started walking again. He scurried clumsily to catch back up to her after doing his best to absorb her words. *Married*?

"I'm sorry," he told her. "I didn't mean anything by it. I just haven't seen many Martians in my lifetime . . . for obvious reasons."

She nodded but did not smile. "Which is why I did not simply challenge you to a duel myself. As your assigned emissary, I am willing to make certain allowances for your newness here, but be advised that others will not be so generous. You must learn our etiquette if you are to survive your time with us."

"Wait." He stopped walking, and she stopped a few paces beyond and turned to look at him questioningly. "What do you mean, *survive*? You mean you *really* duel here? Like, to the death?"

Parvina knit her eyebrows together and cocked her head at him. "Of course. Do you not have such traditions on Earth? How do you keep the peace between citizens?"

He shook his head and could feel his eyes go wide. "Um, we have police and lawyers and stuff. There hasn't been dueling on Earth since, I don't know, the dark ages."

"How strange," she observed, turning back and continuing to walk. "You have much to learn here then. I pray to Mars that you learn quickly."

He didn't know how to respond to that and still wasn't sure if she was messing with him or not, so he kept walking in silence. Parvina led him into a large two-story building. The inside was built from the same concrete and red stone as the outside, and the hallways were tall but narrow, making him feel mildly claustrophobic, especially because the interior passages had no windows or ways out other than closed doors every ten meters or so on either side.

His claustrophobia kicked up to new levels when they entered a tall but otherwise cramped elevator and Parvina hit the button to go *down* three levels.

The elevator finally let them out into an identical narrow hallway. As they walked past door after door, Corey spoke up again. "Will I have a roommate? Or do I have a private dorm?"

To his surprise, Parvina stopped and turned to regard him again with the same quizzical and disbelieving expression she'd worn when he asked her if Martians really dueled. "Were you given the impression that you would have a private room?" she asked him.

"Well, uh, no. But I just assumed that maybe . . . Never mind. I guess I'm okay with a roommate. I'm just curious," he stammered.

She shook her head, turned, and walked on, not answering his question. He jogged to catch up. After another twenty meters or so, Parvina stopped again, this time turning to face a door.

She waved her hand in the air in front of the door, and it slid open. Then she moved aside to allow him to precede her into the room. As he did so, the lights came on, and he stopped in his tracks.

The room was rather large but felt incredibly cramped. And it was immediately clear why Parvina had looked at him the way she had when he asked about a roommate. There had to be at least *thirty* beds in the room, arranged to jut outward from the walls in three-level bunk formats, with five bunks against each long wall and an extremely narrow walkway down the middle between them. On the walls between each bed were strange, multitiered closets that looked as if the people on the second and third bunk tiers would have to climb up and hang on to narrow ladders while grabbing what they needed from their stuff. The closets had no doors, and he could see a wide variety of clothing and hygiene items in most of them.

He wasn't going to have just one roommate—he was going to have twenty-nine of them.

"Your bunk is H1," Parvina told him, motioning to a bunk on the right side of the room. He hoped the number meant he was on the first bunk and was confirmed in his hope when he saw the lowest closet was empty in that row.

"Your classes start tomorrow morning at 0600 hours," she told him, then turned to leave.

"Wait!" he called after her. "What am I supposed to do until then?"

She looked quizzical again—he was really getting sick of that expression on her—and shrugged. "What would you do back on Earth? There is a map on your pad"—she motioned to a data tablet he hadn't noticed sitting on his bed—"and you should be able to find the commissary easily enough. Apart from that, you may visit the sparring gymnasium for exercise, walk the hanging gardens, or begin your studies in preparation for tomorrow. I dare say that you are significantly behind already. Most of your classmates are in class today and have already started their first assignments."

Now, it was his turn to look confused. "But I thought the semester didn't start until tomorrow?"

She shrugged again. "It does start tomorrow, but every professor offers a week of pre-semester lectures and assignments to help students prepare for the first days of classes. They are . . . optional."

The way she said 'optional' told Corey that they really weren't, and he resisted the urge to shake his head in frustration. He watched as Parvina left the dormitory without saying another word, then sat down on his bunk and opened his pad.

Great, he thought, frowning. *Everyone on this planet is apparently a touchy duelist who will kill me if I use the wrong fork at dinner. And to make it all so much better, I'm already behind in my classes! Thanks, Mom and Dad, for sending me all the way to Mars. As if my life wasn't complicated enough.*

Then he had a hopeful thought. *Maybe it's just Parvina. Maybe everyone else on the planet is a lot more relaxed and welcoming.*

Present Day

The punch connected solidly against Tyrus's jaw, and he felt a bone crack and tasted blood in his mouth. That shot had come out of nowhere. He grunted in pain and silently vowed to make his opponent pay for the hit.

He feigned being stunned and shook his head as if to clear it while simultaneously falling backward as though the punch might knock him over. Then, he used the backward momentum to bring his right leg up, and as it passed a certain point, he extended it from the hip and straightened the leg, jamming his foot into the left knee of the man who had punched him.

It was his opponent's turn to grunt as the force of the blow translated even through his powered exosuit. That suit was the only thing that gave Martian a fighting chance against Tyrus . . . Well, that and his longer reach. Tyrus was tall for a human raised in normal gravity—a solid two meters—but the man he was facing was taller still; he had a full five centimeters on him. And that made him only slightly above average height for a Martian.

Tyrus's opponent took a step back to give himself time to recover from the blow to his knee, which he was now favoring. He'd probably managed to tear a tendon . . . or the man was faking, as Tyrus had. Either way, the Martian now circled warily, probably hoping to use his superior reach to land another few blows to his opponent's face before the heavier and stronger Tyrus could land a knockout punch.

Tyrus decided not to wait for any of that. He lunged forward, abandoning the boxing and kicking style of combat they'd both employed up to that point and going instead for a grappling move. He caught the man off guard; the Martian still probably would have been able to avoid the blow. Marcus Parn, centurion by rank and head of the Praetorian Guard by position, was preternaturally fast even without his exosuit. But it was obvious now that he wasn't faking the knee injury, as Parn's leg actually collapsed beneath him as he tried to dodge Tyrus's attack.

The result was that Tyrus reached his opponent and wrapped his arms around the taller but much thinner man, tackling him to the ground. And once there, his arms still encircling Parn's lower torso, Tyrus *squeezed*. He squeezed hard until he heard the satisfying crack of at least two ribs. To Parn's credit, the Martian released a violent breath but otherwise gave no outward indication of the pain he was enduring. So Tyrus kept squeezing.

Another rib cracked, then another, and he could feel the man struggling to move his diaphragm and breathe, but he just kept on squeezing. Finally, in barely a whisper, using the little air he had left, Parn gasped out, "Yield."

Tyrus immediately unwrapped his massive arms from around the lanky Martian. Then he collapsed back onto his butt, rubbing his jaw and a few cracked ribs of his own from earlier in the fight.

"You fight dirty, Visitor Tyne," the centurion wheezed, removing Tyrus's first name in a show of respect and familiarity.

"As do you, Centurion Parn," Tyrus answered likewise. He'd been surprised to learn, after the first sparring session with Parn six weeks prior, that to tell an opponent that they fought dirty was actually one of the sincerest forms of compliments a Martian could give regarding combat skills. The Martians were a strange lot. They valued honor above all else but also believed that it was not just the right but the *duty* of every warrior to do everything possible to win. That meant that even in practice combat, and especially in formal duels, which were still very much a part of Martian tradition and day-to-day life, it was fully expected and even encouraged to fight tooth and nail and use every advantage one could get.

There was one, and only one, exception to that rule as far as Tyrus had been able to ascertain. The groin was strictly off-limits in any engagement. In fact, to hit your opponent—whether man or woman—in the groin was so taboo on Mars that even to do so in a duel by accident meant immediate forfeit of the match and the offender's life. He supposed it had something to do with the low birth rates on Mars, which in turn were owed to the physiological changes the Martians had undergone through several hundred years of evolution to adapt to their low-gravity environment. To do anything that might jeopardize an opponent's ability to procreate was strictly forbidden.

Tyrus was grateful for that rule because Parn fought *dirty*, and he had become Tyrus's most frequent sparring partner since arriving on the red planet. Had the centurion been able to go for the genitals in combat, Tyrus would have found himself in a lot more pain on a daily basis than he already was.

Unfortunately, everything else was fair game, and Tyrus had yet to finish a match with Parn without suffering at least two or more broken bones. At least now, after six weeks of sparring with the centurion, he was inflicting nearly as many breaks as he was receiving, and sometimes even more, like today. In fact, had Parn not been wearing the exosuit that allowed him to withstand the much heavier hits that Tyrus, with his larger and denser muscles acclimated to a much higher gravity, could dole out, then the squeeze move he'd put on the man today would have almost certainly killed him.

An 'immune'—the Martian term for their medics—rushed over to see to Parn while another ambled over a bit more slowly to tend to Tyrus's wounds. Both held nothing more than a simple scanning device, which they ran over each man before analyzing the readings.

"Centurion Parn," the immune tending the Martian said, "you will need an hour in the baths and approximately two hours after that before you see combat again, Mars willing."

"Visitor Tyrus Tyne," the woman tending Tyrus said next, "you will need forty-five minutes in the baths and approximately one and a half hours before you see combat again . . . Mars willing." She added the last part with an almost defiant look into Tyrus's eyes. He had laughed the first time one of the medics had used the strange term at the end of their diagnosis. Having been raised in the Council-controlled 47 Colonies, where religion was strictly outlawed, he had never understood a belief in God nor seen the need for it. He hadn't *meant* to show disrespect to the Martian belief in a supreme being, especially one named after their own planet, but the term had just sounded so unnatural coming from a medical professional that he'd chuckled before he'd known what he was doing.

He'd only laughed the once. That had also been the day Parn had challenged him to a duel to the death on behalf of all Martians for his 'blasphemy'—a new word for Tyrus as well. Only a formal and solemn apology, coupled with his status as a 'godless off-worlder', had allowed him to gracefully back out of the challenge *and* regain Parn's respect. But this same immune had been the one to treat him on that first day, the one he'd laughed at, and it was clear that *she* still hadn't fully forgiven him.

"Well then, Visitor Tyne," Parn said in a tone that was way too cheerful for a man with a severely broken rib cage, "shall we go to the baths as the good immunes have counseled?"

Tyrus nodded, not trusting his voice through his broken jaw, which was now cramping up. But he did stand first and help Parn to his feet, which was just as much part of the ritual as anything else. The winner *always* helped the loser to his feet, unless it was a fight to the death. There was deep meaning behind the act, which Tyrus still didn't fully understand, but it symbolized an end to all animosity that might linger from the fight itself or the events leading up to it.

With Parn's arm around his shoulder, Tyrus helped the man hobble off the sparring mat and toward a door at the far end of the gymnasium. The soldier could barely walk on his injured knee; otherwise, Tyrus's further assistance after helping him to his feet would have been seen as an insult and probably resulted in an immediate resumption of their fight, injuries or no. However, with Parn's knee busted, it was okay to help the man . . . probably.

Tyrus's head was constantly spinning with the intricacies of Martian etiquette, even after two and a half months on the planet, more than half that time spent sparring with Parn and other members of the Praetorian Guard on a daily basis.

They hobbled together to the door and down a short hall before entering another door to their left. As they crossed the threshold into this new space, the humidity hit Tyrus like an additional punch to the face. The baths were exactly what they sounded like: long and deep public baths that every Martian used after training, especially if they were injured. The water was imbued with healing properties that went far beyond minerals or even chemical additives. Martian technology was, in many ways, leaps ahead of that of the colonies and even the other Four Worlds, particularly in the area of nanotech.

The bath water, Tyrus had been horrified to learn after his first foray into it, was teeming with nanites. These incredibly small bots, unlike the ones that literally made up the skin of Martian space stations and warships, were programmed specifically to infiltrate the bodies of anyone who used the baths and *heal* their physical injuries. By telling Tyrus and Parn how long they should stay in the baths, the immunes had been instructing them on how long it would take the nanites to reset and repair their broken bones and torn muscles and tendons.

It had taken Tyrus a while to get used to the idea of letting microscopic Martian robots infest his body, but he had to admit that they *worked.* Breaks and other injuries that would have taken weeks to heal with the best Earth or colonial medicine took hours or even minutes in the Martian baths.

Tyrus helped Parn remove his exosuit and the underskin and then removed his own combat skinsuit. Afterward, he helped Parn hobble down the steps into the bath until the man could float freely.

A figure swam over from the middle of the pool to join them. "My Centurion," Domitia Felix said with a nod toward Parn. "Visitor Tyrus Tyne." Domitia was a near-constant presence during their sparring sessions and had often sparred with Tyrus herself, actually getting angry with him on several occasions when he'd subconsciously, or perhaps consciously, held back because she was both a woman and of such slight build. It had literally taken him breaking her collarbone and femur in the same fight for her to finally forgive him for initially taking it so easy on her.

They'd also gone to lunch several more times, though the conversations hadn't gotten much better than that first time. She was still a woman of few words, at least in Tyrus's presence, and tended toward short, terse answers to all his questions. Being around her was a minefield for him, as she seemed to easily disapprove when he unknowingly stepped on a Martian custom or one of their thousands of social mores. She'd also made it clear, almost painfully so, on every occasion they'd eaten together that she had no romantic interest in him or even desire to be his friend. Strictly professional.

Which all made it extremely strange just how much Tyrus enjoyed being around her and looked forward to it during the times they were apart. He oddly found every second with the woman to be a happy one for him.

With one glaring exception. The baths. Martian men and women shared bathhouses without exception. And while they certainly weren't nude in them, they weren't that far off. Which made it very hard not to stare, especially given the unusual anatomy of the Martians, all long and stretched out in unnatural ways. Unfortunately, staring at someone in the baths violated—as near as Tyrus could tell—at least a dozen different rules on the red planet. Knowing that didn't make it any easier *not* to do it.

Of course, if Tyrus were being honest with himself, the strangeness of the Martian anatomy wasn't the only reason he had trouble not staring at Domitia Felix in particular. She was breathtaking, at least to his eyes, and he found his gaze often lingering on the mostly serious woman's face.

"Good morn, Optio," Parn said. Domitia's rank was akin to a senior lieutenant in the Guard Paramilitary Force back in the colonies. She oversaw twenty-five of the hundred praetorian guards under Parn's command.

"Have you finished identifying the candidates for the hundredth post?" Parn asked Domitia.

She nodded, her long black hair bobbing in the water around her. "I have three candidates for the post and will be presenting them to you for the Trials in forty hours," she responded. Tyrus had learned that the Martian Praetorian Guard must always have exactly one hundred guards, not including commissioned officers, and that anytime a post became vacant, it had to be filled within three weeks. To fill a single spot, multiple candidates, always the elite of Mars's armed forces, competed for the honor via a very dangerous and often deadly series of physical and mental tests known as the Trials.

Tyrus resisted the urge now to ask if he could join and observe the upcoming contest; he already knew that only current members of the Praetorian Guard and the candidates themselves were allowed to be there. But he definitely wished he could be.

Happening to glance over at Domitia as she spoke, he also found himself resisting another urge. Unfortunately, she caught his look. "Visitor Tyrus Tyne," she said in a matter-of-fact voice, adding his first name back into her speech despite dropping it earlier in a small show of familiarity. "Your gaze lingers."

Tyrus felt himself turning red, and it had nothing to do with the steaming water he swam in or the nanites that he could feel painfully reknitting his ribs and jaw—at least they deadened *some* of the nerves first, or the process would have been excruciating. If only he could deaden the rest of his nerves right now.

"My apologies, Optio Domitia Felix," he said, though his words came out slurred from his numb and broken jaw. "As always, your beauty overcomes me."

It was the rote response a man on Mars was expected to give if a woman caught him staring, regardless of whether it was in the bath-house or out on the street, fully clothed or not. It was considered rude to stare at any woman on Mars without being invited to do so. Tyrus, of course, had no idea under what circumstances a woman might invite a man to gaze at her—did the men ask for such a privilege, or was it entirely up to the woman? He hadn't the foggiest. What he *did* know was that Domitia seemed to derive a savage glee from calling him out every time she saw his eyes on her, even for a moment.

Now came the critical part. Having been caught with his gaze on her, he had given the expected response, complimenting her beauty, hoping that she would take flattery over offense and move on. If she didn't . . .

Domitia smiled slightly at him.

"Should I leave?" This question was from Parn and was also part of the social dance. Because now came the most awkward part, at least for Tyrus. If Domitia said yes to Parn's offer to give them some scant privacy, then it was a sign that Tyrus's attentions were welcome, even if they were accidental. Tyrus would then be required to begin courting her—an insanely complex and convoluted series of social moves that made his brain hurt—accepting her will in the matter, even if it was counter to his own. It was the price of being caught even *looking* in Martian society.

Luckily, as she always did, Domitia spared Tyrus further embarrassment. "No, Centurion Parn. Not today, I think," she said lightly. "Visitor Tyrus Tyne, I forgive your rudeness."

Tyrus turned back to Parn, stifling a sigh of relief. His part in the complex social dance was now to pretend that the awkward exchange had never happened. He really didn't know how the Martians got *anything* done with their complex social rules.

"Who are the candidates?" Parn asked Domitia next, ignoring Tyrus's obvious discomfort.

"The first is Triarch Jason Skydancer of the People's Navy, Fleet of the Eagle," she replied.

Tyrus knew that the rank of triarch was equivalent to a battleship captain and technically senior to Parn's own centurion rank. However, Tyrus had also gleaned that, no matter the man's current rank, Skydancer, if he won the Trials, would enter the Guard as a simple celeusta. It was the equivalent of a chief petty officer, and it was the level at which all new members of the Praetorian Guard began. They would even make Skydancer change his last name, thereby suborning familial attachments to his loyalty to the Guard. It was terribly convoluted, as with all things Martian.

"The second," Domitia continued, "is Centurion Alexander Kilnfire of the People's Legion, Saturn Regiment, and the third is Celeusta Vesta Lonesearcher of the Pluto Regiment." The last name piqued Tyrus's attention. For a mere celeusta to be considered for a spot in the

Guard, when so many more senior officers coveted the role even at the cost of a steep demotion, the woman in question must be something indeed.

Mulling this over, he almost missed Parn's next question.

"And the fourth? There must be four candidates—no more, no less, Optio."

Domitia nodded in reply. "There must be four, but we have only three, and only forty hours to the designated start of the Trials." It was a frank admission, but the way she said it made Tyrus think he must be missing something. Surely, there were enough willing and able officers in the whole of the Martian armed forces to fill one more slot.

To his surprise, Parn turned and looked straight at Tyrus. "Visitor Tyne, what say you?"

The question caught him off guard. "What say I to what?" he asked in confusion, annoyed at how his words continued to slur and stumble even as the nanites repaired his jaw.

"What say you to the Trials? There must be a fourth candidate. And you have proven yourself worthy of the contest."

Tyrus froze, sinking a bit in the deep water before starting to churn his feet again to keep his head above the surface. Was Parn really asking *him* to participate in the Trials, to consider joining the Centurion Guard? It was insane! He wasn't even Martian, and he had other obligations, didn't he? Jinny was still somewhere back on Earth, or so he hoped, and she might need him. He . . .

He looked at Parn and saw the expectation on the man's face. Then Tyrus looked at Domitia and saw what could have almost been hope in hers, and in that moment, he had two terrible realizations. First, that this was a one-time offer with a short expiration date. If he did not answer in the affirmative within the next few seconds, the offer would be withdrawn and never extended to him again. Which should have been just fine with him if not for his second startling realization:

That he desperately wanted this.

Ever since breaking his enacter programming almost a year ago, Tyrus hadn't felt like he belonged anywhere. He'd bounced between being Jinny Ambrosa's personal, self-appointed bodyguard and an adviser to the United Earth Navy but never really part of either life.

And the frustrating two-plus months spent on Mars hadn't done anything to help that feeling . . . except for the time he'd spent training and sparring with Parn, Domitia, and the other members of the Praetorian Guard.

But it was crazy! He wasn't Martian, didn't know if he agreed with or even liked their government, or if he wanted to stay on the red planet for a second longer than he had to. However, despite all of that, only one response *felt* right to him, and he did something that surprised even him—he surrendered himself to that feeling.

"Yes," he said, bowing his head to Parn first and then Domitia. "I humbly accept my place as a candidate."

Even more surprising was that after he gave the response, and long after he parted from Parn and Domitia and returned to his guest apartment in the Olympus Mons Government Center, he still felt that the decision—the answer he'd given in the moment—had been the right one. Maybe it was because he so much wanted to *belong* to something after all this time separated from a true purpose, or maybe it was because of the profound respect he'd gained even in such a short time for Parn and the rest of his elite Guard, or maybe it was simply some of that divine inspiration he'd heard about on Earth and again on Mars. Or maybe it had something to do with Domitia Felix.

He thrust aside that last thought. No matter the reason or reasons, Tyrus now found himself less than two Martian days away from his one and only chance to earn something that he hadn't even known he'd wanted just hours before but now *needed* as badly as the oxygen in the air around him.

Forty-Two Years Ago; 689 P.D.

Corey hadn't gone to the gymnasium or taken a walk through the hanging gardens or studied the class material or anything else that Parvina had suggested he do on his first night on Mars. But he did go to the commissary; the food on the passenger liner hadn't been great, and he was hungry from his trip.

When he got to the commissary after a few wrong turns—the map layout on the pad was confusing—he entered to find it was a massive underground chamber full of chattering students, probably two to three hundred of them sitting in close quarters at long tables with benches. As he walked in the door, the tables nearest him stopped their conversations and turned to look at him. That set off a chain reaction, with the rest of the room turning in waves and quieting down to see what had caught the attention of their peers. For a single, agonizing second, the entire room studied him in absolute silence before the wave started again in the same direction, but this time with the students closest finishing their review of his appearance and turning to discuss something—probably him—while proceeding to ignore him otherwise. The rest of the room slowly followed suit.

Well, that was awkward, he thought, trying to brush off the mass encounter. Then, remembering Parvina's reaction when he'd stared at her and all of her talk of honor duels and fights to the death, he made his way with eyes downcast to the line for food. Luckily, it was short. It seemed he'd arrived at the end of the traditional dinner hour, and most of the students either already had their food or were done eating and socializing.

At least that part's like Earth, he thought wryly. After the strange, stilted exchange with Parvina, he'd almost expected the entire student body to be sitting in absolute silence, eyes fixed straight ahead, spooning soup into their mouths in perfect unison to the beat of a drum. *Good to know that college students are social everywhere.*

Once he had his food, he was now presented with the challenge of where to sit. He looked around to see if he could spot any empty tables but found none. Then he looked to see if there were any tables with one end or several seats empty so he could sit in relative isolation. Again, he found none.

Briefly, he considered taking the food back to his room but quickly discounted the idea due to the logistics involved. Was he even allowed to take his tray, plates, and silverware out of this chamber? Once he did, how would he return them? There wasn't exactly an excess of space in his dormitory with twenty-nine other people there; having the leftovers of dinner out and forcing people to step over or around them would be awkward unless he planned to sleep with the tray and dirty dishes in his bunk with him.

Seeing no other option, he steeled himself and walked up to one of the nearest tables, where a mixed group of young men and women talked to each other and where there was a single empty seat. It was blessedly on the end of the table's bench, so he would only actually have to sit next to one person.

He moved up and waited for a lull in the conversation, which came as all eyes drifted to fix upon him. Then he focused his own gaze on the boy sitting next to the empty seat. "Is this seat taken?" he asked.

The boy looked confused for a moment, and Corey realized his mistake. Of course the seat wasn't taken; anyone could see it was empty. What kind of a question was that? Martians were literal—his tutors had explained that at length.

"Sorry," he amended. "I meant to say, may I please sit here?"

The boy shrugged, which looked almost comical, as it had on Parvina, given his incredibly narrow and sharp shoulders. "You may," he answered simply, then turned away and resumed his conversation, as did the rest of the table along with him, ignoring the odd Earther for the moment. Corey sat down and started picking at his food, none of which he could actually identify.

There was a bed of something that looked like it might be rice, but it was red, and the grains were far smaller. Then there was a small bowl of something brown with chunks that looked like a stew and had an aroma that vaguely reminded him of curry. Finally, there was a twisted mass of thin green stalks, perhaps some sort of vegetable.

He mentally resigned himself and used his fork to shove a mouthful of the red almost-rice into his face. Then he dropped the fork and frantically grabbed at his beverage cup—plain water, thankfully—as his entire mouth exploded in gut-wrenching fire.

He downed the entire water cup in one go and sat gasping for breath as the pain slowly abated. He vaguely noticed that the rest of the table was watching him again, and he even heard a few whispered giggles from one or two of the girls.

"First time eating Martian cuisine?" an alto voice asked in an almost melodious tone. He looked up through eyes filled with tears, wiping them away with the back of his hand.

When his vision cleared, he found himself staring at the most beautiful woman he had ever seen, which was far from a seldom thought for him as a young man, but this time he *really* meant it. She had dark brown skin, reminding him of Indian or Latin American origins, but it was offset by hair so blond it was almost white, and eyes of such a startlingly blue color that he couldn't help but stare at them. When she smiled at him, it looked like an easy and natural expression, as if it were her default. The girl was tall and willowy and reminded him of elves he'd seen in a movie back on Earth. She wouldn't have looked out of place wearing a thin metal crown and long, flowing white robes. Instead, she wore a simple headband that held her hair back and a shirt that fell off of one shoulder, revealing smooth skin there. She was mesmerizing.

He hadn't noticed her when he'd first sat down, even though she occupied the seat directly across from him, so intent had he been on *not* staring at anyone at the table. But now he couldn't take his eyes off her.

"I asked," she said in that melodious voice, "if this was your first time eating our cuisine."

Not trusting his voice to make it past the fire in his mouth, he nodded.

"Well," she said without the smile wavering, "I would recommend you *not* start with the ignis rice. The name means 'fire', and it lives up to the name. You would be better served with the curry there." She motioned to his bowl. "It is still spicy, maybe too spicy by Earth standards, but far less so than the rice."

He nodded dumbly again, unable to keep his eyes off her. Then, he abruptly remembered the experience with Parvina and looked back down at his plate. "Thank you," he said shakily, and reached down with his fork to spear one of the chunks floating in the bowl of curry. Unsure he wanted to eat it but not wanting to offend a girl who could have been a stretched-out Greek goddess, he plopped the chunk of meat—hopefully—into his mouth and chewed.

It wasn't bad. It was spicy but about on par with some of the hotter Mexican food he'd had at his parent's home in San Diego. The meat had a texture he wasn't familiar with but took on the flavor of the curry without its own strong taste. He finished chewing, then swallowed, looked back up at the girl, and nodded. "Thank you," he said again, and she smiled once more. He stared again, then looked quickly away and back at his food once he realized what he was doing.

Stupid, he thought as he took the next bite. *You're going to get yourself killed in a duel on your first day if you're not careful, you idiot! I need to call Dad and see if I can get on the next ship out of here before I* am *killed.* But it was only idle thought; his father would brook no failure from his only son. Corey would remain on Mars for the full nine months of the school year. It was as simple as that, even if it might result in his actual death. He felt like he was stuck in one of the video games he'd grown up playing, except in this one, he might die and *not* respawn.

"What is your name?" the willowy, beautiful girl asked, and he looked back up in surprise.

Forcing down the mouthful he'd just taken, he cleared his throat. "Corey. Corey O'Leary," he told her. She nodded as if his name made some sort of sense to her, and he felt himself get irrationally excited at her approval of it. Then he waited for her to offer her own name, but she didn't.

Maybe she was waiting for him to ask, but as he opened his mouth to do so, a chime rang, and every student in the large room abruptly set down their silverware and stood up, taking their trays and straightaway moving toward one of the refuse bins in the four corners of the room.

Corey was left in his seat, stunned, watching them go. Obviously, the break between classes or activities or whatever was over, and just like that, it was back to business. He looked down longingly at his own food, feeling his stomach rumble, but dutifully stood up and took his tray to the nearest bin.

By the time he had disposed of his food and deposited his tray, plates, and utensils in the appropriate places, he was one of the last people left in the chamber. Morose and still hungry, he walked back to his room, following the directions on the pad in reverse and thinking about the beautiful girl and how he hadn't gotten her name. At least she hadn't challenged him to some duel just for staring at her.

Present Day

"You did what?" Corey O'Leary, formerly *Congressman* O'Leary of United Earth, but now considered a traitor to his own people, made no effort to moderate the tone of his voice as he shouted at Tyrus from across the dinner table.

Tyrus didn't shrink from O'Leary's shout; he'd faced down government bureaucrats all his life, though he respected this one a lot more than most. That was especially true given the incredible risks O'Leary had taken both to save Jinny's life and to attempt to get Mars to assist Earth and Europa in fending off the inevitable Council invasion. But now, he met the older man's gaze firmly and refused to back down.

"I am participating in the Trials to join the Praetorian Guard," he said calmly a second time.

"Oh, I heard you," O'Leary said with a sardonic edge. "I just didn't think I heard you *correctly*. Do you realize how insane this is? Do you even know what being a member of the Guard entails, the commitments you'll have to make? Or, for that matter, do you have any idea of what is included in these so-called 'Trials'? I love the Martians, son, but it wouldn't surprise me if there's a fight to the death somewhere in there. Are you ready for that?"

Tyrus nodded solemnly, again surprising himself with his conviction that this was the right thing for him to do.

Corey must have seen the expression in Tyrus's eyes, because he shook his head in disbelief. "Well, isn't that something? This could either be the smartest thing you've ever done or the dumbest, and you'll either give great support to our mission here or tear it apart from the foundation on up. And just when I was finally making some real progress with the praetors."

He stopped, looking thoughtful. "It's a tremendous risk, but having you join the Guard may actually boost our cause by showing our commitment to Mars. Of course, that assumes you prevail in the Trials, because if you don't, who knows what the consequences will be for our mission here. It's not exaggerating, given the intricacies of Martian politics and religion, which are always commingled in ways that an outsider just can't understand, to say that you losing the Trials could even trigger an immediate expulsion of our entire party from Martian territory. I really can't say.

"Tyrus, I wish you would have at least talked with me about it *before* you accepted their offer."

Tyrus shrugged, now somewhat chagrined but still resolved that he'd done the right thing, even if he admittedly hadn't thought through all the ramifications, especially the political ones. "Sorry, Corey," he said sincerely. "They didn't exactly give me the time to consult with you. I had about five seconds to give an answer, and I got the distinct impression that turning them down *would* have damaged our position here."

"Hmmm," the former congressman mused. "Does that mean you did so under some sort of duress? Perhaps I could approach Consul Starshadow about reversing your decision if—"

"No!" Tyrus said the word with such conviction that O'Leary actually jumped a bit in his seat, and even Riggs, who had been trying very hard to pretend to ignore the conversation, startled. The only one who didn't react immediately was Toby, though he did look shocked after a second's delay.

"Listen, Congressman," Tyrus said more calmly now—he still occasionally used the man's former title as a show of respect. "I know this complicates things, but it's something I need to do. I can't explain why, only that it just feels right. I know that sounds a bit crazy, and maybe it is, but Jinny kept trying to tell me to follow my feelings more when we were together on Earth. And I *feel* that this is the best thing I could do here, both for myself and for our mission."

Corey frowned for a moment longer, then let out a sigh and looked up at the ceiling in a clear sign of surrender. "Well, Tyrus, if that's truly how you feel. Far be it from me to stand between you and something you've set your mind to, or to counter Jinny's advice, for that matter. But if you're going to participate in the Trials, you need to *win*."

Tyrus nodded slowly. "I just wish I knew what the Trials entailed."

Corey frowned again and looked back at him. "I tried asking Aphrodite—Consul Starshadow—once, just out of curiosity. Not only did she not *know* the answer, but she was horribly offended that I even asked. It took me a few days to get her to even speak to me again, and this was way back when we were . . . never mind. Few topics of discussion are off limits in Martian society, as you've well discovered, but the Trials of the Praetorian Guard definitely fall into that category. Still, I would hope that your alpha training will serve you well. Apart from trusting in that, all we can really do is hope. How does your body feel?"

Tyrus knew the man was asking about his recovery from the almost daily beatings he and Parn had delivered to each other over the last nearly two months, ever since the centurion had first invited him to spar a month into their sojourn on Mars.

He shrugged in reply. "Exceptionally good, all things considered. Those nanites of theirs are miraculous little things once you get past the revulsion of a million tiny machines crawling inside your body."

Out of the corner of his eye, he saw Riggs physically shiver at the mental image. The ship captain was the next one to speak up, which was unusual for him; even nearly three months after Jynx's death, he was abnormally quiet and introverted. "What happens if you win? Are you a member of this Praetorian Guard for life? Or would it be a ceremonial post offered to you for political reasons?"

It was an astute question, surprisingly so for a smuggler and ne'er-do-well like Cal Riggs purported to be. But Tyrus had found that the man had surprising depths, and Jinny had still never figured out, or at least never told Tyrus that she'd figured out, how Riggs was somehow immune to her reader abilities. The man was an enigma.

Corey answered for Tyrus. "The Martians are big on symbolism, but only insomuch that it enhances the ceremony and procedures already in place. I don't think Parn would offer this if he wasn't dead serious about Tyrus joining the Praetorian Guard as a fully functioning member. Which means"—he turned back and looked pointedly at Tyrus—"that Mars may very well become your new permanent home."

"If that's what it means," Tyrus said solemnly, "then that's what it means. That should bother me, I suppose, but it doesn't."

Corey nodded. "I get it, odd as it is. I was an exchange student here for only nine months when I was younger—a school year, no more. But

I came within a hair's breadth of abandoning everything I had waiting for me back on Earth to stay here. Even so many decades later, I find myself wondering what my life would have been like if I'd made that decision differently. I can't say I regret it, but I also can't say I would have regretted it if I'd chosen to stay.

"Life is funny that way. Sometimes, we're faced with two paths, and either one would work for us, so it's really just up to us to choose the one we prefer. I'll admit that Mars does have a way of getting under your skin. Buried underneath all that symbolism and cultural nuances and formalities, the Martians are a surprisingly warm and welcoming people. I . . ."

He trailed off. He hadn't shared much of his experience on the planet as a young student, but it was clear to all of them that it had included a rather serious romantic relationship with Aphrodite Starshadow, the now ostensible ruler of the Martian People's Republic. It was also clear that the relationship had not ended on the best of terms, which had complicated their mission here to get Mars to throw in their efforts with the rest of the Four Worlds when the Council Navy arrived in the Sol system again. They could all see the conflict in O'Leary's eyes whenever he spoke of Aphrodite, even though the man was happily married to Debra O'Leary back on Earth and had been for more than thirty-seven years.

"I'd like to come and watch the Trials." The words surprised Tyrus, coming from the normally taciturn and quiet Toby. The boy was looking up now, his gaze sharper than usual, conveying his obvious interest.

"That I *do* know is forbidden," O'Leary answered before Tyrus could. "Even to ask would subject you to an immediate duel to the death, so I advise you not to say that where any Martian can hear you," he chided the boy.

Toby shrugged and went right back to examining the table's silverware, something he seemed to do a lot of during their frequent meals as a group. It was as if the boy didn't know what to do with his eyes and hands in normal social situations.

"How long do you have?" Riggs asked Tyrus.

"The Trials start at midnight the day after next. They haven't told me yet where I must go for them, and I get the impression I shouldn't ask—that they'll tell me when they're ready for me to know. I do know who I'm up against, however." He turned to O'Leary. "If I give you some names, can you get me access to their public personnel files?"

The older man rubbed his nose in deep thought, then nodded. "That shouldn't break any rules of propriety that I can think of, especially if we're only talking about the *public* files. I would expect any candidate to do their research on their fellow candidates via those means. I have an early meeting with Consul Starshadow and Praetor Sunsbane tomorrow morning. Sunsbane, in particular, is sympathetic to our cause and genuinely friendly. I should be able to find a way to ask him that won't trigger any social or traditional land mines. I'll let you know what I find out."

Tyrus smiled gratefully and took out his pad, typing in the names he'd heard from Domitia Felix and then swiping toward Corey to send the information to his hand implant; Tyrus's Council-issue watch, which he'd finally stopped wearing a month ago, wasn't compatible with Earth hardware or software, but Martian tech largely was, so he'd taken to using a tablet brought from Earth, connected to the Martian Internet. Of course, they all assumed the Martians watched everything they sent over the network and had probably hacked all of their tablets and even Corey's implant, so they were careful with what they shared via those means.

"Well, now that that's settled," Riggs said gruffly, "can someone explain to me again what in blazes I'm supposed to do when a Martian girl hits on me? Because they won't stop, really."

A chorus of groans greeted him, with even Toby joining in. And Tyrus thought of how good it was to finally hear some of the old captain coming through, even if he knew Riggs was only trying to break the tension in the room.

CHAPTER 10

Forty-Two Years Ago; 689 P.D.

Corey made it back to his room from the commissary, only taking one wrong turn along the way, and found it empty. It was 1900 local time, and obviously, the day's activities were not done yet. He had nothing to do, so he laid back on his bed and used his pad to pull up information on his classes for the next day. He might as well study a bit, so he wouldn't be too terribly behind the rest of the class.

The first subject was environmental science and was mostly the same as what he'd learned on Earth, at least in principle. Based on the pictures in the book, though, the lighter gravity on Mars did some extremely strange things to the flora and fauna on the red planet. Some he could sort of recognize as stemming from plants and animals on Earth, but there were certainly a few that were so foreign he couldn't imagine their evolutionary path.

The second subject was math and really wasn't anything new. Math was math, just as boring and useless, in Corey's estimation, no matter what planet you learned it on. But the third subject was history, and it was full of new material that he'd never read or studied before, all about Mars and almost nothing about Earth or the wider Sol system.

He devoured that, reading for a full hour before he fell asleep with the pad on his chest.

He awoke to the sound of other people chattering and moving about the room. He opened his eyes and was startled to see a tall, thin, brown-haired girl standing next to his bunk, her legs mere centimeters from his head. But what really shocked him was that the girl was wearing little more than undergarments.

He meant to quickly avert his eyes, he really did. But the surprise was just too much for him. Corey had been raised in a conservative family. He was no prude, but he'd never been one for wanton immodesty. Yet near-nudity aside, the anatomy of the girl in front of him was so . . . weird, so long and thin and stretched out, that he couldn't help but stare, and he kept staring dumbly as she proceeded to casually get dressed in clothes pulled from the closet right above his.

He was still staring in dumb shock when she looked down and caught him.

"Your gaze lingers, foreigner," she snapped in an unfriendly tone.

"I, uh, sorry. I just wasn't . . . expecting . . . I don't know. I'm sorry," he stammered, much as he'd done when Parvina had rebuked him for staring, but now even more flustered, embarrassed, and confused.

A boy stepped up next to the girl, staring down at Corey, who was still lying in bed and trying very hard not to look at the girl, though at least she was partially dressed now.

"Do you forgive or welcome his advance?" the boy asked the girl. *What?*

"I do not," the girl said, her voice carrying a hard edge.

"Then," the boy said, "I will see you avenged." He reached down and nudged Corey, who looked back up at him but found his eyes flickering back to the girl as well. The boy noticed and scowled at him.

"Your attentions are unwelcome, Earthling," the boy said, spitting out the last word like a curse. "I demand recompense on behalf of my bonded partner, and I challenge you to a duel."

Corey felt the blood, which had previously been rushing to his face and ears in shame, suddenly drain from his head. He sat up awkwardly on the too-high bed, his feet swinging over the side and not touching the ground, and looked up at the boy in shocked confusion.

"But I, uh, I don't know how to duel," was the only thing he could think to say. It did nothing to soften the boy's scowl.

"Dorrel Farstrider," a familiar voice interrupted, and Corey was shocked to see the elven goddess from the commissary step up next to the boy and the still half-dressed girl. "Do you not know that this boy is newly arrived and a stranger to our ways? The dean has expressly forbidden involving him in any honor duels for at least the first two weeks of his sojourn with us here."

The boy scowled, turning to look at the new girl instead of down at Corey. "Surely, the dean will make an exception for such a gross violation of etiquette. I must have recompense for my bonded partner," he argued.

The elven woman smiled softly. "I have studied Earth," she said calmly. "They have taboos on nudity that we do not share here, and the boy was simply shocked to see it so openly. I am sure he meant no disrespect. But if you are to duel him, then as the challenged party, he is allowed to pick the place, the weapon, and the conditions of combat." She turned her gaze to look down at Corey. "May I suggest tungsten sledgehammers in the UOM commons with the gravity dialed up to Earth standard and no augmentations allowed?"

She continued to look at him expectantly, as if waiting for him to respond. So he swallowed. "Um, sure. That sounds good, I guess."

The boy scowled, but it was the now fully dressed girl who had first startled Corey who spoke up. "In light of this new information, of the foreigner's unfamiliarity with our ways, I hold him no ill will so long as the offense does not repeat in the future."

Abruptly, the belligerent boy's features softened, and his scowl disappeared. "Then I also bear him no ill will and withdraw my challenge." He nodded down at Corey. "My name is Dorrel Farstrider, and you and I will be friends."

Corey didn't know what to say, which was becoming a disturbing pattern, so he just nodded dumbly, which was also becoming a disturbing pattern—the dumbness, not the nodding. The girl and boy left without another word, walking out of the row, squeezing past the elven goddess and then proceeding down the narrow aisle and out through the dormitory door.

"I thank you again," Corey said lamely, pushing himself off the bed and to his feet. He held out his hand to his rescuer, but she eyed it skeptically and did not reach out her own to take it, so he lowered it, feeling awkward. "What's your name?" he asked her, remembering his desire from dinner.

"I am Aphrodite Starshadow," the girl said in her captivating voice. She had changed her clothes since he'd seen her at dinner and now wore loose-fitting pants and a shirt that left her shoulders and neck bare. He fought hard not to let his eyes linger anywhere but on her face —he had learned his lesson already for the day.

"Your eyes do tend to linger, don't they, Earthling?" she asked, frowning. Obviously, he hadn't tried hard enough.

"I *am* sorry," he said as calmly as he could, but inside he was panicking. "I mean no offense."

She sighed. "I know you meant no offense, Visitor Corey O'Leary. But the ways of Mars are different from those of Earth, and you offend here with all you do. If I may be direct, you offend even by being who you are. Earthlings are not thought of favorably on Mars, and there are many in this dormitory who petitioned that you not be granted the honor of staying here with us."

He didn't know what to say to that, but as often happened with him, his mouth started talking before his brain caught up. "Were you one of those," he blurted out, "who didn't want me staying here?"

She shook her head. "I was ambivalent. I neither desired nor shunned your presence. I see now that I was perhaps mistaken. You are so willfully ignorant of our ways that you almost ended up in a blood feud your first evening with us. Either you are monumentally naive or incredibly stupid."

He didn't respond. She hadn't said it in a malicious tone but almost as one recounting the weather or buying a sandwich. Speaking of sandwiches, his stomach rumbled, and he looked down in embarrassment.

"Are you hungry still?" she asked.

"What gave it away?" he asked sarcastically. It was all starting to weigh down on him: the cultural issues, the isolation in a crowd of people, the near-death—or as close as he had ever come—experience with the duel challenge. He was sick and tired of Mars already and wanted to go home.

His sarcasm seemed to be lost on her. Aphrodite cocked her head. "Your stomach gave it away. Come. There is an all-night cafe in the hanging gardens. We will get you something more substantial to eat. And maybe more kind to your weak Earth palate."

He was tempted to say no. How was it possible that she could sound like she was insulting him even as she offered to help him? It was infuriating. At his university on Earth, Corey was considered relatively popular, though he never really knew if it was because of who he was or who his father was. Here on Mars, he was already an outcast, and everything this strange girl—Aphrodite—said to him seemed to reinforce the fact. But hunger overcame pride in this moment, so he stood and followed the elven beauty from the room.

Present Day

Corey entered the meeting chamber expecting to find two Martian Praetors and their retinues already there. No matter how on time or even early he came to these meetings, the Martians always seemed to be there first, waiting for him.

But when he stepped through the door, he was surprised to find only *one* occupant: Aphrodite Starshadow.

He stopped just inside, looking questioningly at his hostess, benefactor, and . . . once something more. Even after nearly three months on Mars, interactions with her continued to be awkward. She was cold toward him, clearly refusing to forgive him for the way things had ended between them but just as clearly refusing to let it come in the way of their discussions and negotiations. She'd been all business, and her attitude was clear: her personal relationship with Corey had ended long ago, and that was that.

"Consul Aphrodite Starshadow," he said with far more uncertainty in his voice than he would have liked. "Have I come at a bad time? I was under the impression Praetor Gale Sunsbane would be joining us this morning." Left unsaid was that he'd also been under the impression that several dozen aides, staffers, and praetorian guards should have been in the room. Every other time he'd tried to meet individually with Aphrodite, she'd ensured at least a half dozen others were always in attendance. The sudden change both worried and encouraged him.

"Sit, Emissary O'Leary," she said in a soft tone. "There is something of which we must speak."

Keying in on her omission of his first name—a clear sign this was to be a conversation of a more personal nature—he slowly walked from the door to a seat opposite her, sitting himself down and meeting her gaze. Corey loved his wife, Debra, dearly and would never consider cheating on her under any circumstances. But every time he looked into Aphrodite Starshadow's startling blue eyes . . . It was useless to even contemplate what might have been.

"I am here, Consul Starshadow," he said, dropping her first name to match her tone as required by Martian custom. "And I listen."

She stared at him for a long moment, and for the first time since he'd returned to Mars, he saw her eyes soften in his presence. "Your companion, Visitor Tyrus Tyne, will participate in the Trials tomorrow morning."

"Yes, Consul Starshadow," he said cautiously. After months of the cold shoulder from her, his mind raced to dissect the import of her new familiarity and her words about the upcoming Trials. "He will participate, and it is a great honor that he has been chosen as a candidate—"

"It is a deadly honor, at least," she said, cutting him off, some unidentifiable emotion creeping into her voice. "One he is unlikely to survive. But I requested that Praetor Sunsbane let me speak with you alone this morning to give you a warning."

Corey knit his brows together in confusion and stared back at her. "A warning about what exactly?" he asked slowly.

She sighed, and all remaining vestiges of formality left her posture and tone. "Emissary O'Leary, so little you still understand of us here on Mars. I know you have grown frustrated with our lack of progress in responding to your pleas for help in defending the system against the Council, but that lack of progress is only on the surface. Under that surface, as the magma roils under the surface of this mountain, there has been passionate debate amongst the Praetors as to what we should do. And while we might have almost reached an agreement early on, now with President Mikael Gorsky's turnabout, there have arisen three distinct factions in the Quorum, each of equal size."

"Go on," he prompted her.

"One faction, led by Praetor Sunsbane, is of the opinion that we should honor your request, even if your own government does not support you, and that we should prepare to add our Navy to the battle when the Council comes. They have even suggested that we would accept the military leadership—for the duration of the battle only, of course—of your Fleet Admiral Horatio Krishna Lopez." That actually came as little surprise to Corey. Sunsbane had been a Triarch—a battleship commander—in the war between Earth and Mars almost fifty years earlier and had battled head-to-head with Lopez and lost. That had immediately elevated the Earth commander in the young Sunsbane's eyes, and he had carried that respect through all these decades.

"The second faction, led by Praetor Moonslayer, argues the opposite, that we must reject all overtures from Earth and stay within our own territory, then take advantage of the situation by attacking both Earth and the Council after they have weakened each other."

Corey nodded. Again, not terribly surprising—and a very Martian way to think about the universe. A lot of his fellow politicians on Earth, including the unlamented former President Luis Pereira, thought the same way and had strongly opposed even asking Mars for assistance.

"And the third?" he asked, genuinely curious now that the two extremes had been claimed.

Aphrodite frowned. "The third is perhaps more troublesome than the second. They, led by Praetor Tiberius, argue that you have no negotiating power on behalf of Earth and that Earth's own attitude toward you and toward us proves that they would never honor any agreement with Mars. So they have turned their sights to an agreement with a third party."

Corey's mouth dropped open. "You don't mean . . . they want to negotiate with the Council? Don't they know that's suicide? The Council—excuse me, the Twenty—doesn't want peace with Mars or anyone else. They want the enhanced surrendered to them, and they want complete and utter subjugation, not even necessarily in that order! They—"

"Emissary O'Leary." She stopped him without raising her voice. She'd always had the ability to do that. "I agree with you." That simple statement surprised him. If anything, he'd expected her to be with the second camp, those who would put Mars first and let the rest of the Sol system fall. But if she was on his side, that meant . . .

"Wait, you said equal factions. But there are thirteen praetors, including yourself. So if you're part of Sunsbane's faction, or even just inclined toward it, as the consul, then shouldn't that put the decision in Sunsbane's favor?"

Aphrodite frowned again and shook her head slowly. "Even after your time among us, Emissary O'Leary, you still simply don't understand. As consul, I am honor-bound to stay above the fray and cannot publicly give my support to any of the factions. Only if one of them achieves a plurality can I then step in and either ratify their decision or dispute it. But as long as they remain deadlocked in equal groups of four, I cannot take any action to tilt the scales in one direction or another."

He opened his mouth to argue but stopped. The way she spoke to him now, almost as a friend, with a hint of the tone she'd used with him so long ago, told him she was sincere. Furthermore, he could sense that she was just as frustrated with the chains of convention as he was in this case. So, instead of arguing the point with her, he asked a question.

"Why tell me all this if there's nothing you can do? Is there something you expect *me* to do to break the stalemate?"

She smiled wanly at him. "Not you, but your companion, Visitor Tyrus Tyne."

And suddenly, it all made sense to him. The invitation from Parn for Tyrus to participate in the Trials, the nearly clandestine meeting alone this morning with Aphrodite, and everything else. He'd learned enough of Martian culture in his time with them long ago that he could put things together when she dropped hints on him like a ton of bricks.

"Tyrus is Praetor Sunsbane's champion, isn't he?"

She nodded with a sad expression. "As consul, I cannot show my support for any position of a deadlocked Quorum of Praetors, but I *can* suggest alternative means, beyond political debate, to break the deadlock. In this case, I suggested that each faction choose a champion from among those who will participate in the Trials tomorrow.

"Praetor Moonslayer chose Centurion Kilnfire. They are cousins of a sort, and Centurion Kilnfire is a favorite to win. Praetor Tiberius chose Celeusta Lonesearcher, who many think is both tougher and smarter than Centurion Kilnfire."

"And what of the Navy captain—sorry, triarch. Skydancer, I think his name was?" he asked her. Four participants and three factions made for some incomplete math.

"Few think he can best either Centurion Kilnfire or Celeusta Lonesearcher, but he would have ended up being the default choice for Praetor Sunsbane—until, that is, Centurion Parn invited Tyrus Tyne to participate."

Corey shook his head in disbelief. "Are you saying that you influenced Parn to pick Tyrus? All so he could be the champion for Sunsbane?"

He knew as soon as the words left his mouth that he was wrong to ask the question, confirmed by the offended look on Aphrodite's face. He was opening his mouth again to apologize when she waved off his attempt before it could start.

"As I said, you still understand us so little. I would never presume to tell Centurion Parn or even suggest to him that he include any candidate in the trials. That is his domain, and his domain alone, along with the officers he delegates. For me to interfere in the selection process would mean my immediate removal as consul and as a praetor, as well as a duel to the death in which Centurion Parn would be honor-bound to end my life.

"No, the centurion was already planning to invite Visitor Tyrus Tyne. He informed me of it so that I could review our laws to ensure that inviting a foreigner did not break any of our codes, which it did not. I simply *suggested* that he wait until a certain point in time to extend the invitation."

Now Corey got it, and he smiled broadly. "You mean after you'd already sold the praetors on the idea of a contest of champions?"

For the first time since he'd arrived on Mars, Aphrodite Starshadow smiled back at him—it was just a hint of a sly smile, but he would take it. "Yes, I admit to that," she said. "That way, Praetor Sunsbane could pick him as his champion, but at a point when it would be too late for the other factions to back out of the contest of honor."

Corey's smile instantly disappeared as further realization dawned on him. "But that means . . . that means the fate of the Four Worlds could very well rest on Tyrus winning the Trials." His mind raced. "But that may be okay because he has a built-in advantage, growing up in Earth-like gravity. He'll be faster, stronger, and more resilient than the other candidates. He . . ." Corey trailed off when he saw the pained expression on Aphrodite's face.

"I'm afraid," she said slowly, "that is simply not true." And as she explained, Corey's hopes fell.

Dinner that night in O'Leary's apartment was a solemn affair. There was little conversation as the four companions silently contemplated what awaited Tyrus just hours away in the Trials.

Several times in the course of the evening, Tyrus caught O'Leary looking at him strangely, and several times, the old man opened his mouth as if to speak but then shut it. Tyrus considered pressing him, forcing him to reveal what he was thinking, but he was reasonably sure the former congressman simply wanted to try again to talk him out of participating in the Trials

It wouldn't work. Tyrus was dead set. He had rarely felt this convinced of anything in his life, and he was even excited.

That excitement would not last long.

CHAPTER 11

Forty-Two Years Ago; 689 P.D.

Eight weeks gone of his sojourn on Mars, and Corey felt like he was slowly getting a handle on Martian culture. Not that he was fitting in quite yet—if anything, things had continued to get more awkward with his classmates. On his second day, he had casually asked where the showers were. The boy he'd posed the question to looked at him in confusion.

"Showers as in rain?" he asked Corey.

Which set Corey on a confusing attempt to explain a very basic concept to someone who looked at him like he was crazy. That was also how he found out about the bathhouses. Every floor in his dorm building had exactly one, and in it was exactly one large bath that *everyone* used, and all at the same time, completely irrespective of gender.

That had been awkward. For two weeks, he had tried to find times that the bathhouse was empty by going late at night or early in the morning, even skipping class once to try and go in the middle of the day when everyone else would be in class or studying.

Despite his many efforts, he'd never once found the bathhouse unoccupied. And he found that being there with fewer people was actually more awkward than bathing with a crowd. The most awkward had been when he'd walked in and found it deserted except for two classmates, both girls. He had immediately turned and walked out, skipping his bath for the day. At least the Martians all wore bathing suits, but that took less awkwardness from the situation than Corey might have expected. As the lone Earther in the dorm hall, he was an object of curiosity whenever he bathed. Whenever he wasn't watching—no Martian would allow themselves to be *caught* gazing at another like that—he could feel all eyes surreptitiously studying him.

The restrooms were even worse. Toilets lined up with no doors and no dividing walls, men and women using them without regard to those around them.

No, things were *not* getting less awkward. But at least he was starting to understand why things were the way they were. His class on Mars history had helped him in that, and it was the one and only class where he was actually *ahead* of the curriculum, reading the textbook ravenously on his pad whenever he got a chance.

Corey had learned that in the early days of Martian colonization, when the outside air was still unbreathable and the soil killed anything planted in it, all the original colonists were relegated to live in small, connected habitats or underground warrens excavated at great expense. The concept of a single-family home was completely foreign to those early colonists and was anathema to the size constraints of their rapidly growing civilization. In those days, everyone lived in communal homes. Adult couples had their own small capsule-like accommodations that at least had curtains that closed but were still barely large enough to fit two grownups lying down. But the children of multiple families, regardless of age or gender, shared a single central room with bunks. By necessity, privacy—and therefore modesty—was nonexistent. The children and even adults lived virtually and literally on top of each other. There was no such thing as a moment alone, a private place to change clothes, or even time alone as a family, given that anywhere from five to ten families or more usually shared a single living area.

This led to the development of a culture that both eschewed privacy and somehow also radically embraced it. Physical privacy was nonexistent, so taboos around nudity and near-nudity were quickly lost by the time the second generation started having children of their own. Most surprisingly, however, the abandonment of those taboos did not lead to the culture one might have expected.

When Corey had first seen the men and women changing in front of each other in the dormitory, he had thought that the Martians must be the most promiscuous culture in human space, which was saying something. He also assumed that in the tight confines, they must be unfailingly polite to each other lest fights should break out.

He was wrong on both counts. The Martian colonists had learned early on that if they were to have their children, especially their teenagers, of different genders live together with no privacy, they *had* to instill in them different norms of sexuality than their predecessors had left behind on Earth. As a result, Martian children were taught from a young age that most forms of physical contact between men and women were to be reserved only for those with whom they'd made a long-term commitment. As such, they were taught that the bodies of their coeds were strictly off-limits until they were ready and able to make such commitments, and this was reinforced by the teachings of their parents as well as in the school curriculum.

What resulted was a society that, with few exceptions, practiced strict abstinence outside of marriage. Even 'bonded partners,' which Corey loosely interpreted as something between boyfriend/girlfriend pairings and engaged couples, limited their contact to chaste and brief kisses. Hugs were rare and never seen in public. It was odd to observe for someone raised on Earth and used to all sorts of public displays of physical affection. But he supposed it made a strange sort of sense. If you were going to be in close quarters with members of the opposite sex, even in your most private moments, you had to be comfortable that they were not going to take advantage of those moments. It also helped, of course, that those who took advantage most often lost their lives via the complex and deadly system of honor duels.

Which led to his second false assumption: that the close quarters and lack of privacy would make the Martians unfailingly polite. They were most decidedly not. In place of politeness was frank and unfiltered directness, along with a culture that embraced the formal resolution of problems via duels of honor. Being in close quarters at all times meant that there was little room for suppressed feelings of dislike or social friction. If someone liked you, they made it known. If they disliked you, they also made it known. If, in either situation, you felt they were over-exuberant in the way they shared their feelings for you, you could seek satisfaction in a duel.

It was so foreign to him, and he still understood so little of it, but he was at least beginning to wrap his head around the basics. Stranger still, because of the duels and the fact that *every* Martian received combat training from a young age, there were no Martian police and still virtually no crime of any kind. Anyone caught even attempting a crime would risk being immediately killed by the witnesses.

Today, Corey was on his way to meet Aphrodite Starshadow—he always called her by her full name, as was the Martian custom, until the woman decided they were close enough to use first names alone. She had invited him to dinner . . . with her parents. The invitation had surprised him. In just a few weeks, he and the strange Martian girl had become fast friends, spending most evenings together, her giving him tours of the areas surrounding the university campus. She'd also been ravenously curious about his upbringing on Earth, asking him all manner of questions. He, in turn, asked her about Martian traditions and culture. It had been a mutually beneficial relationship.

Corey wanted it to be more than that. Despite his popularity back home, he had historically been shy around women. He was hardly what anyone would call a ladies' man and had found few women in his short lifespan whom he would have wanted a meaningful relationship with. But almost from the moment he'd first seen and spoken to Aphrodite Starshadow in the commissary on his first awkward night on Mars, he'd been smitten with the elvish beauty.

That had very quickly evolved from physical attraction to something more. He enjoyed every second of his time with her, finding her to be the most genuine person he had ever met. She was so blunt and honest with him, even by Martian standards, but in a way that never conveyed malice or disdain. She was the opposite of the sycophants he'd dealt with most of his life—those who would cultivate a relationship with him to get to his father's trillions, but not out of any real desire to get to know *him*.

One could say that Aphrodite was refreshingly rude to him. On their second time going to dinner, his third day on Mars, he had dressed in the dormitory in an outfit he'd brought from Earth for special occasions—wool pants and a button-down shirt his mother had picked out for him. Aphrodite, dressing just a few meters away, had laughed out loud at him. "Corey O'Leary," she had said between bouts of laughter, "that outfit is ridiculous. Why would anyone wear such a thing? You cover up every inch of your body. Is it not hot?"

It wasn't hot. In fact, Corey found that most of his time on Mars, he'd felt rather cold. The Martians had adapted physically to their world, and that included its lower temperatures. The 22-degree Celsius weather of the early fall on this part of Mars was considered warm by their standards.

Corey could have been offended or put out by her laughter and statement about his clothes; to laugh at another on Mars was to mortally offend them unless they welcomed the laughter, which he surprisingly did. The magical notes of her laugh—Martians so rarely laughed about anything—and the frankness of her words somehow felt good to him. He walked over to the dormitory's single mirror, looked at himself, and then joined her in laughing uproariously at his clothing.

Every day, he found himself falling for her more. But on the few occasions he had tried to bring it up to her, she had rebuked him gently and stated bluntly that she had no interest in 'pairing with a foreigner.'

So, the invitation to dine with her parents had surprised him greatly. It also made him terribly nervous. Aphrodite did not talk about her family, but he had gathered from listening to others that she was a sort of minor celebrity and that her parents were among Mars's ruling class. He was so nervous, in fact, that he found himself automatically reaching for the wool pants and button-up shirt that Aphrodite had poked fun at before.

Instead, he grabbed an outfit she had purchased for him during his second week on the planet. It was a pair of long, flowing pants that the shopkeeper had needed to hem shorter for his Earther frame. The shirt was a short sleeve with a V-neck that made him subconscious by showing his three or four chest hairs. Still, it was a style he'd seen on many of his male classmates, so he felt it was a safe choice for a night out on Mars.

Aphrodite chose that moment to walk into the dormitory from class. She looked him up and down and nodded her approval but said nothing else. He wasn't sure why, but he got the impression she might have been as nervous as he was for the dinner with her parents.

He pointedly didn't watch her get dressed. Now that the strangeness of the coed dormitory and lack of privacy had softened, he was finding that he really didn't have all that much trouble keeping his eyes to himself. Perhaps it was his upbringing, or maybe it was the casual way in which the Martians conducted themselves in what would be charged situations on Earth. Either way, he was finding it less difficult than he would have expected to respect the virtual privacy of his coeds in a world where literal privacy did not exist.

Aphrodite cleared her throat to signal she was done, and he looked at her and couldn't help but stare. She was wearing a diaphanous white robe that offset her dark skin perfectly. It was open in the front, and in true Martian fashion, she wore a simple pair of shorts and a wrap to cover her torso. The outfit was neither overly revealing nor overly modest, but it looked perfect on her and reminded him of his first impression of her: an elven goddess.

They rode in an aircar together to a restaurant that was perched on the side of Olympus Mons itself. Aphrodite had told him that the mountain, still an active volcano, was hollowed out in places with government and military facilities built in a complex system of tunnels. Outwardly, all one could see of those facilities was an occasional window or balcony carved into the slopes and several landing platforms that jutted out from the mountainside.

Civilian businesses had also been built on the enormous mountain, but they were rarer. The restaurant they were going to on this evening was among the most expensive on Mars and further reinforced the fact that the Starshadow family was well above the planetary average.

When they arrived, they were shown to a table where an older

Martian couple already waited. Corey felt himself growing tense as they approached the pair, and he bowed deeply when they finally arrived at the table before taking his seat. As was tradition, he bowed first to Aphrodite's mother and then to her father. Only then did he open his mouth to introduce himself, but Aphrodite beat him to it.

"My Mother, my Father," she said in that melodious voice he loved so much. "This is Visitor Corey O'Leary of Earth. I wished for you to meet him this evening."

Her mother gave a wan smile, and her father showed no emotion as Corey and Aphrodite took their seats, the ritual of greetings over. A waiter came and took their drink order and then left them alone.

"Visitor Corey O'Leary," her father began without preamble, ignoring a look his daughter shot him. "You are the son of Jameson O'Leary, are you not?"

"I am, Patriarch Johan Starshadow," Corey replied, using the honorific due to all the male heads of houses on Mars.

"Your father is exceedingly rich," the man observed. Corey fought the urge to frown but said nothing. There was no question in the statement and, therefore, no expectation that he would respond. Aphrodite's father continued without waiting for his reply anyway. "He is suspected to have come by his fortune through unethical business practices. What say you to that?"

Aphrodite froze, a look of horror flashing across her face, and even her mother stopped raising the wine glass to her mouth and stared at her husband. While the man's tone hadn't been overly rude by Martian standards, his words represented a direct challenge. To call a man or woman unethical on Mars was one of the highest of insults and would usually be met by the offended party instantly challenging the speaker to a duel.

With monumental effort, Corey didn't flinch. He had lived his entire life with allegations like this against his father. There was always someone who wished to besmirch the name of the fourth-richest man in United Earth, and they usually did so to Corey as they were too cowardly to do it to Jameson O'Leary's face.

He smiled at Aphrodite's father. "There are all sorts of allegations," he admitted. "But a wise man ignores empty allegations and values only hard evidence won by experience."

If anything, the table became even more still. Corey's statement had not been directly insulting, but he had implied that if Aphrodite's father believed the allegations against his father, then he was *not* a wise man. It was a gamble, he knew, but Martian etiquette or not, he wasn't about to let this stranger insult his family's legacy. Corey's father was a tyrant and a hard man, and barely a father to him at all, but he had come by his fortune as honestly as any. He was not about to let Patriarch Starshadow get away with suggesting otherwise.

Now, the ball was in the older Martian's court. Aphrodite's father could choose to take offense and challenge him to a duel, or he could . . .

"So you deny these allegations?" the elder Starshadow asked, his face unreadable.

"I do," Corey answered simply.

The man seemed to consider this. Out of the corner of his eye, Corey could see Aphrodite trying to get his attention subtly, but he ignored her. This was between him and her father, and if there was one thing he'd learned being Jameson O'Leary's son, it was how to deal with bullies.

"Then I will choose to believe you until such 'hard evidence' is presented to me," Patriarch Starshadow finally said. Corey felt the urge to sigh in relief but kept his face impassive.

"As I said," he noted with a nod. "A wise man."

It was the most backhanded compliment he could give, but on Mars, where most everything was taken literally, the older Starshadow took it as a positive only, nodding back at Corey.

"My Father," Aphrodite admonished gently. "I did not bring Visitor Corey O'Leary here to discuss his family or their fortune. But rather, for you to meet him."

"And why is it so important that we meet him?" This question came from her mother, and the tone was one of genuine curiosity, not challenge.

"Because I state now before you that I have decided to make him my bonded partner," Aphrodite said.

For a moment, Corey thought he'd misheard. At no point had Aphrodite given him any indication that any advances toward her on his part would be welcome. Much the opposite, in fact. Now, she had essentially stated, without even consulting him, that he was her boyfriend. Or maybe it was something far more substantial; he still didn't fully understand the dynamics of a bonded partnership on Mars.

Regardless, he found himself only happy at the prospect, and it must have shown on his face as the import of her words finally sank in.

"You find this surprising?" her father asked.

Now, all eyes were on him, and he suddenly felt self-conscious. But he straightened his back in the chair and decided to answer directly and honestly as before. "I do. I find it surprising in that I do not consider myself worthy of your daughter. But I also find it pleasing beyond measure that she would consider me so nonetheless."

The man seemed to be happy with the answer, and Aphrodite's mother did the Martian equivalent of beaming at him.

"Well," her father finally said, "I admit that I am not in favor of my daughter's pairing with an Earthling."

"They prefer the term 'Earther', my Father," Aphrodite said. "'Earthling' is considered derogatory."

The man frowned but made no argument. "I disapprove of my daughter's choice to bond with an *Earther*. This is not a personal offense intended, Visitor Corey O'Leary, but a statement of practicality. Aphrodite has certain obligations to Mars, and a pairing with you will make those difficult to fulfill in full and proper measure."

Corey's mind raced for ways to respond to that, but the man didn't wait.

"With that said, I acknowledge that it is my daughter's choice and hers alone. Even as her father, it would not be proper for me to take that choice away from her. So I will not insist on a duel of honor and instead give my leave to my daughter's desires in this matter."

It sounded like an insult, and it sort of was, but Corey decided to take it as a positive, much as the older man had earlier with his own veiled insult. Frankly, he was so over the moon from Aphrodite's unexpected announcement that he probably would have taken a challenge to a duel with a stupid grin at that point.

The elven goddess had chosen him.

"I presume that this means you are staying here with us on Mars then, Visitor O'Leary," Aphrodite's mother chimed in, removing his first name to show that she accepted him as more of a familiar now. But at her words, Corey felt his heart sink and his mouth go abruptly dry.

He'd given no thought to staying on Mars but realized now that the bonded pairing with Aphrodite might obligate him to do so, which he simply wasn't sure about, as much as he felt he was sure about *her*. It had only been two months, after all, and he had obligations back on Earth. His parents . . .

Oh no, he thought. *Mom!*

"I . . ." he started to say, but Aphrodite saved him.

"We have not discussed this yet, my Mother. Corey has obligations on Earth, and I would see where this bonded pairing goes before I would ask him to give up those obligations."

"But—" her mother started.

"We will leave this discussion for another time, my Mother," Aphrodite insisted. The older woman shut her mouth and frowned. Her husband frowned as well but said nothing.

The rest of the dinner was largely conducted in silence, with Corey switching between anxiety and elation while sneaking glances at Aphrodite. Her father asked him a few less combative questions about his father's business, and her mother made the Martian equivalent of small talk about her daughter's classes, but there was no conversation worth remembering.

Two hours later, as they returned back to their dorm building, but before they entered their actual room, Aphrodite turned to him and lightly kissed his lips. In that small moment, all the evening's anxiety, along with any thoughts about staying on Mars versus going home to Earth, fled, and Corey was simply a college boy in love.

Present Day

Tyrus entered the bathhouse through the darkened doorway. Inside the large space, the overhead lights had been shut off, and the room was surprisingly lit by hundreds, perhaps thousands even, of candles set around the pool at the water's edge. Their flickering light cash shadows around the cavern bored deep inside the bulk of the Olympus Mons volcano.

The water steamed, further diffusing the candlelight, but Tyrus could see waiting by the far entrance to the pool a solemn line of twelve individuals, their lanky Martian frames entirely covered, including their heads and faces, by flowing black robes with deep, shadowed hoods. He began walking around the circumference of the pool toward them.

When he was just a few meters away, the one closest to him raised a hand to stop him. "Halt," the figure said in a deep masculine voice. "Who approaches the Quorum of Judges to participate in the Trials of the Praetorian Guard?"

Tyrus took a breath before answering. Domitia herself had stopped by his quarters just hours before to give him the information on where to meet and the instructions on the proper responses to the ceremony, but she had given him no further details on what the Trials themselves consisted of.

"One who would be worthy to serve Mars," he responded as she had instructed him.

"And does this one have a name?" the second cloaked figure in the line asked.

"He does. Candidate Tyrus Tyne of New Brussels, former alpha, former enacter, and one who would be a child of Mars." That last phrase, Domitia had told him, would be unique to him among the candidates. The other three were *already* children of Mars.

"And what is the sincere desire of your heart, Candidate Tyrus Tyne?" the third figure in the line asked, this one a woman by her voice, though the cloaks gave no hint of gender or build apart from height.

"This one desires to take the Trials and prove himself worthy of serving Mars in the most holy Praetorian Guard, to protect those that serve Mars, to pledge my allegiance to the Guard above all others, and to Mars above even the Guard."

"And why do you feel that you are worthy of the Trials, Candidate Tyrus Tyne?" the fourth figure, another man, asked.

Tyrus took another breath and paused a beat. This was the one and only place in the ceremony in which he was allowed to go off-script and speak from his own heart and mind. And in the hours since Domitia had come to him, he had decided there was only one thing he could say.

"Because once I was among the galaxy's most feared assassins, but I have since pledged my life and my skill to the service of others, violating even my genetic programming. Now, I would stand with those who have done the same and will fight to prove myself worthy of doing so, no matter the cost."

"This is good," the fifth figure said, another feminine voice and one he thought was almost certainly Domitia herself.

The sixth figure pulled back his hood to reveal the face of Centurion Parn. Gone was all familiarity with Tyrus, and what remained was only a stony and formal gaze.

"Candidate Tyrus Tyne," the centurion spoke, "this council has deemed you worthy to take your place in the Trials and prove yourself further worthy of serving Mars. But the cost will be steeper than you know."

Tyrus froze. The first part of Parn's statement had been expected. But the second part, about the steep cost, had not been part of the script Domitia had reviewed with him. What was happening?

"Because you are not of our planet," Parn continued, ignoring Tyrus's stunned silence, "you have advantages that will cloud the results of these Trials, which we cannot allow. We will remove those advantages now."

What was Parn talking about? Did that mean the other candidates would participate in the trials wearing the ubiquitous exosuits that allowed them to operate more or less on par with someone raised in near-Earth gravity—the same suit Parn and others used whenever they sparred with Tyrus?

Parn kept talking. "Candidate Tyrus Tyne, approach the pool."

Tyrus did so obediently, though his mind was racing, considering angles and possible outcomes. When he reached the edge of the pool, two of the robed figures stepped forward and removed the loose robe that Tyrus himself wore, the one Domitia had delivered to him during her visit. He was left standing in only his shorts in front of the twelve members of the Guard, eleven of them still hidden under the cowls of their hoods.

"Enter the water, Candidate Tyrus Tyne," Parn said.

Tyrus almost opened his mouth to question the order but quickly decided against it. He would see where this went. Perhaps they simply wanted to ensure that he was fully healed from his training fights with Parn before he started the Trials. Maybe every candidate entered the water for the same reason. Maybe . . .

Something was wrong. As he stepped down into the water and it reached chest height, he felt his ankles abruptly give way beneath him. He fought to stay standing, but then his knees buckled, and he lost his footing, plunging fully into the water so that it covered his entire body and head. He tried to swim back up and get his feet back under him, but his arms and legs felt weak and sluggish, and he had a moment of panic as he struggled to reach the surface. Even his neck felt weak, and his head flopped around as he fought against the water.

Finally, his face broke the surface, and he gasped in a great breath, the air entering his lungs giving him a small measure of buoyancy, which he used to stay on his back on the surface while he moved his sluggish limps, propelling himself slowly back to the pool's steps. As he reached them, his limbs continued to fight him so that instead of walking out of the pool, he had to half drag himself and half crawl out of the water.

When he was back on the pool's edge, he flopped over onto his back, gasping for breath. The simple act of leaving the pool had drained *all* of his energy and oxygen reserves, and he felt as if he had just run a marathon at a full sprint.

Finding his breath after what felt like several long minutes, he looked up at the stoic Parn and the other eleven hooded figures staring down at him. "What . . ." he gasped. "What did . . . you . . . do . . . to me?"

It was Parn who answered. "The waters of this pool, Candidate Tyrus Tyne, contain a different type of nanite: one that does not grant strength and healing but robs it. The pool has robbed you of your earthly strength and brought you down to the level of the sons and daughters of Mars against whom you will compete in the Trials."

He stopped, and his expression was grim. "Welcome to Mars, Candidate Tyrus Tyne. You are no longer a man of New Brussels or a man of Earth, but a man who would be of Mars. May Mars sustain and guide you through the Trials to come."

"May Mars sustain and guide you through the Trials to come," the other eleven cloaked figures intoned in unison.

Despite their blessing on him, as he labored for each and every breath and struggled to find the strength to move his limbs, Tyrus felt his hope flee with the waters that dripped off his body by the edge of the pool.

"You didn't tell him any of this? Are you trying to get him killed?!"

Riggs was shouting at the top of his lungs at Corey across the breakfast table. At the other end of the table, Toby shrank down in his seat as if he hoped the other two men would forget his presence.

"I couldn't tell him, Captain Riggs," Corey said as calmly as he could. "If it became known that I'd told him, either about his status as Sunsbane's champion *or* about the plan to remove his strength, it would have been grounds to forfeit his place in the Trials."

"So, what?" Riggs asked incredulously. "Instead, you send him blindly into a situation he can't win, not even knowing the stakes? Blast it, man—that's cold, even for a politician. Are you sure you're not an Assembly speaker? Because you're sure acting like one. That's our *friend*, possibly dying, and all for your political gain."

"Not mine," Corey argued lamely. "He's doing this for all of the Four Worlds, maybe for the entire galaxy. He just doesn't know that."

"Do the other champions know about the wager?" Toby's question briefly surprised Corey, but he turned to look at the boy.

"Supposedly not. They'd be under the same risk of forfeiture as

Tyrus. But Aphrodite—Consul Starshadow—said that they will likely be told anyway. Regardless, Tyrus will be watched especially closely. If he shows any sign of knowing what's really going on, his place will definitely be forfeited. Apparently, even among the Praetorian Guard, there are those who are anxious for him to fail, if for no other reason than that he is an outsider."

"Would that really be so bad if he just forfeited?" Riggs argued. "At least then he might survive. Besides, I don't think these Reds are going to help us even if he does win. No one else in this system seems willing to, so why would they?"

Even decades as a politician weren't enough to keep the expression of pain off Corey's face.

Riggs picked up on it. "Wait a blasted second. What else aren't you telling us, O'Leary?"

Corey sighed, and his shoulders slumped. He couldn't meet the smuggler's eye. His answer was so low the other two men strained to hear. "To forfeit after the Trials have started can mean only one outcome for the candidate: death."

Riggs didn't yell, didn't throw his hands up in frustration, and didn't threaten Corey with any manner of evisceration or other bodily harm. He just shook his head and walked from the apartment, slamming the door behind him. A few moments later, Toby left as well with a silent nod of farewell.

Corey couldn't blame Riggs. It was all up to Tyrus now, and the man didn't even know the stakes.

CHAPTER 12

Forty-One Years Ago; 690 P.D.

Corey entered the expansive greenhouse dome through the west airlock. As always, he savored the abrupt change from dry and never-warm-enough Martian air to the hot and humid greenhouse atmosphere. It recalled to him Arizona during monsoon season and was enough to both remind him of how homesick he really was *and* simultaneously alleviate a large part of that homesickness. It also helped that the vast inside of the greenhouse was the largest open indoor space he'd found on Mars, a sharp contrast to the cramped bunk rooms and small classrooms he shared with so many other students.

Many of those other students were around now, strolling through the many greenhouse paths, but Corey ignored them as they ignored him. After four months on Mars, he'd gotten used to the culture, even if it was still somewhat alien and uncomfortable for him.

He quickly made his way down the greenhouse's central path to where a bank of lifts and a small spiral staircase led up the middle of the massive dome to the levels on which the hanging gardens could be found. Feeling strangely energized by the warmth and liquid air, he sprang up the first few steps rather than take one of the faster lifts.

Then, he settled into an easy rhythm that took him quickly up the multistory climb.

After climbing the equivalent of ten stories and ignoring the many paths that branched off from the stairway at various levels, Corey had worked up only a light sweat. Despite the warmth and humidity and the height of the staircase, he found his Earth muscles could still, even after months on Mars, easily climb in the light gravity without too much exertion.

At the very top of the stairway, he chose the path that led off to his right and followed it. The tops of the oversized trees that grew in the greenhouse—a wide variety of Earth species that had been cross-bred with seeds from lighter-gravity colonial worlds prior to the closure of the Castilian Rift and the schism—surrounded him on all sides as he made his way briskly along the narrow path that hung still in the air without any visible supports and only a low railing. Fifty meters or so along the path, he came to an alcove that branched off under the cover of a particularly enormous tree—bred from an Earth banyan tree crossed with a Saudi Centauri whisper willow if he remembered correctly—and which contained several benches set along the round perimeter of the space. Only one of those benches was occupied now, and its resident stood up as Corey rounded the corner.

"My Corey, I was about to give up waiting for you. You are fourteen minutes late." The Martian frankness of the words stood in sharp contrast to the silky sound of the Aphrodite's voice.

"I'm sorry," he replied with the same frankness. "Professor Brutus Lowlander was giving a review for the final exam, and it ran late. Leaving early was not an option, or I would have been here sooner."

Aphrodite smiled and nodded once, accepting his apology without comment. Even the small smile she gave him melted his heart, and he allowed his eyes to take her in more fully now that he was no longer in danger of her righteous wrath.

Her smile deepened as she saw him study her. "Come here, my Corey," she said, holding out her hand. "If you like what you see, then surely you wish to touch as well." It was a monumentally non-Martian thing to do, but ever since he had explained the Earth custom of boyfriends and girlfriends holding hands, she had been willing and even eager to do it, so long as there was no one around to see.

"My Aphrodite," he whispered, grasping her outstretched hand but resisting the urge to pull her into an embrace. *That* would go too far. "As I have always said, your parents named you perfectly."

She laughed and squeezed his hand. Then she leaned into him, slightly downward given her greater height, and brushed her lips against his. As always, electricity coursed through him at even that brief touch.

"What have you decided?" Aphrodite asked as she leaned back and regarded him.

Corey sighed. As always, straight to the heart of the matter. He had been dancing around this issue since the first dinner with her parents, where she had declared him her bonded partner. But now the time had come that he could dance around it no more.

"My Aphrodite, I . . ." He couldn't find the words, and he looked up to see tears welling in her eyes.

"You cannot stay," she said softly, sadly. It broke his heart.

"I must leave, but I will be back. We can still be together," he pleaded. "I just have to return to Earth long enough to convince my parents that this is the right thing. They have rejected all of my pleas over the Net and have threatened to cut me off and disown me if I defy them in this. But I am sure—*so* sure—that I can convince them if I can only sit with them in person."

The tears started to rain down Aphrodite's beautiful cheeks now, and he felt like he had to do something.

"Come with me," he said. It was another topic they had danced around.

She shook her head. "Where would I go? I cannot live on Earth. The gravity would crush me. Or would you have me wear an exosuit at all times? I cannot bear you children there or be part of your life. And you know, my Corey, that I have my own obligations here on Mars. No, it is you who must stay." Now, he could hear the pleading in *her* voice.

"I'll be back, I promise," he said, and in that moment, he knew that even *he* didn't believe it. There was little chance his parents would ever let him return.

She shook her head. "No, you will not. And you dishonor me by lying and saying that you will."

"My Aphrodite, please. Don't say such a thing. I would never do anything to hurt you. I want to stay with you here so badly."

"So stay." She said it with finality, with the certainty of one raised in the Martian culture where a woman decided if and when her relationship with a man started and ended, and the man only obeyed. But *he* wasn't a Martian man.

"You know I can't," he said softly, feeling hot tears now in his eyes to match hers. He *wanted* to stay, but he couldn't bring himself to give up his family. His father, sure. He and the old man had never been close. But his mother? He couldn't abandon her. And what about his responsibilities to the family business? All those people potentially out of work if an O'Leary wasn't there to keep them employed and safe from the vultures who would gladly tear apart his father's legacy and sell it off bit by bit. He couldn't . . .

Despite all that, as he stared at Aphrodite's tear-filled eyes, he almost said he would stay.

But only almost.

She must have seen it in the set of his jaw, for she dropped his hand and returned hers to her side, standing up straighter and looking down at him with a hard expression. "Then go, formerly my Corey. I release you from our bonded pairing."

With that, she turned and ran away, heading farther down the high forest path.

Present Day

It was a problem of momentum and mass because *strength* was no longer an option.

Tyrus stood shakily on the sparring mat, facing off against his first opponent, Triarch Jason Skydancer, who was about his height and far skinnier. He would have been easy pickings if Tyrus weren't using all his strength just to support his own weight.

Domitia had taken him aside again after the pool had sapped his strength and explained that the nanites were adaptive—that they would only take enough strength from him to put him on the same level as a Martian of similar background and exercise regimen. Supposedly, that meant they would leave him a little extra strength commensurate with his much higher body mass versus his Martian opponents. But as far as Tyrus could tell, they hadn't even done that.

Still, as he watched Skydancer live up to his name and dance around on the mat to loosen up before the bout, he kept coming back to two things: momentum and mass.

A lot of fighters and even soldiers thought that strength was everything. But Albert Einstein had proven over a millennium prior that the energy an object released was based on its mass and its speed, or rather, its momentum. Strength didn't really factor into that.

Tyrus had watched a baseball game once on Mendoza. It hadn't been for fun; his mission's target had attended the game, so Tyrus had as well. But he had enjoyed it quite a bit, especially watching the batters. He'd quickly ascertained that the best batters were often the biggest guys, but not because of their strength—or not only because of it. They were the best because they used the mass of their bodies to torque their bats to higher speeds before they impacted the ball. And they didn't do so by gripping the bat tightly and swinging with all their might. Instead, they used the rotation of their bodies and the movement of their hips to create momentum and put their own mass behind the bat, which was then imparted to the ball.

The results were spectacular to watch, and Tyrus had been disappointed when his target chose to leave the game after the seventh inning, forcing him to follow and miss the match's conclusion.

Now, he hoped to use the lessons of that day and countless hours of sparring and training to win this fight.

A praetorian guard optio named Ursus, the most muscular Martian Tyrus had ever seen, though still thinner than him by a good margin, called the start of the match. Skydancer made the first move, lunging toward Tyrus and swinging a thin arm at his head. Not trusting his muscle speed alone, Tyrus used his weight to pull his body downward and let the punch sail overhead. But Skydancer anticipated this and brought up a knee solidly into Tyrus's quadricep, undoubtedly seeking to break his femur and perhaps end the match early. It might have worked on a fellow Martian. But Domitia had let slip—maybe intentionally—that the nanites may have robbed Tyrus of his muscle strength, but they could do nothing about his bone density.

Tyrus took the hit on his quad, grunting in pain but confident his leg could withstand the punishment. Then, he mustered every ounce of strength he could eke out of his overly weak muscles and leaped forward. But he was too slow, and Skydancer jumped back out of his way.

The Martian didn't hesitate but came in again, connecting with a roundhouse kick to Tyrus's right kidney, one that he usually would have blocked or dodged in time, but his sluggish body betrayed him. He felt pain surge, and the blow knocked the breath out of him. He still somehow managed to get hold of the other man's leg before he withdrew it but was surprised when Skydancer was able to wrench it out of his weak grasp.

Three more times, the Navy man moved in and landed a blow on him. The worst part was that Tyrus could see that Skydancer was sloppy—the skills that had gotten him into the Trials were obviously not those earned in hand-to-hand combat. But Tyrus couldn't take advantage of that sloppiness as he normally would, feeling like his own weak body was moving in molasses.

Then, Skydancer went in for another knee to the quad—the same one as before—and Tyrus finally had his opening. He let the blow land again, but this time, he started leaping forward even before the knee connected.

It was awkward and messy. His muscles didn't move with anything near their normal strength or speed. That fact confused his brain, which couldn't understand why his body wasn't reacting properly to the signals it was sending. But awkward and messy for a man as large as Tyrus could still do some damage. His right arm moved forward and locked into place a little earlier—his overall timing was off—than he'd expected, but that was okay, as long as it wasn't late. Because it meant that Tyrus's right arm was held out straight in front of him, elbow and shoulder locked along lines that relied more on bones than muscles, right before the fist of that hand hit Skydancer's sternum.

Tyrus's body mass of 127 kilos might have *weighed* a lot less in Martian gravity than it would have on Earth. But weight didn't matter in lateral movement, where gravity wasn't a factor, and his enter mass, multiplied by his forward momentum, was transmitted to just one spot, or really two—the first two knuckles on his right fist—as they impacted the Navy captain's sternum.

Tyrus felt the satisfying crunch of bone and heard the air whoosh out of Skydancer's lungs. The Navy man was still game and tried to jump backward, doubtlessly hoping to get outside of Tyrus's reach and regain his breath. But Tyrus wasn't done with him. He kept falling forward into Skydancer, this time using the Navy captain's own move against him, bringing up his right knee into the Martian's left quad. And unlike Tyrus's, Skydancer's bones were thin and far less dense from a lifetime in lower gravity.

The match ended there, with Skydancer on the ground, holding his shattered leg and biting his lip hard to keep from crying out in pain. Tyrus had to admire the man's stubbornness. A broken femur was no small matter, and he'd seen otherwise tough men scream like newborns at the excruciating pain of the injury.

"Match to Candidate Tyrus Tyne," Ursus called out in a voice that betrayed no emotion. Tyrus knelt and offered his hand to Skydancer. Still biting his lip and with tears streaming down his face, the man grasped Tyrus's hand and let him pull him up to one leg—a much harder effort for Tyrus now than doing the same for Parn just two days ago.

Two of the Guard judges came forward and took positions on either side of Skydancer, leading him out of the room and toward the healing baths. The man would be fine but would not be able to participate in the rest of the day's activities. And while he wouldn't *lose* any points directly for that, he also wouldn't *gain* any the remainder of the day, allowing Tyrus and the other two candidates to take the lead and leaving Skydancer in a hole he'd have to work hard to dig himself out of.

Of course, the Trials would go on for a full week, so it was still anyone's game. And Tyrus was exhausted from just one sparring match.

At the end of the first day, after multiple sparring matches, Tyrus had three points. He'd lost his first and second matches to Centurion Kilnfire. The gruff man had won every match he'd participated in that day, gaining six points total. Tyrus also lost his first match to Celeusta Lonesearcher, who, despite being a woman, had a body like iron cords. But he identified a few weaknesses he could leverage in that first match and used them to best her in the second, just barely. His third point had come by an automatic win in the second scheduled match against Skydancer due to the man's forfeit of the rest of the day's matches. But that gained Tyrus nothing, as Kilnfire and Lonesearcher also earned automatic points for their scheduled matches with the Navy captain.

That left Tyrus tied with Lonesearcher with three points each, while Kilnfire had six and an early lead.

He went to bed exhausted that first day after a quick dip in the healing bath—a separate bath from the others, with nanites that would heal his wounds but not counteract the other bots still in his system that were keeping him otherwise weak. As he drifted off to sleep, he was genuinely worried about what the second day would bring.

CHAPTER 13

Forty-One Years Ago; 690 P.D.

A week after his final parting with Aphrodite, Corey was packing up the last of his things from the dormitory. There were others in the room, but they studiously ignored him, as he ignored them. He had not seen Aphrodite since that night on the elevated forest walkway. When he'd returned to the dorm that evening, her things had already been gone.

Now, as he put the final clothes into his bag in preparation for the shuttle up to a waiting passenger liner that would take him back to Earth, he missed the dormitory door opening and the entrance of the messenger until the man was right next to him.

"Visitor Corey O'Leary of Earth?" the unfamiliar man asked as if the lone Earther in the room weren't easy to pick out.

"Yes?"

"I bear a message from Praetor Johan Starshadow," the man said solemnly. "He demands restitution from you for bespoiling his daughter and commands that you meet his youngest son on the field of honor in one day's time."

Corey heard gasps from the other Martians in the dormitory. He'd become friends with several of them, but if they believed the allegations, he would just as quickly lose those friendships.

Aphrodite's father had been clever. He had never liked Corey, and had made no secret of it, despite all his lofty talk about honoring his daughter's wishes. However, because Aphrodite had been the one to break the bonded pairing, the senior Starshadow couldn't challenge Corey to a duel based on that.

However, by claiming that Corey had 'bespoiled' his daughter, the Martian equivalent of rape, he could demand satisfaction in a duel. He didn't have to prove the allegation; if he could, Corey would already have been dead. But by simply alleging it and demanding a duel, the old man had painted Corey into a corner. Rejecting the duel would be the same thing, in Martian eyes, as acknowledging that the allegations were true. Accepting it would mean that either he or Aphrodite's youngest brother would have to die. Even Aphrodite was powerless to stop it. Mars had no courts where she could testify that the act in question never happened; they had only the dueling grounds, where Corey would have to prove himself and his innocence.

By pitting Corey against his *youngest* son, the patriarch of the Starshadow family was giving a double insult, implying Corey was beneath the patriarch himself or any of his older sons. It was another carefully calculated insult.

Briefly, he considered getting on the waiting shuttle and fleeing the red planet. After all, what did he owe these people? Was it worth his own death to honor their traditions and stay to possibly be killed just so they would not think ill of him?

His father would have said no. He would have told Corey he owed the Martians nothing and that he was under no obligation to participate in something so silly and archaic as an honor duel. But Corey thought of Aphrodite's face as she had broken their bond. He knew that if he fled, it would not only sully his reputation in Martian eyes, but her reputation as well.

Corey would stay for the duel.

He turned to Parvina, whom he had rarely seen since that first day on the planet but who had come to take him to his waiting shuttle on this, his last day. "Tell the shuttle to return to orbit. If they do not hear from me within two days, they are to return to Earth without me." That would give his father something to think about.

He turned back to the messenger. "Tell Praetor Johan Starshadow that I accept his duel and demand satisfaction for his slanderous words. I will meet his son on the dueling grounds. The weapons are to be only the hands, feet, and bodies of the fighters. No augmentations."

By refusing to let the young Starshadow boy, just eighteen years of age, use augmentations, he was sending a carefully crafted insult back to the Starshadow clan: 'Being of Earth makes me superior to you physically, and I will use that to win the duel'.

The messenger left, as did Parvina, after casting him another one of her signature frowns. Then Corey sat back down on his bunk and began to plan.

Present Day

"This contest will be one of wits," Centurion Parn told the four candidates. He motioned to a table behind him, on which sat six goblets of blue liquid. "Behind me are six chalices. Some of them—I will not tell you how many—contain a deadly poison. The first person to select one of the chalices, drink from it, *and* survive will receive six points. The second to drink and survive will receive three points. The third, one point. The conundrum here is whether you act boldly on mere chance or wait and see how your peers fare, watching them eliminate the possibilities so that you may have a higher chance of drinking from an unpoisoned cup."

He looked pointedly at a clock on the wall. "You have fifteen minutes. Anyone who has *not* drunk from one of the cups in that time will lose two points. You may ask no questions of myself or the other judges. Begin."

The clock on the wall started counting downward from fifteen minutes, and Tyrus watched the seconds creep by for a moment. Something about what Parn had said tickled at the back of his mind. He glanced at his fellow candidates. Skydancer, the Navy triarch, looked like he might be sick. He was still favoring his leg from the previous day's broken femur. Centurion Kilnfire looked resolved, his face stony and hard. Celeusta Lonesearcher betrayed no emotion, keeping her thoughts behind her habitual blank mask.

Then there was Tyrus himself. Despite his nerves, he had slept well the night before—his former life as an alpha allowed him to do so even in stressful situations—and he was feeling slightly better than he had on the competition's first day. But he was still weak, and his muscles were still slow to respond to his mental commands. It felt like he was driving a mech suit that had a time delay built in, a lag between its operator moving its controls and the equivalent movement of the mech's limbs.

Still, he knew this contest shouldn't be a problem so long as he could figure out which goblets did or didn't contain poison. Parn had said 'some' but had given no other indication of the number that were poisoned. And the criteria for winning had been simple: select a goblet, drink from it, and survive . . .

It all snapped into place in Tyrus's head with fourteen minutes and eight seconds left on the clock. He stepped forward, the other candidates eyeing him with a mixture of concern and smug satisfaction. He walked up to the table, selected a goblet at random, and took a single small sip.

Instantly, he felt a fire course down his throat and fill his chest and stomach. Two seconds later, he collapsed to the ground, unable to move any of his muscles. Two more seconds after that, he lost consciousness.

Tyrus awoke slowly, feeling groggy, but he recognized that he was not flying as he had been in his interrupted dream; rather, he was floating.

He opened his eyes, pushing through the pain of the bright lights, and saw what he recognized as the ceiling of a bath house above him. He was floating in the bath, most of his clothes removed. Turning his head, he saw them in a pile near the steps. A splash came from next to him, and he turned his head to look in the other direction, seeing the form of Domitia standing in the shallow water next to him. He quickly averted his eyes, not wanting a repeat of their typically awkward interactions.

"Welcome back, Candidate Tyne," she said softly. It was the first time she'd ever omitted his first name in addressing him. It hinted at a new familiarity and sent a good kind of chill along his spine.

He tried to open his mouth to ask a question, but his throat was dry, and he ended up in a coughing fit instead. Domitia waited patiently for him to finish, then held a bottle of cool water to his lips, which he gratefully sucked down until that, too, caused a fit. A few more tries, and he was finally able to keep the water down.

Finished tending to him, Domitia moved to where she could look down into his eyes. "Tell me," she said, "how did you know?"

He smiled. Until that very moment, he *hadn't* known, just suspected, but it was good to be right. It was good to be alive.

"The way Centurion Parn worded the challenge," he responded in a raspy voice. "The first clue was his refusal to give an exact number of poisoned chalices. The second was that the conditions to win were to pick a cup, drink from it, and survive. But he didn't say we had to drink the *entire* cup. Nor did he specify a condition that we had to pick a chalice *without* poison. Because there weren't any. All of them had poison."

She smiled, something he'd rarely seen her do, and it softened her face in a nice way. "Very good, Candidate Tyne," she responded. "You figured that out in record time. No candidate has ever drunk in the first minute as you did. But how did you know the poison would not kill you?"

"Because there was no way Centurion Parn would want to kill *all* of us. He needs a hundredth member of the Guard, and he's on a deadline. At least one had to survive, and it's only the second day of the trials, so it's too early to start killing us off. Plus, I only took a small sip—the smallest I could manage, really."

Domitia nodded in appreciation. "Had you taken a larger sip, it might have killed you. But the smaller dose was nothing the nanobots in the baths couldn't handle. You chose well, Candidate Tyne."

"And the others?" he asked, surprising himself that he actually cared about the answer.

"All survived," she said, to his relief. "But only three of you passed the test. Candidate Skydancer could not choose within the allotted time period, and watching you and then the other two collapse as if dead convinced him that he would rather take the two-point loss than risk killing himself. Pity, but with his zero points from day one, that puts him at a total of negative two. He has one more day to bring his score positive before he fails the Trials."

She said that last without emotion, and Tyrus found he didn't want to ask what happened to those who failed the Trials. He didn't really want to know, though the answer seemed obvious.

The rest of day two was spent sparring. Tyrus again beat Skydancer, who also lost to the other two. Tyrus lost to Celeusta Lonesearcher again; she had clearly learned from their last match and was ready for him as he tried to use his mass and momentum against her. But, to his surprise, he eked out a win against Kilnfire, pinning the man and holding him down under his greater mass, allowing him leverage to break Kilnfire's nose and jaw despite taking a harsh beating himself. They both required a full hour and a half in the baths afterward. But it gave Tyrus some hope. Despite his weakness, the win in the battle of wits had put him into a tie for first place with Kilnfire, and it made him believe he truly could win the Trials.

He was disabused of that notion later that evening, when the judges introduced a surprise third contest for the day.

"This will be a test of skill, but not of the physical variety." This time, it was Domitia who explained the challenge while Parn stayed silent with the other ten judges in the background. "You will each enter into a simulation in which you will be charged with protecting the life of one of Mars's praetors. May they live long, and may they serve Mars!"

Tyrus and the three other candidates, as well as all twelve judges, echoed the refrain. "May they live long, and may they serve Mars!"

"In this simulation," Domitia continued, "you will be tested. Protect your praetor to the simulation's end, and you will receive a hundred points." Around Tyrus, the three other candidates gasped. Even he couldn't help his eyes going wide with surprise. At the rate that points were being handed out so far in the other activities, a hundred points could end up being worth *all* of the week's remaining challenges combined.

Which meant there had to be a catch.

"Be warned," Domitia said. "Do not take this challenge lightly. Optio Ursus."

The larger man stepped forward and nodded to the four candidates in turn. "You will enter this simulation through the Gladiator interface." Tyrus had no idea what that meant, but the murmured curse under the normally unflappable Lonesearcher's breath clued him in that it was neither expected nor good. "You must know," Ursus continued, "that you will feel every bit of the pain you would feel in the real world, and a fatal wound in the simulation's environment will cause you to miss the next two days of challenges by default."

This time it was Skydancer who sucked in a breath. The man still had negative two points total, and he had only one day to bring his score back to positive. Death in the simulation would spell the end of the Trials for him. Still, to his credit, he voiced no argument.

Tyrus raised his hand, though Ursus had not invited them to ask questions. The big Martian ignored him. "You will each enter the Gladiator interface simultaneously. You will remain in the simulation until you have either completed or failed your mission or until you are dead. And to remind you, your mission is to keep your assigned Praetor alive until the simulation ends. Nothing more, nothing less."

He turned his back on them and returned to his place with the other judges. Tyrus slowly lowered his hand, feeling a bit foolish.

Domitia stepped forward again. "Candidates, follow me to the next room, where we will connect each of you to the Gladiator interface."

They followed her silently, in a single-file line, through one doorway and into a room Tyrus had never seen the like of before. Four metal apparatuses hung from the ceiling. They reminded him of a cross between a climbing harness and a simple exoskeleton, except that, unlike the exosuits the Praetorian Guard almost always wore, these did not enclose the entire body but looked more like skeletons themselves, with straps to attach them to the wearer's limbs.

A judge went and stood next to each of the strange hanging harnesses. Domitia herself motioned to Tyrus to approach. Each of the other three candidates was similarly beckoned forward. When Tyrus reached the apparatus, Domitia started to strap him into it. It was then that he noticed the needles that hung down next to the suit on the ends of two long articulated arms.

"Nano injections," she explained, catching his look. "The Gladiator interface allows you to move within its confines, but the nanobots will make you see, hear, smell, feel, and even taste the environment of the simulation. They will also deliver pain to your body's pain receptors as appropriate. Get shot, and you will feel it as if it were real, though you will live, and the pain fades quickly once the simulation is done."

Tyrus nodded his appreciation to her, noticing that the other candidates were not getting a similar lecture; they likely knew exactly how the interface worked.

Finished strapping him in, Domitia stepped back. Without any further warning, the two articulated arms jabbed the needles into Tyrus, one painfully in the side of his neck and the other in the opposite thigh. He grunted as they injected a thick liquid into his veins and muscles.

Almost immediately, his vision went black, though he could still hear the sounds of the others in the room around him. That faded quickly as well, and he was left in a dark, soundless void that oddly gave him an overwhelming sense of claustrophobia. He remained that way for what felt like a minute, maybe two, though the passage of time in the void didn't seem real or measurable. Then, just as suddenly, he was standing on a sunlit platform, which he recognized as one of the hundreds of landing platforms that clung to the side of Olympus Mons.

This particular platform was high up on the mountain; he judged that he was roughly two-thirds of the way toward the top. He was alone on the platform save one other person, a man he didn't recognize but who was dressed in the distinctive flowing robes of a praetor.

They stood together in the middle of the platform, roughly halfway between a ship on one end—a small star yacht—and a door on the other end, which was carved into the side of the mountain itself.

"Praetorian Guard, attend me," the praetor said in what could only be described as a haughty tone, without meeting Tyrus's eye. The man started walking briskly toward the large door leading into the mountain, and Tyrus had to jog a few paces to catch up.

That was when he noticed his strength. Gone was the artificial weakness imposed upon him by the nanobots in his bloodstream. He was his old self again, and it felt glorious, even if all he was doing was walking. He felt strong, nimble, and fast, and he had to step carefully not to propel himself too far with each step in Mars's low gravity.

He didn't know if giving him his strength back for the simulation was intentional. Perhaps the nanobots that weakened him and the ones that allowed him to experience the simulation were somehow incompatible? Whatever the reason, he was glad. The assignment would be much easier with his full physical capabilities.

He and the praetor had closed only a short distance toward the distant door when all hell broke loose. Ten soldiers appeared on the edges of the platform as if from nowhere, but Tyrus guessed they'd been somehow suspended out of sight below the platform's rim. It didn't really matter—all ten were pointing their weapons at the praetor.

"Get down!" Tyrus shouted, and didn't wait for the praetor to react, shoving him to the ground with his left hand while he pulled the pistol from his belt with his right. Tyrus had worked a protection detail only once in his time as an alpha, so he knew he lacked the instinctual responses in this situation. But he did know one thing: attack.

And attack he did. Leaping into the air above the stunned and fallen praetor, he shot twice, taking down the two closest soldiers. The men facing them—it was hard to tell gender underneath the battle suits they wore—reacted quickly, shifting their aim toward Tyrus, which was precisely what he wanted.

He landed lightly on the ground and let the meager gravity of Mars pull him down into a roll, but not before he squeezed off two more shots, killing one man and wounding another.

Then, a bullet hit him. He felt it tear through his left shoulder, high up by the collarbone, and the pain was excruciating. But Tyrus had been shot before, and he ignored the agony as he fired twice more, watching two more attackers fall, one completely off the platform.

Another bullet hit his thigh, almost exactly where a *real* round had hit him while he'd been rescuing Jinny from the Crater prison. He grunted in pain but made no other move. In the light gravity, and with less weight on the hip, he knew it would be more manageable than otherwise.

He leaped across the platform, shooting as he went, changing direction every time he hit the ground. Two more bullets hit him, one in the lower leg and another in his right arm, but neither was enough to stop him.

He saw the final two remaining soldiers, one of whom he was just lining up in his sights, turn their aim in concert away from him and toward the prone praetor. Tyrus screamed a battle cry to try to distract them while he squeezed off a shot that dropped one of them, but the other fired twice, and Tyrus turned to see that the bullets had done their job. The praetor's head was a bleeding mass; the man was clearly dead.

The simulation ended more abruptly than it had started. One second, Tyrus was standing on the platform, gaping at his dead protectee and preparing to take his revenge on the last remaining soldier; the next, he was gasping for breath and looking into the disappointed eyes of Domitia Felix.

"You failed the simulation," she said simply.

He shook his head in frustration and looked from her to the others in the room. All the contestants were awake, and he could see from the sour looks on their faces that they'd all failed as he had.

"Just one more soldier," he said under his breath. Domitia ignored him.

"All of you will visit the baths to heal from any wounds incurred today," she said, loud enough for them all to hear. "The Trials will resume tomorrow at 0500 hours. Dismissed."

It was a sad and dejected lot that filed out of the room to the baths.

CHAPTER 14

Day three of the Trials brought almost as many surprises as day two. First was another battle of wits, in which the candidates had to view holographic images of ten different people and select, based on nothing more than appearance, which was the assassin who would kill their protectee. Tyrus did well, selecting the right assassin two out of three times. Though he'd rarely been part of a protection detail, he *did* know how to be an assassin and how to read people. Kilnfire likewise identified two correctly. Even Skydancer got one right, raising his score to negative one overall. It was Lonesearcher who surprised them all, correctly identifying three out of three.

Next was more sparring, one round each. Tyrus managed to win all his matches this time, allowing him to take the lead from his previous tie with Kilnfire, who had lost to both him and Lonesearcher. The more he moved in his new, weakened state, the more he was learning to compensate and better leverage his mass and stronger bones to win.

That was all before lunch. After lunch, things got weird.

"Each of you will be placed in a room filled with noxious gas. One breath of the gas is enough to render you unconscious, at which point you will lose this contest," a very tall and very thin optio named Gaius explained. Her skin was as dark as Tyrus's but had a soft, porcelain quality to it that, coupled with her wispy hair and build, made her look almost ethereal, as if she might float away any second.

"You will have as long as you can hold your breath to escape the room. There is a means to escape, but it is not immediately apparent. The first to escape their room will win six points, the second, three points, and the third, one point. Anyone who does not escape will lose two points from their total."

Less than a minute later, Tyrus was locked in the small room with only a single door. Next to the door was a keypad that he assumed unlocked it. A red light burned steadily above the keys. Less than ten seconds after the door closed and locked, sealing him in, gas started to fill the room through a grate near the floor. He took a deep breath and held it as the gas quickly filled the tiny space.

He looked around, his eyes burning and tearing up from the gas but otherwise still able to see. The only thing in the room was a single small desk with a thin archaic paper book sitting on its surface. Tyrus stepped over and picked up the book, flipping through its pages. They were blank. Perhaps the book was a distraction.

He examined the desk itself, kneeling down and looking underneath, searching the edges and the legs for any hidden compartments but finding none. Next he did a sweep of the rest of the room, checking the floor, walls, and even ceiling for anything that broke the uniform reddish brown of the Martian stone. But like most rooms in the Praetorian Guard base deep inside Olympus Mons, the chamber seemed to have been carved out of the mountain itself. He could find nothing that hinted at any secret compartment or clue.

It had been a full minute and a half now, and his lungs were starting to burn. But he wasn't worried. He'd done plenty of vacuum training as an alpha. He'd even held his breath for quite a long time when he'd saved the *Blind Monk* from the Council Navy dreadnought at the Back Door to the Castilian Rift. That had been half a year ago, as he, Jinny, Riggs, and Jynx had fled colonial space.

Tyrus returned to the desk and picked up the book again. He flipped through it more slowly this time—it was only about twenty pages thick—carefully examining each blank page, front and back, searching for any clues they might contain. He saw nothing. He checked the desk again; still nothing. He checked the keypad for any way to remove it from the wall. Nothing.

Two and a half minutes gone, and while he knew he could hold his breath longer, his eyes were starting to burn now, and his vision had become blurred from the tears that he had to keep wiping away. He reopened the book to the first page, hoping for something he'd missed, and he blinked the tears out of his eyes again to see better. In the process, a few tears landed on the book's page, and he was surprised to see them reveal lines of black text. Quickly, he wiped the remaining tears from his eyes and ran his wet hand over the page, revealing more of the text.

Remember to breathe.

He looked at the words in confusion. Why would he want to breathe in the middle of a room filled with noxious gas?

Three minutes gone, and he was really feeling the effects. His head had grown lighter, and he was having trouble focusing his eyes. Frantically, he wiped more of his tears and spread them on the second page, then the third. Nothing!

Breathe. Could it be? Could it be that simple?

In a moment of clarity, he raised the second page of the book up to his lips and blew out a small part of the breath he'd been holding. Then he looked back down at the page. A single number had appeared in its center.

Exultant but quickly running out of oxygen, he blew lightly on the third page, then the fourth. More numbers, one per page! He blew on the back of the second page, just in case, but nothing appeared. OK, so only the front of each page was likely in play.

He went over to the keypad and entered the three numbers he'd revealed. The light turned from red to orange. He hoped that meant progress. He blew on the fifth page and entered that number. Then, the sixth. The orange seemed to fade toward yellow now, which he took as a definite good sign.

He kept blowing on pages, getting through the next five. But every time he expelled his breath, he felt the burning in his lungs get worse at a faster rate. It had been four minutes now, and he was desperate for oxygen. The yellow light appeared to have a greenish tint to it now, but he had nine more pages to go.

Frantically, he started blowing on them. Each exhalation added to his pain but gave him one more number. He blew on several in sequence, stopping when he felt he had no more breath left to give, and entered them in. Only two pages left, and now the light was definitely green, with only a hint of yellow.

Steeling himself and knowing that he had seconds and little air to waste, he lifted the book back to his lips and forced a small amount of air out. Then he entered that number and turned the page. Last one! But try as he might, he had no more air to give. So he did the unthinkable. He inhaled.

It was just a little, but instantly, he felt his muscles start to go even weaker, and his head started pounding. He could feel the oblivion coming for him, but with his last shred of willpower, he blew out the small breath onto the last page. Barely able to read the number as his vision faded, he almost entered it wrong, his finger shook so badly at the keypad. But with one last burst of energy from somewhere, he hit the right key, and the door slid open.

He didn't step through the door but fell through head first. He wasn't sure if it was the gas or hitting the ground that knocked him out.

Tyrus awoke again to find himself floating in the same bath as on the previous day after he'd ingested the poison. Domitia was there again, standing in the shallow water next to him.

"We really have to stop meeting this way," he croaked through cracked lips.

She shook her head at him, but he caught the beginnings of a smile before she turned serious. "You lost that challenge," she said grimly.

"But I got out," he argued. "I made it out of the room."

She nodded. "You did, but you were the last out, so no points were awarded. Skydancer was first, partially redeeming himself; it only took him two minutes. Kilnfire and Lonesearcher weren't far behind. You were in there for just over five minutes. It was impressive in a physical sense. But you lost the battle of wits."

He frowned. "But I don't lose points, right? Because I made it out?"

She shrugged. "That is true, but it does you little good. You are now in second place again, one point behind Kilnfire and only five points ahead of Lonesearcher. You will not win this by merely staying alive, Candidate Tyne. You must compete!"

He was surprised at the conviction in her voice. *Could Domitia be cheering for me?* He'd felt there was a growing friendship between them —perhaps even the potential for something more if he could stop getting caught violating complex social rules whenever he was with her—but he'd grown so used to the almost utter lack of emotion from her and Parn that it had never occurred to him that either of them might actually care if he won or not.

In a way, this changed everything.

"I will win, Optio Felix," he said lightly, watching her face for any signs of a reaction.

She frowned and shook her head. "Do not make promises you cannot keep." Then, she almost smiled. "Your gaze lingers again, Candidate Tyne."

Tyrus smiled in return. "I must apologize, Optio Felix. I am, as always, overcome by your beauty."

Creighton Horvath read the report—the one he wasn't supposed to have—a second time, as if doing so might somehow change the outcome it coldly described.

On the surface, the report was mostly positive. The Navy's 'coming out party' in the Nea Mykonos system had been a resounding success. The pirates, hired by the Keeper to attack the convoy through an intermediary, had arrived and started a legitimate battle with the convoy's Guard escorts. Just when hope seemed lost, and the pirates had almost destroyed the last Guard Space Force ships, Admiral Chen had arrived with a Council Navy task group and saved the day.

Within days, the government's misinformation campaign had twisted the story. The pirates weren't pirates at all, but ships from the rebel fleet—the same fleet that had shown up in orbit of Panamar over four months ago. The propaganda had gone so well, in fact, that even the illegal underground blogs had bought the story and were indignantly condemning the Council Navy and lamenting the loss of the brave rebel freedom fighters. The latest polls showed that not only was the public now aware of the Navy's existence, but most of them thought it was cause to celebrate.

It was perfect—a terrific win for the Council Navy, Admiral Chen, and the Council government. Creighton hated it. He'd been against the plan from the start and now looked foolish that it had come off so successfully. He'd lost a few points in the never-ending dance for power within the Twenty. Worse, Keeper Petrov now had a naval victory to point to as proof that his plan to invade the Four Worlds would be likewise successful, which made it even more likely the impatient man would launch the invasion *before* the Navy was truly ready.

Creighton frowned and turned to the other report on his desk holo. This one was for his eyes only, from an alpha whom he'd convinced to report to him temporarily using his official Council codes. It was Alpha Collins, the same man he'd used to kill Nancy Farnsworth months ago. Collins's report outlined the discovery of a rebel base in a no-name system near the Edge. The rebels had no idea they'd been found out, which made them ripe for the picking. The Navy could have a real victory against a real rebel opponent. Another win would further push the Keeper to accelerate the plans to invade Sol.

Creighton couldn't let that happen. He pressed a virtual button in his desk holo. Moments later, the image of a man appeared hovering in the air above the desk.

"Yes, Speaker Horvath?" Gennady Stewart asked. The man's Guard uniform was tailored and pressed, and he cut an impressive figure in it. But he ducked his head slightly, a subtle show that the man knew his place when talking to a senior Assembly speaker.

It went beyond that, of course. Gennady was a colonel in Guard Intelligence, an almost unheard-of rank for a non-enacter. Even his own exceptional merit hadn't been enough to secure his rise to such a lofty rank; he'd needed a powerful sponsor, and Creighton, recognizing both the man's talent and the opportunity it represented, had stepped in to be that sponsor.

"Colonel Stewart," he began, looking grim. "Have you heard about the rebel base at GX-6607?"

The man nodded. By all rights, he shouldn't have known anything of the sort, but Creighton had learned not to ask about Stewart's sources. The colonel always knew far more than he should.

"Yes, Speaker Horvath, I am aware of it."

"What is your analysis of the situation? How much of a threat does it represent?"

Stewart licked his lips. "I believe it is a substantial threat, Speaker. The rebel forces are far more powerful and crafty than the Guard Space Force often gives them credit for. Far more dangerous than that farce at Nea Mykonos would have us believe."

Creighton hid his surprise. Apparently, the disinformation campaign around the battle at Nea Mykonos hadn't been as effective as they'd all believed. Still, he kept his voice even for his next words. "If Admiral Chen sends her fleet, what are the chances of victory?"

Stewart thought for a moment. "With an entire fleet, almost guaranteed, sir. The rebels likely have better defenses around their asteroid base than we think, but even the best stationary defenses can't stand forever against a large mobile force."

Creighton considered his next words carefully before replying. "Colonel, what would be the minimum size force we could send to GX-6607 to ensure victory?"

The Guard officer cocked his head to one side. "Sir? It's difficult to say, but I'd guess two task forces would be sufficient. Anything less than that would be a terrible risk."

Creighton nodded. It was time to see if all his years of mentoring and shepherding Stewart's career would pay off. "What if I told you, Colonel, that the entirety of the rebel fleet, less the few ships they have at GX-6607, have been spotted near Phoenix?"

Stewart looked surprised. "I've heard no such intelligence reports, Speaker Horvath. Are you absolutely sure? The rebel admiral, Gerald

Williams, isn't one for gathering his forces needlessly where they could all be taken out in one attack. It would be sloppy, and Williams is many things, but sloppy is not one of them."

Nodding, Creighton smiled. "Nevertheless, that is what my intelligence says is happening. They have more ships than we thought they did as well. We believe there are over two hundred warships now in the rebel fleet."

The colonel frowned. "Sir? Our latest intel estimates just over one hundred ships, including those they secured from the GSF at Panamar. May I ask where your intelligence is coming from?"

This was the moment of no return in the conversation—the moment in which Creighton would see if he'd read Gennady Stewart right all those years ago when he'd decided to groom the man for bigger and better things in Guard Intelligence.

"Colonel, have you heard of General Koppel's planned retirement?"

At the mention of his boss's name, Stewart perked up, though he still looked suspicious and confused. The man was smart enough to know that Creighton wasn't one for idle chatter; if he was mentioning Koppel's impending retirement, it was for a reason. "Yes, sir, I have heard word that the general is considering stepping down."

"There are some," Creighton said carefully, "who believe Colonel Peterson is best suited to replace General Koppel. What are your thoughts on the matter?"

"Colonel Peterson is a good officer," Stewart said diplomatically, "though she is not necessarily well liked by the rank and file, sir, if I'm being honest."

Creighton saw the suddenly hungry look in Stewart's eyes and knew he'd judged the man accurately. "I tend to agree," he replied. "Which is why I plan to recommend someone else for the position."

"And who might that be, sir?" Stewart asked cautiously, though the hunger in his expression ramped up a notch.

"That entirely depends on one thing," Creighton said, staring intently at him. "For reasons I cannot explain, I need Admiral Chen's forces sent to Phoenix to investigate the reports of a two-hundred-ship-strong rebel fleet massing near there. With such a large prize, I imagine she'll want to take the majority of her ships, leaving perhaps only a small number—a single task force, I would think—available for the attack at GX-6607."

He stopped, letting his words hang there in the ether between him and Gennady Stewart. The Guard Intelligence colonel wore a tight-lipped frown and was staring off to a point in space that Creighton couldn't see. But after a long few moments, he started nodding.

"I see, Speaker Horvath," he said, looking back at Creighton. "I think I have heard of the rebel fleet massing in the Phoenix system. And I do recall that it's much larger than we thought. If I'm not mistaken, the report came from our local bureau chief there."

Creighton smiled. "That's what I thought, Colonel. I assume you'll pass the intel along through the proper channels so that it reaches the Keeper and Admiral Chen? I would hate for us to miss such an opportunity as this."

Stewart saluted. "Of course, Speaker Horvath. I will see to it personally."

The connection cut out, and Creighton leaned back in his plush office chair. Despite the positive outcome of the conversation with Stewart, it hadn't put him at ease. Too much could still go wrong, and he had to cover all the bases to ensure that the Keeper didn't launch the invasion of the Four Worlds prematurely.

Sighing, he reached out again to his desk holo. It was time to call Hiroto Takahashi. Perhaps, with the scientist's help, he could find a way to speed up the production of enacters from Project Epsilon. Because even if he managed to get Petrov to delay the invasion after a loss at GX-6607, he would still be on borrowed time. Something told him that he'd only be able to delay the Keeper for so long.

Day three ended with the same simulation as day two. Tyrus found himself on the same platform, guarding the same nameless, haughty praetor. This time, instead of pushing the praetor to the ground, he urged the man to run back toward the ship, presenting a moving target while Tyrus again went on the offensive against the attackers.

It didn't work. In fact, this time, Tyrus was only able to kill six of the ten assailants before one of them shot the praetor in the back when he was only halfway to the ship's ramp.

Luckily, none of the other candidates won the simulation either. All lost their protectees, and all went back to their assigned quarters with shoulders slumped in both exhaustion and frustration.

CHAPTER 15

Day four started early, with another test of wits, though a more physical one. This time, they were each placed in a pit that was approximately twenty meters deep and about three meters square on each side. At first, nothing happened. The pit walls were too smooth to climb and too far apart to scale using opposite walls as leverage.

Tyrus had the wind knocked out of him when a thick metal rod appeared from nowhere, jutting out a meter from the wall and slamming its blunt end into his stomach, knocking him to the ground, where he lay gasping for a moment.

Lying there, he saw the rod quickly retract into the wall, leaving no visible trace it had existed. Nanotech, he guessed. Why have holes precut into the wall when you could just create them on demand?

Just before the rod disappeared, Tyrus saw another appear less than a meter away from the first but around the corner from it and about a meter higher. Then that one went back into the wall, and he saw another pop out, again a meter higher but on the opposite wall from the second this time. Again and again, each rod emerged and retracted, but not before the next began its journey.

There was a pattern to them. He could see it.

He stood up. The pattern of rods reached the top of the pit's sides and then stopped. He waited, almost holding his breath in anticipation. Next to him, again at stomach height, a rod came out of the wall. He jumped on it, almost losing his balance, even in the low gravity, but managing to use the wall itself to lean against as he stood on the narrow rod.

Then he looked for where the pattern suggested the next rod would be. As his rod started to retract into the wall, he leaped upward and outward and was gratified to see another rod come out of the next wall over, right where he'd expected it to. He met it in midair, then labored to quickly pull himself up onto it, his weakened muscles screaming for a rest even after so short a time, but the low gravity at least made it possible for him to pull his full mass up, even without his full strength.

He leaped again, catching the next rod across on the other side of the pit just as it made its appearance, again pulling himself up with a grunt of effort.

He repeated the move so many times he lost count. By the time he was halfway up the pit, his arm muscles burned and ached, but he thrust aside thoughts of the pain and kept going. At two-thirds of the way, his leg muscles started to burn as well. Again, he ignored the pain and kept going, knowing that even one misstep, one missed leap, would send him falling painfully back to the floor of the pit to start over again.

Finally, almost without realizing it, his hands found the edge of the floor above the pit, just as the last rod retracted beneath his feet. He hung there for a long moment, gathering his strength, and then pulled himself up and out—where he saw, to his frustration, that Kilnfire had beaten him. The man already stood there, grinning coldly at him, next to his own pit. Based on the grunts from the next pit over, Lonesearcher was also near the top of hers. There was no sign or sound from Skydancer, though his pit was also farthest from Tyrus.

Next came more sparring. Tyrus found that his muscles were still exhausted and sluggish from the pit, and he lost easily to Kilnfire and barely got a win against Lonesearcher. He was so wiped out that Skydancer beat him in his final match. Kilnfire won all his matches and extended his lead, now a full six points ahead of Tyrus, with Lonesearcher six points behind him. Skydancer was so far behind it was doubtful he was still a serious contender.

Something needed to give. Tyrus was losing.

The afternoon of day four had them running the simulation once more, trying to keep their praetor alive. This time, Tyrus pushed the praetor to the ground again and was able to again kill nine of the attackers before the last one killed his protectee. He almost screamed in frustration when he awoke from the interface and found he'd lost again.

Surprisingly, after a short dinner, they were all led back to the simulation room and hooked up once again to the Gladiator interface. The same exact simulation ran again. This time, Tyrus moved as fast as he ever had in his life, using his superior strength and the low gravity to catapult himself all over the platform, spinning and shooting from the air and taking five bullets himself in nonvital places.

And it worked! He managed to kill all ten attackers quickly and keep their attention on him while he did so, and the praetor was still alive afterward.

He stood there, beaming to himself on the landing platform as he helped the praetor to his feet. Any second and the simulation would end, and Tyrus would accept his hundred points, giving him a commanding lead, possibly insurmountable if none of the other candidates won their simulations, and he simply couldn't see that happening if they were operating with normal Martian strength and speed.

To his surprise, however, the simulation didn't end. Without warning, ten more figures appeared at the edges of the landing platform. Caught flat-footed, Tyrus only got four of them before the rest converged their fire, and the praetor died under a hail of bullets.

This time, Tyrus really did scream in frustration when the simulation ended. Domitia gave him a quick look but said nothing. She didn't need to; her eyes showed her disappointment. Luckily, as before, none of the other candidates seemed happy enough to suggest they'd won.

After a soak in the healing baths, this time without Domitia to distract him, it was a tired and dejected Tyrus who fell into bed.

Day five was a bit different than the rest. It started not with a game of wits but with a shooting contest. The four candidates were taken to an underground shooting range that stretched deep into the bowels of the mountain, providing targets as far away as nine hundred meters and as close as twenty-five. Some targets moved; others were stationary. Each candidate was given a pistol, an assault rifle, and a sniper rifle, with a limited amount of ammunition for each, and told to hit as many targets as they could. Each target could only be hit once, and moving targets were worth more than stationary and smaller targets more than larger ones.

Tyrus did well; he'd always excelled at marksmanship. But he was also out of practice after so long playing the diplomat on Earth and then on Mars. He still managed to come in second behind Lonesearcher, who he learned had been her regiment's best sniper. At least he hadn't lost to Kilnfire, but when Parn announced the standings before lunch, Kilnfire still had a four-point lead on Tyrus, and Lonesearcher had closed to within four as well.

But the big surprise of lunch was that Skydancer was leaving.

"You have failed the Trials," Parn said to the man, though not unkindly. "You do not have the minimum number of points required to proceed from here onward. You will return to your fleet with your head held high, and you will celebrate your failure."

Tyrus was confused by that and made a note to ask Domitia the next time he was alone with her, assuming that would happen again. She had refused to meet his eye throughout the morning and most of the previous day, and he wondered if she was still upset that his gaze had lingered two days before in the bath when he'd been half-asleep and drunk on fatigue. It wasn't an excuse, but she had never reacted in this way before, so he was genuinely concerned he'd missed some nuance of protocol and had offended her in some new and unknown way.

Now, he watched with melancholy as Triarch Jason Skydancer saluted Parn sharply and left the room with his head held high, just as Parn had told him to. Maybe there *had* been a deeper meaning to the centurion's words.

He really hoped he got a chance to ask Domitia.

This time, Aphrodite met Corey in the afternoon, and again they were alone together, ostensibly to eat lunch, but he quickly ascertained her ulterior motive.

"The Trials progress well," she said after only a few minutes of silent eating. "Candidate Tyrus Tyne has comported himself admirably, but he does not win. It appears as though Candidate Kilnfire will win."

That took Corey aback, and he struggled to wrap his head around the thought of the big, indomitable Tyne losing at *anything*. More, he struggled with the ramifications of that loss.

"Well, I'm not sure if that's better or worse than Candidate Lonesearcher winning," he said to Aphrodite. "If Candidate Kilnfire wins, then so does the group that wants to sit back and wait to see what happens while Earth and the Council Navy beat each other up. But I suppose that's better than making a deal with the devil."

She nodded solemnly. "At least Candidate Tyrus Tyne has made it this far, and he is only a few points behind Candidate Kilnfire. He may still win, but his weakness gets the better of him at inopportune times, I am afraid. The physical parts of the challenges become far more taxing from here onward."

"What of the fourth man, Candidate Skydancer?" Corey asked, if only to stop dwelling on the image of Tyrus losing.

"He has lost the Trials and is no longer participating in them."

He looked at her in horror. "Then he's dead?"

She returned his look with one of confusion. "No, he lives. Why would you assume he is dead?"

"Because you told me plainly that to quit the Trials after they begin is punishable by death."

Aphrodite shook her head, her long white hair shimmering under the lights of the dining room in which they sat. "You misunderstand, Emissary O'Leary. Candidate Skydancer did not 'quit' or 'forfeit' the Trials. He *lost* them. For a warrior, there is no shame greater than quitting a battle once one has engaged the enemy. In doing so, one betrays his brothers and sisters in arms, his nation, and his god. That is why in wartime, as with the Trials, we punish those who quit with death. They deserve nothing more.

"But to *lose* is an entirely different matter. There is honor in losing, as it means one did not quit but gave all their effort to the end, even if it only buys a few more seconds of life for the men and women to your right and left. There is as much honor in loss as in victory, for many factors outside of the warrior's control determine the outcome. But if that warrior has stayed true and given it their all, then no more can be asked of them."

She stopped, and Corey knew he wore an expression of confusion as he tried to piece together the point she was making. She sighed. "Triarch Skydancer accomplished what few in every generation have done: he proved himself worthy of the Trials of the Praetorian Guard. Even to do so and lose is among the highest honors our military can bestow on a warrior. That is why Triarch Skydancer returns to his fleet as Navarch Skydancer. You would call that rank a rear admiral, I believe. The Europans call it a commodore."

"You promoted him?" Corey asked incredulously. He shook his head. "Consul Starshadow, I do not think I will ever fully understand you and your people, but I appreciate that I have been given the opportunity to try."

With that, they turned their conversation to the dark topic of contingency planning should Tyrus lose the Trials and, by doing so, unknowingly lose the support of Mars in the war to come.

CHAPTER 16

Landon Hartman yawned and started to open his eyes but immediately squeezed them shut again as the sun streaming in through the bedroom window nearly blinded him. Reveling in the coolness of the bedroom despite the sunlight, he stretched and sighed. He cherished these little moments in the morning when he was awake enough to be thankful for another day alive but still asleep enough to forget . . . well, just about everything else.

It was then that he fully registered the sound that had awakened him: a banging on his apartment's front door. Well, not really *his* apartment; rather, the apartment the readers had loaned him to stay in while in Perth.

Frowning, he rolled out of bed and put on a pair of basketball shorts, taking a moment, as he always did, to examine the jagged scar on his left hip. There was a matching one in the middle of his back that he could only see if he twisted himself around in front of a mirror, but both were from the same accident, when an overloaded gravity generator on an assault shuttle had ended his naval career and almost ended his life along with it.

Even though he'd survived the accident, it had resulted in a medical discharge from the UEN and an impossibly small pension that took him away from the one thing he'd always wanted to do most: flying.

That had been before a congressman named Corey O'Leary hired Landon on as his personal pilot, giving him a new lease on life and a new opportunity to do what he loved most. Of course, it wasn't quite as fun as flying an assault shuttle nape-of-the-earth while his gunners decimated anything that got too close, but there had still been plenty of excitement. Plus, he actually had flown an assault shuttle—a stealth one—nape-of-the-earth only three months ago to bring a comatose Jinny Ambrosa to Perth. There was that.

Landon made his way out of the bedroom and across the small living room to the apartment's front door. Bracing himself, he opened it. A small bundle of nervous energy fueled by caffeine and disdain for the rest of humanity barged right through the door and shoved him aside.

"Took you long enough," the girl complained as she plopped down on his couch without an invitation.

"Good morning to you too, Tempie," he said with a smirk.

Temperance Jimenez, known throughout the Four Worlds as the crack hacker 'Neon Mouse,' returned his smirk with a smile of her own. "You have to see this," she said, holding up the tablet in her hand and waving it like he might be able to read it from across the room.

Sighing, Landon moved across the room to sit down next to Temperance. As he did so, she reached out absently with one hand and traced the scar on his back, sending little chills through him.

"What do you want to show me?" he asked, reluctant to pull her attention back to why she'd come.

"Remember how Congressman O'Leary had me hack the Government House servers and send a specific file to a certain IP address?" she replied.

He cocked his head in surprise. Of course he remembered that. O'Leary had thought, or at least told Temperance he thought, that the file was from former President Luis Pereira's personal files. But it had turned out to be a top-secret military file containing the plans for the defense of United Earth from the coming Council invasion. She hadn't known that at the time, but she had dug deeper and figured it out shortly thereafter and had tried to see if Landon could get word of it to O'Leary. Of course, that had never happened because the former congressman had been completely out of communication since he'd fled to Mars. "Uh, yeah," he told her. "I seem to recall something like that."

She gave him a lopsided grin. "Shut up, you. Anyway, I finally tracked that IP address."

He sat up straighter, fully engaged. "I'm confused. Didn't we already know it was Gorsky who wanted the file?" Which was weird because, as the shoo-in for the next president, Gorsky would have had access to the file anyway if he'd only waited a few weeks.

She ignored his question and started talking faster. "It was expertly masked and led me down a multimonth rabbit hole of servers leading to other servers and even a few pretty serious guard dog AIs I had to sneak around or fight, but I finally found its owner!"

"Show me," he said.

She swiped the pad to pull up a new window. When Landon saw the picture and the name underneath it, his mouth dropped open.

Forty-One Years Ago; 690 P.D.

The morning of Corey's final day on Mars was overcast. On a world where the weather was as controlled as the climates of the interior spaces, that was unusual. But even a dry planet needed the occasional rain.

Corey stood at one end of the dueling grounds, in this case a long platform about the size of a soccer pitch that jutted out from the side of Olympus Mons about eight kilometers up from its base. Next to him stood Dorrel Farstrider, the same boy who had challenged him to a duel and then withdrawn the challenge on his first night on Mars. As the boy had promised that day, they had become friends. However, Corey sensed that Dorrel was also here because his family had issues with the Starshadow clan. Either way, he was glad to have him.

Ten meters away stood Antoni Starshadow, youngest son of Praetor Johan Starshadow and Aphrodite's younger brother. The praetor himself acted as the boy's second. Aphrodite was nowhere in attendance, nor was her mother.

The dueling judge examined both of them, verifying that they were both uninjured and ready to fight. Then, with no fanfare, the whistle blew, and the two men started to circle each other.

Corey's heavier musculature and greater bone density, along with the lower Martian gravity, should have made him an odds-on favorite to win. But Antoni was young and quite strongly built for a Martian. He also had a full half meter of height on Corey and, therefore, a much longer reach. If he could use that reach and keep Corey at a distance, he might have a chance against the bulkier Earther, especially given that Corey had no formal training in hand-to-hand combat, whereas Antoni, like all Martian men, had trained since birth to serve in the military and was currently a junior officer in one of the ground legions.

Antoni circled Corey warily, dancing around and moving his hands to a guard position. Then he lunged forward and jabbed a fist toward Corey's face. Corey turned his head in time but was unable to block the jab, and it landed on his cheek instead of his bone. It hurt, but it did not leave behind any damage other than a sore spot.

It was the first time in his life that Corey had been punched, and he'd gotten through it just fine. At that moment, he knew he was going to win, and all fear of being hit again fled him.

The younger Starshadow leaped back, dancing around him again. Then he lunged forward and delivered an uppercut blow toward Corey's chin but found only air as his shorter opponent danced away. In the lower gravity, Corey's Earth-born muscles made him stronger *and* faster than the boy. After stepping back to avoid the punch, he darted forward under the taller man's reach.

Antoni was game and brought an elbow down on Corey's shoulder, but Corey kept moving and ignored the blow. He threw a short punch backed by his own forward momentum that took Antoni in the stomach and sent the boy tumbling to the ground with a grunt.

Corey stepped back, watching Antoni. His opponent was breathing hard, taking in great gasps, either because the wind had been completely knocked out of him or because Corey's single punch had done real damage to his midsection. He couldn't tell.

He waited for the boy to stagger to his feet. Antoni stepped forward and jabbed again at Corey's face. Corey took the punch, ignoring the brief flash of pain in his jaw, and stepped forward again, delivering his own jab to the taller man's chest this time.

Corey heard a crack that simultaneously horrified and excited him. Antoni fell back to the ground, once again gasping for breath. This time he was much slower in getting up. Corey raised his eyes and looked at the boy's father. Praetor Starshadow speared Corey with hatred in his eyes. There seemed little concern there for the man's son, but perhaps he was reading the praetor wrong. He didn't think so.

"Come on!" he taunted Antoni. "Get up." He was feeling strangely excited and craved the chance to hit the boy again, to show his father how wrong he'd been to make up a false accusation as an excuse to challenge an Earther to a duel. This would show him.

Antoni had barely gotten back up on his hands and knees when Corey let loose a wild kick. The younger man desperately tried to block it, but it went right through his outstretched arm, breaking it practically in two before connecting solidly with his stomach with a satisfying crunch.

The boy fell again, writhing on the ground, his face covered in sweat. Corey moved toward him, a strange battle lust coming over him as he planned to go for the killing blow as he'd seen in the few duels he'd watched during his nine months on Mars.

But he stopped. Breathing hard and looking down at the broken body of Antoni Starshadow, Corey knew he couldn't do it. He had never killed a man; he'd never found himself wanting to be in a situation where he even *could* kill a man. And here he was, practically shaking from bloodlust, about to take the life of a man whose only sin was to be born to a domineering father who would stop at nothing to preserve his family's legacy, even if it meant killing a man who had simply refused to stay and marry his daughter.

Suddenly, Corey saw not Praetor Starshadow but his own father standing there on the sidelines, wild-eyed and angry. And he looked back down at Antoni Starshadow and saw . . . himself.

He took a step toward the boy and heard a gasp from the crowd.

Looking up, he saw Aphrodite, a few rows back in the lines of spectators, her hands over her mouth and tears streaming from her eyes.

Corey stepped toward Antoni again, reached down, and grasped the hand of the boy's unbroken arm. Without straining himself, he lifted Aphrodite's brother to his feet. Antoni eyed him warily but made no move to resume the fight. Corey turned and looked at the judge. "I would spare Antoni Starshadow's life," he said, loud enough for the crowd to hear.

"Doing so forfeits the match, and you will be disgraced," the dour female judge said.

Corey nodded. "Yes. I understand that. But I cannot kill this boy. I am Corey O'Leary from Earth, and I do not kill needlessly. It is not my way. I am not of Mars!"

There were gasps and whispered conversations from the crowd now, and all eyes were on him, some confused, some accusatory, and some wavering between the two emotions. Praetor Starshadow watched with triumph in his eyes, but Corey found he didn't really care.

"Visitor Corey O'Leary," the judge began solemnly. "You hereby forfeit this match and—"

"Wait!" All eyes turned to Antoni Starshadow, who grasped his stomach and grimaced with pain, still leaning heavily on Corey. "Wait! Visitor Corey O'Leary has won this match, and I yield!"

Now, the crowd erupted in startled gasps and louder conversation. By yielding before the judge could finish her declaration, the boy had just thrown the outcome into Corey's favor. And by so doing he had practically acknowledged openly that the allegations his father had made against Corey were false. Corey could see Praetor Starshadow's expression turn ugly as he glared now at his own son.

The judge nodded, her own expression bemused. "So be it. I declare this match in favor of Visitor Corey O'Leary of Earth, and hereby nullify the accusations placed against him by Clan Starshadow!"

"Wait!" It was Corey's turn to be the center of attention again, though that hadn't been his intention. But he'd seen the look in

Aphrodite's eyes when she'd watched him looming over her younger brother on the ground. He had one more thing he needed to do.

"Judge," he continued. "I demand that this duel be stricken from the record!"

If he'd thought the crowd was loud before this, they were practically roaring in disbelief now.

The judge turned and eyed him skeptically. "You understand, Visitor Corey O'Leary of Earth, that by doing so, you open yourself up to the accusations against you being levied again? With no record of the duel, Clan Starshadow can make these same accusations against you, and you will either need to duel them again or retire in disgrace."

Corey nodded. "I understand." He looked across the crowd and met Aphrodite's tear-filled gaze. "But some things are more important than my pride and reputation."

With that, he walked off the field toward a waiting air car, Dorrel Farstrider following behind him. An hour later, Corey took in what he thought would be his last sight of Mars through the small porthole of the shuttle that carried him to the waiting passenger liner his father had sent for him.

He knew he would likely never know if Praetor Starshadow ever repeated the false accusation against him, but by the look in both Aphrodite's eyes as well as her brother Antoni's as he'd left the dueling field, he guessed the old man would be heavily dissuaded. Corey also simply didn't care. It was enough that he and Aphrodite knew the truth.

Present Day

The rest of day five had been grueling, with multiple rounds of sparring, another test of wits, this time involving a caged animal that looked like a tiger adapted to the lower gravity of Mars, and a bottle of cologne. It had been a strange one that also required some physical acrobatics, and Lonesearcher had won it handily, with Tyrus taking third behind her and Kilnfire. With that, Tyrus lost his narrow lead over Lonesearcher and found himself in last place among the three remaining candidates. To make matters worse, he'd gone on to lose all of his sparring sessions; both Kilnfire and Lonesearcher had learned how to counter his still-clumsy moves and had negated his advantage in mass and bone strength.

Tyrus saw no hope of winning the Trials now, and it infuriated him to no end. He'd spent the time between sparring matches fuming that they hadn't given him time to adapt to his weakened muscles before throwing him headfirst into the Trials. If he'd had even a few days to get used to his newfound frailty, he likely could have adjusted his fighting style to compensate. But trying to do so literally on the fly wasn't working anymore.

Around then, he started to realize just how *desperately* he wanted to be part of the Praetorian Guard.

However, even Domitia seemed to be distancing herself from him. That afternoon, when he'd been taken to the baths to heal after a vicious knockout blow by Kilnfire, he'd awoken to find an unfamiliar Guard optio attending him, Domitia nowhere to be seen. The man said little, and Tyrus guessed he would be unwilling to answer any of his questions.

Now, the three candidates filed wearily into the simulation room. There, Centurion Parn addressed them.

"This is your *last* attempt at the simulation. As before, anyone who wins the simulation will get one hundred points. Those who die will be unable to participate in any contests for the next two days. Given that this is the fifth day, dying in the simulation today means you will miss the rest of the Trials and will be required to take whatever point total you end the simulation with as your final score.

"Begin."

Tyrus walked over to his Gladiator harness and was gratified to see Domitia moving in his direction. Wordlessly, she started to strap him into the device.

"I have missed speaking with you the past two days," he said quietly as she adjusted the straps on his head.

She gave him a strange look and said nothing in reply but set about checking the various straps. Perhaps it was his imagination, but she seemed to linger longer than normal over that task. When she finished, she stood up straight and looked him in the eyes.

"You must win here and now," she said, her voice softer than even a whisper. "There is more at stake than you know."

She was gone before he could ask her what she meant or, more importantly, just how he was supposed to win a simulation that seemed to be deliberately programmed as a no-win scenario.

Wait, he thought, *a no-win scenario. Could it . . .*

Before he could finish the thought, he felt the jab of the needles into his neck and thigh, and then his vision faded to black.

After a brief stop in the inky void, Tyrus was back on the landing platform. The same praetor, with the same condescending sneer and tone and the same colorful robe, greeted him there. Then, the same ten attackers came up from the edges of the platform, just as they'd done every time thus far.

And just like he'd done in most of the simulations thus far, Tyrus pushed the praetor to the ground. But this time, he went with him, following the man down and lying on top of him, covering the thin Martian patrician with his own sizeable bulk. The man screamed in pain as Tyrus's weight pressed down on him, but Tyrus ignored him, aiming as he could from his prone position, taking out soldier after soldier with his pistol, all the while knowing that some were sneaking up from behind. But he couldn't rotate to see them, or he would risk uncovering the praetor and exposing the man to their bullets.

He managed to take out four of the men he could see before the first bullet hit him, right in the butt, which he imagined was the largest target the men behind him could see. Then another lodged in his left leg, and he felt it painfully sever his hamstring. A third hit him in the back, and he heard, rather than felt, it sever his spine. He lost feeling in his legs and lower torso, but his hands still worked, and he calmly dropped the last two assailants he could see.

Underneath him, the praetor whimpered. Tyrus did his best to turn only his head to look behind. In his state of paralysis, he couldn't have turned his entire body even if it wouldn't have meant leaving the praetor uncovered. He could see, just barely, one of the four assailants approaching from behind, and he squeezed off a shot that nailed the attacker in the chest and dropped him. He felt another bullet lodge in his back and heard the report of the rifle that fired it. It sounded like it came from point-blank range. Painfully, he turned his head in the other direction and found himself looking up at three men standing over him and the praetor with guns.

"Yield," one of the men said. "We want him, not you. He's dead either way, but you may still live if you surrender to us now."

Tyrus smiled at the man. He couldn't raise his arm high enough to shoot him, but he tried to move his gun to his other hand, which would have a slightly better angle and—

Tyrus awoke from the simulation, gasping and crying out in pain as his brain belatedly registered the muzzle flash that had ended his life . . . in the simulation, at least.

Domitia moved over to attend to him, helping him unstrap himself from the harness and interface. He looked over at Lonesearcher in time to see the woman awaken herself with a growl of frustration. Less than twenty seconds later, Kilnfire also woke back up, his face contorted in anger.

"Candidate Kilnfire and Candidate Lonesearcher. You both lost the simulation," Parn said dispassionately. "Neither of you died, though your assigned praetors did. You may return to your rooms or attend the baths as you see fit. We will resume your Trials tomorrow at 0600 hours."

He turned and looked at Tyrus, and neither of the other two candidates made any move to leave, even as their helpers finished unstrapping them from their Gladiator interfaces. They watched in silence for what Parn would say to Tyrus.

"Candidate Tyne," the centurion said in the same even voice. "You died in your simulation, and you will be excluded from the final two days of the Trials. Your point total as of the end of the simulation is your final total for the entirety of the Trials. Dying, even in the simulated environment, can be taxing. Optio Felix will take you to the baths for healing, and she will see that the other nanobots, the ones that weaken you, are removed. You have no further need of them."

Tyrus felt his heart hit his stomach. He had been wrong, and he had failed. He would never be a member of the Praetorian Guard, and whatever other stakes Domitia had alluded to were also lost. His Trials were over.

CHAPTER 17

Tyrus stumbled out of the interface, and Domitia and another judge caught him; he was far too heavy for a single Martian. The two of them supported him as he stumbled from the room, the pain of his 'death' in the simulation still fresh. They led him down the short hall to the healing baths.

There, they both helped him strip down to his shorts. Then Domitia and the other Guard stripped their outer clothing as well and helped him hobble down the steps and into the water.

Once Tyrus was floating in the pool, Domitia dismissed the other judge, who dressed quickly and left the room. She turned and looked down at Tyrus floating in the water while he tried very hard to focus on the rocky ceiling instead of his own dismal failure.

"Congratulations," she said softly.

"For what?" he spat. "For losing with honor? I still lost. I won't be a member of the Praetorian Guard. And I won't be with . . ." He trailed off as he realized what he was about to say. Then he saw the look of hope in her eyes and said it anyway. ". . . with you."

Domitia smiled, a strange expression on the face of a hardened warrior, no matter how feminine and beautiful that face was. "Even now, you still do not understand," she said lightly.

He shook his head. "Understand what? Tell me, Domitia. Understand what?" He saw a brief expression of pain cross her face as the last words came out more harshly than he'd intended. It passed quickly.

"You did not lose," she said simply.

"What, is this another honor thing?" he asked, still unable to keep the acid from his tone. "That even by losing, I'm winning, or some nonsense like that?" He knew that he had just insulted her and Martian society, and she would be within her rights to demand an honor duel to the death, but he found himself struggling to care.

Then he looked into her eyes again, and the anger fled from him. "I'm sorry, Domitia," he said in a soft voice, unintentionally using only her first name. "I should be honored just to have been a candidate. And I am sorry I failed to meet your expectations."

Domitia, to his surprise, only grinned at him. "Tyrus," she said, stunning him by using only his first name in return. "Do you not see? You won the simulation."

That stopped whatever he was about to say next, and he choked on his aborted words and started coughing. He finally recovered and let his feet sink from the surface down to the rocky bottom so that he was standing upright in the pool, water to his neck, facing Domitia from less than a dozen centimeters away.

"What?" he asked in disbelief.

Her grin remained. "You won, Tyrus. A hundred points earned. The simulation ended with your death, but the praetor was still alive at that point, so you won."

"But he would have died as soon as the attackers moved my corpse off him," he sputtered, still trying to process what she was saying.

She nodded. "That is true, but sometimes all we can do as protectors is to give our charges one more second of life, even if it means giving up our own lives to do so. Who knows, but in that second, reinforcements may arrive, or our charges may get to safety some other way. The *only* way to win the simulation was to sacrifice yourself to protect the praetor."

"But I'm missing the last two days of the Trials," he kept arguing, unable to grasp what she was telling him.

She nodded. "Yes, you will, but with your win in the simulation, you have already amassed more points than either Candidate Kilnfire or Candidate Lonesearcher can possibly earn in the last two days. Remember what Centurion Parn said: today was the last chance at the simulation. And you are the only one who won it!"

He let that sink in, finally understanding. He'd been right. He'd gambled, and he'd been right. Tyrus looked Domitia in the eyes, and his face broke out in a grin to match hers. "So I'm in the Praetorian Guard?"

She nodded. "It cannot be official until the Trials end in two days, but you have already won the Trials, Tyrus. You will be a praetorian guard!"

He whooped and thrust a fist in the air in a celebratory cheer, the stresses and even pains of the last five days seeming to flow off him like the water around him. He looked back at Domitia and couldn't stop from grinning like an idiot.

Her smile softened a little but did not disappear. "Tyrus," she said in a formal voice, "your gaze does linger again."

He stopped in confusion. It hadn't; he was sure of it. At least not past the point of impropriety. He was about to argue the point when he saw the hope again in Domitia's eyes.

"Forgive me, Domitia," he said, repeating the same words as always but omitting her title and last name. "As always, your beauty overcomes me." Then he added a part he never would have dreamed of saying before. "If it pleases you, I would gaze upon you longer."

She blushed. Optio Domitia Felix, quite possibly the toughest woman Tyrus had ever met, actually blushed.

"Today, I think," she said, finishing the ritual, "I would have you gaze longer, my Tyrus."

They both grinned again, laughing like schoolchildren, splashing water at one another as the stress of the Trials and the awkwardness between them melted and were carried away by the warm bath waters. When they finally left the pool and dressed, she did not immediately leave. She leaned in where they stood and lightly kissed him. It was a quick peck, barely a brush of her lips against his, but it sent electricity through him. And in a Martian society that placed such a high value on chastity despite their open attitude about privacy and other things, Tyrus knew that single, short kiss meant more than anything any other woman had ever given him.

"Who can we take this to?" Temperance asked Landon as they sat together on the couch in her apartment early the next morning and considered all they had discovered. After her first breakthrough in finding the identity of the recipient of the secret plans she'd hacked, she had quickly been able to locate more and more incriminating evidence. It was enough to make Landon's head spin. As a lowly pilot, he'd never wanted to get involved with matters of system-wide intrigue and politics, but it seemed he was to have no choice.

"I still can't get ahold of the congressman," he admitted to her. That had been his *one* job while she'd done the months of work on her side, and he had failed at it.

"It would have been a miracle if you had," Temperance admitted, snuggling into his side, making him feel slightly better. She was good at that. "But we need to take this to *someone*," she insisted.

He thought hard for a few minutes, though the answer had presented itself to him almost immediately. He just didn't *like* the answer and was desperately searching for another way.

"Lopez," he said simply.

She turned to look at him, eyebrows furrowed in confusion. "The old admiral?"

Landon nodded slowly. "Congressman O'Leary trusts him. He once told me that if I ever got in trouble and couldn't reach him, to go to Fleet Admiral Horatio Krishna Lopez and tell him I worked for the O'Learys."

"Okay," she said with a smile. "So let's tell Lopez."

Landon grimaced. "It's not that simple. I don't exactly have the man's personal comm code, Tempie."

She looked confused again. "Weren't you in the Navy with him?"

"Well, yeah, sort of. But I was a lowly pilot, and he's a fleet admiral.

Plus, the Navy is huge. I never met him. Heck, I never even saw him in person."

"So how do we reach him?"

Landon shrugged at her question. "Not sure." He felt a little chagrined, given that contacting Lopez was his idea, and now he was admitting he had no idea how to make it happen.

She surprised him by leaping to her feet and padding across the room away from him toward her bedroom, the bottoms of her pajama pants brushing the floor.

"Where are you going?" he asked after her.

She turned and looked back at him from the bedroom door. "To put some real clothes on," she said, as if that explained everything.

"Are we going somewhere?"

Temperance nodded. "We need to go find that reader. You know, the one we rescued and all that. Maybe she knows how to reach Lopez."

Then she was through the bedroom door before Landon could ask any questions, such as how she expected to find Jinny Ambrosa in a city of millions of readers.

The bell to Corey's quarters rang for the fourth time in as many seconds.

"I'm coming," he shouted irritably, wrapping his robe around himself and moving groggily through the small living space to answer the insistent visitor.

He yanked the door open and was about to yell at the intruder, even if it meant breaking some cryptic Martian social norm and ending up in a blasted duel, but stopped himself abruptly when he saw Aphrodite Starshadow standing there.

"Aphrodite?" he asked incredulously, forgetting himself in his tired state and using only her first name. If she noticed or took offense, she didn't let it show. "What are you doing here? It's . . ." he looked down at his palm implant. "It's four in the morning. What couldn't wait for our meeting later today?"

She brushed past him and entered the room without waiting for an invitation. He just stood there holding the door in confusion.

"He did it!" she exclaimed as soon as he'd closed the door and turned to face her. Excitement broke through her normally calm demeanor, and Corey briefly had a glimpse of the girl he'd once fallen in love with. "Tyrus Tyne did it! He won the Trials."

Corey blinked in surprise. "But the Trials still have two days left. How did he win them already?"

"It is too difficult to explain, Corey, and I am not even supposed to know."

In her hurried words, he almost missed that she also called him by only his first name, filling him with an unexpected warmth despite the hour.

"I have an ally in the Guard," she continued, "who sent me the message just minutes ago, and I came straight here. I am—" She cut off abruptly and looked around Corey toward the door . . .

. . . the door which was *supposed* to be closed.

Corey looked just in time to see the door ajar and the fleeting image of a face—Toby's—outside before it withdrew. He sprang to the door, almost tripping in the light gravity, wrenching it open and looking down the hall toward Toby's room in time to see its door close as the boy fled inside.

Odd. Maybe the commotion had awakened him, and he'd come to see what was going on.

"Close the door," Aphrodite told him, and he did so, turning back to face her.

"As I told you, Corey," she resumed, "I cannot explain everything. But we will need to move fast. If my spy in the Guard has already told me, we must assume that Praetor Moonslayer and Praetor Tiberius already know as well. They are bound by their oaths to honor the results of the contest of champions, and since Praetor Sunsbane's champion has won, that means that we *will* be coming to the aid of Earth when the Council attacks again."

Corey grinned broadly at her, and for a single, glorious second, she returned his smile, her face lighting up in the way that had long ago made him weak in the knees. For the briefest of instants, the elven goddess he'd fallen in love with returned, no longer as a girlfriend, but now as a friend he'd so desperately missed having all these decades.

Then, her flash of a smile disappeared, and she looked somber again. "This still does not mean they will submit easily. There are still many things they can do to slow down or derail our cooperation. Our greatest hope is to keep the momentum from this win, forcing them into compliance as quickly as we can and creating inertia in our preparations for war and diplomacy that will be difficult for them to stop once begun."

She continued speaking rapidly, pausing only for him to give short answers and ask the occasional question. But after two hours, they had a workable plan.

CHAPTER 18

Jinny was late to her next lesson, jogging across the campus and into the engineering building, where she was due to read a mechanical engineer. The Majko wanted to try something a little more complex than knitting, cooking, or even martial arts. At this point, the old woman was testing the limits of Jinny's abilities, and she had no objections to her doing so. Jinny herself was growing curious as to what she could do with her newfound talents. Even more, she was elated that the nightmares had essentially stopped. Something about her training and the things she was learning had ceased the dreams and, hopefully, her slow descent into madness along with them.

"Reader Ambrosa?" a voice called from behind her as she walked briskly across the engineering building's marble lobby.

Turning, Jinny saw two people she didn't recognize. One was a tall, lanky man around her age who looked embarrassed and nervous to be there. The other was a girl. At first glance, she looked like a teenager, but a closer look showed her to be older, possibly twenty. Her hair was purple, at least on the side of her head that wasn't shaved. She had olive skin and a bright silver nose ring, wore a shirt that bared her stomach, and revealed a large number of tattoos that seemed to flow from her chest all the way down beyond her waistline, thankfully covered by a pair of frayed shorts.

"Can I help you?" she asked the two.

In response, the strange-looking girl nudged the tall boy with her elbow, and he blushed furiously. "Uh . . ." he started. "I guess you don't know us, do you?"

Jinny shook her head.

"Well, we've met, sort of," he continued. "I'm Landon, and this is Temperance. We helped rescue you and—"

"The pilot and the Neon Rat!" Jinny exclaimed, recognizing the names of those the Majko told her had accompanied her on the shuttle to Perth. She'd meant to find and visit them after waking up, but the training schedule the old woman had kept her on had prevented her from doing more than considering it.

"Mouse," the girl said with a frown. "Neon Mouse." She looked genuinely offended.

Jinny smiled apologetically. "Sorry. I'm so glad to finally meet you both. I've wanted to thank you for rescuing me and bringing me here. Listen, I'm late for a lesson now, but—"

"Just tell her!" the girl—Neon Mouse—interrupted, elbowing Landon again.

"We have to talk to Admiral Lopez," the boy blurted out. "It's really important!"

Jinny frowned. "Okay. So why come to me? I've never even met Admiral Lopez."

Landon grimaced again, and the girl looked like she had just bit into a lemon.

"What is this about?" Jinny asked, sensing that they were holding something back.

The Neon Mouse frowned, but Landon elbowed her this time. "Tempie, we need to tell her everything," he urged.

The girl's lemon-sucking expression didn't fade, but she finally nodded. "Fine, but not here. Somewhere private."

Tyrus floated in the bath. A day after his victory, he was still having trouble sleeping. He'd tossed and turned the entire night before, his mind racing, both with the excitement of joining the Praetorian Guard and the somehow even greater excitement of his new—was 'relationship' the right word?—with Domitia Felix.

He hadn't seen her in over twenty-four hours, ever since she'd given him the happy news on both counts. He'd come to the bathhouse again this evening hoping he might run into her after her day of assisting with the Trials had ended, but so far, he'd been the only one in the chamber.

As he was contemplating giving up and going back to his quarters, he heard the door to the healing bath open. He couldn't see the doorway from where he was; the steam was too thick, and he floated at the far end of the pool.

"Domitia?" he asked when there was no further sound.

No answer.

Suddenly, the lights went out.

"Tyrus, Tyrus, Tyrus," said a chiding voice that sounded very familiar yet also very foreign. "Why did you have to go and ruin everything?"

Toby? Tyrus's mind finally identified the voice. *But he's speaking in a New Brussels accent.*

Then, it all clicked.

"I wondered when you would show up," he said, casting his voice toward the far corner of the room instead of toward the door to keep the man from locating him following the sound. "Tell me, how is the Keeper these days? Still a paranoid lunatic?"

Toby laughed, and the sound seemed to come from all sides of the room simultaneously. "Finally figured it out, did you? Took you long enough. But I guess that's what happens with *ex*-alphas. You've lost your edge, old man. I'm here to make sure you don't ever get it back."

"And Jynx, what was she? Just a stepping stone to get to me?" Tyrus kept talking as he moved silently through the water. He couldn't see Toby, but unless the man had night vision, he couldn't see Tyrus either.

"That's far enough. Don't get any closer to the steps," Toby said sharply. So much for him not having night vision—unless it was just a lucky guess.

"Jynx was a fun little diversion," the boy-turned-assassin continued. "She was so easy to manipulate. All I had to do was give her a sob story about being an orphan and having a long-lost brother. She was so obsessed with that dead sister of hers that she fell for it hard. But hey, at least she was fun. I've never been that close to a woman before. At the Enacter Academy, they ordered all the simpering women there to keep away from me. 'Too dangerous', they said. Well, they were right. I *am* dangerous. More than you can ever know."

"Because you're not an enacter?" Tyrus asked, guessing.

Silence. Then, "How did you figure that out?" Toby's voice was a little ragged; he hadn't been expecting Tyrus to have that insight.

"Come on, Toby, don't be dense." Now Tyrus threw a little of the boy's mocking tone back at him as he slowly started moving toward the stairs again. "They knew I would spot another enacter a light-minute away. So the Twenty is training psychopaths now, are they?" Another guess, but now all the boy's delayed reactions to emotional stimuli made sense, as did his attempt to sneak a gun onto Mars.

"Lucky guess," the boy grunted. "And I told you to stop moving toward the stairs."

So, he definitely had night vision—probably implants in his eyes. Tyrus had never gotten those; they'd still been in development when he'd left the Enacter Academy, and he'd never elected to get them after that. He didn't like the thought of letting anyone cut open his eyes.

He didn't stop moving toward the stairs. In this situation, the last thing he wanted to do was what Toby told him to. He wanted the boy off-center, angry, and improvising.

"So, you're not even a real alpha then," Tyrus said casually.

"I am!" the boy snapped back, and this time, he forgot to throw his voice. Tyrus placed the would-be assassin at the edge of the pool directly in line with him, probably following him step-for-step back toward the stairs. "I'm more of an alpha than you ever were! What kind of enacter defies the Council? You failed, old man, and I'm here to make you pay for that failure."

Time to test a theory. Tyrus dove under the water and swam back in the direction he'd come from, away from the stairs. He stayed under for a few moments, then surfaced slowly, listening carefully to the silence in the room.

"Oh, come on," Toby said a few beats too late. "Did you really think you could hide by going underwater?" As he spoke, Tyrus heard light footfalls as the boy also moved away from the stairs and back to a position even with Tyrus.

Just as I thought. We're deep under a mountain, and these bath doors seal pretty tight to keep the moisture from escaping into the halls. Light amplification optics won't work; he has to use thermals. That meant that Toby could see Tyrus now because his exposed head and shoulders were cooler than the warm water surrounding him. But when he'd gone underwater, Toby hadn't been able to track him until he'd resurfaced.

"I think you're in over your head here, Toby," Tyrus said, still trying to antagonize the boy. "I knew you were an assassin this entire time. Never thought you were an alpha; I mean, I still really don't believe you about that. But maybe the Keeper decided to lower the bar for admission. I suppose anything is possible."

"I know what you're doing, and it won't work." Tyrus could hear the sneer in the boy's voice. "I also know about the nanobots that are keeping you weak during the trials. So you can bluster all you want. I'm going to break your neck with my bare hands and then rip your head off your body and show it to Jinny Ambrosa right before I take her to meet the Keeper. Maybe he'll even let me kill her the same way when he's done with her."

Tyrus knew the boy was trying the same tactic on him—to get under his skin by bringing Jinny into it. However, unlike Toby, Tyrus had written the book on using psychological tactics as an alpha. Literally, the boy had probably unknowingly studied tactics in his training manuals and classes that Tyrus had actually written. But he needed the boy to *think* he was getting to him.

"You leave Jinny out of this," he growled. "This is between you, me, and Petrov. And I'll take those odds any day."

Toby laughed, obviously confident that a weakened Tyrus was no match for him, even if he knew exactly where his opponent was.

"Okay, old man," the boy said derisively. "I'll enjoy killing you."

Tyrus heard a sound then—the sound of smooth metal on fabric—and it filled him with hope. He'd worried Toby had been able to somehow smuggle a gun into the Olympus Mons base after all. Despite his taunts, Toby actually had impressed him. The boy had fooled him for so long. But the sound he'd just heard wasn't the solid one of a gun being drawn; rather, it was the lighter, sleeker sound of a knife leaving its sheath.

Tyrus could work with that.

He dove back under the water, swimming a meter or so to his right, just in case he was wrong about the gun. Then he settled in and waited underwater.

A minute passed, then two. Then three. By now, he knew Toby would be getting restless, probably even pacing the poolside in frustration, enhanced eyes searching the water hard for the thermal signature of his opponent.

Now, Tyrus slowly swam, conserving his energy, until his outstretched hand found the side wall of the pool, right underneath where he expected Toby to be standing or pacing and looking for him. Another 15 seconds passed, and Tyrus's lungs were burning, but he still couldn't risk surfacing to take a break. Instead, he cocked his head to the side and, keeping his chest and stomach pressed tightly against the pool wall, he slowly rose until only the side of his head and one ear breached the surface.

His hope was that Toby was still scanning the pool for him and that maybe the boy wouldn't think to look straight down.

But doubt rose inside him, as he couldn't hear Toby at all. Had the boy entered the water already? Or was he standing now and looking straight at Tyrus, readying the knife for a lunge or even a throw?

Then he heard what sounded like a single exhaled breath directly above.

Reaching up slowly and putting his fingertips on the pool's edge, Tyrus gathered what strength he could from his fatigued and overworked—but otherwise now entirely *normal*—muscles and pulled upward in a single heave. He propelled his body up and out of the water, flying up almost a full meter in the low gravity. He extended both arms wide and then wrapped them around like he was giving the air in front of him a bear hug.

Except it wasn't air he grasped; it was Toby.

The boy yelped as Tyrus wrapped his massive arms around him, pinning both of Toby's arms to his side, along with the hand holding the knife. Then Tyrus used his superior weight and his fully restored strength to throw his body backward into the pool, taking his would-be assailant with him.

They hit the water together, still wrapped in the bear hug, but Toby managed to wriggle free by kneeing Tyrus hard in the groin. Obviously, the kid wasn't a fan of Martian combat rules.

Tyrus recovered quickly, and he didn't need to see Toby in the pitch darkness. He could hear the boy frantically swimming away, probably trying to get some distance between himself and Tyrus so he could regroup.

"You made a mistake, Toby," Tyrus called after him. "You came in here thinking I was weak. Well, you're wrong! I'm stronger than you'll ever be."

"Impossible!" Toby yelled back. "I know about the nanobots."

Tyrus felt himself grinning. "You mean the ones they removed from my body within an hour of me *winning* the Trials?"

He could almost hear the smaller man's panic. The water would slow down his use of the knife, assuming he still had a grip on it, and Tyrus's greater reach and weight would be insurmountable disadvantages for Toby in the pool. So he was now trying desperately to get to the steps, to get out of the water before Tyrus could reach him.

Tyrus let him go. He didn't want to kill the boy . . . yet. So he followed after, slowly.

"Tell me, Toby," he said casually. "If you're here and still following orders, that must mean the Keeper has a way to talk to you. Is it quantum entanglement? I heard rumors of faster-than-light comms using that tech. But I didn't know the Keeper had built one on Earth yet."

"Forget it," the boy said, trying to force bravado into his tone. "I'm not telling you anything. You don't need to know. You'll be dead in a minute."

"Come on now, Toby. Is that how you talk to your elders and betters? No wonder you've already botched this little assassination attempt. You know, Petrov really shouldn't have sent a boy to do a man's job."

Toby screamed, and Tyrus heard him moving back in his direction. The boy threw himself the last meter or so, probably swinging the knife. Even without thermal vision of his own, Tyrus could hear well enough to know where Toby was. And they *had* both learned combat from the same instructors. Except Tyrus had years of experience *after* that training.

He threw up an arm, blocking the boy's swing with the knife. To his credit, Toby didn't scream in pain, nor did Tyrus hear anything to indicate he'd dropped his weapon. But he didn't wait for the would-be assassin to recover either. He lashed out with his right hand, delivering a powerful jab that he felt connect with Toby's face in a satisfying crunch.

The boy did scream now, and he swam wildly backward, trying to get out of range of Tyrus's long arms.

"Toby, Toby, Toby. I don't want to kill you. No, that honor belongs to Riggs. And I think he'll get creative with it, in memory of Jynx." Tyrus was actually worried about what Riggs might do if given that chance, but it was all talk at this point. He needed to keep the boy off balance, mentally as well as physically. He needed Toby talking, and he needed him alive.

The boy was their only connection to the Twenty's operations in the Sol system. The mere fact that he was here also meant that the Council had found a second path through the Rift. There would have been no way to sneak him in through the heavily guarded Front Door. Toby would be the key to finding that second path's location. He might also know some of the other Council agents in the system—surely the Keeper hadn't sent just one.

After all, despite Tyrus's taunting dismissal, the kid was an alpha. And alphas always knew more than their masters thought they did. So he needed to capture Toby, not kill him.

Tyrus stopped swimming after the boy and instead swam on a perpendicular course until he was back at the pool's edge. As Toby still made for the stairs at the far end, Tyrus pulled himself up and out of the water onto the edge and started walking swiftly in that same direction, ignoring the oppressive darkness. He reached the far wall before Toby reached the stairs and felt around on it until he found what he was looking for.

By the look on his face as he mounted the first step out of the pool, Toby hadn't expected the lights to come back on. It was a pity the boy hadn't been using low-light amplification. If he had, suddenly turning the lights on could have overloaded his optic nerve and stunned him. But Tyrus supposed he had to be happy that he could simply see Toby now. It evened the playing field, which really meant it gave Tyrus the advantage.

He stood at the top of the pool steps, waiting for Toby to come the rest of the way up to meet him. To his surprise, the boy still had the knife, a wicked-looking, curved Martian blade—they called it a sica—about fifteen centimeters long. But Tyrus had the high ground and the advantage in reach.

Toby tried to lunge up the stairs and swipe the knife at Tyrus's legs, but Tyrus met him with a kick to the face, hitting the boy's already-busted nose and sending him tumbling back into the water, shrieking with pain. Of course, the little nanites in the water were likely already healing and numbing the kid's nose, but Tyrus supposed he couldn't have everything.

The other alpha recovered quickly, lunging up the steps again, this time trying to catch Tyrus's right leg as it came toward him. Tyrus let him reach out and grasp toward it but then pulled the leg back and jumped down the steps, moving his other leg forward so that his left knee caught Toby under the chin. The boy's head snapped back, and he fell back into the water again.

Tyrus moved backward up the steps out of the water once more. He watched as Toby swayed on his feet in the shallow water and shook his head to try and clear the cobwebs. At this point, he almost certainly had a severe concussion, among other injuries, but he didn't seem close to yielding. Tyrus needed to deliver the knockout blow, and soon, but he'd actually expected that knee to the chin to be it. The kid's resiliency surprised him, and he wondered if the magical little healing nanobots in the pool surrounding him had anything to do with it.

"Toby, you can't win. Drop the knife, and I promise you'll be treated fairly as a prisoner of war instead of as a spy. It's more than you deserve, but you have my word."

The boy didn't acknowledge Tyrus's offer, just screamed defiantly at him. He pulled back the hand holding the knife, and Tyrus got ready to dodge.

Then, two things happened in quick succession. The door behind Tyrus opened, and Toby threw the knife. It sailed past Tyrus, directly at the now open doorway.

Tyrus whirled in time to see the long blade bury itself up to the handle in Domitia Felix's chest. She stood there for a second, looking down at the knife in disbelief and then up at Tyrus. An instant later, she collapsed in a heap.

Behind him, Tyrus heard Toby leap up the steps. Inside, he felt cold, and a murderous rage started to build. As he heard Toby leave the water, Tyrus turned and, with all the momentum of his large frame, delivered a devastating roundhouse blow to Toby's temple.

The boy crumpled to the stone floor, either dead or very much unconscious; Tyrus didn't care. All his attention turned back to Domitia, lying on the floor in a rapidly expanding pool of her own blood.

"Help!" Tyrus screamed through the open doorway. "Guard down!"

He reached down to pick Domitia up and took her to the water's edge. Holding her close, he walked down the stairs into the water, submerging all but her head.

And for the first time ever, Tyrus Tyne prayed. He had no idea what he was doing. He didn't know if there was a God or if that God truly cared. But he cried out, invoking the names of Mars, God, Christ, Buddha, and a few others he'd heard on Earth or heard Jinny talk about, pleading with all of them to spare Domitia's life.

Save her! Save her, and I will do anything you ask of me. Just save her!

As he finished the words of his silent prayer, a sudden warmth filled him. Before he could dwell on it, the door to the bathhouse flung open wider, and two figures rushed in: Kilnfire and Lonesearcher.

Taking in the scene with a glance and exchanging no words, Kilnfire darted from the room, hopefully to get help. Lonesearcher made her way quickly into the water and moved to Domitia's side.

"I have field immune training," the celeusta told Tyrus.

"So do I," he rasped out through his tears.

"But yours isn't with Martian anatomy," she said urgently. "I need you to loosen your grip but keep supporting her from underneath so I can examine her."

Tyrus realized he was holding Domitia so tightly that he might very well be causing more damage. He obediently loosened his grip but kept both arms underneath her, holding her head and the top of her chest above the waterline.

Lonesearcher put an ear to Domitia's chest and felt around the knife with both hands. Then, she took the optio's pulse.

"You did the best thing possible by getting her in the bath water immediately," Lonesearcher told Tyrus in a soothing voice as she continued to examine the unconscious Praetorian Guard. "If we get the immunes here soon with their equipment, she might just make it."

"I should have just killed him," Tyrus whimpered. "It's my fault."

Lonesearcher didn't look up but made a raspberry noise with her lips. "You speak nonsense. The choice to throw the knife was his alone, not yours. You could have done nothing, Visitor Tyrus Tyne. But while we are here, congratulations are in order for winning the Trials."

The comment took Tyrus by surprise, and though he knew the woman was just trying to keep him talking to fend off shock, he took the bait. "How did you know?"

Lonesearcher pulled out a knife of her own from a sheath on her belt. "I have to cut another hole to release the pressure from around the lungs so they can inflate," she said as if she were relating the weather to him. Then she started working, slicing away a section of Domitia's skinsuit and making an incision on her upper chest. As she worked, she kept talking.

"I figured it out quickly. You gave your life to save the praetor in your sim. That ended the sim. You won. You received the points, and there's no way either of us can catch up to you. Kilnfire knows too, but he does not want to accept it. And neither of us would ever quit the

Trials early. Both of us will keep trying our hardest, though deep down we know we are fighting for second place."

Tyrus heard movement behind him at the door to the bathhouse but didn't turn. He kept his eyes on Domitia's face, which was slack and still. He felt, rather than saw, the two medics move beside him in the water. "Sir. Visitor Tyrus Tyne," one of the immunes said. "You need to let us take her and put her on the gurney. Do you understand?"

He nodded dumbly but made no move to give up his grip on the woman. Lonesearcher reached out and gently pried his hands from where they grasped Domitia and then helped the two medics lift her gently from Tyrus's cradling arms and onto a gurney that was floating next to them in the water.

They left quickly with Domitia, speaking to each other in hushed tones, Lonesearcher following along and relating what she'd already found and done in treating the optio.

Tyrus stayed where he was in the water, his back to the door and the still body of Toby. He stayed there for a very long time, even as two other members of the Praetorian Guard took the unconscious Toby away. Tyrus waited there, unmoving, until Centurion Parn himself came and, with surprising gentleness, led him out of the water and back to his quarters.

"You're joking?"

From the look on both Landon's and Temperance's faces, they most certainly weren't joking. But Jinny was having a hard time wrapping her head around all they'd just told her.

"You think President Gorsky is a traitor? Really?"

Landon nodded. Temperance just looked annoyed, as if she couldn't understand why Jinny wasn't getting it.

"He convinced Congressman O'Leary to have me hack a secure government server under false pretenses. The file I accessed was the entire defense plan for United Earth against the Council thingy," the girl said, talking slowly as if Jinny hadn't heard her the first time she'd told the story. "But I didn't send it directly to Gorsky. He had me send it to an anonymous IP address."

"Which you traced to Joseph Blackmont, owner of the company running the prison on the moon that you rescued me from?" Jinny finished for her, making it a question because she was still having a hard time swallowing the fantastical story.

Temperance nodded vigorously, and so did Landon after she elbowed him. What an odd couple.

"Can you prove all this?' Jinny asked, the implications racing through her head. She didn't like Gorsky, mainly because he'd so brazenly denounced Corey and the mission to Mars. But she hadn't made the mental leap to thinking the man was a traitor.

"Sure. I have all the records," Temperance explained in a long-suffering tone, as if she found Jinny to be a little slow. "That's why we want to talk to Admiral Lopez, so he can do something about it."

Maybe Jinny *was* slow. She'd been so busy with her training, falling exhausted into bed each night, that she'd spent a surprisingly small amount of time thinking about what was happening outside of the university campus in Perth. Now, Temperance's and Landon's revelation brought her back to the reality of the coming war in a painful jolt.

"But how does Joseph Blackmont having the battle plan for Earth's defense help the Council?" Jinny asked.

The purple-haired girl suddenly looked confused, like she hadn't considered that question up until now. Maybe she hadn't, but it was an incredibly important consideration. To call United Earth's newly appointed president a traitor and Council collaborator just for tricking them into sharing a top-secret battle plan with a mercenary leader was a massive leap. Without a motive—how could Blackmont having the plans possibly help the distant Council Navy?—it would be a tough pill for anyone to swallow.

"Maybe they have a way to talk to the Council," Landon Hartman blurted out, drawing surprised looks from both women. The young man had been largely silent since Jinny had led them to an empty classroom so they could discuss matters in private, letting the odd little hacker, whom he was clearly smitten with, do all the talking. Now, seeing the incredulous looks on both women's faces, he let out a long sigh. "I could go to prison a thousand times over for telling either of you this, but . . ."

He paused, licking his lips and blinking rapidly. When he looked back up at Jinny, his voice was only slightly steadier. "The UEN has a faster-than-light communication method. It's called a Tachyon Telegraph, and it uses FTL tachyon particle bursts to send message across the system instantaneously using a variation of Morse code."

Temperance looked equal parts shocked and excited, but Jinny just nodded.

"You already knew?" the boy asked, exasperated.

"The Navy told Tyrus Tyne so he could help them prepare for the Council invasion," she explained. "He wasn't supposed to tell me either." She shrugged.

"Well, maybe Gorsky figured out how to boost the signal and communicate all the way to the colonies," the boy finished his thought, seeming to shrink a little, as if he believed his own idea too ridiculous to contemplate now that he'd said it out loud.

It was Jinny's turn to sigh. "No," she said, shaking her head. "But they are communicating FTL, and I think I know how." In her readings of Tyrus, she'd learned about the Council's experimentations with FTL comms. It fit with other things she'd learned years before, reading an Assembly speaker. Neither knew everything about the technology, but by putting both of their memories together, she felt she could piece together what was going on.

She turned back to the purple-haired punk hacker. "Temperance, if I gave you some specifications for power consumption, could you run a search of power grids across Earth and find me a match?"

"Sure," the girl said in a petulant tone, seeming offended that Jinny would even have to ask.

Jinny opened her mouth to share what she knew of the Council's quantum entanglement comm system, but then she stopped herself. A shadow at the frosted glass door that led into the room had caught her attention.

She crossed the room rapidly, holding up a hand to forestall any questions or objections from her two guests, and flung the door open, revealing a startled Kelly Martin.

"What are you doing?" Jinny snapped.

"I . . . uh . . ." the girl stammered. "The Majko sent me looking for you. You're late to your next lesson."

Jinny frowned and studied the face of the Majko's assistant. She detected no duplicity in the girl's expression and relaxed her tense shoulders a bit. "Sorry, I didn't mean to snap at you, Kelly. Can you please tell the Majko I'll be along shortly? I'm just catching up with a few friends."

The girl looked around Jinny to try to get a better look at Temperance and Landon, but Jinny shifted her stance just enough to block her. Better safe than sorry. A moment later, she watched Kelly's retreating back moving down the hall while she chewed her lower lip in thought.

Turning back to the pilot and the hacker, she said, "Not a word of this to *anyone*. Are we clear?" She didn't wait for either of them to respond. "Give me your comm codes, and I'll call you as soon as I've figured out a way to help you reach Admiral Lopez."

They both nodded and gave her the codes. Then she left them and headed in the direction Kelly had gone, knowing that the Majko was likely to find her student a little preoccupied as she tried to read and channel an engineer today. The results were unlikely to meet the old woman's expectations.

CHAPTER 19

The Martians called it Nyx, after the Roman god of night. The Earthers had originally called it Scotus, after the Greek god of darkness, but somewhere along the line, they had also adopted the Martian name.

Under any name, it was a hellscape that couldn't sustain life even the size of a microbe, so far away from Sol that it was a barren, bone-dry, frozen wasteland with no hope of ever being terraformed or supporting a colony. Not to mention that its orbit was so irregular and far from the sun that at aphelion, it traveled deep into the Castilian Rift, and was outside the Rift and accessible to mankind only fifteen out of every forty years. Anyone who tried to reach the planet or tried to stay on Nyx's surface when it reentered the area of space claimed by the Rift was never heard from again.

So, in all, Nyx was one of the least hospitable planets ever discovered by humankind. It was also one of the most valuable.

The planet had the highest deposits of otherwise rare metals discovered anywhere in the Sol system. In particular, it was one of the only sources for adamantine, a metal that did not *exist* on Earth, Mars, or Europa, and was otherwise only present in limited quantities on Dione, one of Saturn's moons. Adamantine happened to have extraordinary properties that, when mixed with more pedestrian metals, exponentially increased the strength of starship hulls.

Which made Nyx not only a very valuable planet but also a hotly contested one.

No one was sure who first discovered it. The Earthers claimed to have arrived in 48 P.D. But the Martians claimed to have arrived before that, in 46 P.D. It had been nothing more than a theoretical argument when both planets had been under the Council's rule; the Council simply claimed Nyx for its own and began relentlessly mining the planet for adamantine and its other rare metals.

But then the Council left Sol, taking everything of value that they could with them through the Rift before sealing it up on the colonial side. So, for a few generations, the Four Worlds essentially forgot about Nyx in their daily struggle to survive and rebuild.

In the year 267 P.D., Earth finally sent an expedition to Nyx to start once again mining the planet. By almost sheer happenstance, they landed and established their mining base in the northern hemisphere. Which was good, because they found that the Martians had already arrived in the southern hemisphere and were busy with their own mining.

Multiple battles and wars were fought between the two planets over Nyx in the centuries that followed, but the boundaries between the powers after all of that were much like in the beginning. Earth continued to mine the northern hemisphere while Mars mined the southern, and the two coexisted in a state of uneasy and fragile detente.

Until now.

Centurion Kysto Hearthtender, commanding officer of the MPNS *Ferox*, a liburna—or heavy cruiser—just three years out of the Deimos shipyards, found escort duty for the mining convoys sent to and from Nyx to be simultaneously the most stressful and most boring of any duty he'd ever had.

It was so boring because nothing ever happened; Earth and Mars hadn't fired shots at each other in anger, at least around Nyx, in the almost fifty years since the Six-Month War. But it was stressful because the potential for a battle was *always* there. They perpetually teetered right on the edge of disaster, just waiting for a small shove.

Like now, as the *Ferox* escorted three bulk freighters loaded with adamantine and other mined metals and minerals on the multiday journey from Nyx to Mars. For the first part of the journey, Kysto and his convoy would be on a nearly parallel course with a UEN warship, a battleship of all things, which was likewise escorting a trio of Earth freighters back to their planet. In fact, for the first sixteen hours of the journey, the two convoys would be within weapons range of each other. It was disconcerting, to say the least.

"Optio," he said to his executive officer, Leila Pando, who sat nearby on *Ferox*'s bridge. "When was the last time you saw the Earthlings use a battleship for simple escort duty?"

Pando thought for a moment, then shook her head. "It is highly unusual, my Centurion. Typically, they send nothing larger than a heavy cruiser, and they use battlecruisers as escorts only when they are clearing out the mining stations prior to Rift entry and their convoys are unusually large. We do the same, but never quinqueremes."

Kysto grunted his acknowledgment. Nyx was near the middle of the current seven-and-a-half-year period in which it could be mined before it reentered the Rift. Then, it would be out of reach for twelve and a half years before reemerging on the opposite side of the system for another seven and a half years. So it really made no sense for a ship as powerful as the UEN battleship on their scopes to be on simple escort duty. It also violated several unwritten but no less real rules that governed the uneasy truce Mars and Earth had over the dark planet.

"Can we increase our distance from them?" he asked Pando.

"Sorry, my Centurion. This is the only safe path nearby."

Kysto nodded, and his frown deepened. She was absolutely right, confirming what he already knew.

Nyx had, in its long, sweeping journeys around the outermost reaches of Sol's gravitational field, collected more than its fair share of debris, asteroids, and even small moonlets. So, going to and from the planet was a navigational nightmare. Which today meant that the Mars and Earth convoys would pass very close to each other in an effort to follow the few viable paths through the mess. It was a rare occurrence,

Kysto reflected, for the two powers to not only have convoys leaving at nearly the exact same time but to have them pass so close as well. Regardless, there was no avoiding it. He could slow his own convoy to prevent it from getting too close to the Earth ships, but doing so would symbolically cede additional power to the Earthlings in the endless political dance around Nyx, and he had no intention of doing so. It was the space warfare equivalent of refusing to flinch.

That decision would doom his entire crew.

As they neared the point of closest approach, where the two convoys would be a mere half a light second apart, Kysto watched closely on his scanner display, focusing all of his attention on the enemy battleship. Which meant he almost missed it when two of the United Earth ore freighters abruptly exploded.

"What happened? Pirates?" he snapped at his bridge crew. "Battle stations! We must be ready if there is a threat."

As his crew hastened to fulfill his orders, Cushos Armerum Pica, his tactical officer, spoke up. "No threats on the screens, my Centurion, though I am getting strange readings from the debris. I cannot—"

"My Centurion!" the comm officer interrupted Pica. "You must hear this."

The bridge speakers played static, and then a male voice with what was clearly an Earthling accent began speaking. "Mayday. Mayday. This is UENS *Italy* broadcasting on an open channel. We have been attacked by Martian forces over Nyx. They destroyed two of our convoy and we are firing to defend ourselves. Mayday . . ."

Centurion Kysto Hearthtender didn't hear the rest of what the man said as the words sunk in. *Attacked? Destroyed. We did not fire!*

"Sir," Pica cried again, this time with a frantic dismay. "Missiles inbound from *Italy*. Do you wish to return fire?"

There was only one answer to that question in Martian war doctrine, and Kysto gave it. Regardless, he never had the chance to see if his return volley did any damage. Seconds after his missiles left their tubes, *Ferox* exploded as over two dozen ship killer missiles, fired at point-blank range, slammed into its hull.

Rear Admiral Dalish Connors smiled as the Martian heavy cruiser disintegrated under UEN *Italy*'s blistering fusillade. His battleship, anticipating the Martians' return fire, swatted all but one of their missiles out of space. The only warhead to get through impacted *Italy*'s flanks, gouging but not penetrating the behemoth's armor.

Dalish quietly entered into his console the code sequence that would heavily encrypt and then hide the true records of the battle and replace them with the carefully doctored ones he and the ship's AI had prepared, which the AI would now forget ever having helped him with.

To everyone else on *Italy*'s bridge, it had indeed looked like the Martians had fired first, destroying the two freighters. Now, the official record of the battle would reflect the same, and there would be no record of the planted explosives on either doomed ship.

Dalish wasn't exactly happy that the crews of both freighters had needed to die, ignorant of their part in the grand plans of the Sol system until the very end. But sacrifices had to be made for the greater good, he told himself. And not just for the greater good of Dalish Connors's personal bank account, or the promise of promotions to come from President Mikael Gorsky.

CHAPTER 20

Tyrus sat in the chair, looking at the still form of Domitia Felix on the hospital bed. He'd been crying for a long time, and his face was wet with the tears and the snot that he couldn't seem to find enough tissues to contain.

He looked down at her still face, that perfect face that, just hours before, had kissed his. And now . . . this.

Domitia's eyes fluttered open. "Tyrus," she said weakly, the single word prompting a coughing fit. He moved forward quickly and helped her eat some nanite-infused ice chips from a cup next to the bed to soothe her throat.

"Hi," she said again afterward, looking him in the eyes. She reached up a hand, and he grasped it gently. "Is your gaze going once again where it should not, my Tyrus?"

He laughed despite himself. For hours, they had worked on her, all the might of Martian doctors and nurses, plus the best in nanotechnology, and she'd actually died twice on the operating table. Or so he'd been told afterward. But in the end, she had survived, and the doctors said she'd recover fully as long as she used the healing baths regularly and didn't spar for at least a week. It was absurd how much more advanced Martian medical tech was than anywhere else's, but Tyrus certainly wasn't complaining.

"Forgive me, my Domitia," he said, the tears still falling, though for a different reason, as he leaned down to brush his lips against the hand he held in his own. "As always, your beauty overcomes me."

"Hmm, I like that," she said dreamily.

"Do you wish me to leave?" someone said from the hospital room's open doorway. Tyrus looked up to see Centurion Parn, in full exosuit, standing there, his helmet retracted so they could see his face.

"Yes, I would prefer you to leave," Domitia said, completing the ritual. "But not now," she amended. "Please come in, my Centurion."

Parn obeyed, moving to the other side of the bed opposite Tyrus. "You will be pleased to know, Visitor Tyne," the man said, "that the traitor and spy called Toby survived his injuries. Though your last punch gave him fairly severe brain damage, our doctors are confident the nanobots can repair most of it—enough, at least, for us to question him when he has recovered."

"It's not 'Visitor' Tyne anymore," corrected Domitia. "It's Praetorian Guard Tyne."

Parn smiled. "Not quite yet, Optio. The Trials end today, and tomorrow we will formally welcome Tyrus Tyne into our ranks. And you will be there to pin the insignia on him personally as he speaks the Oaths."

Domitia smiled. Then her eyes fluttered closed, and she drifted off to sleep.

"Tyrus, I would speak with you alone," Parn said, his voice deep and severe. It was the first time the centurion had ever called him by his first name alone, portending a change in the dynamic between them that Tyrus could only guess at.

He nodded, wiping the last of the tears—and other things—off his face and following the centurion out the door and into an empty nurse's office across the hall, closing the door behind them.

Parn turned and regarded him seriously. "Tyrus, do you fully understand the commitment that you have made to Optio Felix?"

Tyrus nodded. "I understand that my fate is now hers to do with as she will. That by initiating the courtship ritual, it is now entirely up to her how our relationship progresses and ends . . . or doesn't."

Parn nodded but did not smile. "I am glad you understand. But will you honor it?"

Tyrus didn't need to think. He nodded. "Yes, my Centurion. Without question. I would cede my will to hers even if tradition didn't demand it."

The other man relaxed a bit, and the corners of his mouth twitched upward in a smile. "Good. You must understand, Tyrus, that Domitia is like a daughter to me. When we join the Praetorian Guard, we forsake all other familial attachments, abandoning our last names and adopting those of the Guard. We still know our parents, siblings, and extended families, but they are no longer our families by law or tradition. Only our fellow members of the Guard fill that role. But even within that structure, I have always felt especially protective of Optio Felix. She reminds me . . ." His voice caught, surprising Tyrus with the emotion in it.

"I had a younger sister," Parn continued in a lower voice, looking away toward the corner of the room. "Anna. She died young in an accident. She fell from a great height. I was the only one with her and was too young to help. I dragged her as far as I could toward home and the healing baths, but by the time they found us only a few hundred meters from our communal dwelling, Anna had been dead for a full hour. I never speak of this, but I tell you now that Domitia has become like daughter and sister to me. I see her as I once saw Anna and as I believe I would see my own offspring were I ever to have any."

He looked back to Tyrus, his face hardening again. "Do you understand what I am saying to you?"

Tyrus met the man's stony gaze. "That if I hurt her, you and I will meet on the dueling field."

Parn nodded. "If it gets that far, you may not survive to reach the dueling field."

He nodded his understanding. "I assure you, Centurion Parn, if I hurt her, I will wield the knife that pierces my own heart." He was parroting what Corey O'Leary had told Praetor Starshadow three months before on their first day in Martian space. It seemed fitting for this moment.

Parn relaxed again, obviously taking Tyrus's pledge at face value, which was precisely how he had meant it.

"Good," the man said. "We have traditions, I know, that are strange to you. But the right of the woman to choose her husband is among the most sacred. The early colonizers of our planet skewed male, and women were scarce for the first several generations. As a result, we did, and still do, treat them as the precious and rare treasures they are, though they now outnumber men on Mars. The traditions hold. You have offered yourself to Domitia. If she accepts your offering and decides to make you her husband, your only choice is acceptance of the covenant or death."

Tyrus smiled. "I would be honored should she choose me, my Centurion. You need fear nothing from me where Domitia is concerned."

"It gives me joy to hear you say it. And it will give me greater joy to see you honor it."

He turned to leave, but Tyrus held up a hand to implore him to wait. "Centurion Parn, may I ask you a question, man to man?"

Parn nodded but said nothing.

"In the bath chamber, after the traitor Toby threw the knife that pierced Domitia, I prayed. I prayed to Mars, God, and a whole host of other beings—any name I could remember, really. I grew up without religion, so I had no idea what I was doing. But I promised that being, whoever they are, that I would do anything they required of me if they helped Domitia live."

The centurion looked understanding. "It is a good thing you did, but a solemn vow not made lightly."

"I know. But what I wanted to ask you . . . Well, I felt something, like a presence there in the room with us, holding a part of Domitia there with me while we waited for help to come. It was only for a moment, then Kilnfire and Lonesearcher arrived to help and the presence was gone, but it felt more real than I can explain. Have you have you ever had such an experience?"

Parn nodded solemnly. When he spoke, his voice was thick with renewed emotion. "Three years after my sister's death, on my twelfth birthday, I felt such a presence at the moment that I raised a dagger to take my own life. It stopped me, and it was at that instant that I pledged my life to Mars. It led me to where I am today."

Tyrus bowed his head. "Thank you, my Centurion. I will never share your experience with anyone, on my honor, but I am grateful to you for helping me understand my own. I look forward to tomorrow, when I can also pledge my life formally to Mars. I will be honored to follow you into battle."

Parn smiled, an expression that still looked strange on the dour man's face. "That is good, Tyrus, for the battle may be great and terrible." He looked in the direction of Domitia's room. "Savor every moment with her now. These may be among our last."

Without another word, the centurion left the room, leaving a thoughtful Tyrus behind.

"Excuse me? You did what?" O'Leary's tone was incredulous but also exhausted, as if he was sick of questioning Tyrus's decisions lately.

"I pledged myself to Optio Felix. We are now a bonded pair."

"That's what I thought you said." The older man shook his head. "Tyrus, has anyone explained to you just how enormous a commitment you've just made?"

Tyrus nodded. "Both before *and* after I made it. Centurion Parn was quite clear in describing to me what would happen if I backed out."

O'Leary blew out a long breath. "You do realize, my friend, that at any moment, Domitia could decide that she wants to marry you, and it would just happen?" He snapped his fingers. "Like that. There's no such thing as a wedding on Mars, not the way we think about them. If she says you're married, then you're married."

Tyrus actually grinned at him now. "I realize that. And I'm hoping she does."

"You really are crazy, you know that?" Despite his words, O'Leary's lopsided grin showed he was happy for his friend.

"I know it sounds insane," Tyrus told him sincerely, "but I believe

I've found my place here. With the Praetorian Guard—and with Domitia. I've felt like a helmless starship for the better part of a year now, and I finally feel like I'm back on the right course."

"That Domitia Felix is a looker," Riggs added around a mouthful of food. "Does she have any sisters, or maybe a hotter cousin?"

Tyrus grinned, but O'Leary shot him a look of disapproval. "Careful who you say that around, Riggs. Technically, Tyrus should challenge you to a duel right now for that comment, but I'm guessing our big friend will let it slide since you and I are just stupid foreigners and not the refined and sophisticated Martian he has become."

Now Tyrus laughed out loud, recognizing the ribbing the two men were giving him. It was good to see more of the old Riggs returning—the pilot had at first been incensed to learn of Toby's betrayal and murder of Jynx. But as the dinner had progressed, a strange calm had settled over Riggs, and he'd begun joking. Tyrus didn't know what any of it meant, but he was glad that he'd agreed to one last dinner with his friends, though it required momentarily leaving Domitia's side in the hospital. He'd only done so, of course, after securing promises from four doctors and half a dozen immunes that they would watch over her in his absence.

And it was a last dinner of sorts. From here on out, he would live, eat, and sleep among his fellow members of the Praetorian Guard. He would even have to forsake his last name and have a new one assigned to him by the Guard.

"So what happens next?" Riggs asked, bringing the conversation back to serious topics. "We won, didn't we? Mars will join the war?"

Tyrus had been upset and had almost gone weak in the knees when O'Leary had told him the stakes of his winning the Trials. If he'd had any idea they were so high . . . Well, he would probably have overthought things even more than he already had and missed the simple solution to the simulation. So it had almost certainly been best to keep the information from him. In the end, everything had turned out well, even if not knowing upset him.

"There is still a lot of work to do," O'Leary replied. "But perhaps the hardest part is over. In fact—"

Whatever he was about to say was interrupted by the chiming of the door. O'Leary told the room's AI to open it, and it slid aside to reveal two praetorian guards.

"Candidate Selected Tyrus Tyne," one of them greeted him. Until he took the Oaths the next morning, he wasn't actually part of the Guard, so his formal title was a little clunky until then.

"Optio Ursus. How may I serve you?" he answered formally, ignoring the big Martian's distasteful look.

"Centurion Parn requests you attend him immediately."

"Then I will do so," Tyrus replied. He started to leave the room to follow the two men, but Ursus turned to O'Leary next.

"Emissary Corey O'Leary, Consul Starshadow requests you also attend her immediately."

O'Leary frowned. "Of course. May I ask what this regards?"

The man shook his head solemnly. "I am afraid that Consul Starshadow must tell you that herself."

Jonathan's face broke the surface of the water next to himself.

That *was* quite strange, he thought, removing his mask and looking over to see an exact copy of himself doing the same as the gentle waves caused them both to bob up and down. It was like seeing himself in the mirror, but when the other him moved differently, it ruined the effect and made it even more surreal.

As do those, he thought, looking down at the front of his wetsuit, just visible under the water's surface.

Careful, a female voice broke into his thoughts. *Those aren't yours.*

Jonathan smiled and barked a laugh, drawing a strange look from his copy a few meters away. *Sorry,* he told the woman in his head—or rather, the woman whose head he currently inhabited. *Just a little weird, that's all.*

He could feel her stern frown of disapproval, though he couldn't see it. He was about to say something flippant to dismiss the concern when someone else's voice, this one from *outside* his head, broke into the conversation.

"Reader Ambrosa, we must speak."

Jonathan looked over at the small boat bobbing in the water nearby, where the Majko stood leaning over the edge, looking at him with a scowl.

That's my cue, Jinny Ambrosa said in Jonathan's head—well, her head—and he gave her the mental equivalent of a wink as he retreated into the fog and relinquished to her full control of her mind and body once more.

Jinny swam clumsily to the back of the dive boat, the unfamiliar weight of the air tank on her back almost making her roll over a few times. Maybe she should have waited to dismiss the persona of her scuba instructor until *after* she was safely on the boat.

As the real Jonathan Meyers reached the boat first and then helped her onboard, she looked inquisitively up at the Majko's face.

"What's up?" she asked the old woman, coming across far more casual than she intended; Jinny was finding that sometimes a few mannerisms of the departed personas persisted for minutes or even hours after she regained control. "Did you get that meeting with Admiral Lopez? Temperance and Landon were very adamant yesterday that—"

"It is not that," the Majko interrupted sharply. Jinny noticed that the old woman's nearly perpetual scowl had a darker quality to it today.

"What's wrong? What happened?" Jinny demanded.

Her answer was a single word. "War."

"The Council fleet?" Jinny looked up at the blue skies above as if she might irrationally pierce the heavens and see the attackers with her naked eye.

"No," the Majko said solemnly. "Mars."

Jinny looked back at her, eyes wide in shock. "What? How?"

The Majko shrugged laconically. "Does it matter? I'm afraid all hopes of a coalition with the Reds have now failed, and the Council will no doubt arrive just in time to sweep up the fragments of Earth and Mars, brush aside Europa, and take the system with ease."

Jinny couldn't believe what she was hearing; she didn't *want* to believe it. All her work, as well as Tyrus's and Corey's, meant nothing now. She was only on day forty-three of her promised ninety-day training with the Majko and the Earth readers, but now even her agreement to that ninety-day period had proven foolhardy. She should be with her friends now, on Mars, but instead, she was languishing here in Australia and . . .

Jinny took a deep breath. *No,* she thought. The last month had most decidedly *not* been a waste of time. The more she learned to summon and dismiss the various personas in her head at will, the less they seemed to pop out when she *didn't* want them. Even the nightmares, which had stopped early on in her training, hadn't come back. For the first time in years, Jinny felt like maybe she wasn't going to lose herself to madness.

Regardless, she looked up again at the sky, this time imagining the United Earth fleet overhead clashing with Martian forces, warships on both sides exploding and falling into Earth's atmosphere as hundreds of ships and tens of thousands of spacers died in nuclear fire—all ships and spacers that would be absolutely vital for when the Council finally invaded in force.

One thing was certain: the Four Worlds could not afford this new war. Unfortunately, the Majko's prediction that the Council fleet would arrive in time to pick through the leftovers of a system-shattering conflict was now a near-certain outcome. Especially given their suspicions that Mikael Gorsky had direct contact with the Keeper and the Council government. They could, together, time the Council invasion just right, for the moment when both Mars and Earth were at their weakest.

Unless . . . She looked back up at the old matron's face. "You didn't tell me that just to let me know that we have no hope, did you?" she demanded.

The Majko shook her head. "No. There may be a way."

"What is it?" Jinny demanded as the old woman trailed off and remained silent for a long count of five.

"It is you," the Majko answered simply.

Jinny huffed in frustration, not believing what she was hearing. Of all the ridiculous times for the Majko to go off on one of her tangents about Jinny being some sort of reader savior. She readied herself to shoot down whatever insane plan the woman had concocted.

"I have considered," the Majko continued, oblivious to or perhaps simply ignoring the flash of anger on Jinny's face, "the things you shared with me that the hacker and pilot discovered and brought to you."

Objections died on Jinny's lips at the mention of Temperance Jimenez and Landon Hartman. She resolved to shut up and listen carefully, for now, at least.

"I have not been able to reach Admiral Lopez through regular channels," the old woman admitted. "He is not on Earth. Now that I have learned of the Martian attack and the UE declaration of war, it does not surprise me. But I also do not believe that telling him of Blackmont's and President Gorsky's potential treachery now will be enough."

She regarded Jinny, her mouth flattening to a smooth line. When she spoke again, she said each word slowly. "You, Reader Ambrosa, must read Joseph Blackmont. We must learn what he and the president are conspiring to do, and *then* we will be able to make Admiral Lopez and anyone else with an ear listen."

Corey entered the room to find that Aphrodite wasn't alone. She stood behind a long table, two praetorian guards flanking her on either side. Praetors Sunsbane and Tiberius were also there, and Corey's heart sank when he saw the morose expression on Sunsbane's face offset by the look of triumph Tiberius wore.

"Consul Aphrodite Starshadow," he said carefully, guessing that their increasing familiarity of past meetings would be inappropriate in this setting. "I came as requested."

Aphrodite licked her lips, her only outward show of emotion. "Former Emissary Corey O'Leary," she said in a hard voice, and the use of the new word 'former' felt like a gut punch.

What happened?

"How may I serve Mars?" he asked warily.

"Praetorian guards, arrest Corey O'Leary!" Tiberius said, almost gleefully, before Aphrodite could respond.

Without hesitation, two of the black-clad guards moved over to Corey and grabbed him by each arm, holding him fast.

"What is the meaning of this?" he demanded, momentarily and instinctively struggling against their iron grip.

"Your United Earth has betrayed us!" snapped Tiberius, but as the man opened his mouth to continue, Aphrodite held up a hand, silencing him. Corey was surprised to see Tiberius obey.

"Former Emissary Corey O'Leary," she said, her voice only briefly catching on his first name. "Seven hours ago, there was a battle between the forces of United Earth and those of Mars at the planet Nyx. I am honor-bound to tell you that the Martian People's Republic and United Earth are now in a state of war. As a former emissary of United Earth, you are to be imprisoned as an Earther spy on Mars, pending your execution."

Corey felt his knees give out. He slumped forward with a cry of dismay and horror, held up only by the strong grips of the two Praetorian Guards. His last glimpse as they dragged him from the room was of Aphrodite's face, and he thought he may have imagined a single tear escaping one startlingly blue eye before she was lost to his sight.

PART THREE
THE NYX WAR

CHAPTER 21

Twenty-Six Years Ago; 705 P.D.

Drip.

Drip.

Drip.

Cal 289 squeezed his eyes shut, trying to fall back asleep.

Drip.

He put his hands over his ears to try and block out the sound.

Drip.

He reached around for his pillow to put it over his head.

Drip.

No pillow. He remembered it had gotten moldy and been jettisoned, along with his mother's last blanket.

Drip.

Fine! I'm awake! He wanted to scream it; he really did. But the last time he'd woken up too loudly, he'd disturbed the neighbors. And then Jenk 312 had pounded him between that day's classes for interrupting his sleep.

Drip.

Cal 289 really had to pee now.

Drip.

He wanted to be especially quiet because he also didn't want to wake up Meera 274. He looked down at her now as he sat up on his cot. She lay next to their mother, the two of them huddled on the same cot for warmth. Proteus seemed to have little enough of that these days. Every day was winter.

Drip.

He actually wasn't sure what winter was, but he'd heard some of the old timers mention it in relation to the cold. And the word just *sounded* glum, especially the way they said it, so it fit. Every day was winter on Proteus, at least for as long as Cal could remember.

Drip.

He tried to tiptoe around the cot Meera and Mother shared toward the small fresher closet they shared with the five other families in this pod. He threw a nervous glance toward the cot where Jenk slept. Luckily, the older boy wasn't stirring. If Cal could just make it to . . .

"Cal?" Meera asked sleepily, and he watched in horror as Jenk turned over on his cot, but breathed a little easier when the boy's eyes stayed closed.

"Go back to sleep, Meera," he whispered. But he knew it was a lost cause. When six-year-old Meera was awake, she was awake. And not even her far older eleven-year-old brother could convince her otherwise.

He ignored her now and lightly took the last few steps to the fresher, where he sat down and shut the—thankfully—soundproof door. There, he did his business, then flushed, waiting as the air sucked his waste down completely before reopening the door. He didn't wash his hands. They'd stopped wasting water on that a year ago, and their supply of saniwipes had run out six months ago.

It was okay. They'd all gotten more or less used to the smell of each other. Mostly. Cal still swore that Jenk had an especially foul odor. He stopped cold; there the boy was, watching him with one eye open. He guessed he hadn't been successful at being quiet enough, or maybe the soundproofing on the door was finally failing. Either way, he'd pay for waking Jenk later, no matter what excuses he tried.

Resigned to his fate, he looked away from the surly thirteen-year-old and back toward Meera, who had extricated herself from under their sleeping mother's arm and was sitting on the edge of their shared cot.

"Cal," she said. "I'm hungry."

He frowned as he felt his own stomach rumble. "Me too, Meera. But you know we can't eat until lunch."

Her eyes got wide and glistened a little. "Please, Cal," she started to whimper, "I'm so hungry."

Cal shushed his younger sister almost frantically, pantomiming to her the need to be quiet as he cast a nervous look over at Jenk, but to his relief, the older boy had turned back over and appeared to be asleep again. Maybe he wouldn't even remember waking up, and Cal could escape another day of being beaten behind the hydroponics lab.

Looking back at Meera, with her wide eyes and—she was sticking her lower lip out now; no fair—pleading countenance, he knew he should be strong and not give in to her. But it was *Meera*. He didn't quite know how to say no to his little sister. Never had, especially when she cheated and used her pouting face on him.

"Fine," he hissed at her. "Follow me, but *be quiet*."

She hopped off the bed, and together, both in bare feet—Cal's last pair of shoes had died four months ago—they made their way carefully between the cots and sleeping Proteans to the door that led out of their pod and into the hall beyond. Once outside, Cal turned left, and Meera put her hand in his and gripped it tightly. That always made Cal feel a little better and stand up a little taller. After all, Meera needed *him*.

Oh sure, she needed their mother as well, probably even more. But it was Cal who got Meera food when there shouldn't be any. As far as he knew, Mother hadn't ever been able to do that.

They tip-toed through the halls, making a series of turns that came as second nature to Cal; he prided himself on knowing where *everything* was on Proteus. Even the stash of extra food that old man Kember kept hidden from the rest of the community.

The best part of stealing from Kember was that the old man couldn't report the theft. Because then Kember would also have to report that he had an extra stash of rations when the rest of the community was nearly always hungry. He also couldn't keep it in his pod, where there was zero privacy and fifteen other pairs of eyes to see him snatch a taste now and again. So he kept it in just about the cleverest place he could think of: the air ducts in the hydroponics bay.

Cal headed there now, Meera still holding tight to his hand. At first, he'd refused to take her with him when he'd go to raid Kember's stash, but after a few times without getting caught, he now let her tag along and play lookout. It made her happy, and Meera's smile was about the only thing that made Cal happy lately in return.

He'd first happened upon Kember's stash two months ago, when he was using the air ducts to sneak past Jenk and his Neanderthal friends, who were waiting for him outside of hydroponics to give him a thrashing. Since then, he'd probably stolen from the stash at least once a week, sometimes twice. Always little stuff—he didn't want Kember to try and find a new hiding place, though he was sure a man as anal-retentive as the old farmer knew exactly how many rations went missing at all times.

Meera started shaking with anticipation as they got closer to hydroponics, and he was about to shush her again when he heard voices from up ahead. Cal stopped, pulling his little sister into him and putting a hand over her mouth. He moved both of them to the side of the hall, behind one of the hatch bulkheads.

"Only three weeks? Are you sure?" Cal strained to hear, but he was pretty sure he recognized the voice. It was Mayor Ula 192. She had a deep, husky voice, like she was always gargling rocks or something.

"We lost another batch of the taters," a higher but masculine voice replied. Kember 202. Blast. They wouldn't be able to steal from his stash if he was already up and about. Still, Cal didn't take Meera and retreat. He wanted to hear more of what they said.

"Three weeks." Ula's words were a statement now instead of a question. "Then what?"

There was an uncomfortably long silence, and Cal started to feel an itch on his back, like he and Meera might get caught at any second. But still, he stayed. Even Meera, who had initially squirmed against the hand over her mouth, seemed to sense his anticipation and stopped fighting him as much.

"Then," Kember said again, "we . . . you know."

"No!" Ula's response was sharp enough to make Cal jump a bit and Meera go wide-eyed. "We're not culling the population."

What does 'culling' mean? Cal wondered.

"Come on," Kember whimpered. "We don't need *everyone.* With fewer people on Proteus, our supplies will last longer."

"No," Ula said, though this time with less force. "There will be a supply ship. Any day now."

"Not likely." Kember's tone was incredulous. "The last ship was more than a year ago. Since then, not even a single sniff of one in the system. You know as well as I do that the blasted guardies are out there making absolutely sure that no ship comes to us. But if we had a third of the population we have now, that might give the farms time to recover and get us to self-sufficiency."

"No." Ula's voice was small now, and its normally deep tone sounded almost like that of a little girl. "Just no. We can't. We won't."

"There's no other way," Kember argued. "Two-thirds of the population are normos anyway. Get rid of them, and our tweaked survive."

Oh, that's what culling means. Cal had heard enough. He started to backpedal and pull Meera along with him, trying desperately to put some distance between himself and the voices. *Culling. Getting rid of the normos.* The words kept revolving around and around inside his head.

Once he and Meera put some space between them and hydroponics, he turned around and started walking faster, stopping only to grab her in a hug and pull her off her feet so he could carry her and move quicker. He shushed her, and she obediently kept still.

Meera is a normo, he thought in despair. Cal himself wasn't. He was a pusher; that was what the tweakers called it. His mother had been proud of him when the tweakers had said that. But Jenk was also a pusher, and Jenk was an idiot. So it couldn't be all that great.

Mother had tried to hide her disappointment when Meera hadn't been a pusher, a wraith, or even a listener. When the Tweakers had declared her 'without mutation'—everyone knew that just meant normo—Mother smiled and told Meera that she was proud of her anyway. But Cal could see the truth in her eyes. Normos got fewer rations; they weren't as important to the community. They represented failures of the tweaker science. They weren't allowed to have mates or have kids or anything like that. No one wanted to pass normo blood along to the next generation.

That day, the day of Meera's testing, Cal had vowed to protect his little sister from anything and anyone who tried to make her feel less of a person because she was a normo. That had started his first fight with Jenk when the older boy, whom Cal had actually looked up to and considered a friend until then, called Meera a normo where she could hear. Cal punched him, and Jenk beat him into the deck.

And now . . . He knew things were bad on Proteus. They all knew. Meals had become lighter, then further between. Water was only served with meals and never for washing anymore. Other supplies—basics like towels, pillows, blankets—had been used until they were so worn out and dingy they were a health hazard, then ejected, and new ones never came anymore to replace them.

Something was very wrong on Proteus. And the grownups wouldn't talk about it, at least not where Cal could hear, but now . . . Now he knew something terrible that they didn't know, but what was he going to do about it?

Present Day; December 10, 731 P.D.

"I am pleased to announce that the rebel base at GX-6607 has been destroyed. Admiral Chen assures me that with a mere single task force, our Navy has struck a blow that has destroyed the rebel threat once and for all."

Creighton Horvath coughed into his hand to hide his reaction to Keeper Ian Petrov's blatant lie. The rebel base had indeed been destroyed. But, just as Guard Intelligence Colonel Gennady Stewart had guessed, the rebel defenses had been far more powerful than Chen had expected, and virtually the entire task force she'd sent had been destroyed. Even worse than losing the ships was losing the thousands of loyal enacters who crewed them. In Creighton's mind, the raid had been an unmitigated disaster, just as he'd hoped it would be.

But it had all been for naught. Petrov was spinning it as a glorious victory, even going so far as to suggest that the small group of rebels encountered there represented the entire rebellion. Creighton had hoped that the loss would make Petrov see reason, or at least allow the other members of the Twenty to pressure the Keeper to delay the invasion of the Four Worlds until the Navy could recoup its losses at GX-6607.

Now, however, as Creighton looked around the table at the other eighteen members of the Twenty, he could see that most of them were frowning and pretending to look at their personal holo fields, refusing to make eye contact with him or with Petrov. They knew, all of them, that the Keeper was lying, but none of them was brave enough to challenge Petrov openly.

Creighton looked at the Keeper next. Petrov had finished his pronouncement of victory and was giving him a hard stare now, a small smile on his lips, as if daring him to call his bluff. Creighton almost did it, even opening his mouth to argue, but then closed it. Without the backing of the other members of the Twenty, all his disagreement with Petrov would accomplish would be to erode his already tenuous power and influence in the group. No, he needed to save that for later—to use it when it really counted.

"That is wonderful news, Your Excellency," he said instead.

"It is, isn't it?" Petrov said with a gleam in his eyes that sent a chill down Creighton's back. "In fact, Admiral Chen informs me that the fleet will be ready to conquer the Four Worlds sooner than expected. The time draws near, my friends."

Creighton gulped and nodded, politely clapping along with the rest of the assembled speakers at their Keeper's words of triumph.

"Now," Petrov continued, "to accelerate the invasion timeline, I've authorized Admiral Chen to pull in multiple Guard Space Force task forces to assist in training her people via war games. You can expect to see . . ."

CHAPTER 22

Twenty-Six Years Ago; 705 P.D.

"And according to the Revised Quantum Entanglement Theory of 581 P.D. it should be possible to use entangled particles to transmit information over near-infinite distances instantaneously. This theory has its roots all the way back in the science of pre-diaspora Old Earth, and was even successfully tested then on a very small scale, though never with the type of consistency to make use practical.

"Subsequent attempts to use quantum entanglement for the transmission of information have largely failed. While it has been shown that it is *possible* to do so in theory, it has not worked in practice in interstellar applications. Not only is the amount of energy required prohibitive—think an independent, city-sized fusion reactor needed, at minimum, for even the transmission of a single bit of information—but in order to make the system functionally usable, we must avoid multipartite entanglement, which means we must have only one possible end point for each entangled particle in the system.

"To illustrate this, we can use the classic example of communicating through two cups on opposite ends of a large string. When you send a message in this manner from one of the cups, there is only one possible destination for that message: the other cup at the end of the string.

That means that if you wanted to set this up for interstellar communication across the 47 Colonies and send enough information to be meaningful, each communication center would need to have thousands of entangled particles assigned to *each* of the other forty-six colony worlds. That grows exponentially if you want to have multiple comm centers on each planet, and so on. Now, add in ships, and the problem becomes one of scale. Modern technology simply cannot . . ."

Cal felt his eyes closing and his neck muscles relaxing as Teacher Harriette droned on about things he really didn't care about. Sure, he enjoyed *some* of his physics classes, but really only the ones related to starship design and navigation. The rest felt like a lot of needless information to him. After all, *he* wasn't going to try to design faster-than-light communication systems.

The whole situation was made worse by the fact that it had been a week since he and Meera had overheard the conversation between Kember and Mayor Ula, and Cal *still* wasn't sure what, if anything, he could do about it.

He'd told Mother, of course. She had just frowned and told him that he'd probably misheard. But he'd expected that. Mother hadn't been the same since Father died three months earlier. She wouldn't even talk about *how* Father had died. The doctor had told them it was a terminal disease, though she'd been vague on exactly which one. Cal suspected it had been something far simpler: Father had died because he'd given up his rations to feed Mother, Cal, and Meera. Cal noticed that their meals had gotten far smaller after Father had passed away.

Since then, Mother seemed to have lost her spark. Once, she had laughed and played with her children. Now, she did little more than go to work at the waste processing plant and stare listlessly at the nearest bulkhead when she wasn't at work. Sure, she would feed Meera and him and make sure they were practicing their hygiene and getting to school, but he could tell she was only going through the motions. The truth was, they had lost Mother on the same day they'd lost Father.

Meera sensed it as well, and she had been increasingly clingy with Cal. She was—

Something hit Cal in the back of the head. He turned slowly, knowing what he would find, and saw Jenk snickering two seats behind and to his right. The boy stared back at Cal with a challenge in his eyes, not even trying to hide his guilt. Cal mentally shrugged and turned back around. Engaging with the older boy would only encourage him. But oh, how he wanted to plant his fist in Jenk's nose.

At the front of the room, Teacher Harriette continued blathering on about quantum entanglement, oblivious to the silent conflict in her classroom, just as she always was. Teacher Harriette was in her sixties, which meant she had already outlived the average life expectancy on Proteus, and she was a normo. Both made her an oddity, but Cal liked her well enough. When she did pay attention to her students, she was reasonably kind.

He looked at the clock on the wall and saw that there were still twenty minutes left in classes for the day. If he could just make it through that time without getting into a fight with Jenk, he might be able to slip out of the class and into the corridors before his bully could follow him and find a quiet place to beat him on the way back to their pod.

Cal's thoughts in that direction were interrupted when the classroom door opened without so much as a polite knock. He was more surprised to see the two people who stood in the now-open doorway. Mayor Ula 192 was there, which would normally have been odd enough, but the man with her was truly a shock.

Chief Tweaker Larabaius stood not more than five and a half feet in height, a full six inches shorter than Ula 192, but his presence dwarfed hers, as did his authority. Everyone knew that, even if the official word was that Ula 192 was the leader of Proteus. All Proteans knew that the mayor served only at the sufferance of the tweakers, and this man, Larabaius, was the leader of the tweakers.

Teacher Harriette had stopped her lecture abruptly when the door opened and was staring in shocked confusion over her archaic reading glasses, one of the lenses cracked, as it had been for the last year or so.

"Ms. Mayor, Chief Tweaker, my, this is a surprise," she said nervously, and Cal thought he could see her withdraw a little into herself as she folded her arms across her chest.

Ula 192 nodded, but Larabaius stepped forward into the room and glared at the teacher, ignoring the fourteen students. "Harriette 164," he said, frowning as he did so. "Would you please accompany Mayor Ula 192 for a moment? She has an urgent matter of which she must speak with you."

Harriette frowned but nodded slowly. Without a word to the class, she gathered up her old half-broken pad and shuffled slowly to the door, where the mayor put an arm around her and led her out into the corridor, letting the door shut behind them and leaving the class alone with the chief tweaker.

Larabaius turned and looked at the children and adolescents in the class, and his frown remained. For a long moment, he said nothing, just looked at each of them in turn. His eyes stopped and lingered on Lola 247, and his frown deepened as if he'd taken a bite of a lemon drop bar—back when they'd had such extravagances. His eyes roved the class again until they alighted on Kenick 291, where he also lingered and made the same sour face. He did likewise for six other students.

This made Cal frown. All eight students the chief tweaker had lingered on were normos, whereas he'd barely glanced at the tweaked in the room, like Cal.

Finally, seemingly with great reluctance, Larabaius spoke. "Students," he said in his nasal voice, "I regret to inform you that Teacher Harriette 164 is retiring, effective immediately. You will have a new teacher tomorrow, and I expect you to give him the respect due his position. You may want to search out Harriette 164 to thank her for her many years of service, but, as you can imagine, this is an emotional time for her, and she has requested privacy. Please honor her request."

Without another word, the chief tweaker turned and left the room as abruptly as he'd entered, leaving a confused and chattering group of students speculating on who their new teacher would be. Cal didn't join in the conversation. He sank lower in his seat as he felt a pain in the pit of his stomach.

Teacher Harriette had been a normo. And unless he was completely off, they would *never* see her again.

Present Day

The UEN base at Waypoint Charlie, stationed about a third of the way between Earth and Mars, had started as little more than a supply depot for United Earth Navy forces patrolling the demilitarized zone between the two perpetually warring planets. But now, hundreds of years later, Waypoint Charlie had been upgraded and replaced with a fully functional battle station, bristling with weaponry and with its own massive drives that allowed it to keep station between Earth and Mars no matter where they each were in their respective orbits.

Of course, its primary mission was still to resupply the UEN forces, which now consisted of the whole of Second Fleet, under the command of Admiral Terrence Lafayette. However, Lafayette was not currently at Waypoint Charlie, nor was the bulk of Second Fleet. The admiral had taken the fleet forward, encroaching into the neutral zone and pointing every active and passive sensor straight at the red planet, attuned to catch the merest twitch of movement from the Martian Fleet of the Bear—Mars's home defense fleet—or its Fleet of the Eagle, arrayed just inside the Martian border and directly facing Earth.

The two massive Martian fleets, each more than a hundred ships strong, were on hair triggers. War had been declared between the two Sol system superpowers, but thus far, neither planet's navies had fired a shot in the two weeks since the scuffle at Nyx.

Which perhaps explained why Vice Admiral Justin Lang on UENS *Belgium* was so on edge. Justin and his task force weren't usually assigned to Second Fleet, but had been sent to reinforce Lafayette and his ships from Admiral Showalker's First Fleet. Justin had been equal parts excited and terrified by the reassignment to the front lines, which made it both a relief and a supreme disappointment when Lafayette had assigned his Battle Task Force 12 to hang back and defend Waypoint Charlie.

It was overkill, really, at least to Justin's mind. Task Force 12 represented fully a sixth of First Fleet's might, anchored by four massive Missouri-class battleships, six battlecruisers, and twenty-six escorts ranging from heavy cruisers down to missile frigates. Given the long line of Second Fleet guarding the neutral zone, anything the Martians might sneak through would be a pittance compared to Justin's forces.

He fully expected the imposed guard duty to be boring and frustrating as they watched the eventual battle take place far away in the neutral zone.

Unfortunately, the Martians had different ideas.

"Admiral?" The voice of Captain Elisheva over the intercom started Justin from his intense study of First Fleet's positioning on the long-range sensors.

"What is it, Tovia?" he replied, stifling a yawn.

"There's something odd on the sensors, sir." It was enough to bring Justin back to fully upright in his command chair. "I'm sending it up to Steven, sir. Maybe he can make something of it."

Justin looked over at Lieutenant Commander Steven Blandid at the flag bridge's sensor station, who nodded toward him to acknowledge receipt of the sensor data. While the man analyzed it, Justin turned his attention back to the intercom. "Any thoughts on what it is?" he asked Captain Elisheva.

"Some erratic thermal readings five million clicks out," she replied. "Way too unsteady to be any kind of ship, even if they were head-on aspect and barely using their drive. Though it could be something cold-coasting in."

"Vector?"

She gave him the numbers, and he studied his system plot. "There's nothing out in that direction," he told her, frowning. "One of our listening posts would have seen the Martians burning on that vector, even if they were going to cold-coast in from way out there."

"Agreed, sir, but I would still recommend we take the fleet to alert status one until we figure out—"

Whatever Tovia Elisheva was going to say was lost to the cry of Steven Blandid at the sensor station. "Martian carrier at oh-four-two mark three! They're launching fighters."

"Incoming!"

Captain Chrysa Aglaia didn't have time to shout out an order before her heavy cruiser, UENS *Churchill*, rocked from the line of rockets impacting its starboard flank. She swore as the Martian fighters evaded *Churchill's* return fire, which missed all three of the enemy craft as they quickly flitted out of range of her defensive lasers.

"Message from *Belgium,*" called her comm officer from across the bridge. "All ships are to concentrate fire on the lead battleship."

Chrysa checked her sensor plot to see that the lead Martian battleship was outlined in orange, designating a squadron target.

"Why aren't they shooting back?" she asked no one in particular. Aside from a few missiles launched at the moment they mysteriously appeared, the Martians hadn't fired a single missile more or even one laser blast. In fact, aside from the fighters, the entire Martian task force had stayed outside of laser range altogether.

Of course, that first volley had been fairly devastating, as had the waves of fighters launched from the two Martian escort carriers. Task Force 12 was a battle task force, meaning it was anchored on battleships and had no carriers of its own. But that didn't mean they were defenseless.

"Captain, *Greyhound* is coming alongside."

Chrysa sighed quietly in relief and began issuing orders. *Greyhound* was a Spruance-class destroyer, purpose-built for fighter defense. With the fast and maneuverable ship next to her, *Churchill* could stop worrying so much about the Martian fighters and fulfill her primary role.

"Helm, take us straight at the lead battleship. Weps, reload forward tubes with ship killers and be ready on the trigger."

Justin couldn't figure out what was happening. Thus far, the Martian task force had hung back out of laser range, using their defensive weaponry to knock down most of the missiles his UEN task force sent their way, but otherwise doing very little to join the offensive fight in the ten minutes since they'd inexplicably appeared next to Waypoint Charlie.

It made no sense. Aside from the two dozen fighter bombers, it was as if the Martians didn't actually want to attack. Even now, as his entire task force burned hard toward the enemy fleet, they refused to engage; they just sat there, waiting.

The one exception was the lead battleship of the Martian formation, which moved forward, separating itself from the rest of the Red battle line. The vice admiral's vanguard force closed with it, six battlecruisers and a handful of heavy cruisers and destroyer escorts upping their acceleration to meet the lone battleship and tear into it with their offensive lasers.

The Martian ship was gone in less than a minute. Even with its thick armor, it couldn't withstand the concentrated fire of so many UEN warships. But now Justin's forward element encountered the rest of the Martian force.

"Sir," called his tactical officer. "The Martian capital ships are opening fire."

The report was redundant; Justin could see on his own battle plot that the entirety of the Martian force had finally let loose with its offensive lasers. Two of his battlecruisers succumbed to the fire quickly, along with four destroyers and three heavy cruisers. Then Justin's four battleships joined the fray with the rest of their escorts, and the battle became a close-quarters slugging match while the Martian fighters harassed the UEN force from behind.

Amid the shouted reports, klaxons, and flashing alerts, Justin watched as the combined weight of the Martian task force and their fighters began to decisively carry the battle. Of his original thirty-six ships, only twenty-two remained, and the Martians had more ships and more tonnage. He watched as another two green dots winked out on the battle plot.

"Sir!" cried Steven Blandid from the sensor station. "*Stockholm* reports a reactor containment failure."

"Tell them to fall back and lock it down!" he ordered, but it was too late, and the bridge fell silent as 25 percent of Task Force 12's battleship contingent exploded, taking two screening light cruisers and a destroyer with it in its death throes.

Justin reviewed the battle plot again, shutting off the pain he felt at losing over three thousand spacers in an instant, and saw that the picture had devolved further in the last few minutes. Down to just seventeen ships, half his original force—it was clear that the battle was lost.

Except that he had an ace up his sleeve.

"Fall back to Charlie Station," he ordered, bypassing his comm officer and sending out the order in person to his entire task force.

Captain Chrysa Aglaia watched the *Stockholm*'s death in horror, wincing when her escorts disappeared with her.

"Message from the flag, Captain," her comm officer reported. "Fall back to Charlie Station."

Chrysa started issuing orders to the helm, feeling an immense sense of relief as her ship turned over and began burning hard back the way they'd come. She even smiled briefly when her destroyer escort *Greyhound* took out two more bombers trying to attack *Churchill.*

She checked the vectors. Admiral Lang had cut it close, but Task Force 12 should have just enough firepower left to get back to the naval supply station they were tasked to protect. And once they did, the Martians would learn a tough and deadly lesson.

The battle raged around her and *Churchill* for another ten minutes as they burned toward the station. Then, Chrysa watched in grim satisfaction as the massive laser batteries of the heavily armed Charlie Station opened up and began cutting apart the Martian fleet. Lang had bought the station just enough time to charge its power-hungry capacitors, and now the enemy was feeling the full wrath of a UEN battle station's redundant reactors.

At the same instant, on orders from the flag, *Churchill* and the other surviving ships of Task Force 12 turned back over to decelerate and present their heavily armored bows to the enemy, adding their own fire to the station's. The battle plot began to tell a different story as the United Earth forces tilted the scales heavily in their favor, and nearly a dozen Martian warships disappeared or went dead in space within minutes.

CHAPTER 23

Twenty-Six Years Ago; 705 P.D.

The afternoon after losing Teacher Harriette, Cal hadn't returned back to his family's pod. Instead, he had given Jenk the slip and headed in the opposite direction, higher up in Proteus, toward one of his favorite spots on the station.

He entered the astronomy bay timidly. He technically wasn't supposed to be here, though he often broke that rule. As always, Chief Astronomer Petra 214 frowned at him from her station on the far side of the bay but said nothing at his intrusion. Cal carefully didn't meet her eyes as he walked to the center of the room, where an empty chair beckoned as if left out expressly for him.

He plopped down and waited patiently for the man at the center station to look up from his telescope's eyepiece and notice him. When the man finally did, he smiled at Cal.

"How's your mother?" Riggs 201 asked him in his baritone voice. It was the same question he always asked first.

"She's fine." Cal gave the same answer he always did. It was part of the ritual. Once, Riggs 201 had let it slip that he and Jessie 223, Cal's mother, had long ago been more than mere acquaintances. It had made Cal always wonder just *how* friendly they'd become and—

to his constant shame—what life might have been like if *Riggs* had been his father instead of the more mild-mannered and timid Gordy 198.

Riggs grunted his acknowledgment and went back to studying whatever he was looking at in his eyepiece. Cal knew that the astronomy bay really didn't look at the stars like they wanted everyone to believe. They had one job, which was to watch for approaching ships. Unfortunately, their job had been largely meaningless for the last year.

Regardless, they kept doing it, though Cal had heard Riggs grumble a few times—strictly when Chief Astronomer Petra wasn't in the room—about just how worthless he felt their efforts were.

"What's on your mind today, boy?" Riggs asked gruffly. Despite the man's tone, Cal smiled slightly. It was more attention than most adults gave him—including, lately, Mother.

"Can we talk?" he asked.

"Isn't that what we're doing?" the older man asked without looking up from his telescope.

"In private, maybe?" Cal asked uncomfortably, casting a glance around the room to see if anyone else was listening. They were, almost certainly, though none of them were being obvious about it.

Riggs looked up, probably reading something in Cal's tone, and frowned. Then he looked over at Petra 214. "Boss, taking a fifteen-minute break." The woman waved a hand dismissively and went back to her own telescope eyepiece.

Cal followed Riggs out of the astronomy bay and over to a small room that doubled as a storage closet and break room for the nearby bays. Riggs closed the door after the two of them entered, then looked down at the boy thoughtfully. "What's on your mind?" he repeated.

"Uh…" Cal wasn't sure where to start. He liked Riggs; the man had become a sort of unofficial mentor to him, often letting him use his telescope. Cal *really* wanted to work in the astronomy bay one day. It was the only place on Proteus where one could see anything outside. And he dreamed, in particular, of working with Riggs.

"I heard something the other day that worries me. I wanted to ask you about it."

Riggs knit his brows together and frowned again but said nothing, waiting for Cal to continue.

"I heard the mayor and Kember talking in the hydroponics bay; they didn't know I was close enough to hear them. But they were talking about . . ." He trailed off, not sure how to put the next part.

"Out with it, Cal," Riggs said, a gentleness in his tone belying the impatient words.

"They were talking about getting rid of the normos," Cal spit out, speaking quickly now. "To, you know, make the rations go further since no ships have come for so long. Maybe to even give the hydroponics farms enough time to catch up and feed us again."

Riggs's frown hardened, and his eyebrows raised in surprise. "Cal, that's a pretty big deal. Are you sure, *absolutely* sure, that's what you heard?"

Cal nodded. Riggs shook his head and looked more troubled. That was the other thing Cal liked about the man; he didn't treat him like a child. If Cal said he was sure about what he'd heard, then Riggs believed him, or at least pretended to.

The man sighed and sat down on one of the frail-looking folding chairs around a rickety plastic table that had been wedged into the corner of the room between two stacks of boxes. He motioned to Cal to take one of the other chairs. "Okay, start at the beginning, and tell me everything."

And Cal did, relating his early-morning mission with Meera to steal some of Kember's hidden rations, and finishing with the story of Teacher Harriette being 'retired' earlier that same day by the mayor and the chief tweaker. Riggs let him finish, though he asked a few questions to clarify along the way. Then he sat back and rubbed his chin thoughtfully, his frown becoming a permanent feature.

"This is troubling," he observed after a few moments of silence. "Larabaius himself wouldn't come down to announce a teacher's retirement, not unless something else was up. And you said that Harriette didn't look like she knew they were coming?"

Cal nodded. Riggs blew out a long breath through pursed lips. "Then that right there is suspicious. Have you told anyone else about all this?"

"I tried to tell Mother about what I overheard in hydroponics, but she didn't believe me. It's like she doesn't care!" Cal said that last part more harshly than he'd intended, and he felt hot tears form in his eyes as the anger and frustration at Mother and her disconnection from him and Meera bubbled over.

Riggs shook his head and leaned forward, spearing Cal with a stern gaze that somehow managed to be sympathetic at the same time. "Cal, you need to cut your mom some slack," he said. "You have no idea how much she's gone through since your father died." Riggs rarely spoke of Cal's father; when he did, he was usually terse. "You need to understand that she's doing the best she can. Do you know that?"

Cal nodded in reply, though he didn't really know anything of the kind. From his standpoint, Mother had just given up. "So what do we do?"

"First, you tell no one else. If what you're telling me is true"—Riggs held up a soothing hand when he saw the look on Cal's face—"and I *believe* that you heard what you did, then we need to play this very carefully."

"But Meera—" Cal started to argue.

"I know, kid. She's a normo, and you're worried about her. But if there is a plot to dispose of the normos, they'll probably take away the children last—they use less food, and there will be more of an uproar when they disappear. If your suspicions about Teacher Harriette are right, then they seem to be starting with the oldest normos first. That means we probably have some time."

"Okay." Cal tried to sound like he trusted what Riggs was saying, but he knew he was failing.

Riggs's face softened as he looked at the boy, and he put a reassuring hand on Cal's shoulder. "Listen, buddy. I need you to trust me. I have an idea that might work, and it will require you to pretend you know nothing. But if you do learn more or see anything else that might help us understand what's going on, you come straight to me. Got it?"

Cal nodded, not trusting his voice.

"Good. Now, get back to your pod. Your mother will be worried. Come talk to me in two days."

Cal left the break room and Riggs behind, making his way back to the pod that he shared with his mother, his sister, and a dozen other people. As he moved through the corridors, he thought about the conversation with Riggs, the strange retirement of Teacher Harriette, and the intense focus on the normos in his class from the chief tweaker. So lost was he in his thoughts that he didn't see the danger until it was too late.

"Look what we have here," a snide voice said, taking Cal by surprise. Jenk, flanked by two of his buddies, Gad and Mor, stepped out from a doorway and blocked the corridor in front of him.

Cal turned in a near panic, ready to run back the way he'd come, but two more boys and a tall girl—Kit, Forrel, and Kinnie—moved out from another door behind. He whirled back to face Jenk, hoping he might reason with the older boy. They had been friends once, but the look in Jenk's eyes made it clear there would be no rekindling of friendship.

"What, poor little Cal lost his way?" Jenk sneered. "Where's your normo sister? Taking up the air and food a tweaked needs, I bet."

Jenk's friends laughed. None of them were normos. "My pa says that it's only a matter of time before we space all the normos," Jenk said with an evil smile, moving forward until he was within arm's reach of Cal, looking down at the smaller boy. "And I bet your sister will be the first!"

Before Cal gave it any conscious thought, his fist was moving through the air toward Jenk's chin. It never found its mark. The older boy stepped out of the way and threw his own fist, low and right into Cal's stomach, causing him to double over and fall to his hands and knees, gasping for breath.

"Big mistake," Jenk said. "Maybe they'll space *you* with your normo sister. We have enough pushers already—we can afford to lose one, especially a worthless one like you."

Despite himself, Cal tried to lunge forward from his knees and grapple the other boy's legs, maybe knock him down and even things out, but Jenk kicked him in the face. Cal saw stars as he fell flat to the deck. The next few seconds were a slurry of pain as Jenk and his friends circled around Cal and kicked him over and over again.

"Hey!" a female voice shouted, and Cal heard Jenk swear and then the sound of running footsteps. A set of heavier footsteps approached him, and he opened his eyes to look up at his savior. It was a woman he didn't know by name but recognized as being from a pod near his. Then he lost consciousness and forgot all about her.

Present Day

Vice Admiral Justin Lang made a fist and hit the arm of his command chair in silent triumph as the Martian forces continued charging forward into the devastating combined fire of Charlie Station and Task Force 12. The Reds' strategy had been good to start, from their sudden and inexplicable appearance already within weapons range to their clever use of fighters and the sacrifice of the lead battleship to lure his task force close. But now, the Martians were well on their way to losing the battle, and . . .

"Admiral!" Lieutenant Commander Blandid called out in dismay. "Another Martian force!"

Justin's thin-lipped smile of triumph turned to a rictus of horror as another thirty Martian ships appeared behind Task Force 12 on the other side of Charlie Station and fired volleys of ship killers straight at the station.

Enough defensive fire poured out of Charlie Station's batteries and gatling guns to destroy a mosquito trying to get through, but it still failed to stop all of the missiles. The Martians had simply gotten too close before launching, and nearly a dozen ship killers slammed into the station, erupting in nuclear fire and destroying a third of Charlie Station in seconds.

The station's fire slackened and then stopped, including from the undamaged parts, leaving Justin's Task Force 12 alone to face the original Martian force, even as the reinforcements circled around the station to join the fight.

The battle plot told the conclusion simply: the battle was over. Charlie Station was lost; secondary explosions were ripping apart the portions of the station that still existed. Soon, Task Force 12 would join the dead station.

"Retreat!" Justin called out. "Retreat!"

Chrysa watched in stunned silence as four more UEN ships around *Churchill* fell out of formation, too damaged to continue even basic maneuvers. Admiral Lang's order to retreat came with no specific instructions, and Task Force 12 devolved into pure chaos as ships tried to break off engagement but couldn't agree on which direction to go.

She called out orders to *Churchill*'s helm and tried to follow the largest group of retreating UEN ships, but the helmsman never got a chance to comply. Six different lasers from a Martian broadside cut through *Churchill*'s damaged port flank like its armor wasn't even there, and all 750 officers and crew either died instantly or were left to tumble out of control in sealed compartments that were no longer part of a fully assembled warship.

Chrysa was one of those who died in that first instant, sparing her the pain of watching her crew and those of half the ships around her suffer the same fate.

CHAPTER 24

Twenty-Six Years Ago; 705 P.D.

"Cal, why hasn't a ship come?" Meera's question wasn't a new one, but it carried a deeper note of worry than it ever had before. Meera may have been only seven, but she was smart for her age, and she could see through the lies of the adults who kept reassuring her and the other children that a ship was due 'any day now.' She trusted her brother to tell her the truth.

"I don't know, Meeks," he said, using the pet name he'd invented for her just a few weeks after she was born. "I heard some of the adults saying that maybe the Council found the routes the ship captains were using to supply us and shut them down." He looked down and saw the expression on her face. "But I'm sure that they'll be back as soon as they can find a new route," he hastened to add.

"But what happens if they don't?"

"Well"—he tried to put confidence he didn't feel into his tone—"we should be okay. We have the hydroponics farms, and they're still making food. Besides, Mother won't let us get hurt. She'll figure something out." That was a blatant lie, and they both knew it. But Meera seemed content to at least pretend to believe the fiction.

"Listen," Cal said, forcing a smile. "Why don't we go to the vid bay after school tomorrow and watch that princess vid you like so much?"

Meera brightened and nodded her head vigorously. At least she was still young enough to be distracted. Speaking of which . . .

Cal looked up in time to see Riggs standing at the entrance door to their pod. He was looking around even though he'd clearly already seen Cal. He looked disappointed, and Cal had the sudden feeling that the man had come hoping to see Mother. But then he focused back on Cal and motioned for him to come out to the corridor.

"Wait here, Meeks," he said, and made his way around the cots in the pod to where Riggs was standing outside the hatch. The older man looked around before speaking to make sure no one was in range to hear.

"Listen, Cal," he said without preamble. "It's worse than we thought. I've heard stories now of a dozen normos of all ages disappearing without a trace. People are starting to whisper, and the mayor has locked herself in her office and canceled most of her meetings. I think I have a plan to save at least some of the normos, but I need you to stick close to Meera until I come and get you, probably in a couple of days. Got it?"

Cal didn't know what to say as the reality of what Riggs was telling him sank in. So he just nodded.

"Good boy. Don't let your sister out of your sight. Stay home tomorrow from school and the next day. Tell your mom you're sick or something like that. But don't stay in your pod where they can find her. Do you have somewhere you can go and hide during the day?"

Cal thought for a moment and then nodded. He would take his sister to the air ducts. It would be uncomfortable, and she would be unhappy about it, but if he took their pads, they could at least watch some vids like he'd promised her.

"Good. I've gotta go," Riggs said. "But I'll check in with you in two or three days." The man turned and exited, leaving a very terrified Cal behind.

Present Day

Mikael Gorsky watched the large vid screen in the apartment and smiled as the vote tallies came in. Sixty-four percent for and 30 percent against, with a few abstaining, easily passing a bill that would cause the UEN to divert further funds to the Martian war effort and away from preparing for the Council invasion. Of course, that wasn't how the bill had been presented in the press or on the congressional floor, but it was an apt summary.

Cecily Johansen knew better. The bill was really just one more nail in the UEN's proverbial coffin when the Council Navy finally arrived.

She knew this because it was common sense, and it shocked her that Congress couldn't see it. Of course, they were all too afraid and worked up by the debacle at Waypoint Charlie to think beyond the war at hand. Cecily also had to admit that she herself might not have seen the truth had Gorsky not bragged to her all about it. He'd boasted of his plans a lot in the over three months since abducting her to extort her blender boyfriend, Jordan Archer. In those months, she had been kept in this same apartment, one that Gorsky visited at least weekly. And when he visited, he *talked*. It was almost as if he needed someone to whom he could safely tell all of his plans, like some sort of cartoon villain.

Of course, Gorsky didn't actually think of himself as the villain. He had some sort of twisted logic that he was doing what was best for Earth—helping the planet and her moon survive the inevitable Council invasion and victory by placating the enemy. He could lie to himself all he wanted about that; Cecily knew the truth, that it was all about the personal power he would wield afterward. Supposedly, the Council government had promised to make him the governor of all the Four Worlds.

Now, the bulky Russian clapped his hands together in joy as the congressional speaker pounded his gavel and announced the bill passed. It would be headed to the president's desk next, and Cecily imagined Gorsky would appropriately express his reluctance at diverting more resources to the war effort with Mars as he signed it. Then he would get good and drunk in celebration and probably force her to drink with him.

That thought made her shudder. Gorsky was a mean drunk. As he looked at her now, he made her shudder again. The big man's cold black eyes had always struck her as reptilian, and he had a cruel smile as he studied his captive. Absently, she rubbed the stub of her left ring finger, the one that Gorsky himself had cut off and used to intimidate Archer early on. She tried not to meet his gaze but knew from experience that if she ignored him, he would hurt her. Finally, after waiting just long enough to be defiant but hopefully not long enough to spark another beating, she turned her head to face him.

"Do you know, Cecily," he asked her in his deep voice, "that your fiancé was instrumental in tonight's vote passing? He got us the dirt we needed on Hollingsworth. Once he was silenced as the bill's chief opponent among the moderates, we had no problem cowing the rest of his voting bloc. Always useful to have a spy like Archer on my staff."

He paused, apparently waiting to see if she might respond, but she didn't. She almost never did; regardless, it was all part of his sick little games, and he smiled anyway. "Come now, Cecily, cheer up. You'll be reunited with Mr. Archer soon. One way or the other."

He probably thought he was being clever by wording it like that. As if she had *any* doubt that he planned to kill both her and Jordan once this was all over. They knew too much. She'd known she was a dead woman the first time he'd monologued at her about his brilliant and devious plans to weaken the Four Worlds ahead of the Council Navy invasion.

Regardless, she played along and pretended to take hope from his words, mostly because doing so might prompt him to give up his game and leave sooner.

This time, it worked. Standing up and adjusting his slacks, Gorsky nodded at his two bodyguards, who started talking to the rest of his team stationed outside, getting ready for him to move. He walked toward the door, passing close by Cecily and reaching out to brush the fingers of his right hand across her cheek. Wanting to avoid another beating, she silently endured his touch but couldn't stop a subtle shudder.

She knew he liked it when she cowered just a bit at his touch. It made him feel powerful, and she braced herself for the hard slap that might follow. Luckily, this time, he seemed satisfied at her reaction, and he turned and left the room, followed by the two bodyguards who watched all and said nothing.

As he left, the door locking firmly behind him—there would, as always, be at least two guards left outside in the hall as well—Cecily let the tears flow. She supposed it could be worse. After all, besides beating her and cutting off her finger, he hadn't done anything else to her. He seemed to be satisfied simply by the fact that he *could* do whatever he wanted to her, so much so that he didn't actually need to do more than hurt her now and again.

Despite all that, she wasn't the least bit grateful, nor was she comforted. She was angry, and she set her mind to thinking through its usual two topics of obsession: Jordan Archer and how she would eventually kill Mikael Gorsky.

CHAPTER 25

Twenty-Six Years Ago; 705 P.D.

Meera hadn't liked hiding in the air ducts, just as Cal had suspected. She also didn't like staying home from school, but Cal had finally convinced her that it was a game, and that the kids who could stay hidden the longest would win a prize of extra rations. That, coupled with her constantly rumbling stomach, was enough to get her to hide out with him.

Mother thought they were going to school, of course, though she didn't ask about what they'd learned or anything else when she returned from work each night. She really never said anything to Cal or Meera these days unless it was an instruction to go to bed or follow her to the nearest food dispensary.

They'd been skipping school and hiding out for almost four days now, ever since Riggs had visited with his warning. And Cal was starting to panic and think about going and seeking out the older man. But he didn't want to leave Meera behind anywhere to do it. Even in his pod, people were now talking in low voices about the strange disappearances across Proteus. Just the night before, two normos, an older man and a teenage girl, had failed to return from their work and school assignments. No one said it outright, but everyone seemed to think they would *never* come back.

Which made Cal all the more motivated to hide Meera and keep her safe. Especially if Mother wasn't going to do it. He'd seen Mother casting somber glances at her young daughter, especially last night after the two other normos disappeared. She said nothing to Meera or Cal, though he knew she'd been fully awake the few times he'd awoken in the middle of the night as his dreams tricked him into thinking Meera was gone. Instead, he found his little sister still huddled against their mother, but Mother herself had her eyes wide open, and even nodded to Cal and said something mildly soothing when he awoke with a start from one of the nightmares.

But in the morning, Mother had gone again, and Cal once again took Meera to the air ducts by the hydroponics bay to hide and spend the day silently watching vids and eating a few ration bars he'd managed to filch from the food dispensary and Kember's stash.

They were halfway through the day and watching Meera's favorite princess vid for the fourth or fifth time when Cal's pad dinged with an incoming message from Riggs.

Meet me. Astronomy break room. One hour.

Cal didn't dare send a response, but he watched the clock carefully from then onward. The minutes crawled by incredibly slowly, especially as Meera somberly watched a vid that they both had memorized by now. Finally, with just ten minutes left to go, Cal led his little sister to the nearest safe exit from the ducts, and they started making their way down the corridors toward the astronomy bay.

At least they didn't have to worry about running into Jenk in the middle of the school day, but they did have to be wary of any adults they might encounter who would question why they weren't both in school themselves. Luckily, most of the adults were busy working, and the corridors were fairly empty. Only twice did they have to duck into doorways or empty rooms to hide from a passing Protean. Finally, only three minutes past Riggs's deadline, they arrived at the astronomy break room.

Riggs was already there waiting, and he ushered them into the small room and shut the door behind them. Then he turned and regarded them with a deep frown. "It's happening," he said. "Today. They're going to announce the culling right after dinner, and by then, they will have already rounded up all of the normos." He didn't say what they were going to *do* with the normos they rounded up, probably to spare Meera's ears. But Cal could guess.

"What do we do?" he asked, his voice cracking on the words.

"I tried, Cal, I really did," Riggs said instead of answering his question. "I even tried to get an appointment with the mayor, but she's avoiding everything right now. The tweakers themselves are doing the rounding up, helped by the enforcers. There was nothing . . ." He trailed off, and Cal thought he could see a single tear forming in one of the man's eyes.

"What do we do?" he repeated, his own voice now more frantic.

Riggs shook his head as if to clear it. "You run," he said. "Not many people know about it, but there are some old escape pods in the lower levels. We go there *now,* and we get you out of here."

"But Momma!" Meera wailed, speaking for the first time. "I want Momma to come with us."

Cal felt tears forming in his own eyes now as the reality of what Riggs was suggesting sank in. "She's right, Riggs, we have to get Mother. She'll come with us; I know she will."

Riggs shook his head sadly. "She'll be safe; she's a pusher. They're not going to cull the tweaked. But these escape pods, they're really old. And they weren't the best to begin with. They're small, and they have limited life support. I already filled one with enough rations for the two of you, but adding an adult means you'd never make it. You'd run out of food, water, *and* air before you'd have any hope of rescue."

"But there are no ships!" Cal argued. "Who will pick us up?"

"There *are* ships," Riggs said softly, and Cal felt his mouth drop open.

"What?"

"There have always been ships, Cal. But they're Guard ships, *Council* ships. They've been patrolling the outer system for almost a year now. Petra ordered us to say nothing. Only those of us working in astronomy know, along with the mayor and Larabaius."

"But why don't we just ask them for help?" Cal asked hopefully.

Riggs looked sadder than he had before. "Because they'll just kill us. They know we're here, but there's so much junk in this system that they don't know exactly where Proteus is. You have to understand—they're not here to rescue us. They came to kill us for what the tweakers have done."

Meera started to cry, sobbing softly, and Cal put an arm around her small shoulders, holding her close. "But why? Why do they care what the tweakers do?"

"Because it's illegal," Riggs said, shrugging. "It's illegal to tweak people—to engineer them—unless you're the Council. So they want us all dead. They see us as a threat."

"Then won't they just kill me and Meera when they pick us up?"

Riggs was silent for a long moment, and Cal was certain the man wasn't going to answer. But when he finally did, his voice was soft. "I don't think they'll kill children. The Guard isn't all bad. Some of them are good people. But some are enacters who will do whatever the Council tells them to." Cal didn't know what an enacter was or why they were so bad, but he nodded as if he understood. "You'll have to convince them you're both normos," Riggs continued. "That means no pushing, especially if they bring in a reader." Cal didn't know what a reader was either but nodded again, not trusting his voice. "If they think you're both normos, I'm sure they'll let you live."

"But Momma!" Meera wailed again, and Riggs gave her another sad look.

"No," he said, shaking his head. "We go. Now."

Two minutes later, with Meera still sobbing quietly and Cal fighting back tears, Riggs led them to one of Proteus's few functioning lifts, keying it to take them down to one of the lowest levels on the station. But the lift opened three levels early, on the floor that Cal recognized as housing the waste management plant that Mother worked at. For a moment, as the doors slid open, he felt a flash of hope.

It wasn't Mother who greeted them at the open doors. It was Larabaius. The chief tweaker looked at them with anger and hatred in his eyes, his fiery gaze scanning first Riggs, then Cal, and then landing on Meera. "Really, Riggs 201? Did you think we wouldn't notice you stocking up one of the escape pods?"

Behind the man, three enforcers in their all-black suits, with mirrored visors hiding their faces, stood ready with stun batons. But Cal couldn't take his eyes off Larabaius himself. He'd always been a little afraid of the tweakers, even though Mother and most of the adults sang their praises. They were the ones who gave them their special powers, after all, and they were revered and practically worshipped for their medical miracles. But now, all he saw in the chief tweaker's eyes was loathing for Cal's little sister.

Before Larabaius could command the enforcers to do anything, Cal sprang forward, kicking with all of his might and catching the chief tweaker on the shin with his heel. Pain coursed through his foot, but he was gratified to hear Larabaius scream in pain as well. The enforcers moved forward, aiming their stun batons at Cal.

Then Riggs was there, whirling, punching, and kicking, taking out one of the enforcers, who hit the ground and didn't move, and sending another to the deck, where the woman tried to get up but seemed to have a problem with her leg. But then the third enforcer hit Riggs with his stun baton, and Cal's friend screamed as high-voltage electricity coursed through him. He fell to the deck, moaning.

Larabaius, who was still standing but favoring the leg Cal had kicked, sneered down at Riggs and then looked back at Meera and grinned wickedly. He took a step toward the girl, and Cal opened his mouth to scream at him to leave her alone.

"Noooo!" The scream that came wasn't Cal's. Mother sprinted out of an adjoining corridor and picked up the stun baton one of the enforcers had dropped. She hit the enforcer who had stunned Riggs first, sending the man screaming to the ground. Then she whirled and leaped toward the chief tweaker, who had grabbed Meera's arm by now and was pulling her toward him as if to use her as a human shield.

"Meeks!" Cal screamed. "Fight!"

Meera turned to look up at Larabaius, who had wrapped an arm around her upper chest and was holding her against him between himself and Mother. The little girl looked down at the arm holding her, ducked her head down, and bit hard.

Larabaius screamed again, probably mostly in surprise and shock, as Meera's small teeth dug into his arm. He pushed the girl down hard to the deck and looked as if he might kick her. But Mother took advantage of both the distraction and the separation of chief tweaker and little girl and lunged forward, planting the end of the stun baton squarely against Larabaius's chest. The chief tweaker screamed one final time before falling to the ground and twitching.

Cal heard another stun baton discharge behind him and spun around in time to see Riggs propping himself up on his hands and knees and stunning the enforcer he'd only knocked down earlier, using the woman's own stun baton against her. Riggs fell back to the deck, wheezing and wincing in pain.

"Go," he said, motioning toward the still-open lift. "Second level. Escape pod 4B. Course already . . . programmed . . . in." He said the last as if running out of air to speak. Then he closed his eyes and passed out on the deck.

Mother looked down at him, and Cal saw something in her eyes that he hadn't seen from her in a long time. She *cared*. There was longing there in her gaze, as well as gratitude.

"Let's go, Cal, Meera," she said and pulled them both into the lift.

Less than a minute later, they disembarked on level two. Mother led them wordlessly to a small round door marked '4B' and then turned and crouched down so she was at eye level with Meera. She looked first at her small daughter and then up at her son. "Riggs messaged me," she said softly. "Told me what he was doing and why. Oh, Cal, I'm so sorry I didn't believe you when you first told me. But I am so proud of you for saving your sister."

She stopped, biting her lower lip as tears sprung to her eyes and quickly began flowing down her cheeks. "Now the two of you need to go. And I can't go with you."

"No, Momma!" Meera cried and flung her arms around Mother, sobbing loudly now into her shoulder and trying to frantically climb onto her body. She slowly pried the little girl from her as Cal watched behind his own hot tears, and then Jessie 223 held her daughter out to look her in the eyes again.

"Don't worry about me, Baby Girl," Mother said, almost choking on the words with her own emotion. "I'll be just fine here. And you have Cal to take care of you."

Cal opened his mouth to try and say something, but nothing came out. He *knew* Mother was lying. She had just attacked the chief tweaker. There was no way she *or* Riggs would be okay—they would space both of them for sure. He *couldn't* leave them behind. He just couldn't.

But then Mother looked at him and seemed to read the thoughts behind his eyes. She shook her head resolutely at him. "I know, Cal. I know," she said softly. "This is just how it has to be. The Guard might go easy on two children alone, but if they read an adult signature on that pod, they might just shoot it first without even asking who's on board. Your best chance is without me." Through her tears, Cal could see that she believed what she was saying.

Jessie 223 reached out an arm and pulled Cal into an embrace, enfolding Meera back into the hug with the other arm and holding her two children tight as all three of them cried. After far too short of a time, she broke the embrace and keyed open the pod door. She lifted Meera up and over the threshold and then pushed Cal inside after her.

"The red button, Cal. Riggs already programmed it. Just press the red button to launch. And take care of your sister."

Voices sounded from nearby, down the corridor. They were angry and getting closer fast.

"I love you both so much," Mother said, speaking quickly now. "Take care of Meera, Cal. Now go!" Then she hit the door control, and the pod door slammed shut and separated her from her children.

Cal almost didn't hit the red button; he almost didn't listen, didn't leave Mother and Riggs behind. But then he looked down at Meera and walked over to the small control panel at the far end of the pod. Before he could change his mind, he slammed his hand down on the one blinking red button he saw there.

Present Day

"I found it!" Temperance cried jubilantly, shocking Landon out of the nap he was having on her apartment's couch.

He'd come over to watch a movie with her. It had become their Sunday evening ritual, and it was normally one of the few times he could tear his girlfriend away from her computer screens. But not tonight. Temperance had barely acknowledged him when he'd come over, so deep had she been into the search for what Jinny Ambrosa had asked her to locate.

It had been almost four weeks since the reader had given them the instructions as to what to look for—instructions vague enough that Temperance had needed to write custom algorithms to filter out the noise of millions of false positives across the planet. The hacker had attacked the search with an almost frantic determination, spending day and night in front of her computer screens and barely noticing as Landon came and went or tried to force her to rest or eat. Even during their Sunday evening movie nights, she'd almost shake with nervous energy until he'd finally relent and let her get back to it.

Landon knew it was selfish of him to resent the time she spent on her search rather than with him. But while she had been working this entire time, he had been simply waiting. His skills as a pilot weren't in any demand here in Perth, and he felt like he'd already watched just about everything there was to watch on the vids.

"Found what?" he asked through his sleepy mind, but then the words registered. "You found it?"

Temperance nodded vigorously, her eyes glued to her screen. "It's in the middle of nowhere in North America, in some desert on the border of Utah and Nevada. But everything matches. This has to be it!"

Before Landon could respond, she leaped up from her chair and threw herself across the room and into his arms, and he decided this was a very good way to be woken up from a nap, especially on Christmas Eve.

CHAPTER 26

Twenty-Six Years Ago; 705 P.D.

It took five days for the little escape pod to clear the debris field around Proteus. Cal had never seen the space outside except through the small glimpses Riggs had given him through the telescope in the astronomy bay. Even that was usually focused on the outer system or distant stars. Up close, the debris field was terrifying.

Fragments of jagged metal floated everywhere as if a hundred Proteuses had somehow exploded here. A dozen times every hour, Cal thought for sure that the pod was going to slam into a piece of detritus and disintegrate around him and Meera, but every time, the little craft adjusted its course just enough to avoid destruction.

For the first two days, Meera had done little more than cry and call out for Mother. Cal felt the same way, but he purposefully buried his own feelings and tried to be strong for his little sister. On the third day, Meera stopped crying and went completely silent, staring out of the pod's small forward window and saying nothing for the entire day, only moving occasionally to use the pod's small fresher. She refused to eat and only drank when Cal held the bottle to her lips.

On the fourth day, she stayed largely silent again but sat next to Cal and burrowed into his chest, holding him tight and occasionally sobbing quietly while he tried very hard not to tense up every time the pod neared a piece of space junk. He even got her to eat a little.

Finally, on day five, just hours after a robotic female voice in the pod started warning them of low oxygen levels—which had made Meera start crying again—they broke through the last of the debris field and into open space. It wasn't long before a pinging noise sounded from the control panel.

"Ship detected," the pod's robotic voice announced. "On intercept course."

Cal didn't know what to do, so he did nothing.

Roughly four hours later, he saw a light approaching through the small window. An hour or so after that, he could make out the outline of a ship.

It took ten hours, all told, from the time the pod announced detecting a ship before Meera and he felt a thump as the unknown craft pulled them in close. Then Meera burrowed back into him as the pod door opened, revealing the face of a woman in a blue uniform frowning in at them.

"And who are the two of you?" she asked sternly.

Neither Cal nor Meera spoke.

"Are you from that station we've been blockading all this time?" the woman asked.

They still didn't respond, which made her frown even more and shake her head.

"Well, we'll figure all that out. But in the meantime, you both look like you could use a shower and a good meal—maybe not in that order. Let's get you out of here."

The next two hours were the strangest of Cal's life. They didn't shower—Meera refused to leave his side to allow for that—but they were fed more food than they had ever seen in one place. During the meal, the woman who they'd first encountered was joined by a man in the same uniform, and they both asked Cal and Meera all sorts of questions. But neither of the children answered them.

Finally, frustrated, the man slapped an open hand down on the table, making them all jump. "You kids need to tell us what we need to know, or we're putting you back in that pod," he said coldly.

"Subcommander!" barked the woman sharply. "Remove yourself at once."

For a second, it looked like the man might argue, but then he raised one hand to his temple and winced before getting up with an obedient nod and leaving the room. Cal and Meera now found themselves alone with the woman and all the food.

"Listen," the woman said softly. "I know you kids have been through a pretty severe ordeal. But we have some pretty strict orders about what we need to do with anyone from that station. I have to know if you were on it. So I need the two of you to talk to me."

Cal considered this. From the tone the woman used, it was clear that she *knew* they were both from Proteus and that the fact they were didn't bode well for them. But Riggs had told him not to push.

"Are you a reader?" he asked timidly. He had no idea *what* a reader was, but Riggs had said he couldn't push just in case there was a reader there. So he figured he'd better be really sure if this woman was one of them or not.

She looked surprised, though he couldn't tell if it was because he'd finally spoken or because of his question. She shook her head. "No, I'm not a reader."

"Okay," Cal said. He reached out across the table and touched her hand before she could react. Then he *pushed* like he'd never pushed before, even during his tests on Proteus, the ones the tweakers had made them all take as part of their classes.

We are not from Proteus, he pushed. *We are from a passing ship that was lost. We are the only survivors.*

The woman's eyes widened in shock, and for a moment, Cal panicked. Had he pushed wrong? Had she *felt* the push? That wasn't supposed to be possible, at least not according to the tweakers. But what if they were wrong?

Then, the woman shook her head rapidly as if to clear it. "You know," she said, "I bet the two of you aren't from that station at all, are you? You must be from a passing ship that suffered some sort of accident. The only survivors, I'd guess. Is that right?"

Meera stared wide-eyed at the woman, but Cal jumped in before his sister could say anything to contradict her. "Yes. That's exactly what happened."

The woman nodded. "Well, that's good. That means I get to do what I think is right in this situation instead of just following my orders. Sucks being an enacter sometimes, if you know what I mean."

Cal most definitely *didn't* know what she meant. He didn't even know what an enacter was, though Riggs had also mentioned that word. But he was just happy that his push had worked. It was the first time he'd done it outside of classes, and he'd been terrified that it wouldn't work like the tweakers had always promised it would.

The woman stood abruptly. "I guess we'll take you to Traverton Station. That's the closest place with a Child Protective Services presence. They can help you either find any living family or get you placed in foster care. Either way, I'm glad we were able to rescue you."

She held out her hand, reaching across the table and down toward Cal. "I am Guard Commander Samantha Lewis, captain of the Guard Space Force Ship *Hephaestus*, at your service. And what are your names?"

"I'm Cal, and this is my sister, Meera," he said slowly, still marveling at how well his push had worked, as he took her hand.

"Well, hello, Cal and Meera," Lewis said. "Do you have a last name?"

"What's that?" Meera asked, speaking for the first time in days as she studied the now smiling woman.

The woman looked momentarily confused, though Cal also didn't know what a last name was. "You know," she said, "your second name, the one that comes after your first name. Unless you're one-namers, but I haven't met many children who are. What was your parents' last name?"

Cal still didn't know exactly what she was asking for, but he knew he had to give her something lest they arouse her suspicions again. "Riggs," he said, giving her the first word to spring to his lips, the one that simply felt right. "Our last name is Riggs."

Present Day

Ramesh Chowdry resisted the urge to bang his fist down on the keyboard in front of him. But he didn't resist the swear word that flew from his mouth.

"What's up?" Veera Larson asked, looking over from the desk next to him. Neither of them was in the best mood, being called in to continue their work after only a single day off for Christmas, but Ramesh's outburst revealed his deeper frustration.

"It's these sensor logs," Ramesh complained, gesturing to his screen in frustration. "They don't make any sense. I mean, one second, there are no Martian forces around Waypoint Charlie, and the next, an entire Martian task force materializes out of nowhere."

"No, they didn't," Veera said, drawing a sharp glance from Ramesh.

"What do you mean? Of course, they did. Look." He reversed the sensor feed records from UENS *Belgium*. "See, no Martian ships in this section of space. But then"—he let the feed play for a few seconds, and a flurry of red dots appeared—"an entire task force. Like magic; they just appeared!"

"No, they didn't," Veera countered. "You're right, of course, that that's what it looks like on the sensor plot, but ships can't just magically appear like that."

"So how do you think they did it?" he demanded, cursing Veera's often pedantic arguments. "Because there's nothing else in the sensor record. No tachyon burst that suggests they did an in-system jump, no thermal signatures to show them moving at stealth, not even latent heat from their hulls like if they cold-coasted in!"

Veera shrugged. "I agree it's a mystery, but there has to be *some* logical and scientific explanation."

"Like what?" Ramesh demanded again, drawing looks from a few other analysts in the Battle Analysis Department—the people who worked here called it 'BAD' for short—deep in the octagon, United Earth's military headquarters in Houston.

Veera chewed on the inside of her cheek as she studied the myriad readouts on Ramesh's screen. Then, she abruptly moved her chair back over to her own workstation and started typing furiously. He waited, pushing down his natural impatience. Veera Larson was a savant when it came to data analysis, and he knew it was better to let her work the problem than interrupt her and demand she explain what she was doing.

Still, after five full minutes of waiting, Ramesh was about to ask anyway when Veera spoke first. "I thought you said there were no tachyon bursts."

He frowned. "There weren't."

She shook her head and turned her screen so he could see on it a graph plot with tachyon particle levels as detected by *Belgium*'s sensors over the course of the hour leading up to and including the appearance of the Martian forces at Waypoint Charlie. Ramesh studied it closely, surprised to see a few small spikes at fairly consistent intervals in the final forty-eight minutes of the recording.

"What the . . ." he started to ask.

"There were spikes," Veera explained, "twenty-five of them, spaced out almost every two minutes. They're just so small that the ship's AI dismissed them as anomalies. Then, our own AI did the same before it delivered you the data. I had to look in the raw sensor logs to find them."

Ramesh shook his head in amazement. "But those are like, what, a hundredth of the strength we would expect to see from a group of ships surfacing from the void?"

She nodded. "Actually, 1.2 percent of what we would expect."

"Wait," Ramesh said, suddenly remembering something. He manipulated his own workstation and then turned his screen so she could see. "Look, here. There was a transient thermal reading 4.5 million kilometers from Task Force 12 at almost exactly two minutes before the Martian fleet arrived."

Veera's eyes went wide. "You don't think . . ."

He nodded vigorously. "Microjumps."

"No," she argued. "That's impossible."

"No, it's not impossible," he said with a smug smile—it was fun being pedantic back to her, "because we're seeing it here. Tachyon's build up in front of ships in the void like a wave. The longer the jump, the bigger the tachyon spike when the ship surfaces back to temporal space, right?"

She slowly nodded her agreement.

"But if you did only a small jump—say a few million kilometers—you'd expect to see incredibly small tachyon spikes, right?"

Understanding dawned on her features. "But we don't have the technology to do jumps that short. We just can't do reliable in-system jumps. The power required to enter and leave the jump is enormous. Even a crash resurfacing—tying the star drive directly to the main reactor—can't surface a ship that quickly after it enters the void. Even if it could, the risk of a reactor overload would be way too high."

Ramesh nodded along but couldn't keep the smile off his face. "But what if the Martians figured out a way to do microjumps? That would explain the thermal reading *Belgium* picked up around the same time as the second-to-last tachyon burst. And it would explain how they seemed to be able to magically appear right next to Task Force 12."

"But—"

He kept going, not wanting her to cast water on the sparks of his idea before it could catch fire. "What if the other small tachyon bursts were similar microjumps? The Martians could be somehow submerging and surfacing from the void very quickly, over and over again, like a rock skipping across a pond."

"I suppose it's theoretically possible," Veera agreed slowly. "But it still doesn't explain how they're able to do it without overtaxing their reactor and blowing their ships to smithereens."

"It sure doesn't," Ramesh said excitedly. "So that's what we have to figure out next!"

CHAPTER 27

Fourteen Years Ago; 717 P.D.

Cal Riggs made his way down the darkened corridor on Traverton Station, in orbit of Mako 7. He'd never actually stepped foot on the planet below them, though he'd lived on Traverton off and on for the full thirteen years since leaving Proteus. He and Meera had been placed with a foster family on the station just a few months after *Hephaestus* had found and 'rescued' them, but the couple that had taken them in had left the station after just three years and hadn't bothered to take their two foster children with them.

It hadn't really been all that surprising when Cal and Meera returned home from school one day to find that Tor and Hetty Shivaram had moved out of their small apartment without leaving behind so much as a note for their two unwanted children. The couple had made it clear from the beginning that they'd only taken in the two orphans to collect the monthly assistance check from the Council government, and when Cal turned fourteen, the size of the stipend for him had actually gone *down*, in some unfathomable twist of the law.

So the Shivarams had obviously decided it was no longer worth the money to watch the two of them and had split. As far as Cal had been able to tell, they'd left the station entirely, maybe heading down to the surface or hitching a ride to another system, though he doubted they could have afforded the latter.

In some ways, it had been a blessing, as it had freed him and Meera, then nine, from their foster parents' oppressive and uncaring thumbs, but it also created a new host of problems for them. Cal had needed to drop out of school and take a role as an apprentice miner on a nearby asteroid, sending the meager money he earned back to Traverton Station so that Meera could stay in a girls' dorm at the school there. From that point onward, he'd seen his little sister only twice a year, sometimes less, though they'd talked almost monthly on the expensive in-system comm for the first year. Later, even that had fallen off.

Now, Cal was returning from a two-year-long mining run to the outer system, where he'd learned how to crew a starship, a long-time dream of his. Unfortunately, it had also meant a longer-than-normal period away from Meera.

Cal, who now went simply by 'Riggs', was twenty-four years old and had seen a thing or two in his hard-fought years. He could drink almost any man or woman under the table and could fight as well as most. More importantly, he was becoming quite the pilot, taking over the helm of his last ship when the normal helmsman died from a virus picked up on one of the outer mining stations.

He'd been excited to step foot on Traverton for the first time in two years earlier this morning, stopping to buy a bouquet of fake flowers—he'd actually never seen a real one, so he had no idea if these were even modest approximations—and making his way to the dorm hall where Meera had been living when he left, and that he still paid for, sending money back to Traverton at every opportunity.

He hadn't spoken to his little sister in almost a year, except to send her a message a few days before to let her know he was coming back. She hadn't responded, but comms were pretty expensive, so he hoped it was only that she wanted to save the money.

However, when Riggs arrived at her dorm room and knocked, a girl he didn't recognize opened up.

"Can I help you, cutie?" she asked, looking him up and down. She appeared to be about twenty, just a little older than Meera, and he couldn't help but notice how cute she was in return or the broad smile she gave him.

"Uh, yeah," he said, hoping the blush he felt wasn't too obvious. "I'm looking for Meera."

The girl's smile instantly disappeared. "Meera hasn't been here in months, and I'm getting really sick of her customers coming around looking for her. So I'll save you the trouble. No, she isn't here. No, she didn't tell me where to find her. No, I don't have any of her supply or know where she keeps it. Any more questions?" She smiled again, though not in a friendly way.

"Uh . . . what?" Riggs asked, confused. "Where is she?"

The girl rolled her eyes. "I don't know these days. Check the down-station district. Last I heard, she was working a few of the clubs there." She went to slam the door in his face, but he held out a hand and stopped it.

"Listen," she said angrily. "You'd better leave right now, or I'll call the Guard."

"B-but—" Riggs started, but the girl pushed his hand out of the way and finally slammed the door shut. He was too stunned to consider knocking again.

Which was why he was now in a darkened corridor, the on-station equivalent of a back alley, looking for his *little* sister.

Riggs was no saint. He'd been a miner and a spacer on tramp freighters. So he was ashamed to admit, even to himself, that he knew the types of joints where he now needed to search for Meera. He knew how to ask the right questions, follow the leads, and find what he was looking for. Which all led him to the Hellfire Club.

Mako 7 was a volcanic planet, barely inhabitable as the ash choked the sky constantly and new volcanoes and lava flows formed on a nearly constant basis. But hidden in those lava flows were rare minerals and metals that made the planet worth mining, even if the life expectancy of a miner on the surface was numbered in years, not decades.

So even though the pay was better to mine the surface of the planet, Riggs had stuck to mining the rocks in the outer system, many of them formed in whatever cataclysmic event had formed Mako 7 itself. The pay was a *lot* less, but there were benefits, like living past the age of 30.

The Hellfire Club played on the theme of mining the planet below. The door was flanked by two fake volcanoes that spewed water backlit to look like fiery lava. The bouncers at the door wore costumes reminiscent of the heat-proof suits worn by the miners brave—or dumb—enough to work the lava flows. Inside, the theme continued. The music bumped too loudly as red lasers flashed through the artificial fog. The bar served volcano-themed drinks for three times the price they were worth, and the DJ wore another reflective miner's heat suit.

There had to be nearly a hundred people gyrating along to the hideous music. After stopping just inside the door to let his eyes adjust to the lower light, Riggs started making his way around the edge of the dance floor, looking hard for Meera. It seemed so wrong that his little sister would be found in a hole like this, much less doing the things her roommate had implied. Despite the solid trail of clues that had finally brought Riggs to this particular club, he hoped beyond measure that he *wouldn't* find Meera here.

No such luck. Fifteen minutes after entering the club, he found her. She was dancing with a man twice her age, and from the vacant expression on both their faces, they had probably liberally partaken of whatever Meera's former roommate had implied his sister was selling.

Riggs's fist connected solidly with the older man's jaw, and the guy fell to the dance floor. The club's other denizens barely took notice, simply dancing around the downed man as he looked up in shock and rage. Meera didn't pause dancing, either completely unaware that her partner was down on the floor or uncaring.

"Hey!" the older guy shouted as Riggs grabbed Meera by the arm and started to pull her away. He got up and started following them, but whatever he was on messed with his equilibrium, and he staggered and fell back to the floor. Riggs didn't look back, leading his strung-out sister off the dance floor and out of the club before security or anyone else could react. The two bouncers at the door didn't give him or his sister a second look.

Finally, down the corridor and around the bend, Meera seemed to realize she wasn't in the club anymore. She stopped, refusing to take another step, staring at Riggs listlessly. "Fifty credits a hit," she said, her voice slurring, and Riggs felt his heart break.

"Meera, it's me. It's Cal," he said, his tone begging.

She looked at him for the first time but didn't smile. Instead, she laughed. "No way! Cal doesn't come here anymore. Nice try, loser. Get away from me or I'll have Jojo find you and mess you up."

"No, Meera, it's really me. It's Cal. I came back to find you and . . ." He trailed off, still in utter shock at the situation.

Meera didn't answer him again. Whatever drug she was on took hold, and her eyes rolled up into the back of her head. She slumped down to the station's hard metal deck before Riggs could catch her.

Present Day

Jordan Archer sat leaning forward on the small couch in the living quarters the Majko had allowed him to use since his arrival to Perth almost four months before. He cradled his head in his hands but made no effort to stop the tears that fell from his eyes and stained the carpet between his feet.

His silent crying was interrupted as his palm implant buzzed. Slowly, dreading what he would see, he lifted his head and looked down at his hand. Projected on the subdermal screen was a picture of Cecily, her face black and blue. Archer screamed in rage mingled with despair as he studied his fiancée's mangled features.

Iasonas: This is what happens when you refuse to answer me.

Archer started typing back his response to Mikael Gorsky, the man who had been his employer for the past two and a half years, first anonymously under the pseudonym Iasonas, and now no longer anonymous. Halfway through his angry response, he looked again at the picture of the bruised and battered Cecily, the love of his life. His rage built, but he quickly deleted the message he'd been typing. Antagonizing Gorsky now would do nothing to help his girlfriend. As much as he wanted to tell the UE president what he really thought, he needed to bury those feelings deep and play the man's sordid game.

He typed back a new reply, still using his own codename the man had given him.

Castor: You didn't have to do that. I was waiting for an opportunity to answer you unobserved.

He watched in rapt anticipation as the bubble appeared that showed Gorsky typing back his response. When it finally came, his heart fell.

Iasonas: I just cut off another finger. Lie to me again like that, and her entire hand will be next.

Archer wailed again in grief, standing and slamming his fist into the wall behind the small couch, immediately wincing as something broke inside his hand.

Iasonas: The time for the next phase is coming. My agent in Perth will make contact with you. Do exactly as they say, or Cecily dies. Acknowledge.

Through tears of rage, Archer typed his reply.

Castor: Acknowledged. Please don't hurt her again.

Iasonas: That is entirely up to you.

CHAPTER 28

Fourteen Years Ago; 717 P.D.

Cal took Meera back to the short-term room he had rented on the station. There, he put her in the small bed and covered her with the threadbare blankets up to her neck. The way she'd been dressed in the club . . . Riggs had been red with shame at the knowing glances other men had shot him, and the angry looks from the women and a few of the men as he'd carried Meera's unconscious form through the station's corridors dressed the way she was.

But on Traverton, no one asked questions. Everyone just minded their own business.

He sat there, silently watching her for about two hours before her eyes fluttered open.

"Ugh," she moaned. "What happened?"

"You passed out," he told her, "from whatever drug you were on, most likely."

At the sound of his voice, her eyes opened wide, and she looked over at him and propped herself up on an elbow. "Cal?"

"Hey, Meeks." He tried to sound upbeat and failed.

Her expression instantly turned to one of anger. "Cal, you blasted . . ." Whatever she was about to call him dissolved in a fit of coughing. When she recovered, she eyed him with a sneer. "Why are you back? And why did you come looking for me?"

He spread his hands. "You're my sister, Meeks. I love you. I wanted to check in on you and found you . . ." He couldn't finish the sentence.

She surprised him by laughing, and not in a nice way. "Oh, don't give me the high and mighty guilt trip, Cal." She spat his name like a curse. "I've heard all about you. You're not pure as the driven snow." It was a strange thing to say, since neither of them had ever seen snow, but he got the point. "You just don't like seeing your sister doing this stuff, even though you left me without enough money to avoid it."

"What?" he asked incredulously. "I've been sending you money every month, Meera. What have you been doing with it?"

"Oh, you mean that little pittance? Do you know how bad it burns to be the poorest little girl at a poor school, to not even be able to afford new shoes? And you're *never* around. I can count on one hand the number of days I've seen you in the last five years! So don't get all protective now, big brother. I've been making money my own way since I was *fifteen*. So you can just turn around and go back to your ship and leave me to it. Okay?"

Riggs was speechless, but Meera saved him from having to reply as she abruptly threw up all over the bed and then passed out again.

Present Day

At least they hadn't thrown Corey in a prison. So far as he knew, Mars didn't have prisons. Most crimes were simply punishable by the injured party challenging the offender to a duel. The offender could then choose to fight to the death or make amends for his crimes that were acceptable to those he or she had wronged.

Oh, he was sure they must have *some* prisons, but he'd certainly never heard of any or seen one.

But even as a declared spy from Earth—one of the worst possible crimes on the red planet—he wasn't in a prison cell. He was in a small apartment in the lower levels of the Olympus Mons Government Center. His door wasn't even locked, though the solemn Martian legionaries who delivered his meals three times a day had made it very clear that to leave his apartment would be to invite death. He didn't test them on that.

There was a knock on that apartment door now. It opened before Corey could invite the visitor in, and Cal Riggs slipped inside, throwing a glare at someone in the hall, probably a patrolling legionary.

"Any news?" Corey asked anxiously.

Riggs shook his head. "Only the same drivel you can watch on the news from here. You'd think such a martial society would have a little more detail in their daily war updates to the public, but . . ." He shrugged.

"And Tyrus?"

Riggs shook his head again. "Can't find him. And every time I wander too far looking for him, some overly tall boy scout with an inferiority complex appears out of nowhere and calmly 'invites' me to return to my quarters."

Corey nodded. "They don't know what to do with you. Your mere association with me tarnishes you, but your association with Tyrus does the opposite. Who knows how they feel about you bringing that monster Toby here. But you're not from Earth yourself, so they don't view you as a traitor or a foreign spy as they do me."

The pilot roamed around the room as Corey took a seat on one of the small chairs at the equally small kitchen table, watching the other man pace nervously.

"And what about . . . you know?" Riggs asked next, pretending to study the apartment's plain walls.

"My execution date?" Corey asked with raised eyebrows. "They haven't told me yet. Knowing them, they'll tell me one day, and I'll be dead the next. So no news is good news on that front."

"This is so ridiculous!" Riggs snapped, turning to face him again. "We come all this way to help these idiots, and now they've turned Tyrus into some zombie soldier who can't even visit his friends—and they're going to kill you!"

He ranted like that for several more minutes, and Corey let him do so. The Martians had weird traditions and rules about privacy. Usually, you couldn't expect *any* on the red planet, but when you had some, they were loath to violate it. Besides, if there were listening devices in his apartment, someone would have challenged Riggs to a duel a long time ago. His current diatribe was far more circumspect than usual.

"Is there anything we can do?" Riggs finally asked, just as he did after every rant.

"If I think of something, you'll be the first to know," Corey assured him, just as he also did every time.

CHAPTER 29

Five Years Ago; 726 P.D.

"Riggs, you sure you want to do this?"

He looked over at the surly but earnest face of his copilot. She'd be pretty good-looking, he often thought, if she wasn't always scowling like she wanted to kill someone.

"I've gotta do it, Jynx," he told her. "She's my sister."

"Your sister, who has made it very clear she wants nothing to do with you," Jynx said, shaking her head and frowning.

Riggs shrugged and turned back to the door and keyed the bell.

After a short wait, the door flung open—no fancy sliding doors on Traverton Station—and Riggs found himself looking at a woman who seemed to have aged far more than the one year since he'd seen her last.

"What do you want?" Meera snapped at him, holding a baby on one hip while an older child could be heard crying in the background. Last he'd seen his sister, she'd had only the one son; the daughter on her hip was new. Had it been more than a year? Sometimes, he lost track of time. It wasn't as if she'd ever welcomed his visits, as irregular as they were these days.

"Hey, Meera," he said lamely as she stared daggers at him. "I was . . . er, we were just passing through, and I thought I'd stop to see how you're doing."

Meera swept her free arm around as if to encompass the dingy apartment and crying toddler behind her, giving him an incredulous look. "Oh, we're just fine and dandy here, big brother. But how nice of you to descend from the stars to check on us out of the kindness of your heart."

She went to close the door in his face, but he got his foot into the gap in time. She sighed and opened the door again, still glaring at him.

"Uh," he started lamely. "I didn't know about the new baby. Congratulations?" He hadn't meant that last word to sound like a question.

"Yeah, right," Meera said with a huff. "Congratulations for what? For popping out another kid, or for raising her by myself because her deadbeat dad left us two weeks into the pregnancy? Oh, sweet joy."

Not knowing what to say, Riggs asked another question. "Uh, Hebron left?" That was the name of her former live-in boyfriend, wasn't it?

Meera scowled even harder at him. "Hebron left a year and a half ago, big brother. Or don't you remember? No, you wouldn't. This little angel"—she nodded toward the girl in her arms—"this is Raymond's spawn. He lasted less than three months and good riddance. Man was no account anyway." Her voice broke a bit, belying her true feelings on the subject.

"I'm sorry." It was all Cal could think to say.

"Great. See you in another year or two." Meera sneered and started to close the door again.

"Wait!" Riggs pushed the door back open and held up his other hand and the watch on that wrist. "I have something for you."

Meera studied him for a moment, still wearing the scowl, but then shrugged and moved the baby to her other hip so she could hold out her own watch and tap it to his. And just like that, ten thousand credits, almost twenty percent of the *Blind Monk*'s profits from the last year plus, transferred from his account to hers.

"Gee, thanks, big brother," she said, though her voice softened slightly. She looked around him for the first time and nodded to his copilot. "Jynx, tell my brother that if he knows what's good for him, he'll make this his last visit."

Then she slammed the door shut in their faces and blocked out the sound of the crying toddler.

Present Day

Jordan Archer entered the darkened movie theater in downtown Perth and proceeded to the exact seat Gorsky's latest message had told him to wait at. The movie hadn't yet begun, but the lights had been dimmed for the previews of coming films, and the theater was only a quarter full. He found his seat and took it, waiting and watching.

The previews ended and the movie began, but no one else entered the theater behind him. He'd been expecting the mysterious spy of Gorsky's to meet him here, but if so, they were running late. He ignored the first twenty minutes of the movie, his eyes fixed on the theater's entrance below and to one side, waiting and barely breathing, but still to no avail.

Sighing, he considered breaking protocol and sending Gorsky an unsolicited message asking if there was any update on the spy's location. The traitorous president would be upset, but he'd likely be more upset if Archer failed to meet with the spy as instructed.

Then, he had a thought. Reaching down, he felt around the bottom of the theater seat, breathing a sigh of relief as his hands found the edge of an envelope. He smoothly removed it and slipped it into one pocket, resisting the urge to read it there in the dark theater or leave early to read it elsewhere. Gorsky would be even more upset if Archer got caught or placed under suspicion because he acted strangely. Then, there would be no hope for Cecily.

Guard Senior Commander Roger Vance looked into the holo field in the center of GSF *Aldrin*'s bridge. The first thing that naturally grabbed his attention was the barren, rocky planet of Moloch III, which took up most of the holo's space. The next thing, however, was the smattering of red dots in orbit of Moloch III.

Two weeks ago, with no warning whatsoever, Vance's Task Force 11 of the Guard Space Force had been issued new orders to proceed to a desolate system in the middle of the Odyssean Waste, the region of space so named because few of the systems within its borders showed even the merest promise of being suitable for terraforming. Upon arrival at the no-name system, he'd been shocked to find an entire fleet already there.

Like most officers in the Guard Space Force, Vance felt almost personally offended that the Council had seen the need to form a new Navy. He couldn't voice that frustration aloud, of course, or even think too long on it, without his enacter gene causing him a splitting headache. But that didn't change what he felt deep down.

For the first two weeks in the system—which an arrogant Council Navy vice admiral had informed him was codenamed Moloch—Vance's forces had drilled in endless wargames against the black-painted naval fleet. While Vance's force was only twenty-five ships strong, the Navy fleet numbered upward of 120 warships, so Vice Admiral Collegio had rotated which of his ships faced Vance's. In every scenario, Vance's GSF ships had played the defenders of Moloch III, while the Navy pretended to launch a planetary assault.

But two days ago, the scenario had flipped. Now, Vance's task force were the aggressors and Collegio's the planet's defenders. It had been a nice change of pace, leavened by the fact that the GSF ships had, on their first try, beaten the Navy's best score on the attack.

Collegio had been furious, and he'd had them run the wargame four times more in just a forty-eight-hour period, each time rotating in fresh CN forces to face the same tired GSF ships and crews. Even with that, and to Vance's grim satisfaction, the Navy hadn't managed to beat the Guard until their fifth and final try.

Now, they were trying a sixth time, against another fresh Navy task force, this one anchored by one of the massive CN dreadnoughts, Collegio's own *Reaper*, which hung above Moloch III like a malevolent spider waiting to catch Vance's ships in its webs. Well, they'd see about that.

"Launch our fighter screen," Vance ordered. "Even-numbered squadrons are to accelerate to flank speed ahead of the fleet. Odd-numbered squadrons hang back behind the forward elements in gamma formation."

The other officers on *Aldrin*'s bridge—most of them enacters like himself—snapped to execute Vance's orders, and he watched as the small green dots of his fighters crossed the holo field in two waves, weaving through and around the larger dots that represented his warships. The first wave quickly outpaced the advancing GSF task force, while the second wave followed their different set of orders and settled into long lines behind the leading GSF destroyers and light cruisers. If all went well, Collegio hadn't noticed that second wave hidden behind the first, and now that the fighters were tucked in behind their bigger cousins, the arrogant CN admiral probably still couldn't see them.

"Fifteen minutes to contact," his tactical officer said from behind him. The man sounded almost bored; the excitement of playing these endless wargames had long since waned for all of Vance's crews. But that didn't stop him from turning and shooting the tactical officer an annoyed stare that had the man sitting up straighter at his post.

Vance turned back to watch the holo field again, counting down the minutes.

Vice Admiral Ricardo Collegio of the Council Navy yawned as the GSF force approached Moloch III behind their meager fighter screen. His own fighters had already launched to intercept the Guard craft, and in greater numbers. Though Collegio's ships only numbered twenty-five—the same as the GSF task force under the command of that upstart Vance—they included a number of battleships and Ricardo's own dreadnought, outmassing the Guard force—made up of nothing larger than a battlecruiser—by an easy 30 percent. More mass meant more bays for smaller ships, and therefore he had little doubt that his far more advanced fighters would easily kill the much smaller approaching Guard squadrons.

He sat up straighter and watched in anticipatory glee as the two fighter forces neared each other. Despite the sterility of watching the entire thing as just so many colored dots in a holo field, Ricardo always imagined the clash of forces to be just like a movie he'd once seen in which foot soldiers of two ancient Earth armies armed with only swords sprinted into each other across a field and met in the middle with an audible metal-on-metal crash.

His smile grew as the red dots of the GSF fighter squadrons began dropping from the display far faster than the blue dots of his own squadrons.

"We've lost 40 percent of wave one," Sub-Commander Jennifer Layton reported, her voice edged with enough anger to tell Vance that at least his task force's CAG was taking this particular engagement seriously. He'd never known anyone to take the losses—even simulated ones—of any of her fighters as personally as Layton did.

"Sir, should we have wave two join the fight?" the tactical officer asked, finally paying full attention to the battle.

"Not yet," Vance said as patiently as he could. The man already knew the plan, so his question was ill-timed and unappreciated. But Vance would wait to rebuke him until they were alone.

"Admiral, our fighters have broken through and are reaching the forward screens of the opposing force," Captain Ferrel reported from Ricardo's elbow.

"Very well," the admiral replied. "Send our destroyers and frigates forward to engage theirs."

"Sir?" Ferrel asked, and Collegio could see the captain wince out of the corner of his eye. He stifled a grin; it was so nice when your subordinates got a little twinge of pain when they so much as questioned an order.

"Just do it, Captain," he admonished. He knew that Ferrel was silently suggesting that they follow standard defensive doctrine, which said to let the enemy come to them and use the sensor scattering effects of the planet at their backs to confuse the attackers' sensors. But Collegio was sick of these wargames already, and the idea of ending this one early and wiping the smug face off Roger Vance's face was just too appealing.

"The opposing force is sending its smaller screening elements forward to engage us."

Vance nodded to show he'd heard the update. What was Collegio thinking? Vance already knew the Navy vice admiral was far too sure of himself, but this was just stupid.

"Order our heavy cruisers and battlecruisers to ramp acceleration by 10 percent," he ordered after checking the vectors at his station. Then he sat back and watched as the two small fleets continued to close the distance between them.

Collegio swore loudly as the enemy force's larger ships surged forward, drawing even with their destroyer and light cruiser screen just in time to meet the Navy's destroyers and frigates. In the holo field, the blue dots of his task force's smaller ships started to wink out as the combined fire of Vance's Guard heavy cruisers and battlecruisers slammed into them.

Still, he tried not to appear worried when his invective brought most of the eyes on the bridge to fix on him. After all, he had his dreadnought and four battleships. When the GSF got close enough, they wouldn't stand a chance.

"Sir! *Billinger* reports simulated reactor failure," Vance's tactical officer called out. "She's falling out of formation."

Vance only nodded. The heavy cruiser *Billinger* got gotten a little too far ahead of the rest of his force, drawing close enough to one of the Navy battleships that it had made short work of Commander Joseph's ship.

He checked the mission clock and the vectors in the holo field, counting down silently in his head. When he finally reached zero, he gave the order everyone had been waiting for.

"Execute Plan Nemo, on my mark. Mark!"

"Admiral, more fighters inbound!"

Collegio looked at Captain Ferrel like he was crazy. Hadn't they already destroyed most of the GSF's fighters in the first clash of this contest? If the man was interrupting him just because Vance had launched some single squadron he'd held in reserve, he was going to . . .

His eyes came back to the holo field just in time to see dozens of small red dots erupt from seemingly nowhere like a vengeful swarm of wasps.

The next ten minutes were simultaneously the slowest and fastest minutes of Ricardo Collegio's life. While the dozens of new GSF fighters harried his own *Reaper* and her battleship escorts, Vance's task force concentrated virtually all their fire on the Navy's remaining light cruisers and heavy cruisers. By the time the ten minutes had passed, Collegio's forces were down to just his dreadnought and three remaining battleships—the battle sim AI had declared that one of the blasted GSF bombers had gotten off a lucky shot against a weak point in *Harasser*'s armor.

He watched in horror then as the surviving warships of Senior Commander Vance's force stood off and began launching missiles at *Reaper* and her escorts from a distance, while the swarm of Guard fighters knocked down almost all of the missiles the Navy attempted to fire back.

It was all over in less than fifteen minutes, with the large blue dot signifying *Reaper* finally turning gray.

Vance's bridge crew cheered as the Council Navy dreadnought died its simulated death, leaving Moloch III totally undefended and decisively winning the engagement for the Guard task force. Around him, even the enacters were breaking protocol and slapping each other on their shoulders. Though they'd won engagements before this one, this was the first time Collegio himself had commanded the opposing force, and apparently every Guardsman in Vance's little fleet was overjoyed that they'd brought the haughty Navy admiral down a few pegs.

"You cheated!" a voice said in Vance's ear as his command chair's privacy field automatically engaged at the private message from Vice Admiral Collegio.

"Excuse me, Admiral?" he asked in surprise.

"You hid those extra fighters from our sensors. You cheated," the man accused. "The engagement doesn't count, and next time you won't try any tricks like that."

"Beg your pardon, Admiral," Vance began, fighting to keep the anger out of his voice, "but all I did was order my second wave of fighters to hide behind my forward screening elements. It hid them from your sensors, as the maneuver was designed to do, but I would hardly call it cheating."

"Silence!" Collegio shouted back, so loudly that Vance involuntarily winced. "Don't try and cover up your actions, Senior *Commander* Vance." The man said the title like an insult, though in the Guard Space Force, a Senior Commander was essentially a full admiral, one rank above Collegio, a fact that the pompous Navy man had utterly refused to ever acknowledge. "As I said, we will rerun the engagement, and this time any cheating will result in your immediate removal from command!"

Vance had had it with Collegio's snobbery and unearned overconfidence. He was about to tell the idiot that he wasn't in his chain of command, and therefore had no authority to do what he was threatening, when another voice broke into the private comm channel.

"Vice Admiral Collegio," a calm but firm woman's voice said.

There was silence for a long few seconds, then Vance heard Collegio's almost breathless reply. "Fleet Admiral Chen! I had no idea you were in system. When did you arrive, ma'am?"

"Long enough ago to see you defeated by the GSF's superior tactics," Chen replied over the channel while Vance held his breath.

"Uh . . . Admiral," stuttered Collegio, "as I was just pointing out to our GSF colleagues, the results of the engagement are not valid, as Commander Vance's forces cheated by—"

"I know what they did." Chen cut him off, her voice harder than before. "And I wholeheartedly approve of *Senior* Commander Vance's actions. In fact, I wish my own forces could exercise that level of cunning."

Vance was grinning now. He could hear Collegio practically sputtering on the line but unable to get any words out.

"Senior Commander Vance," Chen said, ignoring the apoplectic fit her underling was having on the comm channel.

"Yes, Fleet Admiral?"

"Well done. I'd like to invite you to join me on my flagship this afternoon. We'll be meeting your task force and Admiral Collegio's forces in orbit of Moloch III in four hours. I'd love for you to lead a discussion with all our warship commanders on the brilliant strategy you just employed. Is that acceptable to you?"

"Yes, ma'am!"

CHAPTER 30

Four Years Ago; 727 P.D.

Riggs sat sullenly at the bar in the Traverton Station Saloon, studying the glass he held in his hand, his fourth shot of whiskey for the evening. He was still looking at it nearly ten minutes later when Joplin finally slid onto the barstool next to him.

"Riggs," the man said amiably enough as he caught the bartender's attention and ordered a beer. "Long time."

"Long time," Riggs agreed as he knocked back the shot he'd been holding.

'"Heard you were asking around about Meera," Joplin noted with a frown. "She's gone, Riggs. Died about five months ago."

Riggs had suspected as much. When he'd gone to the dingy apartment to find his sister for his annual visit, a florid-faced woman had answered his knock instead of Meera and had pled ignorance to any knowledge of the apartment's prior occupant before slamming the door in his face. When he hadn't been able to find any listing for Meera in the station directory, he had pretty much known. But to hear Joplin announce it so callously, without even any small talk to soften the blow, made Riggs want to punch him as if it were *his* fault Meera was dead.

"Who did it?" he asked instead. He never paused to consider that his sister's death may have come from natural causes.

Joplin shrugged. "No one knows for sure. They found her down on the upper levels. Someone strangled her with their bare hands but burned the skin afterward to hide their prints. The Guard worked the case for a few weeks before giving up. With the rate people die around here, they couldn't afford to stay on it for too long, especially when there was no one here to miss her."

Now Riggs *really* wanted to punch Joplin for reminding him that he hadn't been here for his sister, even to push for the Guard to solve her murder case.

"Any leads or theories?" he asked, his voice sounding robotic in his own ears.

Joplin frowned again. "Some folks think it was Raymond, the guy who knocked her up the second time. She was trying to get him to pay for the baby; even had the Guard put out an arrest warrant for skipping out on child support. Word was he really didn't like that, and he disappeared from the station just a few days after they found her body. So, there you go. Seems pretty obvious to me." He downed a long pull of his beer.

"And the kids?" Riggs asked, dreading the answer.

"CPS took 'em. Off-station somewhere, probably in the foster system. They're young, so it would be tough to track 'em down, even if you wanted to. Looks like you just dodged a bullet, Riggs."

The comment was probably meant to be flippant or was a half-hearted attempt to lighten the dark mood. Either way, Joplin didn't have a chance to explain himself. Riggs reached out with his right hand and grabbed the man by the back of the neck, then slammed him face-first into the bar. Joplin screamed as his nose broke and blood sprayed all over the bar counter.

Shouting erupted all around. Out of the corner of his eye, Riggs saw the bartender brandishing a shotgun—illegal for sure, but the Guard tended to look the other way on minor stuff out here in the Edge worlds. They figured anyone *willing* to live in the Mako system should be allowed to keep on doing so as long as they didn't break any *big* laws.

Riggs ignored the bartender and everyone else shouting at him. His bare hand was still on the back of Joplin's neck, and he did something that had almost become second nature to him in the years since leaving Proteus and making his way in a cold and uncaring galaxy: he pushed. *I wasn't here. You don't remember who hurt you, and you're going to break up with your girlfriend after this because you realize you're not good enough for her.*

The first part was necessary; it had been stupid to hurt Joplin like that over a single callous comment. But Riggs was stupid sometimes, and that was that. The second part was petty and mean, a further punishment for the man, but Riggs didn't care. He suspected that Joplin had been one of Meera's customers. The guy had always seemed to know way too much about his little sister. If that was the case, he couldn't be punished enough.

Riggs waved his watch across the bar surface to pay for his drinks and added a hefty tip. The bartender saw the number and nodded toward him, though the man was still holding the shotgun. Regardless, he didn't stop Riggs as he walked out of the establishment.

"Jynx," he said into his comm once he was in the corridor. "Listen, we gotta leave the station. Yeah, I know, it *was* a quick trip. Let's just say the Guard might be looking for me in a bit. Sure, meet you there. Hey, listen, I need you to see if you can track down a guy named Raymond Henge."

He listened to his copilot's final reply and then made his way directly to the public hanger where he'd parked the *Blind Monk*. Twenty minutes later, he and Jynx were gone, and he vowed to never again return to Traverton Station.

Present Day

Corey paced the cramped apartment that was his prison deep inside Mars's largest mountain. Riggs had visited earlier that morning, and lunchtime had already come and gone. The next human contact he could expect would be an impassive and incommunicative legionary who would bring his dinner.

He'd long since grown sick of watching what passed for popular entertainment on Mars. Some honor duels were live-streamed, especially when a government official or high-ranking military officer was involved. Corey had stopped watching those after the first day of his imprisonment. There were some Martian dramas, mainly of the military variety, but what the Martians called acting wouldn't have made the cut in one of his grandchildren's school plays. People from a society based on radical truth and openness had a hard time pretending to be someone different, even for entertainment purposes.

Likewise, Martian reading material was dry, mostly nonfiction accounts of past battles or the early days of Martian settlements.

As a man who had been busy in either service to his family's businesses or his government for the better part of his life, this was the first time in a while that Corey was genuinely, terribly bored. He should have been grateful the Martians hadn't executed him yet, but he wasn't sure that living like this was ultimately worth it.

The door chimed, interrupting his musings, and he told the AI to admit the caller. He turned and was surprised to find the short—by Martian standards, at least—and broad form of Tyrus Tyne peering in at him.

"Tyrus, come in!" he said, not trying to hide his excitement. This was the first time he'd seen Tyrus since the day he'd been informed of the start of the war. Like with Riggs, he'd begun to think their friend had forgotten all about them.

Then he was further surprised to see Riggs himself enter behind Tyrus, glaring daggers at the back of the tall—for a non-Martian—black man's head.

"Sit down, my friends," Corey invited, motioning to the very small kitchen table with two chairs he'd pushed off to one side of the room to make space for his pacing. Tyrus and Riggs did so, while Corey perched himself on the arm of the small couch, facing them.

"What news from the war?" he asked excitedly before the two other men could get settled. Riggs could never answer that, but maybe Tyrus could.

Tyrus frowned. "Nothing I can share, I'm afraid."

Corey felt his face fall. He'd held out a sliver of hope that the other man would remember his original loyalties to Corey and Earth but knew it had been an unlikely hope. Tyrus wasn't just Martian now; he was a member of their most elite and viciously loyal fighting force. In fact, his name probably wasn't even Tyrus 'Tyne' now that he'd joined their ranks; they would have required him to abandon his old surname and attachments. But it hurt to hear from the man's lips now that he would refuse to share even basic news with his old friend.

"I see," Corey replied slowly. "Then, may I ask why you're here, Celeusta Tyrus Tyne?"

Tyrus frowned again but met Corey's gaze steadily. "We believe that someone on Earth has betrayed the Four Worlds and is in league with the Council."

Corey cocked his head to one side and raised his eyebrows. "And? That's hardly a surprise, Tyrus. We knew that had to be true the instant you exposed Toby as a Council spy. You know as well as I do that if the Council could get Toby into the system, they must have other spies here as well. Which means that they've no doubt also recruited people here in the Sol system to their cause."

Tyrus nodded, and a small part of the solemn mask he'd worn since Corey had opened the door slipped just enough for Corey to see the big man's hesitation at whatever he was going to say next. He decided to save him the trouble.

"You think my old pal Mikael Gorsky is in league with the Twenty."

Tyrus may have learned a lot from his short time on Mars, but he hadn't quite learned to control the outward signs of his emotions as well as those born here. Corey was pleased to see his mask fail completely now. "How did you—?" the big man started, but Corey cut him off.

"It's painfully obvious, really," he said sadly. "This entire time, Mikael was playing me. I have no doubt now that he was the one behind Jinny's imprisonment and transfer to the Crater. He probably set it up to both study her and discredit Pereira so he could remove him from office. Even my coming here to Mars was an idea he planted in one of our many chats, probably so he could get me out of the way and put himself forward as the logical choice for president when Pereira was ousted."

Tyrus nodded along. "When did you work all that out?"

Looking around the small room meaningfully, Corey replied, "I've had a lot of time to think down here." He left unsaid that he'd actually figured it out not long after Gorsky had denounced him as a traitor; he'd just never dared to say it out loud in case the Martians did happen to be listening. "So why tell me this now, Tyrus?"

The big alpha—no, the big praetorian guard—took a deep breath. When he let it out, his shoulders slumped a little. "I've been trying for a while to figure out how to get them to lift the order of execution on you," he admitted, drawing a surprised look from Riggs. "And I think I've figured it out."

"And?" Riggs demanded before Tyrus could take a breath to continue. Corey held up a hand to calm the pilot.

"And it involves Toby. If Gorsky is really the traitor, then Toby would most likely know about it. He'd have to have had some way to communicate back with the Keeper, and my guess is that someone built a quantum entanglement comm on Earth. I doubt they'd have the time or funding to build two of those."

Corey nodded along with the man's logic. "So you think Toby must have been in league with Gorsky so he could use his phone to call home?"

Tyrus blinked at his casual tone but nodded grimly. "But all I have right now are suspicions and leaps of logic. And few people believe me. Domitia does, of course. But few others. However, Centurion Parn has told me that if I can get Toby to talk and implicate Gorsky, he will personally take it to Consul Starshadow and the Quorum of Praetors."

Corey couldn't hide his surprise. For Parn to have offered such, told him that the centurion trusted Tyrus, even after only a short time in the Praetorian Guard.

"So torture Toby and make him talk!" Riggs snapped.

Tyrus kept his eyes on Corey as he shook his head. "We've tried, believe me. Some of the things the Praetorian Guard has done to Toby even crossed some lines for me. But the alpha won't talk. Trust me, alphas don't bend to torture."

"You would know," Riggs said rudely, but Tyrus pretended not to hear.

"So why come to me?" Corey pressed. "How can I help get Toby to talk?"

"You can't," the big man admitted. "But Riggs can."

The room went silent, and all eyes went to the pilot, who didn't look confused as Corey expected, but suddenly wary and guarded instead.

"Why would you think I can make him talk?" Riggs asked cautiously.

"Because I once killed a man named Larabaius."

Tyrus's response seemed to suck all the air from the room, though Corey couldn't figure out what any of it meant.

Riggs bit his upper lip hard and then scowled at Tyrus. When he didn't speak, the big man continued.

"He told me a lot before he died, Riggs."

"How long have you known?" the pilot asked sourly.

"Since Rinali Station. What you did to stop Jinny from reading you—I'd only ever heard of one way that was possible."

Corey watched the two men with bated breath, still not understanding but afraid to speak and intrude on whatever secrets were passing between them. Finally, when he could take the silence no more, he asked a variation of his earlier questions. "So why bring this to me? Why not just ask Riggs to help?"

For the first time, Tyrus smiled. "Because I didn't think Riggs would agree to help without your approval."

Riggs's eyebrows shot up, but all Corey could do was nod appreciatively. Tyrus had just hand-delivered a way for him to make restitution to Mars. Forcing a spy to confess and spill his secrets—however Riggs would ultimately do that—would be the perfect way for Corey to atone for being a supposed spy himself.

"This will really get O'Leary out of being killed?" the pilot asked, studying Tyrus's face hard.

The big man nodded once.

Riggs let out a big sigh. "All right, let's go talk to a psychopath."

CHAPTER 31

"Still no luck finding Admiral Lopez?" Jinny asked wearily as she joined the Majko in the old woman's office. Ever since the war had started, the leader of Earth's readers had attended Jinny's training sessions far less frequently, absorbed in the discussions of the war and what the enhanced on the Australian continent might do to avoid its ill effects… or take advantage of it.

Jinny's training itself hadn't slackened in the least. Kelly Martin had silently but no less forcefully taken over scheduling and shepherding the various sessions with readers from across Perth. By now, Jinny felt that she had read just about every possible occupation and skill set known to man, though she recognized she'd still barely scratched the surface. Still, if the war effort needed someone who could cook a perfect omelet, spar in six different types of martial arts, scuba dive, and knit a sweater while doing it, Jinny was the woman for the job!

The Majko regarded her solemnly across her modest desk. "I'm afraid not. Admiral Lopez has disappeared, and none of my contacts are sure where he is. At least the ones I can reach. Many of them are entirely unresponsive."

Jinny raised her eyebrows in a silent question.

The Majko shrugged. "My highest-level contacts in the UE government will not return my calls. There are things happening in Houston that elude me. Ever since President Gorsky rose to power, my sources of information have slowly begun to dry up."

The woman's frank admission of failure took Jinny by surprise. The Majko noticed and shook her head grimly. "This war, Reader Ambrosa. It grows worse every day, and the media tells only part of the story. After the loss at Waypoint Charlie, the UEN lost another task group in orbit of Venus. I admit it confuses many of us. Fifty years ago, the last war between Earth and Mars ended practically in a stalemate, both powers were so evenly matched. But this war is different. Mars won a major battle at Waypoint Charlie, I know that much, but I cannot find out how they did it."

Jinny spent a few moments trying to take that all in. With the Martians staunchly refusing to engage United Earth in a conversation of mutual defense when the Council came—and still no word on Corey's and Tyrus's mission there to convince them otherwise—a Martian victory in the current war could spell doom for the UE when the Keeper's forces arrived. The realization took only a moment to hit her, and she felt her jaw drop open in surprise.

"Someone started the war on purpose to weaken United Earth," Jinny said, speaking the words slowly, tasting each one's bitter flavor as it left her mouth.

The Majko showed no outward signs of surprise at the pronouncement. "Explain," she ordered curtly.

Jinny frowned, thinking before she spoke. "It should have been obvious from the start, right? The Council's first mission to Sol, their 'reconnaissance in force' as people are calling it, wasn't only a disaster for us. They lost several ships, too, including two of those big dreadnoughts. Maybe we spooked them. So they used their collaborator on Earth, Mikael Gorsky, to engineer a war with Mars for the express purpose of weakening Earth's defensive power—I'm sure to do the same to Mars as well—so that when they do finally attack, we'll have less to throw against them."

She paused, watching for the Majko's reaction, but the older woman's face remained stony. Then it abruptly softened, and the matriarch, usually so spry and indomitable, suddenly looked every day of her age.

"The Council of Factors and I came to the same conclusion two weeks ago," the Majko admitted, drawing a sharp frown from Jinny as she sat forward in her seat. But before the younger reader could demand to know why she wasn't told, the Majko continued. "This theory of yours about Gorsky and Joseph Blackmont having some way to communicate with the Council government was a large piece of the puzzle that made everything else make sense."

Jinny sat back in her seat, somewhat mollified, and nodded. "Great. So just more evidence that Gorsky is in league with the Keeper, and they have one of those quantum entanglement comms somewhere on Earth. Has Temperance made any progress in finding it?"

The Majko nodded. "One week ago, when she couldn't reach you, she messaged me with the coordinates."

Now, Jinny was truly upset. A week! The Majko had known the location of the quantum comm for a week and hadn't thought to mention it to Jinny—when it was Jinny who'd told Temperance Jimenez what to look for in the first place.

"I'm sorry," the Majko said before Jinny could explode. "It was wrong to keep this from you. But I wanted you focused on your training while we independently verified the intel."

Gritting her teeth to keep from screaming, Jinny asked in a low growl, "And have you verified it?"

The old woman nodded. "We have. But from an unexpected source?"

"What do you mean?" Jinny pressed, sick of the Majko's games. "Tell me now or I'm gone. Forget your ninety days. I leave tonight unless you stop jerking me around and tell me everything!" She stood up as she spoke, leaning over the desk and leveling a finger at the Majko. Her voice went deeper as she allowed Tyrus to momentarily take over, using the same tone he'd once used to send high-level Council bureaucrats scrambling for cover.

Tyrus and Jinny were rewarded by finally seeing the Majko flinch back. Tyrus stayed where he was, Jinny's body still leaning halfway across the desk, his gaze burning into the older woman's. The Majko licked her lips nervously, perhaps sensing that it was no longer Jinny Ambrosa, mild-mannered reader, whom she was facing. Just as Jinny had intended when she gave Tyrus control.

"All right," the Majko said slowly. "But I believe it would be best if you hear it straight from the source."

Tyrus was about to demand exactly what she meant when Jinny gently tugged him back and took control again, sensing that the old woman had surrendered. *Don't trust her,* Tyrus warned before disappearing into the fog.

Behind Jinny, the door opened, and she whirled to see a plain-looking man stepping into the room. She was certain he was a blender, and she started to get up, suddenly afraid.

"Hello, Reader Ambrosa," the man said calmly, stopping her instinctual reaction. "It's been a long time since we met at the prison."

Jinny felt herself relax as she caught the reference. Jordan Archer, Corey O'Leary's fixer, had by all reports been instrumental in her escape from the Crater prison. She could trust this man.

Unfortunately, any relief or trust she felt quickly disappeared as Archer sat down and proceeded to explain how he'd been working for Mikael Gorsky from the beginning.

Tyrus led Corey and Riggs deeper into the Olympus Mons volcano than either of them had ever ventured. As they followed him, the corridors through which they traveled became narrower and narrower until Tyrus almost had to walk sideways to keep his broad shoulders from brushing the rough-hewn stone walls.

After what seemed like a long time, they arrived at a small elevator that barely fit the three of them. Corey was surprised when it carried them down.

"I thought the government facilities didn't extend any lower into the mountain?" he asked.

"Most of it doesn't, but this part is special."

Corey was about to ask what Tyrus meant when the elevator door opened and revealed a scene straight from Hell itself, drawing startled cries of terror from both him and Riggs. Just outside the elevator door, there was nothing but roiling fire.

Before either man could ask what was going on or process the eddies and flows of magma around them, Tyrus stepped nonchalantly out of the elevator door and into the fire. Corey gasped again and reached out a hand to hold him back. He stopped when the ex-alpha didn't immediately burn up or disappear in the liquid rock all around them. It was also at that moment that Corey realized what was missing from the scene: heat. The temperature in the elevator was still exactly the same as it had been in the corridors above.

Still, it was Riggs who realized first what was going on. "Who builds a transparent tunnel in the middle of a lava flow?"

Tyrus smiled a little from where he stood just outside the elevator in what Corey could now see was indeed a transparent tunnel through the magma, though he couldn't see around the big man to know what was on the other end. "Martian nanotechnology is a wonderful thing," Tyrus answered. "I've been increasingly amazed the more they've shown me of it. But, to answer your specific question, this happens to be the most secure part of the Olympus Mons Government Center, and you're the first non-Martians to ever see it."

With those ominous words, he turned and started walking down the tunnel without a backward glance. After a shared look of trepidation, Corey and Riggs followed, stepping gingerly on the corridor's transparent floor and trying hard not to look down at the fire that swirled seemingly just centimeters under their feet. Tyrus led them perhaps fifty meters before he stopped at what appeared to be a fairly ordinary-looking door. He pressed a hand against it, and it slid open.

The three men stepped through and onto a metal deck in what appeared to be a large control room of some kind, with a blessedly solid floor, walls, and ceiling, multiple doors on two sides, and a bank of control panels on the other to the right of where they'd entered.

Inside the control room, three others waited, all dressed in the black exosuits used by the Praetorian Guard. One of them stepped forward, his helmet dissolving back into his suit.

"Corey O'Leary," Centurion Parn greeted them in a neutral voice. "And Cal Riggs. Welcome to the Kiln."

"What is this place?" Riggs asked, staring in horror at the magma less than a meter overhead, but Corey already knew. It turned out that Mars *did* have prisons, after all.

"This is where we keep the most secure prisoners on Mars," Tyrus answered. "The tunnel we entered through is temporary, formed as needed by dedicated nanites engineered to withstand the heat of the active volcano."

"We are in the middle of one of the mountain's largest and most stable magma chambers." Another black-clad figure stepped forward, helmet disappearing to reveal the face of Domitia Felix, Tyrus's bonded partner. "And the nanites that maintain this facility can be withdrawn at any time, killing everyone within should a prisoner escape."

Corey gulped. "Toby?" he asked, the question directed at Tyrus.

Tyne nodded. "We have kept him down here for the five weeks since capturing him."

"We doing this or what?"

Everyone turned to frown at Riggs, who stood defiantly.

"That is a terrific question, Visitor Cal Riggs," Parn said dryly. He turned to look at Corey. "Do tell us, Former Emissary Corey O'Leary, will you allow Visitor Cal Riggs to help us interrogate Prisoner Toby Haight?"

Corey shook off his surprise, remembering what Tyrus had told them in his small apartment. From the glint of amusement in Parn's normally unreadable face, the centurion knew as much as he did that the whole thing was a farce. Corey couldn't tell Riggs what to do or what not to do any more than they could. But the fiction that he had that power would be what saved him from execution. He felt a sudden warm gratitude knowing that Parn—or perhaps someone above him—was in on the fiction that would save him.

He nodded. "Yes. Captain Riggs, will you please assist the Praetorian Guard in interrogating Toby Haight?"

Riggs scowled and muttered something under his breath that sounded like 'protean' or 'proteus,' though it didn't ring any bells for Corey. Then he nodded curtly. "Fine. Let's do it."

CHAPTER 32

Four Years Ago; 727 P.D.

It had been a long day in the mines, and the man was absolutely exhausted. Still, the end of the work day brought with it no particular joy. All he had to look forward to was a soggy reconstituted meal and maybe an hour or two of holo vids before he conked out asleep on his horribly uncomfortable couch that doubled as an equally terrible bed in his room that was almost too small for even that single piece of furniture.

He tried not to think too hard about it as he clocked out of the mine with a wave of his watch at the exit and then set down his tools in his locker and trudged down the tunnels—carved out of asteroid rock just like the mine itself—toward his room in the facility's residential wing.

They called this particular asteroid Abaddon, which was actually a religious reference of some kind, though he didn't know that and wouldn't care if he had. So long as they paid him to be here and it wasn't where he'd come from, then he really didn't mind what they called it. Besides, he wouldn't be here for that long anyway; it was best to keep moving when you had a past like his.

Stupid woman, he thought, for likely the thousandth time in the last six months. *All she had to do was let me sell that brat. That Normandy couple would have paid good money for the girl and probably would have given her a better life anyway.* Or maybe not. He purposefully didn't think too hard about why a supposedly well-to-do man and woman from the Expansion Region were in the Mako system of all places looking for a kid to adopt through less-than-legal channels.

Anyway, the baby's mother had objected . . . strenuously. That was gratitude for you. First, Meera had been upset when he'd left her to birth and raise the brat alone. Then she'd sent the Guard after him for not paying child support. And when he'd brought her the *perfect* solution to both problems—no more kid to take care of, plus a whole lot of money—she'd had the gall to call him a deadbeat loser and a score of other things in the middle of the corridor, where everyone could hear.

Well, he had shown her, though she'd put up more of a fight than he'd thought she would, and he'd had to choke her just to shut her up. Raymond hadn't *really* meant to kill Meera. He'd just wanted to scare the harpy and stop her from running that mouth of hers. As usual, she had just blown the whole thing out of proportion, so he'd done the only thing he could do. It wasn't his fault, not really. It wasn't fair that he had still had to leave the station so quickly, in fact, that he hadn't even had time to find that couple from Normandy and sell them the brat. The Guard probably had her at this point, or those blasted meddlers at CPS.

He reached the door to his little hovel, keyed it open, and stepped inside. The small room was dark, which was strange. The lights usually came on automatically when he opened the door. He waved his watch at the light control as the door shut behind him, and the room was suddenly bathed in its usual stark white harsh glow.

Raymond stopped. On his couch, there was a man. At first, he didn't recognize him, which scared him. Then he did recognize him, and that *terrified* him.

"Uh, what are you doing here, Riggs?" Raymond asked while subtly stepping to the left toward the small drawer under his food warmer. If he could just get to the gun he kept there.

"You know, Ray, you're an idiot," the other man said, raising a pistol in his direction and motioning with it for him to step back toward the center of the small room.

"Come on, Riggs. What are you hassling me for?" Unfortunately, he knew the answer, but if he could keep Riggs talking, maybe he could think of a way out of this.

"Ray," Riggs said, ignoring his question. "I'm not sure you realize just how much of an idiot you are. I mean, you didn't even change your initials when you started at the mine here. Rob Henley. Seriously? Not to mention, the fake ID you got was so poorly done that it wouldn't even stand up to a first-level check. I mean, how stupid are you?"

He waited as if Raymond might answer the question, then shrugged. "Anyway, you know why I'm here, don't you?"

Ray shook his head, thinking quickly. Maybe if he stepped toward the gun again, Riggs wouldn't notice. Except—his heart fell—he recognized the gun in Riggs's hand now as his own.

"Why'd you do it, Ray?" The pilot's voice, which had been almost joking, though with a hard edge, suddenly turned dark and stony as the asteroid rock around them. "Why'd you kill her, Ray? Tell me that much."

"I didn't—" Ray's protest was interrupted by the sound of a bullet hitting the stone wall behind him as Riggs pulled the trigger on the pistol. It had an integrated silencer.

"It's a nice gun, Ray," Riggs said coldly. "No one will hear me when I shoot your kneecaps. So why not cut the lies? You're already dead; I just haven't decided how yet. So tell me the truth, and maybe I'll make it fast and painless."

"Riggs, listen, you gotta understand," Ray pleaded as he felt his bladder give way and warmth running down his right leg. "I didn't mean to kill Meera. I swear! It just happened." He was babbling now but couldn't stop himself. "I just wanted my kid back, but she wouldn't let me see her. We argued, and—"

"Wrong answer, Ray," Riggs said, and this time, as promised, the bullet shattered his knee.

Raymond screamed in agony and fell to the hard stone floor, grabbing for his destroyed leg and trying to do something about the excruciating pain, still not quite able to believe he'd been shot.

"See, Ray," Riggs said, now with a preternatural calm to his tone, "I asked around a bit. You and Meera were seen arguing in public. You wanted to sell your own daughter, isn't that right?"

"No. I swear. I've never. I would never! Riggs, you gotta—" His words cut off in another scream of agony as the next bullet took out his other knee.

Tears now ran unchecked down Raymond's face. He couldn't see Riggs clearly anymore, his vision blurry as he wailed and cried and begged for mercy.

"Doesn't matter now, I suppose." The man kept right on talking over Raymond's blubbering. "Because regardless of whatever you were planning with the little girl, you *did* kill Meera. And for that, you're gonna die. There's just no way around it."

Raymond whimpered, straining to see the other man through the tears. Riggs stayed seated on the couch, staring at him, his jaw clenched but no other outward signs of his white-hot rage. After a few seconds, the pilot stood and took a step toward Raymond, leaning down, with the hand not holding the gun, and grabbed Raymond's head like a basketball.

Then, something exceedingly strange happened, and to Raymond's astonishment, Riggs reached out with his other hand and handed him the gun.

"I know you'll do the right thing, Ray," Riggs said, smiling at him. "For Meera."

Raymond wanted to point the gun at Riggs and end him, for the pain and the indignity and . . . Slowly, the gun turned in Raymond's hand until he had the barrel inexplicably pointed at his own head. *That's odd,* he thought, but then it all made a kind of sense. He *deserved* this, and Riggs was being awfully nice letting him be the one to—

Riggs slipped out of Raymond's room, looking around first to make sure the man's screams hadn't carried enough through the rock walls and the flimsy door to draw attention. The corridor was empty, so obviously, people either hadn't heard or, more likely, simply hadn't wanted to get involved. Either way, it meant a clean getaway.

Pushing Raymond hadn't actually been part of his plan. It was a last-second improvisation in a moment of anger, and he tried to ignore the twisted knots in his stomach as he slowly made his way down the corridor. He should have felt good about ending Ray's pathetic existence after what he'd done to Meera. And Riggs wouldn't have had to be the hand of justice if the Guard had just done their jobs in the first place and arrested Ray for murder back on Traverton Station. He'd only given the man what was coming to him. That was all.

But deep down, Cal Riggs knew the truth. A deadbeat like Raymond would have never even met Meera, much less killed her, if *Cal* had just done his job right in the first place. He'd been her older brother, charged by Mother and by Riggs 201 to protect her after they'd escaped Proteus.

He had failed her. Plain and simple. His little sister was dead because of *him*.

When he arrived back at the airlock and made his way through the flimsy air tunnel to the *Blind Monk*, he was in a dark mood. Killing his sister's murderer had not brought a gram of the closure or relief he'd hoped for. Which wasn't to say he regretted it, but it did nothing for the crushing guilt and pain he still felt at Meera's death and his own failure to protect her.

Jynx was waiting for him on the other side of his ship's airlock door. "All done?" she asked impassively, not prompting him to give any details.

"Yep. Time to leave," he told her as he walked past her toward the cockpit. Then, without thinking enough about it, he turned back to her. "Jynx, you still want to head to the Parisian system and try to track down that guy who killed your sister?"

She frowned. "Of course."

He frowned back. "You may want to rethink that." Then he turned away again and kept walking sullenly toward the cockpit. Jynx said nothing, but he could feel her eyes on his back as he left her behind.

Present Day

"Oh look, they sent the loser," Toby sneered as Riggs entered the small interrogation room and tried very hard not to fixate on the lava outside its floor, ceiling, and three transparent walls.

He sat at the metal table, facing Toby, who was chained to the other side with Tyrus and Parn flanking him, both men looking extra imposing today in their black exosuits, especially with the helmets fully deployed.

Riggs looked across at Toby, feeling the blood rush to his face as he thought about this man murdering Jynx. On *his* watch. Just like Meera.

Sure, Toby had manipulated *all* of them from the start, but Riggs should have known better. He should have been able to protect his copilot and best friend. He should have seen the signs earlier and done something to stop Jynx's death. But no, he'd failed her just as he'd failed his sister four years ago and even before that, when he'd left her alone on Traverton Station to her own devices.

He felt hot tears coming to his eyes, and Toby smiled widely at him, sensing victory. The killer and assassin probably thought that his mere presence was terrifying enough to make Riggs cry in fear. Well, he'd learn.

"How about it, Riggs?" Toby taunted him with another sneer. "You're here to make me talk? Okay. Let's talk. How about I talk all about what it felt like to kill that sad excuse for a copilot you had? How about I tell you all about how good it felt to feel the warmth of her blood on my hands, or how—"

"Tyrus." Riggs said just that one word, and behind Toby, Tyrus stepped forward and grabbed the prisoner's head, slamming Toby's face to the metal table and cutting off his speech.

Toby let out a cry of surprise, but even that was choked off a moment later when Riggs reached out and grabbed the man's head like a basketball, just as he'd done with Raymond four years ago. It didn't have to be the head; any skin-to-skin contact would work, just as it worked that way for readers. But the symmetry in doing the same to Toby as he'd done to Raymond was mildly satisfying, even if a detached part of Riggs's brain knew how sick that really was.

He shoved aside any burgeoning feelings of guilt. He suppressed all thoughts of having failed first Meera and then Jynx. And he concentrated everything on the man who had pretended to fall in love with Jynx and then killed her in cold blood.

Cal pushed.

A moment later, his head still held against the table by Tyrus, and with Riggs's hand still palming his scalp, Toby began to talk. They stayed that way for over four hours, with only occasional breaks for Riggs to flex his fingers or switch hands. By the end, Toby told Tyrus, Parn, and Riggs *everything* he knew about the Keeper's plans for the Four Worlds, the existence of the Goat Path's secret route through the Rift—unfortunately, he didn't actually know its exact coordinates—the location of the quantum entanglement comm on Earth, and the identities and names of every Council spy and collaborator Toby knew about.

Including President Mikael Gorsky.

When the interrogation was done, Riggs released his hold on Toby's head and sat back, wiping the sweat from his brow. He'd never before attempted to push someone for more than a few minutes. Every second of his experience with Toby had brought exhaustion mixed with pain, but he'd pushed through it all. Now, he gasped for breath and had to be helped from the room by Tyrus.

Out in the Kiln's main chamber, Corey rejoined them. By the look on the old congressman's face, he'd been watching the interrogation via the room's cameras. "If what he said is true . . ." Corey said, eyes wide as he was unable to finish his own thought.

Riggs nodded, still leaning on Tyrus to stay on his feet. "It's all true, at least so far as he knows. Trust me, he couldn't have lied."

Corey took that in with a gaze of mixed astonishment and fear. Riggs didn't take it personally. The congressman had grown up on a planet where the enhanced were the bogeymen, something to be feared but at least a known risk. However, Cal's ability was something that few in the galaxy knew existed, and it had to be making Corey wonder what *else* might be out there that he and the others weren't aware of. His mind flashed back to Proteus. *If only you knew,* he thought as he met Corey's stare. *You would never sleep again. Pushers weren't the worst thing created on that station—not by a long shot.*

Parn followed them as Tyrus, Riggs, and Corey exited the Kiln through the reformed nanite tunnel and back to the lift. When the elevator opened at the other end, he crammed himself inside the small car with the three of them.

"Will it be enough?" Riggs heard Corey ask the centurion.

"To convince all the praetors?" the dour Martian mused. "Unlikely. They will require independent verification, especially as we cannot reveal how we made the spy talk. But most will believe."

Riggs was grateful for that. He'd assumed that everyone in the Martian government would soon know of his ability, which would likely end up with him sharing the cell next to Toby's in the hellish Kiln. He would have hated that, but he also would have accepted it because it had given him the chance he needed, both to help his friends and avenge Jynx.

"It should be sufficient," the Martian continued, "to approve a mission to get the proof we truly need. That will have to be enough."

Still leaning on Tyrus for support, Riggs saw Parn suddenly go rigid, cocking his head and holding a hand to his ear as if straining to hear something.

"What happened?" Corey demanded, noticing it too.

After a few moments, the centurion frowned and looked at Riggs as he replied. "On his way back to his cell, the prisoner subdued his guard and stole his weapon."

Tyrus sucked in a breath. He'd left Domitia, that scary woman he seemed to be in love with, down in the Kiln with Toby. Riggs winced, hoping none of them saw his reaction.

"Was anyone hurt?" Corey demanded.

Parn shook his head. "None of our people. The prisoner turned the weapon on himself. Toby Haight is dead."

There was a moment, a single beat, between the Martian's pronouncement and the collective instant of realization as three sets of eyes turned to Riggs. He smiled back at them. "How about that?" he said. "Wonder why the guy decided to off himself." He smiled all the way back to the main residential area.

At least now, Jynx's soul could rest.

"The facility's strength is not in its human security, but its structural security," Jordan Archer explained, pointing to the wireframe holo of the fake water tower tank in the Utah-Nevada desert. He'd just confirmed for all of them that the supposedly decrepit water storage facility really housed Joseph Blackmont's quantum entanglement comm array. He'd actually been surprised to find out that they'd already found its location—the Neon Mouse was a better hacker than even he'd given her credit for—but they had all seemed relieved at his independent confirmation, along with his ability to tell them what was actually inside.

He'd been there, after all, summoned like a foot servant to attend Mikael Gorsky lest the traitorous president kill Cecily.

"Here." Jordan indicated a point on the outer surface of the water tank. "The walls of the installation are essentially built like a warship's hull, a meter thick and reinforced with adamantine. Access to the one and only door leading inside is controlled by a human security specialist deep in the heart of the facility, with AI backups that warn him or her of any . . ."

Jinny tuned the blender out as he continued the briefing for the other fifteen people in the room. She'd heard this all before when Archer had initially presented the broad outlines of his proposed plan to her and the Majko. The old woman had then selected twelve readers with the skill sets Archer had asked for, and today's meeting was about letting them in on the plan as well as asking them to poke holes in it to make it better.

It shouldn't have surprised her, Jinny supposed, that the readers in Perth had their own paramilitary. The twelve steely-eyed men and women in the room had mostly been recruited from its ranks, all of them long-time operatives who did off-the-books missions for the Majko and her Council of Factors, the small group of men and women who helped her rule Perth and all of Earth's readers.

In addition to the dozen operatives, today's audience included Landon Hartman, Temperance Jimenez, and Kelly Martin. The pilot was paying careful attention; it would be his job to land the mission team in the stealth shuttle Tyrus had stolen from the UEN, the same shuttle that had brought Jinny to Perth.

Temperance wasn't paying attention. The odd little hacker was busy on a pad, looking for something—some*one*—who both the Majko and Jordan Archer had asked her to find.

Kelly was busy taking notes. Jinny had almost objected to the Majko's inclusion of her assistant in the mission planning. Ever since she'd caught the woman eavesdropping outside the room where Landon and Temperance had first briefed her on the Blackmont situation, Jinny had begun to suspect that Kelly was not what she appeared to be. However, she hadn't quite known how to word that to the Majko, so she'd held her tongue and resolved to watch the old woman's assistant carefully.

As Archer discussed the plan with the twelve operatives, who had several very useful suggestions, Jinny frowned. On the surface, the mission seemed straightforward: break into the secure facility and take control of it, and while some of the operators gathered what intel they could on the construction of the quantum comm, they would capture Blackmont and bring him back to Perth so Jinny could read him here. On the way out, they'd destroy the quantum comm, cutting off President Gorsky's ability to coordinate with the Keeper, and also taking the man's key ally and a valuable source of intelligence away from him.

With what Jinny would read from Blackmont, they should be able to learn everything Gorsky and the mercenary leader knew to date about the Keeper's plans. Then they'd just have to find someone to listen to them long enough to do something about it.

Something about the entire situation nagged at Jinny. Archer had been very upfront about his relationship with Mikael Gorsky, but she had the distinct impression he wasn't telling them everything. She'd considered reading him, of course, but hadn't yet found the opportunity. Besides, the first thing the man had done upon confessing his duplicity was allow the Majko to read him. And while the Majko's reading time of thirty-two hours was extremely impressive for a normal reader, it paled in comparison to Jinny's, obviously. The only problem was that Archer couldn't know that, or at least, he hadn't back when she'd read him in the prison while he posed as her attorney. Unfortunately, that meant she couldn't suggest that he let her read him in addition to the Majko without also implicitly revealing something about her abilities. He would wonder why they were insisting he be read twice.

Still, it would likely be worth it, given the risk of the mission. While the Majko had detected no further subterfuge in her reading of the man, Jinny wouldn't feel comfortable until she could see *everything* and ensure the same. She resolved to suggest as much to the Majko later that same afternoon.

In the meantime, she turned her attention back to the briefing and mission planning discussion to see if *she* could find any holes in the plan.

CHAPTER 33

Two Weeks Later; January 14, 732 P.D.

Forge Lewis ran in a loose crouch across the relatively flat desert ground, still managing to find small gullies and depressions in which to hide his movement from potential watchers. He did so with little conscious thought, letting his instincts—honed over a decade of intense training—take control and guide his feet where to go.

Around him, the winter night air was frigid, negative nine degrees Celsius, but he couldn't feel it. Instead, he baked inside his stealth suit as its internal temperature reached forty degrees, closer to the temperature this same desert would hit on a hot summer day. And it would grow hotter still as he ran because the suit couldn't vent its heat. Not yet.

Forge knew that he wasn't the only member of his unit breaching the perimeter of this particular target at the moment. Another member of his team was on the opposite side of the perimeter from him, but they wouldn't risk communicating and having their transmissions intercepted. This was a fully dark mission with strict emissions control.

After another twenty minutes of overland travel, while the temperature in his suit continued to rise to nearly unbearable levels, Forge arrived at the spot he'd scoped out on the satellite imagery. He looked around and saw the expected slight depression in the otherwise flat ground, sheltered by bushes on two sides and a slight rise on the third. And in front, a full view of the target.

Satisfied, he knelt down and pulled a metal tube out of a special pocket on his stealth suit's thigh. Narrow and roughly as long as a pencil, it would have looked like an odd thing for a recon soldier to carry to anyone who didn't know what it was. With a quick motion, Forge jammed the pointed end into a spot of ground that looked slightly softer than the rest. The other end of the metal tube was connected via a thin insulated wire to his suit, and he held the tube in the ground while he pressed a button on the side. With a thump and a jolt, the pointy end of the tube telescoped and extended down two meters into the desert floor, assisted by a small cutting laser on the end.

The special little extending tube solved the biggest problem of having a true stealth suit. Forge's suit, somehow stolen by the Majko from the UE military, kept him invisible to optical sensors and the human eye. It even absorbed radar and other sensor signals. But the one thing it couldn't do was completely mask his heat signature against thermal optics for any significant length of time. Sure, it could *store* his body heat up and not let it leak out, but then he would literally cook inside of it, as he practically had been on the two-hour trek from the insertion point.

But the tube, sunk deep into the ground and still connected to his suit by the long wire, solved that. It allowed the suit to radiate its heat into the surrounding desert floor, deep enough that it wouldn't show up on any thermal sensors looking at this spot. It was an ingenious invention and would be absolutely perfect, if only it could work faster. Forge would continue to suffer for another six hours before it brought his suit temperature down to his normal body temp. But at least it wouldn't get any hotter than it was now, and the suit would capture and recycle his sweat to replace a good portion of the copious amounts of water he would drink over the next few hours.

Forge settled down on his stomach less than a meter from where he'd inserted the tube into the ground and lifted his optics to get a closer look at the target. Just as the satellite images had shown, and just as that blender, Jordan Archer, had described, it looked like nothing more than a simple water tank, rust-splotched and dusty from years abandoned in the desert. It seemed almost impossible that it could house the most advanced communications system ever invented by humanity.

Now, all Forge had to do was wait, both for the temperature in his suit to come down, and for his target to reveal themself.

Admiral Terrence Lafayette watched the sensor plot that showed his Task Group 21.1 in orbit around Hyperion, one of the irregular moons of Saturn. Hyperion had long ago been claimed by Mars, and the red planet maintained several mining stations on the moonlet's surface. Up until recently, they'd also had a light cruiser in orbit to defend it, but TG21.1 had made quick work of that lone warship.

"Come on," Lafayette whispered under his breath. They'd been in orbit of the moon for six hours now, and their Marine landing parties had already secured the mining stations and had just loaded the few Martian prisoners into a troop transport to take to internment camps set up on Luna for just such a purpose. TG21.1 was running out of legitimate excuses to stay in orbit, and soon, Lafayette was going to have to order them back to rendezvous with the rest of the fleet.

He glanced at the mission clock. Eight minutes left before the designated time at which he would have to call it and take his ship out of Hyperion orbit and back to the fleet. Now, if only—

"Admiral, tachyon bursts detected at one-eight-four mark neg two," Captain Dasgupta reported over the intercom from UENS *Texas*'s command bridge. "Estimated time to arrival, thirty-eight minutes."

Lafayette smiled. At last!

Precisely thirty-three minutes later, he gave the order.

"Reorient the fleet and focus broadsides on the projected exit coordinates!" he ordered, and the dozen warships of TG21.1 started to yaw to port in perfect sync. Just as the Earth ships settled into their new positions, twice as many Martian warships appeared as if from nowhere, just slightly off-center from where the UEN ships were expecting them.

The small deviation wasn't enough to spoil the aim of Task Group 21.1. As the Martians surfaced from their still-inexplicable short series of jumps through the void, *Texas* and its consorts immediately launched every missile in their starboard broadsides.

Lafayette smiled again as the Martians sent back only a meager wave of their own missiles, which crossed with the Earth missiles at just about the halfway point between them. But the UEN ships, expecting the attack, already had their defensive weaponry spooled up and ready. They knocked most of the Martian missiles out of space. Only two got through, and Admiral Lafayette winced as one of his light cruisers, *Jefferson*, went dead in space and started launching escape pods.

The Martian ships did not fare nearly so well. Of the twenty-five attacking ships, fully nine fell to Lafayette's fire within seconds of surfacing, and he smiled grimly to see that the analysts were right about the Red ships not being able to divert much power to weapons for several minutes after surfacing from their strange in-system jumps. Those same analysts called the new Martian capability 'intermittent aborted void submergences,' but everyone in the know who didn't ride a desk had already taken to calling them 'skip jumps.'

No matter. Whatever they were called, they gave the Martians a seemingly insurmountable advantage over the United Earth Navy forces arrayed against them. Except, now that the UEN knew about the capability, they could find ways to overcome that disadvantage.

"Roll and fire second wave," Lafayette ordered, taking advantage of the full ten minutes the analysts claimed he would have before the Reds could charge their weapons and return fire in earnest.

Forge had only been in place watching the water tank in the desert for half a day before he saw activity. The facility's outer door opened, and he watched through his scope as a woman stepped outside. She was middle-aged and very pretty, with brunette hair and a trim figure that Forge could appreciate even from his position nearly two kilometers away.

He watched as she stretched, looking up at the cold and gray winter sky, as if it gave her some solace after being inside the facility for so many days or weeks. Forge knew from Jordan Archer's briefings that the small full-time staff employed by Blackmont Industries to run the quantum comm facility lived onsite, in underground accommodations, the better to not have them seen coming and going to clue in any passing observers that there was more to the decrepit water tank than met the eye.

But Archer had also suggested that this woman didn't like being cooped up around the clock, and she had developed the habit of stepping outside periodically and occasionally leaving the facility altogether. Archer hadn't been sure how the woman got away with such breaches of protocol, but it was enough that she did.

Forge watched her now, willing her to summon a vehicle and leave so he could end this mission. Unfortunately, after a brief period of stretching her legs outside, the pretty woman turned and reentered the facility. Disappointed, Forge settled back in to wait.

"Sir! New enemy ships surfacing behind us!" called the lieutenant commander at the sensor station on Terrence Lafayette's flag bridge. "Two squadrons of battlecruisers. Launching missiles."

The admiral checked the plot to see that *Texas* and TG21.1 were out of position to launch their own return volley against the newly surfaced Martian reinforcements. They'd detected the incoming skip jumps of this second Martian force too late, and now the eight enemy battlecruisers, built for speed and heavy offensive punch, were in perfect position to harass TG21.1 from the rear while the eleven remaining ships of the original Martian force had finally built up enough power in its reactors to start to fire back in earnest from the front.

Swearing under his breath, Lafayette did his best not to look worried, knowing that the crew would take their cues from him and Captain Dasgupta on the command bridge. If they looked calm, everyone else would be far more likely to stay calm, even if Lafayette was feeling massive heartburn despite his trust in the plan he'd laid out.

"Jinny, it's the only way." The Majko looked across the desk at the young reader, her face hard and her tone unyielding.

"It can't be," Jinny argued back, leaning forward in her chair and staring at the older woman. "There *has* to be an alternative. You can't expect me to just sit here and watch from the sidelines as you send these people on what might be a suicide mission!" She'd started out speaking as calmly as she could, but she was practically yelling by the time she finished her thought, and the old woman frowned in response.

"Unfortunately, you have no say in the matter."

The words were so blunt that they shocked Jinny into silence, her mouth working but no words emerging. Always before, the Majko had at least maintained the fiction that Jinny had a choice in her own destiny, but now she was stating the painfully obvious: Jinny was a guest here in Perth with few allies and no power. If the Majko said that she wasn't going on the mission to capture Joseph Blackmont, then there was little Jinny could do to subvert the woman's orders.

"We will capture Blackmont and bring him back here for you to read," the Majko continued, speaking calmly. "That's the plan, and I see no reason to deviate from it. This way, we don't risk our most important asset on a mission that could very well be a trap."

And there it was, the real reason she refused to let Jinny go on the assault against the secret quantum comm facility: the mission stood a good chance of failing, and if and when it did, the results would be deadly for those involved. But how could Jinny knowingly allow others to go to their deaths without sharing the risk with them?

"Not. Going. To. Happen." She made her own eyes as hard as the Majko's, engaging in a staring contest across the woman's desk. "Besides," Jinny hastened to add before the Majko could argue, "if you expect me to be any good in the battle to come, I need real experience, not just what I've read from others. Call it a field test if you want. But I'm not staying here."

For a long moment, the leader of Earth's readers frowned, and Jinny was sure she was going to say no. But then, the Majko slowly started to nod.

Navarch Rufus Ovidius on MPNS *Minerva* showed his teeth as the missiles from his reinforced squadron of quadriremes flew straight and true at the drive plumes of the United Earth force in front of them. When his ships—equivalent to UE battlecruisers—had surfaced from their stitch jump, he hadn't expected to find Prefect Cloelius's larger battle force already cut more than in half. The terse orders he'd received from Cloelius indicated that the Earther force had somehow seemed to know where his ships were surfacing from their final stitch jump. If that was indeed the case . . .

He shook off those thoughts and focused on watching his missiles fly toward the enemy fleet and listening to the countdown from his Nav Phax on when his quadriremes would be able to build up enough power to load another wave and start firing their lasers. No matter how the Earthers had managed to take out so many of the Martian forces in the first group, there was no way such a small number of ships could stand against the combined firepower of two forces of Mars who had them in a perfectly timed pincer.

Rufus smiled. As soon as his ships were restored to their full power, the Earthlings would die here at Hyperion just as their comrades before them had died at Waypoint Charlie. No matter how they'd somehow detected Cloelius's forces, it wouldn't be enough.

His thoughts of the triumph to come were interrupted by a gasp from across his ship's bridge as three massive ships unlike any he'd ever seen before appeared out of nowhere, directly between him and the exhaust ports of the Earther ships. He shouted orders, but it was too late. Fighters poured from the open bays of the three new and very strange vessels while their defensive fire lanced out and destroyed almost the entirety of the missiles he'd sent toward the Earth fleet.

"Nav Phax!" he screamed into his intercom. "I need power n—"

His order died on his lips as four ship-killer missiles impacted his quadrireme and opened *Minerva*'s front third to space in a roiling nuclear fire.

Mary Bol watched dispassionately from the flag bridge of UENS *Enterprise* as her fighters, bombers, and missiles tore into the eight Martian battlecruisers that had appeared at TG21.1's rear, quickly destroying or disabling five of them while the last three turned and tried to limp out of range.

"The desk weenies were right," Commander Lawrence Fish, her tactical officer, said in awe. "The Reds really exit those skip jumps underpowered. Those ships aren't accelerating at even half their full rate."

"You mean half the full rate we *think* they're capable of," she chided. He was likely correct, but bad things happened to naval officers who assumed every piece of intel from headquarters was unquestionably accurate. Still, the analysts in the Octagon had certainly been right about the Martians being unable to fight or maneuver well for several minutes after surfacing from their impossible string of short jumps through the void. They'd seen that twice now already here at Hyperion.

"Tell *Yorktown* to continue harassing those three remaining battlecruisers from Red Force Beta from behind," she ordered. "Leave Blue Squadron to assist them. Order the rest of our squadrons and *Enterprise* and *Midway* to turn and help Admiral Lafayette fight off Red Force Alpha."

As her officers, pilots, and ships hastened to follow her orders, Mary licked her lips in a mixture of satisfaction and worry. Up until this point, her secret squadron of stealth carriers had not been used in any fighting with the Reds. This mission was their coming out party, keeping Second Fleet's admiral—Lafayette had insisted on commanding the TG21.1 personally, arguing that he couldn't ask any other flag officer to act as bait—from getting killed in what would otherwise go into the records as a very successful mission.

And not just because they had essentially validated the naval analysts' theories about the Martians' new skip-jumping capabilities, including their ability to predict where enemy ships would ultimately surface from the void. The mission was also a success in providing a much-needed victory over a superior enemy force, giving the UEN officers and crews both revenge for Waypoint Charlie and a clear and unmistakable demonstration that Earth *could* win this war.

Unfortunately, to do that meant revealing Mary's ships to the enemy. Even if they managed to destroy every Martian ship around Hyperion, they'd no doubt already transmitted their sensor records back to Martian high command. The three top-of-the-line stealth carriers Mary commanded, with their revolutionary singularity drives, were no longer a secret from anyone, really. Assuming the Council didn't already somehow know about her ships, they would find out now as Mary's squadron joined the war with Mars in earnest, which gave the UEN and the Four Worlds one less advantage when the Council Navy finally arrived in force.

Of course, before she could really worry about that, she had to make sure she, her ships, and even her nation survived *this* war.

CHAPTER 34

Forge was bored out of his mind. He knew it was a common misconception in popular media that snipers like him could sit in one spot for weeks on end without ever feeling the emotional drain of the long wait. Maybe some could, but Forge had never been able to do it.

Sure, he could sit here for a week or so if he absolutely had to. He could even stay still for that entire time, using his stealth suit's facilities to eat, drink, and eject his waste. But that didn't mean he *liked* it, even a little. There were only so many breathing and relaxation exercises a guy could do before he ran out of things to occupy his mind. And since Forge's girlfriend, Gayle, had broken up with him a month ago, he couldn't even pass the time thinking about her.

Fortunately, none of the boredom of the last three days kept him from being vigilant. So when the aircar magically appeared from a hidden underground garage, and the pretty, middle-aged brunette left through the water tower's lone door and got in the car's back seat, Forge saw all of it happen.

As he watched the car drive away from the secret quantum comm facility and head in the rough direction of Las Vegas, hundreds of kilometers away, he finally broke comms silence, giving a single click on his comm so that the rest of his team would be ready.

CHAPTER 35

One Week Later; January 24, 732 P.D.

Joseph Blackmont woke to the sound of the car door opening. The chill of the cold desert night hit him, immediately piercing his business suit.

"We're here, sir," Umberto, his driver and bodyguard, announced unnecessarily as he held the door open for his boss.

Joseph rubbed his eyes and emerged from the rear seat of the comfortable car. It was annoying that operational security for the quantum entanglement comm site meant he couldn't just land an aircraft or a helicopter nearby. The nearest Loop station in Las Vegas was a nearly two-hour drive in a low-flying aircar, with an extra hour tacked on as Umberto randomized their route each time.

He stretched as he looked up at the night sky. At least he wasn't here to talk to Petrov again. The colonial Keeper had become increasingly angry each time Joseph spoke to him. Petrov's instructions, as of late, had been more and more erratic, and Joseph and Mikael Gorsky were both of the mind that something was happening in colonial space to delay the invasion. That wasn't necessarily a bad thing; it gave time for the war between Earth and Mars to sap both planets of resources and the will to fight. If all went well, they would simply surrender when the Council Navy arrived in force.

Joseph let Umberto lead him through the gate in the perimeter fence and into the facility's disguised high-security door, his two other bodyguards trailing behind him and watching for threats. Once inside, they took the rusty, rickety stairs down to another door, stepping through this one into the lushly appointed waiting room on the other side.

"Welcome, Mr. Blackmont," Noreen Smith greeted him, sitting in her usual spot behind the room's single desk. Joseph knew that behind that desk with her was a veritable arsenal. Anyone who made it past the facility's exterior veneer and this far would be in for a rude surprise. There was really no reason for a secret facility like this to have a waiting room, but they'd needed somewhere to set up the complex sensors that screened anyone who entered for weapons. Anyone unauthorized to bring one inside would quickly find themselves facing not just Noreen but a full security team waiting just behind one of the room's doors, as well as auto-turrets that would pop out of the ceiling and walls.

"Thank you, Noreen," Joseph said with a smile. "Just here to review some of the latest intel." One of the rules he and Gorsky had agreed on was that nothing the Keeper sent them from the colonies would ever leave this facility, either in physical or electronic form. It was vital to keep both the facility itself a secret as well as to avoid any possibility that anyone could learn that he and the UE president were collaborating with the enemy.

As he passed the reception desk, he stopped and turned to face the woman. Did you get your shopping trip in?" he asked.

Noreen smiled. "Yes, sir. Thank you, sir."

Joseph smiled back. Noreen was no receptionist. She was the best intelligence analyst he'd ever had. She'd almost threatened to quit when he'd told her she would be reassigned to the desert facility. Only permission to take periodic trips to nearby Las Vegas convinced her to stay. It was a risk, but not as big of a risk as losing the one and only person whom he trusted to help him keep up with the massive amounts of intel the Keeper had been sending them that needed to be continuously cross-referenced with that from Mikael Gorsky and Joseph's own people.

"I need your help with a few things," he told her. "My office. Twenty minutes."

She nodded, and Joseph continued his journey toward the elevator that would take him six levels down to his heavily armored office, which also guarded the one and only entrance to the quantum comm control chamber.

Forge Lewis and the other members of his team crept on their bellies toward the fake water tank. By now, the heat in their suits had built up to almost unbearable levels, but they would have to suffer for another fifty meters—and ten minutes—before they could vent the heat, lest they be detected too early.

Timing was everything on this mission. If they moved just a few seconds too soon or too late, they would sacrifice everything they'd come to do. And as the Majko had told Forge time and time again, this plan could not afford to fail.

Joseph was having a hard time focusing on the work in front of him. He was supposed to be compiling a summary of the war between Earth and Mars to send to the Keeper in their next call, but he kept getting distracted and checking the clock on his palm implant. Noreen was usually prompt, but twenty-three minutes had passed. He considered calling up to the reception desk to see what was taking her so long but decided to give her a few more minutes. If she was late, he was sure she had a good reason.

Donna Heinberg watched the clock on her palm implant carefully, trying to calm the churn in her stomach. This wasn't her first mission of this type, but something told her she'd never had, nor would she ever have again, a mission where the stakes were this high.

Of course, she'd also never had the kind of support on a mission like she had on this one. She had no idea how the readers had learned so much about the real Noreen Smith, but they seemed to know *everything* about the woman they'd called upon Donna to impersonate. Right down to what kind of clothes she always wore when Joseph Blackmont came to visit—she had a secret crush on her boss. The extra knowledge had been a massive boon to Donna. Being a blender meant she had no problem taking on the look of Smith, especially after spending a few days with the woman in the hotel room where the Majko's people had been holding the Blackmont employee in Las Vegas, but the trick was always in *acting* like those she impersonated.

Donna checked the clock again, seeing that it was four minutes past the time when Blackmont expected her in his office but still two minutes away from the mission's next phase. If Blackmont grew impatient and called up to her, or worse, sent someone to check on her, everything could fall apart. She just needed *two* more minutes.

Forge and his team lay still in the middle of the road just five meters from the deceptively weak-looking fence that ringed the fake water tank. Ten seconds left. He counted down the time in his head and then rose to his feet just as he heard the click of the fence's single gate unlocking.

"Go!" he cried to his team and the single non-operator among their number, knowing that a verbal command might be picked up on listening microphones, but even a short-range radio signal would *definitely* trigger an alarm.

As one, they rushed to the fence and through the gate, reaching the fake water tank just as the rusty-looking outer door snicked open. Forge made sure their guest got through the door before the last of his men entered and shut it behind them.

Joseph was getting annoyed. Noreen was more than five minutes late, and he needed her eye on a few reports. He pressed the intercom button on his desk. "Umberto," he called. "Can you pop out into the waiting room and see what's taking Noreen so long?"

Donna reached out to press the final button on her touchscreen but jerked it back quickly as the door next to her desk opened. One of the security men, the surly one who had arrived with Blackmont, stepped out and regarded her with raised eyebrows.

"Boss is waiting for you," he said, taking a step closer to stand over her. "You know he doesn't like being kept waiting, so . . ." He trailed off, eyebrows furrowing, and Donna's breath caught in her throat.

"Why did the outer door open?" he demanded, seeing something on the screen in front of her as his hand swept back for the gun at his hip.

Donna forced herself not to hesitate. She reached out and quickly hit the final command.

Five seconds late by the mission clock, the door at the bottom of the rickety stairs unlocked, and Forge pulled it open and rushed through, rifle at the ready. Before he got inside, he heard the boom of a gun. As he took in the scene, he saw the blender member of their team, Donna Heinberg, slump forward in her chair. A man stood above her with a smoking pistol.

Forge put a bullet right into the guy's head, and his team did the same with the four other Blackmont mercenaries who streamed out of the open door to one side of the desk.

It took only another couple of seconds for two of Forge's men to enter through that door and declare the security office beyond it secure.

Forge reached the desk and looked down with a frown at Donna Heinberg's lifeless body, slumped over in her chair. He didn't need to check for a pulse. The blender was gone.

"Plan B!" he called to his men, and two of them came forward and grabbed the corpse, taking it over to the elevator, where she should have enough warmth in her skin to still trigger the biometric palm scanner. Forge himself knew the same codes she had known, somehow secured by Reader Jinny Ambrosa from the real Noreen Smith.

A moment later, the elevator doors opened, and Forge led the way inside. Only once he was confident it hid no surprises did he motion for his guest to follow. The short blond woman did so without hesitation, staying silent and impassive as the rest of the team joined them, leaving behind just two of them to guard their escape route.

A light on Joseph's desk flashed red. He smiled, though his heart was racing. Did they really think they'd gotten in that easily? When Gorsky had passed along the intel from his spy in Perth, Joseph hadn't believed it at first. Did the readers truly think they could infiltrate a secret and secure Blackmont facility? All so they could read him? He was mildly flattered.

Of course, things wouldn't work out for the readers, especially for one of them. The trap was perfect, and the Keeper would be pleased beyond measure.

Forge was surprised that there wasn't a security team waiting for them just outside the elevator when it opened. They'd gotten this far much too easily, and it was nagging at him. He'd expected that if there were a trap waiting, it would be here. Not finding one made him more suspicious.

Still, there was nowhere to go but forward. He led his team across the antechamber and stopped at the single door on the other side. No surprise, it was locked. If it hadn't been, Forge would have likely ordered his team to immediately evacuate to the exfil site. Despite the Majko's insistence that this mission was far too important to fail, he wasn't keen on leading his team to their deaths.

"Jacobs, get the door," he commanded one of his men, and the demolitions expert stepped forward and started affixing a narrow cord of powerful explosives to the locking mechanisms. Then he stepped back and nodded at Forge.

The big operator turned to shield the short, blond woman with his body, his back to the explosives on the door. But when the shaped charge went off, it didn't send any substantial debris their way. He turned and motioned his men through the now-open doorway.

Joseph frowned as the door exploded inward. Sloppy. If they really meant to take him alive, they were surely going about it in a funny way. The charges they'd used to blow the door probably wouldn't have killed anyone inside, but they couldn't have been sure. So unprofessional.

He watched impassively as three large men came in through the door, assault rifles up and sweeping the room. Carefully, he raised his hands from where he still sat behind the desk, showing the attackers that he held no weapon. And he waited.

Another large man entered, his bearing clearly calling him out as the group's leader. The man kept his gun pointed straight at Joseph as he stepped aside to reveal a short young woman coming into the office behind him, the hood of her stealth suit pulled back to reveal her blond hair and brown eyes.

"Ah, Reader Ambrosa," Joseph said as cheerfully as he could muster, "to what do I owe the honor of your visit? Come to read me, have you?"

The leader of the assault team frowned at Joseph's tone, looking around the room carefully, doubtlessly expecting a trap.

Well, thought Joseph, *ask, and ye shall receive.* With his knee, he hit a button under his desk.

Forge saw the flash of triumph on Joseph Blackmont's face and was opening his mouth to call out a warning to his team when his entire world went white in a flash so bright that it overwhelmed his senses, just as it was surely designed to do.

His vision never had time to clear, nor did he feel the bullet that ended his life. Had he been able to register it, it would not have come as a great surprise.

Joseph smiled triumphantly and got up from his desk, the invisible personal shield around it—courtesy of plans shared by the Keeper—fizzling out with an audible buzzing noise as he did so. Those shields were something special, but their short operating life was an issue. He had his own people working on that in one of his research facilities in South America. Still, this one had done its job admirably, protecting him from any strays among the bullets his men had put into the attackers.

The enemy hadn't noticed the doors on either side of Blackmont's office. That was by design; he'd paid good money to ensure they seamlessly integrated into the walls. But it was still sloppy of the reader assault team leader not to be prepared for the ambush. Eight of Blackmont's best mercenaries had come out of those doors the second the stun strobe had gone off to disorient the team of readers. Joseph's own vision was still clearing from that, though he'd at least known to shut his eyes an instant before.

Coming around his desk, he smiled at the crouched form of the one surviving member of the reader team. The blond woman stood up at his approach, glaring at him with a tight frown.

"It is a pleasure to finally meet you in person, Reader Ambrosa," he said with a smile. He could afford to be friendly at this point, now that the woman was his captive. After all, his study of her special abilities would be so much quicker and more effective if he could elicit a modicum of cooperation from her. His false niceties probably wouldn't work to accomplish that, but they couldn't hurt either.

"You knew we were coming," the young reader accused.

Joseph kept smiling as he nodded. "Of course. We have our own spies in Perth, and we knew your entire plan. It was doomed from the start." He was half lying. They'd known the basics of the plan but not the entire thing. Noreen's betrayal had certainly been a surprise, though now Joseph suspected that his real assistant must have been replaced by a blender at some point. It had probably happened on her latest shopping trip to Vegas; he never should have allowed her to leave the facility in his absence. That had been sloppy. Now, the real Noreen was surely as dead as her blender clone was.

Pity.

Gorsky would be interested to know that the blenders were apparently helping the readers. That wasn't a good sign, and it could raise all sorts of complications if even two of the exiled groups of enhanced in Australia were cooperating.

"What happens now?" Jinny Ambrosa asked, still glaring at him.

Joseph shrugged. "Now, you're going to tell us everything the Majko and her friends taught you. And everything your father did when he engineered you. If you're lucky, that will give us what we need to know, and you can live out the rest of your life in relative peace." He studied her. The girl was certainly attractive, and Joseph was down a mistress. No, it would never work. He couldn't have her reading him every time they were together. Another pity.

"And if I don't talk?" she asked somberly. "I held out pretty well against your interrogations at the Crater."

He smiled again. "Yes, you did. But back then, we had to keep you alive and in one piece so that we could use you to discredit Pereira. Now . . ." He let his smile disappear dramatically. "Now we only need you alive. How many pieces you end up in, my dear, is entirely up to you."

"You're right about that part, at least," she replied.

Her hands, held above her head, were closed into fists. Joseph hadn't thought anything of it until the moment she opened her left hand and he saw the small button taped to her palm.

It was the last thing he ever saw before the series of explosions ripped through him and destroyed the delicate electronics in the next room, rendering the quantum entanglement comm useless and cutting off the one and only method Mikael Gorsky and the late Joseph Blackmont had to communicate with the Keeper to plan the downfall of Earth.

CHAPTER 36

Dave was tired. The last hour of his shift was always the worst, and he was counting down the minutes until he could leave and go home. Not that anything waited for him there. A microwave meal and a few hours of TV before he'd pass out on the couch for the evening. Either way, he still hated being at work.

Maybe it was the people who lived in this building. They were mostly the ultrawealthy or politicians, often both. Dave had the typical cynical citizen's view of how unfair it was that politicians always seemed to earn far more than their government salaries while in office. This building was full of those types; there was even a heavily guarded rear entrance for certain high-ranking government leaders to use to come and go as they pleased, hidden from the eyes of the public outside the front of the building.

Which meant that Dave, in his seat at the front desk, only got to deal with those deemed not important enough to use that rear entrance. Like Mrs. O'Doyle and her stupid little dogs that always barked at him whenever they passed through the lobby on their way for their twice-daily walks. Mrs. O'Doyle always gave Dave a look like it was somehow his fault her precious little mutts were yapping at him.

He cringed as the chime of the door announced a new arrival. One more haughty, self-important jerk who would probably either look at Dave imperiously or order him about like he was some kind of servant. But when he turned to see the front door opening, it was a very different type of person who walked through.

She was short and pretty, with long brown hair and bright green eyes, and she smiled at him as she strode across the lobby, straight toward his desk.

"Hi," she said, holding out a hand in greeting. "I'm Becky."

Dave took her hand and shook it, a little thrill going through him as her soft grip lingered.

"You're Dave, right?" she asked cheerfully.

He tilted his head in confusion. How did she know his name?

"It's on your name tag," she said with another smile, pointing to the tag on his chest. "Just like me. See, twins!" She pointed at her own name embroidered on the breast of her blue work shirt.

"Oh, yeah," Dave replied, feeling the blood rushing to his face. Then he remembered he did have a job. "Uh, what are you here for?"

"Just here to do the quarterly service check on the plumbing," she replied, motioning toward the bag of tools in her left hand. Dave peered over the desk to see them.

"Uh," he said lamely, "just one second." He pecked away at his touchscreen and frowned. "It says the quarterly service isn't until next week."

He looked up in time to see the pretty girl's smile disappear. "Oh no," she said. "Did I schedule it for the wrong day?"

He gave her an apologetic smile. "It's no big deal. Just come back next week."

Becky grimaced. "That's just it. I was in charge of scheduling the appointment, and I screwed up. I was supposed to set it for today, but" —she shrugged—"I guess I did it wrong. My boss is going to kill me."

Dave shook his head. "I don't think so. It's not that big of an error, right?"

She bit her lower lip and looked away, blinking rapidly. When she lifted her face back up to meet his gaze, he could see moisture in her eyes. "I just keep doing this. My boss said one more screwup, even a small one, and he'll fire me."

Dave sat there, embarrassed for her and not sure what to say. Luckily, she kept talking.

"You don't know what it's like out there, Dave," she said, motioning with one hand toward the lobby doors and the street outside. "You've got a great job here, but I'm just scraping by. And ever since my last boyfriend left me, it's just me and my little sister, and if I can't make the rent next week, then . . . then . . ." Before Dave could reply, Becky dropped her tool bag and buried her face in her hands, starting to cry in earnest.

Not knowing what else to do, Dave got up from his chair and moved around the desk to stand next to her. He didn't want to be too forward—she was way out of his league anyway—so he awkwardly reached out one hand and lightly patted her shoulder. "Come on," he said in a soothing voice, "it can't be that bad. He'll really fire you for just scheduling an appointment on the wrong day?"

She nodded, face still buried in her hands. Then she looked up at him again, her cheeks wet with tears. "I just keep messing up," she repeated. "And if I lose this job, then I'll lose my apartment and . . ." She put her face back down in her hands and started sobbing again.

"Uh, listen," Dave said, looking around to make sure that none of the building security guards had wandered up from the rear entrance. Finding they were still alone in the lobby, he leaned toward her and kept his voice low. "Your boss doesn't have to know. I can change the appointment in our system and let you in now. Then you can get the work done, and he'll never know you made a mistake."

"Dave, you'd do that for me?" she asked in astonishment, looking up at him again. "But you just met me."

He smiled, self-conscious about it, trying not to look too eager. "Sure, Becky, you seem like a good person. I don't want you to lose your apartment."

"Oh, Dave!" she cried and grabbed him in a hug, burying her face in his shoulder. "Who says there aren't still good men in the world?"

He hesitantly returned the hug. This was uncharted territory for him. His last girlfriend had lasted a week. That had been way back in high school.

Becky broke the hug first and used the sleeve of her uniform shirt to wipe the tears from her eyes and face. Then she picked up her work bag. "Okay, Dave, lead the way."

"Uh, sure. I just need your building access card so I can . . ." He trailed off as she bit her lower lip again, and her eyes welled up once more. "You forgot your card too, didn't you?"

Becky nodded forlornly. "I'm so sorry, Dave. You tried to help me, but I'm just a screwup, and I'm going to lose my apartment and . . ."

"No, you're fine," he said, thinking quickly. He certainly couldn't let her use *his* card. If building management found out, they'd fire him for sure. They probably wouldn't ever find out, but even a small chance was too much for him. He might hate this job, but he needed it.

"You know the worst part, Dave," Becky said, turning to leave. "I was supposed to have a date tonight with some guy I met online. But he messaged and canceled this morning. I should have known then that today was going to be a bad day, right? It was only margaritas at O'Malley's to watch the Rangers game. But it was the first date I've had lined up in months, and I was really looking forward to it. Guess it just wasn't meant to be, like this job. Then I meet a nice guy like you and you want to help me and everything, but I can't even get that right. Sorry. Bye, Dave."

She started walking away from him. Mind racing, Dave called after her. "Wait!"

The girl turned.

"You're a Rangers fan?" he asked, not sure why he chose *that* question to delay her departure.

She nodded. "I really think they have a shot this year with Hernandez bouncing back from his injured shoulder. Tonight's his first game back, and I was looking forward to watching it at the bar, but . . ." She shrugged.

"I could take you," he blurted out. "And listen, I'll let you use my access card, just this once, so you don't get fired."

The smile she gave him brightened Dave's entire week, as did the slightly longer hug she gave him before he scanned his card to open the elevators to let her inside. He didn't stop to think that, with his master card, he'd just given her access to every floor in the building, and not just the ones she would normally need to go to for the maintenance work she had planned.

Don't you think that was a bit over the top? the reader asked the conwoman sourly as the elevator doors closed on the smiling face of Dave the doorman.

Not at all, the conwoman replied. *That was so easy. You know, having you read that poor boy's entire life took all the fun out of it. I had to spice it up a little just to keep it interesting.*

Jinny frowned inside her own head, feeling like she should argue with the other woman but simply grateful that it had all worked thus far. She watched as the elevator climbed to the selected floor, the second highest, just under the penthouse.

Two floors away, she bid farewell to the conwoman and invited someone else out of the fog to take control.

When the elevator doors opened, Tyrus Tyne strode out with confidence, like he belonged there. The two beefy guys guarding the outside of the door halfway down the hall immediately zeroed in on him and watched warily as he approached, though he knew he looked far less intimidating in Jinny's body than he would in his own. The plumber's uniform also helped, he knew. Service people were often invisible in their own way.

"Stop right there," one of the men said, stepping forward but not bothering to put a hand on his gun. "What are you doing here?"

Tyrus smiled at him. "Just here to fix a leak in Apartment 1723," he replied, referencing the unit at the end of the hall. "I have the work order right here somewhere." He reached down and started to rummage through his tool bag.

The guy frowned. "There's nothing on the schedule for that, and this is a restricted floor. You're going to have to turn around and go back—"

He never got to finish his sentence. Tyrus pulled the pistol from the bag and shot twice, hitting both of the men with stun rounds before they could register the gun in his hand or the spit of his silenced shots.

They slumped to the ground, twitching a little, and Tyrus calmly stepped over and pulled the keycard off one of their belts, holding it up to the door control.

The door lock clicked open, and he stepped through. The two men inside the apartment didn't fare any better than their comrades outside, and Tyrus soon found himself looking down at a pretty blond woman sitting tensely on the apartment's couch as Jinny took control of her own body again.

"Cecily Johansen?" Jinny asked, though she already knew this was the woman she sought. She exactly matched the pictures Jordan Archer had shared with her while planning this mission, from her short blond hair and high Nordic cheekbones to her tall, willowy frame.

"Who sent you?" the woman asked, a challenge in her tone. Her eyes flicked to something behind Jinny.

There was no conscious thought involved in switching personalities this time. Tyrus was in control before Jinny even finished registering the movement of Cecily's eyes. He leaped their body to one side and twisted them in the air, pulling the pistol's trigger twice.

The presidential guard who'd been sneaking up on Jinny from behind fell as his friends had before him, but not before pulling the trigger of his own gun, which thankfully spat a bullet too high and to one side, shattering a vase on the table behind the couch but not coming close to either Cecily or Tyrus.

Getting up quickly from the floor, Tyrus whirled on the woman. "Are there any more of them?" At the same time, he cursed himself for not clearing the apartment. He'd been worried Cecily might try to run; so had Jinny. And while the bullet hadn't hit either of them, it had been an unsilenced shot. It would only be a matter of time until someone came to investigate.

Cecily shook her head. "No, only the three. Who sent you?" she repeated

"A mutual friend," Tyrus answered cagily as he quickly searched the doors into the adjoining rooms anyway. "I'm sure there are recording devices all over in here, so I won't say the name if that's all right with you. But he says to tell you he misses cleaning with you."

The woman visibly relaxed at the code phrase Archer had given

Jinny. She stood up from the couch. "We need to go. The guards downstairs will be on their way up shortly if they're not already coming."

Tyrus let Jinny take control again, and the reader shook her head. "We need to change first." She rummaged through the tool bag and pulled out two sets of clothing, throwing one to Cecily.

Dave was in a panic. Four different residents had called down to report hearing a gunshot. Security had already called him from the rear entrance, screaming at him not to let anyone leave the building. Less than a minute later, one of the beefy security guys who usually worked in the back joined Dave in the lobby, facing the elevator doors and keeping a hand on the gun at his waist.

"What's going on?" Dave asked the guy, but the guard just shook his head on his massive neck and didn't answer.

Dave knew he was done for. With something like this, there would be a full investigation, and building management would discover he'd let that cute plumber, Becky, into the building and onto the elevator using his own access card. They'd fire him immediately, even though the gunshots certainly had nothing to do with him or the pretty girl.

The elevator dinged, and Dave almost jumped out of his skin. The bulky guard tightened his hand on his pistol and pulled it halfway out of its holster, tensing as the door opened to reveal . . .

Two beautiful women in cocktail dresses stumbled out of the elevator, supporting each other and looking around in wide-eyed fright. "They're shooting!" one of them wailed. "Who's shooting? We have to get out of here!"

They lurched toward the guard, who looked beyond them to make sure no one else was coming out of the elevator. As he did so, the women closed the distance, running in their high-heeled shoes. One of them stumbled again and fell into the guard, who reacted by pulling his hand off the gun so he could use both arms to catch her. Just as he did, Dave heard a spitting noise, and the guard went limp, falling to the floor and revealing one of the women—a brunette—holding a pistol.

"Becky?" Dave asked in shock.

The pistol-wielding definitely-not-a-plumber smiled apologetically at him as the two women kicked off their heels and raced toward the lobby door. "Sorry, Dave!" she called back. "I found another date for tonight!"

He was so shocked and flummoxed that he didn't even think to follow the two women out the door to catch the license number of the aircar that stopped out front for barely long enough for them to get inside.

CHAPTER 37

Two days after the dual missions to the desert and the city, the Majko strode into a meeting room with Jinny and Kelly on her heels. The factors in the room, along with their aides, stood up as she entered, as was their tradition.

That's where the decorum ended. "What is *she* doing here?" Factor Lamkin demanded, pointing at Jinny. "She's supposed to be dead!" Then, as if realizing how what he'd just said sounded, he stumbled over his next words. "Th-this is a closed meeting. My Majko, I demand that she be removed."

The Majko didn't respond at first, leveling her gaze at the middle-aged Lamkin until he lowered his finger self-consciously. "She is here as my guest, Factor. She brings information that is vital to this council."

The man frowned but didn't argue further. But another factor, Harries, spoke up. "What sort of information, my Majko?"

The old woman looked around the room at each of the eight factors, those she trusted to help her run the affairs of Perth and the lives of every reader on planet Earth. Each of them met her gaze without flinching. Then she stepped forward and took her seat at the head of the table. Only after taking a few moments to settle herself did she respond.

"I'm afraid we have a traitor in our midst."

The simple declaration had the desired impact. Every one of the factors looked shocked and then indignant. "Surely not in this room!" objected Factor Wesley, her face in a frown as she looked around at all her fellow factors and then at the edge of the room, where the various aides sat in shocked silence.

"Yes, in this room," the Majko said calmly, drawing every eye back to her. "Because it was only in this room that we discussed the mission to capture Joseph Blackmont."

"A mission that failed spectacularly," Lamkin interjected. "And one that Reader Ambrosa was supposed to be part of." He looked at the young reader accusingly. "Which makes me think perhaps *she* betrayed us."

"Patience, Factor Lamkin," the Majko admonished him. "I promise that the identity of the traitor will be revealed." Without waiting for the man to respond, she turned in her seat and motioned to Jinny. "Reader Ambrosa, if you please."

Jinny stepped forward to address the gathered factors, standing at the Majko's shoulder. "I'm afraid the traitor is someone very close to this group," she said evenly. "One who knew exactly what our plan was for infiltrating the secret complex where Joseph Blackmont was hiding." Her voice caught on the last part. Jinny had been enraged to hear about the deaths of the entire team sent to capture Blackmont, including the blender who had posed as her. That the mission had met its secondary objective of destroying the quantum comm did little to console her.

So it was no surprise that she had a dangerous edge in her voice when she turned and pointed a finger squarely at Kelly Martin.

All eyes turned to the mousy brunette, who looked just as shocked as the rest of them. "Me?" she asked, edging toward the door.

"Seize her!" the Majko called, and two security men stepped through the door, each grabbing one of the woman's arms. "How could you?" she accused. "After I trusted you, made you my confidant and my friend!"

Abruptly, Kelly's expression changed from one of confusion and hurt to a hard look of barely contained anger. "How could I? Do you even hear yourself, you old crone? All this talk of wanting to free the readers, yet you do *nothing*. When the Council comes, they'll put us back in our rightful place as rulers over the mere mortals who lack our abilities! They'll . . ."

As Kelly Martin issued forth her angry manifesto, no one noticed Jinny stepping away from the Majko's side and working her way around the edge of the room. Only when she was in position did she catch the old woman's eye and see her almost imperceptible nod. At the agreed-upon signal, Jinny reached out with her ungloved right hand and gently brushed the neck of the man in front of her.

The Majko watched as Factor Lamkin whirled at the feel of Jinny Ambrosa's touch on his neck. She could see his entire body go rigid as he realized what had just happened. If that wasn't confirmation enough for her, the nod from Reader Ambrosa certainly was.

"Factor Lamkin!" she roared, her voice cutting above Kelly's rehearsed and entirely fabricated confession. "Why did you betray your own people?"

If the room had gone silent earlier when Jinny had pointed the finger at Kelly, it now went quieter still, as if everyone in attendance were holding their breath.

Lamkin looked back at her, his eyes wide, his mouth working but no words coming out. Then, predictably, perhaps, he bolted for the door.

Kelly got there first, released by the two guards, who were in on the hoax. She whirled in the air, her leg shooting out and the heel of her right foot planting itself into Lamkin's stomach, stopping him in his tracks and doubling him over in pain. An instant later, Kelly wrenched the man's hands painfully behind his back and secured them with a zip tie.

Everyone else watched in shock as the ordinarily mousy and unassuming Kelly Martin showed her true colors for the first time—as the Majko's very secret and very deadly bodyguard.

"Now then," the old woman said, turning back to face the other factors and bringing their attention back to her and away from the gasping Lamkin, whom Kelly had shoved to the floor. "Let us discuss how we recover from the betrayal of one so close to us. And let us discuss what to do next."

To everyone's surprise, Lamkin laughed. "It's too late, you fool!" he cried almost gleefully. His taunt was punctuated by the sounds of distant gunfire. "The president has decided that your run as the Majko ends today."

Kelly put a hand to her ear, listening through an unseen earpiece. "Commandos in the building, my Majko. We have to get you and the factors to safety."

Jinny watched as Kelly grabbed the still-cackling Lamkin with one hand and the Majko with the other, leading both of them out of the room and down the hall. For a second, the other factors milled about in confusion, before they too followed the bodyguard. Jinny trailed the group at a short distance.

Kelly led everyone down the hall and around a corner. There, a nondescript door opened after she entered a code into the control. As it swung open, it was revealed to be a disguised ten-centimeter-thick vault door leading into a panic room.

"Everyone inside!" Kelly snapped, and passed Lamkin off to the two security men for safekeeping. Jinny watched as the leaders of Perth all entered, then Kelly looked at her. "Same goes for you, Reader Ambrosa. Into the room, please."

Jinny shook her head, knowing what Kelly intended. "You'll need help."

The Majko's assistant-turned-bodyguard studied her for a moment, then shrugged. Leaving the door open, she ducked inside the panic room and emerged moments later with two assault rifles, handing one to Jinny and putting the sling of the other over her neck. Then she closed the thick metal door and motioned for Jinny to follow her.

They stopped inside a waiting room right off the elevators, crouching down behind a large marble desk that usually housed the receptionist for the Majko and her Council of Factors, all of whom had their offices on this floor. Kelly listened to her earpiece again and then turned to Jinny.

"There were eight of them. They hit the building hard and fast. Security took out two before they gassed the lobby. I've shut down the elevators remotely to slow them down, but they're in the stairwells."

Jinny nodded at the woman's quick synopsis. Then Kelly shot her a look. "Um, listen, Reader Ambrosa, no offense, but do you mind channeling Tyrus Tyne? You're holding that gun all wrong."

Jinny blushed and looked down at the assault rifle in her hands, held awkwardly with one hand actually wrapped around the barrel. She nodded, and an instant later, Tyrus emerged from the fog and took control. Immediately, he reset his hands on the weapon.

"Call out targets as you see them. I'll cover the door to the east stairwell, you cover the west," he told Kelly, naturally taking control of the situation.

To his and Jinny's surprise, Kelly didn't argue. Any further talk cut off when they heard the sound of one of the stairwell doors opening. Tyrus peeked around the large, solid reception desk to see a man in tactical armor emerge from the stairwell he was covering, the gun in the man's hand sweeping the space between the elevator banks.

Tyrus waited a slow count of two until a second man emerged behind the first. Then he sighted with the rifle and fired twice, both shots taking the second man in the head and neck, dropping him instantly. The first man to emerge quickly returned fire as he tried to backstep to the stairwell door, but Tyrus dropped him with a shot to the head as the enemy soldier's fire peppered the reception desk.

The open stairwell door closed as someone inside pushed it shut. Silence reigned for a few moments in stark contrast to the sound of the gunfire.

"You notice anything?" Tyrus asked Kelly.

"No uniforms. Custom guns. One had a bullpup, but the other had the standard M7 body."

Tyrus nodded, the feel of Jinny's ponytail bouncing with the motion quite strange to him. "Not regular soldiers. And too sloppy to be special forces."

"You're thinking Blackmont's people?"

He nodded again. "Would make sense. Gorsky can't send government resources directly against us without someone asking questions. Mercs are the best alternative." He heard the noise of at least one stairwell door opening a crack. "Brace!" he yelled, then crouched down below the reception desk, putting both hands over his ears and squeezing his eyes shut, trusting Kelly to do the same.

He didn't hear the clattering of the grenades being tossed their way. But he did hear the crash of thunder that accompanied the bright lights visible even through eyelids closed tightly as the two flashbangs went off in quick succession.

Tyrus waited only an instant before he opened his eyes and uncovered his ears, grabbing his assault rifle again and then peering out around the edge of the desk. He had the briefest impression of figures running toward them before he squeezed off two shots and then ducked back behind the desk as bullets slapped the floor all around him.

Through his ringing ears, he vaguely heard Kelly's rifle fire several times. He popped out again, this time looking up and over the desk and firing two more shots, dropping the lead mercenary in the four-man rush. Before he could shift his aim to the next man in line, Kelly's bullets dropped him.

That left only two mercenaries, but they were already too close to the reception desk, just a couple of meters away, and their return fire forced both Tyrus and Kelly to take cover again. Before they could consider popping up to take aim once more, the two mercenaries were there, on either side of the desk, holding their rifles aimed at Tyrus's and Kelly's heads.

"Drop it!" one of the mercs yelled, and Tyrus removed his hands from his assault rifle, letting it hang from the sling around Jinny's neck. "Now come out slowly," the man ordered.

Tyrus stood, hands held high, and followed the direction the merc indicated with the barrel of his rifle, walking out from behind the desk to stand in front of it. Kelly mirrored his movements on the other side, and soon they were standing next to each other, the two surviving mercenaries covering them.

Both of the attackers looked upset, and one kept casting glances toward his downed comrades. Tyrus could see that the men were on a hair trigger, looking for any excuse to kill him and Kelly. But then one of them pulled a printed photo out of his pocket and held it up in front of him, comparing it with Tyrus's—really Jinny's—face.

"It's her," he told his partner. "Kill the other one, then we'll find the Majko."

"Not without my help, you won't," Kelly rushed to say.

The two mercenaries traded looks, and the first one shrugged. "Fine, but you don't need both legs to tell us where your boss is."

Kelly screamed and dropped to the floor as the second mercenary shot her in the thigh. She reached down reflexively to grab the wound, but instead, her hands went to the rifle still on its sling. Tyrus saw the move before the mercs did and took action.

He dived Jinny's body forward, staying low. The first mercenary's rifle barked, but the bullets went over Tyrus's head, and he closed the distance and tackled the man in his midsection. The mercenary cried out and reflexively let go of his gun to grapple with the small blond woman who had just knocked the wind out of him. As they both fell back, Tyrus heard the sound of gunfire. Hoping that it was Kelly who took the shots and not the second merc, he ignored the sound and continued to push the first merc back and down to the hard marble floor.

The man hit the deck on his back, Jinny's fairly light frame landing on top of him. Had it really been Tyrus Tyne who had tackled him, it might have ended the fight right then and there. But Jinny weighed less than half what Tyrus did regardless of what persona was in control of her body.

Luckily, Tyrus had anticipated that, and as the mercenary tried to push Jinny's body off of him, Tyrus reached down and grabbed the pistol at the man's belt. He aimed and pulled the trigger twice, and the merc went still beneath him.

Tyrus pushed himself off the dead man and whirled in a crouch, pistol extended, to see that Kelly's attacker was likewise on the ground, the Majko's bodyguard standing over him.

"You okay?" she asked Tyrus, and he nodded, getting back to his feet. "Uh, do you mind bringing Reader Ambrosa back for a second?"

Tyrus nodded and ceded control of Jinny's body back to her. A second later, Jinny cocked her head at Kelly. "What do you need?"

"Read these guys, will you?" Kelly asked. "We need to know if there are any more of them coming."

Jinny frowned but didn't argue. She first read the man she—Tyrus, really—had grappled with and shot. Then she moved on to the other corpses one by one. Finally, she hit the jackpot, reading the man who turned out to be the leader of the mercenary squad.

She stood up and frowned at Kelly. "They were just the advance team. Their job was to capture the Majko and the factors and hold them hostage until their reinforcements arrived."

Kelly swore under her breath. "How many reinforcements are we talking?"

Jinny grimaced. "A lot. These were Blackmont mercenaries, just as Tyrus thought. But Gorsky convinced the UE Army that the readers in Perth were planning a rebellion—taking advantage of the war with Mars. The Army is going to hit the city hard."

The bodyguard's shoulders slumped even as they heard the whine of multiple shuttles in the distance.

"Thank you, General, and well done," Mikael Gorsky said with a smile at the man on the screen.

General Perkins of the United Earth Army gave his president a sharp salute as Mikael reached out to cut the connection. The instant the screen went blank, the smile on the president's face turned to a scowl.

"Well, that was unsatisfying," the only other person in the presidential office said.

Mikael looked across his desk at Kyle Blackmont, Joseph's oldest son. Only in his thirties, Kyle had always been the heir apparent to his father's empire. Now, that inheritance had become a reality in the worst way possible.

Not that either of them would actually miss the elder Blackmont. Mikael had secretly despised the man. Kyle, despite being his child, had resented Joseph in ways that went beyond a son waiting for his due.

But while neither of them would mourn the man, they would lament the destruction of the quantum comm facility. Now that they were cut off from Keeper Petrov, the president's carefully laid plans threatened to unravel.

"How sure are you that the reader got away?" Mikael asked the younger Blackmont.

Kyle frowned. "My people reported engaging her in Perth before their comms went dark. The blond woman at the comm facility must have been a blender disguised to look like her."

Mikael grunted. He'd been equal parts elated and enraged to learn that Ambrosa had died at the comm facility with Joseph. It meant he didn't have to deal with the impetuous reader anymore, but it also meant he couldn't deliver her to the Keeper as Petrov had demanded. He wasn't sure how he felt now that he knew she was still alive.

"What I don't understand is how could she have gotten out of Perth so quickly," Kyle continued. "You gave Perkins the specs of that stealth shuttle they stole from *Enterprise*. The army should have been able to detect it trying to leave the city, or the Navy should have been able to intercept it in orbit. What happened?"

Mikael frowned. By all rights, Kyle Blackmont shouldn't even know about the stealth carrier UENS *Enterprise*. The entire program was rated above top secret, and most of the Navy's admirals didn't know the ship or its two sisters existed. Even though they'd briefly shown themselves at the battle of Hyperion, that had been far from public view.

But Joseph had known all about every top secret Navy project, including Mary Bol's three ships. Apparently, he'd shared the information on them with his son—or perhaps Kyle had simply hacked his father's files and learned that way.

No matter. Soon, the existence of those ships wouldn't matter.

What *did* matter, unfortunately, was the fact that Jinny Ambrosa had once again escaped. Mikael had already been planning the raid on Perth even before Joseph Blackmont's death and Cecily Johansen's escape. For months, he and Joseph had been planting a breadcrumb trail of evidence that pointed toward the readers in Perth being in league with the Martians. Two weeks ago, Mikael had shared that evidence with his security council.

They'd been planning to send the army into Perth in a month, perhaps two. Mikael had planned to play on the generational fear that most UE citizens already had for the enhanced. Announcing the duplicity of the readers and putting their city—along with the other enhanced populations, eventually—under martial law was intended to make surrendering the enhanced in Australia far easier from the standpoint of public outcry and logistics when Petrov's Navy finally arrived.

But the loss of the quantum comm and Cecily's escape had forced him to move his timetable up. As a result, they'd gone into Perth with less careful planning. And while they'd captured the Majko and her factors, Jinny Ambrosa had been allowed to escape once more. Nor had any of the Army or Kyle Blackmont's mercs been able to find Jordan Archer or Cecily Johansen.

"So, what now?" Kyle asked, his voice a little less confident after the president hadn't responded to his first two questions.

"Now," Mikael said in a low growl, "we crush the Martians on one front, and the rest of Australia on the other."

Neither of the men smiled at the prospect.

"You were right. They knew exactly what to look for," Landon Hartman said from his pilot seat as they watched the squadron of four UEN destroyers shift orbits to chase the stealth shuttle.

They'd avoided trying to launch the shuttle immediately from Perth into the atmosphere. Instead, Landon had brought it low through the city and picked up Jinny from the roof of the government center just before the army's assault shuttles reached that area.

Then it had been nape-of-the-earth flying from there, across the continent first to the east and then to the north through the mostly uninhabited center of Australia. From there, they'd flown low over the Timor Sea to East Timor and then on to Indonesia, where they'd finally landed.

Now, they had lifted off from Jakarta, hoping to get lost in the normal traffic from the major Southeast Asian port.

Unfortunately, that part of the plan hadn't worked. They'd managed to elude the Army's sensors, which were still watching the airspace immediately around Perth. But the Navy, knowing exactly what to watch for and able to watch a wider area from orbit, had caught the stealth shuttle's sensor signature far more quickly than they could have expected.

Jinny sat in the copilot's chair. Besides Tyrus, at least four more of the personas in her head had flight experience. She stayed ready to call upon any of them should Landon need assistance. Now, she watched helplessly on the shuttle's sensor plot as the four destroyers quickly moved to cut off the stealth shuttle's escape vector, and a UEN battle-cruiser shifted into position to support the smaller ships.

"Ready, Reader Ambrosa?" Landon asked from the pilot's seat.

Jinny nodded and channeled Tyrus, allowing him to move her hands onto the copilot's control yoke.

Captain Joe Montgomery of the battlecruiser UENS *Franklin* smiled grimly as the four destroyers dispatched to cut off the stealth shuttle's escape forced the small craft to abandon its desperate evasion maneuvers.

Joe had to admit that whoever was flying the little shuttle was a terrific pilot. At one point, the craft had executed a daring and dangerous turnover in atmo that should have torn it apart or sent it into an uncontrollable spin. But the pilot had expertly used their thrusters to keep his craft together, and the sudden vector change caught the destroyers flatfooted. For a few minutes, it had looked like the stealth shuttle might evade capture.

But then *Franklin* had come over the horizon, putting several blasts across the small shuttle's bow, with Joe's comm officer broadcasting a threat to destroy the craft if it didn't stop its evasion attempts and prepare to be boarded.

He watched now as the four destroyers quickly cut off the shuttle pilot's attempt to reverse direction again to flee from *Franklin*. One of the destroyers got close enough to fire a warning shot with such precision that it burned off one of the stealth shuttle's stabilizers. That finally convinced the pilot that they had no chance to escape.

Twenty minutes later, Joe stood with *Franklin*'s Marine contingent as the stealth shuttle was brought in to land in his battlecruiser's docking bay. The Marines surrounded the small craft before it completely settled to the deck, and Joe nodded to Marine Lieutenant Huan, who signaled to two Navy techs to scurry forward and hack the shuttle's entry hatch.

They needn't have bothered. The hatch gave way to their simple request for access, and Huan led four of his Marines on board while the rest waited outside, guns still pointed at the cockpit windows and the open hatch. Joe waited in eager anticipation. He had no idea who was actually on the little shuttle, but the orders to interdict it had come from the president himself, so the occupants had to be important.

That meant that whoever caught the shuttle would draw the president's attention. Joe smiled at the thought of even perhaps getting a medal at Government House. Or maybe a promotion.

Lieutenant Huan poked his head out of the hatch and yelled, "Clear!"

Excited to see who his prize was, Joe stepped forward, but he stopped in his tracks as the Marine shook his head.

"Sorry, Captain," Huan reported. "It's empty. Someone was flying it remotely, near as we can tell."

Joe's visions of promotions and presidential accolades shattered in an instant, replaced by trepidation about how he was going to explain this to his superiors.

Landon sat back in the pilot's seat with a satisfied grunt. After a moment of flexing his hands and cracking his knuckles, he nodded for Tyrus to shift control of their small cargo shuttle back to the pilot's console. Tyrus did so, then quickly returned control of Jinny's body back to the reader.

"I can't believe that worked," Jinny said in wonder as she watched the four UEN destroyers and the battlecruiser return to their prior orbital paths.

Landon nodded next to her. "Figured that Gorsky must have told them to watch for the stealth shuttle. Sometimes, you give people what they want to see, and they miss what's right in front of their faces." He pulled back on the yoke to move the cargo shuttle they'd secured in Jakarta into a line of similar ships streaming from Earth to Luna. To anyone watching, they'd be just another shipment heading from Asia to Lunar markets desperate for fresh fruit and vegetables on the barren moon.

"That was great flying," Jinny told him honestly.

Landon blushed. "Lot easier to fly a shuttle remotely when no one's shooting at you personally," he said, deflecting the praise.

Temperance Jimenez poked her head into the cockpit from the small crew area. "It worked?"

Jinny nodded. "Your boyfriend did an amazing job. Bought us way more time than we hoped for."

Next to her, the pilot blushed more furiously. He gave a little cry of surprise when Temperance moved up behind him and nibbled on his ear. From the smirk on the hacker's face, Jinny knew the girl was messing with her boyfriend, but it didn't mean she wanted to be there for it.

"I'm going to go back and see what this thing has on board to eat," she said uncomfortably, unstrapping herself.

Landon grunted an acknowledgment, but Temperance didn't appear to have heard her.

Once Jinny was out of the cockpit, she immediately ran into the shuttle's fourth and final occupant.

"Those two being gross again?" Jordan Archer asked wryly, handing Jinny what looked like a freshly made sandwich.

She nodded and eyed the unexpected meal gratefully. "What about you?" she asked the blender. "I'm surprised you were okay to separate from Cecily so soon after getting her back."

Jordan frowned. "Well, you've read me . . . twice now. You know how she would feel if I didn't see this through to the end. But there's no way I'm putting her in a position where she could possibly fall back into Gorsky's dirty hands." He shrugged. "I miss her, but she's halfway to Europa by now, and she's got money and influence there. She'll be safe, which is all I really care about."

Jinny considered his words for a moment, taking a bite of the surprisingly good sandwich and chewing as she thought. Once she'd swallowed, she smiled at Jordan. "Thanks."

"For what?" he asked, eyebrows arching upward in surprise.

"For trusting us to rescue Cecily. For not betraying us. And for saving Tyrus and me at the Crater."

He looked embarrassed. "You shouldn't be thanking me, Reader Ambrosa. It was largely my fault you were in that situation on Luna. But I couldn't let them just kill Tyrus like that or put you back in that cell." He shuddered visibly. "And Cecily would have never forgiven me if I let my feelings for her trump the safety of the entire Sol system."

She smiled again at his attempt to defect the praise. "Regardless," she said. "Thank you for all of that—and for the sandwich, of course."

Before he could try again to downplay his good deeds, she left him and went into the shuttle's small bunkroom, collapsing onto one of the tiny bunks and eating the rest of her sandwich, too tired and hungry to care that she was getting crumbs everywhere. Mere minutes after her last bite, she was asleep.

CHAPTER 38

Five Days Later; February 1, 732 P.D.

Creighton Horvath was extremely unhappy. He'd been trying to get a meeting with the Keeper for the better part of a week. Usually, the small cadre of speakers who formed Petrov's inner circle within the Twenty met at least once a week. Beyond that, Creighton usually met one-on-one with Petrov every few days. All such meetings had been canceled with no explanation, and he knew from speaking with others in the Twenty that he wasn't alone in that. Petrov had refused to see anyone for several days now.

Not even Lara Owens had been able to give Creighton any intel as to what her boss was up to. Petrov had closed out his own people as well, with the exception of Ebby Hall, his chief of staff. And Ebby was an enacter; even if she'd been amenable to telling Creighton or anyone else what the Keeper was up to, she simply couldn't unless he gave her explicit permission.

The sudden disappearance of Petrov from the society of the Twenty and the broader Assembly was concerning in the extreme. Creighton's one-time friend had been getting increasingly erratic lately and seemed to have become wholly obsessed with launching the invasion of the Four Worlds as quickly as possible. He'd stopped listening to reason long ago, but at least he'd still talked with the others about his decisions. Now, he wouldn't even meet with them to do that.

Something had happened that Petrov wasn't sharing. Maybe the man had gotten a message from his collaborators or spies in the Sol system, and learned something that he didn't like. Maybe, just maybe, that meant the invasion would be delayed until the Navy was truly ready to conquer Earth and Mars—even if they joined forces.

Unfortunately, Creighton didn't believe that. Petrov had lost whatever reason he'd once had, and there would be little Creighton could foresee happening that would dissuade the Keeper from launching the attack as soon as humanly possible.

Which meant, perhaps, that the time for more direct action had finally come. Which brought him to the note in his holo from Lara Owens. The wording was cryptic—even the most advanced encryptions couldn't be entirely trusted—but the meaning was clear. The woman was suggesting that another member of the Twenty was equally dissatisfied with the Keeper's behavior of late, though it was a name Creighton never would have expected.

"Kim," he said through the intercom. "Please set a meeting up with Constantina Yenin. Today, if possible. Thank you, Kim."

Yes, he thought after his assistant cut the connection, *maybe the time for action has indeed finally come.*

If Landon Hartman had ever questioned his decision to join Corey O'Leary's staff instead of becoming a commercial pilot, the shuttle flight from Earth to Mars would have cleared those doubts up in an instant. It was one of the longest and most boring voyages of his life.

They hadn't been able to go straight to Mars, obviously. Not only was there no commercial traffic between the two planets, but their standard commercial shuttle was about as stealthy as a flying brick. There would be absolutely no way they could sneak past the two huge UEN and Martian Navy fleets that faced off across the neutral zone.

So they'd had to take the long way around. After Luna, Landon had filed a legitimate flight plan for a cargo delivery run to a small asteroid mining operation on a rock called EB-568932. As the name implied, the asteroid wasn't large enough to merit a nickname, but it was claimed by United Earth, so it wasn't all that strange that a shuttle would haul cargo to it from Luna.

Of course, Landon had never had any intention of actually arriving at EB-568932. But it gave him an excuse to fly past the orbit of Mars and into the asteroid belt. From there, he guided the shuttle through the belt, disappearing in the traffic of mining and cargo ships that hopped from one asteroid to another until he arrived on the leeward side of the red planet. From there, his plan was simple: a run from the belt to Mars, broadcasting as he got close a request to meet with Corey O'Leary and Tyrus Tyne.

He hoped it would work, and thought it should—assuming O'Leary and Tyne were even still on Mars. If they weren't, or if somehow the Martians had thrown them both in prison as spies when the war started, then this trip was going to be far shorter than Landon hoped.

But despite all that, it had taken five entire days to get to this point at the cargo shuttle's glacial acceleration. Five. Long. Days. And though he was now piloting the shuttle through the most dangerous part of the journey, he was bored out of his mind.

A light step on the deck behind him alerted him to the presence of someone else entering the cockpit. Arms encircled him from behind, and someone lightly kissed his ear, making him stifle a giggle that would have been very out of place in the cockpit of a ship hurtling toward enemy lines.

"How goes it, Captain?" Temperance asked as she released her hold on him and slipped into the copilot's seat at his side.

He shook his head but couldn't hide the smile on his lips. "I've told you, Tempie, it's just a shuttle. I'm the pilot, not the captain. Reader Ambrosa is in charge of this mission."

Temperance huffed, pulling her thin legs up so she could sit cross-legged on the seat. "I don't know, Landy, that reader creeps me out. Every time she looks at me, it's super weird, like she knows things about me or like there's some joke about me that she gets, but I don't."

Landon shuddered a little in his seat. He knew exactly what she was talking about. Jinny Ambrosa was around his age, but whenever he was around her, he got the distinct feeling that she was somehow much older and more experienced than he was. He knew some small part of her special abilities—Corey had told him the basics when he'd enlisted Landon's help to rescue the girl from the moon prison—but he felt certain there was far more to it than the little he'd been told.

That was confirmed by the fact that the Majko had prioritized Jinny's escape from Australia over her own, or perhaps the old woman simply hadn't wanted to leave her people behind.

"So, what's new?" Temperance asked, drawing his attention back to her. She pecked idly on the touchscreen console in front of her, appearing bored but, knowing her, probably reprogramming the shuttle's systems in some fundamental way. He just hoped she didn't break it.

"Nothing since the last hour you were up here," he replied dryly.

She eyed him with a raised eyebrow. "I can leave," she teased, "go back there with Miss Creepy Reader and Blender Boy. Do you even understand what it's like seeing a freaky blender changing day to day until he looks like some weird masculine cross between me and a blond girl scout? Have you ever seen a girl scout with purple hair?"

Landon had made the mistake of picking up a water bottle from next to him and taking a sip, which he now unceremoniously spit up all over his pilot's console as her statement drew an involuntary laughing fit.

He was about to scold her for making him do it when the console started beeping at him. His first, fleeting thought was that the water had hit something vital, but the tone of the beep and the image that sprang to life on the screen disabused him of that quickly.

"What the—" Temperance started to yell, but her voice was lost in two more alarms that sounded in Landon's ear as he followed her gaze out the forward viewport and took in the impossible sight in front of them. Reacting quickly, he jerked the control yoke to one side and hit the throttle, instinctively taking evasive action in the sluggish shuttle as a massive ship appeared literally out of nowhere and fired at them.

Mary Bol waited grimly as *Enterprise*'s Marines surrounded the boxy cargo shuttle on the deck of her ship's forward docking bay. Next to her, Commander Trey Kaplan tensed along with three of his SEALs. Mary trusted her Marines without question. But since the war had started, the tall, iron-jawed SEAL team leader refused to allow anyone else to watch after her personal security. She indulged him, if only because it made the man easier to work with and gave the restless SEALs under his command something to do. *Enterprise,* after all, was a *stealth* carrier, appearing and striking usually from close quarters using its fighters and then disappearing back into the dark of space before the enemy could get a shot at it. It made for some exciting naval engagements, but the lack of any boarding actions meant that the SEALs on board were terribly bored.

She watched as Marine Major Thomas gave her a nod to indicate that his men were ready. Then she herself nodded to the two engineers who stood ready to breach the shuttle's hatch. The little craft had tried to maneuver out of range as soon as *Enterprise* had shown itself, but it had been almost laughably slow. The carrier's boarding grapples had stopped its flight and forced it into the docking bay within less than ten minutes of their first warning shot being fired. Unfortunately, several calls to the little ship had gone unanswered, so they really had no idea what to expect on the other side of that hatch.

Mary squared her shoulders as the two engineers forced the hatch open. She had a pretty good idea of who would disembark from that shuttle. She'd received the flash alert from UEN command about the empty stealth shuttle—*her* ship's stealth shuttle—being captured in orbit over Earth. Naval Intelligence had scoured the orbital sensor readings and finally narrowed down the possibilities to three different small craft that could have used the stealth shuttle as a remote-controlled decoy. Two of those craft had been found quickly, regular supply shuttles between Earth and Luna. But the third, *this one,* now in her forward docking bay, had lost its pursuers in the asteroid belt, probably without ever knowing how close the UEN's ships had gotten to it.

Mary had received direct orders from General Cruz himself to watch for the little shuttle's attempt to get to Martian space the back way. Her people had run the vectors, and she had spread her three stealth carriers—already on station in this part of space spying on Red attempts to attack UE assets in the region—across the most likely courses the shuttle could take. It had been almost pure luck that the one the fugitives had chosen had led them by her own *Enterprise*.

The orders from Cruz had not given details on the shuttle's suspected occupants. But given that Mary had last seen her stealth shuttle being 'stolen' by Tyrus Tyne—she'd been complicit in that, of course—she expected to find the big man himself on this cargo shuttle. After all, he had used the same stealth shuttle to facilitate his escape.

She'd heard rumors that the man had defected to Mars with the traitorous ex-Congressman Corey O'Leary, but she hadn't believed them. She hadn't *wanted* to believe them. Tyrus had been assigned to her ship as an observer and consultant on Council military tactics just a few months ago. She'd thought that he might become more in her life. Thinking of him as a traitor stung.

To Mary's surprise, however, it wasn't the large frame of Tyrus Tyne that filled the open hatchway as Major Thomas commanded those inside the cargo shuttle to debark. Instead, it was an odd-looking man with almost feminine features and purple-tinged hair who poked his head out of the craft and made his way slowly down the ramp, hands held out to his sides to show he had no weapons.

Before Major Thomas could demand the rest of the passengers disembark, the man shouted something into the open shuttle behind him. Three more people walked down the ramp after him. The first was a sandy-blond-haired man who looked around the docking bay with appreciation. Probably ex-Navy. Next to him was a girl who looked barely out of her teenage years, with one side of her head shaved and the other dyed bright purple. Her clothing was revealing enough to show that a good portion of her body was covered in tattoos, and she clung possessively and a little fearfully to the arm of the ex-Navy man.

But it was the final person to disembark the shuttle that truly caught Mary's eye. For several months, Jinny Ambrosa had been all over the news and on the covers of magazines and books. She was instantly recognizable now, and by the way that Major Thomas ordered two of his Marines to separate her from the group, he knew who she was just as quickly as Mary did.

The first man tensed as the two Marines approached, but the blond reader said something to him, and he relaxed marginally and didn't try to stop the Marines, who gently grabbed Ambrosa by each arm and led her over to Mary, stopping far enough from their admiral that she wasn't at risk of Ambrosa reading her.

"Admiral Bol," Jinny Ambrosa said with far more calm in her voice than should have been possible for someone under the guns of multiple Marines. "If someone was going to capture us, I'm glad it was you."

"Really?" Mary asked, coloring her voice with skepticism as Jinny Ambrosa debriefed her, *Enterprise*'s captain, George Holm, and a very watchful SEAL Commander Kaplan in Mary's ready room. Only Ambrosa herself had been allowed to come here; the rest of her traveling companions had been taken to a secure holding area that was at least one step up from *Enterprise*'s brig.

"Sounds crazy, doesn't it?" Ambrosa replied with a knowing smile. "But Mikael Gorsky is a traitor. He's been working with the Keeper all along. We don't have all the specifics, mind you, but we know that they've been in contact and that Gorsky engineered Pereira's ouster from office and his own ascension. Unfortunately, we never got the chance to . . . interrogate his co-conspirator, Joseph Blackmont."

Mary frowned. Given Ambrosa's identity, she was sure the girl had been about to say 'read' instead of 'interrogate.' Mary had the typical Earther's fear of readers, though the young woman in her ready room was so unassuming and innocent-looking that it was hard to view her as a danger to humanity. But the story she was spinning was all so fantastic.

"And what do you suggest we do with this information?" she asked slowly.

The young woman met her gaze without flinching. "I've been trying to get in touch with Fleet Admiral Lopez. Tyrus said . . . Well, it's enough to say that both Tyrus and the Majko believe Admiral Lopez is the only person in UE leadership who might be able to do something with this information."

Mary raised an eyebrow. "Yet you've told me without much hesitation."

Ambrosa nodded. "Tyrus trusts you, so I'm taking the chance that he's right about you."

The double mention of Tyne's name made Commander Kaplan wince next to Mary. The rumors of Tyne defecting to the Martian side with Corey O'Leary had made their way through the fleet. Even unconfirmed, many of the officers treated the rumors like fact. For some reason, the SEALs had taken it more personally than most. Mary knew that Tyrus had several times spoken with various SEAL officers about the Council's Alpha program and its tactics, so perhaps the SEALs saw him as something approaching one of their own, which made his potential betrayal sting worse for them.

Mary couldn't afford to think that way, though she also felt the deep sting of the rumors, even if intellectually, she knew that her own nation had betrayed Tyrus first by arresting him and his friends and almost killing Jinny Ambrosa in the process.

"And what do you expect Admiral Lopez to do with this information?" she pressed, repeating a variation of her earlier question.

Ambrosa grimaced and shook her head. "I don't know. I just know that Gorsky is undermining Sol's defenses. He shared the plans for Earth's defense with the Keeper—at least, we're almost sure he did. He's been in near-constant communication with the Council government. And we know he used the services of Jordan Archer to gather dirt on his colleagues to pave his way to taking the presidential office."

Mary frowned, both because of the implications and because she wasn't all that comfortable having both a reader *and* a blender on board her ship.

"But I have no idea how to stop Gorsky," Ambrosa admitted. "I was hoping Admiral Lopez might."

Mary sensed the woman was holding something back. Jinny Ambrosa might *look* like a doe-eyed coed overawed at the size and majesty of the universe around her, but there was something else in her eyes that told Mary she was anything but. This girl was dangerous—Mary suspected she was even more dangerous than Tyne himself.

"I'm sorry," Mary said, meaning the words. "But my orders are to take you back to Earth. We'll leave as soon as *Midway* and *Yorktown* are back in formation."

The reader's shoulders visibly slumped. "Admiral Bol, you're making a huge mistake."

"Perhaps I am, Reader Ambrosa," she admitted. "But my loyalty is to United Earth. I'm sorry it has to end this way."

CHAPTER 39

General Ernesto Cruz read the eyes-only TT message from Admiral Mary Bol on *Enterprise* and scowled. For the fourth time, he checked to ensure that the encryption schema she'd used to send it was keyed only to his personal access codes. If this information got out, it could be disastrous.

He was alone in his large office in the Octagon, United Earth's military nerve center. As chairman of the Joint Chiefs of Staff, he was usually surrounded by aides and junior officers, not to mention the other Joint Chiefs, but he always tried to find an hour or two of solitude daily. It was the only time he could think, though with the war ongoing, even that limited time had been increasingly difficult to find.

Cruz read the message again. He didn't know Reader Jinny Ambrosa as well as he would have liked to, but she'd impressed him greatly in her visit to the Situation Room five months ago when the Council Navy had sent their reconnaissance force through the Castilian Rift and the Front Door. During that tense time, the young reader still had the courage to speak her mind openly and unapologetically to then-President Pereira and his staff. It hadn't done any good in the end, but Ambrosa's gumption had impressed Cruz, as had her earnest and open nature.

Furthermore, Corey O'Leary trusted Ambrosa, and the former congressman was one of the few politicians Cruz had ever liked. No matter what President Gorsky said, Cruz didn't believe for a second that O'Leary had defected to Mars.

He read Mary Bol's message yet another time.

Have acquired Jinny Ambrosa. Claims traitors in command structure. Named MG. Orders?

Cruz had spent his entire adult life wearing his nation's uniform. During that time, he had mostly stayed away from politics and had gained a reputation of being apolitical and strictly obedient to the chain of command. When President Luis Pereira had decided that Fleet Admiral Horatio Krishna Lopez was too opinionated and outspoken—especially against Pereira's own military policies—he'd removed Lopez as chairman of the Joint Chiefs and installed Cruz in his place.

The general knew that Pereira had done so believing he could more easily control him than he could Lopez. Pereira had been right. Cruz didn't like to rock the boat. He was a good soldier who did as he was told. When he'd chewed out Pereira's chief of staff that day in the Situation Room—the same day he'd met Jinny Ambrosa—it had been the first time Cruz had gotten in the face of any member of the executive branch.

He read the message again.

The safe thing to do would be to command Mary Bol to bring Jinny Ambrosa back to Earth. President Gorsky had given Cruz and the other joint chiefs strict orders to do just that if and when the reader was found. He had couched it in the language of 'protective custody,' but the Russian politician wasn't nearly as convincing as he clearly thought he was. Whatever game of backroom politics Pereira had been playing that had put Jinny and her friends in jail the first time was clearly still being played by Mikael Gorsky. And it was wrong. Whatever these men wanted from the pretty young reader—young enough to be one of Cruz's grandchildren—had nothing to do with her protection.

The general licked his lips and read Mary Bol's message one last time. If Ambrosa was saying that MG—Mikael Gorsky—was a traitor, then the last thing Cruz could do was turn her over to the man himself. Not until he could get more clarity.

Slowly, he typed out his return message, using the same encryption schema Bol had used.

Do not return to Earth. Keep JA on Enterprise. Top secret.

He paused and considered what he was doing. If Gorsky or one of his minions ever learned of it, the president could have Cruz court martialed for defying a direct order, and in a time of war, no less. The penalty could be as severe as death.

For a brief moment, he considered not sending the message. But the moment passed quickly, and for the first time in his long life and career, Ernesto Cruz took a stand. He added one last line to the message before he pressed send:

JA to be trusted. Await further instructions, this channel only.

Jinny sighed as the officers in *Enterprise*'s wardroom argued and nitpicked every piece of information she'd spent the last six hours relating to them. Next to her, Jordan Archer sat glumly. Not only had his testimony of Gorsky's betrayal been met with skepticism from Mary Bol and the three captains she'd invited to hear it, but the blender also didn't like reliving all he'd done for the corrupt UE president. Jinny knew that Jordan blamed himself for letting Gorsky manipulate him—and through him, others—to secure his power.

At first, Jinny had been excited when Admiral Bol had told her she wasn't going to take her immediately back to Earth. The admiral hadn't shared her reasons for the change of plans, had actually followed it up by inviting Jinny to make her case in front of her and the captains of *Enterprise, Midway,* and *Yorktown.* Regardless of her reasons for doing so, Jinny had resolved to make the best of the opportunity.

Unfortunately, it wasn't going well. Mary Bol was hard to get a read on, so Jinny couldn't tell if she was swaying the admiral to her side. George Holm, *Enterprise*'s captain, seemed sympathetic, and she thought that he was believing most of what she was telling them.

Yorktown's captain, Gil Forrester, was incredulous at best. It was clear he wasn't inclined to believe that the UE president could possibly be collaborating with the Council government. But the worst was Captain Bettina Kopolov of UENS *Midway*. The way she looked at Jinny and Archer made it clear that she wouldn't believe simply because they were enhanced. Every time anyone in the room used the words 'reader' or 'blender,' the Russian woman visibly winced.

Beyond that, Temperance Jimenez hadn't helped their case. The punk hacker had brought with her most of their hard evidence, in the form of computer records, but had been so rude and dismissive of the questions asked by the Navy officers that she'd almost certainly done more harm than good. Landon Hartman had been more convincing, as an ex-Navy man himself, but he knew so little that it almost didn't matter. Both had come and gone quickly, dismissed by Bol after less than thirty minutes, leaving Jinny and Archer to make the case alone to the four senior officers.

There was a fifth Navy officer in the room as well, but Jinny didn't think he was going to be convinced at all.

He believes you, Tyrus's persona said in her head as she sat silently listening to George Holm and Bettina Kopolov argue over one of the points Archer had tried to make.

Who? Kaplan? she asked him, shooting a glance back at the SEAL commander, who stood immediately behind her and Archer as if he might need to restrain them when they tried to kill Admiral Bol with a soup spoon.

Okay, maybe that wasn't so ridiculous. Jinny had multiple assassins and serial killers in her head, after all.

Yes, Kaplan, Tyrus insisted. *I can tell by his stance. At the beginning of the meeting, he was on the balls of his feet, ready to move at the slightest provocation or sign of treachery from you. Now he's settled back onto his heels.*

Jinny looked back again briefly, met by the SEAL commander's usual hard stare, to see that Tyrus was right . . . probably. Kaplan was standing so ramrod straight that it was hard to tell he had relaxed his stance at all.

What if he's just tired? she argued. *He's been standing there all day.*

He's a SEAL, Tyrus said with a mental smile. *Even if he was exhausted, if he thought you were a threat, he'd be ready to snap your neck at a moment's notice. No, he's relaxed because he believes you're not a threat.*

But I'm not convincing the rest of them, she replied sourly. *And I don't think the opinion of a SEAL commander is going to be enough to sway a room full of admirals and captains.*

Tyrus had no response to that.

Maybe I can help, amiga, a new voice intruded in her thoughts.

Ryder? Jinny had quickly learned that not all of the personas in her head were as active as others. Some, like Tyrus, were vocal even when she didn't give them any control. Others, Ryder included, tended to be silent unless called upon. For her old speaker friend to emerge from the fog now was a good reminder that maybe *she* didn't need to convince the assembled officers.

Who better to do it for her than a genuine speaker—or, at least, the memory-sustained ghost of one? Her head hurt anytime she tried to puzzle through how this all actually worked.

You think you can sway them? she asked Ryder.

Easy, amiga. It's what I do.

Can't hurt to try, Tyrus added.

Ryder's persona almost went away again. He still hadn't forgiven Tyrus for shooting him in the head in real life. Maybe that was the chief reason he was normally so quiet in her head: he was avoiding Tyrus. The entire concept of different personalities in her own mind having conflicts with each other was enough to give her a headache.

Let's try it, she said before Ryder could retreat back into the fog. She surrendered control to him just as a knock came on the wardroom's hatch.

Everyone in the room stopped talking, though an intense argument between Holm and Kopolov regarding the strength of Archer's testimony on the events at the Crater took an extra second or two to fade.

The hatch opened and admitted a young woman with short brown hair, carrying two urns of the foul-smelling coffee that seemed to be the sole staple of the officers in the room. Jinny watched idly as the woman set down the urns and then moved around the room, taking away old cups and replacing them with new ones. This had been a semiregular interruption, and Tyrus had identified the woman as

Yeoman Shelby West, Mary Bol's steward, whom he had seen during his time assigned as an observer on *Enterprise*.

After making sure all three captains had coffee, the steward set down a porcelain cup with a tea bag in front of Bol. The admiral sniffed the drink before taking a sip.

"Hmm," she said absently. "Is that rosemary?"

The yeoman smiled. "Got it in one, ma'am."

Bol smiled at Shelby West, took her first sip of tea, and sent the steward on her way.

You're up, Ryder, Jinny prompted her friend when the hatch shut behind the yeoman and everyone's eyes turned back to her and Archer.

The speaker smiled at Mary Bol. "Now, Admiral, where were we?"

"We must devote the greater part of the Fleet of the Bear to the battle!" Praetor Tiberius argued, standing in the long, flowing robes of his office. "The more we hold back from the fight, the longer we draw out this conflict. We should end it now and end it decisively!"

There were a few nods of agreement around the large round table from the other eleven members of the Quorum, and Aphrodite Starshadow watched them all as dispassionately as she could. However, from the expressions on most of their faces, she could tell that Tiberius's faction had nearly doubled in size in just the last week.

"Foolishness!" called a dissenting voice. Praetor Sunsbane stood and glared at his chief rival in the Quorum. "You would destroy Earth when we know now that their President Mikael Gorsky is a Council collaborator? Who is to say that he did not start this war for the express purpose of weakening us and the Earthers, just as you suggest we do now? A decisive battle will be decisive for both sides, and both sides will suffer! Let us make overtures to the military leaders of Earth and share what we know of their president. If they reject our entreaties and evidence, then we can prosecute total war as you would have us do."

Tiberius scoffed. "You speak of our so-called evidence. You would have us believe the words of one clearly insane prisoner? One who is conveniently no longer around to defend his story? What other evidence do you bring that President Mikael Gorsky is a traitor to his own nation? Forgive me," he said, his tone asking for nothing of the sort, "but as much as I wish ill on the United Earth president, I cannot countenance believing such a farfetched tale of treason and collaboration without more evidence than you can offer."

Sunsbane glared across the table, clearly incensed by the implications of Tiberius's words. Aphrodite knew that her friend and chief supporter was likely to take personal offense at the other praetor's thinly veiled accusation of gullibility at best, lies at worst. And that offense was likely to translate into a duel, which, by the eager look on Tiberius's face, was exactly what the red-faced praetor was looking for.

"Enough!" she snapped before Sunsbane could utter the words from which there would be little hope of return.

Both praetors whirled to stare at her uncharacteristic outburst, Sunsbane looking hurt and Tiberius looking smug as the consul rushed to the obvious defense of her favorite in the Quorum. Before either could speak, however, Aphrodite continued.

"There is a simple way to settle this once and for all." Now, all of the praetors perked up. "What if we were to get the evidence Praetor Tiberius seeks to confirm or disprove the confession of Toby Haight? While also striking a blow to our enemy's capabilities and morale?"

The room was silent. Sunsbane no longer looked quite as upset. But the most marked change was on the face of Kol Tiberius. Aphrodite's main rival in the Quorum was frowning at her as she met his gaze with a cool one of her own. For a long moment, neither of them blinked, but then Tiberius slowly nodded.

"If the consul has a means by which we can secure such evidence, we would be wise to listen," he said, his words a clear surrender as he recognized the corner she had painted him into. By attacking Sunsbane's assertions of Mikael Gorsky's treason by questioning the believability of Toby Haight's confession under duress—not even Aphrodite knew how Corey O'Leary and Cal Riggs had managed that one—Tiberius had to then admit that he would reconsider his position if more evidence were provided to support the claims.

"I am glad to hear you say that," Aphrodite said, stripping all emotion from her voice. "Because Centurion Marcus Parn has formulated a plan that may be able to get us such proof. It is a daring plan—one worthy of the finest traditions of Mars."

Tiberius's face clouded more as her wording further promoted the plan and made it harder for him to argue with it once heard. No Martian praetor could be seen to exhibit cowardice. Now, if Tiberius argued against the plan, no matter how justified his arguments might be, the others might remember Aphrodite's words and have even the smallest doubts about the man's bravery. It was the perfect setup and the best she could do for the truly daring—and slightly insane—plan Centurion Parn had come up with.

The doors at the other end of the room opened, and Parn walked in wearing a full exosuit with the helmet retracted. Aphrodite yielded the floor to him and he began to speak boldly of his plan to the praetors. As she watched their reactions, she was gratified to see several nods and smiles, and an ever-increasing frustration on Tiberius's face.

Mary Bol was alone in her quarters, exhausted but reading through the endless reports that had plagued flag officers since the ancient Greek navies of time immemorial. It had been a trying three days since Jinny Ambrosa had boarded *Enterprise*.

After General Cruz's response to her message about capturing the young reader, Mary wasn't sure what to think. She trusted Cruz, which was why she'd started with him rather than announcing Ambrosa's capture to Fleet Command. Given the girl's allegations against President Gorsky, some circumspection was warranted. But she'd been expecting Cruz to tell her to discount the reader's outlandish story and follow the standing orders to bring her back to Earth.

That he'd gone and told her the exact opposite was concerning in the extreme. As was his admonition to trust the reader. Did that mean Cruz also thought Gorsky was a traitor to his own people? Or was he simply buying time to do more digging on his end? And if the latter, then why tell her to trust Ambrosa?

Either way, it had put Mary in a quandary. So she'd done what any good commander did—brought in her most trusted advisors to give her their thoughts and advice.

She hadn't actually shared with her three ship captains anything about her communication with Cruz. But she had been frank with them that she was having doubts about following the standing orders to return Ambrosa to Earth in light of her accusations against Mikael Gorsky. At first, both Forrester and Kopolov had insisted that they immediately send a transmission to Fleet Command requesting orders. It was a sign of how much they both trusted her that they backed off the demand as soon as she shot it down.

Her hope had been that by asking Ambrosa and her traveling companions to give their testimonies today to her and the three captains, they would reach some sort of consensus. But after the day was mostly over, she could tell that Holm, Forrester, and Kopolov ranged from skeptical to outright disbelieving. The reader and her friends hadn't managed to convince any of them.

Then, something had changed. For the last two hours of the meeting, Ambrosa had spoken passionately and persuasively in a way completely at odds with her performance prior to that point. It had been almost like she could anticipate the captains' counterarguments before they made them, and she spoke with a confidence that had been missing for the first six hours.

By the end, Holm was absolutely convinced by the reader's story. Kopolov wasn't, but Mary had known the Russian woman had some sort of strong aversion to the enhanced, though she didn't know why. Forrester was still more or less on the fence, but Mary guessed he was leaning in Ambrosa's direction after the girl's impassioned speech at the end of the day.

Assuming Forrester was swayed by further meetings with Ambrosa scheduled for the next day, that would put two captains in favor of her story versus one against. Unfortunately, Mary herself still didn't know where she stood. And in the end, her ship captains could advise her, but the ultimate decision was hers, and hers alone.

Either she believed the young reader that her president was a traitor and Council collaborator . . . or she didn't and rolled the dice with Ambrosa's life by returning her to Earth. Because even with Cruz's admonition to keep her on board *Enterprise*, Mary couldn't in good conscience do that unless she had overwhelming evidence that it was the right thing to do. She'd taken an oath to the constitution, after all.

A discrete knock on the door to her quarters interrupted Mary's thoughts and tore her attention away from a report on shipboard stores she'd been pretending to read. Without waiting for admittance, Yeoman Shelby West, Mary's steward of the last five years, entered the room carrying a laden tray. The woman smiled warmly at her boss.

"I thought you might want some refreshments if you're working late, ma'am."

Bol smiled warmly in return. "Somehow, I knew you'd come, Shelby. You seem to have a sixth sense for when I need some tea."

Shelby said nothing more, setting the tray on the small, low table in front of the couch Mary sat on. Mary had never learned to enjoy the caustic coffee that seemed to be the true fuel that powered the United Earth Navy, and had always vastly preferred the tea that her parents had consumed back home in Nigeria. In her early Navy days, she'd choked down the black coffee more as a way to stay awake and fit in than from any real enjoyment, but now that she was an admiral and rated her own steward, she had sworn off the rancid liquid and paid out of her own pocket to keep her flag galley stocked with a variety of teas from all over Earth. There was even a blend grown exclusively on Luna that gained a unique flavor from the low-gravity hydroponics farm where it originated. She'd learned that Martian teas likewise had their own unique and exotic flavoring, but she'd only heard rumors of them, as those markets had long since been cut off as part of the latest cold war with the red planet.

Shelby had a knack not only for knowing when her charge *needed* tea and the small accompanying cakes Mary was also so fond of, but also for knowing which *blend* of tea her admiral needed in any given situation. It was uncanny. Tonight, Mary was not surprised but delighted to see that Shelby had chosen a blend of highly caffeinated English breakfast black. It wasn't her favorite flavor by far, but it was perfect for a night when she needed to be up late to finish the mountain of paperwork that wouldn't wait even for a president's treason. Not that Mary could sleep if she'd not had the work to do. Despite the agreement of the other officers, the responsibility for deciding what to do with the information rested solely on her shoulders as the ranking officer. It was a weighty one.

"How are you doing this evening, Shelby?" Mary asked to distract herself while her steward steeped the tea and put a few small cakes on a plate for Mary to enjoy.

"Quite all right, ma'am," the steward replied in her customary cheery voice, which carried just a hint of her native Irish brogue. "I daresay better than you; something seems to be resting heavy on your mind today."

"The mantle is a bit heavier these days than normal," Mary admitted. "Of course, I can't give specifics, but there are some big decisions to make, and if I'm wrong, some fairly severe consequences. What do you hear from the crew?"

In addition to being Mary's personal steward and tea savant, Shelby West was also her window into the general morale aboard any ship they were assigned to. The cheerful yeoman had a way of quickly making friends and gaining confidences, and people often shared their true feelings about a mission or a ship's operation with her. In some cases, Mary knew they also sought her out specifically so they could complain in a way that was sure to reach the admiral but would be safely anonymized before it did.

It didn't hurt, of course, that Shelby was an attractive woman in her early thirties who, to the best of Mary's knowledge, avoided romantic entanglements for her own reasons but who was often sought out by the eligible bachelors on any ship or station she was on. She wasn't sure if Shelby liked men at all or if she just preferred the simplicity that came with being single, and she'd never tried to pry. Everyone had to have *some* secrets from their boss, after all.

"All seems well in general," the woman responded as she handed the steaming teacup on a tiny saucer to Bol. "There was a fight in the gym yesterday between some Navy folks and some of the Marines, but it ended quickly when the gunny stepped in. Just the normal, to-be-expected stress and nerves from being so close to enemy lines and just *waiting*—likely the same thing that has you on edge, if I may be so bold."

Mary smiled as she sniffed the tea and then took her first sip. Shelby always asked if she could be so bold but never seemed to care if the admiral replied or not. She was just *that* bold all of the time. It was one of the reasons Mary liked her so much; she always knew she was getting the unfiltered truth from her, and she *didn't* walk on eggshells around her superior as so many others did. It was refreshing in a very real way, especially at the end of a long hard day in which the last thing Mary wanted was *another* subordinate carefully considering every word they said to her.

"Well, I think maybe I'll just have to have a word with the gunny after—"

Mary was interrupted by the hatch to her quarters abruptly clanging open. She had always prided herself on having a sharp and quick mind, but it still took her a moment to process the image of Trey Kaplan, standing in her hatchway with his sidearm drawn and pointed squarely at her and Shelby.

The admiral dropped her tea, the hot liquid burning her lap but barely registering in her mind as the realization struck a moment too late. *If the Council has spies and traitors on Earth, why not on* my *ship?* She had just enough time to finish the thought before she saw Shelby fling herself across the small table toward her, leaping in between the would-be assassin and his target, and Mary screamed, not in terror but in a false hope to stop the woman from sacrificing herself.

The gunshot barked in the small space, surprising Mary with the fleeting thought of why the assassin wouldn't use the integrated suppressor to muffle the shot and allow him to possibly make an escape. But all thoughts of that fled when she saw Shelby's body twitch in the air as the bullet struck her.

When the woman landed on top of the hot tea in Mary's lap, the admiral looked straight at Kaplan in horror, wishing she were wearing her own sidearm but never once having thought she might need it, especially in the safe sanctuary of her own quarters. She hadn't worn it aboard ship in years. But her hands formed fists as she prepared to move the surely dead steward's body aside and leap at the imposter SEAL.

Then Mary's mind registered two things. First was the fact that Kaplan's pistol was now sweeping the room instead of pointing at her. Second was the look of relief on the man's face as he finished his sweep and lowered the gun.

She looked at him in confusion and then looked down at the dead steward lying across her lap. That was when she saw the knife that had dropped to the floor from Shelby's outstretched hand.

"Admiral," Kaplan said firmly but with a sense of calm that had always impressed Mary in her interactions with him. "Are you hurt?"

She looked back up at him and shook her head slowly, the realization of events hitting her hard, causing her eyes to fill with tears. She had trusted Shelby, even thought of her in some ways like the daughter she'd never had time to have in her long years of navy service. But she had . . . she had what? Tried to kill her? A part of Mary's brain refused to acknowledge it. Surely, this must be some sort of trick.

But Kaplan had holstered his gun and moved quickly across the room, a small scanner now in his hand, which he waved over the cakes on the table and then, stepping around the small space, waved over the empty teacup that lay on the couch where it had been knocked from Mary's lap.

"Did you eat any of the cakes?" he demanded, his customary calmness replaced by a sense of urgency as his other hand opened to access his comm.

Mary shook her head dumbly, not trusting her voice.

Kaplan visibly relaxed. "I wonder why she only poisoned the cakes and not the tea itself." he mused.

Now, Mary did speak, a part of her professional mind overriding her personal shock at what had happened and the betrayal of a dear friend. "She knew I'd taste anything off in the tea. She would often add special ingredients to see if I could guess them; it was a little game we played. I almost always guessed correctly."

Kaplan nodded. "But the sugar in the cakes would better mask the flavor of the poison, at least the variety she used." He shook his head now in amazement. "Based on what she added to those cakes, if you'd taken even one bite, we'd be trying to resuscitate you right about now."

"How did you . . ." Mary started to ask, but this time her voice broke as she'd feared it would earlier.

"That reader, Ambrosa. She woke me up a few minutes ago with an urgent call. Said she'd felt something off about Yeoman West, then remembered that she'd seen West once in Council space. I didn't want to use internal comms because I might alert the assassin. I got here as fast as I could." He nodded to the prone form on the floor. "Lucky she called when she did."

Mary nodded and felt the hot tears running down her face. Through their haze, she saw Kaplan very obviously notice and then look away just as obviously. SEALS weren't known for their subtlety.

"Let me move the body, ma'am, if that's okay. Admiral, you need to let go."

Mary looked down and was surprised to see that she was hugging Shelby's body, though she didn't remember wrapping her arms around the woman. Shakily, knowing intellectually that she was on the way down to a post-adrenaline crash, she removed her arms and let Kaplan push the small table out of the way and ease West's body off her lap and onto the ground, treating it with a strange sort of respect for a trained killer handling the remains of a traitor and spy.

"I don't know what's really going on here, ma'am," the SEAL commander said slowly after he'd checked Shelby's pulse. Mary looked down but found herself oddly squeamish at the blood from the bullet wound in the woman's chest, blood that she now realized covered her lap and one of her hands from where she'd hugged the dead girl.

"But I don't buy Reader Ambrosa's story for a second," continued Kaplan. "There are trillions of people in the 47 Colonies. No way she just happened to run into Shelby West over there. And how did Yeoman West not recognize her then in return? Something doesn't add up."

"Indeed," Mary said, the word sounding almost robotic. She cleared her throat. "How about we find out together?" She started to get up from the couch, but suddenly felt like her legs couldn't support her weight and slumped back down.

She couldn't be safe anywhere, couldn't trust anyone—the thought overwhelmed her, but the rational part of her knew that was a response to the shock of her confidant's betrayal, and that surely not *all* of her crew could be conspirators and spies.

"Ma'am," the SEAL commander said in a compassionate voice that belied his station as the chief of a group of deadly killers—who at least, for now, appeared to be on Mary's side. "Can I suggest you get cleaned up? I'll stay out here and guard the entrance so you can do so in peace. I've already summoned my squad to join me here, so you'll have plenty of firepower on hand in case Yeoman West had any accomplices."

Mary nodded and slowly levered herself up from the couch, then made her way shakily across the room to her in-suite bathroom, a luxury that only the captain and the flag officer had even on a ship as large as the *Enterprise*. There she stayed for a long time, staring at her red-rimmed eyes in the mirror and mourning a woman who had never really existed.

"Spit it out, Reader Ambrosa," Mary demanded an hour later in her office next to *Enterprise*'s flag bridge. They were alone in the room, except for Commander Kaplan, who stood next to Ambrosa, ready to do violence if the petite young reader turned out to be as dangerous as Shelby West.

Ambrosa frowned and returned Mary's stare evenly, which was something in and of itself. The admiral was using the same steely gaze that usually sent full captains scurrying for cover, and it probably had some extra hardness behind it, given that she'd recently been covered in the blood of someone she'd thought was a friend.

"I told you, Admiral," Ambrosa said evenly. "I recognized your steward from my time in the colonies. We must have crossed paths at some point. As soon as I remembered, I called Commander Kaplan."

"Bull," Mary said with an edge to her voice, though Ambrosa

didn't even have the decency to flinch, "there's something you're not telling me. Spit it out, or our next stop is Earth and Fleet Command. They can figure out what to do with you there."

For a long stretch, Ambrosa stared back impassively. Then, she let out a sigh. "Tyrus trusts you, Admiral Bol, so I'll take a chance. But we should really do this alone."

"Not going to happen," Mary replied instantly. By the look on Kaplan's face, he would have refused a direct order to leave. She was certain she was going to have round-the-clock SEAL protection for a while, even on her own ship, and she wasn't going to complain about it after Shelby's betrayal. "And you're not in a position to negotiate, Reader Ambrosa," she continued. "You're on my ship, and you're here only at my sufferance. Last chance—tell the truth, or we'll send you back to Gorsky, traitor or not."

She actually thought that Ambrosa was going to call her bluff. Then, to her relief, the young woman's shoulders relaxed marginally. "You're right, Admiral. I never saw Shelby West in colonial space. I saw her for the first time when she brought in the coffee earlier today. I had no idea who she was until I heard her speak. Even then, it took me a few hours to realize what I'd heard."

"That's it?" Kaplan demanded. "You knew she was a traitor because of the way she talked? She must have only said half a dozen words."

Ambrosa looked briefly annoyed, and Mary could sense that there was no love lost between her and the SEAL. "Actually, it was five words. And she tried to hide it, but she had a distinct Cigni II accent. Once I realized that was what I'd noticed, I called you to save the admiral. And it looks like I did it just in time!"

Kaplan bristled and was about to snap back at the reader, but Mary held up a hand to forestall him. "Even given that you were right, it seems very hard to believe that you detected a hidden accent in only five words, with enough certainty to send Commander Kaplan to my quarters. You're a reader, not a speaker."

She said the last part almost flippantly, but by the deep blush on Ambrosa's face, she realized she'd struck some kind of nerve.

"What aren't you telling us, Reader Ambrosa?" Mary demanded in a not-unfriendly tone, reminding herself that the girl, for all her evasiveness, *had* saved her life.

Ambrosa studied her for a moment, then sighed. "Can I take a seat, Admiral? This is going to take a while to explain."

Over the course of the next two hours, Jinny Ambrosa proceeded to weave a fantastical story of extraordinary abilities that Mary Bol would have never believed had the young reader not then proceeded to answer every single one of her questions about Tyrus Tyne's time on *Enterprise*. Perhaps sensing even then that Mary was still skeptical, Ambrosa switched from English to Hausa, the language of Mary's native Nigeria.

By the time they were done, Mary had to reluctantly admit two things: that the young woman sitting across from her might just be the most dangerous person she'd ever met, and that under no circumstances could she take Jinny Ambrosa back to Earth.

PART FOUR
TURNING POINT

CHAPTER 40

Two Weeks Later; February 16, 732 P.D.

"We are transferring Guard Space Force Task Forces 23 and 24 to the Brasilia system to safeguard the military supply route to the Delta 3 base. Likewise, GSF Task Forces 12 and 17 will be dispatched to Hazard as a false flag so that anyone looking for Delta 3's location will need to explore both systems."

Assembly Speaker Constanina Yenin paused, looking out over the table and the eighteen other men and women, all watching her with rapt anticipation. Such wholesale movements of GSF forces were rare and concerning. Thus far, the Keeper had transferred a full 60 percent of all available GSF ships and crews to areas in and around the secret Council Navy bases at Delta 3 and Moloch. Each time he did so, it was with a reasonable explanation, but his refusal to even join meetings of the Twenty to discuss the moves was concerning in the extreme, as was the fact that large swaths of human territory would now be bereft of protection from pirates and smugglers with the Guard ships to interdict them.

When the woman began speaking again, her voice was slow and her tone somber. "Keeper Petrov has decided that the time for the invasion of the Four Worlds will be in two months. He believes that will be enough time for Mars and Earth to tear each other to shreds and for Admiral Chen to finish staffing and training the Navy."

Creighton fought not to swear as the rest of the table erupted in shouts and objections. The announcement of the invasion timing *should* have come from Petrov himself instead of from Yenin, the Keeper's de facto number two in the small group of twenty rulers. Yenin, like Petrov, hailed from the colony world Invanov, named after one of the early Keepers. For that reason, among others, Petrov had always trusted her most among the Twenty. Once, Creighton had thought he'd carried similar trust with the man, but that obviously was no longer the case.

Furthermore, this was the first any of them were hearing of a war between Earth and Mars. If it was true, it was a good thing. Weakening the two powerful planets before the invasion was the perfect strategy, and Creighton had to give Petrov credit for somehow engineering the war via his mysterious spies and collaborators in the Sol system. Unfortunately, it also meant that the Keeper had been hiding valuable information from the Twenty. If he hadn't shared his knowledge of the Earth-Mars war, what else hadn't he shared? And why only give them two months' notice of the actual invasion timing after years of preparation?

"Why isn't the Keeper himself here to tell us this personally?" a booming voice demanded over all the others. Creighton looked over at the man who had raised the question, Jerem Pondergast. Pondergast was a study in contrasts. Despite his deep bass voice, he was thin and reedy in appearance, like a stiff wind might easily knock him over. And he was always dressed impeccably, usually better than anyone else in the room, but often in the wrong ways. Today, he wore a somewhat archaic three-piece suit with matching faux leather shoes that couldn't have been very comfortable. Even in New Brussels, where fashion changed and recycled itself almost weekly, the look was severely outdated. It was also quite jarring on the man who was the representative of Malacca, one of the Edge worlds, where *any* sort of fashion was largely ignored as the citizens scraped by on a subsistence existence.

Only a few times in history had there even *been* a member of the

Twenty from an Edge world. Normally on the verge of outright rebellion, the Edge worlds were looked down upon by the rest of the colonies. But when the late and unlamented Nancy Farnsworth had died, Keeper Petrov had felt that promoting an assembly speaker from the Edge might be a way to gain insight into how to placate the rebellious worlds. It had been a politically astute move and one that Creighton had approved of at the time, even if he thought Pondergast a poor choice on a personal level.

Now, he might have to rethink that. After several months in the Twenty during which he'd silently listened and observed, Pondergast had finally found his voice, and he'd quickly become the most outspoken critic of the Keeper's aggressive invasion timeline, putting a voice to what the rest of them were too afraid to say.

Yenin looked flustered at Pondergast's question, and the room slowly silenced as everyone stopped their own objections to see how she would react to this one.

"Why, Speaker Pondergast," she said with false calm. "Keeper Petrov is quite a busy man, and he has entrusted this assignment to me today as a way of freeing up some of his time for more critical tasks."

Pondergast didn't back down. He sneered at the woman. "Right. So what you're saying is that he doesn't believe informing or even *consulting* with the rest of the Twenty about the first real war in modern human history is a *critical* task?"

Yenin opened her mouth to respond, but the man kept right on talking over her. "I'm sorry, Speaker Yenin, but I'm starting to think that the Keeper isn't operating in good faith with the rest of us."

Yenin looked duly shocked, but Creighton wasn't. *If only you knew, Jerem,* he thought. But he couldn't know—not really. Unless Jerem Pondergast's spies were a lot better than Creighton's, which he highly doubted, there was absolutely no chance the man had an inkling of what was really going on . . . because Creighton didn't. Like the others, he had been cut out of all communication with Petrov.

"I'm afraid you'll have to take that up with Keeper Petrov in the next meeting," Yenin said coldly. "Until then," she continued with a raised hand to cut off the man's angry retort, "we have quite a full agenda. So if you'll all please note the proposal for increased tariffs in . . ."

The meeting ended two hours later, but the undercurrent of animosity and worry never left the room. As the other members of the Twenty filed out in small groups, Creighton did his best to appear busy. When the last of the others left, he turned to Yenin.

"What is going on, Connie?" he asked. Two weeks ago, on the advice of Lara Owens, Creighton had reached out to Yenin, feeling her out on a possible alliance to stand against Keeper Petrov if it ever became necessary. Progress had been slow, and Creighton had been okay with that, content to play the long game on the assumption that he had time to do so. But now, with the invasion date set and coming fast, it was time to take the more direct approach.

Yenin frowned. "I'm sure I have no idea what you mean, Creighton."

"Don't sell me any cow pies," he said, letting his voice take on the Nova Tejas country twang he was famous for in the media.

She wasn't amused. "Don't try your lazy charms on me, Creighton. If you have a question, spit it out."

He studied her for a moment, then mentally shrugged. "You know as well as I do that we need more time to crew Chen's ships," he said carefully. "We're several months if not years away from having all six fleets activated and crewed. Right now, we'd be lucky to cobble together four fleets! So why this ridiculous timeline? Two months isn't enough, Connie, and you know it."

Constantina frowned but didn't respond, so he pressed harder. "Why the false urgency? The Four Worlds will still be there in six months, and so will the enhanced on Earth. Plus, if there really is a war between Earth and Mars, shouldn't we let them damage each other more before we go? Why is Ian pushing so hard?"

She kept frowning, and he watched her carefully as her left eye twitched ever so slightly. "You don't know, do you?" he said, revelation dawning on him. "He's not even talking to you anymore, is he?"

Licking her lips and looking toward the door as if to make sure none of the others had lingered to listen, she sighed. "No. I haven't seen or spoken with him in a week. He sent Ebby Hall to inform me of the timing of the invasion. And he's been ordering the redeployments of the GSF as well without consulting me or anyone else."

For a long moment, neither of them spoke, but volumes passed between them as they both contemplated the import of her words. Creighton was the first to break the silence. "Come on, Connie. You must have a theory."

He was hoping she had far more than that. Creighton may have suborned Lara Owens, but she was only a midlevel staffer for Keeper Petrov. Word was that Constantina had *two* spies in the Keeper's office, both of them more highly placed.

"I might have a theory, as you say," she said slowly.

He didn't respond, waiting her out as she considered what to tell him.

"I think something happened to the quantum comm array on Earth."

Creighton's eyes went wide. He knew about the comm of course, but his theory had been that Petrov's agents on Earth had told him something devastating that forced the Keeper to move up the invasion timeline. He hadn't even considered the possibility that the comm itself had been destroyed.

"What makes you think that?" he asked.

Yenin shook her head. "Sorry, Creighton. That's all you get for free." She turned to leave.

Playing a hunch, he stopped her with one final observation. "He's insane, Connie. The man we knew is gone. You know that, right?"

He watched her carefully. Using those words with her was a gigantic gamble. If she reported them to Petrov, Creighton was likely to find himself staring down the barrel of an alpha's gun.

Yenin turned back, regarding him with a thin-lipped, neutral expression. Then, without a word, she turned and left the room.

Admiral Terrence Lafayette watched his flag plot with an outward calm that he did not feel. On the screen, dozens of large blue and red dots moved inexorably closer to each other while smaller dots representing fighters streaked out from both groups.

Up until now, the few battles between Mars and Earth had been mostly isolated affairs, usually consisting of one or two task forces. In those battles, the Martians had made devastating use of their new skip jump capabilities, appearing and disappearing from the battlefield almost at will.

But not this time. For the last two days, Lafayette and the rest of Second Fleet had watched warily as the entirety of Mars's Fleet of the Eagle had massed on the other side of the neutral zone, directly opposite their UEN opponents. Then, they'd watched in further amazement as the entire Martian force had approached them head-on, crossing the neutral zone with no attempt at subterfuge or subtlety. Frantic messages had flown back and forth between Lafayette's command and the Situation Room on Earth, where President Gorsky and the Joint Chiefs of Staff watched the battle from a distance. In the end, General Cruz had solemnly informed Lafayette that the order was to meet the Martians in battle the instant they crossed over into United Earth space.

In the history of the Sol system, no two fleets as large as Earth's Second Fleet and Mars's Fleet of the Eagle had ever met in battle. Lafayette had looked it up. The next largest naval engagement had been between two fleets with a combined mass of less than two-thirds of the tonnage that now flew at each other with intent to kill.

His eyes riveted to the battle plot. He wanted to be issuing orders, making minute corrections to what his ships were doing, but he held his tongue. He had already issued his orders and solidified the battle plan, and now it was up to his individual squadron commanders and ship captains to execute without him micromanaging things over their shoulders.

On the plot, the hundreds of smaller dots representing the fighters finally reached each other. Some broke off their straight course toward the enemy and started spiraling around each other, dog-fighting in small groups. The rest, including the bombers, kept going more or less forward toward their enemy's respective capital ships. At least two squadrons of UEN bombers broke through the melee and homed in on the Martian battle line. But three squadrons of Martian bombers got through and were on their way straight toward Lafayette's *Texas* and her comrades.

Still, the admiral said nothing, listening with one ear to the comm chatter of the battle as one of the carrier CAGs—Commander Air Group, a holdover title from when navies had plied the oceans of Earth instead of the stars—retasked two squadrons of interceptors held back in reserve to go out and meet the incoming bombers. It would be a miracle if they could take them all out, but the enemy ships would still have to break through the UEN's screening line of destroyers and light cruisers, all bristling with antifighter weaponry.

Those lines of screening ships, which had been surging forward ahead of his capital ships, now executed a perfectly synchronized turnover and started burning hard to decelerate on the same vector as the incoming bombers. The move would give them extra time in weapons range of the incoming craft, allowing them to take more of them out before they could reach the lines of heavy cruisers, battlecruisers, battleships, and carriers that the UEN fleet still had accelerating toward the Martian lines.

"Tell CruRon24 to tighten up and not get out ahead of the others," Lafayette told his comm officer calmly. "And tell BatRon21 to take CruRon28 and move forward to defend against the group of Martian battlecruisers trying to flank us on the left."

His orders were obediently relayed, and two of the heavy cruiser squadrons and one squadron of battlecruisers pivoted and moved on new courses to comply. Lafayette settled back in his chair and continued to watch for the inevitable clash of the capital ships themselves.

When it finally came, it was anticlimactic, at least for the admiral and his staff, sitting in the relatively calm environment of his flag bridge and watching two groups of differently colored dots come together and intermingle. He knew it was anything but calm for the young men and women fighting out there under his command.

Then he felt *Texas* shudder as an enemy missile made contact. That wasn't *his* problem. Captain Dasgupta was responsible for fighting her ship, and the last thing she needed right now was for her admiral to take a break from managing the overall battle to manage her as well.

Still, he'd been a Navy man long enough to have a good idea of what *Texas* was going through, even if he made it a point *not* to watch for it specifically on his flag plot. His job was to direct the battle at the macro level, he kept reminding himself. But as he felt several smaller shudders from the deck plates beneath his command chair, he knew that *Texas* had just loosed its own formidable broadsides of missiles.

"Order Admiral Hanover to come to two-two-four mark seven and focus his attack on that small group of battleships," he said, then listened with half an ear as his comm officer relayed his orders to the squadron commander. His tactical officer would also be busy, sending supplemental orders to a few screening elements to accompany the battleships following standard UEN doctrine.

"Sir, there's something happening in sector six," his sensor officer called out. "Sending it to tactical."

A few moments passed, and then the tactical officer added her color. "Looks like a reinforced squadron of Martian battleships has broken off from the main group and is attacking TF26's flank!"

"Move BatRon . . ." Lafayette checked his screen and did some mental calculations. ". . . 22 to support and tell Rear Admiral Cunningham to take *Valkyrie*'s task group to fill the gap." On the plot, a battleship squadron moved to reinforce TF26 while the Fleet Carrier *Valkyrie* and her escorts burned toward the space the battleships were vacating.

He turned his attention back to the battle as a whole. Everything looked largely the same as when he'd diverted his attention to the situation on the right flank. On the screen, red and green dots alike started flashing and turning gray as ships died or lost power, effectively taking them out of the fight. That was to be expected, but something about the entire battle nagged at Lafayette though he couldn't put his finger on what it was.

"Give me an analysis of the fighter and bomber strength of the Martian fleet," he ordered. "I want to know if they have anything in reserve we haven't seen yet."

The response came not from his tactical officer but from the bridge speakers. "Flag, this is the CAG on *Implacable*. Analysis is that all five Martian assault carriers have launched full fighter and bomber compliments, minus a squadron of interceptors from the *Fides*."

"Thank you, *Implacable*," Lafayette said absently, still studying the plot. A single squadron of interceptors wasn't anything to worry about, so the nagging feeling had to be coming from something else. Beneath his command chair, *Texas* shuddered as another salvo from the enemy hit his flagship, but he did his best to ignore it, keeping his eyes on the swirling dance of red and green dots on the screen at the front of his bridge. Then, he noticed something odd.

"Sarah," Lafayette called to his tactical officer. "Where is the *Caesar* right now?"

Commander Sarah Jenkins highlighted one of the red dots on the battle plot. A popup window over it showed an image of the Martian flagship as well as its specifications. All those, the admiral practically knew by heart, but what interested him the most at this moment was the enemy flagship's location.

That wasn't right.

Martian tactical doctrine was that fleet admirals—they called them legatuses—lead from the front. A Martian flag officer was considered a coward if he didn't put his own ship into harm's way. UEN doctrine was a bit more sanguine in that regard, recognizing that fleet commanders needed to survive if they were to direct the overall battle.

So Lafayette would have expected to find MPNS *Julius Caesar* right in the center of the Martian line of battle. Augustus Lightbringer, his Martian counterpart, was no coward, at least by reputation. So why was the Martian flagship accelerating hard for the outer edge of the battle, surrounded by a screening element of two other battleships and a handful of battlecruisers, light cruisers, and destroyers? Where was Lightbringer going?

"Plot the *Caesar*'s vector," he ordered his tactical officer. A new line appeared on the plot, showing that, unless the Martian flagship changed course, it would intercept one of Second Fleet's small outer task groups, TG23.2, anchored by a single UEN battleship. But why?

He quickly pulled up the information on TG23.2. He skimmed

quickly through the task group's order of battle his eyes stopping almost immediately as he read the name of the group's battleship.

Lightbringer was after the UENS *Italy*.

"Reggie," he called to his comm officer. "Tell Admiral Connors that the *Caesar* is heading for him and the *Italy*. I think they may be trying to finish what the Reds started at Nyx. And Sarah, see what we have that can get out to support them in time!" Unfortunately, Lafayette knew the answer before he asked the question. Not much. They'd already committed their reserves to stop the Martians on the right flank. The left flank, which hadn't seen the fiercest fighting thus far, had been allowed to get far too spread out.

Lightbringer planned this, he thought. *He purposefully concentrated his attack on the side opposite* Italy *and her task group to draw us out of position to support them. He's cutting them off from the rest of the fleet. But why? Are the Martians really so upset about Nyx that they'd engineer an entire battle plan just to take revenge? Besides, they fired first at Nyx, not us.*

He might never understand the Martians and their strange sense of honor. But one thing was for sure. *Italy* was in for the fight of her life.

"Fire full spread! Target that battleship!"

Rear Admiral Dalish Connors screamed out orders above the din on the flag bridge. Normally, he wouldn't get involved in the tactical operations of his flagship, but the suddenness and the fierceness of the Martian attack on his task group had caught them all by surprise, and he'd forgotten himself and taken direct control.

Just an hour ago, Dalish had been almost disappointed at the course the battle was taking. The Martian attack seemed to focus all of its offensive power on the UEN's center lines and right flank, virtually ignoring the left flank, where his TG23.2 was waiting. Thus far in the war, *Italy*'s only battle had been at Nyx, and Dalish had been anxious to prove his prowess in a fight since then. Unfortunately for him, he was getting his wish, and he cringed as *Italy* rocked underneath him at the impact of multiple Martian missiles.

But the skin of battleships was thick, and none of the missiles got entirely through.

Now, Dalish watched with satisfaction as *Italy* poured return fire into one of the Martian battleships, her missiles slamming into it and taking chunks out of the red-painted hull. One of them must have gotten through, because when the flash of light cleared, the entire Martian ship was little more than a few pieces of floating debris, the rest disintegrated down to its component atoms. Dalish smiled, showing his teeth in triumph, and turned his attention to the ship he really wanted to kill.

"Signal *Tokyo* and *Lagos* to concentrate their fire with us on the *Caesar*!" he shouted, ordering his two surviving battlecruisers to join him in a full attack on the enemy's flagship. It would be a tough fight, but he could decapitate the enemy Navy in a single strike.

Dalish settled back in his seat to watch the plot as his three ships converged on the Martian flagship, his grin still wide.

"Sir!" His sensor officer's cry of alarm broke through his single-minded focus. "Skip jump detected! More enemy ships, surfacing off our port stern."

Shocked, Connors looked at the plot and saw two more of the hulking Martian battleships and one of their assault carriers appear right behind *Italy*. But how? They should have detected a skip jump well ahead of time. The Navy had recalibrated every UEN ship's sensors just for that purpose.

His heart sank. Unless there had been nothing to detect. No one knew how the Martians pulled off their capability to make several extremely short jumps in a row to move quickly across the system. But no one had ever said those short jumps had to come in sets. What if the Martians had made only one of the jumps, taking all the risks of jump drift and everything else, to simply move three of their ships from one part of the battle to another?

It was insane.

But the sanity of the maneuver didn't matter right now, because they were here.

"Missiles inbound!" shouted his tactical officer. "They're . . . I don't believe this, sir. They're those colonial shock missiles!"

"How?" he screamed at the man as he watched the video feed, which showed a dozen dazzling blue lights moving on a laser straight course from the two new Martian battleships toward his own. That same feed showed the computer-assisted outlines of several dozen regular missiles converging on his two battlecruiser escorts.

"I don't know, sir," his tactical officer replied. "The Martians weren't supposed to have that tech unless . . ."

"Unless someone gave it to them," Dalish finished with a snarl, having a fairly good idea of who that *someone* was.

He'd been in the briefing last year where the ex-colonial enacter Tyrus Tyne had told the assembled command officers of the United Earth Navy all about the vulnerabilities their battleships would have against the so-called shockers the Council Navy would deploy. And the latest word was that Tyrus Tyne had betrayed Earth since then . . . and defected to Mars.

"Send a message to the flag!" he shouted at his comm officer. "Tell them we're about to be disabled and to send urgent support."

But why? Why would the Martians disable him instead of just destroying him? His ship wasn't all that important. Unless . . . No, it couldn't be that.

"Sir, we've lost the *Tokyo* and the *Lagos*!"

He slammed a fist down on the arm of his chair. "Spin up the star drive! We need to make an in-system jump and escape!" It was a desperate order. Even without the serious risks involved in an in-system jump, he knew there simply wouldn't be time.

Suddenly, all the lights and screens on his bridge went out simultaneously, and Dalish felt his stomach flip as the gravity went out beneath him. The Martian shockers had found the weak points on his battleship's hull and done their job.

Emergency lights came on after a second, bathing him and his staff in a dull red glow, and they all looked around at each other in stunned silence. Dalish had been in simulations of a disabling attack before, but the sims hadn't prepared him for the eerie silence that followed, nor for the complete and utter sense of helplessness he felt now.

"Admiral, what do we do?" a young lieutenant, one of his aides, asked in a small voice. He looked at her but didn't answer.

For a long moment, there was further silence. Then, his tactical officer spoke up. "Sir? Orders?"

Still, Dalish couldn't think of anything.

"Sir," the man prompted again. "Sims suggest we have about fifteen minutes left before we regain power, assuming engineering followed protocol and started working to restore it as soon as it went out. What should we do in the meantime?"

That little tidbit of information sparked something in Dalish's mind, and he shook himself. "Send runners with handheld comms," he said. "Tell the Marines and SEALs to prepare to repel boarders. Get NavSec forces to the flag and command bridges."

"Boarders, sir?" the man asked dubiously. He had been there at Nyx, where it all started. But he hadn't been in on it. None of them had been. Only Dalish Connors and *Italy's* captain knew the truth.

"Just do it," was the best response he could give, and the bridge erupted around him as men and women began talking over each other to carry out his orders. He only hoped reinforcements could arrive in time to save *Italy* and, just as importantly, to save *him*.

In the dimly lit troop bay of the assault shuttle, seventeen soldiers waited patiently. Each one was clad head-to-toe in a black exosuit, which allowed them to function in the shuttle's high-gravity environment, already dialed up to Earth standard in preparation for the artificial gravity levels they would face on the enemy ship once it restored power.

One of the soldiers, a centurion by the two red slashes on each shoulder of his exosuit, spoke calmly into his helmet's comms, transmitting to all of the others. "We breach in ten seconds. For Mars!"

"For Mars!" the others echoed. To a man—and woman—they all had the distinctive extreme height and more extreme thinness that was the hallmark of humanity on Mars, except for one of them. A short but hulking giant by Martian standards, he was the only one among them who hadn't been raised on the red planet. It was to him that the centurion now directed his attention.

Marcus Parn switched his comm to private mode so that only two of his troops could hear him. "Optio Felix. Celeusta Decimus. Is your section ready?"

"Affirmative, my Centurion," Domitia Felix replied in her soprano voice.

Next to her, the giant man once known as Tyrus Tyne—now Celeusta Tyrus Decimus—rumbled his own baritone reply. "Yes, my Centurion."

"Then they shall be the tip of the spear. Decimus, you will lead the assault," Parn said, careful to keep any emotion out of his voice.

"Sir?" the big man responded. "Are you sure, my Centurion?"

For almost any other member of the Praetorian Guard, that question would have earned him a reprimand. But Parn understood the conflict that raged inside of Decimus, even two and a half months into the bloody war with Earth. "Do your duty, Celeusta."

"Affirmative, my Centurion."

The shuttle shook around them as it made contact with their target. Then they waited another agonizing twenty-seven seconds, an eternity in an assault like this one, while the specially made nanites on the exterior of the assault shuttle's hull formed a seal with the exact shape of the airlock door on the disabled UEN battleship. Once that was done, Celeusta Decimus stepped forward and keyed open the shuttle's hatch, revealing the dull gray color of the Earth warship's hull, along with a trapezoidal airlock door and a control pad next to it.

He pressed the flashing green button on the control pad, and the airlock door opened without hesitation or complaint, drawing on its own reserve of backup power, kept purposefully separate from the main power systems of the massive battleship. Intel, which Decimus himself had provided, had let them know that one of the automatic responses UEN ships made to losing all power was to unlock every airlock, making it possible for rescue crews to reach any crew trapped inside. Today, it would be to their detriment.

Celeusta Decimus was first through the breach, as befitted the assault leader. Optio Felix was right on his heels. The two were a battle pair, which meant they fought side by side. That they were a bonded pair outside of their duties made them all the stronger when they fought together. Unlike most military units, even on Mars, the Praetorian Guard did not prohibit relationships within its ranks; in fact, it encouraged them. Borrowing a page from the ancient Spartans of Earth, praetorian guards fought in battle pairs instead of individually. Those pairs were mostly inseparable during combat. If one fell, the other often fought to the death over their partner's body rather than leave them behind.

The reasoning was simple. Two soldiers bonded together, training together, learning to anticipate each other's moves and countermoves, made for an efficient and deadly force. Especially because they fought not just for Mars or for their unit, but also for each other. It was all the more powerful if they were bonded together by familial or romantic ties. Decimus and Felix were the latter. They had not married, but they had been bonded together since the very day the war had started.

Parn himself was next through the breach after them. Celeusta Ursus, the other half of the centurion's fighting pair—one of brotherhood, not romance—was on his heels.

Inside the zero-g vacuum that lived between the Earth battleship's inner and outer hulls, Decimus and Felix had already floated to the next airlock door. Its control panel showed red, but only because the outer door was still open. The eight soldiers of Felix's section, four battle pairs, plus Parn and Ursus, crowded into the narrow corridor, and the last woman through hit the controls to close the outer door. Then Felix hit the control to open the inner one. Air rushed into the lock from the ship corridors beyond, and they all held tight to whatever they could as the pressure rapidly equalized around them. As soon as the rushing wind died down, Decimus was again first through the breach, pushing himself off the rim of the hatch and floating down the corridor like a missile, Felix right next to him.

A total of one minute and twenty-seven seconds had passed since they had latched onto the UEN battleship's hull.

"No contact," Felix said through her short-range comm, signaling that the coast was clear for the rest of the assault force to enter. They did so in a typically efficient fashion, and forty seconds later, the entire force of seventeen troops and officers was inside the enemy ship. Just as the last of them entered, the corridor lights flickered back on, and gravity returned gradually, allowing them all to float back down to the deck.

Their suits had two different kinds of integrated comm systems. One was a short-range system that they could use to communicate when standing within a ten-meter radius. It was so low-power that they could use it with little fear of detection, even inside an enemy ship. The second comm system, a stronger one, could have been used to make contact with the other three breaching teams, who by now should have also entered the UENS *Italy*, but contacting them would also give away their presence and positions to the ship's defenders.

With that in mind, Parn had to trust that the other three teams had successfully boarded the battleship before its engineering crews had restored power and the airlocks had likewise resumed their security seals, but he had no way to confirm it. If any of them lost time having to hack the seals or cut through the doors themselves, the mission was doomed.

Two of those teams were tasked with disabling the ship's control systems. That was the second most critical part of the mission—and without its success, the most critical part would be out of reach—hence the redundancy. The third team was tasked with taking the main engineering compartments.

The fourth and final team, Parn's, was heading toward the flag bridge, but that was not their main target. They just needed the UEN battleship's defenders to *think* that was their goal.

They'd been moving through the ship's corridors for only a minute, the stealth features of their suits disabled—lest the power drain of continuous use render the exosuits useless shells—when they encountered their first opposition.

A squad of eight UE Marines had set up at a junction between two corridors, waiting for Parn's team to get close before they opened fire.

The centurion was still directly behind Decimus and Felix when the first shots hit, one taking Decimus in his broad chest and the other hitting Felix in the shoulder. Both of the guards grunted but otherwise did not react, and Felix quickly returned fire. The Marine weapons were designed to have low muzzle velocity so that misses would not punch through bulkheads and hit any critical components behind them. The Martian exosuits were easily up to the task of stopping them.

The same could not be said of the fragmentation grenade that followed the bullets, arcing to land just in front of Felix, a red flashing light showing it was about to blow.

Decimus's move was almost too fast to follow with the human eye. Even as the grenade flew through the air, the big man was moving, throwing himself sideways and forward, landing on his side in front of the optio and between her and the grenade. As the device landed and slid the last meter toward his bonded partner, the big man grabbed the grenade with the arm that wasn't pinned under his body and, in one fluid motion, threw it back the way it had come.

Parn's helmet muted the sound of the explosion that followed but did not do the same for the screams of dying men that came after. As a soldier, the sound pained him, but it also cheered him in that the screams belonged to the enemy and not his own people.

All thanks to Celeusta Decimus. It had been a brave and bold move on the big man's part—impressive, really. *Almost* impressive enough to mask the man's mistake.

As Decimus got himself up off the ground while Felix and Ursus rushed forward with four other men to finish off the remainder of the marines, Parn switched his helmet comm to private mode.

"You hesitated," he said, doing his best to keep his tone that of a clinical observation. "You did not join Optio Felix in returning fire after the Earther's bullet hit you."

Decimus turned his opaque helmet toward his commanding officer. "I did hesitate, my Centurion," he admitted. No matter the man's faults, he owned them, which is what made this next part so much harder.

"We have talked about this, Celeusta," Parn said, his voice hardening. "Your split loyalties are going to get others killed. I gave you the lead today so you could prove yourself worthy of the honor bestowed upon you when you took the Oaths. But you failed on the first test."

There was silence on the other side of the comm. When Tyrus

Decimus finally answered, his voice was low, and he spoke slowly. "I find it difficult, my Centurion, to kill those we will need on our side when the Council attacks and . . . those I once allied with." He admitted the last part after only a short delay.

Parn could understand Tyrus's dilemma, but he could *not* sympathize with it. He didn't have the room to do so.

"If this mission fails, Celeusta Decimus, it will be on your head. And you and I will meet on the field of honor, to the death. Do you understand?"

Again, silence as Tyrus considered his commander's words. Then he nodded his helmeted head. "I understand, my Centurion. And I obey."

Neither said more; there was nothing more to be said. Decimus turned back to the battle and sprinted forward to join the other half of his battle pair, Parn close behind on his heels.

"Admiral, the Marines have pinned down one of the groups outside Engineering, but the other three have blown through our initial defenses."

Dalish Connors swore. He had been watching the battle plot that showed the Martian ships taking up escort positions around *Italy*, just outside the range of his ship's remaining lasers, as she attempted to limp back to UEN lines with only partial power to her engines. She wouldn't make it, and the closest UEN force large enough to make a difference was a good fifteen minutes away at this rate. They just needed to hold off the boarders for that long.

It bothered him that he couldn't decipher the *why* behind the enemy's movements. Two of the four boarding groups made sense. One was heading to Engineering, no doubt to prevent the ship from fleeing or submerging into the void with the enemy on board. And the other was heading here, to the flag bridge—again, obvious. Capture the most senior officer, and you effectively capture the ship. More obvious in that they almost certainly wanted Dalish himself, and not just because of his rank.

But the other two groups made no sense. Both were heading toward noncritical parts of the ship—one toward the hydroponics bay and the other toward the medical center. What were they up to?

"Admiral," interrupted his tactical officer. "You need to see this."

The man flicked something on the screen in front of him to the flag bridge's main forward viewscreen. It was a still image obviously taken from the video feed of a Marine's combat helmet. The Marine in question was lying on the ground, almost certainly dead. A figure clad entirely in black stood over him—or her—looking down and pointing a wicked-looking rifle toward the camera.

Dalish froze. *It can't be!* he thought. Aloud, he said, "Is that what I think it is, Joe?"

"Yes, sir," the tactical officer said, his voice shaky. "The AI has positively identified it as a Praetorian Guard exosuit."

There were murmurs all around the flag bridge at that statement, and the admiral immediately regretted letting the rest of them see and hear that. To win against the intruders, his people had to first *believe* they could beat them. And up until this very moment, everyone on the bridge *had* believed that they held the upper hand.

After all, *Italy* had a crew of just over two thousand, and the internal sensors only showed fifty-four total intruders. Given that *Italy* had an entire company of Marines plus a squad of SEALs on board along with two dozen Naval Security officers, it shouldn't have been a question as to who would ultimately win the battle.

But with this new revelation, that math changed drastically, and it suddenly made sense why three of the boarding groups hadn't even been slowed by the initial Marine defenses.

"Joe, come here," he ordered, and his tactical officer moved up to stand next to his chair. Dalish engaged a privacy field so the two men would not be overheard. The rest of the bridge crew would wonder at and speculate over what they were saying, but that couldn't be helped.

"Joe, what's the latest intel on the Praetorian Guard? Are they still limited to a hundred total members?"

"They are," the man answered, his frown showing that he knew where his Admiral was going with this.

"So we have just over *half* of Mars's entire complement of praetorian guards on board? Assuming all four teams consist entirely of the PGs?"

The man nodded slowly and let out a long breath. "It would seem so, Admiral."

"Any idea what they could be going for on board that would justify them sending half of their most elite fighting force to assault this one ship?"

Both men thought for a moment, and it was Dalish who ultimately answered his own question.

"The computer core. They're looking for . . . our battle plans." He knew that wasn't *actually* what they wanted, but he couldn't tell the tactical officer that without revealing information the man wasn't cleared for. Even Dalish had a hard time believing it, except that he had to admit to himself that fifty-four praetorian guards was overkill if all they really wanted was revenge against him personally—though you never could be sure with the Martians and their twisted sense of honor.

Commander Joe Hammond swore loudly at his admiral's pronouncement. "Sorry, sir," he said quickly. "That would make sense, except that they're not really attacking in the right pattern if they want the core. Sure, the computer center is near the flag bridge, so one team may be on their way there instead of here, but they have to know we can wipe the entire core at any time from here or the CIC. Those connections are hardwired; there's no way to hack them to stop us from sending the command."

The admiral nodded, rubbing his chin in thought. "You're right, but the Martians must know that as well. Which means they have something planned to stop us from doing that. Just to be safe, let's move the SEAL team to the computer center and have them ready to stage a defense there. Tell them that under no circumstances can the Martians be allowed to access an intact core. They are to do *whatever* it takes to prevent that."

"Yes, sir."

"And Joe?"

"Sir?"

"Tell Major Ignacio and Lieutenant Commander Davtyan what

they're facing. They can use their discretion on telling their troops or not." Ignacio was *Italy*'s Marine commander, and Davtyan led the SEALs on board. The men were semifriendly rivals at the best of times but would work together now as if they were brothers.

Dalish Connors turned his attention back to the internal map. He watched four red blotches, representing the four groups of Praetorian Guard boarders, still far outnumbered by the groups of blue converging on them from all over the massive ship, move quickly and inexorably toward whatever targets they were really here for.

CHAPTER 41

"My Centurion, we are thirty-four seconds behind the mission clock," Ursus told his commander on the open channel for all to hear. That was good; let it motivate them.

"You heard him, Guards!" Parn shouted through the helmet comms. "Gemina Team and Hispana Team will move on schedule whether or not we stand ready. Would you let your brothers and sisters down?"

"For Mars!" came the shouted response, followed by an increase in the pace at which they ran down the long corridor.

They had just passed a line of closed hatches, their suits detecting no thermal signatures behind any of them, when the bullets started flying.

Domitia Felix and Tyrus Decimus raised their left arms, and their personal shields sprang to life, taking the impact of the first few shots, but not before one got through and impacted Ursus in the lower leg. The big man grunted and crashed to his knees. He tried to stand, but the injured leg would not bear his weight.

"Armor piercing round, my Centurion," Ursus gritted between clenched teeth. Judging by the blood pooling under him and the way his left lower leg lay at an angle at odds with the rest of his body, his tibia and fibula had likely been shattered by the impact, but he raised his gun anyway and returned fire around the shields his comrade's held.

"Everyone down!" shouted Decimus as his and Felix's shields glowed red, indicating that they were both about to fail. The portable shields built into the exosuits only lasted for a few seconds, and the more impacts they absorbed, the faster they wore out.

The entire team, including Parn and the injured Ursus, fell flat to their bellies. All except for Decimus and Felix, who used the last moments their shields gave them to sprint forward, covering about a third of the distance between their team and the assaulting Marines. Parn could see the enemy now; they had barricaded a corridor with a portable shield and a heavy machine gun peeking out over it. Apparently, they had stopped worrying about damaging anything inside the ship's bulkheads.

The centurion watched as Felix's and Decimus's shields finally failed. But right before they did so, the two soldiers jumped upward. Then, surely to the shock of the watching Marines, they didn't come back down to the deck but flipped, twisted in the air, and fell *up* so that their feet landed on the corridor's low ceiling, where they continued running in a crouch as if gravity had turned itself upside down for them. Which it had, really, given the complex and top-secret antigrav tech in their suits, akin to the antigrav belts that both Earth and the colonies had but at least one generation ahead.

The stunned Marines hesitated for only an instant, but it was an instant too long. Both Decimus and Felix grabbed the assault rifles hanging from their battle harnesses and started firing down—or really *up*—at the battleship's defenders, who at that angle were now fully exposed behind their low barricade and shield. Then, right when the UE Marines finally collected themselves enough to raise their own rifles, their enemy disappeared.

Parn knew that the Earth Marines had seen stealth suits before. They had versions of similar suits that their special forces wore. But they weren't used to fighting against them in a pitched gun battle, at least not outside the odd training exercise against their own SEALS. So, the sudden disappearance of Decimus and Felix confused them for another crucial instant. One of them even stood up, as if by doing so she might get a better view and locate the two stealthed attackers. Parn shot that one through the head the instant she showed herself.

Felix reappeared right in front of the Marines, still standing on the ceiling less than two meters from them but up against the corridor wall, where her thin frame made her a narrow target. She fired calmly into them one after another. There were three still alive with enough time to react and swing their guns to aim at her, but all three in sequence fell forward as bullets took them from behind before they could tighten their fingers on their triggers.

Decimus appeared, falling from the ceiling and spinning in midair to land on the deck behind the now-dead or dying Marines. Parn had to admit that Tyrus was efficient. He may have hesitated earlier to kill the United Earth personnel he had once considered allies, but once he set his mind to a mission, that was that. Especially when Domitia Felix was in danger.

Parn looked down at Ursus, who had retracted his helmet and was sweating profusely and clenching his jaw in pain. "My friend," he told the larger man, "Optio Felix can lead this mission. I will stay with you and guard our rear."

Ursus shook his head emphatically. "No, my Centurion. You will need every guard for the mission. *I* will guard the rear myself, and no one will reach you from behind, on my honor."

Parn nodded. The man's response was expected, and none of the bravado was false. Ursus's suit had managed to administer first aid and stop the bleeding, but it had *not* injected any pain meds into the large man, nor would he allow it to, so that he would be alert to protect his team against any Earth forces that tried to flank them down this corridor.

Decimus had made his way back down the corridor to where Parn was now crouched next to a sitting Ursus. Without a word, the celeusta picked up the big Martian like he was a small child; Ursus had been the largest and heaviest of the Praetorian Guard before Decimus had joined them, but he massed less than two-thirds what Decimus did. Decimus was able to easily carry him to the barrier and machine gun nest the Marines had constructed. The gun was still intact, and

Decimus set Ursus down where he could operate it and have cover behind the portable shield.

"Thank you, Tyrus," Ursus grunted. "It is good to see you do something useful with that slow-moving bulk of yours."

Parn couldn't see Decimus smile behind his opaque full-face helmet, but he could hear it in the man's voice. "My pleasure, Jobe. Leave it to you to find an excuse to sit down during a battle."

Ursus laughed, and Parn shook his head. The two large men habitually poked fun at each other, though they hadn't always been so congenial about it. Ursus had almost challenged Decimus to an honor duel several times in the ex-colonial's first few days with the Guard, and only Parn's quiet disapproval stopped him from doing so. Now, Decimus and Ursus were the best of friends.

He kept his team moving, leaving the other member of his own battle pair behind, which pained him. Decimus and Felix continued to lead the way, and Parn watched them move in concert with each other, almost like two parts of the same body. He checked the mission clock on his helmet's HUD and saw that they were still slightly behind but making up time despite the short battle with the Marines. There was hope that this plan would work.

It had to work. When Parn himself had sold the plan to the Quorum of Praetors, he had promised on his honor they would be successful. He hadn't shared it with the other Guards, but failure in this mission meant his death. Worse, it was the last chance they had to convince the praetors that the Council and its few collaborators, not Earth, were the enemy.

Lieutenant Commander Pyotr Davtyan watched the battle map of *Italy* in his own helmet's HUD display and shook his head in frustration. He had tried to convince Major Ignacio to pull his Marines back to the flag bridge and computer center. Let the Martians come to them and fight against the vastly superior numbers the UE had waiting to receive them. But Ignacio was stubborn and refused to believe that just a relative handful of men and women could stand against his company of Marines, even if they *were* from the vaunted Praetorian Guard.

His exact words to Davytan: "We're not going to let a campfire ghost story get into our heads and change our entire battle plan."

So instead, he had followed the book for defending a UEN battleship from boarders, putting squads of Marines at key intersections to stop the attackers, and allowing other troops to go to their assistance as they made contact with the enemy.

But all that really meant in practice today was that the Martians were able to defeat the Marines in smaller groups, and they were doing so with such speed that reinforcements never arrived in time. Then, the reinforcements themselves got caught out of position in the open corridors rather than in their fortified positions.

The Praetorians seemed to be cutting through anything the Marines could send at them. And it wasn't just their skill—which even Davtyan had to begrudgingly admit was *almost* as good as that of his SEALS—it was also their tech. He'd heard rumors of it being more advanced than what United Earth had, but he'd only half believed them . . . until now.

Fragmented reports were coming in from all over the ship where the Marines had engaged the enemy. Men and women screamed about disappearing foes—stealth suits weren't that uncommon, really—but a few had also talked about enemy soldiers *running on the walls and ceilings*. At the first report of that happening, Davtyan had chalked it up to an overly excited private. But after the third report, he was a believer. He had an antigrav belt on his own battle suit, of course, but about all it allowed him to do was jump extra high or soften the landing if he fell a great distance. Running on the ceiling would be something else entirely.

"Commander Davtyan." A voice broke into his thoughts and his helmet comm.

"Here, Admiral."

"They're breaking through the defenses, son," Rear Admiral Connors said with what Davtyan detected was an edge of raggedness to his voice.

"Yes, sir. I advised Major Ignacio to pull back his troops, but it does appear that the Reds are behind his lines now."

"Never mind who advised who of what!" the admiral snapped. "Are you and your men ready to repel them?"

"Yes, sir," Davtyan responded crisply. "But I must protest again, Admiral. Let me send a fire team to the flag bridge to—"

"We'll be okay here," Connors cut him off. "We have two security teams, and we've sealed the doors behind my personal command codes. I need you to make sure they don't get to that computer core. And if they do, you have your orders."

"Aye aye, sir," Davtyan responded reluctantly. The admiral cut the comm connection.

The SEAL commander looked around the computer center. It was a relatively small room, humming with the sound of the environmental control systems that kept the room at a much cooler temperature than anywhere else on the ship. It was usually staffed by at least two technicians, but those men were now huddled on the flag bridge with the command staff, leaving just Davtyan and his single eight-man squad in the space.

"SEALs," he barked through his squad comm channel. "The enemy is less than two mikes out, and the Marines aren't going to stop them. It's up to us. Copy?"

"Hooyah!" the six men and two women chorused in reply, and they settled in to await the inevitable.

Marcus Parn lost three more guards in addition to Ursus—two dead and one more injured and also left behind to guard their rear. The Marines were starting to figure out that the Martians were behind their lines, but they were slow in repositioning. That was likely in part due to the comm jammers Parn's team had been affixing to the walls and leaving behind them. They didn't impact internal ship hardline comms, but they would wreak havoc with the wireless signals and make it hard for the Marines to coordinate their movements.

He checked the mission clock again. They'd finally caught up to where they were supposed to be, assuming Gemina Team and Hispana Team had made it to their designated positions in time.

"Thirty seconds to Nightfall," he called to the Guards with him, hoping that it would come on time.

"Sir, we've lost engineering." The sour voice of Commander Joe Hammond told Dalish Connors what the internal battle map already had. They'd lost contact with a lot of the Marines around the ship—the Martians were deploying some sort of jamming—but they still had a hardwired connection to the battleship's engineering compartments. Or they had—until about forty-five seconds ago. Hammond had been able to pull up a few of the security cameras in that area, before the enemy had disabled them, in time to see the Martians lining up the still-living crew in that area and hitting them with stun rounds.

Dalish hated the Martians with a passion—even more than most UEN officers. He'd hated them *before* this particular war had broken out. But he was grateful that they weren't killing unarmed crew members indiscriminately. One couldn't always be sure with the Reds.

"What about the other two enemy groups, the ones who were headed toward Hydroponics and Medical?"

His tactical officer shook his head. "It's hard to tell; those jammers of theirs are messing with our internal sensors as well. From snippets we're getting from the Marines, I think we've managed to stop the team heading for medical, but the one going to Hydroponics is likely already there."

Dalish swore. He had no idea why the Martians wanted to take over his hydroponics bay, but he was sure it wasn't good.

"Uh, Admiral," one of the computer technicians who had taken refuge in the flag bridge said hesitantly.

He looked over at the man, who shrank under his gaze. *For all the . . .* "What is it, son?" he barked. "Spit it out!"

"Well . . . uh . . . I think maybe I know why they're in hydroponics. Sorry," he hastened to add, "I couldn't help but overhear, sir."

"Why then?" Commander Hammond asked the man, who now seemed double chagrined to have two officers staring at him.

"Well, sir. Hydroponics needs to be warmer than the rest of the ship. When they designed the Missouri class, they looked for little ways to save money and efficiency. And the main control trunk lines produce a lot of heat. So they routed them through areas of the ship that didn't need to be kept as cool. Like hydroponics. And the redundant control line, sir, goes through the incubation labs near the med bay."

Dalish furrowed his brow at the man, but then it suddenly snapped into place for him. "Hammond, find Ignacio. Tell him to send all of his men amidships to Hydroponics and the medical bay! Do it now!"

But even as he punctuated the last command, he found out it was too late. Two distant explosions sounded, and the lights in the flag bridge, along with every console, display, and touch screen, abruptly winked out for the second time that day. Only gravity remained this time.

Joe Hammond had been wrong. The Marines *hadn't* stopped the Martians headed for the med bay. And with the main control trunk lines destroyed on both sides of the ship, Admiral Dalish Connors had just lost complete control of every one of *Italy*'s systems. And with it, he'd lost the capability to remotely wipe the computer core. Everything was up to Commander Davtyan and his SEALs now.

CHAPTER 42

Lieutenant Commander Pyotr Davtyan heard one of his SEALs gasp in surprise as the lights and every console in the computer core room went dark.

"Sir?" Chief Petty Officer O'Riley asked him.

"I don't know, Chief," he answered honestly. "But it doesn't matter much now. Be ready folks; they're inbound."

Then, the time for talk was over as the door to Davtyan's right blew inward.

Once again, Celeusta Decimus and Optio Felix were first through the breach, though this time they each threw in a stun grenade before entering the dark room, triggering their stealth suits. The overload of the main control trunklines by Gemina and Hispana Teams had done what they'd hoped, and every light in the battleship was out, including the emergency lamps. So were any capabilities for the bridge or CIC to send remote wipe commands to the computer command center.

Though, if Parn was right about who was waiting for them in the computer command chamber, stealth wouldn't matter. It was far too convenient that the only resistance they'd encountered so far had come from Marines and UEN security forces. The vaunted SEALs had been noticeably absent.

The two stun grenades blew, but a wireless connection with his team's exosuits allowed them to dim the helmet face coverings and turn off the external microphones at the exact moment of the explosions. It would give them a slight edge over the SEALs, whose suits would do the same but a fraction of a second late as they reacted to the grenades instead of anticipating them.

That fraction of a second would hopefully be just enough, especially as the other half of the team blew in the opposite door to the chamber right after the stun grenades went off.

Pyotr Davtyan started firing the moment the door blew inward and stopped only when the stun grenades briefly disoriented him and he was worried he might hit one of his own people. But his suit reacted quickly and cut off the worst of the light and noise, and he only stopped pulling his assault rifle's trigger for a fraction of a second.

Then he heard the door behind him blow inward and winced. They had more or less expected the two-pronged assault, but it made things much more complicated. Still, he focused his fire in front of him and trusted that the four SEALS he'd placed watching the rear hatch would handle that side.

For a moment, he thought they might hold off the assault. Only two Martians had come through the door on the heels of the stun grenades, their stealth suits outlined in his HUD based on his own suit's active sonar built just for that purpose. Both of the attackers had hit the floor as soon as they'd entered, hopefully with two or three bullets in them each, courtesy of the United Earth Navy SEALs. That stopped the rest of the Martians, who were firing around the sides of the open hatches but hadn't entered the compartment.

Then, suddenly and without warning, Davtyan saw two red and orange outlines in his helmet's thermal imaging jump up from the floor and fly in a streak toward the computer core's abnormally high ceiling, four meters above. He raised his gun to track them as he realized what was happening, but the two soldiers who had entered the room first, whom he'd thought out of the fight, hit the ceiling feet first and jumped again, now streaking down almost directly over Davtyan's head as they flipped in the air.

One of them fired as they fell, hitting Davtyan in the chest, but it didn't penetrate his suit. It did, however, mess up his aim on the other one, who made it up and over before he could bring his assault rifle back in line. He whirled in time to see the one who had fired on him, a typical long, skinny Martian, shoot point blank into the back of one of his men's helmets, where his neck armor joint was weakest. The SEAL dropped. Then there was a flash of something metal in the wild flashing lights of the muzzle blasts, and another SEAL dropped.

Davtyan wanted so badly to take both of them out, but he could see on his HUD that he only had two effective SEALs left in addition to himself. Between the acrobatics of the first two attackers and the heavy fire from the others now pouring through both doors, the battle was lost.

But maybe not the war.

Davtyan did something he'd never done before in a pitched battle, dropping his assault rifle to hang loosely from its harness as he dove across the room, moving by memory, seeking the one thing he'd been placed in this room to do in the event that they failed to defend it.

With the lights on, it would have been easy. The button was big and red, after all, and even with the ship disabled, its mechanical backups should work. He reached the control panel and crouched down behind it, safe for a moment from the firefight, and started running his hands over the control surfaces, feeling for the 'doomsday switch,' as the technician who had shown it to him had called it.

There!

His hand found the clear, boxy cover that guarded the switch against inadvertent activation. That cover was usually locked in place —it would be catastrophic if someone hit the button while *Italy* was underway; without the computer, the ship would be helpless and ballistic in space. But now, the cover was unlocked, awaiting this very moment, as Davtyan flung it open with one hand and slammed his other down toward the button underneath, a triumphant battle cry issuing from his throat.

But something strange happened. He felt an ever-so-brief tugging on his arm, and then his hand didn't reach the button! *What?* He tried again, but it was like his hand was going *through* the console. In dismay, he reached up with his other hand to feel and found only a stump where his right hand should have been.

Thinking quickly, he darted his left hand toward the exposed button, but something grabbed him and lifted him into the air by his battle harness, slamming him up against the clear armored glass that kept the servers safe from the outside world. He gasped, the wind knocked out of him despite his armored suit, and a light flashed on, mounted on the shoulder of the gigantic figure holding him.

The outcome was never really in question. Marcus Parn had to admit that the UEN SEALs were outstanding soldiers, almost on par with the Praetorian Guard. But they were outnumbered almost two to one and had been trying to defend against attackers on both sides. Even still, they managed to wound three more of Parn's guards and kill another; ironically, the second half of the battle pair of the guard killed earlier. Parn said a silent prayer to Mars that the two would be reunited in Olympus. They'd been a married pair, and it was likely better that they were together now again than that one should continue life without the other.

Tyrus Decimus and Domitia Felix had been spectacular, even by Praetorian Guard standards. They had leaped and flipped and then fought back-to-back, with all the strength of Europan krakens and the speed of Martian attack eagles. Both had been injured, with blood seeping from multiple grazes and a solid hit to the side of Decimus's midsection. The man would be in tremendous pain, but the suit was already pumping its small supply of healing nanites into the wound, and Tyrus barely showed the effects of it even as the adrenaline of the attack wore off.

The battleship's damage control systems had finally kicked in. Less than two minutes after the ship had been disabled, emergency lights started to come on as circuit breakers reset and emergency power rerouted through secondary trunk lines. It would be far longer before primary power or engine control could be restored, and both would require lengthy repairs in spacedock to mend the broken control trunk lines. Either way, *Italy* was out of the fight. He only wished they could finish the job by killing Admiral Dalish Connors, the man who Parn was sure had started this entire war. Unfortunately, they had neither the time nor the tools to cut through the security doors into the flag bridge.

Two of the SEALs at his feet were still alive, though one was mortally wounded, a chest wound that only an immediate full submersion in a healing bath could have a hope of fixing in time. Nonetheless, Celeusta Nero, who doubled as his team's immune, was already tending to the man, administering a small injection of nanites in the unlikely event that they could do any good.

The other surviving SEAL was the team commander, who was bleeding from several grazes and missing a hand but otherwise lacked any serious injury. The man had come within a hair's breadth of destroying the computer core, but Decimus had intervened just in time.

Parn hadn't understood when Tyrus Decimus had asked for two custom-designed swords to augment the normal Praetorian Guard battle kit. The two short gladiuses, with nanotechnology that allowed the self-repairing monomolecular-edged blades to retract into their hilts when not in use, had been wildly expensive to make. But he had to admit they'd been worth the expense. Decimus was good with a gun—with any weapon, really—but he was Thanatos Mors, the Martian god of death, himself with those swords.

Two of the dead SEALs had fallen to those blades, their exosuits barely slowing down the swords as they sliced through bone and sinew. And the SEAL commander had lost his hand to Tyrus's blade right before it would have slagged the servers they'd come so far to infiltrate.

Now, the enemy SEAL commander looked up at Parn with anger in his eyes, though with a certain measure of respect of one elite commander toward another. Most of the anger the man felt, Parn imagined, was likely at himself for failing his mission.

That anger flared, however, and all signs of respect fled the SEAL's features when Decimus stepped up next to Parn to report on the status of the infiltration of the computer core. Upon seeing Decimus, who had retracted his helmet, the SEAL commander spat and swore loudly.

"You traitor!" he growled, drawing a shocked look from the giant of a man. "You filthy traitor. We trusted you!"

Tyrus Decimus said nothing, but Parn could see the sadness behind those hard eyes as he regarded the enemy leader on the ground before him. The SEAL continued, talking in a low and menacing voice now.

"You don't remember me, do you, traitor? We met once, at the Naval Warfare college on Luna, when you came and talked to the SEALs about Council tactics." He spat again, hitting the celeusta's foot. "We thought you were on our side. But I guess once a traitor, always a traitor." The SEAL struggled to get up, almost as if he would fight Decimus weaponless, with only one hand, rather than lie there and do nothing. Only Parn's foot on the man's chest stopped him from lunging to his feet.

The SEAL commander swore more, and Parn looked up at Decimus to see the big man staring down, unmoving. Then, almost too quiet for either of them to hear, he whispered, "I remember you. Commander Davtyan. You asked me a question about colonial personal shield durability."

The man either didn't hear Decimus speak or ignored him. Still fighting to get off the ground despite his weakened state and Parn's exosuit-enhanced foot holding him down, he seemed oblivious to anything other than his desire to kill the bigger man.

"Celeusta," Parn said sharply, breaking Decimus's gaze from the SEAL commander. "Go check on the download progress."

Decimus nodded slowly and turned away, walking with shoulders slumped, a far cry from the indomitable giant that had stormed the computer command center at his bonded partner's side. Parn worried that he might never see that Tyrus Decimus again.

CHAPTER 43

Martian computer techs had programmed a special drive to connect to *Italy*'s computer core. An AI installed on the drive searched the core for its raw log files, downloading all the logs from the day of the battle at Nyx, including those from the two days before and two days after, just to be safe.

The logs themselves were heavily encrypted, and the drive's AI couldn't read them, but it didn't need to. It just needed to make copies. More advanced aIs backed by computer techs on Mars would take on the delicate work of decrypting the files.

The mission was a success; they might now have what they needed to end this war.

It took the praetorian guards only a few minutes to fight their way through the remaining Marines who attempted to cut off their escape. With the ship dead in space, their comms with the bridge cut off, and even the invincible SEALs vanquished, the defense was ineffective and poorly organized at best, and no additional guards were lost, even as they slowed down to recover their wounded left behind during the initial assault.

All four assault teams returned to their boarding shuttles, which quickly separated from the *Italy*. The surviving members of the elite fighting force watched as the large UEN battleship became a distant point in their sensor views, feeling both triumphant at the mission's success and saddened at those they'd lost.

In Domitia's case, however, the feeling of triumph had worn off quickly. Now that the adrenaline had faded and the battle lust was a distant memory, she sat in the shuttle that took Centurion Parn's assault team back to the MPNS *Julius Caesar*, flagship of the Fleet of the Eagle, and she regarded her bonded partner with equal parts love, anger, and sadness.

Tyrus had said little since they'd left *Italy* behind. Outwardly, even with his helmet retracted, he betrayed nothing of the emotions raging behind that impassive face and those hard eyes. No one on the team could tell just how much he was suffering—no one except her.

Domitia knew her man. In the two and a half months they had been together, she had seen him at his best and at his worst. She had known he had struggled with the mere idea of fighting against those he'd once called allies and friends, but it hadn't been until the battle this day that she fully understood just how conflicted he was.

Part of Domitia wanted to grab Tyrus and shake him, even slap him across the face. He was a *Martian* now! He had made that sacred commitment the day he had joined the Guard and sworn allegiance to Mars. The day after he had sworn himself to her.

But her anger wasn't at him. It was at herself. She knew, deep down, that the only reason Tyrus had fought as viciously as he had today was for her. Certainly, he had a deeply ingrained sense of loyalty to the Praetorian Guard and Centurion Parn in particular, but he'd had a similar loyalty to the United Earth Navy before that, even if he'd never technically been a member of their ranks.

No, Tyrus's true loyalty was to Domitia Felix. That was good in a way; it was the entire reason the Praetorian Guard used bonded battle pairs. But it also pained her to no end to see the man she loved rip himself to shreds physically and emotionally for her almost daily since the war had begun—and even more since the consul had ordered the Praetorian Guard to undertake this mission and had moved them to the frontlines. Every time Tyrus joined them in battle or revealed a piece of colonial tech or UEN weakness—like the right spots to hit that battleship with the dozen shocker missiles he had helped Martian techs design and build—she saw a small part of him die.

And now, to find himself face-to-face with a man he'd actually met while he'd assisted the UEN . . . it was destroying him from the inside out. She could see it in his eyes, and it broke past the hardness of her soldier's mentality and was tearing her own heart to shreds.

Domitia had grown up the youngest child and only daughter of a military man. He had raised her as he had raised her three older brothers: to fight and to win. Her father had ingrained in her from an early age that there was no greater honor than to serve the banner of Mars and its legions. And he had cried the only tears she'd ever seen from him the day she took the Oaths and became a member of the Praetorian Guard.

That had been her entire life. Domitia had trained around the clock, even before being admitted to the Guard when she was a simple Optio in the Legion of Charon. Her entire existence had centered around serving Mars and bringing honor to her family and her fellow soldiers.

She had risen quickly in the Praetorian Guard, obtaining the rank of Optio faster than any woman before her and second fastest behind any man in peacetime. She had earned the respect of the soldiers underneath her and had become Centurion Parn's right hand, trusted above his other optios and closer to the man than anyone except his own battle partner, Celeusta Ursus.

Then, she had met Tyrus Tyne. At first, he had annoyed her. Asking her to lunch as he'd done the first time they'd met had crossed so many lines of Martian etiquette that she'd considered challenging him to an honor duel or even killing him there and then as would have been her right.

Instead, she'd decided to be lenient with him as a visitor and foreigner on her world. Besides, Centurion Parn had spoken well of the man, despite meeting him only once, and she respected her centurion's opinion. To her surprise, she had ended up quickly learning to enjoy the large colonial man's company. First, as a friend, who still got slightly annoyed and considered honor duels whenever she caught him trying very hard—and failing—to not look at her as if she were the only water in a desert. And later, as something far more.

Before she knew it, Domitia had found herself looking forward to their lunches, even craving their time together. She started seeking Tyrus out after sparring practice, in part because it was still fun to make him uncomfortable in the healing baths but also because she simply wanted to be around him. Centurion Parn had seen it and said nothing, but he had given her his silent approval nonetheless.

Still, what had held Domitia back was her loyalty to Mars. Surely, Tyrus would someday leave their planet, and Martian women did not bond to a man unless there was a future. Period. She could enjoy his company and friendship, but never more than that, for one day he would leave and she would not go with him.

So her heart had soared when Parn had selected Tyrus for the Trials. She had been ecstatic when Tyrus had won. It meant that they could be together with no worry about it ending with one leaving the other, unless by glorious death in battle. With Tyrus in the Praetorian Guard, they could be a bonded pair in battle as well as in love. She had leaped at the chance.

But now . . . Domitia saw all of that crashing down. It had been coming all along, she realized, though she'd done her best to ignore that fact. Tyrus Decimus—formerly Tyne—could not give up his past. He could not, in good conscience, fight against those who had once taken him in and called him a trusted . . . friend? That wasn't the right word, she reflected, especially after the Earthlings had betrayed Tyrus and his true friends. She had hoped that would be enough for him to break all his ties to them, but it hadn't. Not even *she* had been enough. The man was simply too loyal. Domitia imagined that even when the Council Navy finally invaded—and unlike some other Martians, she believed that they would—Tyrus would weep as he killed those he'd once called brothers and sisters from the 47 Colonies.

He would still kill them, just as he killed the Earthers now . . . for her.

But was that fair to him? Was it fair that he must be a man between worlds, never able to return to Earth or the colonies for the things he had done against them, but never able to completely embrace being a Martian for the things that he must do to be one? Was it fair that he would force himself to do such things for *her*?

No, Domitia thought. *It is not fair. And I cannot let him continue to do this for me. I am what keeps him here. Without me, he can be free. But with me, here in the Praetorian Guard, he will forever be a slave to his pain.*

In a moment of startling clarity, Domitia knew what she had to do, even if it would destroy her and break her heart to do it.

She leaned into Tyrus and gave him a soft kiss on the lips. As a bonded but still unmarried pair, that was all they had ever done; there were strict Martian rules about those sorts of things, and Tyrus had never once argued or pressured her for more than what she gave. He'd always been happy just to have her, as she had been happy to have him.

He kissed her back and then gave her a small smile, but it only lasted briefly as his despair quickly swallowed him again. It strengthened Domitia's resolve.

She gave the silent command, and her helmet reformed around her head and face. She keyed open a private comm channel to Centurion Parn, which he accepted.

"My Centurion," she said slowly. "I must speak with you."

Outwardly, he gave no physical acknowledgment, his own helmet hiding his features and expression as he sat on the other side of the shuttle from her and Tyrus. He answered her simply. "Then do so, Optio Felix."

She almost didn't go on. *Can I really do this? To the man who has given me so much?* But another look at the pain behind Tyrus's eyes eliminated all remaining doubts.

"My Centurion, Tyrus Decimus must leave the Praetorian Guard for his own good."

Now, Parn did react, turning his helmeted head from across the troop bay to regard her. "Do you break your pairing with him then?" he asked, almost in a whisper. He knew how she felt about Tyrus—knew what that would do to her. But she knew he also knew that she was right—Tyrus could not stay in the Guard. He had hesitated in the battle today, and he would do so again, especially after meeting the SEAL commander. Tyrus was broken, and he would put her and everyone else in the Guard at risk. But mostly, he would destroy himself quickly and inexorably.

Domitia Felix took a deep breath and said the words she had desperately hoped never to say—that she had certainly never *planned* to say. But now, she felt herself resolved in a way she never had been before. "Centurion Parn, I hereby request the right of relinquere vexillum."

Domitia waited in the antechamber of the office of the commanding officer of MPNS *Julius Caesar* and the entirety of the Fleet of the Eagle. Though she knew that outwardly she showed none of her anxiety, inwardly she was dreading the exchange to come. Legatus Augustus Lightbringer was a hard man, a man who brooked no disobedience among the crews under his command. And though Domitia was not technically under the legatus's command, and what she had asked of Centurion Parn was not technically disobedience, neither of those technicalities would save her from what was to come in the next few minutes.

The appointment had been for ten minutes before. The legatus had left her waiting, as was his right, but also as a sure and unambiguous sign of his disappointment and anger with her. As the long minutes ticked by, Domitia wondered if she should be reconsidering the fateful choice she had made, the one that had shocked even Centurion Parn and earned her an almost immediate summons from the fleet commander himself.

Surprisingly, she felt completely at peace with her decision, though she knew it would still shatter Tyrus when he found out.

Finally, the outer door to the legatus's office opened, and she watched as a group of senior officers, including two prefects and none more junior than a centurion, left the office in efficient fashion. The celeusta who managed the legatus's schedule frowned toward Domitia.

"Legatus Lightbringer will see you now, Optio Felix," the celeusta told her, nodding his head for her to proceed. Once she was inside, the man shut the door behind her.

The office of Augustus Lightbringer was spartan in its decor. The deck was bare metal, as were all decks in the Martian People's Navy—easier for the nanites to repair that way—and the bulkheads and ceiling matched it. A long plastic conference table dominated most of the room; even on battleships, mass had to be considered. At the far end of the office was a single wooden desk, the only extravagance. But there was no wall of vanity as with the flag officers of Earth, or so Domitia had been told. The only decorated wall in this office was not a shrine to the legatus but to his family. Pictures of his dead first wife, mother to his two oldest sons, and his current living wife, mother to another son and his only daughter, were proudly displayed. As were pictures of his four children, all in various military uniforms.

The three boys pictured all wore the blood-red colors of the Martian People's Navy. The oldest was a navarch, a squadron commander, a flag rank only two steps below his father's, serving in the Fleet of the Bear that guarded Mars herself. Another was a triarch, a ship's captain commanding a trireme in that same home fleet. The final boy was a centurion, helming a bireme in the Fleet of the Eagle under his father's command.

The last picture on the wall, in the place of honor, was that of Lightbringer's daughter, who was the only child not to wear the red of the MPN. Instead, she wore the midnight black of the Praetorian Guard. Domitia's resolve almost broke as she saw her younger self looking out at her from that photo, captured the day she had won the Trials, taken the Oaths, and joined the most elite military unit the red planet boasted.

It had been the greatest honor a soldier in the service of Mars could attain, and her father had cried on that day, tears of honor and joy. Now, she had to tell him she was throwing it all away.

The man himself stood up from his desk, nodding curtly to her and motioning for her to approach. She did, in a perfect march across the metal deck, stopping the regulation one meter from it and standing at rigid attention, throwing a sharp salute and fixing her eyes straight ahead.

"At ease, Optio," her father said gruffly. He remained standing, though, so she did not sit but widened her stance and put her hands clasped in front of her. Most Martian soldiers clasped their hands behind them at parade rest, as did the soldiers of Earth. Only the Praetorian Guard clasped their hands in front, symbolic of their position as the tip of the spear and the ever-vigilant defenders of Mars.

"Your mission was successful," said the legatus. "I have always believed that our trireme did not fire first at Nyx as the Earthlings claimed. Which is why I have viewed this war as a righteous endeavor against the would-be usurpers. But now, with the proof, from their own files no less, we can expose them for the liars they are."

Domitia simply nodded in response. Her father was speaking as if he already knew what the encrypted files they'd captured would contain. It was presumptuous of him, even if the traitor Toby Haight had disclosed the Keeper's plans to start a war between Mars and Earth to weaken both. But she cared little for the politics of the war; she cared only that Earth was trying to kill her and her fellow loyal Martians. That was enough for her to fight against them tooth and nail, regardless of who had fired the first shot. However, she knew that others, including her Tyrus, would take comfort in the confirmation that the Martians had not been the aggressors.

Her father watched her silently, and she felt her back go more rigid as he did so. He was building up to something, and she knew exactly what it was.

"Tell me, Daughter, that it is not true," Augustus Lightbringer said, his voice catching a little at the simple plea. Apart from the day of her Oaths, it was the most emotion he had ever shown, and he only showed it with her, never with her brothers. Perhaps he was softer with his wife, but not that Domitia had seen. Her mother was not one who required nor expected softness.

In her reply, she spoke slowly and carefully, knowing how much her words would sting the man. "I regret to inform my Legatus that I have, indeed, requested the right of relinquere vexillum."

He shook his head and frowned deeply. "And why, Daughter, would you do such a thing?" His voice rose with the question, and she could feel his barely contained anger behind his words.

She swallowed, suddenly at a loss for words herself, and briefly, the idea of backing out of the request flew through her mind once more. However, as before, she pictured Tyrus's face, and all doubts fled. "My

Father," she said softly, breaking formality. "I have found my bonded pair, and the bond must be sealed. I love him, but he is not of Mars, though he has earnestly tried to be."

Her father considered this for a long moment, his face betraying little of the raging emotions she knew he was feeling. When he finally spoke, his voice was pleading once more. "But, my Daughter, he *is* of Mars. He is of the Guard. Has he asked you to invoke this right? If he has, then he is not worthy of your hand, and I will challenge him on the field of honor to the death. If he bests me, your brothers will each take their turn until one of us puts him in the grave. That is my solemn vow."

Domitia shook her head. "No, my Father. Celeusta Tyrus Decimus has not asked me to invoke the right. He knows nothing of this."

"Then why?" His voice broke again, and once again, Domitia almost reneged, but she physically straightened her back as she hardened her resolve and pressed forward with what she *knew* she needed to do.

"He is of three worlds, my Father. He has been entirely loyal to Mars, to the Praetorian Guard, and to me as his battle partner since the day he took the Oaths. But I can see it destroying him. He is a loyal man, but his loyalty is to humanity, and he suffers and dies by measures each time he kills the enemy. He does not stay his hand when the lives of his fellow Guards are at stake . . . when *my* life hangs in the balance. Still, I can see what it does to him each and every time. As his bonded partner, I cannot see him suffer so. It . . . it destroys me as well, though if he knew how much, he would sooner die himself than cause me such pain."

She stopped, regarding her father, who had resumed his characteristic stony expression. He said nothing, so she continued.

"I would be with him always, my Father. He is my anima, my 'soul' as he might say, if he knew of such traditions. And I am his. I will not watch him suffer another day. So, as is my right, I have invoked relinquere vexillum, so that I—"

"It is the way of cowards!" her father hissed, so loudly that it almost made her take a step back. But only almost, and at his words, she felt the anger rise in her.

Domitia stepped forward instead, breaking the proscribed perimeter of his desk, a clear breach of etiquette to answer his. She moved to the edge of the desk, placing both hands on it, and leaned forward to meet his angry glare. When she replied to him, it was in a firm voice with an undertone of anger and menace. "Say that direct, Legatus Augustus Lightbringer. Call me a coward to my face, you who know me so well, and I will kill you on the field of honor as my recompense. And Mars shall lose a legatus and I a father this day!" She almost yelled the last part, and her indomitable father, the scourge of Earth, the supreme commander of fully a quarter of Mars's legions and over half its naval forces, wielder of enough firepower to destroy a dozen planets . . . took a step back.

He licked his lips, and his left eye started to twitch, just slightly. She waited. He had to be the next to speak, and she would not back down. If he answered one way, she would forgive and forget and withdraw the implied challenge. If he answered the other, she would meet him in a duel to the death, blood of her blood though he may be.

To her immense relief, he chose the first path. "My Daughter—Optio Felix—I can see now that my words were in error. I withdraw them. Forgive my brashness and decide my fate."

Even hearing the words, she was surprised at them. They were the proper thing to say at this juncture from someone who had given undue offense. But to hear them from her *father* . . .

"I accept your withdrawal and take no offense. Go in peace." She finished the formal dance of words, and she saw something she never expected to see again in her father's eyes, especially after Earth had attacked and forced him to become the ruthless killing machine Mars needed: the barest glint of tears.

"Tell me, my Daughter," he said in almost a whisper. "Does he fulfill all for you? Is he truly your anima?" She could hear the hope behind his trembling voice.

"Yes, my Father, he fulfills all and more, as my mother does for you," she answered, now fighting to keep the emotion from her voice as well. She stood back up, removing her hands from his desk and looking tenderly at him, all posture of anger and confrontation dissolved.

Augustus Lightbringer nodded, blinking away the tears and looking away for a moment, his eyes lingering on the large picture of her from the day of her Oaths. When he looked back, he smiled slightly. "Then I am happy for you. I disagree with your decision, but I will not stand in its way. Nor will I seek honor from this Tyrus Decimus. Though, now that you have left the Guard and are my daughter once again, I would meet him."

She nodded back. "It is Tyrus *Tyne*, my Father. As he and I will both be leaving the Guard, his name will be once again Tyrus Tyne. So I swear before Mars that mine will be Domitia Tyne. And I would be honored for you to meet him."

Tyrus floated in the healing bath, the nanites mending the bullet wound in his side as he stared at the ceiling and tried very hard not to think about Lieutenant Commander Pyotr Davtyan, the SEAL commander he had bested on the *Italy*. He tried *extremely* hard not to remember the man's words, but he failed at it.

Traitor, he thought morosely. *That's all I am. It's all I've ever been. I betrayed my mother when I let the Council turn me into an assassin. I betrayed the Council when I didn't kill Jinny. I betrayed Jinny when I couldn't keep her safe on Earth. I betrayed Earth by joining the Praetorian Guard and killing the Earthers in battle. And now I betray Domitia and Mars by failing to give my all to the battle.*

I'm nothing but a traitor, and the universe would be better without me in it.

It was the closest Tyrus had ever come to suicidal thoughts. Even at his darkest moments—holding his mother's dead body in his arms and thinking he'd been the one to kill her; realizing all he'd done in the Council's name was *not* righteous; almost losing Jinny—he had never contemplated leaving the galaxy behind. Somehow, even considering that had always felt wrong to him.

Even now, he wasn't thinking of taking his own life. Not exactly. Rather, he was thinking that perhaps everyone he'd ever known would simply be better off without him and that maybe it was time for Tyrus

Decimus—Tyrus Tyne—to simply disappear. For him to stop causing pain by betraying everyone around him.

He was so immersed in his own despair that he didn't hear the door to the bathhouse open. A ship the size of the *Julius Caesar* had several chambers with healing baths spread around its inner corridors, and he had purposefully sought out one of the most seldom-used ones, desiring to be alone with his spiraling thoughts.

But he did feel the disturbance in the water as the other person entered it and then swam in his direction, and he let his feet sink so that he could be upright and face the uninvited guest. He was not surprised when he saw it was Domitia.

Even after being around her for four and a half months and being her bonded partner for two and a half of those both on and off the battlefield—a strange variation of and amalgamation of boyfriend and fiancé—his breath still caught every time he saw her. It was especially hard when they were alone like this. The love and attraction he felt toward her was almost too much for him to bear when little more separated them than centimeters of water.

Regardless, he would never act on those feelings. To do so wouldn't just be a gross breach of Martian etiquette, possibly leading to his death *and* hers, but it would be a terrible betrayal of Domitia herself. He might be a traitor, but in this one thing, he would stand firm; he would die before he ever betrayed *her*. Which was what would make this conversation so difficult

She moved up close to him, treading water and leaning in to brush her lips against his. Then she settled back in the water and began to float, regarding him with a smile.

"My heart," he said, trying to keep the pain out of his voice. The decision hadn't been an easy one. But it was the *right* one. When he entered the battle and hesitated, as he had done today, he put her at risk. If she were to die because of him, he would *never* forgive himself.

He also knew that by breaking their bonded pairing, he was defying close to a thousand years of Martian culture, and the end result would almost certainly be *his* death, either at her hands or at the hands of Centurion Parn on her behalf. Because one or the other *would* challenge him to a duel, and he would let himself die before he would harm either. He would accept his fate and would not raise his hand to fight back.

He opened his mouth to tell her all this, to break her heart to save her life, to give his life for hers, but she put a finger to his lips to quiet him.

"My love," she said, her smile turning sad. "It pains me to see you in such despair. Especially when I bring such glad tidings."

What was she talking about? What could possibly be good? Parn had already told all the Praetorian Guard about the unqualified success of the mission. They'd been there for it. So it couldn't be that. Nor had there been nearly enough time for them to have broken the encryption on the stolen log files. But it really didn't matter what she had to say, especially when he told her what he knew he had to.

She did not wait for him to collect himself. Instead, she smiled again at him. "Tyrus Tyne—my Tyrus—I have decided to seal our bond. I declare you my husband before Mars. And I declare myself Domitia Tyne from this time forward."

Tyrus shook himself physically. Had he heard her right? "My Domitia," he said, feeling the tears rush to his eyes. "Don't do this. I can't . . ." *What is she doing? Why did she call me Tyne? That's not my name anymore!*

She looked at him sadly. "But you can, my love. I know what is in your heart. I know you would break our pairing to protect my life. I know you can no longer serve in the Praetorian Guard—that to do so kills you slowly as you fight against those you once called friends. I can no longer inflict such pain upon you. So I have declared the right of relinquere vexillum for both of us. And Centurion Parn has granted my petition."

Tyrus was so stunned he forgot to swim or float, and his head actually sank below the water before he came back to the surface, spitting out the bath water he had swallowed. "But . . ." Words failed him. *I can't let her do this!* was his first thought. He was opening his mouth to tell her, but she reached over and put a finger to his lips again.

"Silence, my Husband. I know what you would say. This is *my* choice. I can no longer watch you be in such pain, and I choose to never again leave your side. I would choose you above a thousand lifetimes in the Praetorian Guard. Do you deny me the right to choose?"

He thought desperately for a way to convince her not to do what she had obviously already done. A dozen arguments flashed through his mind, and he *knew* none of them would work. When Domitia Felix set her mind to something, no one would talk her out of it.

"Wait," he said, something occurring to him. "You called me your husband. But we're not married yet."

She smiled broadly. "My Tyrus, by Martian law, we became married the moment I declared us so. You are now my husband, and I your wife, until one of us should die. And that is the only way out—death or duel to the death." She paused, and her smile took on a sly quality. He thought he saw a twinkle in her eye before she continued. "And I would really hate to have to kill you so soon after our marriage."

He laughed out loud. It was a sound he hadn't heard from himself since the day Earth had declared war on Mars. And now he let it loose, the months of anger, fear, and doubt all coming forth in a booming laugh that quickly turned to sobs and tears. Domitia swam to him, embracing him and pulling his face into her shoulder. For the first time, they embraced and held each other, now as husband and wife.

CHAPTER 44

"This is unacceptable!" Jerem Pondergast said, standing and slamming a fist down on the conference table to emphasize his words. "If the Keeper can't be bothered to attend these meetings, then perhaps we need new leadership."

Silence reigned over the room and the assembled members of the Twenty. All of them stared in shock at the one person in the group who, as usual, had the courage—and stupidity—to say what they were all thinking. All except for Creighton Horvath. He wasn't watching Pondergast; he was watching Constantina Yenin.

The Russian woman was staring impassively down the long table, her expression betraying none of what she might be feeling at the man's brazen words. For over a month now, she'd been chairing every meeting of the Twenty as the date of the invasion neared and the Keeper continued to work in solitude and ignore the other members of the ruling cabal.

When no one spoke to support or rebuke him, Pondergast seemed to lose steam, looking around the room in something approaching desperation for any sign that he was reaching his fellow speakers. Words, Creighton had long since learned, only had power when they sparked either more words or direct action. In this case, Pondergast's inflammatory words were doing neither. By refusing to engage with him, the other members of the Twenty had robbed his words of any power they might have had.

"That is all for today's meeting," Yenin finally announced, saving Pondergast from the further embarrassment of standing there like a red-faced idiot. "We will convene at the normal time in three days."

Again, Creighton waited for the other speakers to exit the room, leaving him and Yenin alone. When no one else remained, he raised his eyebrows at her. "You felt it, too, didn't you?"

Frowning, she motioned with one hand toward the door and the backs of their departing colleagues. "At least two-thirds of the room wanted to agree with that idiot Pondergast, but they were all too afraid to speak up. It's getting worse."

Creighton nodded slowly. "And what about you, Connie? What would you have said in response to Pondergast's challenge if there weren't any consequences?" It was a bold question—perhaps a stupid one—but Creighton felt he'd had enough time around Connie in recent weeks to know what he could safely say to the woman. That she hadn't turned him in the first time he'd questioned Petrov's sanity was all the sign he needed.

She licked her lips and thought for a long time before answering. When she finally did, her voice was low and breathy. "He's right. Ian has lost his way. He doesn't realize that launching the invasion now will end in disaster." She looked up at Creighton, her eyes wide. "What are we going to do, Creighton? He's our friend."

He smiled back at her, fighting to keep the expression one of sympathy and not the triumph he felt surging through him. "We'll figure it out. But I agree with you; we have to do something."

She nodded slowly, even though she hadn't actually suggested doing anything, and Creighton knew he had her.

Tam Fabius wanted to bang his head against his desk. He'd joined the Martian Signal Corps right after finishing his secondary education. At the time, it had seemed like the perfect way to serve Mars without taking the risks that accompanied a combat position. Because among many other things, Tam was a coward.

He'd known it from an early age. When his classmates had been fighting and bloodying each other in sparring and practice duels, Tam had always hung back, mostly just watching from the sidelines. In a society that valued martial prowess above all else, he'd forever been ashamed of his reluctance to fight and his aversion to even small amounts of blood naturally spilled in the traditional roughhousing of young men.

His mother, sensing her young son's dilemma, had always done her best to comfort him, explaining repeatedly that even a warrior society needed its poets and peacemakers. Tam's father didn't feel the same way. The elder Fabius was a retired celeusta from the Legion, Pluto Regiment. Leto Fabius never understood his son's timid nature, viewing it through the legionnaire's lens that all such behaviors were those of one who lacked a modicum of bravery.

Deep down, however, a small part of Tam knew better. He had never feared being on the receiving end of a fight. Nor did he fear death on behalf of Mars. It was the harming of others that he couldn't stomach. One day, shortly after he'd turned twelve, a larger boy had challenged him to a practice duel over some imagined slight. Tam had met his opponent, as arranged, on the school dueling grounds after class.

Prior to adulthood, boys and girls alike were encouraged to duel to solve any interpersonal problems. However, no one under the age of majority could participate in a duel to the death. Instead, the so-called 'practice' duels the students participated in were held with only nonlethal weapons and ended when either party yielded or was incapacitated and unable to continue.

Tam and the larger boy had squared off within the white lines of a square painted on the school lawn. At a sign from one of their classmates, they'd approached each other. The larger boy had moved first, landing a punch on Tam's jaw that knocked him to the ground. He'd lain there for several seconds, holding his bruised jaw and frowning up at his opponent. Then, Tam had gotten to his feet and closed the distance again. Once more, the larger boy had driven him to the ground with a devastating roundhouse punch.

To this day, Tam could still remember how he'd felt in the course of that duel. He'd feared the first punch. He'd even feared the second. But after the third, he'd realized that the pain wasn't as bad as he'd thought it would be. Time and time again, he got up from each blow and approached the larger boy, only to receive another blow that would just as often knock him to the ground. Then, he would get up again and repeat, never landing any blows of his own.

It went on like this for a full twenty minutes, and Tam lost count of how many times he'd been hit. But he also noticed something unexpected: panic in the larger boy's eyes. It was like Tam's opponent was afraid . . . of him. After another ten minutes, Tam's opponent's panic turned to outright despondency as he screamed at Tam to hit him back —to fight.

Tam didn't accommodate him. By this time, he was so punch drunk that the larger boy's demands and taunts seemed like they were coming from far away, through a hazy fog visible only to Tam. He had no idea what kept him going, but every time the larger boy had knocked him down, he'd gotten up again.

Finally, unable to take it, the larger boy had yielded. The shocked gasps from the crowd, more than anything else, had clued Tam into the fact that he had somehow won the duel . . . without ever throwing a punch.

His mother had been elated. His father had been disappointed. And when Tam reached the mandatory age for Martian military service, he'd chosen a noncombat role, to his father's further chagrin.

The Signal Corps had taken Tam in and been like a family to him, and he'd quickly learned that he had a gift for working with computers and AIs as a code breaker. He was using that gift now, attempting to break the encryption of the log files the Praetorian Guard had captured from UENS *Italy*. But, thus far, he'd been frustrated at every turn. Whatever was in these logs was hidden behind an encryption far more advanced than that usually used by the UEN. Tam could break supposedly encrypted UEN comms transmissions in a matter of hours, sometimes minutes. He'd been working on *Italy*'s log files for the past four days straight.

He wasn't the only code breaker working on the log files, of course, but as the recently promoted optio of his team, he felt obligated to be the first one to accomplish the seemingly impossible task.

"Celeusta Paulus," he called over to one of his subordinates. "Please send me the intelligence packet on that UEN admiral. Connors, the one on *Italy*."

"I hear and obey, my Optio," Paulus answered, and a second later the requested information showed up on Tam's screen.

He skimmed it, not entirely sure what he was looking for, but hoping he would know it when he saw it. Unfortunately, his initial scan found nothing, so he read it again, slower this time, paying attention to every detail. This time, he found something.

Impossible, Tam thought. *Could it really be that simple?*

"Celeusta Paulus," he called out. "Did we not break Blackmont Industries' encryption code last year."

"We did, my Optio," the woman replied. "May I inquire as to why you ask that?"

"It is all here, Celeusta." Tan flicked his current view over to her workstation. "It appears that Rear Admiral Dalish Connors has a brother in Blackmont's executive ranks."

They discussed it for another five minutes, taking in the implications and deciding if their findings were worth calling a superior for, which they finally did. But when the door to their workroom opened another five minutes later, it was not their centurion who entered, but another one.

"Centurion Marcus Parn," Tam gasped as the tall, black-clad figure entered the room, trailed by another large praetorian guard who walked with a slight limp. Unbidden, Tam got up from his seat and stood at attention, saluting the newcomers.

"Optio Tam Fabius, at ease." Parn greeted him with a nod. "Your centurion tells me you have found something of note."

Tam nodded vigorously, his mouth suddenly dry as he confronted one of Mars's greatest modern heroes.

"Will you share it with me?" Parn gently prodded.

"Yes, of course, Centurion Marcus Parn!" Tam snapped out of his stupor. "Rear Admiral Dalish Connors has a brother placed high up within the hierarchy of Blackmont Industries. We thought it significant given Blackmont's known role in some of the events on Earth in the last year." He stopped himself short. Technically, of those on his team, only Tam himself knew the specifics of Blackmont's complicity in kidnapping and torturing Reader Jinny Ambrosa—intelligence shared with the Martians by Praetorian Guard Tyrus Decimus.

But Parn got the point and nodded knowingly at Tam, causing the signals corpsman to stand up straighter.

"This is good intelligence to have," Parn said slowly. "Tell me, Optio Fabius, have you been able to decrypt the log contents from Rear Admiral Dalish Connors's ship yet?"

Tam licked his lips, equal parts thrilled by Parn's show of familiarity in dropping his first name and chagrined at the answer he *didn't* have for the centurion's question. "No, Centurion Parn, not yet. But now that we know of the Blackmont connection, my team has seen similarities between this encryption schema and others we have intercepted and broken from Blackmont Industries. I believe it is only a matter of time now before we can decrypt the log files."

Parn inclined his head. "Very good, Optio Fabius. You do the legions proud. Make no mistake, all our lives may now rest in your capable hands. I would ask that you call me directly the second the logs are decrypted."

Tam felt a smile come to his lips. Always, he had viewed his joining the Signal Corps as an act of cowardice—a way to avoid combat—but now, with Centurion Parn's acknowledgment of the importance of the role he was playing, a surge of pride he'd never before experienced washed through him. "Yes, Centurion Parn," he said, snapping another salute. "It will be done!"

"Praetor Tiberius, you have your additional evidence of President Mikael Gorsky's guilt. Will you now acknowledge that this war may be one we fight not with all of United Earth, but at the behest of only one corrupt man?"

Aphrodite stayed silent after asking her question, carefully studying Kol Tiberius across the round table. Centurion Parn had just finished giving his report, crediting the Signal Corps with not only decrypting the logs, but also pointing out the connection between the attack at Nyx and Blackmont Industries.

Once decrypted, *Italy*'s raw log files had been a platinum mine of information. Not only did they clearly show that *Italy* had sent a detonation command to explosives planted on the freighters it then accused Martian forces of destroying, but they also showed several Tachyon Telegraphs to *Italy* from the president's office on Earth, placed both immediately before and after the battle at Nyx. The information was damning.

However, by asking the question so directly of Tiberius, Aphrodite was taking a large risk. She was effectively backing the praetor into a corner by throwing his own words at him. He could choose to acknowledge the new information and change his stance, or he could just as likely reject it out of sheer, stubborn principle. But Aphrodite grew tired of the games and equivocations. While Mars and Earth continued to fight a sham war, more and more Martians died each day.

It was time to end this.

Slowly, Tiberius's shoulders slumped and he nodded ever so slightly. "I am forced to agree with you, Consul Starshadow. It appears we have all been duped, Martian and Earther alike."

She nodded her thanks to him, knowing how much it had cost him to utter those words. Tiberius might be stubborn and contrary at the best of times, but she also knew he had a fierce loyalty to Mars and her people. She was gratified to see that overcome politics for the time being.

"Very well, Praetor Tiberius," she said evenly, turning from him to the rest of the praetors. "My fellow members of the Quorum of Praetors, Centurion Parn has presented not only this evidence to us, but has also suggested a new course of action, endorsed by Legatus Lightbringer of the Fleet of the Eagle. I put that plan now to a vote. What say ye?"

At first, no one moved, including Praetor Sunsbane, who she knew would support the plan. But Sunsbane, wisely, also knew that if he were the first to vote in the affirmative, Tiberius and several of his supporters might renege if only out of habit of voting against him.

Hesitantly, Tiberius was the first to raise his hand and give a thumbs-up to support Parn's and Lightbringer's plan. Then, several more praetors joined in, thumbs pointing to the heavens above. By the end, no one held their thumb down to vote against the plan. It was the first vote Aphrodite could remember in which the Quorum had been unanimous in a decision.

"The vote carries," she said unnecessarily. "I will inform Centurion Parn and Legatus Lightbringer that they may proceed with all due haste to contact United Earth Fleet Admiral Horatio Krishna Lopez, and through him to challenge UE President Mikael Gorsky. In the end, we will have his blood to atone for the loss of Martian life from his treachery!"

At her last, she stood up and every praetor joined her, anger and defiance on their faces. "For Mars!" they all shouted as one.

"So, let me get this straight," Riggs said with a slow shake of his head. "You want me to 'loan' you the *Monk* so you can . . .what? So you can go on a honeymoon somewhere?"

Tyrus shook his head. Next to him, Domitia flashed a toothy smile at Riggs that was half-happy and half-predatory. The pilot actually leaned back a little in his seat across the table from them after seeing her expression, and she pretended not to notice as she hugged Tyrus's right arm tighter and snuggled into him almost aggressively.

He was definitely *not* used to that, and it sent an electric thrill through him every time she did it or anything like it. He kind of hoped he *never* got used to it. They had only been married for six days, and in that time, they had bonded in ways Tyrus had always thought would forever be unavailable to him in life. It was euphoric, and the fact that they'd never done more than kiss for their entire relationship before made it even more so now, as if a dam had broken and released a flood of love and affection upon both of them.

"No, Riggs," he said, trying not to smile like an idiot as he did so. "Not for a honeymoon. Someone needs to go find Fleet Admiral Lopez, and given the politics involved, Centurion Parn has asked me to be the emissary for Mars."

Riggs harumphed. "What, they think Lopez will be less inclined to blow you out of the sky versus a Martian warship?"

The pilot was likely half joking, but the look Tyrus gave him in return made Riggs sit up straighter and clear his throat. "You really think telling Lopez about that Gorsky guy's treason will end the war?"

"We hope so," Tyrus replied honestly. "Admiral Lopez may be the only one who can cut through the political realities and convince the rest of the UE government and populace not to trust Gorsky. If Lopez calls for a ceasefire, it might actually happen."

Riggs considered this for a moment. A surprisingly short moment. Then he shrugged. "Fine. Where do you want me to take you first?"

Tyrus shook his head. "No way. You can't come. I won't risk your life as well, Riggs. Jinny wouldn't want that. *I* don't want that.

Riggs frowned and shook his head right back. "Sorry, buddy. Me and the *Monk*, we're a package deal. You don't get her without me. You wouldn't leave your wife behind, right?"

"I would kill him if he did," Domitia said in a frank voice. Riggs looked at her for a moment as if trying to decipher if she was kidding or not. Tyrus knew she wasn't; she had already made that *extremely* clear to him. She could be quite scary when she wanted to be . . . as well as quite persuasive. He preferred the latter, so he wouldn't have argued the point even had he wanted to leave her behind. Besides, Domitia Felix—no, Tyne! The thought sent another wave of disbelief and joy through him. Domitia could more than take care of herself in any dangerous situations they found themselves in.

"Okay," Riggs said, giving her a troubled look. "Then you know what I mean. No me, no *Monk*. Period. End of story. Got it?"

"Got it," Domitia said quickly, not giving Tyrus the chance to answer. That was going to take some getting used to as well. He could almost hear his mother saying something about him managing to find the only woman in the galaxy more headstrong and stubborn than he was *and* possibly more dangerous as well.

That thought brought with it melancholy. How he wished his mother could have met Domitia. Instead, he would simply have to keep them all alive long enough so she and Jinny could at least meet. That would have to do.

"Then we're aligned," he said, taking back some modicum of control in the conversation. "You're in, Riggs."

The pilot looked mollified, but then his face darkened a bit. "What would you have done if I'd said no to you taking the *Monk*?"

Again, before Tyrus could answer, Domitia chimed in. "We would break your legs and take your ship while you heal."

Riggs looked horrified.

"Domitia . . ." Tyrus started, looking over and down at her, still nuzzling his arm.

"What?" She sat up and met his eyes, looking at him innocently, and he couldn't tell if it was an act or not. With her, he suspected it wasn't; Martians weren't good at play-acting, though she'd definitely taken on some of his very un-Martian traits in the last three months together. "At least I did not *just* say we would take his ship," she continued. "Breaking his legs lets people know he fought back so he can keep his honor. It is the nicest way we could take this *Deaf Monk*."

"*Blind Monk*!" Riggs corrected her, anger rising in his tone. He leaned forward and pointed a finger at her, using it to punctuate his words. "And listen, sister. No one flies the *Monk* but me. So you'd have to break a lot more than my legs if you wanted to take her from me. And I think you'd find that I'm not all that bad in a fight, myself."

"Look, it's no use talking about hypotheticals," Tyrus jumped in, cutting off the unnecessary argument before his wife tried to challenge his friend to an honor duel. "We already agreed that we'll all go together."

Riggs frowned, but Domitia did something unexpected. She removed her right hand from Tyrus's arm and reached it out toward Riggs.

"What are you doing?" the pilot asked slowly.

"I will grab your hand and shake it," she said. Domitia furrowed her eyebrows and looked at Tyrus, then back at Riggs. "Is that not what you foreigners do to seal an agreement?"

Riggs stared at her for a long moment in disbelief. Then he threw back his head and laughed hysterically.

Domitia looked confused. She turned and met her husband's eyes and the wide grin on his face. "What did I say that was funny?" she asked him, perplexed. "He laughs at me. Is it an insult? Do I need to duel him?"

Now Tyrus started laughing, right up until his wife punched him hard in the ribs. "Ow," he gasped between laughs, unable to stop himself, though he did reach down and rub his side where she had hit him. For a genetically weak Martian, she had a surprising amount of power behind her blows, with or without her exosuit—and especially, it seemed, when those blows were directed at him.

CHAPTER 45

Admiral Terrence Lafayette missed his command chair on the UENS *Texas*. Not only had it been much larger than the simple observer's chair he now occupied in the comparably claustrophobic bridge of the destroyer UENS *Dominant*, but it had been *his* chair, and he had grown quite used to and even fond of its quirks over the years.

He doubted he would ever sit in it again.

Lafayette had no idea what had been on the computer core the Martians had infiltrated on UENS *Italy*. Someone, supposedly the attackers, had destroyed the core entirely afterward, along with any records of what had been copied. But by the nervous way Rear Admiral Connors had avoided his questions on the matter, it had to have been something very serious indeed. That feeling was heavily reinforced by the way President Gorsky had reacted.

The orders had come just days after the battle had concluded. Losses had been heavy on both sides, and neither fleet had emerged with anything resembling a victory. Lafayette had to grudgingly admit that his enemy counterpart, Legatus Augustus Lightbringer, was at least his strategic and tactical equal. But more importantly, after hundreds of years of playing catch-up with each other, the two fleets were almost evenly matched in tonnage and firepower. Sure, the

Martians had some tech that the UEN didn't have, but the UEN had its own advantages, mainly in the power and range of their missiles.

Lafayette had been debriefing his commanders and thinking of ways to improve the outcome in the next battle, just as he was sure Lightbringer was doing on the opposite side, when the orders had been hand-delivered to him by *Texas*'s Marine commander, Major St. Germain.

Lafayette had read the orders in disbelief, then read them again, then a third time. And each time, his heart sank further. St. Germain had stood there, shuffling his feet in embarrassment. The digital signatures at the bottom of the orders were those of General Cruz and Admiral Clancy, but the wording made it clear that the true source was a politician, almost certainly President Gorsky himself. Cruz had later practically confirmed that when Lafayette had briefly spoken to him via a delayed lightspeed comm.

Now, here he was, relieved of his command, torn away from his precious fleet and his flagship, and sent scurrying home to a rushed court martial via a tiny destroyer. The charges were, ostensibly, those of dereliction of duty in allowing the Martians to outmaneuver him and board *Italy* and steal 'strategic information vital to the prosecution of the war'. But in reality, Cruz had intimated, someone, almost certainly Gorsky, was livid over *what* had been taken from *Italy*'s data banks.

If only Lafayette knew what that might have been.

"Admiral," Lieutenant Commander Kim Santos said meekly. She was essentially his jailor for the journey back to Earth. But she didn't seem to see it that way and was unfailingly, if awkwardly, deferential to him.

"Yes, Captain?" he asked, using not her actual rank but her *title* as master of the ship. It was a small breach of protocol for him to do so as a senior officer—it was really just her crew who were supposed to refer to her as 'Captain'—but he did it to remind her again that *she* was lord and master of the *Dominant*, not him.

"Sir, we're coming up on the halfway point. Making turnover to decelerate in fifteen minutes."

"Thank you, Captain." One step closer to his doom. The problem, he knew, was that if politicians were motivating his court-martial, then he suspected they had already decided and arranged the verdict as well.

Lakshmi Dasgupta, his flag captain on *Texas*, and Andrew Porzingas, his chief of staff, had been recalled with him, supposedly as witnesses for the prosecution. However, Cruz had hinted that they would also need to start thinking about their own defenses. They were currently languishing in the small destroyer's wardroom; the bridge was far too tiny for *three* officers with no formal roles on this ship. He only hoped they would escape whatever fate awaited him.

It all sucked, as Lafayette's grandchildren were fond of saying. There was no better word for it.

"Skip jump detected!" the sensor officer cried from his station, and the bridge became a flurry of activity. His presence momentarily forgotten, Lafayette frowned and watched the battle plot as it charted the course and probable emergence points for the incoming Martian ships, while Santos turned her little destroyer to burn as hard as it could away from the soon-to-be battlefield.

In the end, *Dominant*'s rush to flee didn't make a difference. The massive Martian battleship that exited the void practically on top of them wasted no time in firing a spread of shockers and disabling Santos's ship.

Just before the lights went off, however, Lafayette registered the signature of the enemy battleship and swore under his breath.

The *Julius Caesar*.

Legatus Augustus Lightbringer watched solemnly as the little UEN destroyer went ballistic, its engines, weapons, and all other systems dead.

"Optio," he ordered his comm officer. "As soon as they restore power to their communications, send the message."

"Yes, my Legatus."

Lafayette was impressed. It had only taken Santos's engineering department eight minutes to bring some of the basic systems back online after the power surge from the shockers. As soon as some of the lights and consoles on the bridge came back on, however, he had other things to worry about.

"Admiral Terrence Lafayette," said the stern voice over *Dominant*'s bridge speakers. "I would speak with you."

"I'm listening, Legatus Augustus Lightbringer," Lafayette replied, using the Martian's full title and name as he understood their tradition to be. No use antagonizing this man; it was far too late for that.

"You and I must meet in person," the Martian admiral continued. "What I have to say cannot be trusted to a transmission or to the wrong ears."

Lafayette recovered from his shock and asked the first question that came to him. "Mind giving me a hint as to what it is we will be discussing, Legatus?" He winced at the casualness of his words and tone. Martians could be touchy.

He could hear the frown in Lightbringer's voice when he replied. "I am afraid, Admiral Terrence Lafayette, that we have both been duped. This war is not what it appears to be.

"Your navy has dispatched two task forces from Earth's First Fleet to come to your rescue. It appears your young ship commander managed to send a distress call via your Tachyon Telegraph. We have little time. Assuming they do not risk an in-system jump, they will be here in 4.3 hours, but even that may not be long enough for what we have to discuss. I am sending a shuttle. You must come yourself, and you will bring your former flag captain and your chief of staff as witnesses. None of you can be armed. You will be returned to your ship once our discussion has concluded."

"And if I refuse?" Lafayette asked slowly, expecting an explosive answer but needing to issue the challenge disguised as a question nonetheless.

The answer was nothing like he anticipated. "If you refuse," Lightbringer said solemnly, "I will leave you to return to Earth in peace. But, Admiral Terrence Lafayette, I offer you a way to end this war without further bloodshed. I . . . hope you will hear what I have to say."

Lafayette looked over at Santos, and the commander returned his wide-eyed gaze.

"Um," he said, very unprofessionally, "I suppose I'd better come on over then and hear what you have to say, Legatus."

The transmission cut, and the entire bridge crew was silent, contemplating the strange exchange.

Lafayette stood up, looking over at Santos and letting out a long sigh. He tried to put a casual bravery he didn't feel into his tone for the young officer's benefit. "Well, Lieutenant Commander, thanks for getting us this far. Now, I suppose I need to collect Captain Dasgupta and Commander Porzingas and get myself to the airlock. This is going to be interesting."

Santos, despite her charge to bring him back to Earth for trial, didn't argue. She just nodded dumbly and then returned to the task of getting her ship's systems back up and running.

"He never leaves his office," Lara Owens said from her usual place in the overstuffed chair in Creighton's office. "I think he's even sleeping in there."

She looked up at him, her eyes red like she'd been crying, the bags underneath them telling the story of sleepless nights of her own. Unlike most of her visits to him, tonight, she hadn't tried to sell the fake affair they were supposedly having. Lara was dressed for work, not for a tryst or a night on the town, and her hair was pulled back into a severe bun that made the exhaustion and distress even more evident on her face.

"Besides Ebby, has he been allowing anyone else in to see him?" Creighton asked her gently.

Lara shook her head. "No. No one. He still does the occasional holo call, and I've seen him through the open door when Ebby goes in and out, so I know he's there. But it's like he's trying to shut out the world." She looked up, her eyes shining with unshed tears. Spy though she might be for Creighton, he knew that Lara actually liked and respected Ian Petrov.

"Creighton," she said in a small voice, reaching out a hand toward him. "What are we going to do?"

Hesitating for only a moment, Creighton reached out and took her hand and held it tight, the first sign of real affection he'd ever given the woman. As he did so, he told her of his plan and her part in it.

When Lara left his office an hour later, he smiled and sent a message to Constantina Yenin.

She's in. Phase 2 begins.

Terrence Lafayette and his two subordinates had entered the Martian shuttle, which had docked with the destroyer's port amidships airlock, to find four silent figures in head-to-toe black exosuits waiting for them. "Praetorian Guard," Captain Dasgupta hissed, while Lafayette and Commander Porzingas stayed silent but nodded an acknowledgment.

The figures, all standing at the front of the shuttle between the passenger compartment and the door to the cockpit, said nothing as the three of them entered. Shrugging, Lafayette took one of the seats along the port side. Dasgupta and Porzingas hesitated a moment and then sat in two jump seats opposite him.

When the three of them were done strapping themselves in, they felt the slightest of jolts as the shuttle detached from *Dominant*. There were no windows, but Lafayette had been on enough shuttles like this to know the signs.

"This is your pilot speaking," a woman's stern voice said over the internal comm. "I will be slowly dialing down the gravity in the passenger compartment from Earth standard to Mars standard to transition you gradually before you board the *Julius Caesar*."

"Thank you," Lafayette said, but the woman had already cut the line. Still, it was an unusually thoughtful gesture from the Martians.

Then, one of the black-clad figures stepped forward, and his helmet . . . dissolved. There was no other way to put it. Lafayette had heard rumors of Martian nanotech—he'd even seen some of their ships seem to 'heal' from wounds in the middle of battles when given enough time—but no one from Earth had been able to confirm its existence; the little machines seemed to self-destruct whenever the UEN captured a ship or a combat suit. To see it here so blatantly made him worry that perhaps he, Dasgupta, and Porzingas weren't meant to ever make it back to *Dominant*—or to Earth.

But the dour-faced, very tall man revealed by the dissolving helmet didn't look like he was going to kill them yet.

"I am Optio Din Carbo of the Praetorian Guard," he said calmly.

Lafayette raised his eyebrow. They'd obviously suspected who the silent soldiers were based on their black uniforms, but hearing it confirmed was still unsettling. Lightbringer had sent the uber-elite Praetorian Guard to escort them to the *Caesar*; each one of these men and woman was likely responsible for hundreds of UEN deaths, if not more.

"You are Admiral Terrence Lafayette," the man continued. "We have a mutual acquaintance, Tyrus Tyne."

Before Lafayette could answer, Porzingas spit out, "Tyrus Tyne is a traitor and a murderer!"

Lafayette tried to catch his chief of staff's eye and shake his head, but the damage had already been done. Carbo's face turned colder as he turned his head to regard the man. "If you were Martian," he said slowly, "I would challenge you to an honor duel right here and now for those words. As an enemy combatant, it would be within my right to kill you on the spot without giving you the chance to defend yourself. But"—he looked back at Lafayette—"I will defer demanding satisfaction in this one instance only, in the interest of working together against a larger threat. It will be as my legatus has requested."

Lafayette nodded his silent appreciation to the Martian and keyed in on the man's hint about the topic of the upcoming meeting. He also noticed the man's wording. Legatus Lightbringer may have been top brass in the Martian People's Navy, but even *he* couldn't issue a direct order to a member of the Praetorian Guard; he could only *request* things of them. It meant this optio in front of them wasn't just following orders but actually choosing to exert self-control despite Porzingas's untimely outburst.

The man opened his mouth as if to argue the point further, but this time Lafayette cut him off. "Thank you for your understanding, Optio Din Carbo. I only met Mr. Tyne twice, but was impressed by his knowledge. Many of us were disappointed to hear he was fighting against us."

Carbo nodded back. "He did fight against you, and did so honorably. Remember"—he turned his stony gaze back on Andrew, who seemed to now finally realize how close to death he was and shrank under the man's scrutiny—"that Tyrus Tyne only came to Mars after Earth betrayed him and attempted to imprison and murder him and his closest friends. But even now," he said, turning back to Lafayette, "he has left the Praetorian Guard and Mars in the interest of the greater Sol system."

That was news. They'd know Tyne had joined the Praetorian Guard, of course. He'd been seen and recorded onboard *Italy*. The fact that he'd left the Guard in just the few days since that attack was another potential clue to what Lightbringer hoped to discuss when they arrived on the *Julius Caesar*.

Porzingas looked like he might try and say something again, perhaps an apology if he were smart, but Dasgupta put a hand on his knee and threw him a stern look that shut him up.

Carbo shook his head. "I will also give you a warning, one soldier to another. Tyrus Tyne is now married to the daughter of Legatus Augustus Lightbringer. Calling him a traitor in the legatus's presence would be unwise. He is not as patient a man as I am."

Porzingas sank in his chair a little, properly cowed. Lafayette actually shared some of his chief of staff's animosity against the former assassin turned adviser turned . . . well, if not traitor, then something akin to it. Nevertheless, he also understood that Earth had betrayed Tyne first, as Carbo had said. It was a very complex situation at best. And news of the man's marriage to the daughter of a highly placed Martian family made it even more complex.

Carbo was opening his mouth to speak again but then cocked his head. He said something back to whoever was talking to him but he had engaged a privacy field so that the UEN officers couldn't hear him. After a few moments, he looked back at Lafayette and spoke aloud.

"Your UEN reinforcements have arrived sooner than expected.

Most likely, it is a fleet that was waiting at your Waypoint Zulu and received word via your Tachyon Telegraph to submerge and surface here to come to your aid. We will be making a combat landing on *Julius Caesar*. It will be rough."

So, the Martians know about Waypoint Zulu? That wasn't good for Earth, though it wasn't exactly unexpected. Waypoint Zulu was a point in the far outer system, almost to the border of the Castilian Rift, where Earth kept a small reserve force that could do risky in-system jumps when absolutely necessary. Apparently, fallen out of favor though he may be, someone still saw Lafayette as worth saving. Or, more likely, they simply didn't want him and the intel in his head falling into Martian hands.

He felt the shuttle surge forward underneath him and then settle down as its small inertial compensators caught up to its increased acceleration. After a minute or so, he felt it turn sharply and then drop so quickly that his stomach hit his throat. There was a sudden jolt as it stopped moving and contacted something hard.

"We have arrived," Carbo said unnecessarily. Then Lafayette felt something else, the slight swirling of his stomach that he always felt at such times. The *Caesar* had just submerged into the void in another skip jump to escape the attacking UEN task force. With it, it took his last hope of freedom, not that he hadn't expected to lose that anyway upon arriving at Earth.

After disembarking from the shuttle, Lafayette, Dasgupta, and Porzingas were led to a conference room where Optio Carbo and the three other silent, faceless praetorian guards left them, with Carbo's stern admonishment that to leave the room would invite death. None of them doubted his promise. They waited for about twenty minutes. During that time, Lafayette felt his stomach roil multiple times as the *Julius Caesar* skip jumped away from the incoming UEN rescue ships.

None of the UE's scientists could figure out how the Martians managed their so-called skip jumps. The power required for a ship to enter and then again to exit the void was simply too great for the Reds to do it over such short distances and so many times in a row. Unless the Martians had invented some new inexhaustible data source, there was no way it would work. But it obviously did. The prevailing theory within the UE intelligentsia, therefore, was that the Martian ships weren't actually jumping at all, at least not in the traditional sense. Instead, scientists postulated that what the Martians were really doing was *attempting* to jump over and over again.

Lafayette wasn't a scientist or an engineer, but the way it had been described to him was that there were essentially two stages to a ship's submergence from normal space into the interdimensional space they called the 'void.' In the first stage, a ship's jump drive literally tore a hole in the fabric of spacetime, through which the ship then exited its normal dimension and entered the void. Doing that took a tremendous amount of power, but it was only half the battle.

Entering the void was one thing; staying in it was something else entirely. There was a period of time—measured in so many decimal places of a second that he'd only ever seen it expressed in scientific notation—that came directly after a ship entered the void, during which the ship's own dimension tried to take it back, just like a planet's gravity tried desperately to reclaim a lifting shuttle that hadn't yet reached escape velocity. During this infinitesimally tiny instant, the ship was effectively being pulled on by two different dimensions, and it took another surge of power—larger than the first—from the ship's jump drive to stabilize it within the void and prevent normal space from yanking it right back out again.

That second stage of submergence was the real power hog, requiring far more than the first stage. But if a ship's jump drive failed to apply that second power surge at just the right moment, the results would be catastrophic. A ship being pulled on in two different dimensions had to go somewhere, and it usually couldn't make up its mind.

Lafayette had never personally seen the end result of a failed jump, but he'd read about and seen recordings of it at the academy. In one, a patrol had come upon a ship literally ripped in half, but with one half never to be seen again, doomed to exist forever in the void. Not that the occupants cared; the sheer of two dimensions ripping the ship into pieces had killed everyone on board instantly.

But what if—UE scientists theorized—the Martians had found a way to safely abort a jump *before* that second stage? If they had, then their ships would be capable of entering the void in the first stage of the jump, but then almost immediately exiting it when the second stage failed to execute. To anyone observing, the Martian warship would still move millions of kilometers before being jerked back into normal space. But without the power drain of that second stage, it would theoretically be possible to immediately try again. Doing this over and over again could, on paper, result in what looked like multiple small jumps in a row.

Lafayette wished he could ask his Martian captors if the UE scientists had gotten it right, but he knew there wouldn't likely be an opportunity, nor would they be inclined to answer such a question.

Finally, the door to the outside corridor opened, and Carbo stepped back in, this time followed by an impossibly tall and thin man wearing a sharp red and black uniform. Legatus Augustus Lightbringer, one of the top military leaders of Mars and their top strategist, had arrived.

Lafayette stood up out of habit, as did his companions. But they did not salute. Their role here was plain: prisoners to a conqueror, not subordinates to a superior officer. Lightbringer, to his credit, waved them down, which surprised Lafayette after all he'd heard of how the Martians were such sticklers for protocol and decorum.

Sitting back down in a seat so high off the ground—built for the taller Martians—that he had to hop up and back a little to get onto it, Lafayette took the opportunity to closely study his opponent of the last three months. Lightbringer had olive skin but did not look either Latino or Indian to his eyes, perhaps more of a generic amalgamation of races. He had gray hair and lines on his face that bespoke his long experience, though he looked far younger than the more-than-ninety Earth years Naval Intelligence believed to be his age.

Lightbringer took a seat at the head of the conference table, his thin back ramrod straight, and looked at each of them in turn, ending with Lafayette. When he met Lafayette's gaze, he gave a small smile.

"Admiral Terrence Lafayette. I apologize for my delay. I needed to ensure we had truly escaped the rescue fleet that your navy sent to retrieve you. I have often wondered under what circumstances we would finally meet in person. It is regretful that it be in this manner. A warrior like you should be triumphant or die a warrior's death while taking many of his foes with him. And I very much wanted our first meeting to end with my knife in your chest."

"Thank you, I suppose." Lafayette wasn't quite sure how to take the man's statement, but *maybe* it had been a compliment. He'd heard from Fleet Admiral Lopez that the Martians often considered personal death threats to be great honors, so he figured he might as well take it that way.

Lightbringer nodded and continued, so obviously, he was satisfied with Lafayette's response. "You recall our conquest of the *Italy* one week back, do you not?"

"I do," Lafayette admitted dryly. "Your Praetorian Guard teams took the ship but fled when our reinforcements showed up."

Carbo, who had entered the room behind Lightbringer, bristled and looked as if he were about to say something. Lightbringer quieted him with a wave.

"There are two things you must know about the Praetorian Guard, Admiral Terrence Lafayette," Lightbringer said sternly. "First, they do not flee. Second, they kill anyone who suggests they would. In your ignorance, you may be forgiven, but do not tempt Optio Carbo again. Even I cannot command him to spare you should he choose to demand satisfaction for his wounded honor.

Lafayette immediately felt chagrined, recognizing in Lightbringer's rebuke the same one Carbo had delivered to Porzingas on the shuttle ride over. Plus, it probably wasn't a good idea to antagonize one's hosts while being held on an enemy ship. He turned and regarded the tall Martian soldier. "My apologies, Optio Din Carbo. My understanding of the event was flawed, and I did not mean offense."

The man regarded him coldly, then nodded, saying nothing.

Lafayette turned back to Lightbringer. "I am sorry, Legatus Augustus Lightbringer. Please continue."

"Very well," the Martian said. "Our Praetorian Guards left the *Italy* because they had already achieved their mission. As I am sure you have already surmised, capturing the ship was never the goal. Rather, we wanted one specific set of files from the ship's computer core. A heavily encrypted set of raw log files that we had learned only resided in the core of a single UEN ship. The *Italy* was the ship that started this war, after all."

Lafayette thought briefly about arguing that it had, in fact, been the Martian warship out at Nyx that had fired first, starting the war. Connors and *Italy* had fired only in self-defense, but he chose not to risk another threat of an honor duel until he had at least heard the legatus out fully.

"If the files were heavily encrypted, what good would they have been to you?" This question came from Dasgupta, but Lightbringer kept his weary eyes on Lafayette.

"That is not the question you should be asking, Captain Lakshmi Dasgupta."

Lafayette jumped in. "I'm assuming the real question we should be asking is what was in those files that has the legatus venturing so deep into UE space just to have this conversation."

Lightbringer cocked his head in acknowledgment. "That is, indeed, the question, Admiral Terrence Lafayette. But rather than tell you what we found in *Italy*'s logs, I will show you."

The man pressed a finger to the table and its integrated touchscreen. The lights in the room dimmed, and a viewscreen at the foot of the table lit up. A video started playing, displaying authentication codes that showed it was from the *Italy*, with a timestamp from three months ago, the same day the war had started.

As the video played, Lafayette felt his doubts and suspicions of the Martian fleet commander melt away, replaced by both embarrassment and anger. When Lightbringer went on to explain what a Council spy had told them about President Gorsky's role in the atrocity at Nyx and his collaboration with the Council, Lafayette's anger turned white-hot.

"What did they do to my ship?" Riggs yelled as he stomped his way through the *Blind Monk*'s corridors.

The Martian shipwright standing next to Tyrus looked upset watching Riggs march by on his way to and from different parts of the

Monk's interior, and also watching Domitia practically skip gleefully, if those words could *ever* be used to describe anything she did, through the same spaces.

"Look, my Tyrus," his new wife said, pointing through an open doorway. "They installed a healing bath. That will be very useful when we are injured in battle." Then she moved gaily to the next open doorway, admiring the updated medical bay full of Martian tech.

"They ruined her!" Riggs shouted from where Domitia had just left. "Why is there a *pool* on my ship?"

The shipwright looked to Tyrus in horrified confusion. "Don't worry," Tyrus said. "He likes it. That's how they express satisfaction on his home planet." He left out the part that Riggs didn't really have a home planet.

The shipwright seemed dubious but shrugged his narrow shoulders. Then, shaking his head, he walked down the *Monk*'s boarding ramp and left the ship and its crazy crew behind.

"Seriously, Tyrus," Riggs said, stopping his exploration long enough to stand in front of him and shake his fist. "Why is it every time we take my ship to a planet in his Council-forsaken system, they feel like they have the right to take her apart and do whatever they want with her?"

Tyrus had no answer that would satisfy the man. The scientists on Earth and Luna had gleefully taken the *Monk* apart and put her back together, trying to steal whatever colonial tech they could from her.

Those on Mars had taken the opposite approach, deciding that the *Monk* was so woefully unsophisticated that they just had to 'upgrade' her with Martian tech. They'd actually told Corey O'Leary about it, and he had told Tyrus. They had both decided to say nothing to Riggs. Now, they were paying the price for that.

Speaking of O'Leary, the older man trudged up the ramp and came to stand next to Tyrus as Riggs whirled about and stomped away to resume his inspection of the *Monk*. "How's he taking it?" O'Leary asked.

Tyrus shrugged. "Better than expected." Then they both winced as they heard the pilot swear loudly from somewhere deep inside the ship.

Domitia chose that moment to reappear from her own explorations. "Corey!" she cried, and crossed to stand in front of the man, bowing her head slightly. It was the Martian equivalent of a warm hug. "Are you sure you are alright staying on Mars? You won't resent us for leaving you behind?" she asked.

Did she just use her first contraction? Tyrus wondered if he'd heard her right.

O'Leary chuckled. "My dear, I wish I could follow you across the galaxy. You grow more beautiful every day."

Domitia beamed, looking at Tyrus. "You should say more things like that," she told her husband. "I like them."

Tyrus smiled and shook his head. "I tell you things like that all the time," he told her. "Even before we were married."

She shrugged. "Yes, but he says it better." She whirled and left to continue exploring the small ship, though she'd undoubtedly been in every room twice already.

O'Leary looked at Tyrus, a big grin on his face. "My friend, do you even have an inkling of what you've gotten yourself into with that one?"

Tyrus smiled back. "Not even a little, but I can't wait to find out."

"Good answer." O'Leary clapped him on one of his broad shoulders. "I *would* go with you, you know. When you find Horatio, I'd love to be there. But I believe I'm still needed here. The Quorum of Praetors is, for once, wholly united behind the common cause of ending this war and preparing for the real battle to come, but I don't know if they'll stay that way without a lot of prodding."

"So they've reinstated your emissary status?" Tyrus asked in surprise.

He nodded. "For now, at least. Might as well use it while I have it." The former congressman's smile disappeared and he looked away, pretending to inspect the *Blind Monk*'s interior. "How could I have been so stupid?" he asked in a low voice.

Tyrus didn't have to ask to what he referred. "Gorsky duped everyone. He fooled the entire Sol system. You can't blame yourself."

O'Leary looked back and him and shook his head. "True, but I was close to him. And I'm the one he manipulated and used to reach his goals."

"When this is over, he'll pay for all that," Tyrus promised.

The older man just frowned.

"Anyway," Tyrus continued, trying to break the sudden melancholy, "I have the messages you gave me. I'll make sure Lopez forwards them to Debra."

"Good," O'Leary replied with a small smile. "I shudder to think that she might already believe I'm dead. Or back in the arms of an old flame."

Tyrus smiled back. O'Leary had finally told him of his entire history with Consul Aphrodite Starshadow, and it had been surprising. "Do you think Legatus Lightbringer's plan will work?" he asked, grimacing a little at the name of his new father-in-law.

The older man thought for a moment. "If he can convince Admiral Lafayette, and you can convince Admiral Lopez, you'll have two of the most senior and well-respected members of the UE military on your side. Whether that will be enough to sway the public and Congress against Gorsky"—he shrugged—"I don't know, but I hope so." He cocked his head and looked harder at Tyrus. "So you really didn't know Lightbringer was Domitia's father?"

Tyrus shook his head. "You know how the Praetorian Guard works. Domitia forsook her family and changed her name when she took the Oaths; the few times I asked her about her family, she talked about the other members of the Guard and that's it. I'd given up trying to learn about her real kin. But imagine my surprise when it turned out to be the commander of half the Martian fleet!"

O'Leary smiled. "Yes. It seems our little Domitia is akin to Martian royalty. The Lightbringers aren't one of the original thirteen families, or Augustus would be a praetor. But they're only one tier below, and the man, in truth, wields more power than most of the praetors do. I can't imagine he's thrilled to see his only daughter leave the Praetorian Guard, and for a non-Martian, no less." He clapped Tyrus on the shoulder again to take the sting out of his words.

"That's the thing," Tyrus said. "I think he's content to let Domitia do whatever she wants, as long as it makes her happy. But he'll definitely hunt me down and kill me if I ever *stop* making her happy."

"Well, with most fathers-in-law, that's just hyperbole, but with him . . ." O'Leary smiled wickedly.

The sound of booted feet on the boarding ramp distracted both of them, and they turned to watch as a tall, helmeted praetorian guard came up toward them. Centurion Parn let his helmet dissolve and nodded a greeting to the two men. "Tyrus," he said, his voice holding its usual stiff formality. "I come to bid you farewell and to thank you for your service in the Praetorian Guard."

"I'm going to go check on Domitia and make sure she's settling in okay," O'Leary said, rapidly disappearing to give the two warriors some space.

Tyrus bowed his head to Parn. "And I thank you, my Centurion, for your wise guidance, your leadership, and your fierceness in battle." He thought that was the right thing to say in this situation.

Parn's mouth twitched up as if he might smile, but he resisted the temptation. "Tyrus, I wonder if I might speak to you informally?"

"Of course, Centurion."

"Please, Tyrus. I am no longer your commanding officer. It would honor me for you to call me Marcus."

It was the first time Tyrus had heard the taciturn centurion use his own first name, and he had certainly never heard anyone *else* address the man by it unless they were calling him formally by his full name and title. Tyrus overcame his shock at the unexpected honor quickly.

"It is I who am honored to do so, Marcus."

Parn smiled for real now, though only slightly. "Do you recall, my friend, the conversation you and I had the day Domitia bonded you to her?"

"Of course," Tyrus said cautiously. "You promised to kill me if I hurt Domitia. I'm afraid I haven't always been able to keep my promise not to." His thoughts went to his wife's near death at Toby's hands in the baths three months ago, before she was his wife.

The centurion shook his head. "Love is not love without hurt. You cannot taste the sweet if you do not understand the bitter, Tyrus. What counts is that the love outweighs the hurt, always. And you have done your best by Domitia. If she were my younger sister, if she were Anna . . ." His voice caught at the name of his long-dead sibling. "Then there would be no better husband I could wish for her than you."

Tyrus had never thought of himself as a big crier, but he was certainly tearing up a lot lately. Domitia seemed to have had a softening effect on him, which was strange given that she herself was as tough as nails.

His voice caught as he replied to Parn. "Never before has any man given me so much honor with his words, Marcus. I will cherish them and remember them. You always have a friend in me. No matter the hour, no matter the need, you have but to call, and Domitia and I will come to your aid."

Parn nodded. "I know. And the Praetorian Guard remembers our own. You may have left the Guard, Tyrus, but the Guard will never leave you. Remember us proudly and know that we will stand with you when this horrible war is turned to the true enemy. You need only ask and we will be there."

With that, Parn said nothing more. His helmet rematerialized, and he walked down the ramp and off the ship.

"Do you realize what just happened, my Husband?" a feminine voice said in his ear.

Tyrus jumped. "Don't do that, Domitia!" he cried, though he wasn't really angry. He'd never met anyone in his entire life who could sneak up on him; he had prided himself on that when he was an alpha. But his new wife was full of all sorts of surprises.

"He just gave you a blood oath. After you gave him one, of course."

Tyrus stared at her. "I'm almost afraid to ask, especially given the name. But what's a blood oath?"

"It means that the two of you are now more than brothers. If either of you is in trouble, the other will come to their aid, no matter the cost. It is essentially what you said to him, and if he does call for aid and you do not rush to give it, you will be expected to kill yourself as recompense."

"Great," Tyrus said dryly. "I really need to stop opening my big mouth around Martians."

She ignored him and continued. "But what he gave you was even greater. He gave you a blood oath on behalf of the *entire* Praetorian Guard. I have only heard of that happening a few times in our history. It means that the Guard now values your personal safety as equal to that of the praetors themselves. They will not actively guard you like they do them unless you ask for it. But *if* you ask for help, the Guard will come running. And if you are killed in battle, the Guard will not rest until the parties responsible lie dead at their feet."

Tyrus had no idea what to say to that. *Martians and their oaths,* he thought in disbelief. *I'm almost afraid to die now for the hell I'd unleash upon the poor souls unfortunate enough to kill me.*

"Tyrus!" Riggs yelled from somewhere deep in the bowels of the ship. "Why is the wall moving?"

Domitia smiled. "Oh, wonderful, he found the nanites! They will be so useful if the ship takes damage." Her solemn mood abruptly gone, she practically skipped off again to tell Riggs just how excited he should be.

Tyrus laughed and followed after his wife, counting his blessings and maybe watching her butt a little as she pranced down the corridor. He could do that now without having to worry about her killing him for it.

Ebby Hall was exhausted. As she entered her large apartment and set her purse down on the kitchen counter, she signed and stretched, feeling muscles complain and joints pop as the accumulated stresses of the last several months found nowhere to go. The Keeper was increasingly relying on her, and her alone, to communicate his will to the outside world. She wasn't complaining—as an enacter, all it would result in would be a headache—but she did wish for a break now and again.

When she opened her eyes after a massive yawn, she gasped. "Riley? You scared me!"

Ebby's little sister smiled at her from the living room couch, separated from the kitchen only by the edge of a carefully chosen rug from Sharjah.

"What are you doing here?" Ebby asked. Riley was only two years younger than her, so close in appearance that people may have mistaken them for twins growing up had they not both been taken from their parents at the age of five and put into separate campuses of the Enacter Academy.

Still, they had found each other later in life and struck up a friendship. They'd even grown relatively close, but ever since Ebby had ascended to become Keeper Ian Petrov's chief of staff, she'd seen her sister less and less. The last she'd heard, Riley was assigned to the Prefect's office on Cigni II.

"Just here for a visit and thought I'd stop by and check on you, big sister," Riley said, smiling as she stood up from the couch and walked toward the kitchen.

Ebby started to return the smile, then stopped. She and Riley may have created a friendship after they'd both left the Academy, but any familial relationship had long since ended for them. Riley had never once called her 'big sister' or anything of the kind.

Ebby reached for her purse and the gun inside that Keeper Petrov's security team insisted she carry. But before she could reach it, someone grabbed her from behind, a large hand covering her mouth and muffling her scream for help.

Guard Colonel Gennady Stewart looked down at the unconscious form of Ebby Hall and then back up at the woman who resembled Riley Hall. "You're sure one day is enough?"

The lookalike nodded. "She and her sister look enough alike. If I set up a blood transfusion right now, it'll accelerate things. I doubt anyone, even the Keeper, will be able to tell the difference by tomorrow evening. You're sure they won't expect her in the office tomorrow?"

Gennady shook his head. "It's Sunday tomorrow, which is usually her day off. If the Keeper does try and call her in, just tell him you're sick."

The blender posing as Riley Hall frowned but didn't argue, and Gennady looked back down at Ebby Hall's prone form with a frown of his own. When Creighton Horvath had first called to obliquely ask him to falsify an intelligence report about the rebel fleet massing at Phoenix, he'd gone along for the man's implied promise that he'd soon see Gennady promoted to general. That promised reward hadn't happened yet, but doing that one favor for Horvath meant that the senior Assembly speaker now owned him. Over the last several weeks, Gennady had found himself responding more and more to Horvath's demands, the latest being to help this blender kidnap and impersonate first Riley Hall and now her sister Ebby, the Keeper's own chief of staff.

But broken promises or not, he couldn't say no. Each time he did Horvath a favor, the speaker had one more thing he could use against Gennady if he ever stopped cooperating. It was infuriating how helpless he felt, especially because he knew it didn't work the other way around. No one would believe some non-enacter Guard colonel if he tried to go public with everything Horvath had asked him to do. Stewart was well and truly stuck.

Now, he helped the fake Riley move the unconscious body of the very real Ebby into the bedroom, where the blender would hook up the necessary needles and tubes for the blood transfusion so she could transform from Riley into Ebby in time for Monday morning and the next phase of Creighton Horvath's plans.

Admiral Terrence Lafayette couldn't remember the last time he had been so angry. Sure, what the Martians had shown him could have been doctored or even outright faked. But he strongly suspected that was not the case. Admiral Lopez had always tried to impress upon him that the Martians were largely a culture without subterfuge; what you saw was almost always what you got.

Even had he not known that, too much now made sense, including why Mikael Gorsky was so upset about losing this particular segment of data from the *Italy*'s computer core. Now, Lafayette suspected that his own court martial was more about diverting *his* attention from searching for what had been taken.

He wasn't just angry; he was embarrassed. How had he, and everyone else in the UEN, fallen for it?

"Thank you, Admiral Lafayette." Lightbringer had stopped calling him by his full name a few hours ago, and Lafayette thought that might have some significance. He turned to face the man now.

"I should be thanking you for bringing this to our attention, Legatus," he said gravely. "Why are *you* thanking me?"

"Because of your reaction to this," Lightbringer said with equal gravity. "Until our meeting, I was unsure if you had been in on the lie. Now I see clearly that you are not, and it gives me hope that we can end this conflict and focus on the true enemy."

Lafayette considered these words for a moment. Never mind that they came from an enemy commander, who by all accounts was extraordinarily bloodthirsty. There was a bigger issue at hand.

"One problem, Legatus," he said. "I've been removed from command *and* taken prisoner. I have no way to get this information back to my people, nor do I have the credibility to make them believe."

Legatus Lightbringer seemed to consider this for a little while. Then he turned his head and spoke to Optio Carbo, who had never left his position standing by the conference room door.

"Optio," he said. "Tyrus Tyne has left the Praetorian Guard, has he not?"

"It is as you say, Legatus. He has turned his back on the banner, as was his right."

"Tell me, Optio, you served alongside Tyrus Tyne, did you not? What would you do if Tyrus Tyne contacted you now and shared information such as this with you?"

Carbo did not stop to think or consider. He answered instantly. "I would believe him, my Legatus. Tyrus Tyne may have left the Guard and Mars behind, but he is a trusted friend and former guard, and he would not lie to me or to the Guard."

Lightbringer turned and looked back at Lafayette with both eyebrows raised as if he expected his conversation with Carbo to fully settle Lafayette's concerns. When Lafayette said nothing in reply, the Martian fleet commander spoke again. "I believe, Admiral Lafayette, that you will find that a good commander and colleague such as yourself is trusted by the men and women he fights with not *because* of his rank and position, but often *in spite* of it. You may yet have more influence with Earth's legions than you believe."

His face hardened then, and he studied Lafayette closely. "The question now, Admiral Lafayette, is whether or not you will use that influence to help me stop this war between our worlds, so that we may prepare for the true war that is still to come?"

Lafayette didn't have to think, and by the expressions on the faces of Dasgupta and Porzingas, neither did they.

"What do you want us to do, Legatus?" he asked, and forever changed the course of the Sol system with just eight words.

CHAPTER 46

"Admiral, we're picking up something strange."

Mary Bol turned her command chair to face the young lieutenant at the sensor station on *Enterprise*'s flag bridge. "What is it, Fannie?" she asked.

"It's the transponder signal from Shuttle E-442."

Mary cocked her head in confusion, not sure why one of *Enterprise*'s shuttles wasn't in the docking bay and why that shuttle designation, in particular, rang a tiny bell.

"The shuttle we lost transporting Tyrus Tyne?" she realized out loud.

"Aye, ma'am. Bearing three-two-four mark one. Range five light-minutes."

Mary exchanged a look with Captain George Holm, who was visiting the flag bridge for an informal conference with her. He raised his eyebrows, and she gave him a nod.

"Helm," he called down to the command bridge, "bring us about to three-two-four mark one and go to flank speed. Full stealth protocols in effect."

The acknowledgment came over the ship's intercom, and they

watched the forward viewscreen as the starscape displayed there spun dizzily while the carrier came about to its new course.

"Thoughts, Admiral?" Holm asked Mary, who had been silently frowning while he ordered the course change.

"It could be a trap," she said slowly.

"Aye, ma'am, it could be," he admitted. "Shall we signal *Midway* or *Yorktown* to rendezvous at those coordinates?"

Mary shook her head. "No. If it's a Martian trap, then they'll no doubt have enough firepower to account for all three of our ships. Our best bet is stealth."

"And tripling the number of ships springing the trap triples the chances for detection," he finished for her. "Very well, but may I recommend we go to Ready Fifteen now and Ready Five when we're within two light minutes."

"Of course, George, make it so," Mary replied, though she would have hated to be one of the fighter pilots sitting in their uncomfortable flight suits awaiting a possible launch order for the next six and a half hours.

"Should we alert our other guests?" Holm asked next.

Mary looked at him with a flight frown. "Not yet. I'll tell them when we're close enough to ID the ship."

Keeper Ian Petrov scowled at the latest report from Fleet Admiral Tamara Chen. Everything was coming together for the invasion that would very soon kick off, but that didn't mean it was all happening perfectly. Project Epsilon's manufactured enacters could still only be trusted with menial roles on the fleet's ships, and they had a greater shortage of officers than enlisted at this point. In fact, Chen was reporting that some of the ships she planned to use in the invasion would, by necessity, have only skeleton crews.

It was concerning, as was the continued silence from Earth. That someone on Earth had found and destroyed the quantum comm array infuriated him. It meant that Joseph Blackmont and Mikael Gorsky had made a mistake somewhere along the line. Petrov had to assume that Earth and Mars likely both knew about Blackmont and Gorsky working for him, which meant that he also had to assume that, when Chen's fleet arrived, they would face a united Earth and Mars.

Which made the urgency to launch the invasion all the greater. The less time they could give Earth and Mars to stop fighting each other and form a joint defensive plan and deployment, the more likely it would be that the Council Navy would arrive to a Sol system still gripped by chaos. They had to move now—further delays could not be tolerated.

He was just about to call up his quantum comm connection to Admiral Chen to motivate her once again when there was a knock on his office door. He ignored it. It swung open anyway, and Ebby Hall peeked her head in.

"Your Excellency," she said in her usual crisp and professional tone, "Speakers Yenin and Horvath are here asking to see you."

Petrov frowned and shook his head. "Tell them I'm too busy."

"Sir? If I may?" Ebby asked with uncharacteristic timidity.

He nodded but kept the frown on his face.

She came fully into the room and closed the door softly behind her. "Your Excellency, there is turmoil in the Twenty. It's been several weeks since you've attended one of the meetings, and the other speakers are getting restless."

Petrov was about to open his mouth and argue with her. The other members of the Twenty would just have to wait. Couldn't they understand that he needed all his time to plan the invasion? Couldn't they see that this was the only way to ensure that the power of the Twenty remained for generations to come?

But before he could speak, Ebby said quickly, "Sir, I think if you just talk to Speakers Yenin and Horvath, they can assure the rest of the Twenty that you are not ignoring them. Please, Your Excellency, consider it."

He did consider it. Ebby had always been his most trusted and loyal adviser. She'd been playing defense for him with the rest of the Twenty for weeks now. As much as he hated to admit it, she was usually right. Besides . . .

"Fine," he snapped. "Send them in. But you stay here as well in case I need someone to take notes."

If Ebby thought anything strange in the request, she didn't say, and moments later she showed Yenin and Horvath into the office.

"Your Excellency," they greeted him in concert, and he nodded for them to take their seats across the desk from him.

For a while, none of them spoke. Finally, at a silent nudge from Yenin, Horvath started talking.

"Your Excellency, there are concerns among the Twenty that perhaps we are launching the invasion of the Four Worlds . . . prematurely," Creighton said after a long monologue in which he'd acknowledged the Keeper's power and the brilliance of the invasion plans. It was the little dance they all had to do with Petrov, buttering him up before disagreeing with him. It had always struck Creighton as a little silly, but now it was absolutely vital. Based on his wild-eyed gaze, Petrov had indeed devolved further into madness.

In fact, he appeared to be even further gone than Creighton had feared. He was surprised there wasn't drool on the Keeper's chin.

"Do you agree with Speaker Horvath's words, Constantina?" Petrov asked coldly.

Next to him, Creighton could almost feel Yenin squirming in her seat, but when she spoke, her voice was clear and firm. "I do, Your Excellency. No one can doubt the necessity of the invasion or the fact that Admiral Chen has built a fighting force of unsurpassed power, but what of the war between Earth and Mars? Should we not let it continue for a while longer so that, when we arrive, we face a fragmented and damaged defense?"

And there it was, the question they'd hoped to ask by coming here. If the Keeper had indeed lost communication with his spies and collaborators on Earth, he'd hopefully be forced to admit it now. Or he'd throw an angry fit and confirm for them that he had lost his own mind, as they also suspected.

But to Creighton's surprise, Petrov laughed, throwing back his head and roaring in mirth in a way he'd never seen the Keeper do before.

"Your Excellency?" he asked hesitantly, but the man just kept laughing.

Creighton looked over at Yenin, who just met his gaze and shrugged. Then he cast his eyes over to the blender he'd hired to impersonate Ebby Hall. She nodded. Everything was in place.

"I'm sorry, Your Excellency," Creighton said as evenly as he could. "It's clear we caught you at a bad time." He started to get up from his chair, albeit reluctantly. A small part of him had hoped that his old friend and mentor was still in there somewhere, but the more significant part knew the Keeper was insane and that the only hope the 47 Colonies had was if new leadership were found—Creighton's leadership. This visit, short as it was, had only confirmed that for him.

"Sit down, Creighton!" Petrov snapped, his laughter coming to an abrupt halt as he speared first Creighton and then Yenin with a gaze suddenly devoid of humor.

Licking his lips nervously, Creighton complied. This had always been the risk with their plan, that Petrov would be so far gone that he would never let them leave his office alive.

But to his further surprise, the Keeper nodded slowly. "Perhaps you're right. Perhaps it is time that I address the Twenty once more and fill them in on all the plans for the invasion of the Four Worlds."

"I think that would be a wise course, Your Excellency," Yenin said carefully.

"Ebby." Petrov turned to the blender posing as his chief of staff. "Have the Twenty assemble this afternoon for me to address them." He turned back to look first at Yenin and then at Creighton. "Thank you, my friends, for bringing your concerns to me. I promise, in this afternoon's meeting, all your questions will be answered."

Creighton's finger hovered over his watch holo, hidden in his lap where Petrov couldn't see. Slowly, he pulled it back. There would always be time later to execute the final phase of his plan. But first, he was curious to see what the Keeper would say in the meeting to come. *Then* he could decide.

"We've been waiting at these coordinates a whole day, and nothing," Riggs complained sourly. He had the natural spacer's aversion to being this far out in a system, so distant from the primary star and any inhabited planets. For all of their interstellar travel through the void, most ships rarely traveled this far out from civilization and normal commercial routes, where an engine failure or comms failure could leave them stranded in the dark. Riggs was not a particularly cheerful man right now.

"Even if the *Enterprise* got our dummy transponder signal, it could be days until they can reach us without submerging," Tyrus admonished him. It was becoming a very common topic of argument with the dour pilot. "We just have to keep waiting and hope that Martian intel of Admiral Bol's patrol routes was close to accurate."

"Waiting for what?" Riggs looked at his empty sensor holo dubiously. "There isn't a blip on the sensors anywhere near this sector! I hate to break it to you, but the Reds were wrong."

Tyrus was opening his mouth to reply when Riggs abruptly swore and jumped in his seat as a gigantic ship appeared off the *Blind Monk*'s bow just four thousand kilometers away.

The comm system pinged without preamble, and Riggs read the message while Tyrus looked over his shoulder at the comm holo.

The pilot finished reading it for probably the second time and turned to Tyrus. "You sure about this?"

Tyrus nodded. "Send the message." And he watched while Riggs hit the transmit button. A moment later, the comm light lit up again and the pilot put the incoming voice message on the speakers for Tyrus to hear.

"*Blind Monk,* this is the UENS *Enterprise.* On behalf of the United Earth Navy, we accept your surrender. Prepare to be brought aboard."

"I really hope you know what you're doing," Riggs muttered, barely loud enough for Tyrus to hear.

So do I, Tyrus thought. He turned to leave to go get himself and Domitia ready for what would surely be a cold reception.

Jinny watched as the *Blind Monk* slowly entered the cavernous fighter bay of UENS *Enterprise*. Mary Bol stood next to her, her face impassive, and Trey Kaplan was there with four of his SEALs to augment the several squads of Marines already in the bay, ready to both defend their admiral *and* arrest the *Monk*'s occupants if necessary. Jinny hoped it wouldn't be.

The ship landed in the middle of the bay; the deck crew had found just enough space for the *Monk* by practically stacking the fighters on top of each other. Hopefully, they wouldn't have to launch any of the small ships from this particular bay because Jinny didn't think that would be possible with the light freighter there.

Or maybe it would be. She asked the persona of Trey Kaplan in her head—Trey himself had insisted, upon learning Jinny's secret, that she read every one of his SEALs. Jinny had resisted at first, but Bol had urged her to do it as well. She couldn't reasonably read all of the crews of Bol's ships, but she could at least verify that no additional traitors resided among the SEALs, and they could, therefore, be trusted with ships' security.

I've seen them launch fighters from a more cramped deck, her Trey persona replied, *but I'm no bubblehead, so I couldn't guarantee it.*

Jinny snickered at his use of the semi-affectionate, semi-disdainful nickname the SEALs and Marines had for the regular Navy spacers on board, drawing a confused look from the real Trey standing next to her.

"Sorry," she whispered to him, "just nervous."

"Afraid I'm going to have Commander Kaplan arrest your friends?" Bol said from Jinny's other side, one eyebrow raised as the admiral looked down at the much shorter reader.

Jinny grimaced. Was she being that obvious about it? "Are you?" she asked.

Bol shrugged. "The thought has crossed my mind. But I'm willing to hear what they have to say. I make no promises beyond that."

Jinny nodded, satisfied. The very fact that *she* was still onboard Bol's ship despite the standing orders to remand her to government custody on Earth was testament to the admiral's willingness to hear people out. Once Jinny had impressed upon her the urgency of the situation and the betrayal of Mikael Gorsky, the admiral had somewhat begrudgingly admitted that sending Jinny to Earth would be tantamount to a death sentence.

Still, Jinny knew that Bol had complex emotions toward Tyrus, and if it was Tyrus onboard the *Monk*, then things might get awkward at the least.

She pushed that thought aside. She was practically bouncing on the balls of her feet as the *Blind Monk*'s ramp lowered. Two people came down the ramp together, and she bolted toward them before Bol could issue any orders or Trey or any of the Marines could react. Jinny met Tyrus when he was only halfway down to the deck and threw her arms around him. Standing on the lower part of the ramp in front of him, she felt her head only come up to his stomach instead of his chest as it usually did, but she didn't care. She squeezed him as hard as she could and found her eyes welling up with tears.

Jinny heard a growl. She stepped back and looked up—way up—at the face of the very strange person who was with Tyrus. Then she noticed the way the impossibly tall and thin woman gripped Tyrus's arm possessively and realized that this stranger really was *with* her friend.

"Oh," Jinny said as the other woman gave her a dark look. "Where are my manners? I'm Jinny Ambrosa." She reached out a gloved hand toward the Martian woman, who looked at it and cocked her head.

"My Domitia," Tyrus said, turning to the woman and motioning toward Jinny. "This is my good friend, Reader Jinny Ambrosa. I've told you all about her, and you do not need to worry that she hugged me. I explained to you that is a normal greeting among friends on Earth and in the colonies."

He turned and looked at Jinny, who knew that her confusion was showing on her face. "Jinny," he said with a smile. "Meet Domitia Tyne, my wife."

Jinny felt her jaw drop open and her eyes go wide. She looked the tall woman up and down now, noticing that she wore some kind of reinforced suit, and then she smiled widely at Tyrus once she recovered her wits. "Your wife? Wow, we really do have a lot to catch up on." She looked over to her friend's new—or maybe old; it had been almost six months since they'd seen each other, and she'd been mostly unconscious even then—wife and smiled at her as well. "Domitia, it is such a pleasure to meet you. Any woman who is strong and wonderful enough to marry Tyrus is someone I am honored to meet." She held out her hand again, sensing that the other woman probably wouldn't respond well to a hug of her own.

Domitia raised an eyebrow and then actually smiled back and awkwardly grabbed Jinny's hand and shook it as if she were trying to fling water off of a spoon. It was weird, but by the momentary look of relief on Tyrus's face, apparently she'd said the right thing.

"And I," the woman spoke, her voice a high soprano that seemed to fit her slight frame but was at odds with her earlier imposing glare, "am honored to meet you as well, Reader Jinny Ambrosa, the woman who brought my husband to this system and to me, and whose friendship inspires the loyalty of all she meets. I would wish us to become friends as well."

"Of course!" Jinny exclaimed. "Consider us friends. And when Tyrus isn't around, we can talk all about him."

The woman seemed a little confused by that but didn't say anything.

Jinny turned back to Tyrus. "Sorry, let me move out of the way so you can finish getting off the ship. I think Admiral Bol is waiting to arrest you down there. Is Riggs inside?"

"He is," Tyrus said as he and Domitia followed her down the ramp, ignoring the comment about his impending arrest. "He can't wait to see you, but he's making sure his precious ship is properly shut down before he comes out. He's locking all the systems down, too—something about not letting the Navy take her apart again. But Jinny." He looked down at her sharply. "I'm glad to see you up and about, but what are *you* doing here on the *Enterprise?"*

"Oh!" she said with a start. "It really has been a while. I have a *lot* to catch you up on. Which seems to be a theme right now." She tilted her head pointedly toward her friend's new wife.

"Okay, that's fair," he said with a smile that softened his features.

"Is Corey with you, too?"

Tyrus shook his head. "He's still back on Mars, convincing the praetors to . . . Well, it's probably better if we tell the story to the admiral as well.

They reached the place where Bol was standing. Tyrus stopped a meter or so away, just as Trey was about to step forward to block him from getting any closer.

"Admiral Bol," Tyrus greeted her.

"Mr. Tyne," the tall African woman responded coolly. "I should arrest you right here, but I find my curiosity at why you've chosen *now* to surrender yourself to the UEN. I'll give you fifteen minutes to convince me why you shouldn't be back in *Enterprise*'s brig.

Domitia Tyne bristled at this and looked as if she might leap forward and attack the almost equally tall admiral, but Tyrus held out a warning hand to stop her.

"Admiral, I am confident that in fifteen minutes, you'll be utterly convinced not only that you shouldn't arrest me, but also that you should help us."

Bol frowned but said nothing.

"Besides," Tyrus continued, looking back at Jinny, "something tells me that what I came here to say might not be the surprise I expected it to be."

"Very well then," Bol replied. "But first, I'm afraid Commander Kaplan insists that we must check you all for weapons."

Tyrus nodded, but Jinny saw Domitia stiffen next to him. One of the SEALs, Julia Perez—the other SEALs called her 'Perry'—stepped forward and went to frisk Tyrus's Martian wife.

Tyrus held out a hand to stop the SEAL. "Listen," he said, still addressing Bol, "It's considered a mortal insult on Mars to touch someone like that unless you're married. But I can assure you that, besides her exosuit, former-Praetorian Guard Domitia Tyne is not armed."

Jinny noticed Bol wince at hearing Domitia's last name, and the admiral looked like she was about to argue. But Trey stepped forward and beat her to it. "Admiral, if I may?"

His superior officer nodded, an inquisitive look on her face, and Trey continued.

"Visitor Domitia Tyne," he said formally to the tall Martian woman. "I am Commander Trey Kaplan of the UEN SEALs. Are you the daughter of Legatus Augustus Lightbringer?"

Bol stiffened, and even Jinny gasped a little in surprise. *Why didn't you warn me?* she scolded the Trey persona in her head.

I wanted to see the look of surprise on your face, he said playfully.

"I am the daughter of Legatus Lightbringer," Domitia replied.

"And do you swear on Mars that you are unarmed?" the real Trey pressed.

"I swear it," Domitia said solemnly.

Trey turned back to Bol. "Admiral, I've spent a lot of years studying what little we know of the Praetorian Guard. It pays to understand one's enemy." He nodded to Domitia, who nodded back respectfully. "And if a member—or former member—of the Guard swears that they are unarmed, we can take her word for it."

Mary Bol raised an eyebrow and studied the Martian, who studied her right back. "Very well," she said reluctantly. "But we must still search Mr. Tyne and the pilot."

Jinny turned her head to see that Riggs had quietly joined the little group, standing where Tyrus mostly blocked her view of him. She tried to catch his eye, but he looked away, studiously inspecting a spot on the deck instead.

"Tyrus Tyne was also of the Praetorian Guard," Domitia argued. "His word is the same as my own. You need not—"

"Domitia," Tyrus cut her off gently. "It's okay. They can search me if it makes them feel better."

The Martian frowned but didn't argue further, and one of Trey's other SEALs, George Papadopolous—everyone called him Paps—ran a scanner over Tyrus and then frisked him, while another SEAL did the same for Riggs. When they were satisfied the two men were unarmed, Bol resumed speaking.

"Good. Now that that's settled, let's find a place to talk so you can convince me why I shouldn't arrest Mr. Tyne for treason."

To Jinny's eye, Domitia didn't pick up on the way the admiral said

Tyrus's name. But she did. She knew that Tyrus had developed a sort of crush on Bol during his time on *Enterprise*. And the expressions playing across Bol's face confirmed that the feelings had been more than reciprocated. Seeing Tyrus again, with his new *wife* in tow, was obviously throwing the admiral for an emotional loop.

It was good that Domitia didn't notice. Based on her brief interactions with the Martian woman, Jinny worried she might threaten to kill the admiral. But she was too busy now looking around the cavernous fighter bay, not in awe, but with a soldier's evaluating gaze.

Bol started walking toward the docking bay's exit hatch, and the SEALs took up escort positions around the newcomers, including Jinny in the cordon as she fell back to walk next to Tyrus, but not before Trey gave her a concerned look. She threw him a small smile to reassure him.

"Tell me how you two met," she said to Tyrus and Domitia as they walked.

"Well," Tyrus said, "Domitia was sent on an errand to fetch me one day, and I asked her to lunch. Then we served together in the Praetorian Guard, and we were just married last week." Leave it to Tyrus to give her the short, efficient version.

Luckily, Domitia jumped in. "His attentions at first were unwelcome, but over time, he wore me down."

Jinny smiled at this, sensing a joke somewhere behind the words, though the other woman's face remained stoic. Then Domitia continued.

"It eventually reached a juncture where I had to decide to either bind him to me or kill him."

Jinny smiled again, but Domitia didn't. Looking over at Tyrus, Jinny whispered, "She's joking, right? I can't tell."

"I'm not entirely sure myself," he said back with a half grin.

Domitia, who had to have heard their exchange, didn't react, but Jinny caught a slight twitch of one eye that seemed to convey a certain amusement at their confusion. She decided to assume there was humor in the woman's words. It seemed far less strange and concerning that way.

"And how about you and . . ." Tyrus motioned with his head and eyes back toward Riggs, who trailed behind them at a slight distance. Jinny took the hint.

"Um," Jinny whispered sheepishly. "Probably not the best time. I'll explain later."

Tyrus raised an eyebrow but didn't press.

"Reader Jinny Ambrosa," Domitia jumped in. "May I ask you a question?"

"Of course, but please, just call me Jinny."

Tyrus winced for some reason at Jinny's reply, but the Martian actually smiled. "Very well, Jinny. Do you harbor any romantic feelings toward my husband?"

The frank question stopped Jinny in her tracks and drew a concerned look from Trey and the other SEALs.

"Uh, no," Jinny said, perhaps a bit too harshly. "Tyrus and I are friends. Nothing more."

"That is good, Jinny," Domitia replied with a broader smile. "I expected I might have to challenge you to an honor duel for the rights to my husband. I am gratified to find that this is not to be the case. Killing you would distress my Tyrus."

Tyrus and Domitia started walking again before Jinny could respond. Mouth agape, she called after them. "*That's* a joke, right?"

Domitia didn't respond, and Tyrus just hunched his head down into his shoulders and didn't look back.

Creighton sat at his usual place at the conference table as the assembled members of the Twenty quietly awaited the Keeper's arrival. Most of them were pretending to be busy, poking at their watch holos or the integrated holos on the table in front of them, ignoring each other. Only Jerem Pondergast looked around the room, his gaze challenging to anyone unfortunate enough to look up in time to catch it.

The forced tableau ended as the door opened, and the Keeper strode through it, moving toward his seat at the head of the table. He didn't sit down, however, but stopped behind his chair and placed both hands on it, using its back as a support as he leaned forward and stared at each of the men and women in the room.

"It had come to my attention that many of you have grown concerned about my self-imposed isolation," Petrov began without preamble. "So I am here to address these concerns and have an open discussion about the plans to invade the Four Worlds. But first, does anyone have serious misgivings about the timing of the attack?"

It's a trap, was Creighton's immediate thought. *He's trying to see who the malcontents are so he can weed them out.*

"I do!" a belligerent voice cried from near the opposite end of the table. All eyes turned to regard Pondergast, who glared at the Keeper.

"Go on, Speaker Pondergast," Petrov said, his voice cold. Creighton felt an icy hand grip his spine. If that idiot Pondergast just knew how to stay silent, then maybe they could have actually gotten something from this meeting.

"It's clear that the Navy isn't ready," Pondergast said, either ignorant or willfully defiant of the note of warning in the Keeper's tone. "There aren't enough enacters to crew the ships. Epsilon is a failure. We lost too many ships attacking the rebel base, and the battle there exposed how poorly trained and prepared our officers and crews are. We must delay the invasion until we can muster a sufficient force to overwhelm the Four Worlds!" He practically shouted the last part, causing several of the other speakers to wince.

For a long time, Petrov didn't reply as he and Pondergast engaged in a staring contest across the length of the table. "Does anyone else agree with Speaker Pondergast?" Petrov asked.

No one raised a hand or added their voice to the discussion. Not even Creighton. He knew a losing battle when he saw one.

Petrov looked around, however, his eyes boring into each of them. When he'd made a full circuit of the table, he suddenly let his shoulders relax. "Speaker Pondergast is, unfortunately, correct. The Council Navy is not ready to invade the Four Worlds."

Shocked silence greeted the pronouncement, and Petrov actually smiled warmly as he finally pulled out his chair and settled into it. "That is what I came here today to tell you all—that I have decided we are, in fact, not prepared to launch on the schedule I originally set. My hope was, that by giving the Navy and Project Epsilon a hard deadline, it would motivate them to more aggressively ramp up preparations. It did have that effect, but not to the degree I optimistically hoped for."

He peered around the table again, as did Creighton. Relief had replaced the discomfort on the faces of several members of the Twenty. Even Pondergast was smiling a bit.

"Today, I would like all of your thoughts on a new timeline. Let's start with you, Creighton?"

Creighton hid his surprise and nodded toward the Keeper, quickly collecting his thoughts at this unexpected turn. "I'm afraid that the invasion timeline may take some time to finalize," he said slowly. "Project Epsilon should still deliver us a million enacters, but we're perhaps another six months out pessimistically—and four months out optimistically. That said, we may be able to move sooner if we can tell how much of the combined fleets of the Four Worlds were destroyed in the Earth-Mars war."

Petrov frowned again. "I'm afraid I've lost communication with my contacts in the Sol system," he said, the frank admission further shocking Creighton. "But just before, there had been a number of large battles. We can assume anywhere from a 10 to 20 percent reduction in their forces, to be safe."

Creighton licked his lips and nodded. "I'm not a military man, myself, of course. But it seems to me that we will want as much of our force as possible to take out their fleets. That puts us at five to six months out, I'm afraid."

The Keeper nodded, then turned to the speaker next to Creighton. "Constantina, do you agree?"

Casting a quick look over at Creighton, she reluctantly nodded. "I do, Your Excellency. I would suggest setting the new deadline at five months and reevaluating as we draw closer."

Again, Petrov nodded. "As much as I hate to hear it, that sounds reasonable." He turned his attention back to the room as a whole. "All those in favor of the new deadline for the invasion being set five months from today, please indicate."

At first, only Pondergast, Creighton, and Yenin raised their hands.

Then, slowly, another twelve speakers indicated their support for the motion.

The Keeper looked at each of them in turn, his face oddly sympathetic. Then he reached out and manipulated something in the holo in front of him, the privacy settings allowing only him to see what it was.

Without further warning, every muscle in Creighton Horvath's body tensed up at the exact same moment. Excruciating pain shot through him, and he tried to scream at the agony, but his vocal cords, like the rest of him, were paralyzed by an unseen force. He couldn't even turn his eyes, but in his peripheral vision he could see Yenin go rigid next to him, along with at least one other speaker who had raised his hand in support of the five-month delay.

"Ah, my friends," Petrov said, his voice almost light and joking, "how you disappoint me so. Especially you, Constantina. Betrayed by my oldest friend. And you, Creighton. I expected better from you. Did you really think I didn't know about all your plans?"

Creighton tried to reply, but he still couldn't make a sound. Inside his head, he panicked as he heard the room's door open behind him and footsteps approaching over the thick carpet. He expected to next feel the cold metal of a pistol against the back of his head. Instead, he felt a warm breath at his ear, and a gentle kiss of soft lips.

"Hello, lover," Lara Owens purred into his ear. "Sorry about this, but a girl has to take care of herself first."

Creighton's horror ramped up as he realized how badly he'd been duped. The Keeper smiled at him and Yenin. Then Lara walked to stand next to the man's chair, her face a smug smile of satisfaction as she stared right into Creighton's unblinking eyes, which were now starting to burn and tear up.

Surprisingly, another man stepped into view on Petrov's other side. A gleeful Jerem Pondergast smirked at Creighton. "I told you they were plotting against you, Your Excellency," the junior member of the Twenty said. "All they needed was a little push."

"Indeed," said the Keeper, his expression still a little sad. "Some of the others I might have suspected, but not them. Thank you, Speaker Pondergast, Alpha Owens. You've both done a great service here today."

As if his overstressed brain could handle any more surprises, the revelation that Lara Owens was an alpha struck Creighton like a ton of bricks.

"You've disabled the explosives the blender put in my office?" Petrov asked.

Lara nodded. "Right before I killed the blender and rescued Ebby. There was a Guard Intelligence colonel with her. He's dead too, but before I killed him, he had some very interesting things to tell me about Speaker Horvath's role in the disaster at GX-6607."

Petrov frowned and shook his head at Creighton as if silently scolding a small child.

"Should I kill them all now, Your Excellency?" Lara asked, a gleam of excitement in her eyes.

"No." The Keeper stood up, straightening his jacket and continuing to look at his former friends, his face blurry now in the tears gushing from Creighton's unblinking eyes. "It will take a few hours, but eventually, their hearts will give out. This much stress—the human body can only handle it for a short while."

Creighton vaguely saw Petrov turn to address the rest of the room. "For those of you who did not betray me, I am dissolving the Twenty, effective immediately. I no longer have need of you. You can remain in the Assembly, but if you breathe a word of any of what you've learned here today, or since joining this group, you will be dealt with in like manner. Do I make myself understood?"

There were hurried calls of agreement from the few unparalyzed speakers in the room. Then, Petrov turned and left, Pondergast trailing in his wake. Around him, Creighton could hear the rest of the speakers, those few who were able, leave as quickly as they could, until the only ones left in the room were the paralyzed and Lara Owens.

The latter moved to sit in the Keeper's chair, where she was square in the middle of Creighton's blurry line of sight. His vision was so far gone now he could only make out her rough silhouette, but he got the firm impression of a smile on her face.

"So exciting," she said softly, almost as if speaking to herself. "I think I'll just stay here and watch you die, Creighton. This may be even more fun than slitting your judgmental, monogamist assistant's throat on the way here."

CHAPTER 47

When Mikael Gorsky ascended to the presidency, his first order of business was to account for those who might one day oppose him. It was a distressingly common act for new presidents to undertake, so much so that the public barely raised an eyebrow anymore, even when the news deigned to report it.

Most of it took the form of subtly but no less aggressively forcing Congress to replace the heads of certain committees with those more amenable to Gorsky's policy goals. But the most delicate part was rearranging the military leadership to ensure that, when the Council Navy finally arrived in force, those in charge of United Earth's defenses would react in the way that best suited Gorsky's and the Keeper's agendas.

General Ernesto Cruz, chairman of the Joint Chiefs of Staff, was left in place. Going into a war with Mars, the new president couldn't be seen making drastic changes in public-facing military leadership. He would let the success or failure of the war do most of that for him, promoting those who pleased him and reassigning those who didn't on the pretense of some imagined blunder. Besides, for all his Boy Scout morality, Cruz wasn't one to rock the boat, and Gorsky was certain he could manipulate the man when the time came.

But the one man he was positive he could not influence was Fleet Admiral Horatio Krishna Lopez. 'Hunter Killer' Lopez as the reporters and most of the public called him, was a popular figure both among the military and civilians. A hero of the Six-Month War with Mars fifty years ago, Lopez was respected throughout the Sol system. If there was one man who could possibly rally the troops to defy a sitting president, it was him.

Still, Gorsky couldn't simply fire Lopez. Indeed, one of the ways he'd discredited former President Pereira in the Brazilian's final days in office was to point to his effective exile of Lopez to a teaching position on Luna. To leave him in that position or transfer him to a worse station would have exposed Gorsky's hypocrisy. So, rather, he reassigned him to what *looked* like a better assignment.

Waypoint X-Ray had been the UE military's most closely guarded secret for the five decades since the last war with Mars. The UE government had always considered another war with Mars to be a near certainty. In a fleeting and odd moment of setting aside politics for the common good, Congress had overwhelmingly approved a spending bill that gave the executive branch a large sum of money and broad powers to use it toward the UE's defense against Mars. Thus was born Waypoint X-Ray. Nearly forty-eight years later, when a rabid Martian dictator launched nuclear warheads at Luna, Congress had approved another large budget. Part of that had gone to completing the long development and construction of Admiral Mary Bol's carriers. The rest had gone to Project Anvil.

X-Ray itself was unspectacular, a random point in space within the Oort cloud, the big spherical shell of debris, asteroids, and ice that encompassed the Sol system, just inside the perimeter defined by the Castilian Rift. Here, in a place so far from any normal spacelanes that the chances of anyone stumbling upon it were measured with a dozen zeroes behind the decimal, the UE started its most ambitious military building project of all time: Project Anvil.

Gorsky would send Hunter Killer Lopez to be the senior officer for both X-Ray and Anvil. Ostensibly, the transfer was a way to 'get Admiral Lopez back in the fight,' by assigning him to the military's most important secret project. But given that conservative military planners had informed President Gorsky that Anvil was at least eighteen months from completion, he saw it as a convenient way to get Lopez out of his hair and far away from any of his spheres of influence, overseeing a project that ultimately wouldn't be a factor in any fight until long after the Council took over the system. It was the perfect mathematical solution to one of the new president's biggest problems.

But, as politicians often do when dealing with those they considered to be their lessers, Gorsky entirely failed to account for Lopez himself in that equation.

Reunited for the first time in seven months, Tyrus, Jinny, and Riggs sat together in the wardroom on *Enterprise*, eating a late-afternoon meal. Admiral Mary Bol was there, presiding silently over the lunch. Tyrus could see Jinny, across the table, casting surreptitious glances at Domitia next to him. His friend's expression was one of curiosity, not jealousy, which relieved him.

He wasn't sure why. He and Jinny had never even flirted—to his knowledge, neither had ever entertained any romantic thoughts about the other. Tyrus had been the one to kill Alan Daily, whom the young reader had been in the process of falling in love with. That they were even colleagues, much less friends, after that was a miracle. But maybe there had been something beneath the surface, for him at least, that had caused him to subconsciously worry what would happen when his best friend met his new wife.

Either way, it obviously wasn't an issue, though Tyrus was concerned that Domitia might catch a few too many of Jinny's looks her way and decide to challenge the reader to a duel for staring. That would be awkward, to say the least.

"Do not worry, my Husband," Domitia leaned over and whispered in his ear, "I do not intend to kill your blond friend if she continues to study me today."

Tyrus simultaneously felt three emotions: chagrin that Domitia had so easily read him, comfort that his wife wasn't planning an honor killing, and concern that she'd ended her sentence with 'today.' What would happen tomorrow?

Before he could ask her the question, Bol cleared her throat and set aside her plate with its half-eaten sandwich. "Very well, Mr. Tyne. Why not tell me why you've reappeared on my ship after all this time?"

Tyrus winced inwardly. Unlike Jinny, the admiral was *not* taking his sudden appearance with a new wife as well as might be hoped. He'd tried desperately to think if he'd done or said anything while on *Enterprise* previously that might have given the admiral expectations about him, but he also knew he was hopelessly out of his depth. Domitia was his first *real* relationship, and the fact that it was going so well was equal parts confusing and exhilarating to him. But it didn't mean he understood women, even the one he was now married to. *Especially* not Domitia, if he was honest with himself.

"Well, Admiral," he said after only a moment's hesitation. "Where to start? Maybe at the beginning."

He talked for the next thirty minutes solid. Bol and the others in the room listened intently, not interrupting to ask any questions. He gave only a broad outline of his joining the Praetorian Guard—the Trials were a secret to anyone not of Mars, and he wasn't sure that even Domitia's love for him would stop her from putting a knife in his chest should he reveal too much. He hit the high points, including the interrogation of the traitorous alpha Toby—again, he left out any mention of Riggs's role in extracting the information from their prisoner. Then he spoke of the assault in UENS *Italy* from his point of view, including the contents of the drive they'd discovered that clearly showed it had been Earth, not Mars, that had fired the first shots at Nyx. He finished with the evidence in the logs that showed communications between Admiral Connors on *Italy* and President Gorsky's office both before and after the battle at Nyx. Though the contents of those messages had been missing even from the raw logs, their timing was damning.

Throughout his retelling of events, Bol sat impassively, betraying nothing that would tell him if she believed a word of his story or not. When he finished, *Enterprise*'s captain, George Holm, asked several questions, seemingly more for clarification than to challenge any part of his story. After he answered the best he could, all eyes turned again to the admiral.

The tall black woman sat there, eyes hooded under furrowed brows as they had been virtually since Tyrus stepped foot back on her ship. For long moments, no one spoke. Finally, Bol nodded once. "Let's say I believe you, Mr. Tyne," she said matter-of-factly, "and your story does coincide with what Reader Ambrosa and her companions have told us. Unless the two of you were somehow conspiring between Earth and Mars through a solid wall of jamming, it's hard to deny the voices of two witnesses who learned of the president's treachery through their own independent means."

She leaned forward, putting her arms on the table and spearing him with her gaze. "So, assuming you're right and President Gorsky truly is a traitor, just what would you propose we do about it?"

Before Tyrus could answer, another member of the small meeting spoke up. SEAL Commander Kaplan had been silent in the lunch conference until this moment, though the hard glares he'd shot at Tyrus had spoken volumes. He'd probably have to explain to Domitia later why he didn't challenge the SEAL to a duel, given the man's overt hostility. At least when he spoke now, he kept his tone largely neutral.

"Why not just share this intelligence with Fleet Command?" Kaplan asked. "Now that we have this additional evidence to support Jinny's—I mean, Reader Ambrosa's—they'd have to believe us. And surely, there are provisions in the Constitution to remove a sitting president for treason."

Before Tyrus could answer, George Holm jumped back in. "All due respect to Fleet Command, Commander Kaplan, but this is an armed proton bomb waiting to blow. Even with the best encryption, we couldn't afford to transmit this across the system to them. If someone intercepted the message, it would be all over the news within a few days. Worse, what if the wrong person at Fleet Command sees it—one of Gorsky's people? He'd know we're onto him, and he'd dig in and probably find a way to explain away or dismiss the allegations against him. Besides"—he lowered his voice and gave the SEAL commander a look that Tyrus couldn't decipher—"even if Gorsky is innocent, we can't guarantee there aren't any turncoats on his staff . . . or here."

Jinny must have noticed Tyrus's frown, because she jumped in to explain. "There was a Council spy on the *Enterprise*. I'll tell you all about it later."

"Then why not just release the information ourselves to the press?" Kaplan pushed back. "It would be all over the news before Gorsky could work up his defense."

This time it was Bol who answered. "Unfortunately, Commander, we have to assume that Mikael Gorsky already has a defense plan for anything we could throw at him in the courts of law or of public opinion. On top of that, I daresay that leaking this information to the public would likely do more harm than good. We could throw the entire UE into disarray just in time for the Council Navy to arrive and take advantage of it. Plus, if we're wrong, the panic will nonetheless be very real."

She turned to Jinny. "Our plan since Reader Ambrosa came on board was to eventually take her and her information to Fleet Admiral Lopez. I see nothing in Mr. Tyne's report that convinces me to change that strategy."

Jinny nodded gratefully to the admiral. From what Tyrus had gathered, Jinny had already been on *Enterprise* for several weeks; he would have to ask her later why it had taken so long for Admiral Bol to take her to Lopez. Luckily, the woman answered that for him.

"General Cruz has sent us orders to refuel and resupply at Waypoint X-Ray. It means we can finally leave our patrol pattern and speak with Admiral Lopez, without raising any suspicion and without leaving our post open to attack."

Tyrus understood. Despite the explosive information Jinny had brought the admiral—and it had likely taken some time for Bol to believe all of it—*Enterprise* had had a job to do, guarding possible routes of attack by the Martians. The admiral would have felt the urge, of course, to get Jinny's information to Lopez sooner rather than later, but would have also known that simply abandoning her post would leave Earth open to new avenues of attack.

"How far are we from Waypoint X-Ray, Admiral?" he asked.

"We've been accelerating at full military power toward it since we picked you up," George Holm answered for his boss. "In fact . . ."

There was a chime from the wardroom's comm. "Admiral, Captain," a clipped feminine voice said—probably *Enterprise's* executive officer, "we're coming up on Waypoint X-Ray."

"Coming, Lillian," Bol replied.

Two minutes later, all of them stood together on the carrier's flag bridge, which was crowded with Bol's full staff plus Tyrus, Domitia, Jinny, and a silent and sulking Riggs, who had followed them from the wardroom, where he'd also been completely quiet.

Holm, who had separated from them to go to the carrier's command bridge, spoke to them through the comm. "The waypoint is just on the other side of Lucifer, there. Thirty seconds, Admiral."

"Lucifer?" Riggs asked in confusion, speaking aloud for the first time since arriving on *Enterprise.*

"A mythical anti-God," Jinny explained to him. "Basically, this evil guy that tries to make people do bad things."

"I never needed any help with that," Riggs muttered under his breath, so only Tyrus, standing next to him, caught it.

"Not so mythical for those of us who believe," Bol corrected. "But in this case, it's actually the name of that large asteroid right in front of us. Our destination is on the other side of it, safe from the prying eyes of the Martians."

As she spoke, the *Enterprise* changed course and flew in a smooth arc around the large rock, which was big enough to be considered a moon if it had orbited a planet in the system instead of being another faceless asteroid in the Oort cloud. Tyrus assumed that, although he couldn't see them, *Yorktown* and *Midway* were flying in formation with their flagship on the same course.

"What is that?" Domitia said before anyone else could, awe coloring her tone.

Behind the asteroid, now visible, was the largest ship Tyrus had ever seen. Riggs sucked in a breath, and Jinny gasped.

It looked like a extra-large battleship surrounded by a few light cruisers and destroyers, but Tyrus peaked over at Mary Bol's plot display, and his eyes opened wide in surprise.

"It's huge," he said unnecessarily. Those weren't cruisers and destroyers keeping station near the enormous ship, they were *battle-*

ships and *battlecruisers*. The single ship in the center was so large that it filled the viewscreen and made everything look tiny by comparison. He imagined it was more than double the size of even the formidable Council Navy dreadnoughts.

"That, ladies and gentlemen," Bol said with evident pride, "is UENS *George Washington*. The first and only ship of the Constitution-class superdreadnoughts, and the ship built specifically to beat Mars."

Domitia shot the admiral a sharp look, but Tyrus squeezed his wife's hand to warn her against any outbursts. Bol continued as if she hadn't noticed the Martian woman's reaction. "Really, it was built to defend against what many considered to be the inevitable attack on Earth by Mars, just as my three stealth carriers were. What you see here is the result of a twenty-year building program out here in the Oort cloud that was so secret not even Congress was told about it. Even the president's cabinet and staff weren't allowed to know; just the president and the Joint Chiefs and a few hand-picked admirals."

"And now?" Tyrus asked.

Bol shot him a look that wasn't quite as hostile as when he'd first boarded early that same morning. "Now, it's under the personal command of Admiral Lopez himself, but this is where it gets complicated. The ship isn't supposed to be done for another year at least, but as you can see, Admiral Lopez was able to speed things up a bit."

As they neared the massive ship, more and more details came into focus. Its shape reminded Tyrus of a manta ray, with a large flat body —flat at this scale probably still meant thirty or forty decks in the middle—that stretched wide into two large wings. In the middle rear of the body was a stout tower that rose and tilted forward, giving anyone standing at its top a complete view of the space around the ship, except for directly below it. And at the rear, completing the effect, was a long 'tail' that stretched out over the largest bank of drive nozzles Tyrus had ever seen. You could drive a destroyer into one of those nozzles and possibly even a light cruiser.

"Know that just by seeing her, you've all put your lives on the line," Bol said solemnly. "If you tell anyone that she's here, the penalty is death." She looked meaningfully over at Domitia.

"I can keep a secret," Domitia said with a toothy smile that looked altogether too predatory for Tyrus's taste. "Can you?"

Bol nodded but didn't respond, turning back to the viewscreen and pushing a button on her command chair's touchscreen. A moment later, a variety of multicolored symbols appeared, superimposed on *George Washington's* hull. The weapons! There were so many that it took Tyrus by surprise, even given the size of the ship. If he was reading this right, those long wings on either side of the superdreadnought were basically enormous magazines housing capacitors for the hundreds of laser banks and missiles for the hundred-plus launchers on each of the ship's flanks and wings and another hundred or so on its dorsal and ventral hulls. Each wing had its own independent reactor so that its weapons could continue firing in the event that the ship's main reactors were somehow disabled.

At the top of the ship, in its center, just forward of the observation bridge that rose from it, the superimposed symbols showed multiple fighter bays, with the same mirrored on the ship's bottom.

Tyrus counted two UEN battleships orbiting the *Washington,* as well as three battlecruisers, six heavy and light cruisers, and a handful of destroyers and what looked like missile frigates.

"Task Force 15," he said.

Mary Bol looked up at him sharply. "How did you guess?"

He shrugged. "We got intel that the Earthlings—sorry, the UEN—moved another full task force away from their home fleet. But we never saw it in battle like we expected, reinforcing Second Fleet."

Bol nodded. "General Cruz ordered it sent out here to serve as escorts for the *Washington,*" she admitted.

"Then why is it still here and not out fighting the Martians with the *Washington*?" Tyrus asked the obvious.

Bol shook her head. "I don't know. Like I said, last I'd heard, the ship was still a year from completion. It makes me wonder if, perhaps, no one outside of Waypoint X-Ray knows just how far along she really is."

"Ma'am, the *Washington* has responded to our hails. We are ordered to keep station at a distance of ten thousand kilometers and await instructions," the flag bridge's comm officer told Bol just as Tyrus noticed a squadron of fighters launch from the massive ship and set course to arrow-straight at the *Enterprise* and her sisters, no doubt triangulating their location from their comm signal.

"Make it so," Bol noted. "And order the squadron to drop active stealth measures. Let's show we have nothing to hide."

The bridge was a flurry of activity, and they didn't have to wait at the proscribed distance for long. Orders soon followed from Lopez himself—the old man sounded like he'd just woken up—to proceed to close distance with *Washington*. Tyrus watched in silence as the already massive ship grew even larger in the forward viewport. He hadn't quite believed that there could be any ship in the UEN arsenal that was *more* secret than Bol's carriers. Apparently, however, Earth still had some surprises left.

When the shuttle deposited the group from *Enterprise* in one of the *George Washington's* spacious hangar bays, Jinny was among the last to disembark the shuttle. Ever since Tyrus, Domitia, and Riggs had arrived on Mary Bol's ship earlier that morning, she'd been trying to find time to talk to Riggs away from the hearing of others. But they'd been far too busy answering questions for Bol and her officers, getting briefed by Tyrus, and generally being herded around like cats aboard the carrier.

Even with all that, however, Jinny had gotten the distinct impression that Riggs was avoiding her. He'd barely met her eye a single time since they'd been reunited as a group—minus Jynx, of course—and she waited behind on the shuttle now to see if she could catch a brief moment with him.

He appeared to be surprised when he finally unstrapped from his seat and looked up to find himself alone with her in the shuttle's passenger compartment.

"Cal, how are you?" Jinny asked after a brief, awkward silence.

He shrugged. "I'm okay. How about you? All healed from that prison?"

She frowned. It was clear he was trying to distract with small talk, not that her opening question had been anything but. Still, she wasn't going to let him off the hook so easily.

"Cal, I'm sorry about Jynx. Landon and Temperance told me what happened. I was a little out of it when you all rescued me, or I would have said something then."

To her surprise, Riggs suddenly looked angry, but the moment passed, and his face reverted to the same blank expression he'd worn since arriving on *Enterprise*. He just shrugged.

Jinny opened her mouth to try and draw him out again, but a voice interrupted her, calling from the foot of the ramp. "Jinny, Pilot Riggs, are you well?"

Domitia's long body appeared coming up the ramp, her expression inquisitive.

Jinny sighed and turned to face the woman. "We're fine, Domitia. Just catching up, that's all."

Before she could finish her sentence, Riggs practically shouldered past her and gave Domitia a slightly wider berth as he went down the ramp and out of the shuttle without a backward glance. Domitia watched him go and then turned back to Jinny.

"Your would-be bonded partner insults you with his indifference."

Jinny's mind went blank at the other woman's words. Then she shook her head to clear it and frowned. "Riggs isn't my bonded partner, Domitia. He's just a friend."

Domitia's eyebrows went up, having the odd effect of making her long face appear even longer. She was the first Martian Jinny had ever seen in person, and every time she looked at Tyrus's new wife, she almost felt like she was looking at a normal human in a funhouse mirror. She caught how she was thinking of Domitia as 'not normal,' but there it was.

"Does Pilot Riggs know this?" Domitia asked, cocking her head inquisitively to one side.

"That we're friends? Of course he does," Jinny answered cautiously.

Domitia shook her head. "Jinny, I have observed Pilot Riggs for the week since we left Mars. Every time your name is mentioned, it is clear that he wishes to be your bonded partner. You simply must decide if that is your wish as well or if your heart truly belongs to someone else." The Martian nodded meaningfully toward the shuttle's interior.

Jinny blushed and looked at Domitia in a new light. For all the woman's strangeness and seeming rigidity, Tyrus's wife seemed to have a fairly good grasp on the emotional tells of others. If only Jinny could as easily see what *she* was thinking.

And if only she could articulate back to the tall woman the flurry of conflicting emotions that surged through her. To her relief, Domitia didn't stick around to see her response but walked back down the ramp, no doubt to find Tyrus.

Which was good, because at that very moment, the door from the cockpit opened and another person entered the crew compartment where Jinny vacillated. SEAL Commander Trey Kaplan stopped next to Jinny and smirked down at her. Before she could say anything or stop him, he ducked down and planted a kiss on her lips.

Jinny let out a little yelp of surprise and pushed him back gently, ignoring the inrush of memories the kiss brought with it as she read Trey for the . . . she'd lost count of how many times.

"What?" he asked, confused. "Something wrong?"

She licked her lips and looked down the ramp to make sure no one else was close enough to hear. But she still spoke in a low voice. "I haven't told my friends yet about us. There hasn't been time. I'd rather they hear it from me than see us and figure it out for themselves."

He smirked again. "I think most of them have probably already figured it out. You may be hard to read, but they don't exactly teach subtlety in SEAL school, so I'm sure they've caught on. Besides, what are you afraid of, that Riggs will go ballistic?"

Jinny gave Trey a hard look. "What do you mean?"

He shrugged laconically. "Come one, Jin." She felt a little thrill at the nickname he'd given her. "It's clear that guy is head over heels for you. Did you and he . . .?"

"No," she said quickly. "Not really. But you're the second person to tell me that in the last five minutes. I thought *I* was supposed to be the reader."

He smiled at her, more gently now. "Sometimes we're most blind to the feelings of those closest to us. But, hey, if you want me to pretend nothing is going on between us for a little while, I'm game. Just don't wait too long to tell them. I can't stay professional for that long."

Despite herself, Jinny chuckled lightly. "Fine. But no kissing or other public displays of affection until I've had the chance to tell them myself."

"Yes, Admiral," Trey joked, coming to attention and saluting her sharply.

"I'm not an admiral," she said back, swatting his arm. *Did I really just hit his arm?* she thought to herself. *What am I, ten years old and flirting on the playground?*

Do you want me to answer that? Trey's persona said in her head, and she blushed furiously again in real life.

The real Trey raised his eyebrows at her. "What is my mini-me saying now?"

Jinny blushed again. She knew it was almost just as weird for Trey as it was for her to know that an almost exact copy of him lived in her head full-time, refreshed and essentially 'updated' every time she re-read him. For the first week of their time together, he'd tried to simply ignore it. Now, he joked about it, even calling that version of himself 'mini-me' because his copied persona had to be small enough to fit in her head.

But she could tell it still bothered him. It bothered her, too.

"Nothing," she said, quickly changing the subject. "I'm just nervous, that's all. All these months of trying to track down Admiral Lopez. What if he doesn't believe us? What if he turns me over to Gorsky's people?"

Trey's smile turned to a tight-lipped frown. "From all I've heard of Fleet Admiral Lopez, I think you'll be safe with him."

She returned his frown. "What if you're wrong? What will happen to me?" Then, almost without thinking, she added the part that was really bothering her. "What will you do if he orders you to arrest me?"

He sighed. "You know me better than anyone else, Jin. What does mini-me tell you I'd do?"

She shook her head. "I don't want to hear it from him. I want to hear it from the *real* you."

Despite the gravity of the conversation, she saw a fleeting smile pass over his features at her acknowledgment that he and the persona in her head really weren't one and the same. "I don't know."

Jinny could see the surprise on his face when she smiled at him. "Thank you," she said, "for being honest."

"Even if it's not the answer you wanted to hear?"

She got up on her toes and, despite her earlier admonition against displaying their relationship in public, she kissed him. When she was done, she smiled up at him again. "Especially when it's the answer I don't want to hear. I'm sick of people lying and pretending to be what they aren't. Just always be honest with me, okay?"

Trey smiled back. "Sure. Of course, I'm not positive I could lie to you. Mini-me would definitely rat me out."

He chuckled as she hit his arm again to cover up another blush.

"Hey, you two coming or not?" a shrill voice demanded from the base of the ramp, and they both looked down to see Temperance Jimenez glaring up at them, her hands on her hips.

"Coming, ma'am," Trey said smartly, and with another smile at Jinny, he was down the ramp and out into *Washington*'s enormous hangar bay.

Jinny followed behind but stopped next to the hacker. Today the Neon Mouse was wearing fishnet stockings and a shirt that proclaimed the name of some band Jinny had never heard of. "Temperance . . ." Jinny started uncomfortably.

"Yep," the girl responded, not waiting for her to finish. "I saw everything. You and superhot Navy boy smooching and all. Nice going. For a stuffy, self-important reader, you sure can land the big fish."

"Uh, thanks?" Jinny said, thinking that there might have been a compliment buried somewhere in there.

"Don't worry," Temperance said with a smirk. "I won't tell mopey pilot boy that you and soldier boy are a thing." Without waiting for Jinny's reply, she turned and headed back out of the ship and toward where the rest of their group was already gathered at the hangar's far end.

With a sigh of resignation, Jinny eventually followed her.

Admiral Horatio Krishna Lopez waited for them in a pilot's ready room just off the hanger.

Tyrus knew the man was over ninety years old, and that was old even in the modern days of longevity treatments on Earth. But Lopez looked every one of his years as he frowned wearily at Admiral Bol.

"It's good to see you, Mary," he said, shaking his head, "but I really wish you'd come alone." He motioned with his head toward Tyrus, Domitia, Jinny, and their companions. Riggs, Landon Hartman, and Temperance Jimenez all looked as if they were trying to blend into the deck beneath their feet. Even the normally flamboyant hacker tugged on the legs of her shorts as if suddenly self-conscious about them.

"My naval intelligence officers are in a tizzy," Lopez continued with a frown. "They're demanding I let them send word to Earth that our security has been compromised. I've held them off, for now."

He arched an eyebrow, waiting for her to respond.

"It's good to see you too, Admiral," Bol said with a wan smile of her own. "But I think you'll be—if not happy—at least grateful we're all here once you see what we've brought for you."

The old man sighed. "I hope so." He turned his gaze to Tyrus. "It's good to see you, Tyrus, though I wish you'd stayed hidden. The Navy wants your head, and at least a hundred of my crew saw you land on this ship. I'd be surprised if the entire ship doesn't already know you're here."

Tyrus nodded to acknowledge the greeting, but Lopez kept right on talking.

"And Reader Ambrosa, it is a pleasure to finally meet you. And you as well, Captain Riggs. I'm a great admirer."

He turned to look at Domitia, who sat rigid by Tyrus's side. "And who is this exquisite creature? I had almost forgotten the beauty of Mars, but now I see it standing here before me."

Tyrus tensed up, waiting for the inevitable explosion from his wife as he turned to see her . . . blushing? He hadn't even known Domitia could *do* that.

Lopez caught the reaction too, and his expression became a little less morose. "Tyrus, why don't you introduce me to this stunning woman on your arm?"

"Uh," Tyrus started, trying to get his voice back. "Admiral Lopez, my wife, Domitia Tyne. Domitia, this is—"

"Legatus Horatio Krishna Lopez, the scourge of Mars," Domitia cut him off. "It is a great honor, Hunter Killer Lopez, to finally meet Mars's greatest enemy. I wish to one day have the honor of killing you myself."

Admiral Bol shot a panicked look at the Martian woman, as did Jinny and Riggs. Tyrus tried not to roll his eyes. He looked back at Lopez to see the man grinning widely now, as Trey Kaplan also snorted a laugh.

"Don't worry, Mary," the old admiral said with a twinkle in his eye. "My new friend Domitia Tyne here just gave me the greatest compliment anyone has given me in a long time. She just did it in the typical Martian way. You really have to be special for an ex-member of the Praetorian Guard to *want* to kill you."

The words sank in, and Tyrus looked at the man in confusion. "Wait, how did you know she was a member of the Guard?"

"Oh," the old man said without slackening his grin, "we have files on all of the praetorian guards by now. But I also know of your new wife via another means."

Tyrus saw his wife cock her head in confusion while also blushing furiously again, and Lopez continued. "Tell me, Domitia Tyne, how is your father? I have so missed giving him battle."

Now Domitia smiled broadly, showing her teeth. "He is well, Legatus. And he very much looks forward to sinking his knife deep into your chest with his own hand."

"Okay, you people are *all* crazy." Tyrus heard Riggs mutter just loud enough for everyone to hear.

"That may be, Captain Riggs," Lopez said with a nod. "But it's a special kind of crazy reserved for those who have lived life on a razor's edge. A type of crazy I would think you are all too familiar with as well." He looked back at Domitia. "When you see your father next, please tell him that I very much look forward to sinking my knife into his chest as well, and that I would never imagine an ugly old coot like him could possibly spawn such a beautiful daughter."

Domitia practically beamed.

Lopez turned and regarded Admiral Bol again. "Okay, Mary, tell me. What is it that was so important to show me that you're breaking a dozen laws and risking execution by coming here with a ship full of traitors and wanted fugitives?"

She started talking, and Admiral Lopez's smile almost instantly disappeared.

CHAPTER 48

"Okay."

That single word from Lopez was the most unexpected response Tyrus could have predicted from the fleet admiral after he'd sat for two hours listening—not speaking even a single time or asking a single question—to Tyrus, Bol, and Jinny present their evidence of Mikael Gorsky's treason and collaboration with the Keeper and the Council government.

Tyrus had expected the man to potentially argue, or at least ask deep, probing queries to poke holes in their story and see if it stood up. But for him to simply agree? He'd never even considered that would be the man's reply. But something about Lopez's expression tickled at his mind.

"You already knew."

Lopez shook his head. "No. And you haven't even convinced me fully yet. But everything you're telling me answers questions that have been nagging at me for quite some time. Even when Luis Pereira was still president, there were too many things that happened just right to prevent us from preparing for the Council's invasion. Members of Congress and some high-ranking military officers made decisions that were completely out of character, like someone was forcing them or cajoling them behind the scenes.

"And I've never liked Mikael Gorsky. He's always been far too opportunistic for my taste." He blew out air between pursed lips. "So, let's assume that my Intelligence staff's deep checks of the files you brought me all checkout and Mikael Gorsky really is a Council collaborator and the entire war with Mars is a sham. What are you asking me to do about it?"

"Sir, that's what we were hoping you could determine," Bol admitted.

Lopez sighed again, and his face suddenly took on the worry and lines of his over seventy years of military service. "Well, the way I see it, we have three options," he said, leaning back slightly in his chair and looking up at the metal ceiling overhead. "There is a constitutional provision that lets Congress remove a sitting president in the event of a conviction for treason, but not merely on suspicion of such. That could take months, at the very least, to work its way through the courts back in Houston. So, that option is likely out. The last thing we need is an embattled president and the gears of government grinding to a halt when the Council shows up.

"The second option, of course, is to do nothing. We wait and watch, see if we can pick up on his next move now that you've likely cut off the only access he has to speak with the Keeper. If we can figure out his exact plan, we may be able to counter it."

He paused, and his next words were delivered so matter-of-factly that Tyrus almost missed their import.

"Option three is that we stage a coup, take Gorsky out of the equation now, seize control of the government, then deal with the horrendous political and legal fallout *after* we hopefully fight off the Council invasion."

If the room had been silent before, now it was like a graveyard at midnight. No one seemed willing to budge, blink, or even breathe.

Lopez turned his steely gaze to Mary Bol. "Surprised, Admiral? Surely, you knew what our options were before you decided to come here." Gone from Lopez's countenance was the grandfatherly softness

Tyrus had seen from him on Earth. In its place was a man who fit every gram of the description of 'Hunter Killer.'

For the first time ever, Tyrus saw the indomitable Admiral Bol shrink under another person's studying gaze, and he understood. Lopez was calling Bol out on bringing the problem to him without her own proposed solutions—for 'punting the ball', as it were, rather than taking any responsibility for herself. By the look on Bol's face, she recognized the subtle rebuke and accepted his judgment.

"Admiral Lopez, sir," Jinny spoke up. "Any of those options could end up destabilizing the Four Worlds at exactly the wrong time. What if there was a fourth option?"

Lopez raised his eyebrows and nodded for the reader to continue.

Jinny motioned to one of the room's other occupants. Jordan Archer hadn't ridden in the first shuttle from *Enterprise* with the rest of them. Instead, he'd come over to the *Washington* on a later craft with Captain George Holm. It was actually the first time Tyrus had seen the blender since his reunion with Jinny. It was almost as if Archer were avoiding him; even now, he refused to meet Tyrus's eyes across the table.

He probably thinks I blame him for my near death at the Crater, Tyrus thought with a frown. Jinny had filled him in on Archer's role as a Gorsky stooge, but also his redemption by assisting her and the other readers in Perth.

"Mr. Archer here," Jinny continued, "is a blender. What if we were to stage your coup, but do so in secret and, instead of removing him visibly from office, we replaced him with a perfect lookalike?"

Lopez frowned. "Wouldn't the public and his closest advisors quickly see through that, Miss Ambrosa? My understanding of blenders"—he nodded to acknowledge Archer—"is that they quickly lose the appearance of their subject if not in close proximity to them on a daily basis."

Jinny nodded. "Of course, sir, but if we captured President Gorsky and held him somewhere, and gave Mr. Archer access to him on a daily basis, we could—"

"It would never work." Archer surprised Tyrus by arguing against Jinny's plan. He'd assumed Jinny had cleared it with the blender before suggesting it, but apparently, his friend was simply speaking off the top of her head, ad-libbing. "It would raise a lot of eyebrows if I was disappearing for hours, even at night, to reset my appearance with the real Gorsky. Not to mention, I haven't spent enough time around him to pick up his mannerisms or speech patterns. Those who know him well would never buy it."

Jinny frowned, looking deflated, and Lopez picked up the thread. "There is no such thing as a bad idea at this juncture, Reader Ambrosa, but I agree with Mr. Archer. The risk is too high that he would be discovered, and that might do more to undermine our case with the public than a straight-out coup even would. Bear in mind that we believe the Keeper and his cronies wish to conquer Earth specifically to capture and use our population of the enhanced with unmixed and undiminished bloodlines. We already must worry that Congress would quickly surrender the people of Australia if the Council Navy offered to spare the rest of the Earth. If it became known that a blender was impersonating the president, it would likely push even those sympathetic to the enhanced over the edge."

Jinny sat back glumly but didn't argue, and Lopez turned his gaze back to Admiral Bol. "Mary, I can see the wheels turning in that brilliant mind of yours. Why not tell us what plan you're ruminating over?"

Bol, Tyrus noticed, immediately sat up straighter again at her superior's praise. Apparently, even stoic admirals needed the occasional atta-girl from their boss. He understood that. After decades of loyalty to the Council as an alpha and an enacter, few of his so-called superiors had ever complimented his work in any way; when they did, it was usually because they had some ulterior motive. If Tyrus was honest with himself, the rare but straightforward praise he'd received from Centurion Parn was a big reason why he'd agreed so readily to join the Martian cause and the Praetorian Guard.

"Yes, sir," Bol replied crisply. "As much as I hate to admit it, the coup may be our lowest risk option, but we'll need to move quickly, or we risk the Council Navy showing up before we're ready. I may have a way for us to do it that won't destabilize the Sol system too badly and could accelerate our preparation for war. However"—she turned and speared Domitia, sitting to Tyrus's right, with an intense stare—

"it will require support from the Europans as well as from the Martians."

Tyrus's wife sat up straighter in her seat.

Lopez nodded slowly, a small smile breaking out on his face as if they weren't discussing a betrayal of the nation and constitution he'd sworn to protect. Perhaps that shouldn't have surprised Tyrus when the very survival of both concepts was at stake, and it could easily be argued that removing Gorsky from office was the only way to *save* both United Earth and its founding principles.

But when the old man spoke next, his voice was heavy, belying the stress he felt from discussing such matters. "Very well, Admiral Bol. I suppose adding consorting with the enemy to the long list of treasonous activities we're discussing may as well be on the table."

Optio Cadence Benedictus knocked on the hatch of her commanding officer's office, deep in the bowels of MPNS *Julius Caesar*.

"Enter," came the call from within, conveyed via speaker by the ship's AI.

She opened the hatch and stepped inside, looking grimly at Legatus Lightbringer behind his desk. "My Legatus," she said once he'd acknowledged her presence. "I have an urgent message that is for your eyes alone."

Motioning her forward, Lightbringer took the proffered paper from her. The use of a physical copy rather than a simple internal data transfer would have immediately told him that the message was too sensitive to trust to anything that could be intercepted electronically, even by others on the Martian flagship.

"You read this, Optio?" he asked.

Benedictus replied rapidly. "No, my Legatus. But I did find the sender's identity in your personal files."

Lightbringer nodded his appreciation. "Very well, Optio, you may remain while I read it. If the contents can be shared, I will allow you to read after me."

Benedictus stood up straighter and suppressed a smile, which

Lightbringer pretended not to notice as he lifted the piece of paper. She saw the moment the name of the message's sender registered on her superior's face. It was the first time she'd ever seen him look genuinely surprised.

"I did not expect a reply from Admiral Horatio Krishna Lopez this quickly," the legatus observed, almost to himself.

"Yes, my Legatus. It would appear that your daughter's mission was successful," Benedictus said sourly, drawing a sharp gave from Lightbringer.

"You would say more, Optio?" he asked, voice hard.

Benedictus took in a breath and almost lost her nerve. As Lightbringer's aide, she was privy to information that most *prefects* might never see, but she was overstepping her bounds here. Still . . .

"My Legatus, I mean no disrespect, but I do not understand how we can ally with the very planet that attacked us in such cowardly fashion at Nyx and then lied about doing so."

She expected a rebuke. Though she'd worded it as a gap in her own understanding, it was a thinly veiled criticism of a strategy concocted in large part by Lightbringer himself. If he chose to take issue with that, she'd be dead before her next shift—unless she bested him in a duel, of course, but Benedictus was aware of her own limitations.

To her surprise, however, Lightbringer did not look upset. "It is a valid question, Optio," he admitted, "and one that I expect many children of Mars will be asking for years to come. Before I answer, let me, in turn, ask a question of you. If you were on the field of honor, dueling your enemy, and a tiger attacked the spectators, would you continue your duel and ignore the tiger?"

"Of course not, my Legatus," Benedictus answered crisply. "I would help to fight off the tiger before resuming the duel."

Lightbringer nodded. "We may be in the midst of an honor duel with United Earth, but make no mistake, a tiger is coming to rend us all. Only united may we hope to fight off the threat."

Benedictus nodded, realization working its way past her frown. "I hear and understand, my Legatus. But once the Council Navy is defeated, do we continue our duel with Earth?"

The legatus leaned forward onto his desk and steepled his long fingers in front of him. "That, Optio, is a question we can only answer once the tiger is dead. At that point, there may not even be an enemy left to resume the duel."

She watched as he pulled a small lighter from his desk drawer, carefully set the paper communique on fire, and placed it on a metal tray on his desk to burn.

"Get me an immediate secure channel to Consul Starshadow," he said, back to business. "Tell Prefect Angelus that she is to take command of the fleet in my absence."

"Your absence, my Legatus?"

"Yes, Optio. I will shortly tell Triarch Cicero to plot and execute a stitch jump to Mars. Most of what I have to say to the consul can only be said in person."

Tyrus watched as Admiral Lopez entered the long conference room, walking briskly, giving the impression that he might break out into a run at any moment and assault a beach somewhere. Around the table, waiting for him, Tyrus sat with Jinny, Mary Bol, and nearly a dozen officers from Lopez's staff and *Washington*'s command crew.

"Ladies and gentlemen," the old admiral said, not bothering to take his seat but instead moving to the far end of the room and the viewscreen mounted on the wall there. "We now have incontrovertible evidence that United Earth President Mikael Gorsky is working against his country and has allied with the Council government."

There were gasps around the table from the *Washington*'s officers, many of whom were hearing the news for the first time.

"The raw evidence has been provided to all of you in your briefing packets," Lopez continued, waving toward the pads they all carried as they each dinged to signal the receipt of data. "And I welcome any questions or challenges to that evidence once you've had a chance to review it. But I also have no doubt that you will be convinced as I am that our president is a traitor.

"Blackmont Industries is also involved, though that will surprise many of you far less. They, along with Gorsky, engineered the disaster at Nyx as a pretense to start a costly war with Mars and weaken both nations ahead of the Council's invasion."

Rear Admiral Lindy Everston, *Washington*'s commanding officer, a surprisingly young woman whose features and height spoke of Scandinavian ancestry, raised her hand. "With all due respect, Admiral Lopez, have you shared any of this with the Joint Chiefs, or with the Ministry of Justice? This feels like something that needs to go through the proper channels."

Lopez looked at her somberly and shook his head. "I haven't, Admiral Everston. Nor do I intend to, at least not yet. We don't know how deep this conspiracy goes, but there are plenty of signs that the Council has infiltrated our government and our military at all levels. Admiral Bol, do you mind sharing what you told me earlier?"

Mary Bol looked grimly around the table and proceeded to share the story of Yeoman Shelby West's betrayal and outing as a Council spy. Shocked looks greeted her retelling, and some of the officers, including Everston, looked physically ill at the implications.

Lopez took up the narrative again, capitalizing on the outrage at Bol's story. "The simple truth is, ladies and gentlemen, that we cannot trust *anyone*, even in this room. Before each of you are allowed to leave this meeting and return to your duties, you have a simple choice to make." He nodded at Jinny, whom Tyrus knew he'd already prepped for this request over her stringent objections, but she had ultimately and reluctantly agreed. "You can allow Reader Ambrosa here to read you, to ensure you are not a Council spy, or you can be escorted to the brig for safekeeping until we can verify your loyalty."

One of the officers, a captain Tyrus didn't recognize, stood up, hands balled in fists. "Admiral, this is outrageous! You're talking about loyalty screenings? With a reader? Isn't that what we fought to get away from centuries ago? And this whole thing smacks of a coup! Otherwise why not bring the government into the loop? Surely they cannot *all* be Council sympathizers?"

Lopez didn't get upset. In fact, he smiled. "Captain Patel, I appreciate your words more than you know, and your loyalty to the UEN and the civilian leadership. However, we find ourselves in interesting times, and I will fully take upon myself the consequences for my unorthodox actions from here on out. Reader Ambrosa, if you will?"

Patel recoiled back as if Jinny might leap across the table and forcibly read him. But all she did was take up the baton from Lopez and start talking.

"I myself rescued a woman President Gorsky was holding captive to extort the cooperation of a blender in his treason. I can attest, as can the blender in question, as to his guilt. Additionally, I can attest that, working with the readers in Perth, we located and destroyed a Blackmont-owned secret communications station that used quantum entanglement technology for President Gorsky and Joseph Blackmont to communicate instantaneously with the colonial Keeper. Joseph Blackmont was killed in the attack, but Gorsky is the real power behind this. He has been conspiring with Keeper Petrov of the Council government since well before President Pereira's removal from office. We also have proof that he sent the top secret plans for the defense of Earth directly to the Keeper himself."

Captain Patel looked shocked, and a handful of gasps came from the other assembled officers. Jinny forged ahead. "You are also all not yet aware of my full capabilities. Unlike readers here in the Sol system, in fact unlike any other reader alive that I am aware of, I see *all* of a person's memories when I read them, not just their last twenty-four hours. You must know this before you consent for me to read you."

Tyrus watched Lopez carefully, not detecting any disappointment from the man at Jinny's words. This had been the one condition she'd absolutely insisted on when she'd agreed to the admiral's plan. Lopez hadn't liked it then, but he showed no trace of that now.

The table went completely silent. It was Rear Admiral Everston who spoke up first, throwing her gaze across all of the assembled officers and then looking Jinny squarely in the eye. "So what you're saying, Reader Ambrosa, is that you can be absolutely sure that none of us are traitors? And that you will testify that President Gorsky is, in fact, in league with the Council government?"

Jinny nodded solemnly.

Everston frowned and looked up at Captain Patel, who was still standing but now looked far less defiant than he had just a few moments before. "Sit down, Sandeep," she commanded. "We at least need to hear the rest of what they have to say before we choose self-righteous pigheadedness over our admiral's orders."

Patel sat down in his chair and resumed a professional bearing. Tyrus's respect for him, and especially for Lindy Everston, went up several notches.

"Good. Now that we've heard the most salient facts," Lopez broke in, "we have two near-term objectives. First, we need to arrest President Mikael Gorsky." Patel looked like he might object again, but Lopez kept speaking quickly before he could, raising his voice to emphasize his next point. "So he can be tried in a *civilian* court. But he must be removed so that we can prepare for the coming Council invasion. And make no mistake, the majority of our Navy will attempt to stop us from carrying out this coup."

At the word 'coup,' most of the officers in the room reacted as if they'd been slapped. Even Patel, who had already brought the word up in his objections, looked physically sick at hearing it from Lopez.

When Lopez spoke again, his voice was hard. "Our second objective is to end this pointless war with Mars and unite with them to defend our homes. Because make no mistake, ladies and gentlemen, even if we stop Gorsky from further sabotaging the defense of Earth, the Council Navy *is* coming, and it may be sooner than we fear."

Silence reigned once again in the room, and once again, it was Everston who broke it. The admiral stood, throwing a sharp salute to Lopez, and then reached her hand across the table toward Jinny. "Reader Ambrosa, if you will?" she prompted, and Jinny took the hint, standing up and removing one of her gloves and then reaching out her own bare hand to grasp the rear admiral's.

After only a few moments, Jinny nodded and released Everston's hand. "She's as loyal as they come, Admiral," she said to Lopez with a smile, and Tyrus saw the old man relax a small measure.

"Who's next?" Lopez asked, looking around the room.

And that was when the commander moved.

She had been sitting two seats away from Everston and had not stood out throughout the entire meeting, neither appearing overly outraged at Lopez's words or particularly supportive of them. Now, almost before Tyrus even saw her shift, a knife appeared in the chest of the uniformed man next to her. Another flashed in her hand, and she leaped to her feet and made to throw it at Lopez, just two meters away.

Her arm moved forward, and her wrist started to flick to release the deadly knife, but something knocked it to the ground. Then, the commander herself jerked sideways as if receiving a great blow to the head. She crumpled to the floor, the chair behind her moving out of the way as she did so.

For an instant, everyone in the room held their breath in shock and disbelief, looking either at the ground where the fallen woman lay, at the man who had been sitting next to her clutching at the knife in his chest, or at the completely empty air behind where the woman had been, which suddenly had started to shimmer.

The shimmer resolved into the tall and thin form of a fully exosuited Martian, wearing the black of the Praetorian Guard but missing the telltale red slashes of rank that *current* members of that unit sported. Domitia's helmet dissolved in front of the stunned UEN officers as she stepped forward and crouched next to the dying man. Pulling something from her belt, she began liberally applying a nanite healing paste to his chest wound.

"Admiral," she said before anyone else could react, "you must get this man to the bath on the *Blind Monk* before his injury proves fatal. The nanites I have applied will sustain him for a few minutes only. I implore you to hurry."

Lopez nodded to one of his staff, who jumped up and opened the conference room door. Two burly enlisted men and a medic waited there, and they came in and quickly put the injured man on a stretcher and then removed him from the room. Domitia did not go with them, having already given them instructions on where to find the healing bath and how to perform the relatively simple task of immersing anyone injured in it until their wounds healed and their vitals were restored. They left the room with the stretcher, and two more equally large men entered next, moving to the unconscious woman on the ground and putting her in handcuffs and leg restraints before also placing her on another stretcher and removing her from the compartment, no doubt for a quick trip to a more traditional medical bay followed by a long sojourn in the ship's brig.

Before they left, Lopez held up a hand to forestall them and motioned to Jinny. The reader moved around the table and put her still-bare hand on the unconscious woman's cheek, removing it after a few seconds and nodding to the admiral, who motioned for the two men to continue onward.

The door closed behind the security officers and their charge, and Lopez solemnly surveyed the room. "I apologize for that," he said as if it might have been his fault. "I had hoped that the Council's infiltration of our ranks did not extend to this ship, but I had to believe it might after Admiral Bol reported finding a spy on *Enterprise*. It stood to reason that if they'd found and placed agents on her stealth carriers, they would do the same for this superdreadnought."

He frowned. "But I had really hoped to be wrong. Alberta was a promising young officer. It is always sad to be betrayed by one we all trusted.

"Now," he looked squarely at Sandeep Patel, "I *was* asking who would be next for Ms. Ambrosa to read."

In the end, every one of the remaining officers submitted willingly to the readings, and Jinny signaled to Lopez that all of them had passed. There were no more Council spies in *this* room, at least. But Tyrus knew there were almost certainly more on the *Washington*, and there was no way Jinny could read *all* of the seven thousand men and woman who crewed her. They would have to be content with only rooting out the most critical roles.

Jinny slumped back into the chair beside Tyrus, and he could see that she was trembling—and not just with fatigue. He knew that readings took a lot out of her emotionally, but he also guessed that she was envisioning that the assassin's knife could have just as easily been aimed at *her* or any of her friends as at Lopez.

"Admiral?" Captain Patel asked, his tone far less outraged than before. "I think I speak for everyone when I say that your point has been made in the most convincing way possible, even if that's not what you intended. And we're all behind you." Lopez nodded at the man to acknowledge his words. "But," Patel continued, "it's a little irregular to have a Martian commando in full stealth gear in such a high-level meeting, to say the least." Then the man actually smiled. "Especially if we don't even know our savior's name."

Lopez smiled back. "Quite right. Ladies and gentlemen, let me formally introduce you to Domitia Tyne, formerly of the Praetorian Guard, and newly commissioned lieutenant commander in the Free Colonies Navy, under the command of her husband, Tyrus Tyne."

Domitia smiled and nodded to the assembled officers, then winked at Tyrus across the table.

CHAPTER 49

Corey O'Leary was excited, relieved, and a little worried when Aphrodite summoned him in the dead of night. He hadn't seen her or anyone else in power for several days since Tyrus, Domitia, and Riggs had left to find Admiral Lopez.

Thus far, Aphrodite had given no explanation for the unexpected summons, even during the short shuttle ride together from a landing pad on the side of Olympus Mons up to the military base on Phobos, where he'd first arrived with Tyrus and Riggs on the *Blind Monk* so many long months ago.

Despite his curiosity, Corey held his tongue. He knew she would tell him what he needed to know when she was ready. Normally, he'd demand more than that, but he was so grateful just to be out of the small apartment that he was willing to indulge Martian theatrics for a bit.

Regardless, he wasn't prepared when she led him into a small room where waited none other than Legatus Augustus Lightbringer, the supreme commander of the Martian Navy and father to Domitia Tyne. Nor could Corey keep the smile off his face when he recognized the non-Martian man seated next to the Legatus.

Admiral Terrence Lafayette nodded and smiled to acknowledge

Corey as well. Corey had only met Lafayette on a handful of occasions, but the two had always shared a mutual respect. Greetings done, they all turned their attention to Lightbringer, as the legatus shared the text —reciting it from memory—of Fleet Admiral Lopez's message to him.

Corey could barely contain his relief. Finally, things were starting to happen. He could only hope that they weren't far too late to make a difference.

"Sir, how are you so calm about this?"

Fleet Admiral Lopez cocked his head at Tyrus's question. The two were alone in the admiral's office in the middle of the night watch. Lopez was there catching up on the mountain of things that would need to be done before they embarked on their mission. Tyrus was there because he couldn't sleep, and he'd asked the old admiral for a meeting.

"You mean," Lopez said with surprising gentleness, "how can I so readily accept the need to betray my nation?"

Tyrus nodded.

The old man set down the pad he'd been reading and gave Tyrus his full attention. "What is United Earth?" he asked.

The basic question surprised Tyrus, but he gave it some thought before responding. "It's the political entity that encompasses Earth and Luna under the common rule of law, much as the Council does—did— for the 47 Colonies."

"Wrong on all counts." Lopez's kind tone belied the rebuke of the words. "Tyrus, United Earth isn't the government. It's not President Gorsky, Congress, or even the laws they create and enforce. United Earth is an idea: that people on two worlds can live together in peace and work for the common good. Without that shared idea, United Earth ceases to exist."

Tyrus frowned. "I'm not sure I follow, sir."

Lopez sighed. "Tyrus, why did you serve the Council?"

"Because I'm an enacter. Well, I *was* an enacter. I didn't have a choice."

"Of course you did."

The admiral's words surprised Tyrus yet again. "What do you mean?" he asked slowly.

"I mean what I said," Lopez chided. "You were an enacter. So you needed to follow every order the Council gave you, correct?"

Tyrus nodded.

"Did they order you to give your all in every training or sparring session you took part in?"

"No, not exactly. They told me to take my training seriously, but they didn't get that specific with me."

"When they gave you a mission, did they tell you every little thing they wanted you to do for the entire length of that mission?"

"Of course not," Tyrus replied. "I had to adapt to things on the ground that they could have never anticipated. Plans had to change on the fly. Usually—with some exceptions—they gave me the mission objectives and some basic rules for completing it, but they left the details to me."

"Which means you completed every mission willingly, after years you spent willingly training your heart out to prepare yourself for those missions."

The words cut Tyrus to the core. The admiral was right. He'd done terrible things in the name of the Council, and had always hid the worst of the guilt behind the belief that he'd had no choice. When he'd first defied the Council's orders and helped Jinny instead of killing her, the guilt for all he'd done over the years came crashing down on him as he was forced to contemplate for the first time the idea that he could have said no. He'd only overcome that guilt by deferring it, throwing his entire mind and body first into helping Jinny, then into helping United Earth prepare for the Council invasion, and finally into his role as a Praetorian Guard.

But with Lopez's observation, the guilt came crashing back in. Because the old man was right; Tyrus could have done a million little things over the years to sabotage his missions and avoid completing them. He'd actually done so in a few instances, twisting the wording of his orders, like when he let Jet live instead of killing the man along with his terrorist wife, Dax, Jynx's twin sister.

"I can see my words are causing you some distress, Tyrus," Lopez said with a grandfatherly smile. "That was not my intent. Quite the opposite. From my conversations with you, I have grown to recognize the man you truly are. Even more so observing your exploits in the Praetorian Guard from afar. And I have a theory about you."

He paused, eyeing Tyrus until the big ex-alpha nodded for him to continue.

"You never served the Council itself. Nor did you serve United Earth in your short time with us. Nor did you truly serve Mars as a Praetorian Guard. Nor are you simply here serving Mars, Jinny Ambrosa, or me now. My theory, if you will, is that you've always served the same master since the Council took you from your family as a small boy."

Tyrus frowned, not understanding, but his mouth had gone too dry to respond.

"Why did you disobey the Council and help Reader Ambrosa rather than follow your orders and kill her?"

Swallowing and trying to get enough spit in his mouth to answer, Tyrus spoke in a raspy voice. "She showed me I hadn't killed my mother." The frankness of his own reply surprised him.

"And why, when you arrived on Earth, did you try so hard to help us prepare—even though we weren't exactly willing—for the Council's invasion?"

Tyrus shook his head, not knowing how to answer at first. Unfortunately, Lopez didn't jump in and fill the silence, and finally, Tyrus couldn't take the admiral's gaze anymore. "I couldn't let the Council do to Earth what they did to me."

Lopez nodded as if that was the exact response he'd been looking for. "And why did you agree to take the Trials and join the Praetorian Guard?"

Again, Tyrus hesitated before answering. When he finally did, he felt the unexpected sensation of tears forming in his eyes. "I couldn't let the Martians—or the people of Earth—all die when the Council came. I couldn't sit back and just watch it happen. I needed to do *something*!" Despite his dry mouth and throat, his voice rose as he spoke.

Lopez smiled. "As I suspected, Tyrus, there is one thing and one thing only that has driven you to do everything you've done in life: guilt."

The single word had the effect of almost physically knocking Tyrus back in his seat. "I don't understand," he said, though he knew it was, at least partially, a lie.

"You served the Council at first because that's what was expected of you. But after they tricked you into thinking you'd killed your mother, you served them because to do otherwise would have been to acknowledge that she had died for nothing—that there was no greater ideal at work.

"Then, when Jinny told you that you hadn't killed her, you stopped serving the Council and served her and the rebellion, again because you felt guilt for all you'd done in the Council's name and you desperately wanted to atone."

Tears were now falling freely from Tyrus's eyes. "Why are you doing this?" he asked.

The old man just smiled again. "Because you need to hear it, Tyrus. When you got to Earth, it was no longer the guilt for what you did as an alpha that drove you—at least, not entirely. It was the guilt you knew you'd feel if you didn't do everything to stop us from being enslaved as you'd been.

"When we betrayed you and kidnapped Jinny, you went after her because she was your friend, but also because you felt you'd let her down. The guilt was tearing you apart, so you executed the impossible and broke her out of the Crater. Then, when you arrived on Mars, you did your best to help them, again to avoid the guilt you knew you'd feel if you allowed them to fall to the Council's totalitarian rule.

"Everything you've done, Tyrus, boils down to guilt in one way or another."

Lopez paused, and Tyrus looked up and shook his head. "Am I that shallow?"

The old admiral leaned forward across the desk, his gaze fierce. "Who said anything about shallow? Too often, we dismiss our guilt as an unwanted emotion, one that we should ignore in the interest of simply feeling good about ourselves. But I'm telling you now, my friend, that the best people don't suppress their guilt; they use it as a fuel that keeps them ever striving to do better—to *be* better. Because there's another side to guilt."

"What is it?" Tyrus practically demanded.

"Love."

Tyrus shook his head, again not understanding.

"You served the Council, not just as an enacter, but as an elite alpha, far beyond what genetic obedience could have possibly forced you to do. And not just because of the guilt over killing your mother, but also because you loved her. The entire reason you felt that guilt is because you loved your mother and couldn't bear the thought of having lost her for no reason.

"Then you came to love Jinny Ambrosa in a different but only slightly less powerful way, and you couldn't bear the thought of harm coming to her, so much so that you were willing to almost kill yourself at the Back Door to fix the *Blind Monk* and allow it to jump to the Sol system.

"When you got here, you loved us, not because you knew us, but because you *wanted* to love us. And even when we betrayed your trust, you kept loving us, Tyrus, just as you went on to love the Martians. Just as I did all those decades ago when I fought against them and killed them."

Tyrus, who had buried his tear-streaked face in his hands, looked up in surprise.

"That's right, Tyrus, I love the Martians, just as you still love the people of the 47 Colonies and the people of United Earth. I imagine you even love both the willing and unwilling enacters who will crew the ships that pour from the Front Door to subjugate us all. I've seen the vid logs from *Italy*. I know you could have killed far more of the battleship's defenders, including SEAL Commander Davtyan. But you stayed your hand more than once. Because you loved them. But you also killed those you needed to because you felt you had to in order to save even more of the people you've grown to love.

"This entire time, you've only felt guilt because you love everyone around you more than you love yourself."

Lopez paused again, studying Tyrus across the desk. "You asked me why I'm so calm about executing a coup against the government

I've sworn my allegiance to," he continued. "Because I share the same reasons you do, Tyrus. I love the people of the Four Worlds, and I would feel crushing guilt if I didn't do *everything* I could to save them. And if that means betraying some of them, then I'll do it. But I'm not calm about it, Tyrus, not at all. Inside, I'm a roiling storm of guilt and love and everything in between. Does that answer your question?"

Tyrus nodded, again not trusting his voice.

"Well then," Lopez said, his tone and expression softening. "I'm done with my religious sermon for the day. And you have someone waiting for you back in your quarters—someone who loves you as much as you love her and all the other people you've grown to love in your lifetime. Go be with your wife, Tyrus. Because none of us can know exactly what tomorrow brings."

After leaving the admiral's office, Tyrus practically stumbled back to the temporary quarters he and Domitia had been assigned in *Washington*'s officers' country. He opened the hatch and almost stumbled again at the change in gravity, which the superdreadnought's engineers had helpfully dialed down so that Domitia could be out of her exosuit while in their shared room.

His wife was waiting for him, sitting in a chair.

"Did Fleet Admiral Lopez help you reconcile the conflict within you?" Domitia asked.

Tyrus gaped at her. "You knew?"

She smiled. "I guessed. Did you find solace in his words?"

He nodded.

Domitia stood and crossed the small room to him, enfolding him in a hug as the tears came once more.

PART FIVE
TREASON

CHAPTER 50

Two Weeks Later; March 13, 732 P.D.

The Martian courier ship surfaced from a skip jump less than thirty light-seconds from Earth but on the Solward side of the blue and green planet. The ship broadcast exactly one message, transmitting the data packet it had carried from Mars to the outer system, then to Earth. Exactly six minutes later, as a pair of UEN destroyers on patrol burned hard to intercept, it submerged back into the void, its mission completed.

The message was broadcast in the clear, with no encryption, so Mikael Gorsky actually heard it a few minutes later than the news services. When he did receive it, he was sitting in his office having a meeting with the Europan ambassador, who had requested an emergency session with him to discuss the escalating conflict between Earth and Mars. Mikael's palm implant pinged him at virtually the same time as Ambassador Trevor Caspian's, and they were both silent for a moment as they watched the recorded message.

"People of Earth and Luna, I am Consul Aphrodite Starshadow of the People's Republic of Mars. Recent evidence has come to light that the war between our worlds is a sham, perpetrated by a traitor to the Sol system in order to weaken us before the Council Navy invades. It is my sad duty to report that the traitor of which I speak is your president, Mikael Gorsky. I have attached evidence of his treachery to this message. If Mikael Gorsky agrees to relinquish power, I will immediately call upon my forces to cease fire in our war on United Earth. For Mars . . . and for the Four Worlds!"

The short message ended, and Ambassador Caspian frowned at the UE president.

"Lies, all of it," Mikael said gruffly. "A thinly veiled attempt to destabilize United Earth's government in a time of war."

"Of course, Mr. President," Caspian said slowly, and Mikael could tell the man didn't fully believe him.

He cursed the Martians in his head. Could they possibly know that their allegations were true, or did they simply suspect? Without knowing whether or not they were bluffing, he couldn't figure out the right response.

A knock sounded at the door to his office and it opened almost simultaneously opened. His chief bodyguard poked his head in. "Mr. President," the man said, ignoring the Europan ambassador. "Fleet Command has detected multiple skip jumps inbound to Earth. We need to get you to the command bunker and the situation room right away."

Mikael swallowed and nodded, then seemed to remember Caspian's presence. "If you'll excuse me, Mr. Ambassador?"

"Of course, Mr. President," the Europan said with a solemn nod. "I look forward to resuming our conversation when the current emergency is over." The man's words were innocuous, but his tone conveyed his serious questions about whether or not Gorsky was truly a traitor to them all.

Mikael wanted to snap the puny ambassador's neck, but he smiled. "As do I."

Ambassador Trevor Caspian settled into the back of the armored aircar that would whisk him home to the Europan embassy and its own underground bunker just four blocks away from the UE Government

House. Subconsciously, he wiped the hand that had shaken Gorsky's on his pants as if to cleanse it.

"Do you think he suspects anything?" his chief aide, Monica Firth, asked from the seat next to him.

Trevor shook his head. "If he does, he's hiding it well. No, I don't think he realizes we know what we do."

Monica licked her lips nervously. "I don't buy it. He's smart—too smart not to suspect us."

Trevor smiled softly at the woman who was young enough to be his daughter—indeed, he'd always thought of her in that way. "That's the key. Mikael Gorsky *is* an incredibly smart man. But smart men often cannot conceive of a world where others are smarter or more resourceful than they are. Gorsky is likely to think he's fooled everyone until the moment everything comes crashing down around him."

"You're beginning to sound a lot like Professor Tichner," she chided gently.

Trevor would have laughed had the overall situation not been so grim. "I'll take that as a compliment." He greatly admired the former professor-turned-power broker who had come from Earth to Europa almost a year ago to unofficially negotiate an Earth-Europa alliance when the Council Navy finally arrived. Most Earthers took for granted that Europa would ally itself with them; Tichner didn't, which was why Trevor respected him.

Monica didn't respond, turning instead to look out the window at the passing buildings and cherry tree-lined streets of downtown Houston. He sensed a melancholy from the girl but let her ride along in silence for several moments.

They were less than a minute out from the embassy when she finally spoke again. "How can you do it?"

"What's that?" he asked, brow creased.

"Betray Earth like this," she said in a voice so small he had to strain to pick out the words. "I'm not from here, but we're all *from* here. It's the homeworld."

"I suppose," he answered honestly, "that I don't feel I'm betraying Earth. I'm helping them get rid of someone who *has* betrayed them. In the end, they'll be stronger for it." He didn't add on the last words—*at least I hope*. Then, suddenly worried, he looked at her sharply. "Did you send the signal?"

Monica frowned but nodded as well. "The second you got in the car. There's no turning back now."

No, there isn't, Trevor thought with a frown of his own. *I just hope we did the right thing.*

Mars and Earth had last conducted a joint military exercise seventy-eight years before, and that had almost ended in a war. It had also been only a training exercise, but the nearly catastrophic outcome was enough to convince the commanders and politicians involved that trying anything else would be inadvisable. Martians and Earthers just didn't mix.

Today was to be the first new attempt since then, and it was decidedly *not* a mere exercise. To add to the anxiety Horatio Krishna Lopez was feeling, it also had abnormally, devastatingly high stakes. Not to mention that it was completely illegal.

After all, staging a coup against a sitting president was strictly defined as treason. But when it became known he'd enlisted the *Martians* to help with that coup . . . Well, he wondered if they'd figure out how to execute him *twice*.

Regardless of the risk of undertaking the mission, he knew that the risks of *not* doing so were far greater. He'd meant his words to Tyrus Tyne two weeks prior in his office. Lopez knew that if he didn't do this—if he called off the coup—he would be following the law. But he'd never forgive himself for knowingly letting Gorsky continue to waste lives and hulls in a war of his own making, all so that the Council Navy could arrive and clean up the pieces.

A successful coup likely meant a firing squad for himself and a few of his most trusted senior officers and friends. *Failing* the mission would mean the death of millions, if not billions, of innocents.

The morality of the choice was clear, even if the legality of it wasn't.

"Admiral," Commander Jancery at the helm reported, "course is laid in for an in-system jump to Earth. AI is warning of a 15.4 percent chance of catastrophic failure."

Lopez almost snorted. 'Catastrophic failure' was the computer's way of saying, 'You'll be dead along with your entire crew *and* the largest and most expensive warship ever built.' Fun. Still, AIs tended to be pessimistic about such things. The real risk was probably no higher than 15.1 percent.

"Understood," he said to the commander. Everyone on the bridge was of that rank or above; there was no need to expose any junior officers or enlisted men and women to the charge of being on the bridge during their treason. Then he turned his attention to all of them. "Ladies and gentlemen, we have Ambassador Caspian's confirmation that President Gorsky is headed to the bunker. Our part of the mission starts now. The order is: submerge."

With a single-word command, Fleet Admiral Horatio Krishna Lopez became the first military leader in the history of United Earth to initiate a military coup.

Commander Kinsey Phillips had been on her fourth cup of coffee, and six hours into her eight-hour shift as Earth Home One's watch commander, when her world went straight down the tube.

The news of the Martian fleet skip jumping toward Earth, especially hot on the heels of the inflammatory and surely lie-filled message the Martian courier ship had sent their way, had put Earth Home One at full alert status. With Captain Judd on leave Earthside, Kinsey was the massive battle station's most senior officer at the moment.

"Ma'am." Her sensor officer called her over, and she went to peer over the man's shoulder.

Earth Home One's sensors were far more powerful than those of even a UEN battleship, powered as they were by a dedicated, albeit small, reactor of their own. Kinsey had bragged to her colleagues that the station's sensors could pick out the scratch on a destroyer's hull paint from twenty light minutes away and almost tell her what the ship's captain had for lunch. Now, those sensors showed the entire Martian Fleet of the Eagle, over a hundred ships strong, closing on Earth.

"Why did they surface so far away?" she asked no one in particular. There was nothing to prevent the Martians from skip jumping nearly all the way into Earth's orbit. Close proximity to a gravitational source like a planet did little to pull a ship out of the void, though it did prevent ships from submerging until they'd reached a suitable distance. But the Martian fleet had surfaced almost five light seconds away, nearly four times the distance between Luna and Earth. It just made no sense. It made even less sense when the Martians quickly turned over and decelerated to a zero relative velocity with Earth, then just sat out there, waiting.

"All First Fleet ships," a voice said on a military-band comm channel, piped through Earth Home One's command center speakers, "this is Admiral Showalker. Do not, I repeat, do not approach the Martian fleet. They may be trying to draw us away from Earth orbit so that another force can come in behind us. Set Condition One throughout the fleet and prepare for battle, orbital defense pattern Omicron."

Kinsey quickly returned to her station and pulled up the details on plan Omicron. Unlike the mobile units of First Fleet, Earth Home One and the other orbital defense platforms couldn't move themselves to take up new positions around the homeworld. But it was important for her to understand where the fleet would be deployed so she could identify her station's area of responsibility and likely engagement.

Navy Lieutenant Rashid Bakir jogged toward the cargo shuttle that had landed an hour before in the middle of Ellington Field, southeast of downtown Houston. The shuttle had already been on the tarmac when the order had come down from Fleet Command to lock down everything and allow no ships to land or leave without a direct order from the Octagon. Ellington's control tower had ordered the shuttle's pilot to keep the hatches and cargo ramps secure, not allowing anyone to leave the craft, and had then dispatched Rashid and a squad of UE Marines to inspect the crew and contents before clearing them.

As they approached, one of the outer hatches opened, and a single man stepped out and climbed down the ladder to meet them a few meters from the shuttle. At the sight of the man's uniform, Rashid stopped in his tracks and immediately saluted. But at the first sight of the newcomer's face, his jaw dropped open in shock.

"Ad-Admiral Lafayette!" he exclaimed a little too loudly. "We thought you'd been captured, sir."

Admiral Terrence Lafayette smiled sadly, and Rashid heard the quiet but unmistakable sound of multiple silenced weapons spitting fire from the shuttle's open hatch. Around him, the four Marines dropped their rifles and fell to the tarmac, twitching from the effect of the stun rounds.

Rashid fumbled for the pistol at his belt but stopped when two figures literally materialized out of thin air to either side of the admiral, each pointing a wicked-looking assault rifle right at Rashid's chest.

"I'm sorry about this, Commander," Lafayette said sadly as it belatedly registered in Rashid's mind that the two black-clad figures with him were too tall and thin to be natives of Earth or Europa. "But trust me, we're actually the good guys."

Rashid made a snap decision and drew his pistol. It almost cleared the holster before the stun rounds hit him.

Kinsey was running on pure caffeine and adrenaline as the Martian fleet continued to simply sit in space, light seconds from Earth. They hadn't even fired any long-range missiles, instead only using a screening force of destroyers and fighters to block and destroy the waves that Admiral Showalker had commanded First Fleet to send their way.

How strange.

"Commander!" The loud shout broke her from her study of the sensor plot. "Ship detected surfacing at oh-one-five mark zero, range 500,000 kilometers! It's . . ."

"Spit it out, Spacer," she barked at the man when he didn't continue.

"Ma'am, it's massive! I've never seen anything like it, but the AI says it's one of ours."

She felt herself relax by only a small measure. "On screen," Kinsey ordered, and the command center's main viewscreen switched to a magnified camera view of the largest ship she had ever seen, bristling with weaponry that was already setting off alarms at the stations around her.

"What is that?" she allowed herself to ask in awe.

"AI says it's the *George Washington,*" another one of her people answered in a voice colored by obvious confusion. "But all details on it are classified. That's all the system will give me, the name."

Kinsey opened her mouth to order her comm officer to hail the ship, but the man's voice interrupted her. "Commander, comms coming in from the *Washington.*"

"Answer the hail," she ordered.

"Uh, ma'am, it's not a hail," the young man said, chagrined. "It's a general broadcast on all channels. Unencrypted."

"Then put it on the screen!" she snapped, watching the officer scramble to do so.

The image of the massive ship on the main viewscreen shrank to a small window in the bottom left corner, and a new larger window popped up, one that showed a very familiar face.

Admiral Horatio Krishna Lopez stared solemnly into the camera and started speaking.

"People of United Earth and fellow citizens of the UEN. This is Fleet Admiral Horatio Lopez of the United Earth Navy, broadcasting in the clear. I regret to bring with me evidence that supports the recently broadcast Martian claim that our president, Mikael Gorsky, is in direct violation of seventeen articles of the UE penal code and stands accused of treason against United Earth for his role in knowingly falsifying information that led to the war between United Earth and Mars. He has also broken another twenty-seven articles of the UE espionage act by collaborating with and providing sensitive information to the enemy Council government. I am here to serve an arrest warrant and take him into custody pending . . ."

Kinsey didn't hear the rest. She looked around the command center and saw everyone else staring open-mouthed at the viewscreen along with her as Admiral Lopez repeated and expanded upon the obvious lies spouted by the Martian consul less than an hour before.

One word came to Kinsey's mind: *coup*.

"Message from Fleet Command," her comm officer spoke up, his voice unbelieving now. "We are to destroy the *George Washington* with prejudice." He looked up from his console and stared at Kinsey as if hoping a mere commander relegated to space station duty in the middle of a war would have some special knowledge or insight to make sense of this unthinkable situation.

She had nothing for him.

" . . . if fired upon, we will defend ourselves." Those were the last words she caught from Lopez before his transmission started over again, repeating on a loop.

"Uh, Commander?" the station's tactical officer—a mostly boring post until right that moment—asked. "Do we fire on the *Washington*?"

Kinsey had stood up when the alert first came through. Now, she sat down slowly in her command chair and shook her head. "I don't know," she almost whispered. "I just don't know."

CHAPTER 51

"*George Washington,* you are ordered to heave to, power down all weapons, and decelerate now to a zero approach velocity with Earth. Failure to comply will result in deadly force."

Horatio Lopez frowned as he heard the completely expected message from the UENS *Congo,* flagship of Earth's First Fleet, delivered in the passionless voice of his longtime friend and confidant, Admiral Hank Showalker, the home defense fleet's commander.

"Do we send a reply, Admiral?" Commander Lisa Bortis asked from the comm station.

"Send the second buffered message," he told her calmly. It wasn't a direct reply to the demand from *Congo,* but it was a personal missive to Showalker himself, a plea from a friend. Knowing his friend as he did, it almost certainly wouldn't work.

"*Congo, Laos,* and *Georgia* are charging weapons, Admiral," Captain Naomi Rossi said with preternatural calm from the tactical station. She was a steady one, even if she was way too senior to be manning the tac station in a battle herself.

"Understood," he said. "Fire up the jinns and lock our offensive weaponry; defensive measures only for now."

"Sir, open channel from Admiral Showalker directly to you," Commander Bortis told him.

"On screen."

A window popped open in the viewscreen and showed the face of Hank Showalker, frowning deeply. "Horatio. Don't do this. Whatever you think the president has done, a coup is *not* the answer. I don't want to destroy you and the thousands of spacers on that behemoth, but I will if you don't immediately surrender. If you turn yourself in, I will guarantee you get a fair hearing. Do the smart thing for yourself and your people. Even that monstrosity cannot stand up to the combined force of First Fleet."

"Hank," Lopez responded, "read the evidence I've transmitted. Mikael Gorsky is in league with the Keeper and the Council government. If we don't remove him from power now, he'll keep pulling us deeper into war with Mars until there's nothing left to stand against the Council Navy when it arrives."

Showalker frowned. "If this so-called evidence is so compelling, then take it to the courts, Horatio. This is the *wrong* way to do things."

"I'm sorry, Hank. I really am."

"So am I, old friend. You have one minute to surrender. Showalker, out."

The window disappeared, leaving behind the battle schematic that showed roughly half of First Fleet adjusting their orbits from where they'd been lobbing missiles at the Martian fleet to intercept *Washington* instead. Even if Showalker's first attack failed, there would be wave after wave of UEN warships bearing down on Lopez and his ship.

Which was exactly what he wanted, and exactly why he'd jumped his ship to this side of the planet, directly opposite Houston.

"Anyone who wants out," he said to his bridge crew, "grab an escape pod now, and we'll cover your retreat."

No one spoke up. A few frowned and shook their heads, but none took the offer.

"Very well then," he said with resolution. "Now, we wait."

Showalker's one-minute deadline passed quickly, but the First Fleet admiral didn't give them a second of grace period. At exactly sixty seconds from the time Showalker had ended his call with Lopez, *Congo* and her cohorts launched full broadsides of missiles directly at *Washington*.

At near point-blank range, and with no screening elements to protect her from the barrage, *Washington* should have been done for. But that was not to be.

"Launch the jinns," Lopez ordered calmly.

'Jinn' was the unofficial code name for a special new toy the UEN had developed and installed first on the *Washington*. Now, four specially designed missile tubes disgorged their payloads.

"Jinns away," reported Rossi from the tactical station.

Over a hundred missiles fired from three battleships were only 2.4 seconds away from impact when abruptly, the *George Washington* disappeared from in front of them and reappeared ten thousand kilometers to the starboard, away from Earth.

The tiny brains in the missiles didn't wonder at how the ship had moved or consider that movement like that had been physically impossible—no star drive in existence, not even the Martian skip drives, could execute a jump anywhere close to that short a distance. Instead, the missiles simply relocked on the new location and veered to intercept.

"It's working," Rossi said, excitement tinging her professional tone. "The jinns have spoofed the missiles."

In its most simplistic form, a jinn was just a jammer and a decoy, designed, with three or more units working together, to mimic the radar, magnetic, and heat signatures of even the largest warship. In that regard, it was centuries-old tech—so old, in fact, that most ships didn't carry jammers and decoys, given how easily modern warships and missile sensor suites could see past them.

But the beauty of the jinn system was in the *fourth* unit launched. That one didn't follow the other three to spoof a new *George Washington* one thousand kilometers away. Instead, it moved to take up position directly between the incoming missiles and its mothership. And at the exact moment that the other three decoys started broadcasting, it did as well, but in a very different way.

Ironically, what the fourth jinn did was based on even older technology than the other three. Like the noise-canceling headphones that had been standard on Earth before the invention of privacy fields, the fourth jinn took in the radar pings and other active sensor scans of the missiles and broadcasted its own signal that completely *offset* their waves. It was the same technology that allowed Admiral Mary Bol's three stealth carriers to move undetected even through active sensor pings.

When the radar returns from *Washington* reached the small AI brains in the missiles, they were completely canceled out by the broadcast from the fourth jinn. The big ship's thermal signature was still there—no amount of jamming could hide that—but it was enough.

The instant the radar and magnetic signatures of the missiles' target disappeared, they reappeared, along with another huge heat signature, ten thousand kilometers to the starboard. That made the AIs in each missile retarget, classifying the remaining heat signature of the real *Washington* as an anomaly now that it wasn't confirmed by the radar and magnetic signatures.

Lopez smiled as all hundred-plus missiles veered off course toward the decoys. He knew the jinns were a one-time thing; as soon as he realized he'd been duped, Admiral Showalker would remove the safeties on First Fleet's remaining missiles, allowing them to home in on just the *Washington's* true heat signature. But it bought them time, nonetheless, which was really the entire point.

It was ironic, he thought, that the most powerful warship ever built by humanity was going to play the simple role of providing a distraction for the other components of today's mission.

There were about a dozen different personas in Jinny's head that she could easily channel right now, all of whom would be better conditioned to take the stress of the moment than she was. Regardless, she channeled none of them, instead allowing most of them to be only casual observers of what was to happen next in case she needed their insights or direct intervention later.

She'd expected a pitched fight for Ellington Field, especially after the squad of praetorian guards had stunned the Marines and the lone Navy officer who'd been sent to inspect their cargo shuttle. But Admiral Lafayette had quickly transmitted orders to the base's commander, including a detailed file of the evidence against President Gorsky, and signed orders from Fleet Admiral Lopez to drive it all home.

In the end, it hadn't convinced the base commander, but the confusion had bought their landing party enough time to unload their armored aircars and fly right over the base's fence and toward Houston proper.

Once inside the city, she watched on her helmet's HUD as four of the armored vehicles, including her own, made a beeline toward the downtown government district, while four others peeled off—three in a similar direction and a fourth on an almost tangential course.

She gulped. Talking about a coup was one thing; executing it was something else entirely. But it was too late for second thoughts now. And even if she hadn't wanted to come, the mission couldn't possibly be a full success without her involvement. She just hoped she could survive long enough to do her part.

"We're two minutes out from the drop zone," Tyrus's voice said in her helmet as he broadcast the update to everyone in their set of four aircars. "All teams report ready."

"Fretensis Team stands ready. For Mars!" came the calm voice of Centurion Marcus Parn. Jinny had met the dour Martian commander—Tyrus's former boss—only briefly as they'd taken the Martians on board Admiral Lopez's *Washington* to prepare for the mission. But she'd been able to tell quickly that he and Tyrus had a strong bond, which made her immediately trust him.

"SEAL Team Six is a go. Hooyah!" Trey's voice added, and Jinny smiled to herself as the version of him in her head—his 'mini-me'—added his own battle cry to that of her real . . . boyfriend? She'd never had one of those before. Not even Alan and she had gotten to that point, and she wasn't sure she felt the same way about Trey as she had for Senior Guardsman Alan Daily. But there was definitely something forming there. Of course, having the man's mini-me as a constant resident in her brain made things a little weird.

"Ahem," a figure next to her elbowed Jinny in the ribs.

"Oh, right!" she exclaimed. "Saturn Squad is ready too, Tyrus—I mean, Commander Tyne."

A few laughs greeted Jinny's late response as Landon Hartman's nudge reminded her that she'd been inexplicably put in charge of the small team of noncombatants along for the mission. Or maybe they were chuckling at the squad's name, assigned almost jokingly by Trey as he'd noted that the civilians on board *Washington* seemed to gravitate toward Jinny like they were the moons to her gas giant.

She'd made him pay for comparing her to a gas giant, but the name had stuck.

Jinny looked to her left, opposite Landon. "You okay?" she asked Jordan Archer. She couldn't see the blender's face behind his helmet—they were all armored up for their protection—but she could tell from the way his entire body was tensed up that he was worried about something.

"I'll be fine," he almost snapped, but she kept her own helmeted head turned toward him expectantly. After a few moments, she heard his sigh over their direct comm connection. "Okay, maybe not so fine. I can't help but wonder if any of this would be necessary if I'd just figured out sooner who I was working for and somehow put a stop to Gorsky's plans."

Jinny considered the blender's words. As ridiculous as it was to think that Archer alone could have stopped someone with the drive and resources of Mikael Gorsky, she could tell the man really believed there was something he could have done.

"Forget about it," she said at last. "You can't do anything about the past—trust me, I know—so just focus on what you can control here and now."

She saw him nod his helmeted head, and she was about to say more when the aircar came to an abrupt halt.

"Go! Go! Go!" Tyrus called over comms, and light filled the interior of the aircar as its back ramp slammed down on the paved streets of Houston.

On the flag bridge of the *Enterprise,* Mary Bol looked down on Earth. She hadn't been home in almost two years, nor had most of her crew. Even the existence of the three stealth carriers was such a closely guarded secret that the Navy hadn't felt it could trust the traditionally loose lips of spacers on shore leave.

Now, she was so close, having surfaced her carrier almost in Earth's orbit, about as close as one could safely surface from the void near a planetary body. Below her, she could see the outline of the North American continent, specifically the Gulf of Mexico and the southern coast of what had once been the United States of America.

Houston was down there, the seat of the United Earth government for the last 575 years. And hers was about to be the first military force in longer even than that to invade it.

"Admiral," George Holm's voice came to her via the internal comm. "Looks like they're taking the bait."

"It does, indeed," Mary agreed, looking at her battle plot and watching the majority of First Fleet move away from their normal orbits toward the eastern hemisphere, where Admiral Lopez and the *Washington* were providing the perfect diversion for the on-the-ground portion of the mission taking place in Houston below them. In fact, only a single battlecruiser had been left above Houston to guard the capital.

Unfortunately, she knew that diversion wouldn't last, and she already saw several of First Fleet ships coming back toward the Western Hemisphere as no-doubt panicked calls from Fleet Command alerted them to the presence of hostile forces near Government House.

"Message the squadron," she said reluctantly. "Launch all fighters and bombers, arm all defensive weapons, and prepare for a blocking action."

Up until seconds ago, Captain Joe Montgomery had been terribly disappointed. Something big was happening on the other side of the planet, but he and his UENS *Jakarta* were stuck in stationary orbit over Houston, while most of the rest of the fleet got to go and defend Earth from an attack by—if it wasn't some kind of sick joke—Fleet Admiral Lopez himself in a massive prototype superdreadnought.

It was incredibly frustrating to be left out of that. Joe had spent most of the *war* on the sidelines. *Jakarta* had been rotated to Second Fleet and the front lines with Mars for just four weeks in the middle of the conflict but had been put back on Earth watch afterward and had stayed there ever since. It was almost as boring as the time he'd commanded a frigate on close lunar patrol, much earlier in his career.

Besides, battlecruisers like *Jakarta* were meant to run and fight, not to stay stationary and defend. It went against every one of their design principles, but no one had asked Joe Montgomery his opinion when they'd written UEN fleet doctrine. So here he was, stuck while almost every other UEN ship was in on the action today.

When the word came in of hostile ground forces in the streets of Houston, it didn't improve his mood any. As powerful as *Jakarta* was, a battlecruiser would be no good for support of an urban battle. None of her many weapons had the pinpoint precision to provide air support from above.

It was—

"Sir!" The stunned cry of his sensor officer broke him from his wallowing. "Three ships, practically on top of us! One orbital level down on nearly the same longitude antispinward. Range less than a thousand kilometers!"

A thousand kilometers! Montgomery thought in shock. *How did they get so blasted close?*

"Identify!" he ordered.

"Markings are UEN, but no IFF squawk."

"On screen."

The forward viewscreen resolved to show the image of a large ship, carrier size, sitting so close to *Jakarta* that they were solidly in laser range of each other. There was something strange about the ship; it looked like no carrier or battleship—UEN or otherwise—that Joe had ever seen. The image zoomed out to show two identical ships flanking the first.

"Charge all weapons. Hail them!"

"Ma'am, the *Jakarta* is hailing us."

"No response," Mary ordered. She checked her mission clock. *Enterprise* and her sisters had been visible now for thirty seconds as they'd opened the launch bays to disgorge their fighters. And the First Fleet reinforcements rushing to *Jakarta*'s aid were only minutes away.

"Reading multiple fighter launches from the target ships!" *Jakarta*'s tactical officer said from his station behind Joe Montgomery.

"No response to our hails," his comm officer chimed in.

"Ready the forward chase armament. Fire even laser banks on my command."

He hesitated, wondering if he should wait for orders from Admiral Showalker or another senior officer, but they were all engaged on the far side of the planet, and the closest flag officer, Rear Admiral Morris, was still out of sight over the horizon in the Southern Hemisphere. Besides, his standing orders were clear. Defend Houston against any threat, even if he was drastically outnumbered and outmatched.

"Fire!" he said with far more confidence than he felt. On the viewscreen, six twenty-four-centimeter lasers lashed out toward the middle enemy—he hoped—ship.

To his shock and surprise, the target seemed to *jump* out of the way of most of the lasers, moving impossibly fast to a higher orbit and jinking to the side. They must have detected his lasers readying to fire and tried to time the move to dodge without giving him time to retarget. They'd almost been successful, but he watched in mixed satisfaction and horror as two of the lasers hit the dorsal armor of the large ship, burning holes right through it.

Mary swore. Those hits had been the closest thing to glancing blows, but they had still done their damage, burning off the ablative plating on *Enterprise*'s dorsal hull in two spots and, with it, the ship's ability to deflect and cancel out light and sensor signals in those areas. In essence, that had always been the big carrier's greatest weakness. It only took one solid hit to ruin its ability to go to full stealth. From now forward, she'd be visible if she got within a few thousand kilometers of an enemy ship, or from farther away if the enemy sensors got lucky.

"Do we fire back?" her tactical officer asked, though he already knew the answer.

"No. Hold fire but keep jinking us and send a squadron of fighters to harass *Jakarta,* low-power lasers only. Hopefully, we can spoil his aim . . . and hopefully, he won't be inclined to launch ship-killers this close to the atmosphere."

She checked the mission clock again and silently prayed for the ground teams to hurry up.

CHAPTER 52

The scene on the Houston streets was one of pure chaos. Everywhere, civilians ran from the group of black-clad Praetorian Guards and their shorter but no less imposing SEAL companions. Sandwiched in the middle of the formation, Jinny wanted to yell to all of the screaming people in the streets not to be afraid of them, but she knew it would be no use.

She also knew this was part of the plan and why they'd taken the risk of exiting the armored aircars two blocks from their target. They wanted the civilians to have enough time to flee the area. There was no guarantee that there wouldn't be collateral damage, but everyone, even the Martians, had insisted on taking every measure available to them to prevent civilian casualties.

Still, as a squad of Trey's SEALs was forced to fire back on a group of Houston cops who had set up a hasty roadblock, she knew that this coup would be anything but bloodless. As the police officers fell to the bullets from the reluctant SEALs—the range was too great for stun rounds—Jinny started crying in her helmet.

I got this, amiga, said the persona of Julia Perez, one of the SEALs she'd read on *Enterprise* and who was only a few meters away in real life. *Let me drive for a while. And trust me, this is nothing. You should have been with us when we dropped on an insurgency over Kazakhstan a few years ago. They used human shields to try and stop us. This is a cakewalk by comparison.*

Jinny tried to take comfort in the words, but at least with the SEAL persona in control, her breathing had slowed, and she no longer felt the suicidal impulse to remove her helmet and scream at the police to stop shooting at them and run for their lives.

"Sir! Another hit amidships on Target One."

Joe Montgomery smiled fiercely. The strange ships—they didn't even appear to have drive nozzles!—had jinked and juked all over the place, but that could only do so much against lightspeed weapons at near hand-to-hand combat range. Still, they weren't firing back.

He opened his mouth to issue a vector change and bring his broadside lasers to bear on the second target, but he never got the words out.

"Captain!" his sensor officer cried out. "New contacts surfacing, bearing one eight four mark three. They're . . . they're Martian!"

"What?" he whirled to look not at the sensor officer but at his tactical officer behind his command chair. "Just what in blazes is going on?" he demanded of the man.

Lieutenant Avery Castro looked nearly panicked as he swept his gaze over his station's screens. "Sir," he said with a look of shocked horror. "It's the *Julius Caesar*. And it's firing on us!"

Mary cringed as she watched the Martian flagship open fire on the smaller *Jakarta* and the small group of light cruisers and destroyers who had arrived first to aid the battlecruiser. This was the part of the plan she hated the most.

"Direct hits!" called out her tactical officer. "*Jakarta* is out of the fight. So is *Perseverance*!"

Mary closed her eyes and shook her head. When she opened them again, she manipulated her own display to zoom in on *Jakarta*'s last location, just five hundred kilometers off *Enterprise's* bow. There, she saw the battlecruiser with no outward signs of damage.

"Report!" she barked.

"Martian shockers hit right on target, ma'am. Estimate seven minutes until they can restore enough power to maneuver, and another two minutes after that until they have weapons capability."

"Any danger to their orbits?" she asked, dreading the answer.

"No, ma'am." Mary felt a massive weight come off her shoulders at the man's words. "They should have no trouble restoring power before there's any risk of orbital degradation."

It's all up to you now, Tyrus, Mary thought to herself as the Martians continued to fire the last of their hastily manufactured shockers at the remaining UEN ships. *We've done our part, terrible though it was.*

Then she turned her attention to the battle plot to make sure she could get her squadron away before the rest of First Fleet arrived to duel with her.

Mikael Gorsky had been literally shoved down the small corridor to the huge metal door that hung open, beckoning him to enter the underground bunker, commonly called the Situation Room, under Government House in Houston.

He'd been receiving by-the-minute reports since the *George Washington* had first arrived in Earth orbit, but hadn't allowed his bodyguards to take him to the bunker until the reports had come in of ground troops in Houston itself. By the time he'd reached the bunker, he was also hearing frantic updates about a battle taking place between UEN ships and a mixed UEN-Martian force in orbit right above the city.

Mikael wasn't quite sure what to think of that. Part of him was mildly afraid, but another part was nearly giddy with joy. In one fell swoop, the attack had given him fodder to use both against the Martians and Fleet Admiral Lopez. With Lopez discredited by his own actions, any influence he might have had to challenge the president's leadership was now gone.

All Mikael needed to do was survive the attempted coup, and then he could spin the Martian involvement in the effort to strengthen the resolve of Congress and the people of United Earth to fight against the filthy Reds. He'd ride that wave of anger all the way up until the Council Navy arrived in orbit and demanded the surrender of Earth. At that point, a suitably 'reluctant' President Gorsky, absolved of the patently false charges levied against him by a group of traitors, would do what was best for his people and accept the Council's gracious terms to take the enhanced and leave Mikael himself in control of the entire Sol system. He'd enjoy that, even if it were as a vassal governor under the Keeper's rule.

Inside the Situation Room bunker, he saw a beleaguered General Cruz barking orders to Earth's defenders.

"Mr. President," the general said, only turning briefly to nod at his commander-in-chief before turning back to the battle plot on the massive screen at the front of the room. "The situation is fluid," Cruz continued as Gorsky drew closer, "but there's a reasonable risk to Government House from those ground forces. We're getting reports of a mixed force of UEN SEALs and what looks to be perhaps the entire Martian Praetorian Guard."

Mikael felt the first vestiges of real fear at Cruz's words, but he kept it out of his expression and voice. "I am sure, General, that you will see to our defense and ensure that we remain perfectly safe here."

"That's what I intend to do, Mr. President," the man said before calling out another set of orders to the officers sitting in stations around the room.

CHAPTER 53

"Sir, decks four and six open to space, bow sections seventeen through twenty-one!"

Horatio Lopez gritted his teeth as the damage reports rolled in. *Washington* was big, and the jinns had done their jobs several times—more than he'd expected. But First Fleet had closed to laser range, and now he risked losing one of the few ships that might actually be able to make a difference when the Council Navy arrived in force.

Saying a silent prayer for his compatriots on the other side of the planet, he gave the inevitable order all too soon for his taste.

"Helm. Get us out of here!"

Washington turned to burn directly away from Earth, and her massive engines ramped up to full military power seconds later, putting her on course toward the waiting Martian Fleet of the Eagle, which still hovered well outside laser range and had never fired a single offensive shot toward Earth or First Fleet.

"I don't understand," General Ernesto Cruz said, watching the SEALs and praetorian guards on a video feed from cameras on the streets of

Houston. Most of the UE did not have state-run surveillance, but the capital was the exception. After all, if terrorists were to attack anywhere, the seat of the government was a very appealing target.

"You do not understand what?" the deep voice of Mikael Gorsky rumbled next to him.

"Why did they get dropped off a full two kilometers from Government House? If they're after you, Mr. President, why not just come right to the Mall or Government House grounds? Now they have to fight their way through a chunk of the city before they even get to the bunker entrance."

"It is confusing, yes," Gorsky replied, though his tone was neutral. "Though maybe they know that you've called in all available Marine and Army units to defend the Capitol and Government House, and they are trying to find a weak point in the lines."

Cruz turned and looked at his commander-in-chief. He was purposefully trying to not think about the messages from Consul Aphrodite Starshadow and Fleet Admiral Lopez. But it tickled at the back of his mind nonetheless, and so much of Gorsky's behaviors since taking the presidency made more sense in a world where he was a traitor to Earth.

Still, it was Cruz's job to defend the planet, the capital, and the president, and he had always prided himself on being a good soldier and doing his job.

But he hated morally gray areas. He preferred simple wars, where all he had to worry about was how to kill the enemy and keep the good guys from dying. If the revelations from Admiral Lopez were true, then Cruz wasn't really sure *who* the enemy was anymore.

He stifled a sigh and hid his roiling doubts as best he could. "Not to worry, Mr. President. We have additional Army units inbound to their location, ETA two minutes. Hopefully, we can take a few of them alive to see what their plan was and make sure there are no more surprises waiting for us."

"My Legatus, the enemy's line of battle is breaching the horizon."

Augustus Lightbringer smiled in predatory fashion as four battleships ringed by two squadrons of battlecruisers poked their bows over Earth's disc, flying straight at his *Julius Caesar* as his flagship and her escorts covered the retreat of Admiral Mary Bol's carriers. Behind those coming battleships, he knew, would be at least one of the UEN's large fleet carriers, filled to the brim with fighters.

"Launch a full broadside," he ordered, knowing it would do little good. A wave of smaller but faster destroyers was now visible scattered among the larger Earth ships. Those escorts would easily swat his missiles out of the sky before they could do real damage to their larger cousins. But that was okay. Sadly, it was even preferred. The missiles were meant to slow down First Fleet, nothing more. Had he had more shockers left in his arsenal, he would have used them instead. Unfortunately, Mars had only manufactured a few dozen in the time since Tyrus Tyne had first revealed their general plans.

"Send the message and withdraw," he ordered, the final word tasting sour in his mouth. And with that, *Julius Caesar*'s part in this phase of the battle was done.

CHAPTER 54

Graham Coltrane was a cop because his father was a cop and his grandfather was a cop. Even his sister was a cop. It was sort of the family business. And most days, when he walked his patrol beat, he felt like the most powerful person out there, defender of the weak and scourge to Houston's criminal element.

He didn't feel that way now.

Crouched behind his squad car, Graham couldn't stop his gun hand from shaking as he tried to steady his pistol against the car's hood. With the panic in the streets, it had been hard to even get the car into position on one of the parallel avenues the strange invaders might take to get to Government House, and he knew that the Capitol Police were on their way to reinforce him, but slowed by the crowds.

Until they arrived, he and his partner, Shelly Mahtani, were all that stood in the invaders' way. Two of them against, by all reports, over a hundred enemy Martian troops. The frantic calls from other cops also reported UEN SEALs among the attackers, but Graham didn't believe that for a second. No way the SEALs were part of this.

"Coltrane, you in position?" his precinct's captain asked over his radio.

"Yes, sir," he replied, his voice trembling almost as bad as his gun hand.

"Well, stay there," Captain Wayne said. "They've stopped for some reason a block ahead of you. Drones can't tell what they're up to; blasted Reds keep shooting them down!"

Archer led them all into an ice cream shop, of all things. It was deserted, though the lights were on, and there were some half-eaten ice cream cones melting on the tables and floor, showing that the place had evacuated on a moment's notice.

The blender didn't stop to survey the scene. He just walked back behind the counter and opened a door marked 'Employees Only.' Tyrus followed him.

The back of the store looked as ordinary as the front, with a giant walk-in freezer and what looked like a small office and a supply closet off a short hallway. Archer opened up the freezer door and went in. Tyrus shivered as he followed; Houston was a relatively warm place, even in the late winter, and the contrast between the balmy air outside and the dry, icy freezer air was startling, even though his exosuit covered all but his face at the moment.

Only five of them could fit in the freezer at a time, but they'd already chosen the advance team. Archer was there, of course, as was Tyrus. Domitia had utterly refused not to be at her husband's side for every step of the mission, so she was present as well. With her was Parn, but he left the other half of his battle pair, Ursus, outside, making room for the fifth member of the advance squad, a jovial SEAL master chief named Papadopoulos, whom everyone called Paps and who seemed to be particularly protective of Jinny. Tyrus suspected the SEAL had developed a crush on the pretty young reader at some point on *Enterprise*. He wondered if the man knew or cared that his commander had already stolen Jinny away.

Jinny herself was not part of the first group, nor would she be in the second. She and the rest of the civilians would be spread out across the middle groups for safety on both ends.

Archer walked to the back of the freezer and slid aside a tall shelf laden with ice cream without help. The blender had been spending a lot of time with the SEALs on *Enterprise,* who had adopted him as sort of a mascot. Right now, he was tall and muscular and seemed to be enjoying his strength.

Behind the shelf was what looked like an ordinary metallic freezer wall, but Archer knocked on a seemingly random spot, and a small hatch opened in the wall. It had been so flush with the rest of the structure that Tyrus hadn't even noticed the seams. Now that it was open, he could see an old-fashioned keypad inside.

"Now we'll see if Gorsky was smart enough to change his codes," the blender said. "This whole mission could be over pretty quickly."

Tyrus knew that Archer had only been this way once, when Gorsky had demanded the blender meet him in the presidential office in the underground bunker code-named the Situation Room. There had been little practical reason for Archer to come this way; Gorsky had simply wanted to show off by demonstrating he could sneak his agent in and out, even under the military's nose.

As Archer finished typing the ten-digit sequence, a light above the pad turned green. The entire back wall of the freezer slid aside, revealing an elevator door behind it that opened after only a slight hesitation.

Jordan Archer stepped into the elevator first and then turned and looked at the rest of them.

"Going down?"

Admiral Hank Showalker swore as the Martian Fleet of the Eagle closed ranks around *Washington,* cutting First Fleet off from Admiral Lopez's superdreadnought. Though, a small part of him was relieved. He hadn't actually wanted to kill his friend, but he had tried his hardest to do so nonetheless. Showalker was a loyal soldier, and in his mind, loyal soldiers followed even the orders they disagreed with or didn't understand.

Part of his relief was also that he hadn't been forced to destroy the

Washington. Showalker had been aware of Project Anvil, of course, but like the rest of the Navy, he'd thought the superdreadnought was at least a year away from completion. Whatever magic Lopez had worked to push through eighteen months of construction in a third of that time, it had sure been a sight to behold the massive ship that made even some of Earth's orbital defense platforms seem small by comparison.

"Message from Houston." His comm officer interrupted his thoughts. "General Cruz reports enemy ground troops near Government House and orders us to maintain overwatch from orbit."

Showalker resisted the urge to swear again. What he really wanted to do was pursue the Martian Fleet of the Eagle and call in Second Fleet to be the hammer to First Fleet's anvil. If they could catch the Martian Fleet—which couldn't skip jump away if they wanted to continue covering the *Washington*—between them, they could wipe out half of Mars's Navy in one fell swoop.

But as the good soldier he was, Showalker acknowledged the order and began the process of moving his fleet into a geosynchronous orbit over the UE capital, but not before launching a few dozen more missiles after the fleeing enemy ships just for good measure.

Less than fifteen minutes later, with the *Washington* safely out of First Fleet's range, the Martian Fleet of the Eagle disappeared from normal space as they skip jumped away, leaving behind the superdreadnought to make its way solo back toward the outer system.

Mikael Gorsky was angrier than he had been in a long time. That idiot Cruz might have been flummoxed about why Tyne and the other invaders had stopped advancing where they had, but Mikael knew. And the fact that the invaders also knew filled him with rage.

Archer, he thought sourly. *That stupid blender; I should have killed him a long time ago.*

He would have to tell Cruz and his security team about the secret passageway, typically known only to UE presidents themselves. Or maybe not. It was entirely possible the tunnel itself would take care of them. He decided he'd wait and see.

Ernesto Cruz looked across the room at the president and frowned. The big Russian was worried, though there seemed to be little reason to be all that concerned. The invaders, most of the 140 they'd counted, had somehow packed themselves into an ice cream shop, and no one had left the building since while the rest took up defensive positions outside it.

It made no sense, which also worried Cruz greatly. Something was up, and he had the feeling Gorsky knew more than he was letting on.

He looked down at his palm and reread the message there. It had come just minutes before, and he was still digesting its contents and what they meant to him. As the chairman of the Joint Chiefs, his duty to his country was usually very clear, but now he just didn't know.

He read again the digital signatures at the bottom of the message addressed directly to him. Cruz knew and trusted every single person who had signed the missive; in fact, he trusted Admirals Lopez, Bol, and Lafayette a lot more than he trusted Mikael Gorsky. And Corey O'Leary had always been one of the few politicians Cruz had ever liked and respected. The congressman had always been an especial friend of the military and, more importantly, a straight shooter in a city where most people felt it was their duty to lie for a living.

If all of them swore to Mikael Gorsky's treason, could he afford to doubt it? Always, before, he'd known that his orders from the civilian chain of command—even the ones he disagreed with—were essentially in the service of the greater good. But now . . .

Cruz squared his shoulders and looked back at the battle plot, which showed Admiral Lopez's massive ship now safely out of First Fleet's missile range, though damaged. The Martian Fleet of the Eagle had left, as had the *Julius Caesar*'s smaller task force once Admiral Bol's carriers—also damaged—were out of range.

Could they really afford to continue doing this? To continue tearing each other apart when the real enemy was out there, just waiting for them to be weak enough to conquer?

His frown deepened as President Gorsky waved him over for a conference on Earth's defense.

CHAPTER 55

Jinny hadn't been allowed to come down the elevator in the second group, but one member of her civilian team had. Temperance Jimenez —she was still upset that she couldn't get anyone else on the mission to call her by her Neon Mouse moniker—stepped out of the elevator after Commander Kaplan got the all-clear signal from the advance team outside. Even then, he insisted she stay behind him while he moved carefully forward, his assault rifle up and scanning the room.

They were in an underground space. That would have been abundantly clear by the *long* ride down in the elevator, but the walls here were of a gray brick that screamed 'deep in the Earth' to her. She shivered a little bit. Temperance had never liked enclosed spaces. And the feeling here of being buried alive was nearly overwhelming.

"Temperance," Tyrus Tyne barked, and she almost jumped. Even though it had been almost seven months since that fateful day on Luna, she hadn't ever been able to shake the memory of him moving like an angel of death through the corridors of the prison to rescue Jinny Ambrosa. Even before that mission, the big man had equal parts excited her and terrified her. But afterward? Now, he just scared her, even if she knew he was one of the good guys.

"Here," she squeaked out, and that SEAL commander who'd been making out with the reader, Kaplanis . . . Kipling . . . something or another—she just thought of him as the soldier boy with a nice butt—let her move ahead of him to where Tyrus was standing with Jordan Archer.

"The control panel is right here," the blender told her, "but Gorsky didn't give me the code to this one; he deactivated whatever automated defenses this place has from his office in the bunker."

He motioned to a physical keypad embedded in the brick wall. She examined it for a moment and then nodded.

"Can you hack it?" Archer asked.

She threw him a look. What a stupid question. She wasn't going to answer that.

"Temperance, is this going to be a problem for you?" Tyne's baritone rumbled.

"Uh, no. I've got it . . . sir." So much for being the silent and disdainful hacker. Around the big ex-assassin, she felt like she was ten years old again, cowering under the kitchen table and listening to her stepfather smack her mom around.

It wasn't that she actually thought Tyne would hurt her, but she'd seen him burn with a cold rage before. She also knew what he was capable of, even if he seemed to have far more control over himself than Chad, her mom's loser husband, ever had, at least until that day that Temperance had hacked police records and evidence files and gotten Chad arrested and convicted for an unsolved murder. That had also been the day her mother finally kicked her out of the house.

She shuddered. Thirteen-year-olds didn't fare well on the streets of Phoenix, Arizona. Temperance had survived the ordeal, but she'd known plenty who hadn't.

She played with her pad for a while, attacking the keypad via all sorts of different means. None of them were working. She couldn't even get the stupid thing to establish a wireless connection to her pad.

"Anyone have a screwdriver?" she asked, and someone slipped a small electric one into her hand. Moments later, she had the keypad's cover off, and she frowned.

"What's wrong?" Tyne demanded.

Temperance stood there, staring at the mess of wires and circuit boards, not a quantum matrix in sight.

"Temperance, what's wrong?" Tyne repeated, more forcefully this time.

"I can't do it," she almost whispered.

"You're sure?"

She nodded dumbly. "It's too old. This has gotta be at least two hundred years old. I mean, it's practically analog! I can't hack it when there's nothing to hack." She looked up at the tall, scary assassin and waited for him to scream at her, to tell her she was as useless as her mother had said she was the day Joe went to prison.

Temperance winced as Tyne's big hand enveloped her shoulder and squeezed . . . and then just as quickly released.

"It's okay, Temperance," he said, his tone reassuring and soft. "You're the best. If you say it can't be hacked, then no one can do it. Stay in the rear; we'll need you alive when we get to the bunker."

She blinked back tears as Tyne motioned to one of the tall and skinny Martians to take Temperance and lead her to the back of the assembled group. As she followed the praetorian guard, she heard Tyne raise his voice to address the assembled soldiers and civilians.

"Listen up, folks! We can't shut down the automated defenses, and we don't know what to expect. We have a timetable to hit. Our noncombatants don't have stealth suits, so we can't rely on those, either. That means we'll have to move at a moderate pace, trip the defenses, and deal with them as they hit us."

To Temperance's surprise, there was no disagreement from the group. Her Martian escort dropped her off with Landon at the rear, and her boyfriend put an arm around her as she stared in embarrassed silence at the floor.

Tyrus peered down the long, dark tunnel with his flashlight. It reminded him of the Loop tunnels he'd often traveled through in his short time before on Earth, except that the walls were made of the same rough stone as the chamber they were currently in instead of smooth metal.

"Okay," he said to his troops. "I go first, with Centurion Parn, and—"

"No!" His wife's voice cut him off, and he looked in confusion at Domitia, who had retracted her exosuit's helmet so that her eyes burned into his. "You will not take point, my Husband, nor will Centurion Parn."

"Optio," Parn growled warningly, though she technically was no longer an optio or under his command.

"Silence!" she barked at her former commander, and only because Tyrus knew her so well could he see the brief flush in her cheeks as she spoke in such a tone to a man she respected so greatly. "Centurion Parn and my husband are too valuable to this mission, as are the reader and the hacker. None of you will be the tip of the spear. Celeusta Ursus!"

The big praetorian guard, the other half of Parn's battle pair, stepped up beside her and looked as resolute as she did. "My Centurion," he said in a voice that was very deep for a Martian but still slightly higher than Tyrus's. "Celeusta Cassius and Celeusta Tiberion demand the right of extremum hastae. Do you deny their right?"

Something passed in a flash of the eyes between Parn and Ursus, and the centurion shook his head. "You know I can deny no praetorian guard this right, even if it is not theirs to take."

Ursus nodded resolutely as if the matter were entirely settled, and two male praetorian guards whom Tyrus knew but had not grown close to in his time with the Guard stepped forward and started down the tunnel.

"Now that ain't fair!" another voice drawled from behind Ursus. "Why do these Reds get to have all the fun? I reckon we oughta join 'em, eh Murdock?"

The speaker, a wiry SEAL who called himself Tex, stepped around Ursus and started down the hall after the two celeustas. Behind him, a stockier SEAL followed, gun at the ready.

"Well, I guess that's settled," Tyrus said in resignation. "But I'm next. Centurion Parn, shall we?" He turned and studied his wife. "You follow right behind us, my Domitia." He saw her eyes flash with anger and her mouth open to retort. "I need you to keep Jinny, Temperance, and Archer safe and alive, and I trust no one more to do that," he quickly added. The anger didn't leave Domitia's eyes, but she closed her mouth and nodded her consent. Still, he knew she'd make him pay for that later, assuming they both survived.

"Okay, let's go," he said and started down the hall, Parn at his side as they followed the four members of the advance team.

Mikael Gorsky had made an excuse to leave Cruz's side and make his way into his private office in the Situation Room bunker. There, he pulled up the desk's integrated touchscreen and entered his private code into it. A map came up, very different from the big map of Earth and the surrounding space that dominated the command center. This map was of a single tunnel that stretched two kilometers under the city.

He watched solemnly as at least fifty red dots moved down the tunnel, already much further along than they ever should have gotten. But then he grinned as he watched them reach the first weapons emplacement.

SEAL Chief Petty Officer James Fenimore Jones—his mother had named him after her favorite ancient author, but he just went by 'Tex' anyway—trailed closely behind the two spindly Martians, his partner Chief Kyle Murdock at his side. The two SEALs swept their guns across the tunnel walls around them, being sure never to point them directly at the Martians' backs but covering as much as they could from the rear.

Murdock opened his mouth to say something, but a loud *brrrp* sound interrupted Tex's buddy, and he watched in horror as Murdock simply broke apart, barely registering the scream of one of the Martians in front of him.

His shock lasted for only the shortest instant; then, his training kicked in. As the surviving Martian leaped to one side to avoid the auto turret's stream of fire, Tex took advantage of the gun's track on the other man to aim his own rifle and put a round right through the turret's optical sensors.

The cacophony and stream of death ceased, and Tex heaved a deep breath as the lone Martian turned and nodded to him.

"What is your name, Earthling?" the Martian asked.

"James Fenimore Jones," Tex answered, not sure why he was giving his full name.

"I am Celeusta Brutus Tiberion," the other man said. "We have both lost our battle pairs this day. I would be honored if you would consent to be my battle pair for the remainder of this fight."

"Sure thing, Stretch," Tex drawled, surprised to see the tall Tiberion smile rather than take offense at the unintentional, habitual racial slur.

Mikael Gorsky at first watched in glee as the turrets and mines in the presidential escape tunnel whittled down the fifty infiltrators to forty-eight, then forty-five, then forty-three. But his excitement turned to anger when the next segment of defenses failed to kill even a single attacker. Nor did the one after that.

His foe had learned how to anticipate and defeat the tunnel's automated defenses.

He swore. It was time to flee the bunker, which meant he needed to tell Cruz what was coming.

Just as he was about to leave his office to do just that, his palm implant pinged him. He looked at the simple, innocuous-sounding message on the screen. Unbidden, a smile sprang to Mikael's lips. It turned out that the attackers were too late. Now, all he had to do was survive.

CHAPTER 56

"Hey, Captain!"

Govinder Nelson practically jumped out of his uniform as the squad of fellow Marines jogged around the low wall and approached his guard station at the entrance to Government House and its grounds.

"You idiots almost got a bullet!" he yelled at the four men, the most senior of which was a captain like himself. "Give a guy more warning next time." Then he settled down. "You those reinforcements I was promised?"

The invaders had stopped their advance a full two kilometers away from Government House, but that didn't make Govinder feel any better. There were still a few of the enemy's armored aircars that had somehow disappeared from the city's sensor grid, and no one quite knew where those had ended up or how many enemy troops had been inside them.

"Sorry, Captain," the other Marine captain said with a wry grin. "Where do you want us?"

"Over on the south wall," he said, his tone making it clear he'd forgiven them. "Head on over, and Lieutenant Dexter will give you the lay of the land."

"Roger that," the other officer said with a nod and motioned for the eight Marines following him to move out.

But as they passed, Govinder reached out with a hand and stopped one of the enlisted men. "Hey," he said, confused. "That don't look like no unit patch I've seen around here. Where'd you guys say you were—"

Even as he spoke, he read the unit designation under the unfamiliar patch insignia, and his free hand was already flying toward the pistol at his belt. It never reached it, and the stun round that slammed into his lower back just beneath his flak jacket sent him crashing to the concrete.

However, it didn't knock him out completely, and he lay there paralyzed as the rest of his squad fell around him, taken completely by surprise by the other Marines, before any of them could even call it in.

"Sorry", he heard the other captain say, "but you'll understand later why we did this."

Footsteps jogged away as the enemy Marines moved out of his view and toward the front door of Government House. Then, another flurry of footsteps as dozens of additional Marines streamed in from the street outside. Govinder's eyes were out of focus, but he knew that they likely all sported the same unit patch as the first group, that of the Marine contingent of UENS *Enterprise.*

"Why are you only just now telling me this?" General Cruz practically screamed in the face of his president.

The man had known all along that the enemy was headed for an escape tunnel. A secret escape tunnel, apparently, because it didn't show up on any of the maps or schematics for the Situation Room bunker.

"That's not important, General," Gorsky insisted, his tone dismissive. "What is important is that we have to get out of this bunker. We can go back up to the main house and escape from—"

Cruz's comm pinged him, and he held up a hand to cut off Gorsky as he listened. When the call ended, the general glared at the president again. "I'm afraid sneaking out through the main entrance is no longer possible," he growled. "Unless you think me and the dozen armed Marines down here can fight our way through the entire *company* of hostile Marines who just took over Government House!"

The color drained from Gorsky's face, giving Cruz a minor flash of satisfaction before he started shouting orders to his men and women to prepare for the defense of the bunker.

Sergeant Timothy Park had never wanted to be a hero. He'd joined the United Earth Army mostly as a way to escape the small town he'd grown up in. At the time, it had seemed like an easy way to both see the world and maybe get a free education along the way. Earth and Mars weren't at war, and local dustups from the odd insurgency or terrorist cell on Earth were usually quashed quickly and with minimal casualties on the UE side.

But as he and his squad and the rest of Fox Company approached the exterior of the ice cream shop that the enemy had inexplicably decided to invade, Timothy quickly learned that the men and women he faced were far different from the half-starved and poorly armed rebels he'd fought in the past.

The first indication was the private to his right, who fell hard to the asphalt roadway when a bullet took him in the face. As Timothy threw himself to the ground to seek cover, the corporal to his left likewise fell.

On his stomach now, he rolled over a few times until he was behind a thick concrete bus stop bench. Around him, his fellow loyal UE soldiers returned fire toward the entrenched enemy, and Timothy sighted down his rifle and joined them.

For the first several minutes, it seemed that the invaders arrayed both inside and outside the ice cream shop would prevail. The Reds—if the rumors were true and there had been SEALs with the Martians, they were nowhere to be seen—were crack shots, downing three men for every one the Army got of theirs. But slowly, surely, their losses mounted, and the UE Army and their superior numbers began gaining ground toward the ice cream shop as Golf and Charlie companies arrived to reinforce Fox.

Tyrus called a halt as they reached the last two hundred meters of the tunnel. Ahead, he could just make out a large, vault-like hatch that he knew led into a smaller tunnel that would, in turn, open into the president's office in the Situation Room bunker.

Installed secretly when the bunker had been built, this tunnel was meant as a last-ditch escape route for the president should the bunker's main entrance be blocked or fall to enemy forces. Tyrus thought it ridiculous; the whole point of a bunker was to be impenetrable, and the secondary entrance with only automated defenses was a major point of vulnerability. But he was grateful for the poor judgment of the designers now.

Still, they'd lost a dozen of their number to the attacks of the tunnel defenses, despite their early learnings on the patterns and vulnerabilities of the same. Now that they were near their goal, he expected the defenses to be even more thick and insurmountable. Which was why the very fact that every sensor in his Praetorian Guard exosuit insisted that there were *no* defenses in these last two hundred meters had all sorts of alarm bells going off in his head.

"You sense it, too?" Centurion Parn asked, coming up to stand next to him and peer down the darkened tunnel.

Tyrus nodded. "This is where the defenses should be heaviest. But nothing."

Parn nodded. "It is as you say, Tyrus. A trap of some kind. Yet our rearguard on the surface has been engaged by superior numbers. Time grows short."

"I will go," Tyrus said. "I'll draw the fire of whatever there is ahead, and you can—"

Before he could finish his sentence, Tyrus watched in horror as, by some unspoken agreement, Marcus Parn himself, and his battle pair, Ursus, sprang forward at a full run down the tunnel.

Domitia Tyne, nee Felix, nee Lightbringer, had entered the Praetorian Guard five years earlier after quickly proving herself in the People's Legion, Saturn Regiment. Upon completing the Trials and taking the Oaths, she had immediately fallen in love with Centurion Marcus Parn.

It wasn't a romantic love, though she'd briefly mistaken it for such at first. Rather, it was the same love she felt for her older brothers and her mother and father. It was a love that transcended physical attraction and ran in many ways deeper even than that which she'd at first felt for her new husband. And, to her surprise, Parn had reciprocated that love, taking her into his tutelage despite her junior rank in the Guard, and growing her quickly into one of his optios and, from there, into his trusted right hand.

Now, she watched as the man she loved like a brother, father, and mother ran full tilt down the tunnel toward certain death. At first, nothing happened, and she felt a brief hope that Parn and Ursus would make it to the far end unscathed. But that hope was short-lived.

Their first indication that something was wrong was a blood-curdling scream from Ursus as his entire right leg separated from his body. As the large Guard fell forward, his torso inexplicably split into two almost right down the middle, cutting off his cries.

Domitia leaped forward, irrationally intending to go to her former comrade or perhaps to save Parn from the same baffling fate, but Tyrus caught her as she passed him. Enraged, she fought against her husband, cursing him and promising death if he didn't let her go. At any other time, the blatant show of emotion would have made her ashamed. But now, she fought tooth and nail against one man she loved in the hopes that she might save the other.

She screamed, echoing Ursus's prior yell, and watched helplessly while Marcus Parn lost an arm and then the entire lower half of his body. With one last push, she almost freed herself from Tyrus's grasp to go to him, but her husband held fast to her.

"Domitia, no! Monofilaments!" Tyrus cried, and the words barely pierced the rage and despair coursing through her mind as her hand shot toward the knife at her belt so that she could cut her way free, if necessary, from her husband's grip.

But her brain finally processed his words, and she felt her legs go weak beneath her, Tyrus holding her up and preventing her collapse as she sobbed into her helmet and beat her fists against his chest.

General Cruz watched in solemn silence as another two life signs in the escape tunnel winked out. It brought him no satisfaction. He was still upset almost beyond reason that Gorsky had kept the tunnel a secret until the last possible moment. And he was . . . conflicted. Every ounce of his training told him that it was his responsibility to see that none of the men and women moving through that tunnel made it to the Situation Room.

But his humanity? His honor? Those were different stories. Never before had the general faced such an ambiguous and difficult decision. As he watched the tunnel's defenses do their worst to the attackers, he had no idea what he was going to do.

Jinny heard the screams as Parn and Ursus died, both from the dead men and from the survivors left behind. As one, the other members of the Praetorian Guard in the tunnel wailed through their helmet comms and external speakers as their centurion was cut in two by the strange, invisible threads that somehow crisscrossed the tunnel in front of them.

She recovered her senses just enough to hear Tyrus yelling orders. Briefly, she considered handing over control again to Julia Perez or maybe even to the persona of Tyrus himself living in her head. Surely, they could be more helpful than she could in this or just about any other situation. But something stayed her, as if surrendering control now and retreating in her own head would cheapen the sacrifice so many others were making around her.

Gritting her teeth, she stayed in control of herself and let the wave of grief at those lost wash over her.

When Tyrus had first requested swords as his close melee weapon of choice upon joining the Praetorian Guard, the other members of the Guard had thought him mad. After seeing him in action with the implements, many had reconsidered, which would be what saved them and their mission now.

Five of the guards with them in the tunnel had adopted similar swords—gladiuses by Martian tradition—as those Tyrus carried, with a charged, monofilament edge that included nanites for a self-healing blade. Now, they hacked through the invisible chords of death in front of them, monofilament threads designed to cut down anyone foolish enough to walk into them and spaced no doubt so close together that—even if they could detect them—there would be no way to simply go around them.

Of course, he knew intellectually that the threads could be retracted somehow—there had to be a way for the president to do so in order to escape along this route—but the act of using his swords along with the other Martians to cut his way through them allowed him to channel his rage and intense pain and guilt over the deaths of Parn and Ursus.

He approached the bodies of the two men now, only wielding one of his swords as he almost blindly hacked the air in front of him, feeling rather than seeing the broken threads as the barest sense of resistance against his blade. Next to him, Domitia held his second sword, doing the same, refusing to leave his side.

He almost screamed in shock when a hand grabbed his ankle.

Domitia felt her husband stiffen next to her and kick out in surprise. She grabbed Tyrus and stopped him from doing more, then fell to her knees next to the torso of Centurion Marcus Parn, who had somehow reached out and grabbed Tyrus's ankle.

As she did so, Parn's helmet dissolved, and he looked up at her with nearly vacant eyes. Any momentary hope she might have felt at her friend and mentor surviving instantly disappeared. Parn was seconds from death, if that, and no amount of nanites could save him.

"Fulfilled," he said through frothy lips, reaching out with his one remaining hand to grab Domitia's. "My blood oath . . . fulfilled."

She nodded at him, dissolving her own helmet so he could see her face in return. "Yes, my Centurion. You saved my husband. Your oath is fulfilled. All of Mars will rejoice in your glorious death."

Parn opened his mouth to say more, but no words emerged. With one last burst of strength, he pulled Domitia closer so that her ear was almost to his lips.

"Daughter."

That one word, whispered with the centurion's dying breath, shattered any remaining composure Domitia retained, and she pressed her forehead to the dead man's, sobbing in great gasping cries of pain and rage.

Jinny watched as Domitia Tyne wailed and cried into the dead body of Centurion Parn. She'd known the leader of the Praetorian Guard for only a short time since they'd rendezvoused on the *Washington* to plan and execute the joint mission, but she knew from Tyrus that he had been like a second father to Domitia.

Her friend now watched in helpless despair as his wife mourned Parn at his feet.

Propelled by an unknown force, Jinny stepped forward, brushing off Riggs's half-hearted attempt to hold her back, and moved carefully and slowly toward where Tyrus stood over his grieving wife. As she moved past Trey Kaplan, he fell into step beside her, somehow grasping that she would not be stopped, yet refusing to let her continue onward alone.

She oddly wasn't worried. If Tyrus, Domitia, and the other Guards had done their job cutting the filaments, she would be safe. If not, then none of them were likely to leave this tunnel alive. No one had told her directly, but she knew from the tense postures of the soldiers around her that things on the surface behind them weren't going well. It was only a matter of time before Earth's defenders entered the tunnel behind them and their mission came to a tragic end.

Reaching Tyrus and Domitia, Jinny ignored her friend's questioning gaze and crouched down next to the Martian woman, resisting the urge to put an arm around her. Instead, she reached out and put her gloved hand on top of Domitia's as she continued to clutch Parn's lifeless hand in return.

"May I?" she asked simply.

Domitia didn't respond. But she did something on the exterior of Parn's exosuit gauntlet, and the glove covering the dead man's hand dissolved into the sleeve. Jinny removed her glove as well, then replaced her bare hand lightly on top of the centurion's, even as Domitia's still-encased hand refused to let it go.

The memories flooded into Jinny, and she welcomed them, unlike so many before. In those few moments, she learned more about Martian culture and honor than a hundred of Earth's scholars could have in a lifetime.

"He loved you so much," she heard herself whisper before she broke the connection. "He thought of you as the daughter he never had, like . . . the sister he lost. His love for you is why he welcomed Tyrus into the Trials in the first place. And why he did not challenge you or Tyrus when you chose to leave the Guard."

She paused, unsure of how to say the next part. Then she decided to let Parn do the talking himself. He smiled gratefully in her head as she surrendered control to him.

"Daughter," he said through her, and Domitia finally looked up, her gaze sharp but showing a measure of her surprise. "You bring honor to me, Domitia. You . . ."

Jinny retreated into the fog of her own mind, feeling that even she couldn't be a witness to the private words that now passed between the memory of Marcus Parn and the still-living Domitia Tyne. For the first time ever, she willingly surrendered control so entirely that she was no longer even an observer in her own head. Only a few seconds passed, however, before she felt a tug, and Parn pulled her from the fog and restored her control.

Thank you, she heard him say. Then, in an experience that was, for Jinny, entirely new and unexpected, he was gone. Not back into the fog with the others, but simply gone. Parn's memories remained like an echo of the man in her head, but his persona was nowhere to be found. Unbidden, Jinny felt tears spring to her eyes as she reached out, in dire violation of every Martian cultural norm, and embraced Domitia, who returned the embrace as the two women cried together for only a few moments before wiping their tears and proceeding forward with their mission.

CHAPTER 57

Cruz cursed. If he'd been the one to design the escape tunnel, he would have planted demolition charges to collapse the tunnel if the enemy ever managed to infiltrate it. But driven by the same paranoia at being trapped underground that had surely prompted the building of the tunnel in the first place, its architects had installed no such mechanism. And with the main Government House entrance to the bunker covered by an entrenched company of *Enterprise*'s hostile Marines, there was nowhere else to run.

Still, he waited outside the door to President Gorsky's office, the dozen Marines tasked with Situation Room security joining the six members of the president's security detail, weapons drawn and aimed squarely at the closed door, ready to catch any force that attempted to exit in the crossfire.

When the door finally opened, only a single individual stepped through. At the sight of the pretty young blond woman holding her empty hands high over her head, even the security men hesitated.

"Hold fire!" Cruz shouted as Jinny Ambrosa waited patiently under the aim of nearly twenty sidearms and rifles.

It had always been the plan. Sure, originally, both the Praetorian Guard and the SEALs—the latter far more reluctantly than the former—had suggested hitting the Situation Room fast and hard, taking down anyone who stood between them and President Gorsky.

But reason had quickly intervened. There would be enough death on both sides already. So Jinny had suggested—in fact, demanded—that she be allowed to try to stave off those deaths.

Now, she felt herself almost slump in relief as General Cruz commanded his troops to hold fire. Except, she saw out of the corner of one eye, a man in a suit—surely one of Gorsky's personal guards—tighten his finger on the trigger of his pistol.

The gun barked, and Jinny winced, shutting her eyes reflexively in anticipation of her death. Then she opened them, watching in fascinated silence as the bullet fell to the ground in front of her just as the personal shield Tyrus had given her winked out. The strange moment took her back over a year to an alleyway in the Alpha Centauri system, when a similar shield had stopped Alan Daily from killing Tyrus Tyne—and changed the entire course of Jinny's life.

She almost physically shoved the thought aside and stared a challenge at the assembled UE officers, Marines, and bodyguards.

"I said hold fire!" Cruz shouted and moved to wrench the pistol out of the offending bodyguard's hand.

Jinny looked around, expecting to see Gorsky countermanding his general's orders, but the president was nowhere to be seen. For a moment, her heart sank, and she thought that they'd failed after all—that Gorsky had never been in the bunker or maybe that he'd escaped before the contingent of Marines sent to take Government House had sealed off the bunker's main entrance. But she discarded that worry. His guards were here, so he must be as well

"General Cruz," she said, keeping her voice as calm as possible given the circumstances. "I'm here to discuss a peace accord between Mars and Earth. And I'm here to convince you that it's time to arrest Mikael Gorsky for treason."

Mikael couldn't believe his ears or eyes as he watched the vid feed from inside the conference room across the command center from his office. Jinny Ambrosa was here! After so many months of trying to recapture the stupid little reader, she had come to him. But in the worst way possible.

And to make a bad situation worse, she was being allowed to talk.

He pushed his way through his most loyal four bodyguards, who had accompanied him into the conference room—using the space as a last bastion in the event that the invaders got past the men at his office door—and stepped out into the main command center.

"General Cruz!" he cried. "Arrest that woman, now!" Maybe he'd get to deliver the Keeper's prize to him after all.

Jinny watched the general's face harden at the order from his commander-in-chief, and he started to open his mouth. She had no idea if he was going to echo his president's order to arrest her or perhaps argue with the man instead, but she decided not to wait and find out.

"General, before you do anything," she said loudly, "I need you to listen to me!"

General Cruz couldn't believe his ears. Things already contained in the message from Aphrodite Starshadow, the transmission from Horatio Lopez, and the personal communication from Lafayette, Lopez, Bol, and O'Leary, somehow seemed all the more real when delivered in the simple, confident speech of a twenty-something girl who had seen all too much killing and suffering in her short life.

As she spoke, Cruz vaguely registered Gorsky yelling behind him, ordering him and the others to shoot the girl, but none of them obeyed. Even the president's bodyguards started to look back at their boss with horrified expressions.

Still, Cruz wasn't sure what he was going to do. It all seemed so wrong, so fantastical, it had to be some kind of trick. Maybe Jinny Ambrosa herself had been fooled. Maybe *this* was all just part of some Council plot to destabilize the UE before the invasion, maybe . . .

Abruptly, every screen in the Situation Room went dark. An instant later, they came back on, all showing the exact same thing, the battle plot and sensor records from a UEN warship.

Temperance smiled in triumph as the computer in Gorsky's office allowed her to override the feeds of every screen in the bunker and play the unaltered recording from UENS *Italy*'s actions at Nyx. While Ambrosa had been just outside the office door, holding the attention of the bunker's defenders, she and two SEALs had snuck into the room behind the reader, and the Neon Mouse had made quick work of the hack, aided by the root access Gorsky's workstation had over the entire facility. And she needed to hack only one simple password to awaken his console.

It was the ultimate irony. Deep underground in the most secure facility in all of United Earth, with some of the strongest security of both the physical and cyber varieties, all that stood between her and total control was a ten-digit password.

Too easy.

When the video showing UENS *Italy* firing first stopped playing, and after the log files that showed transmitted messages between Admiral Dalish Connors and Mikael Gorsky immediately before and after the battle, all eyes turned to the president.

"Lies," he said, his voice lacking its usual bluster. "All lies."

Jinny watched General Cruz's face carefully. She saw the moment he finally accepted the full truth and the import of that truth, detecting it in the way his jaw tightened and his eyes burned as they stared at his no-longer commander-in-chief.

"Marines!" the general barked. "Arrest President Gorsky."

Cruz wanted nothing more than to shoot Mikael Gorsky right through the heart. But he wasn't that kind of man, so he ordered the Marines to arrest him instead. He would see to it that Gorsky got his day in court for his crimes . . . after they'd restored order to United Earth and stopped the needless war with Mars so they could—

"No!" the president yelled, and Cruz watched in horror as the big Russian produced a gun from somewhere in the folds of his suit coat, pointing it squarely past Cruz and right at Jinny Ambrosa.

Around Gorsky, his personal guards moved as well. Whether it was to help their president or restrain him, Cruz couldn't tell, and neither could the Marines, who leaped forward to stop them either way.

But all Cruz could focus on was Gorsky himself. And as the president finished raising his pistol, he knew what he had to do.

The report of the gunshot echoed in the enclosed space, and for a moment, Cruz thought he'd failed. Then he looked down at his chest, seeing the blossoming of red there where he'd thrown himself between Gorsky and Jinny Ambrosa. The general looked back up at Gorsky in time to see him knocked to the ground by a black-clad, preternaturally tall figure who materialized out of nowhere next to the traitorous president.

Ernesto Cruz smiled as he slumped to the ground.

CHAPTER 58

Landon Hartman wasn't entirely sure why Jinny Ambrosa had chosen him for his particular part in their mission, but he was here and doing his part. The strange black suit he wore hid him from the eyes of everyone in the room, even from the similarly invisible Martians who had snuck with him into the command center behind Jinny while she spoke to General Cruz and the others.

Landon's stealth suit was an identical twin to the one that Tyrus Tyne had worn in his assault on the lunar prison, the Crater, over seven months before. Both suits had been supplied by Osiris Arms, a military contractor and subsidiary of O'Leary Industries. They'd been designed for the SEALs but had ultimately proved too expensive for the Navy to order more than a few prototypes.

The one Landon was wearing, unlike the one Tyrus had previously worn, had a special modification: a high-resolution camera, which was currently capturing everything happening in the Situation Room and piping it through a broadcast channel Temperance had hacked before the mission started.

Yasmine Peralta dropped the dish she'd been holding for the last several minutes, frozen in the act of drying it, as she watched in horrific and rapt attention the broadcast that had taken over the show she'd been watching while cleaning the kitchen.

She cried out in shock when General Ernesto Cruz, a native of her own Bolivia, was shot in the heart by his own president. Her husband came running in from the other room to see what was going on and stopped next to her, wordlessly watching as their national hero lay bleeding on the floor while a strange, tall figure tackled the president-turned-murderer.

They were still standing there, mouths agape, when the video feed faded to black and was replaced by the grim face of a man they only vaguely recognized.

"People of United Earth," the newcomer said solemnly into the camera. "I am Corey O'Leary, former congressman and former friend of Mikael Gorsky. I am broadcasting to you from the offices of the Sol News Network in Houston, where forces loyal to the Constitution have brought me to be able to speak to you today.

"As you've just witnessed, our president has fooled us all, including me. He has been collaborating with our greatest enemy, the Council, while fomenting war between Earth and Mars to weaken us ahead of the Council Navy's return in force.

"Please do not take my word for this. Trust what you have just seen yourselves. Beyond that, I have transmitted to every news service and station, as well as for all of you to see on the Internet, every shred of evidence that Reader Jinny Ambrosa alluded to and more. You will find files and testimonies outlining a long history of deceit and manipulation by Mikael Gorsky, including . . ."

Yasmine sank slowly into the closest chair by her small kitchen table, almost missing it in her shocked state as the man—O'Leary—gave further details of the president's treason. Her husband still stood there, shaking his head in silent dismay.

Another man joined O'Leary in the shot, this one wearing a military uniform. "Citizens of United Earth," continued the former congressman, "we have an opportunity ahead of us. Fleet Admiral Horatio Krishna Lopez, the highest-ranking member of the UE military, has asked me to take temporary stewardship of the civilian government so that we can ensure the removal of the traitor Mikael Gorsky from office and the peaceful transition of power. In turn, I have asked Admiral Terrence Lafayette, with me now"—the second man nodded—"to immediately enforce a ceasefire of all UE military forces so that we may negotiate with Mars and Europa to jointly defend our system against the Council Navy when it arrives. Even now, a peacekeeping force of ships from the Europan Navy is on its way to Earth to oversee these negotiations and agreements so that we may . . ."

Yasmine shook her head in disbelief but found her shock mixed with an odd sense of hope as she continued to listen to the broadcast, ignoring and forgetting the shattered remains of the plate she'd dropped until hours after the message had ended.

Corey ended his broadcast and looked up at the eight Navy SEALs who had gotten him safely from the drop zone to the Sol News Network offices on the other side of Houston. One of them nodded at him to indicate that the studio crew had cut the feed as ordered.

"Do you think it worked?" Corey asked Admiral Lafayette.

He would never get the chance to learn the answer to that question.

Admiral Hank Showalker looked around *Congo*'s flag bridge as the broadcast from Earth's surface ended. Every member of his staff was staring open-mouthed at the now-blank forward viewscreen, which a moment later reverted back to its normal display of a battle plot.

Showalker had always hated politics. Whether the Red Party, Blue Party, or Green was in office, the Navy never got the full funding it needed or the support and recognition it deserved for keeping the Martians at bay for over half a millennium. He respected few politicians and didn't particularly care for Corey O'Leary any more than he'd cared for Mikael Gorsky. He viewed them all as various levels of evil.

But even Showalker had to admit that the evidence against Gorsky was damning in the extreme. Furthermore, he *did* respect Horatio Lopez and Terrence Lafayette, just as he trusted his own eyes and ears and what he had just witnessed on the live feed from the Situation Room.

"Admiral, the fleet is requesting orders, sir," his comm officer said, the man's voice almost shaking with stress.

Showalker opened his mouth to answer, but he couldn't find the words.

"Multiple ships surfacing!" screamed the tactical officer. "There's so many. They're firing!"

Whatever decision the admiral was about to share with his crew and his fleet was burned from existence as the nuclear fire of a dozen ship-killer missiles, fired at point-blank range, engulfed UENS *Congo*.

PART SIX
INVASION

CHAPTER 59

Guard Senior Commander Roger Vance winced as return fire from Earth's First Fleet peppered GSF *Aldrin*'s hull around him.

He'd argued against the Guard Space Force being the first stage of the attack on the Four Worlds, all the way up until the pain his enacter gene drove into his skull was too much to bear. Then, he'd shut his mouth during the treacherous journey through the Goat Path's shifting gravity fields.

He'd considered arguing again when his Guard fleet—designated Echo Fleet—had surfaced in Sol's outer system. But he knew then that it would do no good. Even as his Council Navy overseer, Vice Admiral Henri Townsend, ordered Vance and his fleet to undertake an extremely risky in-system jump to Earth orbit, Roger had kept his mouth shut, like a good little enacter.

Now, he regretted all of that. Despite outnumbering the Earth defense fleet almost two-to-one and having the element of surprise, he knew it was only a matter of time until the tide turned against his GSF forces. Not only were the Earth ships larger than his Guard fleet, but they were also crewed by men and women experienced in fighting wars against evenly matched military opponents, not just the smugglers and pirates usually engaged by the GSF.

Silently, he cursed himself for being so effective in the war games at Moloch that Admiral Chen herself had decided to place him in command of a hastily formed combined GSF fleet for the first strike on Earth. Using Echo Fleet as the vanguard allowed the Keeper and his minions to meet the insanely aggressive invasion schedule they'd refused to be swayed from.

"Move TF54 to the left flank," he ordered, shoving down his traitorous thoughts and ignoring the pain they brought to his head. "And tell TF52 to concentrate fire on that carrier. Broadcast to all fleet units: launch fighters."

He watched on the battle plot as his orders were carried out, most ships moving quickly to comply. But a few of his units, mostly smaller escorts, hesitated just slightly before moving into their new attack patterns.

Next to Vance, Henri Townsend cursed. "Your people are slow to obey," the Council Navy admiral accused.

"Not all of them are enacters," Vance shot back in a much sharper voice than he intended. "Not all of them want to destroy Earth!"

Townsend sneered at him. "Then it's a good thing that they will have the honor of clearing the way for the forces that will."

Vance did his best to ignore the man, turning back to watch the plot and call out orders and adjustments to his cobbled-together but still impressive fleet as they poured their fire into Earth's defenders.

Mary Bol stared in shock as the fleet of unidentified, mostly smaller ships tore into First Fleet.

"Helm! Turn us about and signal *Midway* and *Yorktown* to make all haste back to Earth. We need to help with the planetary defense."

Mikael Gorsky smiled in triumph as the large viewscreen at the front of the Situation Room showed the massive Council fleet destroying several ships from UEN First Fleet in just the opening moments of the battle. He'd never liked Hank Showalker—the admiral had always thought politicians were a sub-breed of humanity, certainly not on par with the lofty flag officers of Earth's military. Too bad he hadn't had a chance to survive to see just how wrong he was.

The only thing that would make watching the invasion live any better would be if Gorsky's hands weren't securely fastened behind his back and if he didn't have a Marine holding him by each arm. But that was only temporary. No one else in the room knew it, but soon they would be begging his forgiveness as Keeper Petrov arrived and handed him control of a battered and defenseless Sol system.

He heard a choking cough from nearby and looked over to see two Martians in their black exosuits leaning over the prone form of General Cruz. Gorsky's shot had taken the general through the chest, but the Martians had almost instantly applied some strange paste to the wound, and Cruz wasn't dead . . . yet. Maybe that wasn't such a bad thing. With Showalker gone and that fool Lopez and traitor Lafayette soon to follow, *someone* in the upper ranks of Earth's military needed to be around to witness just how outmatched they were by Mikael Gorsky's cunning.

"More enemy ships coming through the front door!" one of the UEN officers in the Situation Room cried out, switching one of the chamber's viewscreens to show the long-range sensor feed of the exit from the Castilian Rift, over thirty light-minutes from Earth but still far too close.

Tyrus watched helplessly as wave after wave of Council ships surfaced from the void, quickly destroying the combined UEN and Europan Navy forces stationed to defend the Front Door—understrength forces after so many of the United Earth ships had been pulled to help in the war with Mars.

He'd tried so hard to warn them—to tell them how outclassed their ships were, to help them see their weaknesses, to convince them that only together could they stand against the Council's might—but they hadn't listened. And as more and more ships in orbit above died in the flash of nuclear fire or by the white-hot knife of lasers, Tyrus knew that the worst was yet to come.

Fleet Admiral Tamara Chen did not smile as she surveyed the wreckage in the cone of space that was aptly named the Front Door, the only place where—until today—citizens of the Four Worlds had thought it possible to travel through the Castilian Rift.

Chen took no pleasure in the death and destruction all around her. While a certain part of her—the clinical part—felt relieved that she had thus far been able to fulfill her orders and spare herself the pain of disobedience, the human part of her silently mourned the men and women lost in the brief battle against the token force Earth and Europa had guarding the Front Door.

No one would be surprised to learn she mourned the spacers lost under her command; she had a reputation as a leader who cared for those in the ranks underneath her. But many would have been surprised to learn that she also mourned the lost enemies her fleet had been forced to dispatch.

Still, she only gave herself a moment to lament their collective deaths. Then she turned and began issuing orders as the last stragglers of the Council Navy's Alpha Fleet surfaced from the void. Minutes later, the entirely of Alpha Fleet was burning hard toward Earth, leaving room for Bravo and Charlie Fleets to come through the Rift behind them.

"Admiral, we'll be back within weapons range of Earth in twenty-seven minutes."

Horatio Lopez nodded from his command chair on *George Washington*'s flag bridge. "Lindy," he called to Rear Admiral Everston on the command bridge. "I need you to get me more speed on the drives, or there won't be an Earth to return to."

"Peters says that more power to the engines and we risk burning out the impellers, Admiral," replied *Washington*'s commander. From the tone of her voice, she had probably already argued the point with her chief engineer.

"Tell him to remove the drive safeties, on my authority," Lopez said, and he watched a few moments later as the mission clock went from twenty-seven minutes to twenty-three as his superdreadnought surged forward.

Then he started calling out orders to the remnants of First Fleet through the comm.

Commander Kinsey Phillips lost her footing as a missile strike shook Earth Home One around her. Looking up from her hands and knees, she saw a flashing image on a secondary viewscreen that showed the station's D-ring open to space along an eight-hundred-meter section, with alerts that another similar stretch to either side was irradiated past survivable levels.

One of the enlisted women helped her to her feet, and Kinsey made her way to the weapons station she'd been headed toward. Pushing aside the lieutenant commander there—the man was frozen with fear —she slid into his place and began keying in targeting commands. Seconds later, Home One's leeward broadside fired at a squadron of Council battlecruisers that had come within range, killing two of them and damaging several others with the station's volley of missiles.

Killing two battlecruisers in one volley was a small win, and there was a hoot of triumph from one of the other officers in the station's command center as the surviving battlecruisers broke off their attack run, but Kinsey didn't join in the celebration. On the battle plot, she saw the truth: First Fleet was barely holding its own. Even with backup from Home One and Earth's other orbital defense platforms, it simply wouldn't be enough. The enemy ships seemed to understand her station's range and weapons capabilities far too well, staying outside of effective laser range and hammering her with their missiles.

She keyed in another firing solution and unleashed another flurry of missiles aimed at a distant enemy heavy cruiser squadron. The targets' smaller escorts moved to block the wave, but Kinsey was already turning her attention to another squadron of cruisers, silently willing them to move just a little bit closer as they punched it out with a UEN battleship and its escorts.

All the while, she maintained a silent countdown in her head, knowing that soon, inevitably, she would be faced with a terrible choice: abandon the station or go down fighting.

CHAPTER 60

"Sir, *Laos* is gone!" the nearly panicked voice of UENS *Turner Joy*'s tactical officer called across the heavy cruiser's bridge.

Commander Greg Winters swore under his breath as the battleship his smaller ship had been playing escort to disappeared under the onslaught of fire from eight Council heavy cruisers and their destroyer escorts. He swore again when the Council force turned its considerable combined firepower on their formation's second largest ship, the battlecruiser *Paris*.

The Council fleet had only surfaced from their in-system jump forty minutes ago, but already their superior numbers and the element of surprise—they'd caught First Fleet entirely flatfooted with their attention on the happenings in Houston rather than their sensor screens—had cut down Earth's defenders by almost a third. All around *Turner Joy*, burned out and disabled hulks of UEN ships began slow but unstoppable spirals down Earth's gravity well.

With Admiral Showalker dead, Admiral Lopez had started transmitting orders to the fleet. At first, some of the squadrons had ignored him—they'd just been fighting *him* hours before—but soon the hurt feelings and legal ambiguities of the coup were set aside, and more and more rear admirals, captains, and commanders had recognized in

Horatio Lopez their one chance of living through this and maybe even saving their planet.

"Move us to support *Paris* on her starboard flank," Greg commanded the helm, doing his best not to let his own panic bleed through his tone. Deep down, he knew the truth. Even with Lopez's leadership, Earth was already lost. The Council fleets would just keep coming and coming until no one remained to defend the planet. But he'd be cursed if he wasn't going to make the Council pay for every centimeter of this battlefield.

There was a cry of triumph from the other side of the bridge, and Greg turned to see his sensor officer smiling. "Sir, she's back. The *Washington* is back, and she's engaging the Council fleet!"

Rear Admiral Lindy Everston bared her teeth as every ventral laser bank of her superdreadnought concentrated fire on the Council battlecruiser in her sights. They weren't the most powerful shots—*Washington* had drained its power stores cutting a few precious minutes off her travel time back to Earth orbit—but the sheer volume of fire blew the Council ship to smithereens.

"Message relayed from the surface, ma'am," her comm officer announced. "Commander Tyne reports that the attackers aren't Council Navy. It's the colonial Guard Space Force."

"And what does he expect us to do with that information?" Everston snapped more harshly than she intended.

"He said their primary weapons are their shocker missiles, so—"

The warning came too late. Across the battlefield, UENS *Georgia,* the anchoring battleship of First Fleet's Task Force 18, exploded in a brilliant flash of light as one of the cursed shockers hit an overload point. Almost a year ago, Tyrus Tyne had warned the UEN that specific vulnerable points on their battleships' hulls, when hit directly by a shocker, would allow the missile's electronic charge to overload and blow the reactor. Apparently, the Council had figured out the same.

Or rather, Mikael Gorsky had told them. Everston cursed the man in her head.

"Launch all fighters and target the enemy battlecruisers," she ordered aloud, and the CAG at his station behind her acknowledged the command. On the plot, dozens of smaller craft began pouring from *Washington*'s hangar bays, their own capacitors fully charged even if their mothership's weren't.

"Admiral Lopez just ordered the remaining survivors from First Fleet to form up on us, ma'am," her comm officer reported. "Defensive pattern Foxtrot-4."

Everston nodded to herself. Gamma-4 would put *Washington* and First Fleet's surviving battleships in the center of a sphere of smaller escorts. It would help protect the larger ships from more cheap shots like the one that had destroyed *Georgia*, but would also effectively take their lasers out of the fight—they'd be forced to engage with missiles only.

Oh well. She trusted Admiral Lopez to know what he was doing, and she watched as the blue dots on the battle plot slowly moved into formation around her superdreadnought.

Unfortunately, the enemy moved faster, and Everston winced as a squadron of Guard battlecruisers and heavy cruisers began an attack run on her ship. With *Washington*'s laser capacitors still charging, they couldn't hit all of them, so she ordered fire concentrated on the closest ships, leaving the rest to be harassed by her fighter screen.

Roger Vance frowned as GSF *Sentinel* started a death spiral toward Earth's surface below. Its loss left Vance's forces short one more battlecruiser. On paper, they still had enough ships to finish the job, but the battle-hardened UEN forces were simply better trained and more experienced than his fleet, and it was showing.

Plus, there was that superdreadnought to consider, though it appeared to have surprisingly understrength lasers, perhaps from its mad charge back to the planet.

Either way, the massive Earth ship was on the other side of the battlefield from Vance right now. Calmly, despite the red-faced Council

Navy Admiral Townsend behind him, Vance issued more orders to his ships.

"Concentrate fire in this sector on that station at oh-one-four mark two!"

Kinsey Phillips felt momentary elation when her missiles knocked out yet another of the Council battlecruisers. But any exultation died on her lips as more than twenty *other* enemy warships turned and began burning in Earth Home One's direction.

"Where are the blasted Martians?" she screamed to her crew. She'd seen the Martian Fleet of the Eagle leave Earth's vicinity just three hours before, but why weren't they coming back?

So much for a joint defense against the Council Navy! she thought acidly. *Reds betrayed us, just like we always knew they would.*

Gritting her teeth, she forced herself to accept reality as nearly a hundred missiles took flight from the approaching Council ships straight at her station.

"All hands, abandon station! Get to your escape pods."

Around her, junior officers started to panic and senior enlisted salts barked at them to get ahold of themselves, all while Kinsey ignored them and commanded the station to launch everything it had at the approaching enemy ships. There was little chance Earth Home One could stand up to the enemy armada—not without support from the UEN's mobile assets, and they were in no position to help anyone, not even themselves—but she would at least take as many of the enemy as possible with her before she died.

CHAPTER 61

Vice Admiral Jessica Monroe knew that there was no way they were going to save Earth. Maybe if Admiral Showalker had survived the opening salvoes, he could have rallied First Fleet to mount a credible defense in orbit, even against the much larger Council fleet that had magically appeared on Earth's doorstep.

And maybe if Lafayette were still commanding Second Fleet, he would be able to find a way stop the three *additional* Council fleets that had come through the Front Door, one of them burning toward Earth while the others made for Mars and Europa, respectively.

But Showalker hadn't survived, though Admiral Lopez had arrived in time to hopefully shore up First Fleet. And Terrence Lafayette was no longer in command of Second Fleet; Jessica was.

"TT from Fleet Command," her comm officer reported on the bridge of UENS *Harrier,* Jessica's fleet carrier. "We are to interpose ourselves ahead of the second Council fleet headed toward Earth and prevent them from reaching the planet."

Jessica considered that for a moment. Second Fleet was indeed in position to catch the Council invaders before they reached Earth orbit and reinforced their considerable forces already there. But catching the enemy and stopping it were two entirely different things.

"Who signed the order?" she asked.

The comm officer frowned. "No signature, ma'am. Just says it's from Fleet Command."

Jessica let out a frustrated sigh. Without a signature, she had no idea if the order came from General Cruz—doubtful based on the bullet they'd all seen him take in the live broadcast—Chief of Naval Operations Admiral Clancy, or some civilian intern in the Octagon or anyone in between. With the turmoil on Earth *before* the Council Navy showed up, she had no idea who was even in command down there.

Which left her in a quandary. She could follow her orders and perhaps delay the reinforcement fleet headed to Earth, with inevitable heavy losses to Second Fleet. Or she could try to find another way to help the situation that didn't result in losing Earth's only remaining fighting force now that First Fleet was almost certainly doomed.

She knew what she *should* do. She should set course toward Mars, hoping to catch the *third* Council fleet headed there from behind just as the Martian home defense fleet met them from the front. Together, they could destroy that fleet in detail, assuming the Martians would coordinate with her. Then, perhaps she could lead a combined force to retake Earth. But she couldn't do that, could she? Especially since the Martians weren't sending either of their fleets to aid Earth.

"We'll follow the order from Fleet Command," she informed her command staff. "Order all ships on an intercept course toward these coordinates." She transmitted from her station a vector that would place Second Fleet right between Earth and the approaching Council reinforcements.

Her officers began shouting back and forth as they repeated her orders and followed them, and Jessica hoped that she hadn't just doomed them all to a senseless and futile battle out of sheer, stubborn principle.

Mary Bol slammed a hand down on her command chair's arm as she read the message from Fleet Admiral Lopez a third time. It made her just as angry as the first two times.

"How can he order us to stay away from Earth?" George Holm demanded, or maybe pleaded, from where he stood next to her on the flag bridge. He'd made record time coming up from the command bridge, too stunned to discuss the orders over the intercom.

"He wants us to hang back and harass the Council reinforcements," Mary said with acid in her tone. "We are to slow them down as much as possible to give First Fleet time to defeat the GSF and regroup."

Holm shook his head. "But we can't just abandon Earth, Admiral. Can we?"

Mary blew a violent breath out her nose. "We're going to follow orders, Captain. Signal *Yorktown* and *Midway* and then bring us about. We need to buy First Fleet as much time as we can give them."

"What's this I hear about you wanting to commit the Fleet of the Eagle to the battle at Earth?" Praetor Tiberius demanded as he walked into the Chamber of Praetors. "Consul Starshadow, the agreement was for them to support the removal of Mikael Gorsky from power, *not* to do anything more! They have done their part, and you have no right to change their orders."

Aphrodite eyed him from her seat at the table. Tiberius had been the last praetor to arrive at the emergency meeting she'd called, and she could see now it was a deliberate and calculated sleight on his part. He'd always chafed under her leadership, fancying himself a far better choice for consul than she could ever be.

"Praetor Tiberius," she responded as evenly as she could, but she knew the despair was evident in her voice, "we *must* honor our commitment to United Earth. The Fleet of the Eagle must come to Earth's aid."

Tiberius scowled at her as he arrived at the table, standing behind his seat rather than taking it. "And leave Mars uncovered? I think not, Consul Starshadow. No consul or praetor may refuse to defend our home. With an entire fleet of Council Navy ships bearing down on Mars, we must use the Fleet of the Eagle to reinforce the Fleet of the Bear and defend our world!"

Aphrodite looked around at the other praetors for support. None of them would meet her gaze. Even Gale Sunsbane, her longtime mentor and fiercest supporter, looked away, abandoning her when she needed him the most.

The worst part was that they weren't wrong. Already, the Council ships in the Sol system vastly outnumbered the combined fleets of the Four Worlds. Committing the Fleet of the Eagle to the defense of Earth would doom Mars to suffer the same fate as the UE faced now.

Could she sacrifice her own planet in the name of honor alone? To fulfill an implied commitment never formally made? Negotiations of joint defense with the UE—slated to take place after the successful coup—had never even commenced. Despite the agreement from the Quorum of Praetors in this very room just weeks ago that such joint defense was necessary, was it still the right thing to do?

Yes, it was. Mars needed to honor her commitments. *Aphrodite* needed to honor her commitments.

She squared her shoulders and glared across the table at Kol Tiberius. "Praetors of Mars!" she shouted, refusing to let them ignore her any longer. "Would you sell your honor so cheaply because you are afraid? Or will you fight?"

CHAPTER 62

Jinny felt the tears running down her face as she watched the battle plot in the Situation Room. On the screen, dozens of UEN ships perished as the Guard's onslaught continued. Admiral Lopez's return in *Washington* had changed the dynamics of the battle, and now, for every blue dot that went dark, two or three red dots representing the GSF fleet did the same. But in the jumble of attacks and counterattacks, she couldn't tell if it would be enough for Earth to win.

Briefly, she considered channeling the persona of Horatio Lopez himself to give her his analysis of the battle. No one else knew that she'd read the old fleet admiral; he'd insisted on it, wanting the knowledge in his mind to be available to the defenders of the Four Worlds if the worst should happen to him. But Jinny didn't channel him now; she wasn't sure she wanted the bad news he might report after seeing the battle plot.

A choking gasp drew her attention away from the large screen, and she turned to see General Cruz fighting to sit up while two Martians held him down, one of them inspecting his chest wound with some kind of device. Whatever strange paste they'd applied to it—Tyrus had mentioned nanites—it seemed to have not only kept him alive, but to be slowly healing his mortal injury. Already, the blood flow had slowed to a trickle, and some color had returned to the general's face.

He must have sensed her eyes on him because he rotated his head slightly to one side to look at her directly. Moving one of his arms weekly, he motioned for her to approach. She took a few steps over, wincing as she saw the open hole in his chest, covered in the strange reflective gel of the nanite paste. Jinny tore her eyes away from the bullet wound and met Cruz's. One of the Martians moved out of the way slightly so that she could kneel next to the man.

To her surprise, Cruz reached out and weakly grabbed one of her hands. She looked down at it and then back at him.

"Glove . . ." he gasped, the word taking great effort, " . . . off. Read . . . me."

Jinny shook her head. He had no idea what he was asking her—that she would see everything he'd ever done in his life. But he nodded as much as he could. "Read . . . everything."

Her eyes went wide with shock. How did he know? The answer presented itself to her mind as if she'd already read him: the Majko. The old woman seemed to have connections in all the halls of UE power, and it should have come as no surprise that if the old woman knew Admiral Lopez, then she would also know General Cruz.

His expression silently pleaded with her, so she reluctantly removed her hand from his and then tugged off the glove she wore over it. Both of the Martians reflexively shied away, but she ignored them, reaching down tenderly to take Cruz's hand in her own.

Ten seconds later, Cruz lost consciousness, and Jinny let his hand fall back to his side and stood up. The two Martians moved back to keep up their ministrations, and one of them met her eye and nodded to Cruz's chest, which she saw was still rising and falling. Relieved that the general simply slept, Jinny turned to face the rest of the room.

Taking a deep breath, she invited the new persona of General Cruz in her head forward to take control.

"Everyone!" he shouted through her. "We have to leave now."

Some of the assembled mix of Marines, Praetorian Guard, SEALS, and assorted UE military officers peered at her curiously, but the majority of the room ignored her. Turning his attention to the main viewscreen, Jinny's Cruz persona immediately saw why.

One of the largest green icons on the battle plot had changed to a flashing orange. Earth's defensive stations were starting to die.

Kinsey watched in a strange sort of disconnected curiosity as the enemy fleet sent ship after ship into close weapons range of Earth Home One. Thus far, the Council ships had batted away many of the missiles she'd sent their way, whereas her station, short-staffed and half-destroyed, hadn't managed to do the same to their return volleys. Even now, most of D-ring and half of C-ring were just gone, fields of debris where steel bulkheads and decks full of people had been just hours before.

Around her, most of the command center crew had already left, heeding her orders to abandon the station and take escape pods to Earth's surface. She prayed that none of them would land in the ocean—it would be a long time before anyone thought to retrieve them, if at all—but she'd done all she could for them. Three Navy spacers remained in the command center with her, one lieutenant she'd barely gotten to know and two older chiefs she'd come to rely on. None of them had so much as responded to her second order to leave, so she'd given up.

Now, while they did their best to manage the station's defensive weapons and automated damage control systems, Kinsey put all her focus on the approaching enemy armada. Lasers started to spear out toward Home One from the Council ships, carving into the station and causing more alarms and flashing red lights throughout the command center. But still, Kinsey waited, luring them closer by her refusal to return fire.

Then, at the exact right moment, she struck, hitting the command that sent a crash burn to every rotational thruster that remained, spinning the damaged and dying station in place at a speed it was never meant to sustain. She imagined already stressed girders and supports snapping under the inertia of the rotational maneuver but didn't even glance toward the damage control board, trusting her companions to monitor things there.

As the station rotated in place, wobbling and cavitating due to its lopsided, damaged structure, Kinsey entered a second command just as the largely undamaged side of Earth Home One—the side that had, until now, faced *away* from the enemy—came to bear on the fast-approaching armada.

With her final command, sixty-four thirty-centimeter laser projectors roared with every bit of power the station's redundant reactors could muster, causing the lights to flicker overhead and the artificial gravity to give out for an instant before crashing back on, roiling Kinsey's stomach but not piercing her stubborn refusal to be distracted from her task.

She smiled as the concentrated laser fire vaporized all six of the enemy battlecruisers on approach, leaving their escorts to scramble like so many ants fleeting a rainstorm. Her smile didn't disappear as the lasers finally gave out, and the lights and gravity flickered off for good. Nor did she change her expression when the belated return salvo of enemy laser fire from the Council force's remaining heavy cruisers lashed out and hit Earth Home One's central sphere, its hull already weakened from the nuclear fire of missile salvos.

Commander Kinsey Phillips kept smiling until the instant the command center was incinerated by sun-hot beams of light.

CHAPTER 63

It had taken Jinny less than a minute to convince Tyrus of the 'orders' General Cruz had issued her and the rest of them in the seconds she'd read him before he passed out. From there, Tyrus had made it clear that everyone in the Situation Room—Martian, Earth loyalist, and rebel traitor alike—was now under the command of Reader Ambrosa.

Under anything approaching normal circumstances, she knew, they would have argued, but with Gorsky disgraced and arrested, Parn dead, and Cruz lying in a near-coma, there was a gaping vacuum of leadership, and most of the Situation Room's inhabitants were glad that *someone* was stepping into it. They needed anyone at this point to save them from the torture of watching from front-row seats as the birthplace of humanity fell to a fleet so massive the outcome was never in doubt. Even the Martians seemed to prematurely mourn Earth's demise.

Within fifteen minutes, the Situation Room had been emptied out, Jinny and Tyrus leading everyone out through the same tunnel by which they'd infiltrated the bunker. At the other end, they encountered the small rearguard force of two SEALs and two praetorian guards they'd left to secure the elevator's underground entrance. Then Tyrus took a small team up the lift and called down to report that the ice cream shop was empty and the coast was clear.

When Jinny finally emerged back into the rear of the ice cream shop, through the false door in the freezer, she was greeted by the smell of battle and death. Everywhere lay the dead and dying, their own Martians and SEALs languishing next to the UE Army officers who had thought they were defending Earth.

Those still able to leave under their own power had already done so, no doubt to report back to their barracks for orders against the invasion in process. Four medics had stayed behind to treat the still-living wounded from both sides, but they made no move to stop Jinny and her ragtag force. They did try to take over the treatment of Cruz, only to be met with the visages of the two glowering Martians who had thus far been doing quite alright in keeping the general alive.

A squad of SEALs and another of Praetorian Guards insisted on staying behind with the medics to guard their still-living wounded. There wasn't time to argue with them.

Gorsky, throughout the flight, had been taunting and teasing them, promising great pain to those who opposed him and boons to any who freed him as soon as the Keeper's forces landed and restored him to his rightful place. His mad jabbering had gotten on everyone's nerves, so the tape that one of the Martians finally affixed over the man's mouth was welcome by all, even the former president's surviving bodyguards.

"Where to now?" Tyrus asked Jinny, who studied the mental map in her head supplied by Cruz.

"This way!" she guided them, running down the street directly away from Government House and the secret tunnel entrance.

Above them, they heard the roar of aircraft, the deep, throaty rumble of Earth's atmospheric fighters almost drowned out by the higher pitch but much louder whine of the colonial Guard's space and air superiority fighters and assault shuttles descending on the capital.

Jessica Monroe watched the plot nervously. Her ships of the UEN's Second Fleet were still hours from intercepting the large Council Navy reinforcement fleet burning toward Earth from the Front Door. Three and a half hours, to be precise. But more and more, it was looking like none of it would matter. The Council Guard Space Force ships already at Earth—the ones who had somehow infiltrated the Sol system via some *other* route through the Rift—had already destroyed much of First Fleet and Earth's military orbitals. Defenses that had been built up over centuries to dissuade even the militaristic Martians from ever attempting a direct attack on humanity's homeworld had crumbled in hours under the relentless onslaught of the Council's GSF forces.

She took solace only in the fact that First Fleet—regrouping under Admiral Lopez's leadership—had given as much as it had taken, whittling down the Guard force to near parity with the beleaguered UEN forces. *If* Monroe could stop the other Council fleet—this one a true naval force with massive, black-painted dreadnoughts in its vanguard—the remaining defensive forces at Earth might have time to fight off the first attack. But if she failed . . .

"Admiral, are you all right?" a voice next to her asked, speaking softly so that no one else on *Harrier*'s flag bridge could hear.

"What?" she asked, startled, as she looked over to see Captain Cunningham, *Harrier*'s master. When had he come up from the command bridge?

"Your face," he nudged gently.

Surprised, Jessica realized for the first time that her cheeks were wet with tears. Chagrined, she reached up and wiped at them with her uniform sleeve.

"It won't mean anything, will it?" Cunningham said, voice still low for her ears only.

This time, she didn't have to ask what he meant. Jessica shook her head in response. Even if, by some miracle, they could destroy the larger Council fleet on approach to Earth, there were still two other enemy fleets in the system. "But can we do anything else?"

Cunningham frowned, showing his displeasure at the catch-22 they found themselves in. Earth was *home*; it was as simple as that. To not defend her would feel wrong to every one of the nearly 200,000 officers, spacers, and Marines of Second Fleet. None of them would be able to look at themselves in the mirror for years, if ever again, should they abandon their planet to the Council conquerors.

But if they met that fleet, none of them would likely ever look in the mirror again anyway. The dead couldn't care for their consciences or their appearance.

She mulled this over, torn by indecision, when her old commanding officer came to her rescue.

"Admiral Monroe, there's a message being broadcast to you directly," cried her comm officer. "It's Admiral Lafayette!"

"Put it on speaker."

"Admiral Monroe," Lafayette's voice came through, "I'd join you up there, but things are a little hot here on the surface. However, I'm ordering you to stop your advance to block the Council Navy reinforcements."

There was a pause on the recorded message—they were still too far from Earth for real-time comms, and Lafayette had too much to say for a Tachyon Telegraph—before the admiral continued in a more somber tone. "Jessica, I know that you are no longer obligated to follow my orders, but the Martians *will* come to our aid. So, if you still trust me as you once did, then here's what I need you to do."

As he explained his plan, every eye on *Harrier*'s flag bridge looked at her expectantly, and Jessica knew that whatever she said next would be spread across the fleet almost as fast as if she simply broadcast her response in the clear.

"Chelsea," she said to her comm officer, "give me a channel to the fleet."

Vice Admiral Henri Townsend smiled broadly as the final thirty-four ships of Earth's doomed First Fleet formed a last-ditch defensive cluster over the planet's southern hemisphere, encircling the heavily damaged superdreadnought that had *almost* turned the tide of the battle in Earth's favor.

Even Henri had to admit that the Earthlings had put up a good defense—masterful even. Watching that superdreadnought direct the battle had been like taking an advanced course in strategy and tactics from Delta 3's naval academy. But ultimately, it wouldn't be enough. Even if Henri's GSF forces—Roger Vance only *thought* he was in command—were ultimately bested, more ships from the far superior Council Navy would be arriving shortly. There was nothing the Earthlings could do.

Even now, Guard Paramilitary Force assault shuttles were descending on Houston, Earth's seat of government, overcoming the meager planetary defenses by the sheer weight of their numbers. Within minutes, thousands of loyal men and women, most of them enacters, from the GPF would secure Houston and all of United Earth with it.

At this rate, by the time Admiral Chen arrived, Henri would already have accepted President Gorsky's formal surrender.

He frowned at the thought. Repeated attempts to contact the UE president—they'd all been surprised by the Keeper's revelation that Gorsky himself was the spy he'd had in the UE government—had gone unanswered. Echo Fleet's GSF ships had picked up scattered comm signals and news reports from the surface that indicated some sort of coup had taken place. If so, Henri wasn't quite sure who to call upon to demand Earth's surrender.

No matter. They would find someone to surrender to them eventually. Until then, Henri enjoyed watching them die.

"Admiral!"

Fleet Admiral Tamara Chen turned to regard the overly excited tactical officer on CNS *Excelsior,* her Ivanov-class dreadnought and the flagship of the Council Navy's Alpha Fleet. "What is it, Gorman?" she asked, keeping her own voice more firmly under control.

"That United Earth fleet, ma'am. They've turned over."

Chen looked toward the holo field in the center of *Excelsior*'s bridge, where she saw that the UEN Second Fleet had indeed turned over and was decelerating, moving itself off of an intercept course with her fleet.

"Where does that new vector take them?" she questioned aloud.

"Mars intercept, ma'am," the tactical officer answered.

Chen frowned. "Contact Admiral Gregorovich and warn him that he's about to have company from behind." Studying the plot, she shook her head and muttered to herself. Never in their mission planning had they considered that Earth's fleets wouldn't all rally to their homeworld's defense. Even though the UEN Second Fleet was understrength after the costly war with Mars, Chen had expected it to bravely cut off her larger force and die valiantly in a vain attempt to stop her from reaching Earth and Luna.

But now, she had a decision to make. She could continue onward toward Earth, easily overcoming what was left of the planet's defenders—even that very interesting and unexpected superdreadnought wouldn't be able to stand against the combined might of her CN Alpha Fleet. Or she could go after the UEN Second Fleet and support Admiral Gregorovich and his Bravo Fleet in their attack on Mars.

In thc end, her enacter gene made the decision simple. Even thinking about abandoning her flight toward her primary target—Earth—was enough to give her a piercing headache. She and Alpha Fleet continued onward toward the mottled blue and green world that grew larger and larger in the external cameras.

"I demand that we restore our honor," Aphrodite said, her voice still laced with anger. Despite her earlier impassioned plea to the praetors, they had made little headway in agreeing upon a course of action.

Before anyone could respond to her latest challenge, the doors at the chamber's far end opened and a Navy navarch marched in, moving around the table as the silent praetors watched until she stood next to Aphrodite and whispered something in the consul's ear.

As the navarch made her retreat, Aphrodite turned back to the twelve men and women who sat around the table with her. "Praetors of Mars," she said, then paused to collect herself. "The Navy reports that, even now, Earth's Second Fleet has turned away from the defense of their homeworld to come to the defense of ours. They chase the Council fleet sent to conquer Mars. With them catching the enemy from behind as the Fleet of the Bear meets them from the front, can we doubt that we will emerge triumphant?"

"How can we be sure they're coming to our aid?" Tiberius said before any of the other praetors could react. "What if they sense an opportunity to join the Council in their attack? What if this is a ploy to draw away the Fleet of the Eagle and leave us open to conquest?"

Aphrodite couldn't believe her ears. Could Tiberius really be that deluded? Why would Earth ally with the very fleet that was even now destroying her defenses? It was ludicrous, so much so that she didn't carefully consider her next words.

"How can you be so foolish, Praetor Tiberius? How can you be so devoid of honor that you would stoop to such lies?"

She realized her mistake the instant the last word left her mouth. The eyes of every one of the praetors was now riveted on her, so that all but Aphrodite missed the cruel smile that sprung to Kol Tiberius's face.

"You dishonor me with your slanderous words, Consul Starshadow," he hissed. "I demand recompense on the field of honor!"

On the flag bridge of UENS *Washington,* Horatio Lopez studied the battle plot and frowned. His sincere hope had been that his superdreadnought alone could turn the tide of the battle sufficiently in their favor. And for a while, he'd thought it would. But losing Earth Home One and the other defensive platforms had been the turning point, and now he saw few ways he and his fleet could emerge victorious without help.

The Martians had never arrived as promised. Legatus Augustus Lightbringer had abandoned them in their hour of need. Not that he could blame the Reds; their own homeworld was under threat as well. But he'd sincerely hoped that they would have banded together with him to defend Earth, after which Lopez would have also taken every surviving UE ship to defend Mars.

But his hopes had been in vain. Even Second Fleet, burning to aid Mars under Lafayette's orders, was out of reach to help defend the homeworld. And Lopez's few remaining ships clustered together against overwhelming odds, with an entire enemy reinforcement fleet just hours away.

"Send the signal to the Martians again," he said to his comm officer, and the man somberly pressed the transmit button on his touchscreen. None of them had any hope it would be answered.

CHAPTER 64

Augustus Lightbringer slammed a hand down on his command chair's display console, shattering it under his fist. The latest plea for help from Horatio Lopez made it clear that the Earth admiral did not believe he could win the battle. And Lightbringer should have already come to the old man's aid.

Unfortunately, he'd been ordered back to Mars to aid in his own planet's defense. It may have been the prudent thing to do, but it lacked honor. The fact that Earth's own Second Fleet had turned from its defense of Earth to come to the aid of Mars only added insult to injury. Lightbringer couldn't remember a time in all the history of humanity in which the Earthers had shown more honor than the Martians.

"My Legatus," Triarch Cicero said from Lightbringer's shoulder. "We have not returned to Mars as ordered."

The man was correct. Lightbringer's orders were to stitch jump back to Mars, joining the Fleet of the Bear in orbit to defend the planet. Instead, however, he'd brought his Fleet of the Eagle only to the edge of the neutral zone. From this position, he could jump his fleet back to Mars in minutes, long before the attackers arrived. He could *also* jump his fleet back to Earth, to honor their commitments made to the Earthers.

Because at this moment, Augustus Lightbringer could do nothing but pray to Mars that the leaders of his planet had honor. And when he got the—hopefully—inevitable command to stitch jump back to Earth, he wanted to be as close as possible.

Aphrodite knew that there was no time. Earth's fleets were mere minutes from annihilation, and she had made a grave error that even the most naïve schoolgirl knew to avoid.

When she'd accused Tiberius of lacking honor and truth, turning the argument into a personal one rather than a political one, she had stepped right into the man's trap. Now, she had to either apologize and hope for his mercy—a move that would dishonor her and almost certainly result in her removal as consul at a critical moment—or agree to duel him, which would simply take too much time.

Either way, Earth, and the Sol system with it, would die.

By the grin on Tiberius's face and the horrified look on Sunsbane's, they all knew she had lost. Her mind raced desperately for a way out, but it was as if her thoughts were too jumbled to organize a response.

Then, her decades of studying Martian law, even the more esoteric rules and procedures, came to her rescue.

Standing up from her seat and squaring her shoulders once more, she addressed Tiberius with a firm tone and a snarl on her lips. "I accept your challenge! And I demand the right of proelium immediatum."

"Impossible!" Tiberius shouted after only a short delay. "The right of proelium immediatum was stricken from Martian law four centuries past. You are grasping for straws in the wind, Consul Starshadow."

Aphrodite smiled. "I suggest a check of the official records, Praetor Kol Tiberius," she growled. "For you are mistaken."

Every set of eyes in the room besides those of Aphrodite and Tiberius fixed on the displays in front of them. It was Sunsbane, predictably, who found it first. "The consul is correct! The right of proelium immediatum can still be invoked in time of war and imminent threat to Mars."

Aphrodite jumped in before anyone could argue the point. "What say you, Praetor Kol Tiberius. Are you brave enough to face me now?"

The man's expression fell. He had no doubt been planning to appoint a champion to the duel, a right held in Martian society only by the praetors that ruled it. It was the same rule Aphrodite's father had once used to force Corey O'Leary to fight her younger brother rather than facing the Earther boy himself on the field of honor.

But now, challenged by immediate combat, Tiberius had lost that option.

Rear Admiral Oswaldo Martinez had given up all hope. The Council forces had encompassed the few survivors of First Fleet—just twenty-five ships, including Admiral Lopez's damaged and bleeding *Washington* and Oswaldo's own *Dallas*—with over forty enemy GSF warships, cutting off their escape from Earth orbit and keeping them deep in the planet's gravity well.

Maybe it had been losing Admiral Showalker in the first seconds of the attack. Or perhaps it had been the quick deaths of First Fleet's carriers. Two of the three behemoth ships died before they could launch a third of their fighter squadrons, allowing the GSF's fighters to harass the remaining UEN ships almost unopposed. Or perhaps it had been inevitable either way, and no fleet could have stood against the sheer numerical advantage the enemy had brought with them, even if the Guard Space Force sported nothing larger than a battlecruiser.

Either way, it didn't matter now. Despite the hope and resurgence of confidence they'd all felt when Admiral Lopez and *Washington* had arrived, they'd lost that hope quickly when the blasted Martians had betrayed them by not following the superdreadnought to their aid.

It was over now for the UE. The only decision left was whether to surrender and save what they could or go down fighting. Oswaldo couldn't decide which option he hated more, and Admiral Lopez hadn't responded to his latest hail, the fleet admiral's comm officer informing Oswaldo that the old man was otherwise occupied.

"Orders, sir?" his flag captain, Ericka Chambers, asked from the captain's seat next to him. He thought about his response for only a moment. If Admiral Lopez wasn't going to do the right thing, then Oswaldo would.

"Signal the fleet on an open channel," he ordered his comm officer. "Tell them and the GSF forces that we surrender!"

The knife came within centimeters of Aphrodite's throat as Tiberius used his longer reach against her.

They hadn't even left the Grand Hall of Praetors to conduct the duel, and the boundaries of their field of honor were formed not by lines on the ground, but by the silent circle of the other eleven praetors themselves, most of whom watched with outwardly dispassionate expressions.

Aphrodite tried a counterthrust with her own blade, but Tiberius jumped out of the way. He was ten years her senior, but stronger both by gender and build. She was slightly faster, but with his superior height and reach, it wasn't enough.

She was going to lose, and so would the entire Sol system.

"My Legatus!" the optio at the comm station reported, grabbing Lightbringer's attention. "We are receiving a message of surrender from a portion of Earth's First Fleet. It has thrown their forces into disarray."

"No new messages from Mars?" he demanded.

"No, my Legatus," the optio reported, his own distress mirroring his commander's.

CHAPTER 65

"All units, regroup around *Washington*!" Horatio Lopez cried into the comm in vain, watching as his small remaining force scattered and was destroyed in detail by the GSF forces, who had staunchly ignored Admiral Oswaldo Martinez's desperate pleas for a ceasefire.

Martinez had never found anyone to accept his surrender. Almost the moment he'd broken formation, a squadron of GSF heavy cruisers had pounced on *Dallas*, and the small bits that were left of it would light up the night sky over Mumbai with their trails of fire.

The end had come.

"Admiral Everston," Lopez ordered through *Washington*'s intercom. "Take us straight at the enemy flagship. Flank speed. Have any surviving fighters and bombers follow us in."

The blade drew blood from Aphrodite's cheek as she was too slow to dodge another swipe of Tiberius's knife. At the sight of the crimson line on her face, her opponent showed his teeth. It was the fifth time he'd bloodied her, and she'd barely managed to scratch him once.

She wasn't going to survive this duel. Aphrodite knew now with a certainty that she couldn't do it. But maybe she could die in a way that still brought honor to Mars and, if she was extremely lucky, still saved what was left of the Sol system.

Watching Tiberius carefully—her timing had to be perfect—she waited for his next strike. When it came, a low thrust toward her midsection, she did not dodge.

She stepped forward.

Tiberius's knife sank deep into her stomach, bringing with it a burning pain such as she had never before experienced. But she fought through the instant of agony and clenched what remained of her long abdominal muscles, twisting her entire body as she did so. The blade went with her, wrenched from Tiberius's grasp, just as her left hand shot out and grabbed the man behind the neck to hold him close.

As Tiberius's eyes went wide, Aphrodite used her last bit of angry energy to move her right hand, thrusting her own blade through her opponent's neck.

Tiberius fell first, dead almost instantly, ending the duel in a win for Aphrodite, though she followed him to the hard stone floor mere moments later. As her eyes closed for what she knew was probably the last time, she heard Gale Sunsbane cry out to the other praetors. "The consul has won. We must honor our commitment to Earth!"

Aphrodite Starshadow's world faded to black, a smile on her lips.

Council Navy Vice Admiral Henri Townsend had frozen with fear less than a minute after the massive UE superdreadnought had begun its suicide run straight at *Aldrin*. Luckily, Roger Vance did not startle so easily.

Unluckily, even his competent and relatively calm orders weren't enough. It had taken them precious seconds they didn't have to realize what the giant UE ship intended, and any elation he and his crew had felt at the Earthers' disorganized surrender turned to terror quickly as they saw their own death coming.

Even with two dozen GSF ships firing point blank into the superdreadnought's hull, the enormous ship just kept coming, its own lasers clearing a path of death and destruction through the GSF fleet.

By the time the massive ship reached *Aldrin,* it was little more than a giant floating hulk. But in one last gasp of terrible power, its few remaining lasers tore the GSF flagship apart.

Captain Kim Verity, commanding officer of the battlecruiser UENS *Warsaw,* watched the suicidal run of the UENS *George Washington* with something approaching both horror and awe. Goosebumps formed on her arms as she realized the sacrifice the thousands of spacers on the superdreadnought were making, all so a few of their comrades might survive.

"Who is the surviving senior officer?" she asked her bridge crew.

"Uh, I think you are, ma'am," her tactical officer reported. "There aren't any admirals left, and *Warsaw* is the biggest ship left."

Kim only considered that for an instant. She supposed it was as good as any reason for her to be in command. "Signal the surviving UEN ships," she ordered, knowing that it was worthless to call the half-dozen remaining warships a fleet. "They are to regroup on us as we burn to Luna. Send a message ahead to Lunar Command. Tell them to get their orbital defenses ready to back us up."

She didn't know if the GSF forces would try and follow them to the moon or if they'd just remain and continue the conquest of Earth. But it was the only strategy she could think of that stood even a quarter of a chance.

Kim never got the opportunity to see if it would work as the battle plot in front of her erupted with a new influx of red.

Council reinforcements had arrived, almost to add insult to injury against a UEN force so small it couldn't even hope to fight off the enemy ships already in Earth's orbit.

Then, something strange happened. "Are those enemy ships firing on each other?" she asked in dismay.

"No, ma'am!" her tactical officer cried in something approaching triumph. "It's the Martians, Captain. The Fleet of the Eagle finally came!"

Legatus Augustus Lightbringer had grown sick of waiting. He'd chafed under his orders *not* to come to Earth's aid, waiting on Consul Starshadow to send word unleashing him to save their erstwhile allies.

That word had finally come, mere minutes *after* he'd commanded his fleet to stitch jump back to Earth.

After this battle, someone in the Martian Navy's vast bureaucracy would put the timeline together and realize that the Fleet of the Eagle had jumped back to Earth *before* receiving the orders to do so. Lightbringer didn't care. When faced with the choice of dishonor by disobedience and dishonor by abandoning comrades in arms to their fate, he had easily chosen the former.

Though, to his ever-lasting shame, he hadn't arrived in time to save Horatio Lopez. So now, he would have to do what he could to save Earth in the old man's stead. It was the only way to atone.

CHAPTER 66

Fleet Admiral Chen tried her best to remain stoic as the Martian fleet routed the GSF forces of Echo Fleet in orbit of Earth. She knew that all of the men and women on CNS *Excelsior* would be looking to her for her reaction, and a poor reaction would make its way through the fleet like wildfire.

Inside, she seethed. The Keeper had assured her repeatedly that there was zero chance Earth and Mars would work together to stop the invasion. She'd seen the first sign of that being a lie when the Earth fleet on an intercept course with her had turned and fled to reinforce Mars. Now, she was seeing the final proof in the Martian's short jump to Earth orbit to join the mere handful of UEN ships that were trying to flee with their lives.

Her head throbbed as she railed against the Keeper's hubris internally and watched helplessly as the Martian fleet hammered the few dozen surviving GSF ships that hadn't fallen in the UEN superdreadnought's suicidal run. And she vowed that she would destroy every vestige of that Martian fleet when her Alpha Fleet made it to Earth in mere hours.

Quickly, however, she was distracted by other things.

"Admiral, incoming missiles!"

She turned in surprise to regard her tactical officer. "From where?" she demanded, turning back to check the battle plot. Had the other Earth Fleet—their Second Fleet—turned back and launched an attack without her noticing? No, it was still there, burning hard toward Mars and the rear of Bravo Fleet and well out of weapons range of her Alpha Fleet.

"Three ships, ma'am, battleship size but unknown design," her tactical officer reported. "It's like they appeared out of nowhere!"

Mikael Gorsky had told the Keeper, and he had told Admiral Chen, about the three stealth carriers in Earth's arsenal. But up until now, Chen hadn't stopped to wonder where those ships were. Now, she knew.

Mary Bol slammed a fist on her command chair's arm as *Enterprise, Yorktown,* and *Midway* emptied their missile tubes on one broadside and then spun on their long axes to empty the other. Dozens of ship-killer nuclear warheads flew toward the Council Navy fleet as it moved to reinforce the Guard forces around Earth.

It reminded Mary of her surprise attack months before against the Council Navy's recon force. Then, she'd destroyed two of the CN's dreadnoughts. Like then, she targeted the massive ships now.

Unfortunately, unlike the last time, the commander of the Council forces hadn't gotten sloppy. The recon force's commander had allowed his escorts to outpace his dreadnoughts, so they hadn't been able to help defend against Mary's missiles. But the current attacking force was not out of position in the same manner, and CN destroyers and light cruisers batted her missiles from space before they ever got close to the largest Council ships in the formation's center.

It would have been frustrating in the extreme had the Council ships not been so focused on the missiles that they missed the true threat. On the battle plot in front of her, Mary watched in breathless anticipation as the entire fighter and bomber complements of all three of her carriers—launched nearly simultaneously with the missiles—cold-coasted toward a spot in space ahead of the Council fleet.

Corey ducked as the stone facade of the building next to him crumbled, large chunks falling within meters of him. One of his SEAL guards shoved him out of the way just before a piece that would have crushed him clattered to the street. The man cried out as it glanced off his shoulder with a sickening thud, knocking him to the ground in place of Corey.

"Landry!" cried one of the other three SEALs, but the downed chief petty officer waved his squadmate off.

"Get . . . the president . . . admiral . . . to safety!" he gasped through clenched teeth. Then he passed out.

Petty Officer First Class Peyton looked like he might ignore his superior's final orders, but he squared his shoulders and cast Corey an almost angry look as if it were somehow his fault that Landry was dying.

Corey sympathized; the SEAL wasn't all wrong. And Peyton had to be furious at not being in the thick of the battle to defend Earth from the blue-uniformed Guard Paramilitary Force troops that had landed all across Houston. They'd already narrowly avoided one group of the enemy ground troops, and one was closing in behind them and would catch them if they didn't hurry. They could hear, seemingly just around the corner, the tromping of massive GPF mech suits as they moved inexorably through the city, destroying anyone and anything that got in their way.

Next to him, Admiral Terrence Lafayette grabbed Corey's arm and urged him onward.

Their target destination was the Third Street Barracks, a Marine base, where they hoped they could take shelter in the command bunker and assert control over Earth's defenses. Assuming, of course, that the base commander didn't order Corey and Lafayette executed as traitors, much less accept Corey as the new interim president.

Either way, it would be safer than being out on the streets, so he and Lafayette followed Peyton and the other two surviving SEALs as best he could keep up, Corey huffing and puffing as his old legs, unaccustomed to Earth's gravity after months on Mars, threatened to give out with each step.

Commander Richard Ingram, call sign Thrasher, hated the waiting that was so often an unavoidable part of space battles. For over an hour now, the seventy-five fighters and bombers under his command had cold-coasted from Mary Bol's carriers toward a spot of space ahead of the approaching Council fleet. Now, they'd arrived at that point at almost the exact same time the enemy did.

Admiral Bol had been adamant that no matter how much *Enterprise, Yorktown,* and *Midway* harassed the Council forces, the enemy was unlikely to slow their approach to Earth. She'd been right, and the perfect timing their plan had required became a reality.

Richard watched the mission clock slowly tick down to zero. Then he transmitted the go order, a single click of his comm that would likely sound like background static to the Council ships but told all seventy-five of his small craft to go hot at the same time.

Tamara Chen watched in confusion as dozens of new red dots appeared in the holo field, most of them already inside her formation.

Beneath her, *Excelsior* rocked as proton bombs exploded against her flagship's hull. Then she started barking orders.

"Wingo, Killmonger, concentrate your squadrons on that leftmost dreadnought," Richard Ingram ordered.

"On it, Thrasher," Jay 'Killmonger' Bhardwaj answered quickly, and his squadron of fighters moved to escort Kelly 'Wingo' Jefferson's bomber squadron as they made an attack run on the enemy dreadnought in question.

"Watch your six, Thrasher!" his wingman's voice yelled in the comm, and Richard slammed his thruster control to jink upward and narrowly miss the antifighter missile launched by one of the Council destroyers.

"Enemy fighters launching!" announced another squadron leader, and Richard changed course to take his fighter straight at a new cluster of small red dots that appeared on his sensor display.

"Hooligans on me!" he ordered, and his own squadron mates swung around to form up with Richard's fighter. "Take out those bogeys before they can get to the Jolly Rogers," he ordered, reaching out a hand to highlight on his display and for his squadron mates an enemy fighter formation moving to attack a group of bombers from *Yorktown* just as they poured their bombs into a Council battleship.

"Admiral, we've lost the *Decimator,* and *Indominable* is under heavy attack," reported Chen's tactical officer.

"Move the fighters from *Devastator* to cover *Indominable,*" she ordered. "And tell DestRon17 to move into position with CruRon13 to shield our battleships on the port flank."

Around her, *Excelsior*'s bridge was a scene of controlled chaos, with both her and Captain Jacobs's voices shouting out orders. She'd heard from intel reports that the UEN separated its command and flag bridges on capital ships to avoid this type of overlap, but that idle thought was gone almost as soon as it entered her head. There was a battle to fight, and she did her best to ignore it as her dreadnought once again shuddered beneath her command chair.

"Thrasher, I've got one on my six!"

Richard hit his port nose thrusters and goosed his main drive to change course and go to his wingman's aid. "Looper, come about to oh-one-two and break left on my mark!"

He counted down as his wingman did as instructed, and the Council fighter followed. "Mark!"

Looper hit his own nose and tail thrusters to spin his ship and then put full power to his main drive, momentarily leaving his pursuer behind. But the Council fighter didn't let that last, changing its own course to follow Looper after only an instant's hesitation, which brought him right into Richard's crosshairs.

The Council fighter exploded from within as twin laser blasts from Richard's craft hit its drive nozzles and burned forward through the fuselage, igniting the enemy craft's fuel tanks. There was no great flash of fire to mark its death—not in the vacuum of space—but the ship broke apart nonetheless.

Richard watched in satisfaction as Looper escaped unharmed. Then, he brought his fighter around to survey the battlefield. An alarm screeched a warning at him in his cockpit, and his eyes went to his display just in time to see the antifighter missile an instant before it exploded against his craft's starboard side.

Mary Bol blinked back the tears. Of the seventy-five fighters and bombers launched by her squadron of carriers, only thirty-four had survived running the gauntlet of the Council Navy ships. The survivors now waited in the wake of the Council fleet for *Enterprise, Midway,* and *Yorktown* to come and pick them up. They left behind them the destruction of fully a dozen enemy ships—more than hoped for, but not nearly enough.

"Admiral, our magazines are dry," George Holm reported gently over the intercom from the command bridge. "It's time to withdraw."

"Make it so, George," she said hoarsely. "Let's go pick up our people." Inwardly, she cursed the earlier damage to her ships' hulls, damage that had weakened their stealth capabilities and forced them to stay out of laser range of the enemy. If they'd just been able to get closer—

She shook her head to stop the futile train of thought. Their combined fighter and missile attack had forced the Council fleet to slow down a bit, and it would add another thirty minutes to their timeline to reach Earth. They'd have to be happy with that delay and with what they'd accomplished in weakening the enemy just slightly.

Except Mary wasn't sure if she'd ever be happy again.

CHAPTER 67

The tide was no longer turning; it had turned. The last ships of the Guard Space Force in orbit of Earth died in streams of fire as they spiraled down into the atmosphere. Captain Kim Verity had ordered *Warsaw*'s comm officer to stop listening to the horrified broadcasts from Earth as falling debris destroyed towns and cities below them.

There was simply little they could do about it right now, though at least the Martian fleet was helping her few remaining ships cut apart some of the larger pieces of debris.

Nor could they do anything about the thousands upon thousands of Council troops that had landed on the surface. All they could hope was that Earth's armies would be able to eventually take back Houston from the enemy.

"Ma'am, we're being hailed by the Martian flagship," her comm officer called hoarsely.

"Put them through," she ordered, then spoke into the open channel before the ship calling her could say a word. "Legatus Lightbringer, you sure took your sweet time coming to help!" She knew her voice was far harsher than she'd intended, but she had a hard time caring right at the moment.

"Your words are true," came the somber reply. "Mars has dishonored herself this day."

The frank and self-critical reply surprised Kim so greatly that she couldn't think of a response. After a few moments of silence, the Martian legatus prodded her.

"Attention, Captain Kim Verity. Have you lost our transmission?"

"No, just thinking," Kim hedged. She turned to her tactical officer. "How long until that second Council fleet gets here?"

"Three hours, ma'am."

"Captain Kim Verity," Lightbringer prodded again. "As this is your planet and you are the senior-most surviving officer of its defenses, what are your orders in regards to the fleet that comes? If you so order, Mars will stay and fight."

An unusual mix of emotions swirled within Kim, the anger at the Martians' late arrival at war with a warm gratitude at their offer to stay and take on a second, much larger, Council attack force. But all of the emotions were overshadowed by a sense of futility.

"I appreciate that, Legatus Lightbringer," she said, her voice trembling. "But I'm afraid it won't be enough."

There was another long silence before Lightbringer replied. "That may well be so, Captain Verity, but Mars stands ready nonetheless."

Tyrus jogged alongside Jinny and forty mixed praetorian guards and UEN SEALs, augmented by a company of UE Marines they'd intercepted along the way and managed to convince they weren't the enemy. They had no idea where the company from *Enterprise*—the ones who had seized Government House—had ended up.

By some miracle, or rather by the blood of the military men and women, the civilians had all survived. Jinny, Riggs, Landon Hartman, Temperance Jimenez, and Jordan Archer were still with them. Unfortunately, so was Mikael Gorsky.

Two of his former bodyguards dragged the ex-president along. Tyrus had long since given up worrying that they might be more loyal to their erstwhile boss than to the coup forces who had deposed him.

They hadn't betrayed them thus far, and he simply couldn't spare anyone else to force the recalcitrant Gorsky to keep pace with them. Everyone else with a gun was too busy fighting off the Guard Paramilitary Forces they kept encountering.

Part of Tyrus wanted to just leave Gorsky behind, leave him to his own fate. The plan had always been for Jinny to read him as part of the coup; they'd all hoped that doing so would reveal more about the Keeper's invasion plans. Even though that was now a moot issue, she had still read the former president. By the look on her face when she did it, Tyrus imagined it had been like eating a slimy eel or dipping her head into a vat of crude oil. But he was grateful she'd done it anyway. Now, even if Gorsky failed to survive their flight—such a pity that would be—they would still have all of his knowledge and memories of his conversations with the Keeper. Those might help when they set up the inevitable resistance to Council rule on earth.

Tyrus was under no illusions. Even if the navies of every one of the Four Worlds combined to defend Earth, the Council Navy would just keep coming, especially since Keeper Petrov had so clearly reinforced them with the Guard forces. Eventually, they would entirely overwhelm the homeworld's defenses, and then Earth would fall.

He'd warned them. He'd tried so hard to make them take the threat seriously. He'd failed.

"Commander Tyne," one of the Marines, the company's captain, called over to him. "We're picking something up on the civilian bands. You might want to hear this."

Tyrus didn't stop jogging as he pulled out a handheld comm and searched the airwaves to find the channel the Marine captain provided. What he heard on it almost did make him stop in his tracks.

". . . surrender. Repeat, this is Congressman Dorian Hastings of the legitimate government of United Earth. We surrender! We accept the Council's terms and will deliver up the enhanced on the Australian continent. All UE forces are commanded to immediately cease fire and surrender to the nearest Council—"

Tyrus cut the feed, sick to his stomach and unable to listen any further. It was over. Even if only half the military listened to the congressman, in the absence of a counterorder from Corey O'Leary or someone else in charge, eventually, everyone would be forced to consider Hastings's word as the law. And no one had heard from Corey for over an hour, despite several attempts to raise him, Lafayette, or their SEAL escorts. Tyrus wasn't even sure the old man was still alive.

Nearby, Jinny talked between labored breaths—they'd been running for so long, and it was clearly getting to her. "Just as Gorsky planned," she panted. "But the Council won't stop with Australia. The Keeper's plan was always to take over all of the system and supposedly install Gorsky as the puppet leader. I doubt, though, that Petrov ever intended to honor the agreement. Tyrus, we've lost."

The despair in her voice awakened something in him, pushing aside his own sense of impending doom and lighting a fire that he'd feared had almost died down. "We haven't lost yet," he told her. "And we won't. No matter what."

Next to him, Domitia grunted her agreement.

Captain Kim Verity briefly considered trying to countermand the surrender order from Congressman Hastings, broadcast from the capital to the ships in orbit, as well as the forces on the ground. But she couldn't reach anyone at fleet command to tell her whether or not she had the authority to do that, and she doubted that any Army or Marine general on the surface would listen to a mere captain anyway.

Nor did she have much time to even try it. The Council Navy reinforcement fleet was only two and a half hours away from Earth's orbit now. But if Kim wanted to run and save her surviving ships and Lightbringer's, she had a much smaller window than that to do it. Otherwise, the Council fleet would carry more than enough speed to stop the retreat in its tracks.

She studied the long-range sensor plot again, frowning to herself. Admiral Bol's ships had done a good job of slowing the reinforcements down, and they'd even destroyed a dozen of the enemy ships, including two of their dreadnoughts. But it wasn't enough. Almost two hundred Council Navy ships were bearing down on Earth, and even with Lightbringer's Fleet of the Eagle, the planet's defenders numbered less than a hundred. They'd simply all taken far too many losses fighting off the GSF fleet, and they'd entered the battle under-strength as it was after the bloody conflict between Earth and Mars.

"Legatus Lightbringer, do you read?" she asked through a private comm channel, putting up her command chair's privacy field so that no one else on *Warsaw*'s bridge could listen in.

"I listen, Captain Verity," came the stoic reply.

"We can't win, can we?"

"We can always win, Captain." Lightbringer's voice was hard.

"But the probability is low, isn't it?" she insisted.

There was a pause, and when the legatus replied, his voice was somber. "You speak truth. Our chances of victory are small."

Kim sighed loudly. "Then we really don't have a choice. Earth is lost, and the Four Worlds will need your fleet to take her back."

Another long pause. "What are your orders, Captain?"

Kim steeled herself as best she could to keep her voice from trembling. "You and your fleet should leave. I'll stay back with my ships to see if we can buy some more time. Maybe we can—"

"No." Lightbringer's one-word response stopped Kim midsentence. "You have but six ships, Captain Verity," he went on. "You will not buy your planet any time. Earth is conquered, and Luna will soon follow; if you stay, it will make no difference. You must come with us. We will need heroes like you in the battle to come."

Kim felt the tears running down her cheeks. She knew Lightbringer was right, even if she didn't consider herself a hero. Dropping her privacy field, she spoke to her bridge crew as a whole.

"Signal the fleet," she said, her voice not much above a hoarse whisper. "Retreat. I say again, retreat. Earth is lost."

EPILOGUE

Vice Admiral Jessica Monroe looked down from orbit at a planet she'd never expected to see in person this close. It felt wrong to see that much red interspersed with the green and blue that could almost be Earth's landscapes.

Mars. Before, when she had imagined herself this close to the red planet, it had always been in the sights of a battleship's bombardment weaponry. Never in her wildest dreams had she considered the possibility that she and her carrier might be in orbit above Mars as one of its defenders.

Admiral Terrence Lafayette had ordered Second Fleet to help the Martian Fleet of the Bear to pincer the Council fleet attacking Mars between them. But the enemy hadn't cooperated. The CN fleet had veered off their attack vector about the same time Jessica had listened in despair to Earth's surrender. But she'd ordered the fleet onward to Mars, ignoring the cowardly orders of Congressman Hastings.

Nearly half a day later, the *very* few surviving ships of the UEN First Fleet had arrived in Mars orbit under the escort of the Martian Fleet of the Eagle. Noticeably absent was the superdreadnought *George Washington,* and its commander. Instead, the still-flying UEN ships had been under the command of a nearly hysterical battlecruiser captain.

Jessica had relieved Kim Verity of her command and sent her down to the surface of Mars to recover. The battle at Earth had broken the young woman, and Jessica wasn't sure if Verity would ever be okay again.

Frankly, she wasn't sure if *any* of them were ever going to be okay again.

Jessica felt a tear run down her cheek as she studied the red planet below her. Soon, she would board a shuttle to the surface, where she would join a war council of the surviving military leaders from Earth, Mars, and Europa. Just a few days ago, she would have felt honored to join such a gathering, content to sit at the edge of the room while admirals like Horatio Lopez and Terrence Lafayette represented her world.

Now, she was terrified, because *she* was the second most senior surviving officer of what was left of the United Earth Navy. No one had heard from Lafayette since he'd sent her the orders to turn and support the Fleet of the Bear instead of taking on the second Council fleet headed to Earth.

At least she wasn't the most senior admiral, she supposed. She didn't envy Mary Bol one bit. She didn't envy any of them. Everything had gone so wrong. Everything.

Jessica bowed her head. She couldn't remember when she'd stopped praying as a child. It had probably happened sometime after her father's death and before her mother had left her with her grandparents. When she was a teenager, they'd tried to get her to continue going to church, but she hadn't seen the point. If God could be so cruel as to take her parents from her, then she felt she owed him nothing.

Now, she prayed for the first time in years, not sure if anyone was listening but hoping desperately for a miracle. They were going to need one.

Aphrodite Starshadow cast her eyes over the assembled group of weary men and women in one of the larger meeting chambers of the Olympus Mons Government Complex. Her midsection, still sore despite two days submerged in a healing bath—the immunes told her she'd died twice in just the first hour following her duel with Tiberius—twinged with a sharp pain as she turned her body to take in the entire room.

The eleven surviving praetors were there, of course, with their retinues. No one represented the family Tiberius, nor would they for quite some time, until the man's heirs did something heroic or selfless enough to atone for the sins of their patriarch.

Apart from the Martians in the room, UEN Admiral Mary Bol was there, sitting at the main table with the praetors, several of them casting furtive and very un-Martian-like glances at the African woman. Aphrodite had met with Bol briefly ahead of the conference and been impressed by her, as she had been by Vice Admiral Jessica Monroe, Bol's second, who stood just a meter or so behind her superior.

Next to Bol, looking extremely out of place and nervous, was Commodore Kent Knoll. The Europan man, built like an Earther—Europa made liberal use of artificial gravity set to Earth standard in their cities and habitats—tried to look everywhere and nowhere all at once. Apparently, he'd been quite happy as fourth in line for command of the Europan Poseidon Fleet and was content to never rise higher by playing the political games that further promotion would have necessitated. Well, he was in the thick of it now, whether he was prepared or not. Admiral Jason Namor and his second and third in command had died in the desperate and ultimately failed attempt to defend their world from the Council fleet sent there.

In the outer reaches of the chamber sat the staffs for the foreign admirals, including a strange Earther named Harold Tichner, some sort of professor on Earth but for some reason part of the Europan delegation. Legatus Lars Moonslayer, cousin of Praetor Kahn Moonslayer and commander of the Fleet of the Bear, was also seated at the table next to Legatus Augustus Lightbringer, whom Aphrodite had newly promoted to be the commander-in-chief of all Martian military forces.

Everyone was here. The assembled crowd represented the top military and political leaders of the Four Worlds. They were painfully few, and those absent were conspicuous. Aphrodite would tell no one, not even those closest to her, of the silent tears she'd shed for hours when no one had brought knowledge of the survival or location of Corey O'Leary.

Somberly, she addressed the assembled crowd.

"Praetors of Mars," she began, her voice ringing out and quelling the side conversations in the chamber, "Defenders of Mars and Friends of Mars, I call this session to order to plan the liberation of the Four Worlds. Our situation, in all honesty, is dire. The Council Navy outnumbers us by over two hundred ships and outmasses us by more. Furthermore, we must assume that they have more forces in reserve in colonial space.

"Earth has surrendered, and the status of her interim president, Corey O'Leary"—she barely kept her voice from catching as she uttered her old love's name—"is unknown, as is the status of Reader Jinny Ambrosa, former Praetorian Guard Tyrus Tyne, and their allies."

All they really knew was that Marcus Parn, centurion and commander of the Praetorian Guard, was dead. That transmission had made it off Earth before the Council conquerors had taken over all of the planet's communication networks.

"As consul of Mars, I declare the war with United Earth is over. But the war with the 47 Colonies has just begun. And I declare this council of war opened."

Fleet Admiral Tamara Chen did her best to ignore the cold, biting wind that cut right through her coat as she stood on the roof of one of Houston's tallest buildings, chosen as the temporary seat of the occupying government of United Earth. Next to her, UE Congressman Dorian Hastings likewise shivered, though no doubt from more than just the cold. Together, they silently watched the lights of the shuttle descend from the clouds above.

Underneath them, the skyscraper shook as a squadron of fast attack fighters screamed by overhead, escorting the shuttle down from CNS *Dominant,* flagship of Delta Fleet, which had arrived through the Front Door three weeks after the battle for the Sol system had concluded.

Those three weeks since Earth's surrender had been busy for Chen.

Luna had fallen quickly. Even with its orbital and surface-based defense platforms, it hadn't taken much to convince the moon's governor to agree to Congressman Hastings's call for surrender. But several armies on the surface of both Earth and Luna had needed more convincing.

At first, Chen had sent the divisions of the Guard Paramilitary Force and her own CN ground forces to take on the remaining defenders on both worlds. But despite some early successes, Keeper Petrov had grown impatient, issuing her a direct order via her dreadnought's quantum comm array.

That had forced Chen to reluctantly begin the orbital bombardment, destroying entire cities and killing millions upon millions of civilians until the last of the UE ground force commanders finally broadcast their surrender. Europa had likewise fallen. There, it had taken only the destruction of one of their cities for their prime minister to yield.

Mars, however, was a different story entirely. All of the surviving UE Navy and Europan Navy ships had fled to Mars, reinforcing the red planet's already strong fleets and creating a combined force that Chen was loathe to attack head-on. It was made worse by the fact that, unlike on Earth and Europa, the Keeper had been unable to send any spies to Mars—their different anatomy made foreigners stand out far too much—nor had he been able to cultivate any local sources of intelligence. So Chen had no idea what the Martians were planning or where the weak points in their defenses might be.

Regardless, she'd half expected Keeper Petrov to order her to take her fleet and attack the red planet anyway. It had been a surprise and a relief when he hadn't done so, instead instructing her to await his special emissary, the same emissary who was in the shuttle now settling to a rest on top of the skyscraper upon which she stood.

As the shuttle's ramp descended, Chen went to one knee, and Dorian Hastings awkwardly and belatedly copied her move. A skinny man wrapped in a winter coat walked down the ramp, surrounded by bodyguards with drawn weapons. She and Hastings waited patiently —mostly—for the man to approach them.

"Admiral Chen," the thin man said, smiling but not offering her his hand nor inviting her to rise from the hard surface of the roof. "You have done well, despite your failure to bring Mars into the fold of the Council's enlightened rule."

Chen had prepared herself for this line of challenge. "Vice Keeper Pondergast, we have concentrated our forces on securing Earth and the enhanced populations here. I am pleased to report that we have conquered nearly the entirety of the continent of Australia despite firmer-than-expected resistance there."

"Nearly?" Pondergast asked with a deep frown. "Admiral Chen, are you telling me that you have yet to subdue a single continent?"

She licked her lips. "Sir, the speakers surrendered early. And we have brought the readers and blenders under control. But it is the enacters in Australia, Your Excellency, who still resist. They are scattered throughout the continent's interior, and they fight us guerilla style, disappearing into the 'bush' as they call it whenever our forces get close, then popping up and attacking elsewhere in unexpected ways."

Pondergast looked like he was contemplating whether or not to send her to the guillotine.

"Of course, we could bombard Australia from orbit, but Keeper Petrov did not want us to risk destroying the enhanced population," she quickly added, lest Pondergast suggest such a course of action himself. Chen was still getting to know the strange Vice Keeper; the entire position was a new one in the Council government, and she still wasn't sure about Pondergast as an individual, either.

When he spoke again, his tone was acerbic. "You also failed to capture Jinny Ambrosa as ordered."

Chen swallowed with a suddenly dry throat. "Yes, Your Excellency. It is reported that she likely died in the battle to take Houston. But," she added before the storm clouds building in Pondergast's expression could unleash their fury, "I have another gift for you that I believe will be almost as good as having Ambrosa herself."

She touched her watch, and the door that led up onto the roof opened behind her. Two burly enlisted spacers thrust an old woman out onto the roof so roughly that she fell to her knees beside Chen, drawing a sympathetic wince from the admiral that she quickly hid lest Pondergast see it.

"This, Your Excellency, is the one they call the Majko, the leader of all Earth's readers. Our intelligence confirms that she personally trained Jinny Ambrosa in unlocking the full use of her abilities. She has, as of yet, not told us what we want to know, but it is only a matter of time before she breaks."

A smile meaner and more predatory than Chen had ever seen spread across the Vice Keeper's face as he eyed the old, bruised woman kneeling on the hard deck. The woman looked up and eyed Pondergast, defiance in her eyes despite the two burly enlisted men standing just behind her. "So," she said in a raspy voice, "you're the mythical Keeper? Or Vice Keeper, was it? For a man with your reputation, I didn't expect someone so short and ugly."

Whatever the old woman might have said next was choked off when Pondergast delivered a kick to her face that sent her flying. Her back hit the roof with a sickening thud. Without so much as another glance in her direction, Pondergast turned his attention to Hastings, who stood up on shaky legs to greet the Vice Keeper.

"You're the one who has asked to be the occupation ruler of United Earth?" he asked, cocking his head at the congressman.

Hastings nodded vigorously. "Yes, Your Excellency. I wasn't privileged to be in on President Mikael Gorsky's plans, but I saw quickly that the best thing my government could do was work *with* the Council, rather than against it."

Pondergast raised his eyebrows. "Is that so? Tell me, Mr. Hastings, do you have any suggestions as to the best way to subdue Australia?"

"Of course, I do, Your Excellency. We should . . ."

Their voices faded from Chen's hearing as Pondergast put an arm around Hastings's shoulder and led him to the low railing that spanned the perimeter of the building. She watched from her still-kneeling position, ignoring the pain in her joints, as Pondergast pointed to a few areas of Houston, as if seeking Hastings's advice on different things. Then, Chen winced and stifled a gasp as Pondergast reached down and grabbed Hastings by the legs and flipped him up and over the railing, the wind capturing all but a hint of the congressman's scream as he fell toward the distant streets below.

The Vice Keeper walked back to where Chen still kneeled, a small smile on his face. "Now, Admiral Chen," he said almost casually. "Let us discuss the subjugation of Australia, and then Mars."

Jinny Ambrosa looked out across the pristine mountains of the range the Earthers called the Rockies. The early spring air was freezing here, with snow down to the bases of most of the tall peaks, and the cold bit through the coat she wore as she surveyed her surroundings.

A crunch in the snow behind her alerted her to the presence of someone else. Cal Riggs stepped up beside her. "Tyrus is looking for you," he said, his voice almost robotic. He'd been that way ever since she'd first seen him again onboard *Enterprise*, before they'd gone over to the *Washington* and planned the coup against Gorsky.

The coup that had succeeded just in time for them to fail entirely.

"I'll come back inside in a few minutes," she replied somberly. "I needed to get out of that place."

Riggs nodded slowly. "I get it. Who knew a secret bunker inside a mountain could be so stark and uninviting?"

She looked at him in surprise. His tone had been deadly serious, but his words hinted at the old Riggs, able to joke even in serious situations. She'd thought that man surely dead and gone after the death of Jynx; he'd withdrawn even more into himself when, one week after arriving at the bunker, he'd stumbled upon Jinny and Trey Kaplan stealing a private moment together. This was the first time he'd spoken to her since, and if he noticed her startled gaze, he gave no sign of it.

"So, what now?" he asked instead.

She knew he wasn't referring to whether they'd head back inside the bunker or not and find Tyrus. She shrugged. "I don't know. The Council forces destroyed most of the comm arrays on the surface and in orbit. They control the rest. We don't even know if Corey is alive." That part really bothered her. She knew from the way he winced that it also bothered Riggs more than he was willing to admit.

"What if he's dead?" the pilot asked.

Jinny choked up. She hadn't allowed herself to consider that her friend and surrogate father had died in the battle. They'd all hoped that somehow they'd find Corey on their mad dash across the streets of Houston to the underground secret Loop station Jinny had read from General Cruz's memories. It had carried them north and west, depositing them just a few kilometers from this mountain base, deserted when they'd arrived. Most of them had made it here; Cruz hadn't. Even with the Martian nanites, the stress of the hurried escape from Houston had been too much.

That had been a month ago, and there was still no sign of Corey, Lafayette, or anyone else they'd been forced to leave behind. That they only caught snippets of comm traffic made it hard for them to know if the former congressman turned interim president was dead, alive and hiding, or a Council prisoner.

"Tyrus thinks we should fight back—form some sort of resistance to Council rule on Earth."

Jinny turned to look at Riggs. By the way he said it, it was clear he disagreed with Tyrus. She swallowed her silent sobs, licked her lips, and chose her next words carefully. "We have to fight, Cal. If we don't fight, then it's all been for nothing."

He didn't respond, just stepped away and started to make his way back to the mountaintop entrance that let out into this camouflaged observation post. Without thinking, Jinny reached out and grabbed his hand to stop him from leaving.

Riggs turned in surprise, his eyes going to their clasped hands. Jinny followed his gaze and then gasped. She'd forgotten she wasn't wearing gloves, and her bare hand grasped his. But she felt . . . nothing.

There was no inrush of memories. Nor was there the shout and push from his mind that he'd used against her so long ago on Rinali Station. There was simply nothing.

"Is this what it feels like?" she whispered. "To touch someone without being a reader?"

He shrugged, yanking his hand out of hers and heading into the bunker without a backward glance.

Jinny watched him go, wishing she could figure out a way to reach him. Tyrus had alluded to something that had taken place on Mars that had made Riggs even more sullen but had refused to provide any details, telling her that Cal would tell her himself when he was ready. Thus far, her friend had been wrong.

She turned back to look again at the mountains, only to turn around once more as another step crunched the snow behind her.

Expecting—hoping—to see Cal returning or Trey coming to check on her, she opened her mouth in a greeting but stumbled on her words when she recognized the tall, thin figure of Domitia Tyne. The Martian wore her powered exosuit, as always, lest the higher gravity of Earth crush her. Jinny thought it had to be horrible for her and the other praetorian guards with them to never leave their suits, though Tyrus had told her that Domitia could take hers off for short stints to clean it. But then she could only lie down and couldn't walk or otherwise move much at all. It sounded like torture.

"Domitia, did Tyrus send you to find me?" she asked, recovering her wits.

The tall, olive-skinned woman shook her head. "No. My husband does not know I come to see you."

"Uh, okay," Jinny said uncertainly.

"I am here about the many people in your head."

Jinny grimaced but nodded. At this point, her special abilities were no secret. Just about everyone in the base—everyone who had left Houston with them—knew all about what she could do. She'd even channeled General Cruz in several meetings with the various officers of the surviving SEALs, Praetorian Guard, and Marines. She'd never channeled Centurion Parn. His persona hadn't reappeared since he'd left her in the tunnel immediately after delivering his message to Domitia. Jinny still didn't understand what had happened to him.

"What exactly do you want with them—the people in my head, I mean?" she asked Domitia.

"These people in your head. My husband is one of them, is he not?"

Jinny nodded uncomfortably. Did Domitia take offense that Jinny had a version of Tyrus in her mind? Was the Martian woman here to ask the impossible, that she somehow purge Tyrus's persona as she had done with Parn's? She wasn't sure how any of this worked.

"Good. This is good," Domitia replied. "You will read me then, as well."

Jinny's mouth fell open in shock. "Uh, you want me to read you?"

Domitia nodded vigorously. "Yes. You will read me. Right now."

Shaking herself as if trying to wake up from a dream, Jinny fought to find a response. "But why?"

Tyrus's wife surprised her even further by smiling. She'd seen Domitia smile only a few times before, usually a toothy, predatory grin when she was contemplating battle or killing someone—or messing with Tyrus. Martians were extremely strange, Jinny was quickly learning. But this time, Domitia's smile was far different. It seemed almost normal.

"Because," the Martian woman replied, "we are all likely to die in the battle that comes." Before Jinny could argue with that, Domitia held up her hand and continued. "On Mars, we believe in the anima—the soul—of every human being. As I have learned more about your strange abilities, Jinny, I have come to believe that when you read someone, you take a part of their anima, and it lives inside you from then onward. I would have part of my anima live within you so that it may be with the anima of my husband even when we are both gone from this plane of existence."

A tear ran down Jinny's cheek, and she hastily wiped it away. "Domitia, that was beautiful. I'm not sure I agree with your interpretation of my abilities, but it's a nice way to think of it."

Domitia smiled at her again, taking the compliment.

"If you really want me to read you, I will," Jinny said. In response, Domitia pressed a bare hand to Jinny's forehead. A few moments later, the Martian woman was gone, leaving Jinny once again alone on the mountainside—alone save for the hundreds of people who lived in her head, now one more than before.

She turned back once again to the mountains, contemplating Domitia's words. Could they survive what was coming? Did they even stand a chance? She knew they couldn't sit back and wait forever while the Council subjected Earth to domination and slavery. But they also couldn't fight a battle alone. There was little the few dozen of them here in this remote mountain range could do against the hundreds of thousands of Council Navy and Guard troops that had landed in the last month on Earth's surface.

Still, they had to at least try, didn't they?

Of course we do, replied Alan's voice in her head. It brought with it an unexpected warmth. Ever since she'd woken from her coma in Perth, he'd been largely absent from her thoughts. To hear him again, right now, was far more comforting than she could have imagined.

But he was gone in an instant, disappearing back into the fog and leaving her alone and facing the same insurmountable problem she'd been contemplating before his appearance. Then he sent her one last thought, an impression more than words—a suggestion. Maybe, he implied, there was something to the other thing Domitia had said. And if souls could exist, then why not a God?

Jinny had long since given up her search for religion. What had become a simple quest to honor Alan's memory had quickly turned into a futile effort. Only a few times had she felt anything beyond herself at work, and she couldn't understand why any God would allow the horrible things that had happened to them over the last several months.

But there, on the top of a camouflaged mountain peak, on a planet consumed by her enemies, Jinny Ambrosa closed her eyes and uttered a silent prayer.

It couldn't hurt, and she'd take whatever help she could get.

THE END

Don't ever miss a new release!

Sign up now for Skyler's newsletter and get access to new release updates, free content, and great deals.

Just go to www.skylerramirez.com/join-the-club

BOOKS BY SKYLER RAMIREZ

DUMB LUCK AND DEAD HEROES

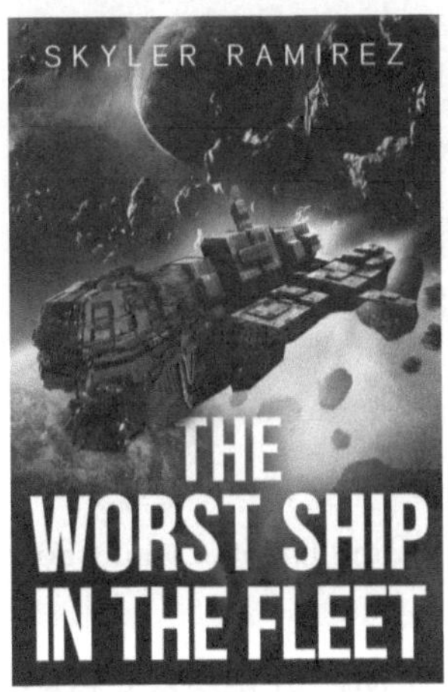

The Worst Ship in the Fleet

The Worst Spies in the Sector

The Worst Pirate Hunters in the Fringe

The Worst Rescuers in the Republic

The Worst Detectives in the Federation

The Worst Traitors in the Confederacy

The Worst Fugitives in the Star Nation

The Worst Mercenaries in the Border Systems (Coming Soon)

A STAR NATION IN PERIL

Set in the same universe as Dumb Luck and Dead Heroes

Rogue Agent

Suicide Mission

Assassin's Flight (Coming Soon)

THE BRAD MENDOZA CHRONICLES

Set in the same universe as Dumb Luck and Dead Heroes

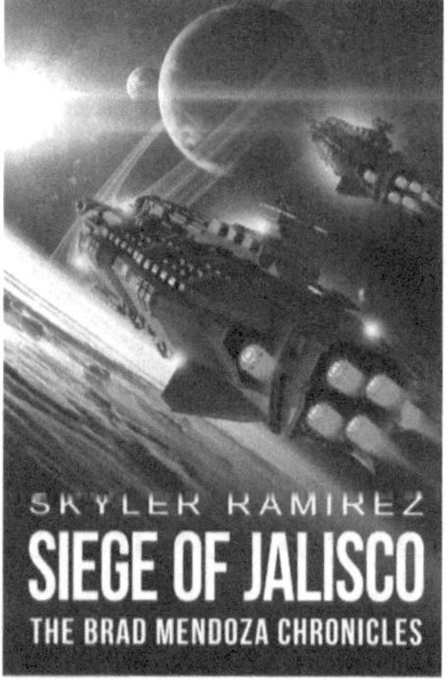

Saving the Academy

Battle for Poe

Siege of Jalisco

THE FOUR WORLDS

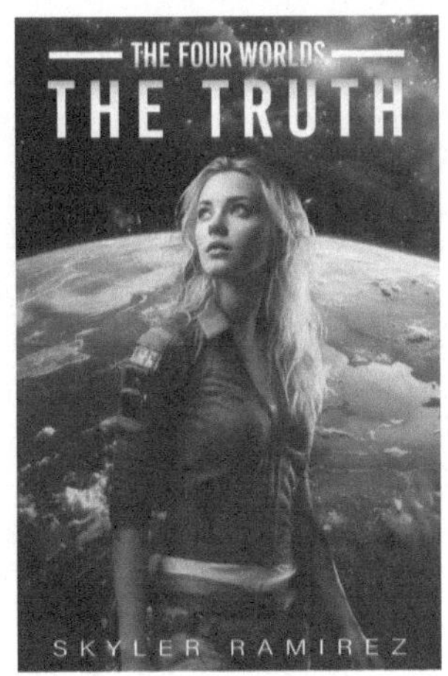

The Four Worlds: The Truth

The Four Worlds: Subversion

The Four Worlds: Wrath of Mars

Revolution: A Four Worlds Story

ANTHOLOGIES

AI Apocalypse: A Collection of Science Fiction Stories (with Jonathan Yanez, Andrew Moriarty, Anthony J Melchiorri, and Stephen Gay)

ABOUT THE AUTHOR

I just love writing. My goal is to write books that my readers enjoy and that celebrate everyday imperfect heroes. I want to show that everyone, no matter how life has dealt with them or how they've dealt with life, deserves a second chance and can go on to do amazing things. Just look at Brad and Jessica in Dumb Luck and Dead Heroes or Jinny Ambrosa and Tyrus Tyne in The Four Worlds.

It's important to me that everyone be able to read my books, including my teenage children, so I purposefully leave out any swearing or graphic scenes, though I don't shy away from serious topics. In this, I follow a tradition set by many (far better) writers before me, most notably in my life, Louis L'Amour.

As for the personal side, I live in Texas with my wife and four children (and often a revolving door of exchange students), and I work for a major tech company in my spare time. But writing is my passion, and I often toil into the early hours of morning, especially on the weekends, and it's all worth it when I see people enjoy my books.

Thanks for reading!

Skyler Ramirez

amazon.com/author/Skyler-Ramirez

facebook.com/skylerramirezauthor

instagram.com/skyler.ramirez.author

tiktok.com/@skylerramirez_author